Come Sing with me my People

Steven Baker

The Book Guild Ltd

First published in Great Britain in 2017 by
The Book Guild Ltd
9 Priory Business Park
Wistow Road, Kibworth
Leicestershire, LE8 0RX
Freephone: 0800 999 2982
www.bookguild.co.uk
Email: info@bookguild.co.uk
Twitter: @bookguild

Copyright © 2017 Steven Baker

The right of Steven Baker to be identified as the author of this
work has been asserted by him in accordance with the
Copyright, Design and Patents Act 1988.

All rights reserved. No part of this publication may be
reproduced, transmitted, or stored in a retrieval system, in any form or by any means,
without permission in writing from the publisher, nor be otherwise circulated in
any form of binding or cover other than that in which it is published and without
a similar condition being imposed on the subsequent purchaser.

This work is entirely fictitious and bears no resemblance to any persons living or dead.

Typeset in Aldine401 BT

Printed and bound in Great Britain by CPI Group (UK) Ltd, Croydon, CR0 4YY

ISBN 978 1911320 517

British Library Cataloguing in Publication Data.
A catalogue record for this book is available from the British Library.

For the unsung heroes and helpers of the less fortunate

Courage, brother! Do not stumble,
Though thy path is dark as night;
There's a star to guide the humble –
Trust in God and do the right

Norman Macleod

One

1983

Nathan Palmai rolled to one side of his bed as the buzz of his radio alarm clock broke the deep sleep he had been in. He opened his eyes slowly as the tune of 'Waltzing Matilda', played in a rather different fashion by a Russian musician on a Balalaika, drifted from the soft music station his radio had been tuned into. Nathan stretched his arm to the dial and turned it through several stations. One of them was a loud blaring rock station. From another came a flowing classical music concerto. Then he paused at a soft music station where the voice of the legendary singer Nat King Cole, brought back a few minutes of nostalgia. He turned to one from which he found a bubbly, bright and breezy voice saying, "Good morning, Sydney town! It's a beautiful morning in the sweetest city in the South Seas." He settled for the cheery talk on the radio, rubbed his eyes, stretched his arms and moved out on to the balcony of his home unit to perform the same exercises he had been carrying out every morning for the past seventeen years. It was indeed a most beautiful morning. The warm sunshine seemed to soak everything in a glorious light.

When he had stretched his muscles and limbs into life, he stood still and stared at the beautiful view from the balcony. Darling Point was a good vantage point for gazing at the panoramic view of Sydney Harbour. Every morning Nathan stood in his dressing gown after exercise and breathed the air deeply and looked at the multitude of boats of all kinds berthed down below on the sparkling blue waters. He always appreciated how lucky he was to live in such affluence, and his home looked every hard-earned dollar it had cost to buy.

Nathan went back inside to his bedroom and looked at himself in the mirror: tall with dark eyebrows, serious eyes, and a shock of silver-grey hair. He had the looks of a very distinguished man about him. He was a distinguished man; something he never ceased to remind himself of. Although he lived and breathed in an aura of opulence, he had known troubled times in his life and an unsettled youth, that now in his later years he felt more than compensated for. Nathan's features seemed to blend well with the faith to which he belonged, of which he was fiercely proud. Tonight was a special occasion as he had been invited to speak at a large gathering of leading representatives of the ethnic community.

On Nathan's dressing room table, next to two photographic portraits of his late mother and father set in enamelled gold frames, there was a diary that he flicked through quickly. The next few days were going to be a very busy time for Nathan; he had important appointments on each day, and did not have time for relaxation. Still, the exhilaration of it all thrilled him a little. Nathan had a shower, breakfasted and then drove to his city law practice at his office location in the centre of Sydney's business district in Elizabeth Street, just down from the Great Synagogue and opposite Hyde Park.

The drive to work along the Bayswater Road past Rushcutters Bay and Kings Cross was always slow with the build up of traffic leading into William Street. He always enjoyed the comfort of his large Mercedes Benz. Being a people watcher in the slow traffic, he would study the looks of the other people passing him by in the busy streets. The expressions of their faces always interested him. There were the old diggers who had probably seen Gallipoli in the First World War; those who may have seen Kokoda in the last conflict; the young men in their smart shorts and short-sleeved shirts on their way to the office; and the mass of beautiful women, so abundant in Sydney, of all ages wearing light cotton dresses and broad-rimmed sunglasses. Nathan was so immersed in watching people that he did not see the Rover that drew up beside him in the lane of traffic that was beginning to move, nor the swarthy bearded man of his own faith inside the car who called out to him.

"Nathan, my boy! How are you?" He beamed, a beautiful smile. Nathan turned his head and smiled in recognition as the man tipped his Borsalino hat in courtesy. It was an old family friend of Nathan's, David Hertzel, whom he had known for years. Nathan smiled back and made the letter O with his fingers to indicate he was well. David Hertzel was in the fast-moving lane and moved into second gear swiftly and drove off while Nathan languished in the armchair seat of his Mercedes listening to the talkback programme on the car radio.

At the office, Nathan sat down at his leather-topped desk and performed his morning ritual, when he wasn't in court, of setting aside correspondence in order of priority and drafting a timetable of events that he would have to cram into his working day and his leisure hours beyond. It was going to be an ultra busy time. Nathan was just pondering how he was going to rework his schedule when the door of his office opened and in strode the partner of his legal firm, Harry Masters, whose ebullient presence and larger-than-life personality became the nucleus of any atmosphere of which he was part of. Harry was a big corpulent man, wearing broad-rimmed spectacles, the possessor of a rich, Noel Coward-like voice that had been demonstrated to its full oratorical prowess in the courtroom on many an occasion. He was also a lover of good food and wine, which were well reflected in his physical characteristics. He had a fine sense of dress; today he was wearing a light tan suit, a mid-blue silk shirt and a cream tie. It was almost as if he had worn the suit to compliment his grey hair. He puffed on his Havana cigar and adjusted his spectacles.

"Good morning, Nathan," he said in a gentle tone as if he was about to begin an oratory.

"Good morning, Harry. I'm just trying to sort out my programme for the next few days. I've exceeded myself. Would you care to hazard a guess as to how much I've got to get done in the next couple of weeks?"

"I would say it would be frightening myself, knowing the workload and the number of engagements you try to cope with. I've always thought, Nathan dear boy, that you have an appetite for work paralleled only by my gargantuan appetite for a tasty morsel or two."

"Well, Harry, for starters, tonight I'm going to be speaking at an ethnic dinner and tomorrow, Saturday, is my godson's bar mitzvah, to be followed the next day by my attendance at the opening of a new kosher restaurant. I'm addressing a dinner at the New South Wales Law Society the following night – that's just the beginning."

Harry took a long drag on his cigar. He was the perfect complement to Nathan as a legal partner; Nathan invariably wore dark suits of a fine cut, whilst Harry preferred lighter more casual clothes of flamboyant shades.

Nathan had a more serious air about him. He could be the one to provide a sense of drama and pathos in any discussion. He was a quietly spoken man, but every word he spoke was effective and direct in its emphasis.

Harry, on the other hand, was a great character. His wit could be biting, his voice sounded as if it belonged to a Shakespearian actor rather than a leading lawyer, and he was always a rather jovial man, unlike Nathan who permanently gave the impression that he was constantly serious minded and in deep thought. Although this was not always an accurate picture of the man who, in reality, had much thoughtfulness for others, and was a compassionate and friendly man, once a person grew to know him well.

"My dear Nathan, as they say in the acting profession, you need a good stand-in. It all comes with the prestige of being one of Sydney's leading lawyers and a highly respected member of the community. Can't say I envy the task of attending all those boring functions too much though, but I must say that a bottle of wine or two and a seven-course meal would be an enticement for a *bon vivant* such as myself. Personally, I'm glad to get home to my garden to tend the roses or to go out for a night at the opera."

A wry smile broached Nathan's lips. "Tell me, Harry," he enquired, feeling slightly guilty that external activities were imposing on his working life. "Can you cope all right with the workload for this week. I'm sorry that all these things seem to have cropped up at once."

"It's no problem at all. From what I can see, I think it's just a case of clearing a backlog of paperwork for the next few weeks. No court attendances for at least two. Should anything really important come up, I'll give you a ring at home or wherever you happen to be."

"Thank you, Harry," Nathan said with an expression of relief. "I knew I could rely on you."

Harry took a puff on his cigar and said pleasantly, "As always, dear boy. As always."

After the day's work Nathan returned home, showered, changed, and prepared for his appearance at the ethnic dinner. He had rehearsed and re-rehearsed his speech for weeks now examining every meticulous detail for double meanings or phases that could be taken out of context or misinterpreted. Nathan studied and prepared everything in only the way a member of the legal profession can.

Delivering the speech was an easy task for Nathan. Having been the veteran of many a courtroom skirmish or airing, passionate opinions was a skill he had well acquired. Speechmaking to a peaceful crowd was simplicity itself.

The ethnic gathering was held at the Sydney Town Hall. It was a meeting that had been organised by the Department of Immigration to show the enormous contribution that had been made to Australia by the wide variety of migrants from Europe and elsewhere.

To represent each group and nationality, traditional dances were performed. The Italians, as with the other migrant's, wore the traditional costumes of their homeland and performed the national dance, the Tarantella. The Greeks, complete with bazouki's, performed Zorba. This was then followed by representatives from Spain, who performed some particularly fiery Flamenco dancing. Then there were the Yugoslavs, the Dutch, the Swiss, the Lebanese, those from the British Isles, the Scots in full Highland regalia, the Welsh, the English and the Irish. There were also Hungarians, Czechoslovakian, Austrian, Maltese, French, German, Danish, Swedish and Sicilian. Every nationality it seemed had some representation. From the Pacific region there were islanders from Fiji, the Cook Islands, Filipinos and Samoans, and from South-Eastern Asia there were Vietnamese, Cambodians and Thai's. Such a huge mix of so many varied nationalities, religions and races that seemed to blend together that night in splendid harmony.

There were even the descendants of migrants in evidence such as the great-great grandchildren of Irish, Scottish and Chinese prospectors, who generations before had come to Australia to work on the Victorian goldfields of Ballarat and Bendigo, just another example of Australia's mixed heritage.

Also in attendance were the descendants of the first settlers, who had travelled to this great southern continent with the First Fleet in 1788. Nearly two hundred years after the colony's beginnings, many of the original settler's descendants had assembled, representing each of the square-riggers that had pioneered the founding voyage. They came as a family member of several generations before who had arrived on each of the eleven vessels: the *Sirius, Supply, Alexander, Lady Penrhyn, Charlotte, Scarboro', Friendship, Prince of Wales, Fishburn, Golden Grove* and *Barradale*. From those early beginnings the nation had progressed to a varied cosmopolitan and multicultural society.

It was a spectacular occasion. The meeting was addressed by the Minister for Immigration, who, prior to introducing someone of a particular nationality, spoke of the areas of life to which they had contributed. The distinguished guest nominated the arts, the theatre, the restaurant business, catering, the law, private industry evolving from risk-taking speculative entrepreneurs, consulting work, textiles, carpet design, the medical profession, notably in the area of research and explorative surgery, and sports where he seemed pleased to point out that many top Rugby League players and a few notable Boxing champions had names of an ethnic origin.

When it came to introducing the point where Nathan would deliver his speech, the speaker made mention of the fact that, in a world where there was much strife related to religious and sectarian differences, Australia was unique in the fact that on all of it's capital city councils, it's representatives had mixed-descent from all denominations and religious groups, including Protestant, Catholic, Arab and Jewish which was relevant in Nathan's case.

Nathan smiled to himself at the speaker's zest in describing how the Jewish people, who throughout the ages had been a race constantly downtrodden, rose again and again and showed a great penchant for survival. The Minister, obviously well versed in this subject, spoke of the Jews throughout the world; namely those who had fled Germany at the time of the rise of the Third Reich in Germany in the far off days of the 1930s, and Nathan felt his heart sink as this particular reference encompassed the circumstances of his early life. It set his mind racing for a moment and it was only the realisation that he would be called upon to speak at any minute that stopped him from drifting away on a cloud of memories. Nathan listened as he heard the guest speaker talk of the wide range of talents of prominent Jewish people, whose entrepreneurial skills in show business, finance, banking, commercial enterprise and the arts had made them worldwide names. It was at that point that Nathan heard the words introducing him to speak.

"Ladies and gentlemen, it is now my very great privilege to introduce to you, one of the most respected leaders of the Jewish community, a gentleman immensely regarded by his colleagues in the law profession, and admired and liked by many of his friends amongst the ethnic community of New South Wales. He is a man who has had a chequered life that began in Berlin, who was taken to Austria at the time of the rise of the Nazis in Germany during the 1930s, who began his working life in a kibbutz in what was then known as Palestine, and who served with the British Army as a volunteer in that country and in North Africa during the Second World War. After the war, he studied Law at London University before coming to Australia, where he has lived ever since, rising to prominence in the field of the Law, to directorship positions with several companies and whose service on many community committee's has proved to be invaluable. Men and Women of the migrant community, my fellow Australian citizens, may I present Mr Nathan Palmai."

To polite applause from the audience, Nathan strode from his chair to the front of the auditorium, feeling quite humbled at such an ebullient introduction. He looked at the entourage of mixed races before him and began his speech.

"When I was a young boy in an Austrian mountain village so many years ago at a time of rising concern in Europe, my father, who had taken my family from Berlin, expressed the hope that one day soon all lands would live in absolute harmony, regardless of race, creed, belief, denomination, political persuasion, religious belief. My father was not to live to see this hope realised. If he were here today he would be delighted that his son could live in a country like Australia where harmony amongst races can be found. Amongst my friends and acquaintances, I can number those of most nationalities, those of most religions including" – he paused before continuing – "those of Hindu, Muslim, Islamic and of my own faith. It is one of the great things that here in this land friendship knows no boundaries. We are a lucky land – a lucky people – to live in this country of a good and outgoing people, where our work and leisure can be enjoyed with equal enthusiasm. Perhaps I may sound to some of you that I am waxing lyrical. I do not deny that for one moment I am glad that I was given the opportunity to live here for it has been the making of me as a man. It was not the success of my life that benefitted me, it was the struggle and the hardship that I learned from. Meeting other migrants from different nations, those that I see before me tonight, opened my eyes and my mind to the contribution that a mixed population has made to the fortunes of Australia. In this land that encompasses so many professions – be they the trades of tradition, the sheep shearer, the miner of coal or mineral, the fishermen who traverse our coastlines, the jackeroo on the cattle stations and properties from Brunnette Downs to Haddon Rig, every boundary rider on a lonely outback trail, the oil drillers on our offshore stations, the executive in financial, commercial, technical engineering, architectural trades, and those on the factory floor or the bricklayer or the restaurateur – there has always been the feeling that even in the most difficult times, even in recession when unemployment and redundancy strike people of all ages " – Nathan raised his hand and clutched his fist as a sign of emphasis – "that we are being prepared to lay the foundations for even greater things to come. That there is at least hope here." He spoke with real optimism now. "That we at least have the chance to achieve, and to go on achieving. We are indeed privileged to be able to live here. Thank you all, ladies and gentlemen."

The huge audience in the Sydney Town Hall needing no prompting and burst into applause, for in Nathan's mention of various trades, every member of the meeting had felt that he had been talking to each of them individually and they had felt the pride swell up in their hearts.

At the end of what had been a stunning evening various people got together and shook hands. True to Nathan's statement that he had friends of diverse backgrounds, he found himself constantly shaking hands.

"*Theodorakis*," he said with genuine feeling as a Greek businessman, whom he had not seen for some time, clasped his hand. "*Yassou! Kah-Lees-peh-rah!* Tee-Kah-nis?" Nathan asked him in one of the few phrases of Greek he knew, "How nice to see you again, Theo," and then turning to someone else he said, "Come sta Mario?" asking politely in Italian to the proprietor of a pasta restaurant he was known to frequent. Not being totally without a sense of humour, he joked with a turban-clad friend of his originally from Calcutta, who worked as a physiotherapist. "Your headdress is more colourful than mine, Ali," Nathan said, referring to his own yarmulke he had worn. It had been a very warm and friendly evening and Nathan had felt genuinely happy when he returned home late that night.

★★★

The next day, a gloriously sunny Saturday, Nathan drove to the synagogue at Bondi Junction for the bar mitzvah of his godson, Nicky Hertzel. This too was a very warm occasion. Rabbi Jacob Presch, a man always beaming with joy at every family occasion, conducted his duties in such a way it always brought out the feelings of utmost joy or ecstasy.

The haunting thrilling voice of the cantor echoed throughout the synagogue, moving even the most unmovable, emotionally-stilted of people by its immense clarity. Nathan observed the looks of little Nicky's parents, David and Mira Hertzel, who gazed at their boy in loving adoration, not wanting to suppress their pride and love.

Nathan admired the beautiful women that existed in the Hertzel gathering. There were ladies with jet-black hair, sparkling eyes and clothes that matched, black skirts and jackets and dark shiny patent leather stiletto-healed shoes. The Hertzel men and friends were all bearded. In a moment of realisation Nathan stroked his chin gently, thinking to himself he should have worn a false beard this morning.

Gazing at the innocent young face of Nicky Hertzel, with the outside sunlight deflecting from the stained glass windows on the lad's serene composure, Nathan felt a sudden twinge of overwhelming sadness as he thought of his own youth in such different conditions. But that had been in a time of fear, confusion, prejudice and the prospect of a war.

So different for this boy; Nathan thought that Nicky was growing up at a time and in a land where one could be proud of their own faith and not be repressed or persecuted as the Palmai family living in the Germany and Austria of the 1930s had been. The years had marched on and things had changed, the moods and attitudes of the world had changed innumerably since the days of the frightening storm clouds over Europe. Young Nicky was a lucky boy, thought Nathan, but even more so, he had the best moments of his life to come.

After the ceremony friends and relatives gathered at the Hertzel's beautiful, but not extravagant, home in Drumalbyn Road, Bellevue Hill for the traditional reception.

"Thank you for inviting me, David. It has been a lovely day," Nathan said in a quiet aside to his friend. "Days like this make me reflect on how lucky we are. Thank you my friend."

"Not at all, Nathan. You're welcome at the Hertzel household anytime. Mira and I would be pleased to see you whenever and your godson, Nicky, looks forward to your visits, I know. Our door is always open to you. We know you get lonely. Tell me, have you ever thought of marrying again?"

Nathan laughed, genuinely amused. "At my age?"

"Why not?" queried David. "At your age, you ask. You still have life pulsating in your veins. Early sixties you may be, but you are young in spirit and still energetic. Still with much to offer a good woman."

"I had a wonderful marriage to a fabulous woman. I was so lucky to have had her love. I'm single, true, but I am not lacking in friends or company. My work on committees keeps me busy. My career in law has always been immensely satisfying and demanding. I am also a company director of a large enterprise. These things keep me occupied and, as for love, well, I only have to turn to friends such as you and your wonderful family for that. I am lucky."

"That may be so. The friendship and the comradeship is always there. It is the emotional warmth, the depth of real love that counts. Those private moments."

Nathan thought deeply for a moment before coming up with the right reply. "My marriage to Francine was all that. It could not have been bettered," he replied, with what appeared to be a reflective smile at the memories of such happy years. "It was Francine who gave me such support and love. When I was at my lowest ebb, in one of my *Oy Vei is mir* moods, she would bring me out of it and, when we were both happy, life was so wonderful. No, David, I will never marry again. I will be a happy man with the memories of such happiness." His eyes clouded momentarily. "Francine was truly wonderful."

The two men stood in silence for a short time before David acknowledged Nathan's comment with a smile and a nod of his head. David knew that Nathan's late wife had indeed been a rare gem. Francine's own life story would have made a great book.

★★★

Over the next few days Nathan's busy schedule continued. But the next day was going to be one in which he would relive much of his past life and indeed the lives of people who had been so important and influential to him throughout the years.

The next evening, Nathan arrived for the opening of a new kosher restaurant at Double Bay. After the usual introductory formalities and a cocktail party with kosher wine, the various guests made their way to the tables. Nathan was seated at one of the round tables and chatted amiably to the people alongside him. There were a mixed group of guests from all walks of society.

A drum roll from the band on stage signified an announcement was about to be made, and the people became silent as the compere came to the front of the stage and took the microphone in his hand. He was a well-known television personality who needed no introduction and the guests automatically applauded.

"Ladies and gentlemen," he began. Nathan thought to himself that he would be hearing those opening words quite a lot this week. "To open the cabaret of this newly opened kosher restaurant, distinguished guests will you welcome a professional dancing group from the Hakoa Apia Club of Bondi. Will you put your hands together for these wonderful dancers."

To enthusiastic applause the dancing group took the stage and performed in an acrobatic and energetic fashion. Nathan paused at this stage, in-between watching this very professional performance, to look at the people around him. Next to him a charming divorcee had been conveniently placed. In the audience he noted many prominent people, not only of his faith, but those who had shown a keen interest in it. There were members of the theatrical world, performers and entrepreneurs, a Labor MP, a Liberal MP, a noted historian and lecturer of Jewish affairs. Also in attendance was Bob Hawke, who would lead the Australian Labor Party to victory in the general election that year.

Nathan shook hands with a former Prime Minister, Gough Whitlam, who was an eminently newsworthy figure and of huge political stature, but was a warm and friendly man in person. Whitlam was a colossus of a figure in Australian history.

Nathan failed to notice the dark-haired beautiful woman who was gazing at him intently from a few tables away. She had strong commanding features, wore expensive glittering jewellery, and had a certain aura of warmth and presence about her. For a moment, if one had observed her closely, the look she was directing at Nathan resembled more of a surreptitious study. She had known Nathan long ago and her feelings towards him were those of warm affection.

The dancing group from the Hakoah Club performed traditional numbers that had the whole of the audience clapping and stamping their feet, before everyone in the restaurant decided that this was the time to join in. Nathan was enthusiastic and responded to the spirit of the evening, joining in throwing his arms up and loving every minutes of it. When the people decided to leave the dance floor and return to their tables after the number had finished, the dancing team stayed on demonstrating their abilities in Rock n'Roll, Swing, Jitterbug, Jazz and a few modern day numbers. They finished their act to a standing ovation and then the next act was introduced. The atmosphere that night was one of near nirvana.

This time a platinum-blonde Russian lady of the faith in a stunning sequined gown took the microphone. Well-known in cabaret and theatrical circles, particularly for her treatment of traditional Jewish songs, she sang in a beautiful rich tone, every word crystal clear, every note calculated to the finest degree and every chord strong and vibrant. Her voice control was as fine as a skilled musician's dexterity in playing an instrument.

To a hushed audience who were completely mesmerised, the words of 'My Yiddische Momma' drifted high into the air with only the spartan accompaniment of a piano and clarinet. Somehow the words of a popular song when sang by the right person, the phrases and notes enunciated to perfection, could always move people to their most emotional. Nathan always felt moved when he heard this song. He thought of his own mother, lost in memory, and a tear rolled from his eye. Such was the emotion engendered in her voice.

On conclusion of the song, the audience again gave a standing ovation and the compere announced that there would now be music for dancing. The band played a softer and easier style of music and couples, clinging tightly, swayed together. Courteously Nathan asked his date next to him to dance. They moved out onto the dance floor.

"I think that earlier bout of dancing wore me out," Nathan smiled at her. "They tell me you've recently been divorced. Is that a taboo subject?"

"No not at all," she replied. Her face had a sparkling gaiety about it. "I'm quite enjoying my independence and evenings like this. It's a pity I have to go soon."

"Oh," said Nathan, "So soon? It has been a pleasure to meet you tonight."

"Yes. I have two teenage daughters. I can't leave them alone too long. Perhaps I may see you again." She sounded hopeful. "I have enjoyed meeting you and talking to you." Nathan looked into her eyes. She was very beautiful; a lady in her mid-forties, who looked very much younger, she was a very bright and intelligent talker. "My name's Marguerite," she reminded him, "I'm afraid I shall have to go. You are a nice man, Nathan."

"I'll escort you to your car, Marguerite," Nathan said, and they left the restaurant. *So many attractive women in the world,* thought Nathan. He had wondered about his friend David Hertzel's words about remarrying. The music inside distracted him from his train of thought and he went back inside to his table.

"Ah, Nathan," someone said as he walked back to the table. "This is my new business partner, Abe Mathias. Have you two been introduced?"

"I don't believe so," he responded. "My very great pleasure to meet you, sir."

Abe thrust his hand out immediately. "I am delighted to meet you. I have heard so much about you. I heard your speech at the Town Hall. It was a fine speech."

"Thank you, Abe. I hope to see you again." Nathan smiled politely and made his way back to his table. All of his acquaintances were up dancing and Nathan sat alone at the table. He poured himself another glass of kosher wine. He did not see the women who had been gazing at him earlier approaching his table. Nathan sipped the wine gently and then heard a soft voice call out to him.

"Hello Nathan," she said, staring at him from a short distance away. He turned his head slowly, the voice from his past registering not only familiarity but a whole string of memories. He looked up at the woman hardly believing his eyes. "May I join you, Nathan?" she asked pleasantly. Her smile was encouraging.

"Of course," he stammered. At this point he stood up and embraced her and kissed her cheek. "Melissa – it must be over twenty years. I can't believe it."

Melissa sat down. For a moment they just sat quietly, each one waiting for the other to speak, until Nathan found the words that he was desperately groping for.

"Over twenty years. Must be close to twenty-eight years, I think. We haven't met since... I can't remember when. How good to see you, my dear friend."

"No, not since I went to Hollywood, Nathan," she said. "My, you look so well. You look handsome as ever – and you've done good things. I've read some of your work in community affairs and your work with the law. There were articles about you in the *Sydney Morning Herald* and the *Age* last week. I was most impressed. I saw you talking to Bob Hawke and Gough Whitlam tonight. You have come a long way. I believe you've been recommended for the Order of Australia."

"I've heard rumours of it. Nothing even remotely certain." Nathan said modestly. "You're a fine one to talk of my doing good things. I read the papers too. Mellissa, my dear, you've come a long way too. From those radio plays you used to appear in when you first came to Australia. Hollywood, the West End Stage, and Broadway. Twice nominated for the Oscar for best supporting actress. And now you're back here for a film?"

"Yes, all too briefly. And then back to Los Angeles to star in a new television series. I didn't know you were going to be here tonight. Believe me, it is good to see you." She had spoken very sincerely. "Tell me, is dear old Harry Masters still your business partner?"

Nathan nodded with a smile at her mention of Harry. Melissa had always liked him. Years before Melissa had acted with Harry in Melbourne. During the 1950s Harry had been a law student by day and an occasional radio actor.

"Dear old Harry. Still on his seafood diet, I expect. Eats everything he sees, no doubt." Melissa smiled at him. "You know, you're still one of my favourite people." There was a warmth in her voice, and in the last sentence was a hint of regret for a love and friendship that had once been very strong. Nathan knew that this conversation, with a woman who had once meant so very much to him, wasn't just an amiable chat. It was a build up to something more. "How is Francine? She's not here with you tonight?"

The question had come out of the blue and Nathan felt sadness engulf him for a moment before he answered.

His voice was low and tinged with sadness. "Francine died four years ago." He paused in reflection. "Cancer – I am sorry to say, and I miss her terribly. I loved her deeply."

"I didn't know, Nathan." Melissa looked disturbed by the news. "When my career took off and I went to Hollywood, and I married the first of my three husbands, I was so happy that you married Francine. I hoped for your sake it would last forever. I sometimes wonder how life would have treated us if we had married. A silly speculation, I know."

Nathan looked at her, realising that so much old ground was about to be covered. "I think our careers probably split us apart and probably would have done so in later years if we had married." He smiled at her, not wanting to sound too stern or as if he was condoning her. "Besides," he continued, "life has treated us both well, has it not?"

Melissa smiled politely. "Of course it has," she said gently. "Through my career I have travelled the world. It has been nothing short of exhilarating. I have met a lot of famous people, American Presidents, for example: Kennedy, Johnson, Nixon, Ford, Carter and Reagan. I have met the immortals of the screen and stage: Frank Sinatra, Judy Garland, Henry Fonda and Humphrey Bogart. I have performed on stage in Warsaw, Israel, at the London Palladium, Moscow, Tokyo, Las Vegas and so many other places. I'm happy in my career. My third marriage to Dick Allyson has lasted well. It's happy. Dick and I are content. I have great children. I could not wish for more. Dick is a good man."

"Dick Allyson?" Nathan remembered. "The bandleader?"

"Yes," Melissa answered. "We have a daughter of eighteen who will be going to the University of Hawaii. I also have a son of twenty by my second marriage. He lives in Florida though, and I only see him occasionally. He's training to be a civil airline pilot."

"And where is Dick? Is he here in Sydney?"

"No, he's still over in California at the moment. He and his band are just finishing a record album in the studios, but he should be here in a week or so."

Melissa looked at him warmly with what appeared to be a hint of a long ago love. In-between conversation they looked at the band playing and people dancing in the very packed restaurant. The atmosphere was one of affluent people who had worked hard but knew how to enjoy life without inhibitions.

Melissa oozed warmth and attraction. It was a mixture of emotions for Nathan to see her again. She had been the first real love of his life. Now a woman in her early sixties, with only a slight accumulation of weight around her hips and a few minor facial creases and lines, Melissa had aged well. She wore jewellery on her hands and expensive armbands with what appeared to be crystalline gemstones set in them. Her voice, like Nathan's, still carried slight inflections of her early Austrian/German background, although her diction and her mastery of English was impeccable. Once, a lifetime or so ago, Melissa had been the girl that Nathan had wanted to marry. It was hard to believe now she was an international film star.

Nathan had adored her, but he knew that as her career took an upward swing in the 1950s it would have been difficult to maintain a permanent relationship let alone to keep a possible marriage alive. To think this girl once worked with poultry on a kibbutz.

With Melissa's career taking her from radio plays to Australian films and eventually a Hollywood offer of a seven-year contract with one of the big studios, Nathan conceded that the relationship did not have a future. It was fortunate for Nathan; he was later to marry Francine to whom he would have a happy marriage until her early death.

Melissa had gone to Hollywood and begun a sparkling screen career. She had married three times. Her first marriage, to a matinee idol called Gary Markel, had ended in divorce after barely a few years. Her second marriage to a New York theatrical producer called Irvine Strasselki had produced a son, and also ended in divorce after a few short years. Melissa remarried once more, this time to a bandleader and film score composer called Dick Allyson. The marriage had endured happily for nineteen years.

Occasionally Melissa had come back to Australia, but this was the first time she had encountered Nathan on one of these journeys. Now, at least twenty-eight years after the last time they had seen other face to face, here she was again; someone with whom he shared so many memories of his past life with. She was still a proud Jewess, with her Star of David gleaming from beneath her dark two-piece suit, and as charismatic as ever.

"We've travelled a long road from Berlin, haven't we, Melissa?" Nathan asked her casting his mid back to their first meeting. "Who would ever have believed the progress of our journey?"

"A long way indeed, Nathan," she agreed. "Do you ever think back to those days? Do you ever dwell on the memories? The bitter-sweet years, the difficult years, and the good years."

"I often think back to those days." Nathan took a photograph from his wallet and showed it to her. "The older I get, the more I remember. That's my mother and father, Marlene and Arthandur Palmai. It's hard to believe that I last saw them in 1938. I still miss them so terribly."

"My parents, too. God knows how they suffered with the war and the concentration camps. Even now it affects me emotionally if I think too much about it. We are a passionate people, us Jews, passionate in our loves, our traditions and our causes, passionate in our professions – even in our business affairs. We are also protective towards our families. Perhaps the greatest passion of ours is for our families. From birth to bar mitzvah to burial, we love so deeply our kinfolk, don't we, Nathan?"

Nathan nodded his head in agreement and put his elbows square on the table, resting his head on his hands that were clasped together. He admired her eloquence and gave her a warm smile of acknowledgement.

"And our friends, and those we loved more than friends," Nathan added. He looked down at his watch quickly and then cast his eyes back to her. "Look, Melissa, it's a quarter to ten. We have so much to talk about. Would you like to come back to my home unit for a while? It's only round the corner in Darling Point, and it would be much quieter there than here."

She smiled and said, "Fine. Yes, that would be a good idea," and they left the noisy, crowded and smoky restaurant. There was so much they wanted to catch up on.

★★★

Melissa stood on the balcony of Nathan's home unit gazing at the lights of the Sydney skyline, while Nathan made some coffee. He came through to the lounge, adjacent to the balcony and put a tray down on a table. How stunning the city looked at night with the lights on the harbour bridge and the huge metropolis of glass and light from the skyscrapers in Sydney's central business district. In the distance, gently cruising along the harbour waters came one of the big white P&O cruise boats being guided by some tugboats. A gentle breeze sprang up in the air slightly ruffling Melissa's hair. She turned around and came inside. Melissa looked around at the antique furniture and a picture of Arthandur and Marlene Palmai with their young child Nathan taken in the 1930s against an Austrian Tyrol mountain backdrop. *Every picture tells a story*, she thought.

From the Austrian mountains to the harbour-side luxury of Sydney, and the span of years between those two places had covered much ground for Nathan. Melissa studied the lines of character engraved in the man opposite, now seated in the armchair pouring two cups of coffee. Melissa sat down and sank into the cosy warmth of the armchair and the security she had once felt with her old friend. Nathan had seen

Melissa examine the photograph and took a look at it himself. Even now it was evocative of another age.

It was an interesting photograph in a frame, yellowing with age, but still managing to capture the atmosphere of the time. Nathan's father, Arthandur, was tall and striking with almost smouldering features. His mother was so like the women in his life – Melissa, Francine, Marguerite – dark-eyed, dark-haired, with a stunning presence to match, but even in the photograph, warmth was evident in her lovely face. It must have hurt Nathan to look at the picture so many times and think of how their lives had come to an end.

"Yes, Nathan we have travelled a long road from Berlin," Melissa said, sipping her coffee and studying the books on Nathan's shelves. "Arthandur and Marlene were a beautiful couple. I can see where you get your looks from. What were they like? As people, I mean. In their characters and in the way they did things."

"Arthandur and Marlene? They were both devoted to each other. Father was a very strong man, both physically and mentally. Quiet but strong, intelligent and learned. Sometimes very witty. Mother was beautiful," He hesitated before saying the words of flattery, he had been looking for as an excuse to direct at Melissa. "She had the same kind of beauty that is so evident – in you for example – and she was warm. Deeply warm. That is what I remember about her so strongly. In all the years that have passed I still remember she never spoke ill of anyone or anything. I never heard her say deep, angry words, yet she controlled me as a boy; disciplined me without causing pain. I make no pretences to be vain or to sing my own praises, but if I have any qualities, then the finest have been inherited from my parents: Love, kindness, courtesy, to constantly learn. All great qualities."

"They sound such fine people. That photograph," Melissa nodded towards it, "that was taken in Austria? When your parents first moved from Berlin presumably?"

"Yes, in 1933. I was about eleven or twelve there. My father had always been wary of the designs of the future Chancellor, as far back as the Beer Hall Putsch in Munich in 1923. Arthandur's fears were only justified when a few years later *Mein Kampf* came out. From then on it was an inevitability that we would move. When the country became possessed by the Nationalsozialistiche Deutsch Arbeiter Partei and put them in power in 1933, we left. Arthandur and Marlene urged my aunts and uncles to go too, but they all felt it was a passing phase. A momentary phenomena. But no one could foresee the unspeakable horrors ahead. Most of them thought our move to Austria, first to Vienna and then a quiet mountain village, would be a mistake. They were right. As you know, the Nazis came in 1938. People of our faith lost their homes, their businesses. If both our parents had not sent us to Palestine more weeks – in my case a matter of days – before the Anschluss then perhaps we would not be here today. Arthandur regularly slipped into Berlin quietly. He worked with a Baroness, Baroness Christina von Harstezzen, to get people of our faith to other countries. Arthandur was one of the Companions of the Circle, at one time the deputy leader of that group. You remember that group of course?" Melissa nodded and smiled in response. "It's strange really Melissa how our lives can be affected by the spiral of events that happened long ago. I think the turning point of my family's life came in 1936 when my father was in Berlin at the time the Olympics were held." Nathan's thoughts drifted back to that time before the storms. He recalled that time in quiet tones that hinted at the sombre chapter it held in the world's history. "Europe was rather hedonistic in those days, wasn't it? Although there were changes going on all around, I would say. In the British Isles, for example, there were the effects of the Great Depression; many, many unemployed without work. In Spain there was the Civil War, Italy was going through changes with Mussolini – the Duce with his Fasci di Combattimento. Nowhere though, as you and I know, would there have been the wide-ranging changes that Germany experienced after the burning of the Reichstag. One would only have to have seen the crowds at Nuremburg to know that something chilling was in store in the coming years. My father, the Baroness Christina von Harstezzen, the Englishman Freddie Miller and their associates in the Companions of the Circle had much to do. I often think that the chance meeting between Freddie Miller and Arthandur in Berlin in that summer was so fatalistic." He looked at Melissa who was absorbing every word reliving an important time of her life too. "To my mind," Nathan continued, "Germany and Austria are not only far away in terms of miles, but those two countries in the 1930s, under the conditions that then applied, are like places beyond time and dimension. It is all so vivid, and the years since have been so full. Even now, I can still see so clearly the Berlin and the Austria of my youth." He appeared pensive. "Ah, those memories, those splendid memories." Nathan and Melissa could visualise the city as it was so long ago, steeped in the euphoria of the 1936 Olympic games.

It was no longer a warm night in Sydney, Australia, in the summer of 1983. Instead they were travelling back in time through painful and ecstatic memories to the city of Berlin in Germany over forty-seven years before and, as they spoke that night, remembering so many people who had been prominent in their lives and the incidents that had affected them, they could almost feel the times, the sounds and the atmosphere. The memories and the emotions once more came alive with such an overpowering vibrancy.

Two

1936-1939

Berlin, Germany, in the summer of 1936 had undergone a metamorphosis for its presentation of the Olympic games. There was an unbridled enthusiasm and nationalism about the city that had reached an amazing pitch. Chancellor Adolf Hitler had made no secret of his desire for a complete victory at the Olympics, both mentally and physically.

An abundance of overseas tourists, Olympic supporters, journalists and news camera teams had arrived in the city. The government of Hitler, fully aware that it would be the centre of the worldwide attention, saw this as the supreme opportunity to expound its propaganda to the limit. A few token Jewish athletes had been allowed to participate in the German team. This was merely a gesture; it was not in any sense a concession.

One of the visitors to Berlin that summer was an Englishman named Freddie Miller, who had come with a newsreel camera team to film the events. Before the games commenced he had spent some time as a tourist, walking around the city. Freddie was not a stranger to Berlin and had been there on several previous visits. This time he felt very conscious of history in the making, but the future on the horizon line had a worrying effect. He had studied the defiant looks of the military men who wore the swastika in proud arrogance. They were in stark contrast to the craggy, friendly faces of the flower sellers near the major railway station. The women of the city had a quality of beauty and allure that Freddie found enticing. Their very bearing and sense of fashion, preceded by a bow wave of perfume, constantly made his head turn. They walked with a confidence and independence for all to see.

Freddie Miller looked at the architecture of the fine old buildings; the character of Berlin engraved into every nuance of stonework. He strolled around the city that would one day be divided by a great wall into West and East sectors. Being an ardent student of history and always highly knowledgeable of places he visited in the course of his profession, Freddie took careful notice of every thoroughfare and colourful building he passed by. Gazing at the German State Library, he realised that inside Albert Einstein had formulated the theory of relativity. At Humbolt University, Karl Marx had once been a student. Further down the same avenue, Unter Den Linden, he rested his gaze on the imposing structure of the State Opera House, a reminder of the reign of the Legendary King of Prussia, Frederick the Great. All around him there seemed to be pages of history.

On the other side of Berlin where Freddie's hotel was situated there were just as many palaces and museums that indicated Germany's dynastic heritage. Each one had its own story of a prominent member of the hierarchy who had resided there at one time. Bellevue, constructed in 1785, was the palace where Frederick the Great's younger brother had dwelt. Grunewald belonged to the Elector Joachim II. Its Renaissance style architecture had been upgraded almost two hundred years after its original design to a baroque character.

For such an obviously beautiful city, a place where the ordinary Berliner was on the surface jovial and friendly, there was an undercurrent of tension. Soon, Freddie Miller thought, there would be events occurring here that would cause irrevocable damage. Many people to whom he had spoken both at home and here in Berlin had predicted that the 1936 Olympic games may be the last time that so many nations could participate in an athletic competition in peace and friendship.

Just the year before Freddie had visited Germany with a camera team to film the Nuremberg Rallies. To massed crowds and a display of military strength, Hitler had given a powerful and frightening oratory. Although Freddie could speak little German, the tone and emphasis of every syllable had come through with a terrifying effect.

Now, a year later, he was back and his fears were being fully realised. The people of Germany, convinced that Hitler was a messianic leader bringing the country back from being badly defeated in the 1914-1918 war and the Depression years, had responded to the hysteria of it all. They had allowed themselves to be swept along with it, not realising the terrible consequences their passions would engender.

At a pleasant outdoor cafe Freddie stopped to ponder things for a while. He ordered a cold beer in his amateurish knowledge of German and relaxed in his chair watching the people. The café was full that day: businessmen wearing Homburgs, fashionably dressed women, tourists with cameras, and a sprinkling of Nazi officers. Freddie gazed at the people and reflected on Germany's chequered history. It was curious how the present day cycle of events had evolved. From 500 BC a mixture of Germanic tribes had dwelt there. During the era of Charlemagne, the King of the Franks, it had become part of his empire that encompassed much of Western Europe. After Charlemagne's death in 814, Germany became a number of individual principalities. During the time of Saxon inhabitation, the territorial boundaries of Germany extended. Otto the First ruled the Saxon dynasty and became Holy Roman Emperor crowned by Pope John XII. In the centuries that followed, as Germany grew, there were many internal conflicts, some religious, some to do with boundaries. The Thirty Years War of 1618-1648 had one such divisive conflict that left the country in sectarian difference. In the early part of the nineteenth century the military aspirations of Napoleon Bonaparte led him to Germany where he dismantled the shaky Empire. But unfortunately further rifts were to develop in later years. Prince Leopold von Bismark was determined that the chief state Prussia should set the pattern for the rest of Germany. Under the Iron Chancellor's rule Germany entered Austria and France, gradually expanding a dominant rule. This manifested itself throughout the years as the wheels of industry turned and developed and the arms race grew with frightening pace. Then came the First World War in which Germany was defeated. It dissolved its Empire, and established the Weimar Republic. The Depression of the years after the war precipitated the rise of Hitler and once again aggressive territorial claims were being pushed that would almost certainly lead to another World War. To many observers it was clear that this was only a matter of time.

Freddie shuddered at the thought of it. He knew there were politicians abroad who were fearful of the things that were happening. For a moment Freddie thought of the words of a speech that Anthony Eden had made in Bradford, the year before: "There is a spirit of violence abroad in Europe today which bodes ill for the future unless all the restraining and responsible influences in humanity are brought to bear to check it".

"*Ist dieser tisch frei?*" A voice spoke to him suddenly. Freddie was lost in thought and raised his eyes to look at the person who had asked him in German if the table was free. He found himself facing a well-dressed man with jet-black hair, dark eyes and features that strongly indicated he was of the Jewish faith.

"Please feel free," Freddie replied in English, not knowing the words in the German language. The man smiled at him pleasantly, and ordered a coffee from a passing waiter.

"You are an Englishman, of course?" the man asked Freddie, revealing a well-spoken German-accented English. He stretched out his hand to Freddie.

"Of course," replied Freddie, taking the handshake.

"I always think of you English as a gentle race of people. Taking tea on green lawns; and playing polo and cricket."

Freddie's eyes sparkled in amusement. "I suppose that is the imagery one sees in the cinema. A very glossy picture – not the true portrait of the ordinary working man in the factory in Lancashire or the tin mines in Cornwall. We are a gentle people, at least until we're provoked and then we roar like hungry lions."

"What is your name, sir?" the man opposite him asked.

"I'm Freddie Miller," came the reply.

"And I am Arthandur Palmai. You are here for the Olympics?"

"Yes, I'm here to film them." Freddie noticed an interested look in Arthandur's eyes. "I'm a cameraman, I have my own newsreel team. I provide the direction and sometimes the commentary."

"You must be a busy man, Mr Miller," remarked Arthandur.

"I am constantly on the move. Wherever there is news, I have travelled. Even as far as India. I filmed Gandhi – a most remarkable man."

"I agree," Arthandur concurred. "I have great admiration for men of love and peace." He paused to sip his coffee. "Do you know anyone here in Berlin?"

"I have a lady friend here that I'm going to see," Freddie answered.

"Really!" a surprised Arthandur exclaimed. "Where did you meet her?

Freddie appeared reflective. "I was a British Army officer for many years. I did service in India, Saudi Arabia and Malta for much of those times. When I was in Malta I went to Paris on leave from time to time. I met her on one of those leaves. When I left the army I formed my newsreel team, and I have occasionally seen her on trips to Europe." Freddie's face took on a grave appearance. "I am trying to convince her to leave Germany, I have great fears for the future of this country."

"Your thoughts are an echo of my own, Mr Miller," Arthandur said, building himself to release a pent-up outlet now that he had an impartial audience.

"In some villages in this country, many people of my own faith, my kindred Jew, cannot buy milk or medicine. You know I love this country. I love its cultural history, the nation's passionate music, the great strides in industry and incredible progress in science and medicine. But the acceptance of Hitler and the enormous prejudices towards my race appals me. From the time of his rise in 1933 I have feared for Germany. I am a doctor. I took my family to a lovely village in Austria some years ago. All my patients are of my faith. And I feel that even there in seclusion our lives may not be as secure as we would hope!"

"You don't have to tell me, Arthandur," Freddie said reassuringly. "I filmed the Nuremburg rallies with my news team."

"You understand then. You too are concerned?" Freddie shook his head in reply.

"Do tell me though, Mr Miller, would the English rise up in the event of Hitler trying to build up his empire?"

"I'm still on the reserve of the army," Freddie replied. "There are many of us in England in the future possibility of any invasion who would be called up to defend our nation."

Arthandur looked deeply concerned. Freddie had been on the point of leaving, but now he felt inclined to stay. There was something about Arthandur that intrigued him; he was firm with his words and spoke with conviction.

"Mr Miller," Arthandur said after digesting Freddie's words, "perhaps your men and women may rise up. Your leaders though, why are they not more vocal in their criticism of the regime? I've heard talk of the British Bulldog spirit – defiant and independent – but why does it not rear its head when it is so badly needed to do so now?"

Freddie was wondering how such a quiet tourist walk around Berlin on a sunny day in July had become a political lecture in an open-air cafe. There was something impatient and a deep sense of concern about Arthandur. Freddie sought to reassure his acquaintance. He quite liked

Arthandur. Always an admirer of men with genuine compassionate causes, Freddie was in sympathy with him, but he was slightly suspicious of him, for he felt that there was more to Arthandur's character than the immediately obvious.

"It's true that the leaders of our government have not come out with as much condemnation as they could have. But there are detractors, believe me. There are men in our government who will be future leaders, people such as Winston Churchill and Anthony Eden. No one wants war. The last one was horrific enough. Oh yes, Arthandur, the critics of Germany's rulers are growing."

The two men got up from the table and walked down the street, chatting amiably about things. Before going to their various destinations, they stopped at a crossroads in the city. Arthandur took Freddie's handshake with a warm affectionate grip.

"It has been good to meet you, Mr Miller," he said sincerely. "I think maybe you are a man of compassion."

Freddie felt flattered although he was a modest man to whom criticism or praise hardly registered. He reached into his pocket for a pen and paper and wrote down the name and number of his hotel.

"And you, sir, are a man of concern. This is the telephone number of my hotel. I am here for a few days after the games. Perhaps we could have lunch together, will you call me?"

"Indeed," replied Arthandur, taking the note and then they went their separate ways.

Three

August 1st 1936 was the official opening of the Berlin Olympic Games. Arthandur sat in the stadium audience with so many people of mixed nationalities supporting their home countries. Next to him sat an American couple in dark sunglasses extolling the virtues of their Olympic team. On the other side a French couple enthused over their honeymoon trip so far. Arthandur understood every word, being fluent in that language.

Cinecameras were being moved into position at various points around the stadium to record the historic opening ceremony and Arthandur saw his friend Freddie Miller lining up his lens and shuffling into position.

At that very moment thirty thousand boys of the Hitler youth movement were on formation at the Lustgarten. A staggering display of how the Chancellor's influence had reached down to even the very young of Germany. It was a sight that cameramen and photographers recorded knowing a new chapter of history was being recorded. Chancellor Adolf Hitler, observing the sight from an open top car, was on his way to the stadium.

In the stadium the music of Handel and Beethoven, stirring in every note, built the audience to a feverish pitch. Freddie Miller and his news team swung their cameras to all points of the vast auditorium to capture the varied looks of the people. Arthandur sat in his seat, feeling uncomfortable and disturbed by the huge ovation the Germans gave to Hitler as he and his deputies took their seats. The swastika, the sign that had been on display in every Berlin shop window was now so evident in the audience.

Chants of, *'Sieg Heil'* constantly thundered throughout the crowd, arms were raised in that particular salute could be seen everywhere. The music of the 'Hallelujah Chorus', such a splendid piece of orchestration seemed oddly out of place amongst the propaganda and the pomp and circumstance of the occasion. The various competing teams walked or rather marched the traditional Olympic circuit with salutes varying as they passed the Chancellors box.

Hitler stood erect, firmly holding his arm out, never flinching as the teams of fifty-three countries walked past, the standard bearers of each team dipping their flags in courtesy. They were all there, from the Swedes to the Americans. The differing Olympic teams, clad in their respective colours, strode past with dignity, many refusing to respond to the Chancellor's salute and responding with their own rather than add a dignified verification to the Nazi regime.

The British, at their most upright and stiff upper lip, maintained their independence as ever. At the sight of his home team Freddie Miller called out to his fellow newsreel cameramen, "Come on, lads, there's our boys. Give 'em a cheer and some applause." Freddie began the 'hip-hip' of each hoorah and found many of the English spectators joining in on each of his calls. They were in much competition with the cries of '*Sieg Heil*' and a mixture of provincial Yorkshire, Mancurian and London accents could be heard singing 'Land of Hope and Glory'.

There were members of the military everywhere, many of whom were there for no other reason than nationalism. 600 men and women, all clad in the white of the German team, marched past, the swastika dipped by the standard bearer to a tumultuous response from the Germans in the audience.

Arthandur Palmai watched in dismay. Freddie Miller recorded through his camera lens the whole scene. He was not so much dismayed, but utterly fascinated and intrigued that one figure could command so much power and sway a crowd to such levels. The American couple who were sitting next to Arthandur felt moved to comment.

"Gee, honey, that guy has one hell of a hold over the crowd," the man said to his wife in an audible voice. The Chancellor went through the motions of formally declaring the Berlin Olympic Games open. Thousands of pigeons were released as a symbol of peace and they flew upwards.

The Olympic flame was taken down the steps of the stadium by a single runner to the refrains of the 'Hallelujah Chorus', and he then ran a complete circuit of the auditorium. With the flame taken to the appropriate point to blaze as a beacon for the duration of the games, the official opening ceremony was now complete.

August 2nd 1936, the first competitive day of the games. Arthandur was again amongst the spectators and Freddie with his newsreel team. It had been an exciting day with the audience in full cry for their home teams. Already some of the featured athletes, although they didn't realise it, were on the crest of becoming immortals in the history of the Olympics. Arthandur in his youth had been a sprint runner and was naturally interested in the track events. Being of a razor sharp mind one point had stuck in his thoughts.

Several of the leading athletes were African-American. Realising Hitler's strong prejudices, Arthandur pondered with fascination how the Chancellor, so unshakeable in his beliefs, would handle the presentation of a gold metal to one of them should they win. It was more than a distinct possibility. The outstanding abilities of Ralph Metcalfe, Cornelius Johnson and Jesse Owens made them a force to be reckoned with.

The test came on the third day. It had been raining before the semifinals and the track was heavy. There were no starting blocks, which made it difficult for the runners to get their secure footing. It began to drizzle slightly and then for about ten seconds the rain was extremely heavy, not exactly helpful to the those in the racing in the 100 metre sprint, which would be run so much better on a hard track. Then the runners took their positions. The man at the starting point raised his starting gun, uttered the words of commencement and then fired.

Arthandur leaned forward in excitement. The sleek black athlete, Jesse Owens, had taken the lead over his nearest rivals, Metcalfe, Whitehead, Stormberg, all unable to keep the pace. In Arthandur's heart he was hoping that Owens would storm home. The normally placid Arthandur found himself bouncing up and down in his seat shouting, "C'mon, Jesse!" along with all the Americans and as Owens shot through the finish line in first place, he laughed happily. Arthandur jumped up and down and, with his right fist clenched, he raised it in victory. He could not help but look at the Chancellor's box.

A modest man despite his enormous athletic talents, Jesse Owens made a short speech followed by the playing of the American National Anthem and a wreath was placed around his neck. He was given the gold metal for his achievement in the 100 metres.. Jesse Owens was now an Olympic champion.

The reaction to the win by Owens became evident later on. Owens,

Metcalfe and Osendarp were presented to Chancellor Adolf Hitler; however, it became abundantly clear that Hitler wasn't going to make any concessions. Instead of showing any display of courtesy, Hitler turned his back on Owens and Metcalfe and spoke only to the Dutchman, Osendarp, The event brought a sourness to the Olympics.

Jesse Owens' talent knew no bounds and the next day he was to break even more records. Not only could he sprint, but he was a competitor in the broad jump. On his first attempt he cleared a remarkable 25 feet 9¼ inches. If that had not been an achievement enough, on his second jump he bettered it by clearing 26 feet 1½ inches. There was only one jump left. Owens soared to legendary status when he successfully defeated his opponents clinching a convincing victory by setting a record in the broad jump of 26 feet $5^{1}/_{3}$ inches.

When it came to the presentation, Jesse Owens' opponent put his arm round him and congratulated him on the achievement. Neither of them, standing on the platform while the United States national anthem played, gave the Nazi salute – yet another blow to the German Chancellor.

During the course of the Olympic Games another African-American athlete, Cornelius Johnson, in addition to Jesse Owens and Metcalfe, had been snubbed by Hitler. His actions had not been ignored by the Olympic committee, they felt compelled to reprimand Hitler for only congratulating the German athletes. The end result was that Hitler refused to meet anyone at all.

Strangely enough it was those very actions that compelled many of the German athletes to make friends with their counterparts. Owens went on to become a four-time Olympic champion, which included an outstanding performance in the 400-metre relay. With the possibilities of a war not so far away, many of the athletes had joined hands in friendship with their opponents of the other nations, for it was clear that this may be their last chance to do so. The Second World War was tragically only three years away.

Then after the competition, the gold medals, the tears and the exaltation, the pride and the nationalism, and the demonstration of international athletic skills, the controversial 1936 Berlin Olympic Games came to its final conclusion.

The closing ceremonies, every bit as grand as those that opened the games, signalled almost a sadness poignant in the parting of friendships.

A total of fifty-three countries marched the circuit of the stadium. The standard bearers of those countries dipped their flags as they passed the Chancellor's box. A trumpet sounded as darkness fell over the stadium. It echoed into the memories of the many people who had been privy to the event, including Freddie Miller faithfully recording the events on his cinecamera and Arthandur Palmai from his seat in the stadium analysing the whole thing in detail. The Olympic flame was extinguished and the Olympic flag was lowered by the Marathon Gate. The games were officially over.

★★★

It was in a beer hall a couple of nights later that Freddie Miller and a couple of his news team colleagues had their first time off for relaxation that they had managed to grab for a few days. Freddie looked around him with a cameraman's study of people. The looks on people's faces always intrigued him. There were people of all ages enjoying themselves in a smoke-filled tavern where cigarette smoke spiralled around, and the smell of beer and of a crowded place full of too many people permeated throughout.

A German band on stage struck up a rousing beer drinking song and soon the whole of that tavern joined in enthusiastically, banging their steins on the table in time with the music. Freddie and his two colleagues sat quietly watching the people. When the band had finished and the audience had applauded, the conversation that had been interrupted was resumed.

"Wonder if it'll last, Freddie," a cockney colleague of his mused.

"By the looks of these people it will," said Freddie, noting in his mind's eye how much support the people around him had given the singers on the stage. The other colleague, a quiet voiced man from Yorkshire, leaned across the table and came into the conversation.

"We've just about finished here now, haven't we? I mean, we've filmed the whole lot really, from opening to closing ceremonies. We have filmed the city, the people and interviews. We've cut, spliced and edited all the film we've had. We could go home now, couldn't we, Freddie? Nothing much more, is there?"

Freddie sighed gently. "Not for you, lads. At least not until our next assignment in Spain. You can all go home for a while, if you like. I'll be in touch with you. I'm going to stay here for a bit longer. I've got a couple of people to see."

Freddie thought instantly of the girl he wanted to see. The music started up again from the band, this time just an instrumental of a popular romantic melody. The tune seemed to match the mood of his thoughts. He thought of a tall, slim blonde whom he had met in Paris so many years ago when he had been a younger, impressionable army officer. There had been many rendezvous since that first meeting. They had danced together in top London nightclubs. They had swum in the warm blue water of the Mediterranean bordering the coasts of France and Spain, and walked in the sun in romantic places such as Pamplona, Biarritz and Andalusia. On their next meeting Freddie was going to make a big decision: he was going to ask her to marry him.

Returning to his hotel that night, he was walking through the lobby when the desk clerk called out to him very sharply, *"Herr Miller! Einen Augerblick! Wir maben einen telefonanruf fur sie von Herr Arthandur."*

Freddie stopped in his tracks to try and interpret the message. It was a telephone call from Arthandur of course. He took a slip of paper from the porter and noted the telephone number, which he promptly proceeded to ring from a nearby phone booth. Arthandur replied and the two made arrangements to meet later in the week. Both had commitments they needed to attend to.

For Arthandur it was the fruitless task of trying to convince his numerous relatives in Berlin to leave Germany. Despite his pleas they somehow remained convinced that the current euphoria would soon pass.

The next evening Freddie prepared himself for his big moment. Tonight he would propose marriage to the German girl, Tillie he had long harboured such strong feelings for. He gazed at himself in the full-length mirror. He was not a man given to vanity but was given to wondering how well he held his thirty-one years. Freddie stood just under six feet tall. He had fine, well-conditioned mid-brown hair and clear eyes but distinct signs of an interesting tiredness lined his high cheekbones. He was graceful, not muscular in build or light in physique, probably just about the right stature for his height and weight. His chaotic lifestyle in recent years had not been beneficial for good health, although in recent times he had made a genuine effort to temper some of his less healthier habits.

He put on a chequered sports jacked, pulled his tie into the shape of a Windsor knot and on his head he placed a broad, creased hat that gave him the air of a man around town. Then he made his way across to the other side of Berlin where the girl that he had thought he loved, lived alone and would be surprised at his unexpected visit.

Tillie Kern lived in a large apartment block. At thirty-five she was a girl of independent means; she was educated at the Sorbonne, fluent in four languages and strong in spirit and stubborn at heart. Freddie was probably more infatuated with her than in love. If he had been a little older and a little wiser, he would have been able to clearly distinguish the difference.

The apartment block was just an average home. It was not gaudy, nor cheap, and not on the other side of the scale ostentatious or luxurious. The area of Berlin that the block was situated in was respectable and middle class with pleasant parkland close by.

Freddie did not take the lift up to the third floor apartment. He walked slowly, deliberately. The block was obviously badly soundproofed: From one flat, he could hear the music of Mozart bring played very loudly, in another, the sound of Hitler's voice, echoing from a radio broadcast, came though. Then he came to Tillie's flat. He raised his hand to knock, hesitated, and then gave two loud knocks. In the pause that followed, he took his hat off and held it to his chest.

The sound of someone inside scurrying around could be heard. Then the sound of a latch being drawn back came swiftly after the unlocking of the door. Freddie found himself staring at the object of his attentions between the door and a chain attached to an inside lock.

"Hello, Tillie," Freddie said gently, smiling with real affection at her. A look of surprise registered in her attractive brown eyes. "I'm here for a short visit. I hope you didn't mind me calling."

"Freddie?" she queried. Tillie rubbed her eyes sleepily. "I've just woken up. I went to sleep early." She undid the latch in her apartment and opened the door to reveal a pleasant, liveable abode. Tillie was wearing a nightdress and looked attractive in a daring sort of way. She had long blonde hair, the rose complexion more affiliated with English girls and gentle clear white skin. She stood tall and slim. It was her eyes that were the most captivating feature about her. They seemed to gleam and flicker with a touch of humour.

"My darling, I am so surprised to see you." Tillie put her arms around Freddie and kissed him. She stepped back, looked at him and smiled. "How good to see you. Let me get you something. A glass of wine perhaps?"

"That would be nice, thanks, Tillie," Freddie replied. While Tillie went into the kitchen Freddie looked around the apartment, noting the position of the settee and armchairs, the paintings on the wall, the wireless set and a few dolls placed strategically at different points around the room.

Tillie came back into the room and handed a glass to Freddie. "Take a seat, Freddie. Obviously you're here for the Olympic games?"

"Yes, I've a lot of newsreel filming to do," he answered, removing a doll from the armchair to sit down. He smiled as the sight of it brought back memories. "I bought you that one in Biarritz."

"Pamplona," Tillie corrected him. "You ran through the streets with the bulls."

"That was a wonderful leave," Freddie recalled with pleasure. "You still have a passion for collecting dolls." Unwittingly he was furthering the conversation away from its original target.

"Yes, Freddie. We had so many wonderful times together. Whenever you were on leave it was so good to spend time with you travelling through Europe. I remember when we used to drive along those country roads and we would stop at a café or a vineyard." She lit a cigarette and inhaled, blowing out a ring of smoke. Even when she smoked a cigarette she did so with a seductive manner. "Freddie, I know this is strange, I almost sense you are here for a reason."

"How perceptive you are!" Freddie exclaimed. There must have been tell-tale signs about him that gave the true meaning of his visit away. "Tillie, I've known you since 1930. I'm sincere when I say that I have always had strong feelings for you." Tillie looked perturbed. "I've decided that after six years of knowing you, that perhaps it's time for me to—"

"Freddie!" Tillie interrupted. It was as if she had anticipated what he was about to ask. She could almost sense he was about to propose marriage.

"Let me finish, please," Freddie persisted, determined to finish the task he had set himself. "I've loved you for a long time. I am in a good financial position. I own the newsreel team. It's been very successful latterly. Tillie, would you come to England with me, and – and would you marry me?"

"Would I marry you?" she repeated, aghast.

"I didn't mean to shock you," Freddie said almost apologetically. "I thought I would come straight to the point rather than beat around the bush."

"You have certainly shocked me. Freddie, it's been some months since we last met." The alarm bells rang inside Freddie's mind. He knew she was going to refuse him. "We have always been good friends, nothing more. I liked you a lot and I know we had our romantic times. I never thought of you as a potential husband."

"Don't spare my feelings. Say what you have to say," Freddie said with obvious disappointment.

"We are so different, you and I. You have a love of travel and a very busy life. I have rarely seen you this part year. Besides, Freddie, in the past few months something has changed in my life."

Tillie had spoken in slightly sombre tones almost preparing Freddie for what he had fully expected.

"You've met someone else?" He said quietly, trying hard to maintain a show of grace.

"I am involved with someone," Tillie replied, her words spaced evenly and coldly.

Freddie seemed resigned to what had happened in the long periods between times when he had met Tillie. "I guess I'm not surprised really," he said matter of factly. "It was silly of me to think that I could court you at intervals of several months."

"Can we still be friends, Freddie?" Tillie said in a humbling tone, taking his hand for reassurance.

"For as long as you like," Freddie answered in a quiet voice that could not hide his disappointment. "I wish you well." He stood up suddenly. "I must go, Tillie." Hurt was clearly evident in his eyes. He strode quickly to the door and then turned around. "Are you going to stay here in Germany?"

Tillie rose from her chair to open the door for Freddie. She looked at him quizzically. "Of course I am. This is my home and I think the future here now holds interesting developments. This is an exciting time to be a German."

Freddie looked down at the floor for a moment then he raised his eyes to face Tillie square on. "It's such a misguided notion to think the future under your present leader bears good." He paused to study her reaction. Tillie's face was just blank and expressionless. "Perhaps we are so different," Freddie said repeating her own words. He left quickly.

He felt very despondent as he travelled back through Berlin that night to his hotel. He sat in the tram thinking about Tillie. He remembered the time he had first met her. Tillie had always possessed a coolness and sophistication about her that appealed to Freddie greatly. She was also a passionate woman, enticing, sensual, yet combining these characteristics with an above average intelligence. Freddie felt at a loss to understand why his relationship with Tillie had not blossomed in to a happier ending. He was surprised, too, that a lady of Tillie's strong will and independence could support the government of Hitler. Freddie felt bitterly disappointed and sad that his judgement about Tillie had not been sound.

Originally after the end of the Olympic games, Freddie had intended to have a few days rest before preparing for his next assignment to Spain where Civil War was erupting. His schedule there would be hectic and dangerous. He wanted to luxuriate in the relative peace and security of freedom from responsibility, even if only temporary; however, after a chance meeting in the lobby of his hotel with a German journalist closely allied to the Nazi party, Freddie was given the opportunity to film at a function that Hitler would actually attend.

Freddie felt personally inclined to give the event a wide berth, but, realising it would be a first rate scoop in journalistic terms, he reluctantly accepted the invitation and geared up several members of his newsreel team into action.

It was a strange feeling to be at the centre of such an event. Filming the Olympics had been dramatic enough. this particular function was a real close-up of the awesome power of the German dictator whose presence seemed to tower over a huge banquet room of specially invited guests. Amongst them there were many of the German Olympic athletes, the hierarchy of the Nazi party and an assortment of lavishly dressed ladies. Disliking intensely being at this reception Freddie wished that he could be somewhere else. He had a job to do and he continued focusing his camera.

The room was filled with some of the leading national figures on which Freddie concentrated the lens of his camera. Filming was a difficult task. Freddie considered that the general public viewing cinema newsreels did not realise that filming was a great skill; a blend of the arts and sciences. Whenever, Freddie embarked on an assignment he always attempted to capture in each frame of every reel simple human mannerisms, expressions, reactions, responses and the effects that situations create.

Freddie swung his camera in the direction of the doorway as the German Chancellor made a carefully staged-managed entrance. Under a significant close-range camera study, Hitler seemed an unremarkable figure. The applause that the German leader received was near deafening. It was frightening that he could engender such support. When Hitler spoke to his audience, the rhetoric, persuasive and powerful in its influence, was explosive in every phrase. Freddie had been at Nuremburg and had seen the power of the oratory there. He was seeing it again at its most awesome. Somehow he would let the camera lens capture the story: the reactions, responses and the effects.

The men at the banquet were introduced to Hitler one by one, bowing cordially and shaking his hand. The women made curtsies to Hitler and he in turn responded in an unprecedented show of diplomacy by kissing their hands. Expressions now, thought Freddie, adjusting his camera lens for a long shot on to the face of one woman stepping forward to be presented to Hitler. Freddie's heart missed a beat. It was Tillie Kern.

Just as quickly Tillie stepped back and sidled up to a Nazi officer. Freddie, in fascination, continued focusing on Tillie. Then to his dismay he saw the girl he loved, wrap her long bejewelled fingers around the hand of the officer.

Despite his shock and a feeling of betrayal, Freddie continued to film the event. A little later many of the guests, including Tillie and her officer beau, took to the dance floor. Aware of the camera Tillie swung round and faced the full onslaught of the camera lens. It was at that precise moment that Freddie raised his face from behind the viewing point to look at her.

Tillie, stunned by Freddie's presence, released her grip on the officer and stared back at him. The two looked at each other, recalling how much they had once meant to each other. After a few minutes of bewilderment and appraisal, Tillie began to dance again with her partner. Her face looked blank and cold, her eyes steely in their gaze.

This time Freddie just stood and watched. His feelings of dismay and sadness were indescribable. The evening had certainly been a revelation.

Four

Freddie spent several more days as a tourist in Berlin that summer. They were pleasant leisurely days spent walking in the park, going to museums and concerts just like any other overseas visitor. The thought of Tillie Kern constantly occupied his mind. Somehow he would try and forget her. At the moment it hurt, but Freddie was not given to dwelling on romances that did not come to fruition. It was strange but his social conscience troubled him more. He felt great concern at many of the things he had seen in Germany on this trip. The direction that the country was taking could only in time affect the rest of Europe.

In a pleasant area of parkland, Freddie sat on a bench watching some happy children playing with toy boats on a lake. With so much drum beating and continual propaganda flooding the newspapers and airwaves, Freddie was given to wondering how it would influence these children growing up in Berlin in future years. He thought about it in great detail for a long time.

Arthandur Palmai joined Freddie for lunch in the outdoor restaurant of a tavern during the same week. The two men conversed on a wide range of subjects for much of the afternoon. Arthandur was a sympathetic, compassionate man and a good listener; he was also an amusing man who could tell jokes and anecdotes, often against himself. He was in his forties, a man with a rich mellow voice, and someone who was very expressive and demonstrative in his affections for others. In so many ways Arthandur was quintessentially Jewish. He bore all the finer traits: love of his family, a sincere dedication towards his profession and a firm commitment to his faith.

During the course of the afternoon the conversation took on a more serious note. Arthandur and Freddie had talked about their lives in their respective homelands. One thing that came across so abundantly clear was the immense love Arthandur had for his family. The way he spoke made it seem as if the prime reason for Arthandur's existence was his family.

"My family mean everything to me, Mr Miller," he expounded. "It is their future as much as my own that concerns me. I have a son, his name is Nathan and he is fourteen. Very mature for his age. My wife, Marlene, and I have discussed his future. We would like him to go to Palestine on an agricultural scholarship when he is sixteen to work on a kibbutz. Marlene and I, we think that maybe we will follow him later."

"I see, and your son Nathan is at school in Austria?" Freddie was genuinely interested.

"No. In our small village community there is not an established school as such. Most of the people in my village are all of my faith. My wife, Marlene, was a schoolteacher in Berlin. She gives Nathan private tuition at home as well as the children of our friends. Marlene is fluent in English and French, as I am. Our son, Nathan, can already speak English quite well. Marlene's influence on him has been good. She loves classical music, you know. Bach, Strauss, Wagner and Mozart. Her appreciation of music has passed on to our son. I am pleased that he has developed well at such an early age."

"Your life seems to be very independent from what is actually happening here. What brought you back here, Arthandur? Was it purely the Olympics?"

Arthandur looked at him with a wry smile before answering. "I did have a motivation, I must be honest with you in that respect. I am deeply concerned about my relatives here. I have many of them, cousins, aunts and uncles. And I have plenty of friends here too. I am trying to convince them to leave Germany. Do they listen to me? No! They say to me, 'Arthandur, it won't last. It will pass soon'. I argue with them constantly. Something terrible is going to happen here, Mr Miller. I feel it in my bones."

"You and I both have the same feelings, Arthandur. The lady I visited here was someone I've known for years and who a few days ago rejected my proposal of marriage. I feel that the hypnotic influence of this almost daily propaganda has affected most people. Even her. I do not like the prejudices shown towards your people. Sometimes I wish there was something I could do either as an individual or even in my role as a newsreel cameraman."

Arthandur leaned back in his chair and stared straight at Freddie. He quickly flickered his eyes to the left and right as if to ensure that no one else was listening and then he leaned forward and spoke in hushed tones.

"This may surprise you, but there is something you could do. Forgive me for speaking so quietly. I am wary of possible eavesdroppers."

"How can I help you?" Freddie murmured, aware of the sincerity in Arthandur's voice.

"My visits to Germany are not just purely to persuade my relatives and friends to leave here. I have another mission in life too." He paused as the waiter came over to fill up their glasses. When the man had gone, Arthandur continued. "I think it might be a good idea for me to talk to you in quieter surroundings."

∗∗∗

In the privacy of Freddie's hotel room Arthandur expounded the details of a cause he was personally committed to. Freddie was astounded. He could not believe just what he was listening to.

"I have a friend here in Germany – a Baroness. We are working together with various hand-picked contacts in Europe. Our aim is to establish links in other countries for the Jewish people who may wish to leave here. Hitler will surely push into other countries if he is not stopped. Almost certainly he will take Austria, move on into Hungary, Poland, France, and he will not stop there. Then I feel the lives of Jewish people will be threatened across the continent. This is not wild speculation, Mr Miller. Naturally, the organisation we have founded is known only to a few and works under a code name. If war begins we would also be able to act as a resistance group with the emphasis on transporting many of my faith to safety. We are attempting to save lives from persecution. In peacetime we need to found a network of reliable people, sympathetic to our plight, who could help us."

Freddie looked startled. At first he felt inclined to dismiss it out of hand as some enormously ridiculous clandestine scheme. He could not believe that a man he had only met casually some days before was now imparting such details of an intricate nature to him.

"Why have you told me of such things, Arthandur? You only met me a short time ago. This organisation you speak of sounds like something from a fiction writer's pen."

"My group is seeking to establish a wide circle of sympathisers who can lobby their governments to bring pressure to bear on the Third Reich. We need people who can act as sponsors for refugees. If you are unable to help us, Mr Miller, we could simply forget we ever met."

Freddie looked up sharply. "Don't write me off quickly, Arthandur." He poured them both a cup of tea. "I must think deeply about it. I have a deep social conscience. From my early days as an army officer to the present time as a newsreel cameraman, I have always been interested in causes that champion the underdog and the minority."

Arthandur smiled warmly at him. "Believe me it is an important cause. As to the role you would play the Baroness would be able to advise you. I am leaving for my home in Austria soon. She has an estate near the border. Would you like to come with me? I could introduce you to her."

Freddie nodded, He was not sure exactly what he was letting himself in for but at the moment, there were so many things clouding his mind. Somehow he felt prepared to throw caution to the wind. The next day Freddie and Arthandur proceeded to the Baroness's estate.

The drive was long and Freddie sat back enjoying the view. The day was grey and rain was beginning to fall in fine droplets. He looked at the people working in the fields and at the pleasant countryside around. It was going to take a while to get to the Baroness's estate, where Arthandur had told him was actually situated in a lush agricultural area. The crops for the harvest that would yield wine were nurtured there. Freddie, always a connoisseur of a bottle of fine wine looked forward to the arrival with the thought of his palate sampling a deluxe vintage.

It was interesting for Freddie to note that there had hardly been a car on the road that day. The only moving vehicle he had sighted had been an itinerant horse-drawn gypsy caravan slowly clip clopping towards its destination.

After an overnight stay at a country hotel, they continued their drive. They approached some winding hillside roads. After a drive through much undulating countryside Arthandur pulled the wheel of the car tightly as he drove the car on to a narrow road. Up in the hills could be seen a huge brick and stone edifice. Freddie was quite unprepared for what he saw. It was a castle. Its imposing structure was like something out of Plantagenet times. Gazing at it one would have almost expected knights of an old English tale to come galloping out on huge white steeds in bright shining armour with all the valour and strength to protect a Princess in a secluded fortress.

"That's it!" cried Arthandur exuberantly. "That is where the Baroness lives."

Beyond the castle were some attractive rolling hills. The sun played off the domes and turrets of the castle as the car wound its way up a spiralling road. By now Freddie was feeling very tired from the journey and stifled a yawn. He was impressed by the size and grandeur of the monstrosity. To an Englishman of a modest upbringing, old buildings, mansion houses, stately homes, castles, were all part of a history he had been educated with. When Freddie was a child his parents had taken him to the Royal Pavilion at Brighton and to Windsor Castle near London, both highly impressive structures steeped in history, with stained glass windows and the bric-a-brac of another age. Now he was about to visit a German castle. For a moment Freddie began to consider just what he had let himself in for coming on this journey. What private world of secrecy, intrigue and espionage was he about to be admitted to?

Freddie looked on in awe as Arthandur moved the car forward into the enormous grounds surrounding the castle. Behind them the vast extent of the estate could be seen. The car began a long drive up a spiralling road and very soon they were parked outside the building. Freddie leaned forward in the car, gazing through the window. Arthandur eyed him in amusement. His new English friend was obviously impressed, even amazed!

"Come, my friend," Arthandur said softly, and the two left the car. Arthandur handed over the keys to a servant who got into the car and drove it round to another side. Once in the interior of the castle, Freddie and Arthandur were greeted by a butler, who led them to a huge drawing room adorned with trophy heads on the walls, a library of books – most of them with red velvet covers and golden manuscript paper. There were maps and charts on the walls, paintings of another age in mahogany frames, a pair of crossed muskets over a doorway and a set of shields that would have made an interesting study in heraldry.

The butler beckoned to Arthandur to come with him, but motioned to Freddie to stay in the room. Shortly afterwards the butler returned, obviously well-rehearsed in this routine, bringing with him a tray of sandwiches, some cakes, coffee and a small bottle of wine. The butler also handed Freddie some newspapers, indicating that it would be some time before he met the Baroness.

Eventually after half an hour the butler came back. He spoke in German to Freddie which he in turn understood to be the invitation to join the Baroness and Arthandur. They walked along a narrow corridor to a room with big arched double wooden doors. The butler opened them and with a sweep of his hand told Freddie to go inside.

At a long highly polished fine wooden table with silver candelabra positioned at evenly spaced intervals sat Arthandur with a striking woman of a Nordic appearance. She rose to greet Freddie and stretched out her immaculately gloved hand, which he received in a gentlemanly fashion.

"I am" – she paused to glance at him from top to bottom – "Baroness Christina von Harstezzen."

Her voice was a mixture of a Swedish-German dialect. She was slim but well rounded beneath a long gown. She looked every inch the epitome of a European Baroness. Freddie was aware that the mind behind those blue eyes was working hard in analysing his suitability for her organisation. The Baroness, Freddie considered, was not a woman to be underestimated. First impressions on meeting people, he thought to himself, are often illusory. He considered that beneath her soft beauty lay strong character.

Freddie sat down at a table next to Arthandur, facing the Baroness. She lit a cigarette in a long holder and moved into the first stage of her analysis of Freddie.

"Arthandur has told me about you in great detail, Mr Miller. You are an ex-British Army officer. Still on the reserve, I have been led to understand. May I ask you in which capacity did you serve?"

"I was an intelligence officer," Freddie replied. He noticed that his inquisitor cast a swift glance to Arthandur, almost suggesting that this was of positive interest to them. "In the event of war I would almost certainly be called up. I served in Malta, India and Arabia."

The Baroness appeared to be interested, although she was already well versed in Freddie's history from her discussions with Arthandur.

"And I understand you are a newsreel cameraman? You have filmed all over the world, everywhere from Nuremburg to Rome. Generally where news takes place, Mr Miller. And there is a lot of news these days, is there not?"

"Most eloquently put, Baroness," Freddie said, with a smile at what an obviously retentive memory she had for detail. "Arthandur has obviously told you to the finest degree my life history. I understand that I could be of aid to you in your assistance to future refugees. In what way I am yet to be fully advised." Freddie turned to look directly at Arthandur for some reassurance that he had not been misinformed or misinterpreted the conditions of the role he was going to carry out. "Arthandur has told me that you are expanding a group of selected helpers, who can help the Jewish people in the future,"

Baroness von Harstezzen revealed a momentary nuance of warmth and empathy in her eyes. She was prepared to admit Freddie to her group.

"In answer to your question, we are eager to organise an overseas network of sympathisers, people who are genuinely caring and understanding of the problems that are faced by the men, women and children of Arthandur's faith. We need people who will lobby their governments to bring pressure to bear on Hitler's regime. Also we require to make contact with people who may be able to provide a centre for refugees, perhaps even a claim to relatives."

Freddie appears puzzled by this. "A claim to relatives?" he quizzed. "By this do you mean pretend relatives?"

Arthandur answered for the Baroness, "Yes. People who could sponsor, perhaps even provide documents of identification – passports if it is possible."

Freddie thought hard. It was very intriguing. Yet he could see how it would be possible for him to pay a pivotal role in a wide and complex network of specially selected people who would work together to help refugees. The one thing that constantly bemused Freddie was – why him? What particular quality had Arthandur espied in him that he considered would be so vital to an organisation of this nature? He pursued this point.

"Arthandur, the scheme that you are hoping to establish – it's pretty ambitious. I would be at the centre of some pretty extensive cloak and dagger work. Forgive me for sounding suspicious, but why are you so trusting of me? What is it about me that you see as being beneficial to this?" He waved his hands for expression as he groped for words to describe the group which he would become involved in. "This – er – this clandestine organisation."

Arthandur's reply was swift. "From our conversations together in

Berlin first of all, it became clear that your background – to quote you, ex-army intelligence – and secondly, from my own personal observations of you; your sympathy and feelings of compassion to people of our race was in our favour. But more importantly, you mentioned that you were still on the army reserve."

"That was the main thing that swung the balance, Mr Miller," the Baroness emphasised. "Obviously you would, as a former British army intelligence officer, and as an officer still on the reserve, know people in high positions militarily."

"Certainly," replied Freddie. He had been singularly interested in the Baroness from the outside. He was impressed by her, not just because of her ash-blonde hair and vibrant Scandinavian looks, or her obvious sensuality, so finely developed in this women somewhere in her late thirties. It was the authority combined with the acute acumen of her wholly refined senses, never failing to interpret correctly an emphasis on intonation or syllable made in their conversations that intrigued.

"Mr Miller," Baroness von Harstezzen continued, "in a time of war our group and the intelligence sections of the army could be of advantage to each other. By helping us you can help your own country."

The words made an impact on Freddie. He could sense the value in being a participant in this group. Over a sumptuous meal in a candlelit dining room the Baroness continued explaining to Freddie the priorities he would be required to perform if he decided to join them in their venture.

"On your return to London you can begin by approaching a member of your country's parliament and bring his attention the strong feelings you have for the safety and the right of freedom for the Jewish people in Europe. Constantly lobby him at every opportunity."

"That will be no problem at all," replied Freddie. "My local member of parliament in the electorate I live in happens to be a close friend of mine. I don't particularly subscribe to his particular brand of politics, but I do know he is a strong supporter on causes like this."

"Naturally," Arthandur felt inclined to add, "you will not mention to anyone of this organisation, or the names of either myself or the Baroness here."

"Of course. I realise the need for secrecy." Freddie gulped back the remains in his wine glass. The Baroness responded diplomatically by immediately filling up his glass again.

"If I can just reiterate, Mr Miller," Baroness von Harstezzen said with emphasis, "to sum up the objectives of your tasks again: lobby your government, alert your contacts in the army and the intelligence service, organise petitions for presentation to your government, be of assistance to any future refugees from the European Jewry as to accommodation and possible sponsorship. They are difficult missions I agree, but I and the Jewish people would be eternally grateful to you."

"I take it then, Mrs Harstezzen, that you are pretty certain that there will be refugees."

"There already are," she replied with firmness. "The trickle will become a flood. We will need contact with people who can house refugees, temporarily at least, providing them with accommodation until they have adapted themselves to new lives

"I will do what I can in that area," promised Freddie. He appeared pensive as he considered how he would tackle this aspect. "Acting as a concerned individual – yes, that's the best way of putting – it as a concerned individual but acting for this group in secrecy, I will approach leading members of the Jewish community in Britain."

"Please do so, Mr Miller. And keep in touch constantly. If whilst you are travelling abroad on your news assignments you meet people who you think may be able to help us, inform either Arthandur or myself."

"We have agents also in Holland and France," Arthandur pointed out. "All of them carefully selected. People who believe in freedom for the individual, whatever their race or religion."

Freddie had listened quietly and courteously. He had pondered for a moment if there was some well-concealed conspiracy here whereby the Baroness may have been a double agent. An alarming thought crossed his mind. Was it possible that the Baroness may have been working for the Nazis, but by her involvement with this secret organisation was in reality trying to infiltrate any opposition? He decided to tackle the subject head on.

"Baroness von Harstezzen, there is something I must ask you." She looked up at him with a directness that equally met his challenge. "In our conversations tonight you've shown a finesse and, if I may say, a remarkable firsthand knowledge of activities and ideas designed to defend the welfare of the Jewish faith. But why you? Why do you show such concern? You are not even from this country. I have to know more about you and your intentions?"

The Baroness smiled at him. "I understand your questions. Obviously, Mr Miller, you have deduced from my accent that I have had a Swedish upbringing. In fact I am Austrian. I was born in Vienna. I am a diplomat's daughter. My father was posted to Stockholm when I was young, a year old to be precise, and that is where my family spent many years. I was educated there, although I have also lived with my family in Italy, England and France, hence my fluency in the languages of those countries. After university I worked in Berlin as a secretary to Baron Rieber von Harstezzen, my late husband. He was heir to the von Harstezzen wine estates and an industrialist with a variety of factories and interests in coal and steel; also armaments and vehicles."

"A massive industrial empire," Freddie said, almost with a gasp of incredulity.

"Yes, it is indeed. When I first began to work in the Harstezzen industries, I was staggered by the magnitude of it all. I would never have dreamed that one day I would be controlling the entire empire."

"I still don't understand why you involved yourself with this group."

"I didn't involve myself, Mr Miller," the Baroness retorted almost haughtily. "I initiated it. I began it. You see, when I was younger the wanderlust held a fascination for me. I left the Harstezzen industries and I travelled. First to Palestine where I formed my feelings for the Jewish people. Then, later, I went to Africa, to places that brought out in me all the senses of being thrilled, bewildered, saddened by the poverty and amazed by the scenery and the animals. Places such as Tanganyika, Dar-es Salaam, right through to South Africa, wherefor some years I lived in Cape Town. I had kept in touch with the Baron and when I returned to Europe, he offered me a job again. He had been widowed for some years and he proposed to me. We married and we ran the industries together. Some of our closest friends were of the Jewish faith. Often they expressed their concern at what was happening under the Reich. It was from there that I began this idea of a wide-ranging circle of people who could help our cause. I am ideally placed to know what is going on in the military. Although my husband had no taste for politics, because of his factories he found himself dealing with some of the leading government figures. Since my husband's death I have taken over and with the knowledge that I have gained, I am even more devoted to this cause than I have ever been."

Just purely by the expression on her face, Freddie no longer had any doubt.

"Are you with us, my friend?" asked Arthandur, clasping his hands together and leaning forward. The Baroness also leaned forward slightly.

Freddie rubbed his chin and then replied, "Absolutely. I will do my best."

"It is good to have you with us," Baroness von Harstezzen said with a sincere degree of warmth. "One thing, Mr Miller, I realise you are a busy man with your newsreel business. I am just curious to know when you will commence your tasks for us. Where is your next assignment?"

"Spain," replied Freddie. "My colleagues and I have a daunting task before us. The storm clouds of the civil war are gathering with some virulence I'm afraid."

"I see," Arthandur pontificated. "You are going to film Franco and his forces, no doubt."

"Both sides, if it is possible," Freddie emphasised. "I will be splitting my camera team in two and in the name of impartiality we will be attempting to film the Loyalists and the Fascists. After that I will return to England. Next year I intend to spend some time in America filming events over there and the way of life. I have contacts with Warner Brothers, Metro Goldwyn Mayer Studios, and British Pathe News. All have expressed that they would like me to do some work for them."

"You will be a busy man in the next twelve months," the Baroness acknowledged. "I too hope to visit the United States next year. My aim will be to establish new markets for Harstezzen industries, but my prime purpose will be in keeping with our cause here. Perhaps we could meet in America if our schedules allow, and you can advise me of how your tasks have progressed."

"Certainly, I will," agreed Freddie, and he was now casting an admirable study over her. The thought of a future rendezvous with this fine woman was certainly an enticement. "I will write to you and keep in touch, Baroness."

They stayed talking for some time changing to other subjects on a more natural level. Arthandur seemed relieved to be able to speak of his wife, Marlene, her natural domesticated talents and her attributes in the areas of music and the arts, of which she was very conversant. Arthandur positively glowed when he spoke of his young son, Nathan. It was almost as if Arthandur had invested all of his energies and enthusiasm in his son. He spoke with a definite certainty that his son would grow up in a free world and with something to offer in whatever capacity he chose to devote his future career to.

Arthandur retired early and the Baroness took Freddie to a guest room overlooking the vast beauty of the estate. They were halfway up the staircase when she noticed Freddie studying a portrait handing on the wall. It was a picture of a regal looking man with dark hair and a fiery moustache. He wore a dinner jacket, a bow tie and a sash. Freddie guessed who it was, but before he could ask, the Baroness told him.

"Rieber, my late husband," she sighed, almost in a tone of sadness. She too paused to look at the portrait although she must have looked at it many times before. "He was a good man." Then she turned and looked at Freddie, and asked him a question that had not been relative to their previous conversation that night. "Are you a Christian, Mr Miller?"

Freddie thought before answering. His words were well chosen, but most of all they were unerringly modest. Although he was curious as to why she had posed the question.

"In the sense that I was educated at a Church of England school, I am perhaps, too, in terms of my own family upbringing. My parents were of the old school. The great values of honesty, loyalty, sincerity and grace under pressure were the most important things to them. By my own chaotic lifestyle in recent years, I've not lived as a Christian. I have the belief but not the conviction."

"I have tried to believe in the time since Rieber died," said the Baroness in a voice so low Freddie had to strain his ears to listen. "I do hope there is a wonderful place where I can be reunited with Rieber. I miss him so terribly. He was my life. My inspiration."

"I concur with you, Mrs Harstezzen. It would be so good if at the end of this life there was another time span to go to where we could say the things to our loved ones we never had the chance to. Such as 'I love you', simple things that count for so much."

"I know that too, Mr Miller," the Baroness said sympathetically.

They continued walking up the stairs and to Freddie's room. At the door the Baroness stopped and opened it for him revealing a pleasant bedroom. There were French-style shutters across the window space, which she unfastened. Even at night the view was magnificent.

"Your bags will be here. I'll have the butler bring them up for you. Tomorrow you might like to look over the estates before you and Arthandur leave."

"I'd love to, Mrs Harstezzen."

She faced him squarely, in a look that indicated a directness about her. At times it could be quite discerning, it was as if her eyes stared right into his as if she was trying to define the soul of the man.

"I think you are genuine, Mr Miller. I have no doubt that we will be able to work together. I would like to welcome you."

"Welcome me?" Freddie inquired.

"Yes. To the Circle."

"The Circle?" Freddie was even more bemused. Then he realised what she meant.

"Our organisation is known to its members as the Companions of the Circle. This is the working name of the group, known only to its members, and not to be quoted in public, by letter or even in the slightest utterance."

"The Companions of the Circle," murmured Freddie. The words seemed to sink in. The secret organisation had its own title and the members, their own designation. Freddie was now a member.

Baroness von Harstezzen left him to the privacy of the room and Freddie looked around him. He concluded that the room was a creative work of art; all around him were examples of a great wealth, he had never been previous acquainted with. Exotic tapestry, mahogany and redwood cupboards, cedar wood bookcases, carpets and rugs of a Persian origin, no doubt with a wild conglomeration of colours. Every colour in the rainbow, it seemed, and a passionate artistic mixture: there was a huge Elizabethan four-poster bed, there were porcelain and china vases and glittering solid silver ornaments. It was a room evoking expense. The Baroness in her private activities was certainly advancing from a strong financial position.

The next day with Baroness von Harstezzen acting as a guide, Freddie and Arthandur were driven round the countryside in a British bull-nosed Bentley. The car was bright and shiny, and in near mint condition. It cruised comfortably around the estates where the crops for the wine were grown.

"My pride and joy, Freddie," the Baroness beamed pointing out some lush pasture with one hand and steering with the other. Freddie felt delighted. It was the first time since they had met that she addressed him by his first name. Freddie felt half inclined to ingratiate himself more into her company by calling her Christina. But the closeness and the warmth of her real womanly qualities became more evident as the day grew on. This woman, who technically led a secret life and who would have been accustomed to cunning and devious planning where her organisation, the Circle, was concerned, still had so many enticing qualities.

The wine-growing areas of the von Harstezzen estates were certainly impressive. During the course of the day the three of them sampled the delights of the vintages. They talked very affably on that sunny day about so many things.

It was later on in the day that the time came for Freddie and Arthandur to move on to their next destination, Austria, where Arthandur lived with his family in a little village. They took a meal in the dining room of the Baroness's castle. Freddie soaked up the atmosphere of that room and indeed the moment in time. He had the distinct feeling that for the rest of his life, he would always remember that summer. He considered his knowledge and intellect enriched enormously by knowing Arthandur and Christina. They talked of literature and music, but always came back to their common cause. No one could expound on it with as much clarity as Arthandur.

"The Jewish people," Arthandur began, as if he was about to make an oration and symbolically of his race he always moved his hands demonstratively for emphasis. He repeated himself. "The Jewish people throughout history have always been a people who have known great perseverance. They are resilient, resourceful, optimistic when they should be pessimistic, and pessimistic when they should be at the heights of optimism." For a moment his eyes gave way to sadness, as he thought of the consequences facing his race at this time in history. Then, just as quickly, they flashed with humour and confidence. "But!" he continued, waving one finger sharply, and now there was defiance in his voice, "I am proud to be part of a race of people whose faith is the very backbone of their strength. We are a people who by virtue of being who we are, and of the race and religion we are gain faith from our very origins. Our cultural and social distinctiveness and our claim to be the chosen people separates us from other races – for tragedy often it would seem, but perhaps for the ultimate reward: survival. By that I mean not only the survival of our race in Europe, but also the principle of survival of all humanity."

The weight of Arthandur's words sank in. For in such a crystal clear fashion this intellectual doctor of medicine had put forward so admirably the real reasons for the existence of such a group.

After that stay at the Baroness's estate, it was time for Arthandur and Freddie to leave. Baroness Christina von Harstezzen arranged to meet up with Freddie in America the following year when they would confer on how their individual tasks had been achieved. There was obviously a great rapport between Arthandur and the Baroness. The warmth between them was very evident in conversations they had talked deeply and knowledgeably on a number of subjects. Yet the basic theme that allied these two interesting people was a fundamental and unwavering belief in the rights and freedom of all men.

When the car started up with Arthandur at the wheel, Freddie turned around in his seat and gazed back. The Harstezzen castle was an impressive fortress soaring above the gigantic estates. Baroness von Harstezzen waved from the doorway. Freddie thought that undoubtedly she was the most intelligent and authoritative woman he had ever met. Next year after having lived a very full twelve months Freddie envisaged that he would again meet the Baroness, in the very different surrounds of the United States. Although the exact location, and date, were still to be determined.

On the drive to Austria, Freddie thought of his additional responsibilities now that he was a Companion of the Circle. This strange designation sounded more as if it was the sort of lifetime honour that was bestowed on a private citizen by the King at Buckingham Palace. But this was a very different title and in a sense it was an honour of a different kind.

Five

Austria was the beautiful country that Freddie had imagined. Coming across the border he had thought it stunningly attractive. He was now looking forward to a pleasant stay in the village where Arthandur's family lived. This was a place of peace and tranquillity, of lakes and mountain streams. Before getting involved in his new activities, he wanted some peace, a world away from responsibilities and politics. At the sight of the little village with the cuckoo clock-style houses, set amidst snow-capped mountain scenery, Freddie knew he was going to find it.

The village could have been painted in a backdrop used in the sets of a Hollywood film. It was as much in contrast to the Harstezzen castle as could possibly be presented. This little village had a charm and a quiet that was only broken by the chugging of the pistons in Arthandur's car engine.

It consisted of little houses with sloping green roofs, green chalets, a few stores and shops and narrow winding streets that were not so much thoroughfares, but a semblance of roads distinguished only by the buildings situated on each side. The mountains soared above like gigantic monoliths in the background and the air was fresh and clear.

"This is my home now," Arthandur said proudly, and he waved to one of the local villagers sitting outside a store drinking coffee. "Hello, Hans," he called, and turning to Freddie he remarked, "That's Hans the greengrocer. He's a nice fellow. Poor man comes to see me for treatment for his arthritis."

They drove on through the sprawl of the Austrian village until they came to the outskirts where the buildings and houses became less and less, tapering off into an infrequent ribbon development. Arthandur slowed the car down and gently applied the brakes, bringing the vehicle to a halt outside a pleasant chalet with a long stretch of garden in front of the house.

"Ah," sighed Arthandur. "It's so nice to be home again." From where the house was situated a superb view across to the mountains could be seen. Freddie gazed at it wistfully. "This is my Shangri-La, Freddie. This is my Avalon." Arthandur opened the car door and stepped out. Almost as if on cue the front door of the chalet opened and there stood Arthandur's wife and son, Marlene and Nathan. Marlene was a dark-haired, dark-eyed woman with an engaging smile and genial matter. Her clothing consisted of what Freddie presumed would have been typical of an Austrian village women's national dress. There was nothing ostentatious about Marlene that would suggest that she was the wife of a doctor, nor was there anything immediately obvious about her that suggested a privileged upbringing. There were strong traits inherent in her that indicated her religious upbringing. She greeted Arthandur warmly with a hug and drawing back with a face that seemed to be tired and resigned, she gave Freddie a puzzled look.

Nathan, Arthandur's fourteen-year-old son, quite tall for his age and already outwardly showing signs of growing into a strikingly handsome boy, smiled charmingly at his father who in turn gripped his shoulders with deep affection.

"It is good to see you both," Arthandur spoke with deep honesty. He looked with a real sense of love at the two of them and then with a sweep of his hand, he introduced Freddie to them. "Marlene, Nathan, I would like you to meet Freddie Miller. Mr Miller is an Englishman who I met in Berlin. He is a cameraman filming newsreels."

At the mention of Berlin, Marlene's eyes drifted sharply towards Arthandur. It was a look of recognition for she was only too well aware of Arthandur's private work, but casting a sharp glance to their young son who, it was obvious, was not aware of the real reason for Freddie's presence, she could just make a play of courtesy.

"Please come in, Mr Miller. You are most welcome." Marlene said politely. Freddie smiled back, but knowing human nature he felt like a privileged guest, more or less just a nuisance to be borne with.

Nevertheless, if Freddie had thought that was the way he was going to be treated, he couldn't have been more mistaken. He was soon to find out that the Palmai family were generous with their hospitality and warmth to a great degree. In the days that followed Freddie was to find that Arthandur had spoken to Marlene about their first meeting in that café in Berlin. Not wishing to impose too much on the Palmai family, he spent his time walking around the local countryside.

Just for a while one day Freddie luxuriated in the quiet on a mountain crevice. Far below him in the valley was the pleasant little village spread-eagled in all directions. Above him were the peaks of the surrounding mountains. There was stillness, not a sound of anything mechanical like a car engine or a train approaching. Freddie could not identify any living creature in close proximity, like a bird or livestock. How wonderful to be away from responsibility, it seemed. This moment should be treasured. Like so many times lately Freddie had considered that every moment, experience and event should be treasured.

Winding his way down to the valley below, from out of a cluster of rocks came a jolly-faced, chubby-looking Austrian wielding a stick, who nodded to Freddie saying, *"Guten Tag!"* in a pleasant jovial fashion, even removing his hat. Just as quickly, from around the corner came a multitude of mountain goats. The man was obviously a goat herdsman. Freddie could well have imagined the man breaking into a yodel across the valley. The goats raced past with a boundless energy, leaping and sprinting, with the herdsman keeping them all in line by gently swaying his stick to and fro.

Going downhill Freddie was surprised to see young Nathan Palmai coming up and not far behind were Arthandur and Marlene. From his early conversations with Nathan, he realised the little boy wasn't too conversant in English as yet, but was willing to try and speak something other than in his own native tongue of German.

Freddie stopped to wait for them and looked out again at the valley, a view he much admired. The aspect that Freddie found so enchanting about this part of Austria was the amalgam of colours that seemed to be so prevalent. The mountains were almost iridescent, combining a mixture of blue, mauve and silver with the cool glistening sparkling white snow creaming over the tops and falling down unevenly like the gushing overflow of ice-cold water from a frozen tap in winter. The sky was cloudless and a generous mid blue in the soft sunshine. There were exotic greens from the vegetation that grew on the mountain slopes in shades of varying degrees. Lush green where clumps of trees and grass grew thickly together, faded and brown where rocks prevented the growth of any form of plant life. Down in the valley the chalet roofs of the houses were all green mixed in with auburn brickwork or red stone. The roads leading to the little settlement were yellow and fawn and sandy in colour. So from Freddie's vantage point he could view a diverse array of colour and he prided himself on his sensitivity and appreciation of such splendid scenery.

"You are admiring our valley, Mr Miller," Marlene called out to him. He turned to face the Palmai's as they approached. "In a way the situation in our homeland may have been good for us. It gave us the chance to live here, in such a peaceful place."

Turning to the young boy Freddie asked, "How does Nathan like living here?"

The young boy flashed a quick smile but it was his father Arthandur who answered for him, almost defensively.

"Nathan – he is a good boy. He has adapted well to his life here and he studies hard. Marlene teaches him you see."

"What's your favourite subject, Nathan?" asked Freddie, interested in the younger member of the family.

"I like English, History and Music."

"Do you like music, Mr Miller?" Marlene asked.

"Yes, but I have a feeling that my musical tastes might be a little different to yours," he smiled, knowing from previous conversations that Marlene was interested in classical music, and not the sort of swing music he enjoyed. "I like Harry Roy, Glen Miller, Al Bowlly, Duke Ellington, Bing Crosby and Ambrose. Not classical."

Marlene and Nathan smiled at each other as if they were sharing a private joke. "You have just named all our favourites!" Nathan exclaimed.

They all smiled and then went walking together on a route that Arthandur chose, knowing all the ins and outs of the beautiful high ground. At one point they had a picnic in a lovely stretch of green grass high above; isolated it seemed to Freddie, from the worries of the world. Freddie noticed how calm and serene the three members of the Palmai family were together. It was hard to believe that Arthandur was the second in command of a secret organisation called the Circle. Here on a sunny day in Austria, Arthandur was just an ordinary family man enjoying some wine and sandwiches in an open-air picnic.

They talked quite easily about simple things like the weather, the subjects Nathan was learning in his private tuition and if the conversation ever touched events in present day Germany, Arthandur and Marlene were quick to veer the conversation on to another subject. Freddie listened politely and savoured the view. There was one mountain in the distance with a peak that was shrouded by clouds and mist. It had very steep cliff faces and for any budding mountain climber it would have presented a vast if not virtually impossible challenge.

"That mountain you are starting at," remarked Arthandur, almost as if he could read Freddie's mind. "When I was younger I climbed to the top."

"You did!" Freddie gasped, surprised, thinking how even a younger man would have found the scaling difficult. Marlene and Nathan looked at Arthandur proudly. He has obviously told them the story many times before, and now he had found another eager audience.

"In 1912," Arthandur nodded. "At medical school I befriended someone who was a mountaineer and I climbed several mountains with his team in the Alps on different vacations. In my final year at the school, before he was due to leave for America and I to take up private practice in Berlin, he suggested I might like to join him on the big one." Arthandur pointed to the mountain. "Eicherel it is called. We stood at the top in 1912. On the day we ascended the Eicherel, the British ship *Titanic* hit an iceberg. That was a note in history. We went to the top and the *Titanic* touched the bottom of the sea."

Freddie, always impressed by man's achievements, pursued the subject further.

"It must have been a treacherous climb. Those cliff faces – they're so steep."

Arthandur's face changed from one of serenity to deep thought as he pondered the memories. If everyone had a 'time' in their life they often recall then that was Arthandur's.

"It was a real challenge. We were all young men, full of spirit and energy. The Eicherel had never been scaled before. When we climbed it, I began to curse myself. I had no idea how tough it would be. The team was well prepared, but it was so difficult. We were halfway up when our leader slipped. We were all behind him, the rope connecting each of us was strung out like an elastic band across the crevices, and I, Mr Miller, was suspended in mid-air, unable to get my footing. I couldn't reach the rocks to grab on, so many thousands of feet in the air, nothing below or above my boots. The agony of the rope top stretched out across my back and the weight of the climbers below. *Oy Vei*! I nearly passed out. I thought at the time, *I know I am one of the chosen people*. But I thought, *Why choose me now, Lord, when I still have so much life to live*."

"What happened then, Arthandur?" Freddie, by now engrossed, asked. Arthandur grinned. Beneath his often-serious façade there was always great humour that revealed itself so suddenly it could surprise the onlooker.

"I heard one of the mountaineers cry out to me. 'For God's sake, Arthandur, don't go to sleep now!' I was in such pain but that one joke almost broke me up with laughter. A joke, believe me. As if I was going to sleep nearly a mile and a half above sea level!"

Freddie and the others had to smile at Arthandur's recollections of that incident. He continued, obviously recalling this high point of his life with a sheer delight. "Then I began to sway and sway until I got some footing and soon the others were in place. We climbed the most icy of pathways and such steep cliffs. We had to push and pull ourselves to our utmost. See the peak, Mr Miller." Arthandur pointed and Freddie nodded. "We had estimated how long it would take us to reach the top allowing for delays. I had asked the bell ringer from the village church to ring in the valley below when it was carefully assumed we would have made the peak. Would you believe it? When we stood on the peak with the valley and the whole world below us the only noise we could hear was the quiet. Then as we stood in silence – far off in the distance, yet so faintly, the church bell was ringing to celebrate our success. When we finally got down again, the villagers treated us like heroes. I have always loved this place since then."

He sighed at the conclusion of this memory. For if every man remembers something in his life that he would live through unchanged then surely this would be that special time for Arthandur.

"And Arthandur is still scaling mountains of impossible proportions," Marlene pointed out. Freddie caught the double meaning in her statement, and raised his eyebrows acknowledging that he understood her.

It was in the village the next day that Freddie saw Arthandur hard at work on his other profession, that of a Doctor of Medicine. This was an area totally removed from the impression that Freddie had gained of Arthandur in the brief time he had known him. Now this was the real man fully revealed. Here in his private work as a doctor, Freddie could see him as a man of real human warmth and compassion, showing great love and concern for the children, the elderly and anyone who was sick or in need of medical help.

Arthandur's surgery was in his home. People trod the garden path to see Doctor Palmai who greeted each patient with a handshake or a hug. Freddie sat by his desk and was introduced as a "friend of the family" which indeed he now was. There was often wit or small chat about each other's family and Arthandur would tell Freddie the history of each patient after they had made an exit from the surgery.

"That was dear Mottie," he smiled at Freddie after one consultation. "He is a nice fellow you know but every time he comes to see me, he has a different complaint. Sometimes I test his blood pressure. No problem there. Then it's his hearing. Then his vision – his vision! A joke! Finest eyesight for any man of his age. Complains that he might have arthritis, rheumatism or thrombosis. He is built like a log. Mottie only suffers from one illness, Freddie. Chronic Hypochondria, I call it. I didn't know how old he is. I said to Mottie, 'You will live well over seventy years'. He says to me, 'Arthandur, this is the only true thing you have told me all morning. I am eighty on my next birthday!'"

With the children, he spoke to them in soft affectionate tones in a warm fatherly voice. To the adults he was a good friend. Freddie was in turn introduced to the locals in Arthandur's village, people such as the greengrocer, the butcher, the storekeeper and some of the farmers in the valley. It was obvious that Arthandur was greatly loved by them all.

These people were all obviously proud of their faith. Whenever Freddie met any of them, he would look at their characteristics, which were so evident of their religious discipline. In the event of the Reich expanding its territorial claim, the very privacy and freedom that this small exiled community were experiencing would come to an end.

Sometimes Freddie would wander down to the local tavern and mingle with the ordinary Austrian villagers. In the evenings they would often sing when one of them would render a tune on the accordion. The happy people would burst forth into song and bang their beer glasses on the tables in time with the music. Freddie would smile at their enthusiasm, the ordinary villager's love of life. He enjoyed just being there in the camaraderie of their company, and the atmosphere that pulsated happy music and laughter.

When Freddie had first arrived in Berlin that summer, using his trained cameraman's eye, he had scrupulously made the study of people's faces in the city. Looking around him in that Austrian village tavern he could see, in every nuance and crevice of the elderly, people who had lived lives on the land in all kinds of weather, snow, sunshine, wind and rain. The younger people had the fresh-faced soft skin, white and pink, smiles of youthful exuberance, and the appearance of innocence and naivety yet to be tarnished by the ardour and experience, torment and success that only years of living acquire.

There was warmth in their rich voices. When they sang together in the tavern, the blended harmonies of the young and the old vocalising a rousing song created a sound that was to be indelibly stamped in Freddie's memory. He would always recall that night in the tavern: the old goat herdsman slapping his thigh followed by a bellowing infectious hearty belly laugh. The elderly men in their felt hats and mountain jackets; the charming girls in patchwork dresses and clothes that sometimes seemed indistinguishable from that which a Dutch girl might wear. Then there were the young men: some dark in appearance, some with blonde hair and gleaming eyes. All of them smiling, all of them happy.

At this point, Freddie's train of thought was disturbed by the accordionist striking up a polka and a few people in the tavern considered it the ideal opportunity for a dance. Freddie began clapping his hands with the other revellers in time to the music. He turned to one man he had met at Arthandur's surgery and said cheeringly, "These are fine people," to which the other clinked his beer glass with Freddie's.

Eventually the time came for Freddie to leave Austria. He had an assignment to carry out. The Spanish Civil War between the loyalists and Fascists had brought about great changes to that nation. Freddie had always loved his visits to Spain. In his days as an army officer on leaves in Spain, he had ran in the streets at the Festival of the Bulls in Pamplona. He had visited Madrid and Barcelona, swam at Torremolinos and Malaga and walked to the top of Mount Igueldo in San Sebastian on the mountain path well worn by visitors from other countries. Spain had always held an indefinable magic and magnetism for him.

Freddie had written to the other members of his newsreel team advising them to meet him in Bilbao on a certain date. It was now time for him to proceed from Austria across Europe to meet them.

It would have been so easy for Freddie to have stayed on longer in that peaceful, friendly village but his next assignment beckoned and reluctantly he had to leave. At their suggestion Freddie agreed to let the Palmai family show him around the sparkling city of Vienna, before he caught his connecting train. Arthandur adored Vienna and he pointed out the old buildings and places of historical interest for Freddie's attention.

For the newcomer to Vienna it was easy to see how the richness of its soul had been the very basis of so much beautiful music that this city was famed for. There was a rhythm almost about its movements in the traffic and the people. The sounds of the trams rolling along and the tintinnabulation of church bells intermingled with the cacophony of car horns could have been the inspiration for a Viennese concerto.

Vienna was, at close hand, a city that seemed to evoke an essence of grandeur. Arthandur pointed out some of its most famous cultural landmarks such as the Vienna Opera House, The Volksoper, and the Musikverein Concert Halls. Marlene with her great love of music mentioned the names of some of the composers who had lived there in centuries past. Beethoven had composed his Pastoral Symphony here inspired by the tranquil beauty of the hills, the famous Vienna Woods. And there were many more besides.

To the magical tune of Vienna, Wolfgang Amadeus Mozart had woven his spellbinding music. Johann Strauss had created his waltzes here. Schubert had composed his sentimental lieder and a number of symphonies in the city. The talents of Gluck, Brahms, Haydn, Hugo Wolf, Bruckner, Mahler and Schonber had also been borne to full fruition in this creative atmosphere. Freddie thought to himself that one day he would return here and make a newsreel of Vienna accompanied with a soundtrack of the historical music of its composers.

In the company of the Palmai family, Freddie took in much of the city. They strolled happily together in the Karnestrasse. Architecture always fascinated Freddie and during that visit he absorbed the sights of St Stephen's Cathedral, the Hofburg Palace, the Schloss Belvedere and the Cappuchin Monastery which within the church's crypt was housed the sarcophagi of the Hapsburg.

At the train station Freddie shook hands with Arthandur and young

Nathan. Marlene embraced him warmly. For a moment he gazed at the three of them with affection. He felt such empathy for this warm and loving family. There are times in a person's life when a certain feeling of love can be experienced without words being said or a demonstration of affection. This was one such time in Freddie's life. He seemed to receive feelings of love merely by being in their presence.

"I don't know what the future holds for you all," Freddie said in a gentle, hushed voice, "but my thoughts for you will be those of great goodwill and love." He was almost moved to tears and he turned towards Nathan. "May I wish you, young man, all the best that life can offer. If you grow up with the strength and humour of your father and the warmth of your mother, life will be wonderful for you."

The words moved the Palmais, particularly Marlene, whose eyes showed a momentary flash of mutual compassion. Freddie smiled warmly at her. He straightened his sports jacket and tie, and picked up his suitcase. He felt such sadness leaving them.

"I will walk with you to your carriage," Arthandur said. Freddie looked at both Marlene and Nathan again and then turned quickly and began walking along the platform. Arthandur walked beside him.

"You know, Freddie, I like you," he said in a jocular manner.

"And I you, Arthandur," replied Freddie. "You have a fine wife and son." He stopped outside the door to his carriage. "Through our mutual contact, the Baroness, I'm sure we will hear from each other. I hope that one day we may meet again." He lowered his head for one moment, thinking hard for anything further he could add. "If at any time you consider coming to England let…"

At this point the train guard blew his whistle and people started to scramble aboard. Freddie was not able to finish the words he had begun. Arthandur shook his hand and gripped Freddie's shoulder fiercely in that familiar gesture of his.

"Goodbye, my dear friend," he said to Freddie. There were clouded mists in those eyes that were streaked with red veins. The two men hugged each other in the manly embrace more pertaining to a father and son than close friends.

Smoke started to stream over the train carriages. Freddie made his way inside and seated himself at the window. When the train started to pull out of the station, Freddie stood up and pulled the window down.

He stared back at the main platform. Smoke from the train funnel swirled and swirled about obliterating any final view of the Palmai family. Almost in an unexpected instant a breeze blew up lifting the smoke. Freddie could see Arthandur, Marlene and Nathan waving to him. He returned the wave. Then the smoke returned and as it did, his last view of the Palmai family together was lost. He slumped back into his seat sadly.

Soon he would have to begin the work of the Circle. First of all there was the assignment in Spain to contend with. – that in itself would be a difficult accomplishment.

Six

For the Palmai family in Austria life continued in only the way that it could in such traumatic times and difficult circumstances. While Arthandur attended to his surgery, Marlene concentrated on domestic matters at home and the education of Nathan.

Marlene would be seated at the piano occasionally in the quieter moments of her leisure playing classical pieces that she had learned in her youth. The music of Strauss or Beethoven would be featured as her fingers glided across the keys. Nathan would listen attentively. Sometimes he would enjoy the excerpt of music that his mother would play. There were definitely times in his music lessons that Nathan would find a certain piece droll and lacking in anything that he could appreciate. Marlene would notice this and there would be flashes of humour in her eyes. It was on occasions like this that she would stop in the middle of a concerto, walk across to the phonogram and put a record on by someone like Al Bowlly or Bing Crosby.

"Is that better, Nathan?" she murmured, and then she would teach Nathan to dance in slow ballroom style. "Come, I will show you how to dance. One day you may dance with someone special the way your father and I used to dance." She was recalling far off memories when she and Arthandur used to glide around the dance floors in the time before the rise of the Third Reich. When she danced with Al Bowlly's voice rising from the gramophone speaker in the corner, there were memories of the times she had danced with Arthandur when he had held her close and love had been so evident in the depths of their eyes. Marlene saw her son Nathan as a younger version of Arthandur.

In reality Marlene knew that this was a mistake, for every human being on this earth has an identity of their own. There may be certain traits of character inherent from one's parents in every individual but each person has a talent or a personality that is their own creation. Marlene looked at her son warmly. What would this young man develop into with the passing of the years? Would he be as compassionate as his father? If that was all that he became – simply a man with compassion for other people, a man that strove to love all human beings – then she could not ask for anything more.

When the tune had stopped, Marlene walked to the phonogram and turned it off. She took an atlas from a bookshelf, thumbing through the pages.

"That's the end of your music lesson, Nathan. Today you have listened to Tchaikovsky, Beethoven, Mendelssohn and Strauss. And you have danced to Al Bowlly singing 'On a Steamer Coming Over'. "Should all young men be that lucky with their music lessons!" Marlene took the atlas and sat next to Nathan in an armchair in the drawing room. "Palestine," she exclaimed suddenly. "What does Palestine mean to you, Nathan?"

Nathan thought before answering the question. He came up with the answer that Marlene had envisaged.

"It is to be our future home!" he replied. "The land where all people of our race will be able to settle.

Arthandur appeared at the doorway, having finished his day's work in the surgery. Nathan and Marlene both looked up as he walked into the room, seating himself at a seat close by.

"Go on. I'm listening," he said pleasantly. "Tell me about Palestine, Nathan. I want to know what you have learned."

Arthandur really was intently curious as to how his young son's education had progressed in the matter of such an important subject as to the geographical and historical content of the Promised Land.

Nathan thought hard as if he was trying to measure his words. It is a difficult thing to talk of a land that one has never been to, but which one is so well acquainted with by details of knowledge. Marlene and Arthandur keenly looked at him. To both of them Palestine was truly the Promised Land.

"Palestine is the land that one day all our people will be able to call home. It will be our traditional home. It is made up of many areas: Naphtali, Zebulun, Galilee, Samaria, Judaea, Peraea, Decopolis. There are more. I can't remember them all."

He looked up at his parents who were beaming with pride.

"That's all right, Nathan," his mother reassured him softly. "You've done well to remember those names. What else do you know?"

"There are three seas: the Mediterranean borders the coastline by the villages of Caesarea, Joppa and Ashdod; the Dead Sea is between Judaea and Reuben, and is one of the largest inland seas anywhere; then in the North there is the Sea of Galilee or Gennesareth, around it are the towns of Bethsaida, Capernaum, Magdala and Tiberias."

"I'm impressed," Arthandur said, his surprise at his son's obvious deep knowledge of Palestine so evident. "Tell me the name of the land that bounds the areas of Galilee and Samaria."

"That is Syro Phoenicia, Father," came back the reply. Arthandur had asked in jest. He was further astounded. "From Phoenicia, it is said that the world's first sailors came. They were known as the Phoenicians. It is said they put to sea in the first boats with a sail mast; they were a great maritime people who brought back the treasures for the Kingdom of Solomon and David."

"To us believers – those that deeply believe, Nathan – what does Palestine really mean to us?" The boy's mother asked.

This was a question that required a more definitive answer; Nathan wasn't as quick in replying as he had been describing Palestine in geographical and historical terms. What did Palestine really mean to the believing Jews? A more spiritual answer was to be the substance of his reply. He thought deeply in his memory and considered the knowledge that he had gained from his Talmudic studies.

"When the Second Temple was destroyed in 70 AD and the Jewish people lived throughout the world, it meant to the believers, a place of…" Nathan groped for words. He wasn't sure how to complete his answer, but it was his father who felt inclined to take the senior role in this teacher-pupil situation. "You tell me, father. I'm not sure how to describe it." Nathan asked Arthandur.

"A place of dwelling, Nathan, for all our people." Arthandur gladly replied, tapping his son on the shoulder with gentle affection. "Indeed, the land of Palestine is one that we call Eretz Yisroel. It is, to us of our faith, the Promised Land. It was promised by God to Abraham and his descendants, and it is the Land of the Kingdom of David and Solomon."

Marlene felt inclined to add her own comments. "The holy city of Jerusalem was built there. Jews pray at the Wailing Wall. Our teachings tell us that all Jews buried in the Diaspora will be brought to life again. One day too the Messiah will appear before all of us in Eretz Yisroel. There are such dreams for that land that sometimes I think that we base our aspirations on a scale of such grandeur that in our lifetime may never reach fulfilment. There are many people there now attempting to bring their dreams to reality, Nathan; people on the Kibbutz, for instance."

Marlene had cast a glance at Arthandur, indicating that it was time to talk of their combined plans to send Nathan to a kibbutz. It was not a subject that could be avoided. The present climate politically in Europe was such that the kibbutz had to be mentioned again. To think of the separation of their only beloved son was heartbreaking.

"You know we have talked of the kibbutz before, Nathan." There was a concern in Arthandur's voice. "You are an intelligent young fellow, my boy. Still with a great deal to learn, I may add! But you know what is happening in Europe today. There will be time soon when we must send you to the kibbutz."

Nathan was not yet fifteen. Yet, although he had already reached an admirable stage of maturity both in his studies and appearance, he was still capable of grief. His parents were moved emotionally as the tears clouded Nathan's eyes.

"I don't want to leave you both," he said in a gentle faltering voice.

"Oh, Nathan," his mother expressed sorrowfully. "We don't want you to go. But things – things are happening. We will come soon afterwards."

Arthandur looked stern and saddened. He lowered his head sadly, his heart broken. He consoled himself that it would be a while before this would happen. Then looking up at the ceiling as if he was looking up at the heavens and asking 'Why'. That history was on the brink of unforeseeable uncertainty made him query why such momentous decisions would have to be taken in so many individual persons lives.

The contrast of the future and present seemed to penetrate his spirit like the sudden changes of temperature from hot to cold. He knew that his work with the Circle was a dominant feature of his life, but he could not ignore the responsibilities that he had to be of assistance to so many people. Yet in terms of his own family he wanted nothing more than to be able to keep them all together.

He thought about the Englishman, Freddie Miller. How was Freddie getting on in war-torn Spain? He thought of Baroness Christina von Harstezzen. What were her next moves in her vast chess game of the Circle? Who were the pawns and knights on her chessboard of what would ultimately be a resistance group?

Seven

Freddie Miller was in the centre of the action in the Spanish Civil War. He was an Englishman in the middle ground, not of the upper classes or the working class, but just an ordinary mild-mannered son of a Hampshire farmer. This mild manner and gentle upbringing did not hide his enthusiasm for life, and being in the midst of all things exciting. He had a gregariousness that would occasionally surface, a love of excitement and, more importantly, a sensitivity for others. Despite being a farmer's son who had won a scholarship to Sandhurst on his own academic and personal abilities; he had never felt happier than when mingling with the men from the counties in his regiment. He had a great rapport with the Liverpudlians and the East Enders.

Here in Spain, he was again working well with a team of men in his newsreel capacities. But as shells exploded around him and rubble was thrown into the air, Freddie was beginning to wonder what on earth he had let himself in for.

Several months of fighting between opposing forces had already passed by towards the end of 1936. It was a state of friction, compared to the hedonistic days of leisure and wine drank at outdoor cafés with laughing dark-haired Spanish girls that Freddie recalled from only a few years ago

En route to one of the major cities, Freddie and his news team had stopped in what seemed to be a quiet Spanish village far removed from the sounds of gunfire they had earlier experienced. They had sat in the shade of a café in a village of white buildings and an imposing monastery. It was dusty, and brilliantly warm. The peasant villagers rode past on their bicycles and did their daily chores in an unhurried, casual fashion that befits a sleepy Spanish village. It was midday and before the siesta period, and still curiously warm.

The scent of peppercorn and sand seemed to hang over the air. There was also the aroma of burned embers and ashes, as if there had been a fire earlier in the day that had coated the tepid atmosphere.

The wine they were sipping was pleasant and refreshing. It was quiet and still and the sun flickered gently through the treetops. Birds squawked gently. The spokes of a passing bicycle made a tiny sound as they thrashed by, and a dog barked in the background.

One of the cameramen had set up his lens and was adjusting it. The others sat quietly in the sunshine just soaking up the peacefulness of it all.

Freddie contemplated the world through his wine glass like an elder statesman reviewing life's varied events. He thought of the present predicament in Spain.

The Spanish Civil War had begun in earnest on 18th July 1936 when a number of army divisions based in Spanish Morocco suddenly and without warning proclaimed a revolution against the government of Spain. The instigators of this revolution were General Francisco Franco and Emilio Mola. In the few months since its commencement the uprising had become even more widespread, with the majority of army units joining forces and swinging their full support behind General Franco.

In fierce opposition to the Franco forces were the numerous numbers within the Government's Popular Front. Amongst these forces even women of varied ages and capabilities were taking up arms and entering what was becoming an increasingly bloody fray.

The strange thing about this particular revolution was that it was attracting widespread foreign intervention. In addition to this there were people of different nationalities joining different sides, and an influx of mercenaries ranging from the politically concerned to the soldier of fortune seeking a battle to fight and an experience to gain.

For Freddie Miller reporting on these events with a newsreel team was a difficult task before even getting one reel of film into the camera. To begin with he had to overcome opposition to the team's presence in Madrid and Barcelona, where envoys and contacts seem prepared to accuse him and his men as being representative of one side only. This had not been the case, but to film both Loyalist and Fascist forces had created an obviously difficult task from the outset.

In Barcelona the newsreel team had finally settled for filming events as they happened. They were driven round the city streets filming the ruins of different buildings now devastated and bullet-ridden. Filmed interviews had been conducted with priests, nuns, ordinary people, other foreign journalists in the middle of the action and wounded people in the crowded hospitals.

Freddie had not liked this assignment from the first day of arrival, nor did he like seeing this fabulous country ripped asunder that he had great affection for, acquired from the times he had spent his army leaves there in the late 20s and early 30s. Oh, how he remembered the time of the bulls in Pamplona when the German girl Tillie had been waiting for him with passion in her eyes. Now there was rubble, bombing and bloodshed in Barcelona, and Madrid was the same.

Here in a tiny Spanish village vaguely reminiscent of something from the Byzantine era when Don Quixote may have come riding through to do battle with the windmill, it was so pleasant. There was not the hint of trouble to come. Freddie sipped his wine. He looked at some of the villagers in straw hats and cool scruffy white clothes, so casual in their warm almost sleepy lifestyle. For a moment, a dazzlingly sensuous Spanish señorita, with jet-black hair and eyes that evoked a hypnotic stare, caught his full attention. *My, what a girl*, Freddie thought with admiration, casting his eyes down the full scope of her slim, well-rounded, most alluring figure. What is it about European women that intrigues and bedazzles?

Other people sat in the open air café gazing at the slow, apparently quiet, world through the tint of their sunglasses. Down south there was turmoil. Here there was just sunshine and shadow.

The cameraman was running some film capturing the looks of people seated at the café. In the background the monastery bell gently tolled and that seemed to be the only noise. Freddie looked around, reached for his glass, drained the contents and gently replaced the glass on the table. It had just gently clinked against the metal surface when there was one almighty roar and fragments of brick and rubble soared high into the air, as the monastery building burst forth into flames of soaring red and yellow from a massive explosion.

Freddie had been thrown forwards by the impact of the affects that dynamite could provoke. Smoke, fire and dust soared into the sky.

In just the space of a few minutes this quiet village had become a blazing inferno. People all around him were scrambling for cover, others were giving help to each other. There were a few bodies lying in pools of blood with a limb missing, and Freddie could hear an agonising cry in the background, people shouting, a baby crying, dogs barking and the sound of a building collapsing.

The first thing Freddie did upon raising himself from the dusty ground was to check for all members of his newsreel team. Apart from bruises and one of the team being hit on the back of the head by a piece of debris, all of them had emerged miraculously virtually unscathed.

Amazingly, all this time the cameraman, who had originally set up his lens to capture and make a photographic study of people in a quiet Spanish village, had been unwillingly privy to some bloodcurdling photography. The camera had been running all the time. The cameraman too had narrowly missed some flying debris and had stayed in control during the events. Such was his concentration and dedication to the task in hand.

Freddie came over to him as soon as he checked the rest of his team. He was covered in dust and soot.

"Are you all rright?" he asked the cameraman.

"I am," came the reply and then he pointed at a few strewn out people. "But not that lot." Freddie turned and looked. "This is really what you call being on the spot." The cameraman looked ashen and distressed. It was then that Freddie saw his colleague shaking.

"Calm down, old friend," he assured him, and stopped the camera running. "I think that'll be enough of that reel. Let's see if we can help these people."

During the next few hours, Freddie and his colleagues did whatever they could to help the less fortunate victims of that particular incident. The team drove some of the injured to a nearby hospital while Freddie assisted some of the locals in trying to move the rubble of the burned out buildings.

Freddie walked out into the centre of the main street of what had earlier been a peaceful and tranquil idyll. He clutched his head in his hands and looked at the cameraman who had unknowingly recorded the whole scene.

In full view of the camera lens, a picture of carnage and devastation had been fully recorded. It was not going to be a worthy newsreel for public consumption. It was, however, a very accurate and frightening portrait of the harsh reality of civil strife.

"You've been with me on a few assignments, eh, Sam?" he said to the cameraman in a quiet but well-controlled voice. "Never did we see anything like that." Freddie looked deeply disgusted and angry. "War! It's so futile. It's madness, immoral and destructive!"

The flames had burned themselves out now and all that remained of that part of town were charred remains and rubble. With a bit of luck the newsreel team could get the hell out of there and home to some sanity. Freddie's home in Hammersmith, London was to be a welcome escape. He was so tired, all he wanted to do was to go home and sleep for a week.

Eight

Baroness Christina von Harstezzen carried out her duties on her vast wine estates with all the enthusiasm and aplomb of a South American coffee plantation overseer. Her soft alluring beauty did much to disguise her authority and intensions. On the same day that Freddie Miller had been witness to the destruction of a Spanish village, Baroness von Harstezzen was working quietly in her study at the castle in the Rhineland of Germany. She had been pondering over a list of the Companions of the Circle in Holland, France and Belgium. So far she had received favourable replies from them all. Each concerned individual had lobbied their government and the Baroness was pleased with the response.

In a number of instances, provision for sponsorship for many families had been made and through any one of a number of avenues support was forthcoming. There was a knock on the door and the butler entered.

"Baroness, you have a visitor," he expressed. The look in his eyes was wary and indicated it may not have been someone of a welcome nature. Baroness von Harstezzen blew a ring of smoke and eyed him. He continued, "It's a Colonel Burnhoff." The Baroness knew instinctively that Colonel Burnhoff of the Nazi High Command would be seated outside.

"Very well," she signed reluctantly. "I will be there shortly."

The butler nodded and left the room. It was about fifteen minutes later that she left her study to walk down the stairs to where she knew the German officer would be waiting. With the expansion of her circle it was of constant worry to her that one slip on behalf of one of her associates would betray the activities to the military. But, although the presence of a military officer was an unexpected event, she would remain calm and in control of the situation.

Through the Harstezzen Industries, the Baroness had to deal with many of the leading Generals in conjunction with the armaments that were required by the defence forces. Certainly Baroness von Harstezzen was in a privileged position to know how technical rearmament was advancing in Germany at that time.

The Baroness left her study and walked down the stairs to greet her guest. Who was Colonel Burnhoff? Certainly the name Burnhoff set a bell ringing in her memory. *Surely it could not have been…*, she pondered. Then she realised. Colonel Verner Burnhoff was a boyhood friend of her late husband Rieber. Perhaps and hopefully this was only a social visit.

For one moment she paused to gaze down from the staircase at her guest who was gently pacing around the auditorium with his hands clasped together behind his back, and looking at ornaments, trophies and books. His uniform and officer's cap fitted him to perfection.

There was definitely something familiar about him. Even from the back it must have been his stance. The way he walked. An air of arrogance and authority seemed to exude from him.

Then, totally unexpectedly, he seemed to pivot on the soles of his brightly polished boots and turned to meet the Baroness as she descended the stairs. Baroness von Harstezzen recognised him as being the man who she had suspected. He was indeed a childhood friend of Rieber. He smiled a most engaging smile to her that could only initiate a feeling of friendliness and warmth in return.

The Baroness beckoned with her hand outstretched to the colonel to take a seat in one of the comfortable armchairs. Although the uniform that Colonel Burnhoff wore was repellent for the ideology and politics that it represented, the man beneath it was handsome and the possessor of great charm. It was hard not to be enveloped by the charisma of this man's presence.

"It is good to see you again," he said, taking her hand in a gentlemanly fashion. When Colonel Burnhoff spoke, his voice had a friendly timbre about its tone, "I have not been here since your late husband died."

Baroness von Harstezzen nodded. "I remember. You grew up with Rieber, didn't you? I could not recall your name at first, now I recall, though. When Rieber and I first married, you were a frequent visitor here."

He smiled at the memory "Yes. They were wonderful days. That was at a time before the euphoria of politics and ideals separated us. I always cherished my friendship with Rieber." There was understanding in his voice and sensitivity in his deep brown eyes. "Of course, I know that he did not have much time for politics, particularly my party, but I do recall that he loved this country with much devotion. He was a proud German, but dare I say a technocrat. I believe he thought that scientists and engineers were more equipped to run the country than mere politicians."

"That is true, Colonel Burnhoff. My husband did not like involvement with politics or politicians and I certainly do not either. I believe that Rieber vastly preferred the Weimar Constitution that was adopted by Germany in 1919. He did not like the changes made in later years. Primarily, he was an industrialist who believed in innovation, invention, manufacturing and wine production. He was always interested in new technological advances in every field of enterprise, particularly telecommunications and aeronautical progress."

"When I first became involved – truly involved as an officer in the German Army, I talked much to Rieber on that subject." Colonel Burnhoff pointed out. "We used to talk frequently on the reasons for that. The way in which the constitution established a democratic federal republic and made provision for a parliament of two houses and a president. It could be said that the Weimar Republic had very little strength to begin with. A great proportion of the German population found it difficult to understand the strengths that self-rule brings to a nation. Also many preferred the monarchy towering above politics; Rieber was amongst them, I know. Yet, in the massive price increases and the problems that the depression brought, even Rieber's financial concerns took a downturn. It could not be denied that the Chancellor improved the economy through his new constitutional powers".

"Do you think that Germany in the three years since the republic was dissolved in 1933 is a better place? Is that a naïve question, Colonel?" She was genuinely curious as to the man's real opinion. Did Colonel Burnhoff constantly follow the party line or did he have an alternative view?

"No, that is not a naïve question, Mrs Harstezzen," he answered politely. Then, in a direct manner, he said, "Nor was it a question innocently asked. I know many people in Germany ask the same question. I believe that the fruits are only just beginning to bear."

A feeling of coldness enveloped the Baroness. *The fruits are only just beginning to bear*. The words were more of a prophesy of doom, rather than a premonition of hope.

"Why are you here, Colonel Burnhoff," she asked him without betraying any signs of anxiety or impatience. "Is this a social visit? Or do you have some business to discuss regarding the Harstezzen factories?"

"Partly social – partly on business. For the party you understand." He reached into his jacket and produced an envelope. "In here you will find a request from Headquarters for armament parts. I trust you will pass this on to the manager of your munitions factory."

Baroness von Harstezzen looked at the requests in the letter, a shudder going down her spine as she realised the consequence of the use of such weapons.

"I shall pass the details on," she said coldly. But she felt that if it were possible every power within her grasp would create a slow manufacturing job before the appropriate people could put such armaments into use.

Colonel Burnhoff seemed eager to talk about other things more than mundane and official business. His interest in her extended beyond professional boundaries.

"I thought, too, that I could use this opportunity to visit the Harstezzen estate again and to see you. I often think of the times that I spent with you and Rieber. I always admired him as a man, the way in which he built his industries up after the end of the war. You know he and I grew up together, served as young soldiers in the trenches and married within weeks of each other after the armistice. His first wife and, I am also sad to say, my now late wife were friends. We both had our separate lives to lead. Mine in the military. Rieber as an industrialist." It was almost as if Colonel Burnhoff wanted to relate the memories to an audience. The Baroness sat transfixed, fascinated by the recollection of this man. "I think after Ypres, Paschaendale, and Villiers Bretonneaux that life in peacetime was a time for inspiration for us all in the depressed spirits of this country which was bitter in defeat. When Kaiser Wilhelm abdicated it was not the end but the start of a new resurgence." He paused changing the subject. "I always remember a film I saw made by a director called Fritz Lang – *Metropolis*. Did you ever see it, Mrs Harstezzen?"

"Yes, I did. It was about a time in the future. It was set in an underground city, in a time when mechanical inventions ruled over human beings."

"But did you not think that the Germany we live in could lead the way for the rest of the world? That it is rich in talent? It could lead through its scientific advancements, for example, rather than through creating a metropolis as we saw in the film. Under the Chancellor's guidance, who knows what kind of society we could create."

The Baroness sat in stony silence for a few moments. Her long cold look answered the question for him. She felt as if he was trying to convince her of his politics, which she thought of as distasteful and dreadful.

Then she answered, "In some ways I can understand why, in a country like Germany – defeated and dispirited after the end of the war – the people would cling to dreams of nationalism. Anything that would lift their spirits, in fact. Colonel Burnhoff, have you considered the rights of all men to be free? Would you deny any man that? Would you deny a man his own free rights because of his religion?"

He looked slightly confused and glanced at his watch nervously. Sensing that Colonel Burnhoff was now on the defensive, the Baroness pursued her conversation.

"In years to come history will judge this time very harshly, Verner." It was the first time she had used his first name, although now there was a slight edge of friction in her voice. "I remain, like my late husband, apolitical. It's a pity you did not learn more from Rieber. A society can change for the better without being prejudicial"

A smile surprisingly crept over Colonel Burnhoff's lips.

"There was much I could have learned from Rieber. I wish I had done so. Perhaps we could speak as old friends above politics. But as an old friend, please take a little advice: don't express your thoughts in a crowded place."

The Baroness smiled too. "Why, Verner? Would they think I was working against the national interest?"

They both laughed, but it was the Baroness who was laughing the most inside.

"What with your interests?" chuckled Colonel Burnhoff. "Your factories and the wine estates would keep you busy beyond the length of a normal working day. Speaking of wine—"

"Of course!" she interrupted him. "I have not forgotten, Verner, of your love of wine. If we have differences in views on politics, I know one thing that we will be agreed upon: Germany produces the greatest wine in the world." Verner nodded in agreement as the Baroness went to a cabinet and unlocked it, producing a bottle of a fine wine and two glasses. She poured from the bottle and gave the colonel a glass.

"Before you leave here," she said politely, hinting that he should make his departure shortly, "as one old friend to another, would you join me in a toast?"

"I would be most delighted to, Mrs Harstezzen," the colonel replied, raising his glass. "A toast between friends is always welcome. Long may our friendship continue."

The Baroness spoke, "To our future as individuals, Colonel." They clinked their glasses and then she continued, "And to the rights of free men throughout the world and freedom for all."

There seemed to be a pause as Colonel Burnhoff absorbed the words and then he appeared to concede to her without saying anything at all and joined in the toast. For in his heart deep down he knew she was right and, despite the doctrine he felt so compelled to espouse to all those who appeared willing to listen, he could not deny and question the rights and freedom of individuals.

The colonel stayed only a short time after that before making his exit. In her mind the Baroness looked at this soldier as he strode to the car outside of the window and she recalled him from several meetings years before. She had felt half compelled to tell him of the activities of the Circle and the private work she was involved in. There was just the glimmer of a chance that this old friend of her late husband could have been won over to her cause and acted as an inside informant on the hierarchy of the ruling party in power.

Somehow, though, Colonel Burnhoff seemed to be possessed of the burning zeal of a fervent nationalist, for all the wrong reasons it seemed. His thoughts and aims would not be open to persuasion easily. Such a shame. Colonel Burnhoff was similar in some respects to Rieber von Harstezzen. Just for a moment, and only a brief moment, Baroness von Harstezzen thought it possible that he may well have been a man she could have loved. If only he did not wear that uniform or believe in the policy it purported to represent.

***

For the rest of the year Baroness von Harstezzen maintained her role, keeping in contact with the various people carrying out their allotted tasks in neighbouring countries. In Holland a small group had been established who were pursuing their intentions quietly. It was evident that this small and pleasant country in the circumstances of war could easily be taken and occupied.

The Baroness was satisfied that much work had been carried out so successfully in the high and low countries of Europe. Her thoughts now turned to England where Freddie Miller was in charge of the organisation of the Circle activities.

Nine

Freddie had been swift to pursue his new mission in life on his return from Spain. He had been active in beginning the work of the Circle in England. There had been no joy in his last filming assignment in Spain.

During this assignment they had got a great deal of historical footage in the can. Some of it was explicit bravado of the opposing Spanish forces and some of it was of explicit violence: a monastery blowing up in a quiet village and then other buildings close by, a hotel blowing up in Madrid, whole streets shelled, a fire raging out of control, troops and mercenaries in bloody combat, children crying, lost in the street, innocent people caught in a crossfire. Such were the results of the turmoil of the civil war.

Now in a private studio in London, in the suburb of Shepherds Bush, not far from Freddie's home in Hammersmith, the cinematic footage of these events of battle and terror were being cut, spliced and edited. They were run and rerun on a projector until the full extent of events in the Spanish Civil War were being shown for full effect. In order to provide a dramatisation of merit, a commentary describing each incident was added. The commentator was Freddie.

He had always begun his commentaries saying, "This is Freddie Miller reporting from —." The list of places and incidents was impressive: Nuremburg, Pamplona, Rome, Abyssinia, India, Paris and Berlin. The people Freddie had seen and recorded on film, included dictators, royalty and statesmen. He had once walked with Gandhi in the rain in India and been stunningly impressed by this figure of peace and love, whose very character puzzled and intrigued the Western world.

He had travelled briefly to Abyssinia and seen Mussolini's pretence to military victory. On film, Freddie's news team had captured the true story.

Coming from Spain where he had seen more tragedy in the making, it seemed so peaceful to be watching the changing events of the world isolated in a warm film-editing studio in West London. Yet it was also immensely worrying. How long before the net of war would stir England from its isolation? Would events in Europe escalate without warning?

Even at home in England there were problems. The Depression had taken its toll on the country. Unemployment had broken the back of the working people, but not the spirit of the British people who in times of trouble pulled together like no other nation on earth. The government of the day, headed by the authoritative figure of Prime Minister Stanley Baldwin, had much to grapple with in its economic problems. Soon it would also have an unexpected constitutional crisis to deal with coming from within the monarchy itself.

Far from the world that was referred to as 'Up West' by the East Enders and the outer suburbs, the real side of Britain in the difficult period of the 1930s was epitomised by the men who marched in the Jarrow Crusade and the coal miners who worked in abysmal conditions and the unemployed people who searched endlessly for work in a depressed situation that seemingly had no light at the end of the tunnel. The other world 'Up West' was one where the music of Ambrose or Harry Roy played, champagne glasses clinked over tables at the Ritz or the Savoy, the Café de Paris or the smart hotels around Knightsbridge and Mayfair where all talk seemed to be around the King's relationship with Mrs Simpson.

Freddie and his news team had once filmed King Edward VIII at Buckingham Palace. The King had amiably mixed with the cameramen afterwards shaking each of their hands with a warm affable manner. He was far from aloof and very approachable.

Freddie, who was by his own political tastes a man of issues rather than either a conservative or a socialist, admired the king greatly. However he thought that the king in his exalted position was often radical in his views, not that this was a disqualification of course for such a high office. Some of the greatest heads of state in history had been radical and forward thinking. If anything perhaps that was what set a great leader apart.

When Freddie in his role as the director of a newsreel team had met King Edward VIII, he had found the man in person to be genuinely concerned about the welfare of his people. It seemed that the expected long reign of this popular and much loved monarch was going to come to an ignominious end, with the prospect of abdication looming, so that he could be constitutionally free to marry a twice-divorced American woman, Mrs Wallis Simpson. His good intentions were being obscured by his romantic desires.

During the era of the 1930s since Freddie had left the army he had recorded all the events of historical importance through the lens of a cinecamera. From the agonised faces of the unemployed and the despairing caught up in the Great Depression to the rise of the Third Reich and the turbulence of the Spanish Civil War, he had been witness to it all. He had not only lived through it all, he had become part of it.

When the film of the Spanish troubles had been edited and spliced, and put into documentary footage, the assignment had virtually been completed; Freddie had given a commentary throughout the newsreel that had been recorded against particular sequences. There were some scenes where words were better unsaid. For effect, a guitarist playing flamenco-style music accompanied some scenes. Somehow the instrumental played against the background of the cold, stark, barren reality of war was more descriptive in its mixture of musical notes than a thousand words of commentary.

With the job over Freddie began the work of the Companions of the Circle. Writing as a 'concerned individual' he sent letters to every national newspaper in England expressing his fears for Europe. Many of the press barons had already expressed their views privately and were now well aware of the growing voices of dissent amongst the British public. They began to reflect their own concern through a number of editorials. Some parliamentarians, notably Anthony Eden and Winston Churchill, campaigned with vigour against the situation. Tragically, their warnings were vastly unheeded.

Freddie's various letters to newspapers under his pseudonym certainly aroused interest if not quite inflaming the passions about the harsh treatment of the Jewish people under Hitler's regime. Several more concerned papers made a point in their editorials of referring to letters from the public and as a result kept their journalists based in Berlin and Munich very busy sending back highly detailed despatches. Once Freddie had written to a certain newspaper, a flood of letters from other members of the public would pour into that particular publishing house expressing similar views. By constantly writing letters incognito Freddie managed to keep the issue alive and continuously in the news. He made a point of sending copies of the newspapers to Baroness von Harstezzen who read them with constant interest. Such a relatively small task as writing letters in fact provided an enormous impetus to the functions of the Circle.

The next stage of his assignment for the Circle was to organise a huge petition to present to the British government for them as incentive to oppose the policies of the Third Reich. In order to do this Freddie had established a network of sympathisers throughout the United Kingdom on his behalf to collect signatures. Once this had been achieved Freddie forwarded the massive petition through his local member of parliament. The man who was a personal friend of Freddie's saw to it that this reached the Prime Minister and his government's ministers. Certainly this action prompted by Freddie never let the matter waiver at this stage,

With these tasks accomplished the remainder of the assignment could be carried out. It was nearing December 1936 and in January Freddie would be leaving for the United States to do some newsreel work there. He had very little time to advise his contacts in the army and the intelligence section of his newfound association with the Companions of the Circle. These were the only people in England that Freddie was to advise at this stage of the existence of such a group. He thought of the prospect of revealing the details with trepidation. There was always the possibility that he would not be taken seriously. That may well be the case, however, Freddie did have a couple of aces up his sleeve. Before he had left Baroness von Harstezzen's estate, this lady had given Freddie the names and addresses of numerous members of the Circle, which could prove to be of great importance to the British intelligence groupings in Europe in future years.

There was a certain colonel in the Special Operations Group whom Freddie had served with in the Middle East. His name was Colonel Francis Brindmarsh, a stalwart soldier's soldier as they say in the services, who could inspire feelings of enmity and dislike or respect and admiration.

Freddie rang Colonel Brindmarsh's office to make an appointment and found himself speaking to his former friend and colleague. In order that a crossed line did not give away the real meaning for this meeting, Freddie arranged the appointment on the supposition that as the prospect of war was now a distinct possibility he wanted to discuss rejoining the service. Colonel Brindmarsh was puzzled, but agreed to see him the next day at his office in Whitehall.

At Whitehall, Freddie sat in a waiting room when a civil servant came to take him to Colonel Brindmarsh's office. The corridors of the building echoed with the footsteps of people striding along them. They stopped at an office. The man knocked on the door, opened it and allowed Freddie to enter.

Colonel Brindmarsh rose to greet him with a firm handshake. To look at him, he was every inch a military man. He towered well over six-feet in height. His physical build was that of a man who had been used to rigorous exercise. Although he was balding with grey temples and a jet-black wiry moustache streaked with silver, his face looked considerably younger than his forty years.

The two men faced each other over a desk and reminisced about times in the Middle East and Malta. Then it was down to business.

"So, you want to come back?" he quizzed Freddie. The colonel's accent betrayed his early upbringing in Edinburgh.

"Not right at this very moment," Freddie replied, "but I do have a little story to tell you. It's not fiction, a fairy tale or fantasy, but one of fact."

Freddie then began to tell Colonel Brindmarsh the whole of the story beginning with his visit to Berlin for the Olympics. He went on to explain about the work of the Companions of the Circle, the people involved, the names and addresses of the various agents that Freddie produced in a list, and Baroness von Harstezzen's association with the organisation. Colonel Brindmarsh sat intrigued and silent but his eyes indicated surprise.

In order to clarify the story even more, Freddie produced various letters from the Baroness and Arthandur as legitimate proof of the existence of such an organisation. The colonel was mystified in one sense and enthralled in another. These sorts of valuable leads were the stuff that the backroom boys dreamed of. Before he could use the information in a functional basis there were many more important factors that needed to be taken into consideration.

Colonel Brindmarsh listened to all the details intently. He could make the distinction between truth and pure fantasy with little trouble. He was a past-master at the art of intelligence work and he was impressed by Freddie's revelations. If it could be proved to be factual, there was much substance in the information on which useful foundations could be built in the coming years; the implementation of this knowledge could be of paramount importance to any future undercover work.

Brindmarsh lit his pipe, inhaled and listened carefully to every word uttered by Freddie. It was all so compact, it was all so neat; he had to allow himself some leeway for deliberation.

"Am I really expected to believe all this?" he asked Freddie in the manner of a doubting Thomas. Privately it was his careful act that actually concealed his true delight at this newfound knowledge. "It's a most fantastic story, you know."

"Can you afford not to?" Freddie riposted. "I'm certain this will be of positive benefit."

"We can certainly use this information. As you know I'm a believer that prevention is better than care. I hope that war can be stopped before it is started, There are regrettably warmongers who'd relish it. The fact is, Freddie old son, I and some of my colleagues are already working with organisations that one day may provide resistance should it be necessary to do so." He ran his finger down the list looking through the names and addressed. "And you say all these people are working for the Circle already?"

"Yes. Right throughout the length and breadth of Europe, Holland, Belgium, Austria and France. All carefully negotiated. Need I go on?"

Brindmarsh twisted his moustache. "What about Hungary, Poland and Czechoslovakia?"

"That's an interesting point," Freddie said, realising it was an area that he had no knowledge of whether the Circle actually operated there or not. "I think they may still be trying to establish leads there."

"And this Baroness?" Brindmarsh was not only curious but also genuinely fascinated by the sound of this woman.

"Baroness Christina von Harstezzen."

"Yes. She is the mainstay of all this? The pivotal compass in the circumference." The colonel grinned at Freddie. "No need to be alarmed, Freddie. I wasn't being sarcastic, I was just thinking of some code name for this particular lady. We have operatives under various code names you know."

"What happens now Colonel Brindmarsh?" He was undoubtedly concerned at the almost blasé manner of such a brilliant man who was known for his organisational work. He seemed unimpressed. Yet Freddie knew that this man's very casualness hid his real mission in life; weaving complex intelligence networks.

"Naturally I'll have to get the backroom boys to look into this. There's a great deal of the information you've given me that will need verification. I'll get back to you on this." Brindmarsh thought hard for a moment, "Now!" He raised his finger to make a point of emphasis. "The subject of providing sponsorship for Jewish refugees. That's a sticky one. It's going to depend on the government's office policy on this."

"In what sense? If I or any of the people I may make contact with can provide a halfway house or lodging and are willing to look after the refugees while they establish themselves – well, what could possibly be the problem there?"

The colonel was quick to reply. "There may not be problems with refugees from Belgium, France and Holland. If we are going to think in terms of countries that we may be involved in should there be any future declaration of war, let me say now that any refugees would have to be carefully screened." He tapped his pipe gently on the table. "For obvious reasons," he felt inclined to add. "There's always the probability that in wartime, agents disguised as refugees could infiltrate the networks in this country."

"I see." Freddie slumped back into his chair. "I'm sure that many of the countries in the Empire are already taking many refugees, America and Palestine naturally, and here of course. The Circle was looking at taking people through the back door, unofficially."

Colonel Brindmarsh looked concerned. "That's it, Freddie. By all means operate within the Circle on an official basis. Don't attempt – don't even think about doing anything underhand or illegal – like providing false passports for instances, documents that are forged."

"I understand, Colonel," Freddie replied almost meekly. "At this stage I think the main aim has been to organise sponsorship and homes for some of the refugees to go to. If there is a great deal of pressure applied to them later on we can't abide totally with the laws of bureaucracy. We will need to save as many German and Austrian Jewish lives by any means that we can if they are threatened. And that may mean falsifying documents of identity and passports. Baroness von Harstezzen and Arthandur Palmai have already done this in the cases of a few people who were being constantly frustrated in their attempts to leave."

Brindmarsh wrote a few notes then looked up at Freddie. "The Circle is very expansive in its role," he said quietly. "Let me get this absolutely straight. It's a possible resistance group?"

"Yes,"

"And it's attempting to detour many migration procedures? By providing documents, the Circle is finding homes and contacts for refugees?"

"That's absolutely right, Colonel Brindmarsh."

"And—" he said with strong emphasis, "and its operation and agents are spread throughout Europe."

"You've memorised the complete breakdown," Freddie said with a smile.

The colonel stood up offering a handshake to Freddie as polite dismissal.

"I have much to do now. I'll be in touch with you before you go to America. Remember, Freddie, don't do anything unofficial." He hesitated. "At this stage do everything within the bounds of secrecy for the Circle on a legal basis. Oh, and continue to keep me informed. Ring me to make an appointment. And thank you for your confidence. I look forward to working with you again."

Freddie left the office and made his way out into the London Street. Colonel Brindmarsh walked to the window. What a great asset to special operations, the knowledge and aid of the Circle would provide. Brindmarsh asked his secretary to obtain a file on Freddie Miller's military history, and in due course a bundle of papers were deposited on his desk. It was more out of curiosity than anything that he wanted to browse through Freddie's history, although it was a course of natural routine when establishing informants and contacts..

There was no doubt that Freddie was an interesting man. The file was well detailed: Frederick Robert Miller, born April 10th 1905, Alton, Hampshire, the son of Thomas and Jean Miller, now both deceased and formerly dairy farmers. At the age of twelve Freddie had sat for the entrance examination to Somerset Grammar School, a fairly well-to-do establishment, and on his high marks and academic ability had won a scholarship there. From there he had entered Sandhurst Military College as an Officer Cadet in 1924 and after training he had been on active service in intelligence work in India, the Middle East, Saudi Arabia and Malta. By this time he had become conversant in Arabic, some Indian dialect, French and German. His personal interests had revolved around cinematography. Whilst on service he had often filmed for army documentary use, particular operations and areas of scrutiny. When Freddie had left the army together with a friend of his from a British film studio, they had established a newsreel team together, which travelled the world to major news spots.

Brindmarsh wondered about many of the tasks that Freddie had carried out for the Circle so far. Certainly Freddie Miller was in a good position to work incognito. He was constantly on the move; undoubtedly he could continually make fresh contacts in other countries for the Baroness's operations. In truth Brindmarsh was quite impressed with what Freddie had achieved so far: The huge response and the petition to parliament. Perhaps, thought the wily colonel, he could convince Freddie to come back into the armed services again, if only for a short time, to help the operations under way.

While Colonel Brindmarsh set the wheels in operation using the information he had been provided with of the workings of the Circle, Freddie tried to establish links with the Jewish community in England. His objective was to sound out families and leading figures such as Rabbis in the Golders Green area and also much of the market areas like Whitechapel, Aldgate and the East End where the rag trade proliferated. By meeting people in these areas he could find out if any of them would be willing to resettle German and Austrian Jewish refugees.

With a list of addresses he had obtained by detailed research in reference books and old newspaper files, he began the difficult task. Freddie had forgotten the bustle of the East End of London. Walking around Petticoat Lane there was sparkle and life, stalls with everything on sale for everyone's taste or so it seemed. 'Violets – lovely Violets', trinkets, fruit, vegetables, puppy dogs and textiles. The people always seemed to smile here and be so consistently cheerful despite the brisk December weather. It was a joy to be here, he thought, in this area of London where he believed the friendliest people on earth must live and the most down to earth salt of the earth artisans dwell, but it was back to business.

For the next few days Freddie, acting alone as in the guise of one of many concerned individuals, spoke to a huge number of people in the communities around London who would be willing to sponsor a family or individual refugees. By contacting the editors of different Jewish publications and different synagogues, he managed to compile a list of addresses of people offering sponsorship. He would at once return to his flat in Hammersmith and advise Baroness von Harstezzen of what he had organised. He also took the trouble of ringing Colonel Brindmarsh and letting him know, as he had promised to do so, of the various stages of his work for the Circle.

On December 11th 1936, Freddie sat by his wireless writing a letter to Baroness Christina von Harstezzen. In it he wrote about what he had achieved so far. There was always the chance that, in the cloak and dagger world of evasion and half truths and double meanings relative to intrigue and intelligence work, some aspiring Nazi could have established a link between the Baroness and her secret operation work. Therefore in the fear of his letter being intercepted, Freddie had written it in a carefully worded fashion that would indicate to her his accomplishments. He also chose to mention his address in the United States where she could write to him prior to her arrival there.

When he was writing the letter he stopped for one moment to listen to the wireless. He put his pen and paper down and listened keenly: it was the King's speech to his people. The crisis over the King's relationship with Mrs Simpson had been building up to its final constitutional crescendo. King Edward VIII was abdicating and his younger brother would then take over as the reigning monarch.

There was a silence. Even the street outside of his flat window seemed to be devoid of traffic. Then the King's voice came across from Winsor Castle over the air. Freddie listened to this poignant note of history and noted the date at the top of the letter he was writing. December 11th 1936.

The King spoke in a voice that phrased each line carefully and slowly. The wording was spaced without signs of emotion, but in a couple of syllables, his voice quivered slightly suggesting that there were feelings below being kept in control. Across the airwaves that day where people in all parts of the British Isles listened, they heard Edward VIII speak. "At long last I am able to say a few words of my own," Freddie listened as the words, making history, came over the air. "But until now it has not been constitutionally possible for me to speak." The speech was effective, but certain phrases made more impact than others and stayed in the mind. There was something very surreal about this day.

"But you must believe me when I tell you that I have found it impossible to carry the heavy burden of responsibility and to discharge my duties of King as I would wish to do without the help and support of the woman I love." It was the final words that seemed so powerful. "And now we all have the new King. I wish him and you his people happiness and prosperity with all my heart. God bless you all. God save the King."

Very shortly the ex-King, now the Duke of Windsor, would be saying farewell to the Royal family, staff and servants at Windsor castle. Then he would be on his way to France where he would marry Mrs Simpson. The new monarch would be King George VI who was married to Elizabeth Bowes-Lyon. They would become the most loved King and Queen in many years. They were fine and gently spoken people, who would in time inspire great love.

After Freddie had listened to the radio broadcast and finished his letter, he crossed to the window of his flat and gazed out. This was a strange age, an era of happenings. History seemed to be made every day. He glanced back at the table where the letter he had been writing to the Baroness lay on the surface. In a way he was contributing in a minor way to history by his involvement in that group of supporters for the cause of the Jewish people in Europe. For much of the decade Freddie had studied the newsworthy events through a cinecamera. The thought struck him that he was in the throes of being a participant by his recent actions. Not an observer or a recorder of history, but perhaps even a creator of history.

Freddie came back down to earth again. If he got carried away by his own enthusiasm he would lose sight of reality. Strange, he thought, how the Duke of Windsor now on his way to exile in France could give up being the reigning monarch of England and the Dominions for the security of marriage to an American woman of obscurity. The Duke of Windsor and Mrs Simpson. Well good luck and God bless them both, thought Freddie. May they find the happiness they seek. Then he thought of the new King and his charming wife.

Perhaps it was all fate that these things happened. Maybe they were unwittingly destined to be the King and Queen and that by their accidental ascension to the throne their direct descendants would prove to be great and well loved titular heads in the future. Yes, it was probably fate, like the fate that inexplicably drew Freddie to the work of the Circle, like the fate that seemed bound for the Palmai family and many similar families

Next year he would enjoy meeting the Baroness again. That would be a pleasant experience. In the meantime he thought now that it was nearing Christmas he would try and enjoy the festive season. There was a girl he could ring if he could find her telephone number. Perhaps she'd like to go to the Hammersmith Palais one night.

There was a time, thought Freddie, that some of the finest things could be found in the simple things of life. With all the talk of war, the Nazis forever pushing themselves to the forefront of European power and the chaos that was Spain, Freddie wanted to enjoy himself before more turmoil. It was nearing Christmas and no one seemed to be sure what prospects that the new year would bring. Better enjoy this one, at least what was left of it.

For a moment all those seemingly glamorous travels with a news team, encounters with a German Baroness and being part of a secret organisation, could all go to the background. It would be nice to enjoy the atmosphere of a London dance hall and the company of a pretty girl.

The next day Freddie rang an old friend. "Cynthia?" he asked.

"Hullo, Freddie, you old rascal." The voice at the other end sounded delighted to hear from him. He knew she would be. Cynthia Field was one of those girls a man could always be friends with without fear of deep involvement. They both had their relationships with others, but were platonic friends who would meet up from time to time and talk about recent occurrences in their lives.

Cynthia seemed pleased to talk to him. "I see you've been a busy boy, Freddie. I was at the Curzon the other night and guess who came across the screen between features reporting live from the Spanish Civil War? How many Spanish girls did you chase between explosions, Freddie? Damn dangerous if you ask me! I'm glad you're home, darling."

He laughed at her wit. Cynthia was always flighty and fun to be with. She was also provocatively flirtatious without intent.

"Cynthia, are you free over the festive season?" He asked.

"Darling, for you I'm always free. You still haven't taken up the opportunity to marry me. And after I went down on one knee and proposed too!"

Freddie felt happy to be the recipient of her wit. "Well, Cynthia, I'm totally free. No close family ties. No permanent lady in my life. And I've just got a bit of free time to early January when I leave to do some news work in America for a while. You name the night, Cynthia, and perhaps we could go to dinner and dancing!"

"New Year's Eve, Freddie. I'm just dying to kiss you passionately. What better excuse than New Years Eve?"

"You've talked me into it, Cynthia. I'll pick you up at seven o'clock. This one's on me, lovely."

He heard Cynthia laugh happily at the other end of the phone. She was a nice uncomplicated girl, and, in this world and his own life that was becoming increasingly complex, it would be nice to enjoy a few simple pleasures.

He had hardly put the phone down to contemplate a few moments of gaiety when it rang again sharply. He hesitated before answering it. Then when he did the unmistakeable tones, not sharp but mild and dour voice of Colonel Brindmarsh came on the line.

"Freddie. Your leads have been verified," he said, referring to the list of the Companions of the Circle that Freddie had provided him with. It would seem that Brindmarsh had access through his intelligence networks to a wide field of acquaintances that could immediately confirm the existence of agents of any resistance groups. In Europe they could gain access to files of the local populace or just merely by placing an observer on the person in question.

"I'm glad, sir," Freddie acknowledged him with respect.

"Get in touch with me as soon as you get back from the States. Anyway, Freddie, merry Christmas, and may the new year be a peaceful one for us all."

The phone disengaged. The Circle agents had been confirmed by intelligence forces, now Freddie considered that one part of his mission had been successfully completed. There would be the question of assistance to future refugees to be answered, but that was a subject he would discuss with Baroness von Harstezzen when they met up in the United States in the next year.

Just a few days before his imminent departure on an ocean liner for New York, Freddie kept his appointment with Cynthia Field. The streets of London on the last night of 1936 were already filled with many revellers going out to celebrate in style.

By midnight there would be crowds in Trafalgar Square and Piccadilly. He had always loved the feel of New Years Eve and the handshakes from complete strangers wishing them all the best and the expectations of good things to come in the next year.

Freddie arrived at the flat in Earls Court where Cynthia lived and they greeted each other affectionately and then proceeded to a dinner dance at a London hotel not far from Piccadilly.

Cynthia was a striking young woman in her mid-twenties. She had long, well-kept auburn hair, bright sparkling brown eyes and a cheery smile. Considering her fine womanly qualities and her pleasant personality, it was a wonder that she had not been married off long ago. In truth, she had always wished that Freddie would fall madly in love with her. Yet, knowing the nomadic ways of Freddie Miller and his love of excitement, she had given up trying to snare him and was contented for the moment just being a close friend of his.

People were up dancing on the hotel ballroom floor wearing party hats, singing in tune with the music and participating in the 'Lambeth Walk' while the band played in a jovial mood. Freddie and Cynthia talked of things that had happened in the past year. They were at a quiet corner table and watched the dancers.

"So it's all over with that girl in Germany then, Freddie?" Cynthia said very sympathetically. She was always sincere, but not serious in her manner.

"I don't think it ever really stood a chance if truth be known," said Freddie in a matter of fact way. "Tillie was a girl I had a blazing infatuation for. She was independent, beautiful, intelligent, everything but loyal and loving. Now she's infatuated with the politics of her country. She actually believes all that rubbish. Anyway, that's enough of my story, what about you, Cynthia?"

"Oh, I'm still a simple Civil Service secretary. There was a chap I was seeing for a while, but I think I was a bit too boisterous for him! I think my personality was a bit overwhelming! I scared him away. It was no loss, he couldn't dance the tango anyway!"

They both smiled at her admission. She was undoubtedly gregarious and an extrovert.

"Do you remember where we first met, Cynthia? Your personality even in those days was bubbly, breezy and bright. A bit too bright for some of those officer types."

"How could I forget, darling? At a military ball, on an unbearably humid night at the height of an Indian summer, when monsoon-type rains drove us all inside. All those upper class army officers from rich family backgrounds kept asking me to dance, and then I plucked up the courage and asked you! And to my delight you accepted. I was so pleased too when I found that, although you were an officer and spoke nicely, you were a farmer's son and down to earth like me."

"Now it's my turn to remind you, Cynthia. You were an eighteen-year-old Straits born, Bournemouth girl, just arrived in India for a fun time. It's funny how the course of life takes us. I was just getting to know you and then I was posted to the Middle East and then to Malta. If I hadn't we could have had the most fabulous passionate love affair!"

"I always enjoyed your letters, particularly about your leaves in Paris and Spain. It's a pity though."

"What's a pity, pretty lady?"

"Oh, if you hadn't left India and not met the German girl, you might have accepted my marriage proposal," she said jokingly. "I was serious, you know. I don't do things by halves! I need your help to get pregnant. I can't do it on my own with a smile on my face!"

"Well there's still time, Cynthia. Why don't you accept my proposal of a dance? By the way I know how to dance the tango!"

"I won't turn you down like those officers at Jawapindoo in that case. We'll show them what we can do, shall we?"

It was a happy night. The people on the dance floor were going to make sure of that. Freddie and Cynthia threw their inhibitions to the wind, put on funny paper hats and joined in on the crowd.

They waltzed, they danced South American style and kicked up a storm dancing in such a professional style, that the other dancers made an enclave around them. Cynthia was dazzling and vivacious, and in her tight gown she was a real head-turner, a complete complement to Freddie, who himself caught a few admiring glances from various girls.

Much more than anything, it was a fun night. All the talk of war in Spain, the growing concern of Germany and the abdication of a popular King had overly contributed to 1936 being a year of frightening change and a time when nothing seemed certain anymore. There was this universal feeling that tonight should be enjoyed and it was contagious. Everyone was laughing and joking.

Cynthia tossed her head back and laughed. She stood to one side while Freddie shed himself of his dignity, rolled his trousers up above his kneecaps and linked arms with a happy group dancing and singing along to 'Knees up Mother Brown'. Cynthia could not help but adore Freddie. He could always be a surprise.

Pretending to be exhausted after the dance, he crawled over to Cynthia on all fours and then, standing up and straightening his clothes out, he took her in his arms as the music changed, and the lights dimmed as the mood of the evening changed from one of amusement to romance.

The band was playing a softer tune now, it was an instrumental version of a popular romantic ballad of the day. With a mixed brass combination and string sounds, the couples on the dance floor glided around holding each other in a manner befitting lovers,

The music that swirled around the hall was instantly recognisable: 'The Blue of the Night', 'Please', 'On a Steamer Coming Over', all popular songs of that era.

The dancers in their dinner suits and ball gowns looked spectacular with the different colours of their outfits blending together.

Cynthia looked up at Freddie occasionally as they danced. She relished being in the hold of his arms. The lights were dim to create the atmosphere that seemed to tie in with romance, and occasionally the gleam from one of the beams in the overhanging chandelier would catch the twinkle in Cynthia's eyes.

Freddie was letting his mind drift. He was thinking of everything that had happened this year. The girl in his arms was aware that Freddie's thoughts were elsewhere. She could sense it.

"What are you thinking of?" she whispered. "Or more to the point, where are you?"

"Oh, Germany and Spain. And you set my memory back to Jawapindoo of all places. Normally I think of Valetta, Riyadh, Paris, Bordeaux and Biarritz, and do you know what? I couldn't be happier being here tonight."

Freddie had actually been thinking about the Baroness in her estate with the castle surrounded by the finest wine crop in Europe. He felt a sense of guilt dancing with a girl who he had always known deep down really loved him. There had been Tillie, the girl in Berlin he had been in love with but who had never really had any true feelings for him. He had seen her from time to time over the years. She was now something of the past. The Baroness was a woman some years older than him who represented the type of woman he had never really been acquainted with. Business-minded, strong, authoritative and beautiful with skills in running industries and a network of agents. She was unattainable, a distant dream.

The girl he was dancing with was a freewheeling happy person, light years removed from the women of the world he had known. She was fun and a loving person to be with. He felt pressed to talk about days he had known with her in Jawapindoo, India.

"I always think of the oppressive heat when I remember Jawapindoo, you know, Cynthia," he spoke in a voice barely a whisper. "I think of the faces of the beggars, the holy men, the market place, the different castes and the cattle in the street. I always remember some of my brother officers, so pompous they thought that they were a cut above everyone else, and the way they used to treat the Indians with such disdain. I couldn't bear it at times."

"That was why I liked you, Freddie," Cynthia said in a rare moment when she really appeared serious. "You're the son of a poor farmer, darling, who rose in life through his own ability. A man with respect for others. I adore men with compassion and gentility."

Freddie felt quite flattered by her comments. He looked up at a clock on the wall. There were five minutes to go before midnight. Everyone was on the dance floor now ready to see the new year in. A compere stood by the microphone. 1937 was merely minutes away.

"That was the nicest thing anyone has said to me for a while." He stopped swaying and pulled her really close. "I don't think we need to wait till midnight for that passionate kiss." He embraced her and kissed her warmly.

From the compere's microphone a voice came across the hall in a broad North Country accent filled with a sense of humour for the occasion.

"Well there's a couple who can't wait for the new year, ladies and gentlemen," the compere said, referring to Freddie and Cynthia who looked up and smiled. "Everyone on the dance floor for 'Auld Lang Syne'."

Soon everyone poured onto the floor of the hotel ballroom and as the countdown began towards midnight, the revellers linked hands.

"It's 1937, ladies and gentlemen! Happy New Year!"

Champagne corks popped. Strangers shook hands and embraced. 'Auld Lang Syne' was sung by everyone as balloons rose to the roof.

Freddie and Cynthia left soon afterwards and mingled with the crowds around Piccadilly Circus. There were people mounting the Statue of Eros and forming a human pyramid. People were doing a Cockney knees-up. It was curious how this particular New Years Eve was one that Freddie really felt he needed to celebrate. This year had been indicative of things to come.

Looking around at the happy revellers heading off down into Regent Street it was interesting for Freddie to speculate just how many of those young men would be members of the armed forces in the not too distant future. He put his arm around Cynthia and walked along in the cold night air to the car.

Outside of Cynthia's flat, Freddie declined the invitation to go inside for coffee – an invitation that may or may not lead to a romantic interlude. Instead they just sat inside the warmth of the car talking for a while. Cynthia lit a cigarette. She seemed pensive as she spoke.

"I suppose you've seen it all this year, Freddie, haven't you? The Nazis and the troubles in Spain."

"That was part of the reason I wanted to get out tonight. This year might be one of the last that we'll have the opportunity to celebrate News Years Eve in peacetime."

"You seem certain there'll be a war then?"

"Unfortunately, yes. There'll be problems in Europe if Hitler decides to move his forces. He will, I'm certain. I saw all the signs there. Oh I know it's the new year now and it's probably morbid talk, but I'm a realist and war is not only inevitable, I regret to say it is certain."

"What will you do if there is war?"

Freddie turned to look at her directly. He felt safe in this girl's company. "I'd join up again on active service."

"You always did look good in uniform. You seem so convinced. I get the impression that you saw a lot more than you are willing to admit."

"I met this chap in a café in Berlin one day, a Jewish doctor from a village in Austria: Arthandur. He has a wife called Marlene and a young son about fifteen called Nathan. Well I stayed with Arthandur and his family in this lovely village and where they lived they were surrounded by many other – I suppose you'd call them self-imposed exiled refugees. They are restricted in their freedom of movement, their choice of work, even certain shops won't serve them. I wondered what sort of world their young son, Nathan, would grow up in."

Cynthia leaned across and slipped her hand around Freddie's, "You think that because of the oppression of people like them that will lead to war. Surely the government will try and avoid it. They don't want another fiasco like that fourteen-eighteen thing."

"Perhaps they will but I could not imagine a civilised country like ours standing and watching things happening across the water that may eventually threaten even our own way of life here."

Cynthia puffed on her cigarette. Even in the car the chill of the night could be felt. They sat in silence for a while. Then she spoke in a soft voice.

"I've always had feelings for you, Freddie. We've been friends since 1928. Quite some time, isn't it? I know you've had your girlfriends – particularly Tillie – but all these years did you ever think that maybe you could have loved me?"

There had been almost an element of sadness in her voice. It seemed to indicate an expected disappointment of her long secretly held hopes for marriage to him. Freddie knew this. He gripped her hand strongly.

"Often," he replied to her. "My life was never straightforward, I've always had feelings for you too, Cynthia. Sometimes I think I was too wrapped up in my own work. I've been going through my own life with blinkers on. Trying to see everything and missing out on much of the best of it."

"Well I'll be here when you come back, Freddie. I always have been."

Cynthia moved her arms up around Freddie and kissed him slowly, passionately and luxuriously. She let herself out of the car and moved up the steps to the entrance of the house where her flat was situated. Freddie watched her through the window. She waved her fingers at him and he in turn blew a kiss to her. One day soon, he considered, he would have to weigh up the balances of matrimony.

Four days later he sailed from Southampton aboard a liner bound for New York. His entire news team was on board, thrilled to be heading off on an assignment in more peaceful conditions. The voyage across was pleasant although the North Atlantic was very cold at this time of the year. It was to be his first visit to North America. He had been looking forward to the journey enormously. People had told him so much about travelling in the United States. Freddie was not to be disappointed.

On the huge liner he made acquaintance with a number of people who offered him invitations should he ever come to their towns. Some of the Americans that Freddie met seemed interested in his recent travels. They wondered what a newsman's close observations were of the current European situation. Even across the waters of the Atlantic Ocean, the thoughts of war and the possibility of it occurring in the near future were a worry to the people of the United States.

Freddie's first view of New York from the deck of an ocean liner was one that would stay in his memory forever. The huge white skyscrapers against a blue sky on a bitterly cold day provided an impressive backdrop on first viewing. It was here that Freddie would meet up with the contacts he had made in some big film companies for whom he would be working with for the next few months. Once his itinerary had been planned, he would forward a copy of it to Baroness von Harstezzen. Then they would work out a date and place to meet up somewhere in the United States where they would discuss the progress of the Circle's activities.

The United States that Freddie's news team were going to film for the benefit of British cinema-goers was a land, even in the aftermath of the Great Depression of the 1930s, that still captured much of the world's imagination. It represented to so many people a land where dreams thought to be unattainable could prove to be a reality. Many migrants in the European countries under threat from any future occupation by Hitler's forces saw the USA as a country representing freedom and safety.

Franklin D Roosevelt, the President of the United States, had come to power at a time of great economic depression pledging a new deal for the people of America. Slowly his new deal policies were leading the people out of an economic abyss.

Hollywood was a sparkling dream factory with film studios such as Warner Brothers and Metro Goldwyn Mayer producing movie after movie making it one of the most prolific industries in the country. From movie posters all through the country the faces of glittering stars of the magnitude of Clark Gable and Errol Flynn gazed down at movie patrons escaping from the hardship of the economic times for a night out at the cinema.

The hopes and aspirations of the oakies and the sharecroppers and itinerant workers were being realised in the orange groves and the fruit farms of California. Baseball and Grid Iron Football were prodigiously played, supported by thousands of gum-chewing fans and with an introduction to the games being enhanced by the presence of cheerleaders, and pneumatic-thighed drum majorettes twirling their batons with precision. Large Cadillacs dominated the streets. People were confident, friendly and brash with a strong patriotic aura about them. For Freddie Miller, the next few months in this wonderful country were to be jam-packed.

On one occasion Freddie and his camera team filmed the run up to a football match. Before the game the spectators had joined together and sang the words of the 'Land of the Free' in a rich and wonderful manner. Yes, it felt good to be here.

Ten

The goat herdsman in the little Austrian village where Arthandur Palmai and his family lived was a very jovial man. Often he whistled or sang to himself as he walked up and down the hills each day. He would stop occasionally and breathe in the air that he was convinced was perfumed by some heavenly fragrance blown in by the mountain winds. In his lifetime in this picturesque place, from which he had rarely departed, he had seen great changes in the little community.

Although he wasn't of the 'chosen people', he was not indisposed to the small band that had fled to the secrecy and seclusion of his home village. Just as long as he was able to tend his goatherd and enjoy a glass of good beer in the local tavern, he would be content to live his life here in peace. Like many people who disliked and did not want to understand politics, he would turn his radio off when the music turned to political commentary.

People were people, the goat herdsman believed. Let them live, work, sing and yodel if they felt the compulsion, and enjoy a stein of beer. What more could a person want out of life? He was fond of Arthandur. He thought of him as a good man and an affable doctor. Arthandur's dry wit and quiet strength seemed to gel with the goat herdsman's own joviality and humour. Often a visit for a check up or a nagging complaint would turn out to be a period of joy as they mutually enjoyed each other's company. Never having experienced the pleasure of a family of his own, he loved talking to the young boy, Nathan.

One cold but beautiful morning, the type of day when the cold bites into the bones and gives a hardworking man a healthy appetite, the goat herdsman wandered up the narrow winding pathways singing happily to himself. Just for fun he thought he would give out a friendly yodel across the valley. The resonance of the valley was good that morning as the timbre of his vocal tones echoed and rebounded across the hilltops. He smiled as he realised the power of his own lungs.

Turning to continue his steep mountain walk, he was surprised to see young Nathan Palmai sitting on a rock some way away from him staring out across the valley towards the Eicherel, which the boy's own father Arthandur had once climbed in 1912, in a passion of youthful exuberance. The boy turned his head and smiled at him in that glorious expression of youthful happiness yet to be soiled by the difficulties of growing up in a world becoming ever difficult to live in. In a fit of fun, the goat herdsman yodelled at Nathan, knowing the young boy would laugh again.

"You're waiting to see your friend Wilf, the old goat man." He laughed. It was a lovely contagious laugh that always made his cheeks seem to flush red with joviality.

"I have to leave here soon," said Nathan. Now the young boy's lovely smile had gone so quickly. It was a dark shadow on such a young face. "I am going to leave this country."

"Oh! Where are you going?" The man was quite concerned.

"I have to go to Palestine. My father says it may be very soon. I don't want to go, Wilf. I like it here. I like these hills, the mountains and the valley."

It saddened Wilf to see the unhappiness in his young eyes. A tear rolled from Nathan's eye, running down his cheek and down the end of his chin. Wilf reached for a handkerchief in the top of Nathan's jacket and wiped his face.

"Now, now, young fellow," he said softly. "You tell old Wilf all your troubles. I will listen. Me, I only have the goats to talk to."

Nathan looked up at lovable old Wilf. He was a delightful character in this lovely setting. One could be cheered immensely just by looking at this colourful local.

"You tell me, Nathan. I'm your friend," the old goats man persisted, sitting down by the young boy.

"Father says there are difficult times coming and that I must go to a kibbutz in Palestine." He rubbed his cold hands together. "But I am happy here. So are my parents. Why should we all be split up?"

Old Wilf grabbed a reed of grass, put it in his mouth, and chewed it. How could he answer young Nathan's question? How could he answer the young man honestly? He cast a glance back at his goat herd who, without any direction, were feeding on scraps of clumped grass.

At last he answered. "Your father, Arthandur, I like him. He is a good man. He is a wise man too. Do you ever listen to the wireless?"

"Sometimes."

"What do you hear? Do you hear that man in Germany who rants and raves? Old Wilf does. Old Wilf turns him off and goes out for a nice beer. That man in Germany," Wilf looked at Nathan sternly.

"Yes."

"That is why you go away." Wilf looked more sad now than stern. "Listen, Nathan, to your friend, old Wilf. I have been goat herder here for many a year. Before me my father was goat herder and before him my grandfather, and before him his father. I have been to Salzburg once; to Vienna just a few times, but you are so young and you are going all the way to Palestine. You are a young man going across a big world." Old Wilf was smiling now. His cheeks were bright red, almost crimson in colour. "Perhaps you come back one day and you see your old friend Wilf. I will still be here. I will be here always, walking up these mountain slopes till the day I die." He looked at his goat herd. The goats were beginning to disperse. It was time to take charge of them before they all ran away, "Come, the goats are getting restless. We will walk with them for a while."

There are times in everyone's life where a certain moment is never to be forgotten. It may be a splendid moment of enlightenment or self-education, a brief period of joy or awakening, the remembrance of which lays dormant in the mind to be recalled years later with an afterglow attached to it. Nathan Palmai would always recall that cold day when he walked and talked with Wilf. The memories of this happy man who sought nothing but the simple pleasure of living life could always evoke a smile on Nathan's face.

They walked up the steep slopes with Wilf taking a real delight in pointing out details of the psychology of goats. There was an art in Wilf's fascinating observations of the habits of goats. At an age approaching sixteen, young Nathan made the assumption from the goat herder that no matter how humble a man's trade, there is something to learn from every occupation.

Wilf pointed out how one goat always seemed to assume the lead as they clambered to wherever they were going. The rest of the goats would follow on from behind. However, one goat would force his way in front of the others to try and take over the leader of the herd. Wilf had an explanation of this.

"See the goat at the head of the herd, Nathan?" The boy nodded. "He is the leader. He is the self-appointed leader. He is the goat who thinks he was born to lead, the one who takes charge. See the goat who is barging through all the others." Nathan smiled at him. "Now he is the ambitious one. He knows where he is going and as you can see he steps on all those who are blocking his way. But he will get to the top of the herd no matter who he steps on. Now look over there, Nathan."

Wilf pointed to a ledge where a solitary goat looked out at the valley. There seemed to be a look of puzzlement about the goat. Which way to go? Which direction to take? It wandered away from the mainstay of the herd trying to make a pattern of life on its own.

"Now that goat – he is the one I like," said Wilf. "He is the one I admire most. Do you know why, my young friend? Because he is a real mountain goat. He is the loner who goes his own way. He is the goat who is stubborn and goes the way he wants and leaps from edge to edge, till he finds where he wants to be. I learn a lot about human beings from watching my friends, the goats. Old Wilf, some people think he's silly, but old Wilf is wise. Wilf sees in goats what we are as human beings. There are the natural leaders who the flock follow. There are the ambitious who fight to lead. Then there's my old friend, the mountain goat. He's the one that climbs and climbs. He might not make the peak of the mountain. Believe me, though; wherever he arrives that's where he wants to be. He will be the happiest of them all."

Nathan studied the goat. True to its own individual nature it leapt from crag to crag. If one could identify any outstanding characteristic about the mountain goat in comparison to a human being, then it would be that of a little boy seeking his destiny.

Wilf talked to the young fellow about the little village. He had his memories of the people who had lived here. The visitors. The elderly people who were slices of local colour and who had seen it all. He talked of his family and how proud he was to be the descendant of an historical line of goat herders and how sad he was too that he would be the last of his family line to follow that profession.

"God has given me so much to be thankful for," he said. "But if I had been blessed with a wife I could have had a son to be the seventh goat herder in the family."

The young boy listened to Wilf who was a fascinating storyteller. Wilf told Nathan of an opera singer from Salzburg who had come to the village for a visit thirty years before. Her voice was clear and powerful. She could sustain high notes for an awe-inspiring length of time. She had recently performed in Verdi's opera.

"I remember this fine lady so well," said Wilf, the sparkle of the memory of her visit so apparent in his eyes. "She was a beautiful lady who sang opera in Salzburg. She was the finest opera singer in all of Austria. Maybe even in the world. Who is to know? Nathan, my good friend, she walked this very path we are walking now every day that she stayed here."

"Along here!" Nathan exclaimed. The boy was genuinely excited.

"Oh yes. Just along here. And one day I am feeling really good. One morning I feel really good to be alive and I give a great big yodel across the valley – so loud they hear me far away in Palestine, I bet." He laughed at the memory. "She was sitting over there and she says, 'Good God, what is that?'" Wilf slapped his thigh, laughing, and Nathan began to laugh too. "Anyway she says —" He wiped his eyes and lifted his hat to scratch his head. "Any way this lovely lady says valley is like big concert hall – maybe like one in Vienna or Salzburg, I don't know – and then," Wilf paused as he seemed to remember a breathtaking day of his life, never to be forgotten. "Then, she starts to sing, Nathan. Oh, Nathan, you never heard in all your life such a beautiful voice. In all your life! Oh it was voice full of riches. It echoed around this valley, across the mountains. I stopped to listen all day. Even the goats gathered together to listen! Down in the village everyone comes to town square to listen. They think this lady is angel sent by God. Oh she was very fine singer. I bet even on the Eicherel mountain top birds stop to listen."

Wilf loved to talk of the past. He was really a happy man, happy in his memories of the simple things. Just the mere memories of his life were his most prized possession.

They as they walked Wilf found another happy memory to relate to his young audience. He was so happy just talking to Nathan.

"See this muscle," Wilf roared with laughter as he pulled his sleeve up to reveal a huge muscle, powerfully strong. "One day into this village comes big wrestler from Berlin. He was big!" Wilf made a gesture with his hands to indicate the immense size of this man, he was recalling. "At the tavern he sits down to talk to me. He was a big man with a big shiny head; so shiny I could see my face in it! After many a beer and many laughs together, he challenges me to an arm wrestle! All night long and next morning we sit in the tavern arm to arm. For ages Nathan, and then he starts to push really hard. The veins in his arm, they look like they bulge. I push and I push back, but he is strong. And then I feel my arm shaking; I am pushing back so hard. I give him long cold look back and do you know, Nathan, I am beating him! I feel him loosening his grip. He is weakening. I push with all my might. Then I beat him. I push his arm down. He is beaten! The whole of the tavern cheer me. One of the greatest days I have known. I beat a man who they say is unbeatable! Afterwards he buys me beer after beer. Do you know Nathan I am the first man to beat him in arm wrestle and he and I – we became best of friends."

Nathan could see the pride swell up in the goat herder as he recalled a high spot in his life. There were more stories that he told to his young audience with a great degree of enthusiasm. They laughed together. Nathan would gasp with amazement at some incredulous story that Wilf would tell him. He did not realise and perhaps was too naïve to realise that Wilf, aware he had a captive audience, was embellishing some aspects of his life for effect. Wilf was a complete extrovert. He was not inhibited in any sense, he would laugh loudly and boisterously. His most common manner was to slap his thigh and bellow at the remembrance of some humorous incident. Yet for a man who might be considered brutish in his outward appearance by others, it was a veil over a very jolly man's real sensitivity and feeling for others, and a simplistic happiness in just being alive.

On the way home down the slope, as Nathan relived a myriad of Wilf's most cherished memories, Arthandur and Marlene waved from down below. Wilf waved back. His face was as bright as a newly ripened tangerine orange. Arthandur and Marlene looked up happily. Marlene had one arm tucked through Arthandur's and there was deep love in her eyes for him and great affection for her son. She saw her son laugh at something old Wilf had said. This had fired in her an emotion of happiness as she cherished the remaining times she would know with her son.

"You have been storytelling again, Wilf, you ancient jolly goat herder," Arthandur joked in jest.

Wilf slapped him affectionately around the shoulder and laughed that hearty laugh of his. The two men greeted each other affectionately sparring imaginary punches in fun. Marlene laughed too. She had always liked Wilf since she had first come to the village; so long ago it seemed.

Often Nathan would walk with Wilf along the mountain tracks. It was a case of the old man and his young protégé. Wilf invested his humour and energy in talking to Nathan. The two spoke often about Wilf's life in the valley. The 'ancient jolly goat herder' as Arthandur had nicknamed him had a seemingly inexhaustible round of stories he could tell. It obviously delighted him to be able to talk to someone who was such an eager listener. In true fact Wilf, although happy on the outside, was in fact a very lonely man. He enjoyed a beer in the old tavern with friends, but with time many of his old drinking partners had gone. In the tavern there was much talk of politics, which he did not want to know about. It seemed that as the atmosphere of the village changed with the times, he had much more in common with the small Jewish émigré community that had established itself there. He often found that young Nathan Palmai was like the son he had never had. He could communicate with the young boy entertaining him like the clown in a circus that fascinates a small child with his mischief and magical performance.

When Nathan had to leave Palestine, Wilf decided he would find peace in his solitary life He would add to his list of memories. He would remember the young boy, Nathan, who listened in fascination as the old man spoke of days gone by. Who knows, maybe one day Wilf may find another protégé – someone different. Someone full of naivety and innocence, who would keenly listen to the old man with the goats.

Nathan woke one morning to a sound like a curious whistling noise. He opened his eyes blearily. The strange musical sound filled his bedroom. He rose slowly sitting upright in his bed. Then he found he wasn't alone. Through a half opened window a bird had flown inside. It sat poised making a musical noise. Its eyes went up and down looking at its new surroundings that it had become captive to by its own making. There was something funny in the little bird's actions. The way it twitched its beak and rolled its eyes up and down like roller shutters. The young boy laughed.

Nathan made a clucking sound with his mouth trying to emulate the bird. He outstretched his hand rubbing his fingers against his hand. The bird eyed him strangely. Then it flew onto his arm as if it were landing on a perch in an aviary. Nathan felt delighted. At the age of fifteen he was learning how to charm total strangers!

"So you have become St Francis of Assisi now," his mother laughed as she walked unexpectedly into his room. Nathan stroked the top of the bird's head gently. "He was lonely, Nathan. He wants someone to talk to." She looked lovingly at her son. "Now you are learning to love all of God's creatures. You must let him go, Nathan, and you must get dressed. We have a visitor, an important lady who has come to visit us."

Marlene walked to the window and opened it fully. From the window the snow-capped mountains could be seen in their full splendour. "That is where he belongs. High in the sky." She beckoned to Nathan and he stepped out of bed still balancing the bird on his arm. He came across to the window. "Fly, little bird," said Marlene and almost as if it understood the command, it took flight and soared into the sky. "One of God's messengers, Nathan," she said wistfully. "He came to show us there is beauty in the world."

They both looked up at the sky where the bird had flown. It was a wondrous sky, so blue, the air so clean, and so high above the worries of this troubled world.

Nathan washed and dressed smartly. He was quite unprepared for the person he was going to meet. He walked into the lounge room and there stood a lady of such an aura and presence about her. It was hard to absorb it all. She stood with her back to him. Arthandur and Marlene entered the room from another door. It was Arthandur who made the formal introductions.

"My boy, I would like you to meet a fine lady," he said. Dressed in a fur coat Baroness Christina von Harstezzen turned around and smiled at Nathan. "So you are Arthandur and Marlene's son. I have heard much of you."

Nathan was a bit perplexed. He took Mrs von Harstezzen's hand where she held it out to him. Nathan had certainly never known of his mother and father's friendship with this woman. Nor was he to know for many years what was really going on beyond the surface of this highly intelligent woman.

"Nathan, this lady is Baroness von Harstezzen; a very dear friend of ours for some years" Marlene added. It was then that the Baroness spoke to Nathan, discussing his schooling and his interests in her gentle manner. In years to come Nathan was to be surprised to learn of her real mission in life. They spoke for a brief while before Marlene took Nathan out on what was supposedly a 'nature walk'. In reality the Baroness wanted to talk to Arthandur privately about the work of the Companions of the Circle. Nathan warmed to this lady considerably in the brief time he met her. His everlasting memory of her was somehow connected to the expensive perfume that seemed to cling to the room for a long time after she had gone. When Nathan and his mother left the house, he espied a huge car parked opposite their chateau where a chauffeur stood waiting for the Baroness. The size of the car was indicative of this woman's wealth and status.

Inside the house Arthandur and the Baroness discussed the various operations of the Circle. She was a little dismayed that more pressure had not been brought to bear upon the leaders of the German government. For all of the strength that the many Companions of the Circle had begun to muster, it was still falling short of its goals in fuelling the international debate into action more than mere words.

"I have heard from Mr Miller," she pointed out with great delight. Arthandur was equally enthusiastic and looked up from some notes he had prepared with interest. "I thought you would be pleased, Arthandur. He has succeeded in all of his tasks. However, on advice from British Intelligence, refugees can only be taken in on an unofficial basis from everywhere except, I regret to say, Germany and Austria. Officially, yes. That is fine for those who are materially independent and have contacts."

"*Oy Vei,*" Arthandur exclaimed, and he sank back into his chair with a look of disappointment inscribed on his every feature.

"But, Arthandur, that was on an official basis. Providing the Circle screens the people here who wish to leave, Mr Miller and his contacts in London will take them on an unofficial basis. But if we are to smuggle them in unofficially, we run the risk of agents breaking into the British Isles."

"Unofficially… Perhaps I can understand why," said Arthandur. "There is always the possibility that there may be some colluders."

They both stared at each other at the realisation of it.

"If there were," the Baroness pointed out, "that would mean the end of the work of the Circle. Now, Arthandur, I have some documents for you. She reached into an attaché case and gave him a bundle of papers and notebooks. "I will be going to the United States shortly on the *Hindenburg* – you know the airship we have heard so much of. I will be meeting Mr Miller on my arrival there. I have written to him and he will be at the airfield with his news team to meet me. Those papers you have Arthandur. They are the names and addresses of all the Companions of the Circle. Should anything happen to me while I'm away, should my life end in unexpected circumstances, Arthandur, you must burn all those papers. I am already under scrutiny by a Nazi officer. He was a boyhood friend of my late husband. His name is Colonel Verner Burnhoff. He has visited the estate several times on the supposition that he is procuring munitions from Rieber's factories. He knows of my dislike of his policies, yet I believe his friendship with Rieber, and the fact that I think he may be in love with me, have stopped him from going any further."

Arthandur had listened carefully to his instructions; however, there was a point he felt needed to be clarified.

"What of the people in the rest of Europe?" he asked. "Baroness, I hope you'll not meet a fate that will end our friendship and our very important work together, but if anything happens to you, how will they continue to operate without your guidance?"

There was great concern for the rest of the European agents. They were an absolute necessity in the operations of the Circle. The people who had been recruited would, in the event of a war, prove to be the backbone of any important resistance group. Baroness von Harstezzen had made provision for this factor and in consultation with Freddie Miller that part of the operation would be able to carry out its work without fear of hindrance. It was an eerie preparation she had made. There was almost a spectre of some foreboding fate about her as if she had a premonition that something catastrophic was about to occur.

The Baroness was able to allay any fears that Arthandur possessed for the safety and survival of the agents of the Circle who remained incognito in France, Belgium, Holland and Switzerland.

"Mr Miller's contacts in British Intelligence, a special operations area headed by Colonel Francis Brindmarsh, will take over the running of the European section. Colonel Brindmarsh is a very sharp man. Freddie visited him one day and Brindmarsh's men were verifying the existence of all our agents, and not only their existence but their reliability in the same week."

"My, my, such a heinous job, is that the right word I am seeking! No! Arduous – difficult, that is what I mean. To think we are working hand in glove in this secret work."

"Therefore, Arthandur, it would seem that much of our work is now well organised. You and I can more or less disappear into the shadows for a short time, until the need for more urgent work arises." The Baroness hesitated for a few moments. She felt a great desire within her to change the subject. The subject that Arthandur always felt happy to talk about was his own family. She seized on this point. "I like your son, Arthandur. He is a nice boy. Your wife, too, is very fine." Arthandur glowed with pride. He secretly hoped that their reflection was from his own mirrored-image. "I hope that your son will be able to lead a good life, in an untroubled world."

It was now Arthandur's turn to seize on a point that she had made and to express his own feelings in that wonderfully lucid tongue of his. Although Arthandur was a quiet man, words were his strength. He could always take centre stage on any occasion and make himself understood with an admirable clarity.

"My hope, Mrs von Harstezzen, is that one day this will be a world where all people, whatever their race, their religious following, their class or status, will be able to live freely without any discrimination whatsoever. I dream, perhaps as all men dream, of great beauty in being able to live in a land – any land – where there may be a mixture of religions and denominations, and a mixture of races, where we can all live together as friends and fellow countrymen. There should not be segregation, discrimination or altercation! Just pure harmonious living, in which we could all learn from each other. Each race has much to offer the other. In medicine, for example, I, as a doctor, read many journals. The Chinese have been practicing acupuncture for many years. One day it may well be considered a serious form of therapy. We could learn from them so much. Just imagine how much better a world this would be if each race, instead of being at an alternative view to each other, were to work together and help each other, then we would not have such huge divisions."

"A dream, Arthandur, purely a dream," mused the Baroness, "But, without a doubt, a worthy one. Regrettably such differences, such divisions are those that have created history. There has always been a leader, be they Napoleon Bonaparte or Attila the Hun, who creates such circumstances.

We are just merely passengers of history – people swept along and swept against the things we do not care for and wish to change. You and I, and the Companions of the Circle, must always continue in our defence of defenceless people. Then, maybe in another lifetime, the world may be cohesive and understanding. It is my dream and my hope too."

The two of them had a deep mutual respect for each other and a love that is only shared by people fighting for the same cause. They had a common affinity that people enjoy when they believe in a cause with a deep conviction and an absolute righteousness.

It was later in the afternoon that Mrs von Harstezzen drove away from the village in her chauffeur driven car. When Arthandur and his family watched from the gate he must have known that he would never again see this woman. She had helped mould his fervent beliefs and place him at the nucleus of an extensive network. In that year of 1937 many people must have held widely suspect views about each other's destiny.

The Baroness smiled to herself as the car winded its way up and down the mountain roads. She had done much through her work with the Circle to take the drabness out of so many ill-favoured lives. The recruits of the Circle had been a curious lot, representing people from a diversity of professions. In Holland her associates included a banker, a miller, a watchmaker and a policeman. In France she could count on the support of several public servants, a librarian, several café owners, a town clerk and some high-ranking gendarmes. The biggest coup of all had been in meeting Freddie who had enlisted the help of British Intelligence.

Arthandur Palmai and Mrs von Harstezzen were unusual allies; an unusual soufflé made of odd ingredients, which had risen with the right mixture and created the Circle. Undoubtedly much of its operations were working, but the response to its drive was not as good as it could have been. There was still much to be done.

In the village there wasn't anything resembling a synagogue for the community of the faith. However, a house of prayer and worship had been established in the home of one of the faithful and it had been lent out for bar mitzvahs, weddings and other ceremonies. The Palmais attended one on a bright and beautiful day. Probably because the bar mitzvah was held in an unusual surrounding, the ceremony was not of the significance of one held in a huge brick built building, which would echo with the Cantor's voice, could give to it. If anything, that an ordinary home in a picturesque surrounding opening its door to, such an occasion made the ceremony a more warming and easy going affair.

Most of the small community of Jewish families were there. Although not directly related by an immediate birth-line, this small group could not help but be a family of its own. At an occasion like this they would get together with zest and in tradition; always enjoying each other's company like blood relatives at a family wedding. They would gather afterwards at someone's house for the particular diet that is so unique to the Jewish people. Yet the food was so nourishing and deliciously tasty that in the village some of the non-Jews had become converts to it.

From the small expatriate community that lived there, Nathan could identify all the finest qualities evident in the human race: thoughtfulness, love of all people and devotion to the family, gregariousness, charm and friendship.

One bright afternoon at the home of one of the oldest expatriate Jews, the families were gathered in the garden taking prayer. Arthandur spoke the traditional prayer in a beautiful voice, with such an audible clarity. The community enjoyed food cooked in kosher style, pure and succulent to taste. There seemed to be love and charity in abundance. The Austrian mountains looked dynamic against the clear sky. It seemed so good to be alive. *Better enjoy it. Remember this day. Savour it, it is a special time.* The words seemed to come from nowhere and flood Nathan's mind. He knew there would come a time when he would have to leave here. *Yes,* he thought. *Enjoy it, remember it and savour it. It is a special time.*

Eleven

The inaugural flight of the airship, the *Hindenburg* to North America in 1937, was to be a special journey. It was to be a flight that would commence in Frankfurt, Germany and finish in Lakehurst, New Jersey in the United States, crossing miles and miles of the Atlantic Ocean far below. For its passengers it held the promise of something really thrilling. The chance to be among the first to participate in what was envisaged to become a regular trans-Atlantic run. A previous round trip between Frankfurt, Germany and Rio de Janeiro, Brazil had been successful. Now it was time to test the potential of a long-distance flight to the United States.

Baroness von Harstezzen had written to Freddie Miller. With his news team he was now comfortably ensconced in Hollywood, California filming the lifestyles of the movie stars. A newsworthy event such as the arrival of the Hindenburg had prompted Freddie to bring across his entire team to record it on film. It would give him the opportunity to combine work and his personal commitments.

Freddie had read the Baroness's letter as he sat by the poolside of a famous actor's mansion. He felt enthusiastic at the thought of seeing her again. He would be delighted to tell her of his work for the Circle in full detail.

Sunny California was a welcome respite from the battleground-style news he had usually covered on the politically controversial spots he had visited. Somehow life in that glossy world of movies seemed so far removed from the rest of the problems other countries were facing.

Freddie had enjoyed his time here. He had filmed the homes of such people as the newspaper magnate William Randolph Hearst, who lived in an extraordinary abode of palatial magnitude called San Simeon. He had personally met Douglas Fairbanks Senior, Gloria Swanson, Henry

Fonda, Humphrey Bogart, Wallace Beery, Gary Cooper, Clark Gable, Jean Harlow, Ingrid Bergman and Joan Crawford. He had taken tea with the English actors, including David Niven and Errol Flynn, who made up the Hollywood Cricket Club led by a former England test player and now a distinguished character actor of note called Sir Charles Aubrey Smith. He had danced with several starlets at an open-air restaurant with the stars illuminating the dark night sky like a romantic chandelier.

There had been other jobs in this trip to the United States: Freddie had put together a documentary for British moviegoers on the splendours of San Francisco. Once this city had been virtually ripped asunder by an earthquake in 1906. Now it had been rebuilt and thirty years later was one of the world's most attractive cities. He had left his little hotel at the corner of Powell and Market Street, and taken a tram to the bay. It was easy to fall in love with this city.

In New York, on the other side of the United States, Freddie's team had filmed baseball and gridiron football matches and they had caught the magic of these games. The huge concrete metropolis was a cameraman's delight, whether the cameraman was concentrating on a long shot of New York from the very summit of the Empire State Building or just a medium close shot of the daytime traffic in Fifth Avenue or Broadway, there was so much to be seen that the work of the news team was virtually inexhaustible.

The letter Freddie had received from the Baroness was very warmly written in its approach. It was more like receiving a letter from a cousin than a colleague of the same cause. Mrs von Harstezzen had written in a beautiful style of italics in a fine nib pen that had obviously been dipped in navy blue ink. There was even an aroma of perfume about the letter. Was it a suggestion on her part, or could Freddie have been simply hoping for finer things to come? Besides, he reminded himself, it was just purely a professional relationship at this stage.

With an alarming thought he realised that he had not thought of Cynthia Field for a while. The last time the two had met, she had at last made true her real feelings for Freddie. He pondered over Cynthia for a moment or two. Now there was a girl who had always genuinely loved him. For years it would seem, ever since he was an impressionable young army officer in the North-West Frontier of India.

He gazed down at the letter from the Baroness again. He could just imagine Mrs von Harstezzen in that incredible fortress style-castle of another age in the Rhineland by the wine estates, at that very moment preparing for her journey. Freddie had always enjoyed meeting the prominent people that his work had brought him into contact with. Yet this particular woman seemed to exert a peculiar fascination for him. Mrs von Harstezzen carried with her all the hallmarks of a woman of mystery and intrigue, but she was ahead of her time in the manner of independence she possessed.

Freddie put the letter down, luxuriated in the sun and took another sip from his wine glass. His host, a debonair film star, swam several laps in the pool while several of Freddie's cameramen chatted to a bevy of beautiful American girls in swimsuits and sunglasses. He reminded himself that he must write to Cynthia before he and his team departed for New Jersey to film the arrival of the *Hindenburg*.

★★★

There must have been some sixth sense that made Mrs von Harstezzen turn around in the car and gaze at her home as they drove to Frankfurt. The chauffeur was told to stop by his lady employer. *This amazing place,* she thought, *has been my life*. From here she had inherited vast wealth, industries, prestige, position and indeed as a widow of great resource she had also acquired admirers whose affections she had spurned. The truth was in fact that she still missed her late husband, Baron Rieber von Harstezzen. Oh, but life was cruel when such a man as dashing and colourful as he could be cut down in his prime.

Just for moments of reflection, she surveyed her vast wine estates. She could feel sadness as she thought of the times of her life there. But there were things to be done in the future, ideals to be achieved, and the past must not be dwelt upon. The good memories must be cherished. The bad memories recalled for whatever lesson was learned from them. The future must be faced with realism, energy and enthusiasm. That had always been her philosophy on life. It was too easy and defeatist to lapse into nostalgia and re-assessment of years gone by.

"I shall miss my lovely home," she remarked in a tone of resignation to her chauffeur. "Drive on."

The chauffeur revved the engine and the car began its journey, spiralling down the twisting roads. It felt exciting to be travelling again. In her younger days she had seen much overseas. Now she was going to the United States where, under the guise of establishing a market for some of the Harstezzen industries, she was intending to attract some sympathisers and lobbyists for the work of the Circle.

The drive to Frankfurt in itself was a chance for Mrs von Harstezzen to recall parts of the country she had visited with Rieber. She was just a young lady of would-be eloquence when she had first met the Baron and worked as his secretary. Her genteelness and fluent knowledge of languages had impressed Rieber no end. So too had her capacity for hard work. Her other positive attributes that he noted could be found in her memory of facts, details and other intricate points such as mathematical calculations scientific formulae.

With Rieber, she had once driven to some of the places they were passing through now. *There is much nostalgia in this day*, she thought, *so many things to be remembered*. Christina felt lucky to have such treasured memories of happy years with her late husband.

The city of Frankfurt soon came into view. It would not be long before they reached their destination and the start of the journey on the *Hindenburg*. She had remembered much in her journey down, now it was time to make new memories. From her coat Mrs von Harstezzen took out the letter that Freddie Miller had written to her. She enjoyed Freddie's literary style and re-read it over and over again.

Freddie had spent much of it enthusing about the United States and his words of description had whetted Mrs von Harstezzen's appetite for travel considerably. He had previously written various letters to her describing what he had achieved for the Circle so far. He had mentioned in his letter that he looked forward to pursuing their 'common goals' together. The Baroness too was looking forward to meeting Freddie again. At first she had not been sure of him, but now she was convinced he had been a real find.

At the airfield there was a band playing. Mrs von Harstezzen could see the imposing airship from the window. Spectators had gathered to see it off on its flight across the North Atlantic route. There was almost a carnival atmosphere about it that day, mixed in with a military display of strength.

From the car the Baroness studied the zeppelin airship with a degree of knowledge for she had read all the details and the specifications in advance. Mrs Harstezzen knew that, originally, the *Hindenburg* was to have been named *Hitler* after the Chancellor, but after some considerable dispute by the designers the new name was retained. The length of the Hindenburg was some 800 feet long and weighing approximately 242 tonnes. Its actual physical capacity was contained within seven million cubic feet. Already it was being hailed as a great aeronautical achievement.

The operations of the *Hindenburg* were to be a joint venture between the United States and Germany; however, for this particular air journey the United States, who were to provide helium gas for the fuel of the airship, had declined to do so and instead it had been filled with hydrogen. It was anticipated that the *Hindenburg*, travelling in the westbound direction, would complete the total journey in an estimated time of sixty-four hours and eastbound fifty-two hours. This was to be the first of many scheduled flights from Frankfurt.

After Mrs Harstezzen's travel documents had been examined she had a while to wait before boarding the *Hindenburg* with the other travellers and crew. It was a good feeling to be travelling, even better to be travelling aboard an airship on an historic flight. While she waited in a reception centre specially laid aside for the benefit of the passengers, she looked around at the people milling together. There were Nazi officers, photographers, reporters, ground staff and onlookers, all bubbling over with enthusiasm.

The temptation to sit back, relax and think about nothing was so strong. In recent weeks the managing of the Harstezzen Industries and the organisation of the Circle's strategies had caused great pressure upon her nerves. Now she was able to feel free of the heavy burdens of responsibility that she had to bear, if only for a short time. Then coming towards her she saw the smile of a familiar friendly face. There was no mistaking that old charm, the dark features and the arrogance, nor the rank of colonel on his uniform. She gazed in amazement at him.

"Why, Verner! Are you travelling on this flight?"

Colonel Verner Burnhoff stopped and sat down at the seat next to her.

"Unfortunately not, I am just here for the ceremony," he replied amiably. "You are travelling purely for pleasure?"

"A business trip on behalf of the Harstezzen Industries. I am hoping to make contacts in the United States, particularly to market our wine produce. I could not resist the opportunity to travel on the *Hindenburg*. It seemed to be something of historic importance not to be passed up."

"Quite," he agreed. There was something of restraint about Verner. He had remembered their last meeting and he felt he wanted to say something about it. Finally after a short pause, he felt inclined to bring the subject up. "Christina, I feel that I may owe you a slight apology."

Mrs von Harstezzen looked up surprised. To hear Verner talk of an apology was the humbling of an arrogant, albeit charming, man.

"Yes. On our last meeting I may have imposed my strong political beliefs on you. I am an ardent exponent of our cause. I realise other people are entitled to disagree in a free world." It was half a concession at least, not quite a severe humbling. Verner still managed to express his faith in his sour beliefs. "Sometimes one can be overwhelmed by the passion of it all. Often we who believe in something with such devout conviction find we need an audience to impart our passions."

It was hard not to be affected by his clever wording. It did not disguise anything or conceal the man's inner self. The Baroness was familiar to such circumstances. Her ability to scrutinise people was of paramount importance to her. However, she did regard Verner Burnhoff as a friend. His company, when politics did not enter his conversation, was always agreeable. She could afford to make some concession.

"I understand, Verner," she smiled at him lightly. "I know what you mean when you say 'one can be overwhelmed by the passion of it all'. Let's not talk of such things though. This airship I am about to travel on, now this is really something that Germany can be proud of. It is a great achievement for the workers who built it and for the aeronautical industry. Something that other nations will envy, and may well strive to emulate."

Verner smiled. "The aeronautical industry in England will be watching with interest. Certainly the Americans will be giving it an enormous welcome on arrival. There will be cameras rolling from many countries."

Now the Baroness thought of one man she knew would definitely be there with cameras rolling. Freddie Miller and his team, at present working on contract to an American studio, would be waiting.

She turned towards him and as a matter of curiosity asked him, "What do you feel for the others nations such as…?"

"Such as the Swedish? The English? The Americans?"

"I would be most interested."

"The Swedes I have great affinity with. Americans – I do not really understand them. What exactly drives them to their successes and failures. They are a great people, I believe, pioneering people with great drive."

"And the English?"

"The English? I like them. That may surprise you that an ardent German patriot such as myself could like a race of people with whom I was in confrontation with in trench warfare. But yes, I like them. I wish they would be our close allies. I would rather have them with us than against us. Do you know, Mrs Harstezzen, during the Great War when I was a young soldier fighting for the Kaiser, I was one of those in the trenches who stopped fighting the British Tommies for a few hours to play football with them? Have you heard that story?"

"I have not, Verner. Is this true? This is not an exaggerated war story?"

Verner smiled as he recalled the event. His eyes sparkled as he thought of one cold Christmas day in the fields of battle-scarred France so long ago.

"My dear Mrs Harstezzen, it is not an exaggeration, I assure you. It was Christmas day 1914 and bitterly cold. We had been involved in rifle fire for what had seemed an eternal period of bullets flying backwards and forwards, backwards and forwards. Then there was silence. We stopped firing in our unit. Our trenches were so close we could hear the British Tommies talking. They were all saying what we felt: they were cold and hungry and they wished they were at home for Christmas, eating a roast dinner with their families and sitting by a warm fire. Then our officer in charge called us to stop firing. When the Tommies realised this they thought we were going to surrender." Verner stopped for a moment and looked at Mrs Harstezzen who was hanging on to every word with an absolute fascination. Knowing his audience was keyed up he continued his story without embellishing it, although he had the urge to do so.

"Anyway, I heard one of the Tommies say to his comrade, "ere what's up with them, guv'nor? They're 'aving their blinkin' Christmas dinner or something.'" Both the Baroness and Verner laughed as he did his imitation of a cockney soldier.

"My officer in charge heard this and he called out to the British. 'Hey, Tommy, do you hear me?' Then we heard a voice call out from the other side, 'We hear you, Hun. What is it?' 'It is Christmas day, Tommy. It is

Christmas. Will you join us in a truce today? Today only, Tommy, then we carry on tomorrow as we were before.' Well, the next thing we heard were all the English in their trench saying things like, 'Cripes, mate, I reckon summat's up. Are they pulling our leg?' and then a well spoken voice, the sound of one of those aristocratic British gentleman officers who probably went to Eton or Oxford spoke to us. He said, 'We will join you in a truce if the officer in charge of your section will meet me halfway between the trenches. Unarmed, of course.'"

"And did he?" the Baroness asked still intrigued by this revelation from the past.

"Yes!" exclaimed Verner. "My commanding officer strode to the centre of the two trenches. I was so amazed at such a thing happening in this place they called No-Man's Land. The next thing I knew I saw the officer in charge of the British troops come up from the other trench. He was a tall man in khaki and a peaked hat – a colonel, if I remember rightly – and he had a moustache that curled upwards, and yes, a monocle too. To my surprise our officer said, 'Merry Christmas, Tommy,' and shook his hand. Then some of our men joined them and some of their troops came up. From out of nowhere someone found a football and we played against the English – can you believe such a story? Christmas day, 1914. And after all that—" He broke off for a moment, reflecting on the memory.

"And after all that what happened, Verner?" the Baroness asked.

"The next day," he continued, "After we had played football with the British. After we had sung Christmas carols with them and drank warm mugs of tea with them, the next day we were shooting at them. Isn't it sad?"

"Yes. It is sad."

"And they were such likeable fellows. I met men from Manchester, Birmingham and Yorkshire and we talked about all common things that interest men like football and girls. It was a night I shall never forget. Such a strange thing. How we could enjoy them as friends and yet fight against them as opponents. They were such good men too."

"Such are the divisions of war, Verner. People make enemies of those they would benefit from in friendship."

Both looked at each other, momentarily agreeing in thought if not openly. All around them in the waiting area, people were getting ready for the departure. There were Americans, different European nationalities and a sprinkling of naval officers. A journalist was talking to different people, finding out their impressions of the *Hindenburg*.

Verner, who felt relaxed in Mrs Harstezzen's company, continued the conversation.

"Who will be running the industries in your absence?" he asked.

"I have reliable general managers to look after each section. I am lucky that I am able to delegate so easily."

"And how are the industries faring?" This was a question of intent actually. Verner knew that Mrs Harstezzen's business interests covered a wide variety of concerns. He was curious just to be reminded what they were and exactly how financially successful they were. He was intrigued to know just how rich she was.

"Oh, the Wine Group is ever profitable. We have a good market for red and whites, naturally. I understand that our vintages are to the palate of everyone from the aristocracy of Europe to the villager, which is the way it should be. Wine should not be a rich man's drink."

"I agree wholeheartedly, Baroness. What of your other industries? Are they still in demand as much? Are the levels of production as high as demand?"

Mrs von Harstezzen was puzzled to Verner's questions. She still wondered about the motives of this man. Although he was a friend, she still felt that she was under a sort of polite and well-mannered inquisition. To keep the level of conversation on an amiable basis, she resorted to a touch of humour.

"Perhaps you would like me to employ you one day?" she remarked. "In the wine fields, maybe, when your career in the army is over." They both smiled at her comment. "In answer to your question, Verner, the von Harstezzen factories manufacturing car parts have never been busier. We are currently at an all time high. In fact, Verner, the highest level of production in the history of our companies."

Verner looked impressed. He had not realised the extent of the manufacturing empire that Mrs von Harstezzen commanded.

"So, despite the depression there is still high demand for vehicles," he added.

"Oh yes, and what is more our car parts, be they pistons, headlights or the chassis, are always first class and highly efficient. Our work has very little faulty produce. Our tradesmen are the finest, and most hard-working, I have ever encountered anywhere." She was obviously proud of this area within her control. "You, of course, are well aware of armaments being the bulk of my other concerns. The last time we met you gave me a list of demands for a huge rearmament of the German forces." There was a slight tone of distaste in her voice, although she had not yet passed the list to her factory managers, she could recall the extent of the order. "It included quite an arsenal, did it not? U-boats, weaponry and tanks."

"All in the name of defence," remarked Verner. Then he added as an afterthought, "If you thought that order with the Harstezzen Industries was large, the one we placed with the Krupp family was even larger."

Christina von Harstezzen knew of the Krupp family. The Krupps were in charge of a huge consortium of blast furnaces, mines, shipyards, armaments, foundries and countless factories that covered a multitude of different goods, produced for an ever-obliging market. The combined industries of the Krupp family were a vital tool in the German economy providing employment for much of the populace.

Bertha Krupp was the heir to her late father's, Friedrich Krupp's, many industries. She had inherited a colossal amount of shares in the Krupp empire, believed to be 159,996 out of a total of 160,000, and, at only seventeen years of age in 1902, she had ascended to a position of great status. With a team of advisers she found herself in command of a massive business empire.

Kaiser Wilhelm II had virtually taken control of the industries, but remained quietly in the background pulling the invisible strings. Upon Bertha Krupp's marriage in 1906 to the German Ambassador to the Vatican, Gustav von Bohlen und Halbach, the name Krupp had become synonymous with armaments as they acceded to the Kaiser's wishes and produced weaponry at a frightening pace on the outbreak of war in 1914.

Bertha Krupp's life was similar to some extent to that of Mr von Harstezzen. Christina shuddered at the thought of the Krupp arsenal programme and was fearful of the purpose that the weaponry might be implemented for. Sensing the conversation was on dangerous ground, about to slip into a political discussion, she moved rapidly to change the subject but as she opened her mouth to speak, the Flight Director of the *Hindenburg* beckoned to her to board the airship.

"Well, Verner, it is time for me to go." She said, rising from her chair and smiling at him pleasantly. Verner, always the gentleman, rose too, and took her hand kissing it gently and bowing slightly. The two of them were silent for a moment. Then he smiled that old charming engaging smile, his face brilliantly lit up and full of warmth.

"Goodbye, Mrs Harstezzen," he said with finality. "Have a wonderful trip." He paused and watched her walk away to board the airship. He looked at her wistfully and then thought of something to call out to her. "I hope the Americans like your wine as much as I do."

Shortly afterwards, in a flurry of excitement, the *Hindenburg* took off from Frankfurt. The feeling of flying in an airship was invigorating for her. It seemed to rise at a surprisingly fast rate. The vessel seemed to ascend against the air pressure outside like the cork in a shaken up bottle of champagne being ejected.

Soon they were up amongst the clouds. Down below she could just make out the shapes and rectangles of the airfield and the people moving around looking like ants sprawling together over a pot of jam. Then Mrs von Harstezzen gazed in awe at the beautiful fields, lush and densely green, squared off in boundaries. It felt wonderful to be high up above everything.

This floating palace, as she had heard one man describe it, continued to move higher and higher and further and further out towards the ocean. Its huge motors gave an added thrust and lift, and successfully counteracted any drag and turbulence that it encountered. The interior of the airship boasted a splendid dining room, a lounge, writing room, promenades and cabins. It was indeed a palatial and luxurious vessel.

Mrs von Harstezzen returned to her seat after a tour around the *Hindenburg* and just sat there with her arms clasped together viewing the clouds and the ocean.

It was a privilege for her to be aboard, she considered. She wondered what the sight of the *Hindenburg* would be like to the people toiling in the fields of Europe, or to sailors on fishing vessels far out in the sea.

A sleepy feeling seemed to swamp her. Against her better judgement she had joined the flight director and some passengers in sipping a few glasses of wine. She had not slept well for the past few nights, having been a keeper of late hours and arranging for the Circle's activities to carry on unhindered in her absence. There were also documents concerning her factories and the wine corporation to be signed, and her long hours, hard work and the high degree of mental concentration she had applied to her work, were beginning to take effect. The glasses of wine added to her lethargy. Soon she was sleeping peacefully as the motors of the *Hindenburg* throbbed carrying her across the Atlantic Ocean to North America.

Mrs Harstezzen was dreaming. She was dreaming of her late husband. She could see the very regal face of Rieber as he once was, handsome, arrogant but warm and authoritative. What would he think of her independence and her skilful running of the multi-million mark industries? Furthermore what would he think of her passionate involvement in the activities of the Circle? A group specifically established to form an incognito defence of the chosen people and to be, at a time of war, a virtual underground resistance.

Her dreams were prolific that day. There were fjords, lakes, mountains and clean white faces with friendly smiles. These were the memories of her childhood in Sweden, of happy days lost beyond a myriad of experience-filled years, and an accumulation of wisdom, cynicism and acceptance that only the passing of time brings – a mixture of sorrow and regret, nostalgia and ecstasy, and disappointment and fulfilment.

Then there were curious colours of every shade and texture swamping her mind, the sound of crashing water, and surging, rushing foam. Overpowering waterfalls, huge rocks and crevices apparent in her gaze. She was dreaming of a time when she had been lost as a child in Sweden, separated from her parents for an alarming period, and in her wanderings in the fjords she had been caught in the rain. When the rain had cleared there was a rainbow, hence the colours of every shade, and somehow the sun's rays had played trickery on her viewing. The colours of the rainbow intermingled with the suns rays playing on a waterfall, and a fjord had created a fascinating array of viewing through a child's eyes. A sight that would always stay imbedded in the patterns of memory. After many hours her parents found her but that short time alone in a world of wondrous childhood vision of light and colour and nature's own creation, made her so very appreciative of beauty in all its forms.

The crash of natural water onto the rocks became the heavy throbbing of man-made engines. The breeze rustling through the pine trees and the sound of water trickling in an estuary became the sound of a huge airship pushing and forcing its way through heavy air turbulence and currents.

Mrs Harstezzen raised her eyelids slowly. Slowly, very slowly, she contemplated on her dream and considered how her childhood had returned for a brief dream. A brief journey back to such an easy time in one's life. Then she twisted in her seat and looked through the window. She had been asleep for longer than she realised. Below her on the Atlantic Ocean, a liner, with its funnels blazing with smoke, glided majestically along.

America, it seemed, was merely a seagull's flight away. The *Hindenburg* hurtled on and on like a time capsule, propelling its way into the history books.

Twelve

Lakehurst, New Jersey on May 6th 1937 was abuzz with excitement in anticipation of the arrival of the Hindenburg. The townsfolk were out in full throng in that American town, preparing for sight of the airship coming into land. A number of people who had relatives and friends aboard the oncoming airship were waiting in the hanger by the mooring mast where the airship would be berthed when it finally set down at the Naval Air Station in Lakehurst.

The world's press were on watch, as were different camera crews, setting their lenses and equipment in place. Freddie Miller organised his team and directed the positions of the various cameras. Newspaper journalists mingled freely with the crowd eagerly writing down people's opinions about the airship they were yet to view. Different comments varied between 'exciting' and 'a great day for aviation progress'. Cameras were already rolling and journalists scribbled furiously.

An American radio commentator called Herbert Morrison, due to describe the arrival of the *Hindenburg* for another news team, casually walked around talking to people about the flight of this airship. He amiably chatted to Freddie Miller for a while, who was quite thrilled, although for totally different reasons. His thoughts were on his reunion with the Baroness Christina von Harstezzen. He considered her the most fascinating and talented woman he had ever met. In just a few short hours the *Hindenburg* would be landing. He would be able to cast his eyes on her again; the prospect of what this way might hold was a thrilling thought.

Freddie told the American news commentator, in a friendly conversation, of his many different assignments over the years. The American was genuinely impressed by Freddie's accomplishments. He commented on his courage in going to battle-scarred places to film the events as they occurred. He was also swift to commend Freddie on his initiative in recording historical events and he wished him well in his future endeavours. Before the commentator moved on to talk to other people he remarked to Freddie that on this day, a special day in aviation history, the newsreel shots would be breathtaking. Freddie did not disagree with him. It would be very memorable, but not quite for the reasons they were anticipating.

He directed his camera team to swing their lenses around and conferred with his colleagues, the best method of capturing the event on film. With every previous event Freddie had filmed, in order to obtain the most detailed and descriptive footage of his newsreels, he always took great care in preparing long, close and medium shorts well in advance. Finally, after consulting his team members in order to get the best shots possible, Freddie decided on the prime use of three cameras.

One camera was to be strategically placed at a position directly in front of the Hindenburg as it came in to land. This camera would film the full frontal view of the airship capturing the power behind the propellers as it descended towards the mooring mast. Another camera would be positioned towards the end of the airship. This one would be mounted on a movable platform, which would be pulled back by a motor vehicle as the airship progressively dived towards the ground. From this angle the full length of the *Hindenburg* could be emphasised on film. With a bit of luck and cinematic skill, if the airship came in close enough, they would be able to capture the looks of people peering through the windows as they approached. The other camera would be placed close to the crowd and would switch backwards and forwards between the looks on the faces of onlookers – always important to register people's impressions on screen – and the landing of the airship. The other cameras in Freddie's team would operate on the guidance of a second director.

When Freddie was quite satisfied with the arrangements he relaxed, happy in the thought that he was going to capture another stunning newsreel achievement in his professional career.

High over the clouds and the ocean Baroness Christina von Harstezzen smiled. Soon they would be coming into land in a country she had never visited before, but one that she was especially interested to visit. She had been impressed with Freddie Miller's letters of his travels across the United States. The mention of wine grapes in California had stirred her palate considerably. She would be interested to try some of the vintages just to see if they measured up to the high standards of the Harstezzen estates. Perhaps she might even learn something from their qualities.

For a moment she felt a shock wave pulsate through her. The Circle. Mrs von Harstezzen had been so carried away by the exhilaration of the flight she had put all thoughts of the Circle out of her mind. In fact she had relaxed her mind so much on this issue, she had found herself talking quite amiably to several Nazis and listening to them espouse their doctrine without realising she was a silent participant to their cause.

There would be work to be done in the United States. A new market for the export of her wine; sympathisers and supporters to be sounded out who could possibly be of beneficial advantage to the Circle. Oh, but that was a while away, she thought. For the moments remaining of this journey she would just bask in the serenity of it all. Tomorrow's worries could wait. Enjoy the peace and freedom of today.

In just over two days of flight the Baroness had savoured all the luxuries of this aeronautical achievement. She had drunk wine and champagne and dined well in-flight. Through her contacts in the air industry she had felt privileged to be on this particular flight and pleased that her status in life was highly regarded enough for them to allow her a place aboard. She considered the possibility of investing money in the Zeppelin industry.

Several people on board had engaged her in conversation. Among them a rather eccentric millionaire, an elderly company director and a Baroness, whom she had met before in Berlin with her late husband, Reiber. They were interesting conversationalists who talked eagerly of their own lives and professions. It had been a while since she had met so many different and varied people beyond her own professional and private arena.

The flight director kept coming back at different intervals to talk to her. So much so, that the millionaire pondered as to whether the polite gentleman was her suitor or not. She merely conceded that he was just dong his job in an overly efficient manner and that perhaps in future flights politeness, courtesy and efficiency would be normal on such long journeys.

Soon they were over the United States. The *Hindenburg* in all its majesty and significance was flying over cities and towns, and neat rectangular fields of corn, wheat and barley. From the airship window different colours could be identified. There were greens of light and shade texture, yellows, pale auburns and gold-bright orange flaring up separately from the rest.

People in the airship were getting excited and returning to their seats to take in their air-born views of the United States. The time was passing quickly. The pace of the airship seemed to be gathering rapid movement, its engines pushing hard against the oncoming air currents flaring up against its huge outer shell. The propellers swivelled around and around, never losing motion, never struggling against the prevalent conditions that surrounded it.

The *Hindenburg* began its decent. The most apparent thing that was obvious on the faces of all the passengers was the look of enthralled travellers. Mrs Harstezzen considered in her mind that the airship would become a regular means of flight from now on.

"It has been a momentous flight, Mrs Harstezzen," the millionaire remarked to her. She in turn nodded and smiled happily as the airship lowered and lowered. From the window that was her vantage point she could see the outline of Lakehurst, New Jersey in the distance. She felt happy and excited.

Freddie started signalling to his news team colleagues on the ground to take up their positions. They moved promptly at his request. The cameraman on the soon-to-be-moving platform stood poised and alert, while the rest of the team ran last-minute checks on their equipment. Freddie moved across to his position behind the number one camera and stood in expectation of the first view of the airship.

People in the crowd gazed through binoculars up into the sky. The journalists shuffled around, pens at the ready to write down details, and a whole array of professional and amateur photographers were ready to set their shutters in motion.

In the hanger, the American radio commentator, Herbert Morrison, who had earlier been talking to Freddie, started to deliver his own description of the event. His own colleagues began to move out at the expected time of arrival of the *Hindenburg*.

Taking a deep breath he began his delivery. "The *Hindenburg* left Frankfurt, Germany, yesterday – er, Thursday evening rather – at 7.30 their time, and for the best part of the past two and a half day's they've been speeding through the skies over miles and miles of water here to America."

All around Lakehurst on that day people were waiting with baited breath. Then it came into view. Camera shutters closed and opened frantically as the *Hindenburg* came down towards its landing point. The cinecameras rolled, the crowd gazed up in awe. Freddie Miller caught the full view of the airship as it gave the impression of floating down like a pillow on a cushion of air. The other cameras in Freddie's team operated in coordination in the manner they had been instructed to do so.

On board the airship the full effects of its rapid descent could be felt. Mrs Harstezzen, full of childlike curiosity, along with other passengers looked down enthusiastically as the *Hindenburg* came in to land.

The commentator on the ground was keyed up. There was a real skill in describing an historical event as it happened. He employed his talents in that area to a fine art.

"Now they're coming in to making a landing and I'm going to step out of here and cover it from the outside. So, as I move out, we'll just stand by for a second."

Without losing continuity in his description, he stepped outside of the hanger from where he had been broadcasting his commentary. Freddie was so close to the man that the words of the American commentator were practically ringing in his ears.

Mrs Harstezzen looked down at the people surrounding the landing strip. She pondered as to where Freddie Miller and his newsreel cameramen would be. What sort of sight would this appear to Freddie through the lens of a camera.

"Well here it comes, ladies and gentlemen. We're out now. Outside the hanger and what a great sight it is. A thrilling one. It's a marvellous sight. It's coming down out of the skies pointing directly towards us and towards the mooring mast. The mighty vehicle motors just roared, the propellers backing into the air and throwing it back into a gale like whirlpool."

Freddie's camera whirred. What a tremendous site! He controlled the speed superbly and the focus of the lens caught the full effect of the airship as it slowed down.

"No wonder this great floating palace can travel through the air at such a speed with these powerful motors behind it. Now the fields that we saw active when we first arrived have turned into a moving mass of cooperative action."

Freddie was now applying his full concentration to the job that he was performing. The commentator was speaking close by and the words seemed to drift over the air as Freddie swung the lens towards the people working furiously as the Hindenburg approached. Freddie could only hear occasional phrases, as the American commentator delivered his description in glowing terms. 'Last minute preparations' almost signalled the man behind the camera to capture the actions of the men close to the mooring mast ready to berth the vessel.

"The ship is gliding majestically towards us like a great feather." *It was an apt description,* thought Freddie. He had that incredible shot square on now. He moved the camera forward on a trolley with wheels to obtain a medium to close shot. He was still within earshot of the American commentator and could hear his words, "Now the ropes are being dropped from the nose of the ship." He moved the camera forward even further. It was an exciting picture that he had within his view.

Freddie could feel the droplets of rain on his face. The commentator's words reflected everything that day including the weather.

"It's starting to rain again. The rained backed off earlier today." From the windows of the *Hindenburg*, Mrs Harstezzen stared down at the field seeing the men rushing around the base of the vessel attempting to moor it. The weather certainly wasn't the best. No sunny skies in America to welcome her, it seemed.

The commentator on the ground continued. Freddie adjusted the lens while half listening to him, half concentrating on his view. Was that a blue flame he could see coming from the tail of the airship?

"The back motors are holding—" Then, in the space of a mere second or so, everything changed. Freddie could just hear a maze of words that he couldn't absorb. His mind went into a spin; his eyes froze in horror.

"It's crashing! Oh, it's crashing!" Freddie almost lost control of his camera. "It's burning into flames – four or five hundred feet in the sky." The commentator's voice was breaking. Flames and smoke surged high into the air. The *Hindenburg* had exploded before his very eyes. The vessel was incinerated, ashes and wreckage strewn in front of him. Oh my God. The people on board. Mrs Harstezzen. Throughout the horror of it all, as Freddie drew back his camera, the film still rolling, the American commentator, thoroughly broken up by the tragedy, carried on speaking. "It's a terrific crash, ladies and gentlemen. There's smoke and there's fire. Oh my God." Freddie put a hand over his mouth as the smoke swirled and swirled around him. He was so shaken, so horrified, that he had not realised his eyes were streaming with tears. The last words he heard from the commentator were, "A mass of smoking wreckage and we can hardly breathe." There was smoke and there was fire and then—

★★★

The next day the full revelations of what had happened were unleashed on an unsuspecting public. Of the ninety-seven on board, comprising thirty-six passengers and sixty-one crewman, there were thirty-five fatalities – thirteen passengers, twenty-two crewmen and one member of the ground staff died.

★★★

A mass of smoking wreckage. Freddie opened his eyes. What a nightmare. Then he realised he had not been dreaming. He was in his hotel room in New Jersey. How he had got there, he had no idea. The last thing he remembered was the smoke and the fire and the commentator clearly broken up and the screams of the onlookers. Those cries of horror – so many of the people had friends on board.

A bolt hit him like a thunderous streak of lightning. Mrs Harstezzen had gone. Freddie rolled over in his bed and sobbed like a child. He thought not only of that gallant, noble woman who had initiated the Companions of the Circle, but he thought too of all the other people who had been lost when the *Hindenburg* had exploded.

Freddie tried to contain himself. He wiped his eyes. Still the tears came. In all his years in the army, and afterwards as a newsreel cameraman, he had never witnessed anything quite so horrifying before.

He reached across to the wireless and switched it on. There was music playing by a jazz band. Getting himself out of bed and moving across to the sink, he washed his face in cold water. Then he heard a news bulletin. Naturally the details of the events surrounding the explosion of the Hindenburg provided the main topic. The name of Mrs Harstezzen was listed among the victims who had died. He listened as the horrors, to which he had been witness to, were graphically described. Finally, he could stand it no longer and turned if off sharply. He ran his hand through his hair. His face was a picture of shock. His thoughts were a mixture of so many things. He couldn't think straight or recall everything clearly and he set about rectifying the problem by pouring himself a whisky from a bottle he obtained from a cabinet in his hotel room. He had scarcely raised the glass to his lips when there was a loud knocking on the door. He heard someone call his name. He recognised the voice belonging to Sam, one of his cameramen, and he moved across the room to open the door.

Without saying a word they acknowledged each other with a glum look. Sam came in and closed the door behind him. Freddie poured his friend a drink and they both sat quietly for a moment, sipping their whisky. "Shocking. Absolutely horrendous." said Sam quietly, his voice hushed, his tone that of disbelief. "The moment I saw that slight blue flame at the tail end, I had an inclination something disastrous was going to happen."

"I have never ever—" Every word Freddie spoke was spaced out as he trembled inside at the memory. "I have never been a witness to such horror. I don't think I will ever be able to forget it."

"Nor me, mate," Sam agreed with him, and then as a thought of concern he added, "Fred, are you all right?"

"No, I'm feeling terrible." Freddie replied softly. Even though Freddie was still in a deep sense of shock there was not a hint of aggression or anger about him. He was still in good control of his temperament. His emotions were a different story. He wanted to burst out sobbing and weeping and to unleash a flurry of tears. He could feel his eyes flooding with tears and he wiped his eyes. The two men, close friends from their years as working colleagues together, felt deep empathy for each other. Tears between friends were no embarrassment. There was still something playing on Freddie's mind. He felt compelled to ask Sam. "What happened to me? How did I end up back here?"

"You passed out – fainted. We brought you back here. Oh my goodness it was chaos on the airfield. People running around, people crying and weeping, and that poor yank next to you who was describing the event broke up completely. He had a tough time of it."

Freddie could still hear the man's faltering voice in his mind. "I listened, at least I started to listen, to a broadcast but I couldn't take it. I switched it off. They haven't any ideas I suppose?"

"Ideas? How it started you mean, Freddie?"

"Exactly. I can't believe how the *Hindenburg* could come all the way from Frankfurt here to America and explode on arrival. Any there any theories being touted?"

"It would appear to be a mystery. I talked to a journalist in the lobby and there was a bit of speculation going on, he reckoned. All kinds of things. You name it, Fred. Whatever is a possibility they're speculating on it."

Freddie sipped his whisky as he considered the possible causes. He shook his head from side to side slowly in gloomy dismay. It had all been so dreadful. He couldn't bear to think of Baroness Christina von Harstezzen. Such a loss to the world.

"I knew someone aboard," he pointed out to his friend who had been completely unaware of this. Sam looked at him in shocked amazement. "I heard on the wireless – she was a victim."

"I'm – I'm sorry," Sam stammered. He had a look of genuine surprise. "I didn't know."

"Yes. A lady I met in Germany." He wiped his face with a handkerchief, drying up the dampness of his tears. "One of the most fascinating, talented and intelligent ladies I have ever had the privilege to meet. She was a fine lady. I had arranged to meet her here. She was a widow. A business woman, you know, and a very capable one at that."

"I'm truly sorry, Fred," said Sam, completely taken aback by his friend's appearance. "Look, mate, I didn't realise just what you'd gone through. I mean it was a shock to us all. I'll never forget the horror of it." He looked embarrassed at Freddie's plight, but inside he felt saddened. "I just came to see that you were all right, Freddie. Shall I leave you alone for a while?"

"If you wouldn't mind, Sam," he said, quietly topping his whisky glass up again. Sam started to move to the door. Freddie suddenly called out to him. "Listen, how would you and the rest of the boys feel about going home? Do you think it would be a good idea?"

Sam stopped in his tracks. He rubbed his chin pondering what to do. "It might be a good idea at that."

"Would you put it to them? Let me know tomorrow, will you?"

"Sure thing," replied Sam, and he left the room.

Freddie sat alone. He wondered now about the Circle. The complete workings of the Circle in Europe would now be handed on down to Arthandur Palmai. Arthandur would by now have heard the news of the Hindenburg disaster. There was Colonel Brindmarsh too of British Intelligence. He would have to be informed. It would mean a complete reorganisation of the networks that were operating in Europe. But all that seemed immaterial as he sat there motionless, frozen in the shock and the aftermath of such a devastating aeronautical tragedy in which people had lost their lives in front of him.

Poor Freddie had witnessed tragedy before. In the previous year he had experienced firsthand the trauma of the Spanish Civil War. This tragedy was different. The whole of the airship was a man-made design and considered a triumph in modern engineering. That this vessel of flight together with its numerous passengers and crew should have turned into debris and ash strewn across the airfield at Lakehurst, New Jersey, was unthinkable. It was so hard to fathom just what he had seen. There is so much value in human life. The loss of so many lives was tragic. Loss of life is irreplaceable.

After a period of solitude in his hotel room, during bouts of drinking whisky Freddie gathered his thoughts together and sat down to write letters. Straight away he would write to Arthandur Palmai at his home in Austria, expressing his sorrow and grief and then proceed reluctantly to the subject of the Companions of the Circle. Arthandur would now be the one who would coordinate the various agents throughout Europe.

Colonel Brindmarsh of Special Operations for British Intelligence would be the recipient of another letter, his own undercover men and associates would have to be informed. This would be another monumental task in itself.

Freddie gritted his teeth and in a mood that was composed of a mixture of melancholy, grief, confusion and shock, he sat down and wrote these important letters, relating what had happened. He wanted to get this matter over with quickly; then he could be alone in his grief and solitude. Yesterday the explosion of the *Hindenburg*, today the aftermath.

He had fully expected the rest of the cameramen to comply with his wishes. They came back to see Freddie the next day and, under the guidance of Sam, they all expressed their wish to go home as soon as possible. The event of a couple of days before had put a blight on the whole trip. What had begun as a wonderful introduction to a fine country, and a fine people, had ended on a sour and sad note. Freddie began the task of ringing the studios to whom he had been working on contract for, expressing the wish to finish up and return to England. He had little difficulty there. The studios had been delighted with the footage on the American way of life that the newsreel team had compiled. The executives of the various studies were sympathetic to Freddie's request and, rather than retain his men at the present time, they issued an invitation to the British news team to return again and pursue more work.

When Freddie had finished talking to the studio executives over the phone, he sat alone in his room thinking about things. Filming the news was a wonderfully invigorating life. Rather it had been. Perhaps the past tense definitely applied now. It had not been without its rewards. He had met many famous and infamous people. He had seen people who had made the news. He had travelled. He had gathered a wealth of experience, the value of which could not be measured in material gain. From his own experiences he had seen the diversity of people's natures.

He recalled with pleasure the spiritual love of Gandhi. He thought of the regal eloquence of the now abdicated King of England, Edward VIII, and the humility and decency of the new King George VI and the delightful Queen Elizabeth. He had seen much but as times changed so had his own personality. There were different things he wanted out of life. Things that money could not buy. Although he was reticent to admit it to anyone but himself, he knew exactly what he was looking for.

It must have been in that little village in Austria that Freddie finally made the realisation about himself. He had sat with Arthandur and Marlene Palmai many times at a meal table and seen the obvious joyous pride that they had in their son, Nathan. The family was the focal point of love. From good family unity, love and warmth could radiate at a scale of which Freddie had not known for years. Such a thing as family life could provide the security he had not known throughout his years as an army officer and a newsreel cameraman.

He seriously considered that his lifestyle was becoming chaotic. Perhaps it was time at the age of thirty-one to resign from the news team and let his next in line colleague, Sam, take over the running of things. Freddie would look for a different line of work, a different lifestyle. After all there was a girl in London who had always loved him from the time of their first meeting in an Indian location called Jawapindoo; a twenty-six-year-old flighty, flirty girl, with auburn hair, and brown eyes that could flash with impish humour. Cynthia Field. Freddie planned his line of attack and as soon as he got home to London, he would bombard Cynthia with flowers and presents and, strictly to comply with tradition, he would go down on one knee and propose to her. He had better do it fast, he considered. A jewel of a girl like Cynthia would not wait for ever.

It was just a few days later, a short time before he and his friends were due to leave aboard an ocean liner from New York to Liverpool, that he misguidedly took in a movie in a town called Hoboken in New Jersey. Freddie was horrified when a news documentary came up on screen between features. He had risen from his seat at the mention of the *Hindenburg*. He had felt compelled to leave but some fatal fascination, some hidden inner force seemed to pull him back into his seat like the effect of the earth's gravitational pull, and he found himself transfixed to the footage that an American camera team had pieced together.

This news documentary was all the more powerful and haunting, for this one featured the voice of the commentator who had been standing so near to Freddie at the time of the incident. The man's vivid description followed leading up to the explosion on arrival. Freddie's legs went numb. His whole body shuddered. He could not move. He was captive to the terrifying sight. And within him he was reliving it all. He could virtually smell the smoke and the fumes and he was again experiencing the full-pulverised shock of it all.

When Freddie left the picture theatre, he gazed into the sky and looked at the stars. He remembered that once the Baroness had asked him if he was a Christian. It was a question he had to think about deeply before answering. Yet he did believe deeply. He was exhilarated to realise that he had a genuine belief in life itself and a life hereafter. For if we are here on this earth and our very existence is so precious then surely that must be the ultimate proof of any belief.

Perhaps the Austrian-born, Swedish-raised Baroness, a lady of prodigious talents and a deep concern for the under-privileged, and the persecuted, was in fact watching him from a wonderful place beyond the realms of human comprehension, where real love flows in abundance. From his jacket Freddie took out a photograph he carried. It had been taken on the vast wine estate in the Rhineland. In it Freddie, Arthandur Palmai and the Baroness posed in front of a bull-nosed Bentley, one of Mrs Harstezzen's prized possessions. He glanced down at it and up again to the stars. At least he was here to enjoy this night.

Hoboken was to become well known in future years. It was the birthplace of a singer who in the next few years would become one of the most popular balladeers of the century and whose monumental talents would earmark him for recognition as a fine dramatic actor in motion pictures. It was 1937, but in two years time a young singer called Frank Sinatra would make the town of Hoboken well known. On that particular night Freddie wandered with the crowds as he had done so in many cities. He did a tour of the drug stores and the bars, talking to people with an easy art and confidence that he had acquired over the years. Freddie always prided himself that he could talk to people anywhere about anything. He did so here, talking to people that night about baseball, gridiron, English cricket, and life in general. He concluded that the Americans were a people he could develop a great affinity and fondness for.

Taking the bus to New York he wondered if some day he might return. Life is strange. Sometimes he pontificated, 'we return through fates that we have no control over'. He and the rest of the newsreel team took in a show on Broadway on their last night in New York after which they dined in style at a French restaurant just off Times Square. A bottle of red wine, a superb steak and succulent vegetables, and all was right with the world. Truly a good life could be had in this land.

The next day the liner moved out from New York. It was a beautiful clear day, so much warmer than when they had arrived and, as with all departures, there is always an element of sadness. If only the Hindenburg had not ended its flight so disastrously on that sixth day of May in 1937. Mrs Harstezzen has gone, he reminded himself. The Companions of the Circle have a new leader. For one moment he thought of Arthandur Palmai. He wondered just what Arthandur would be doing at this moment far away in the mountains of Austria.

He paused for reflection then cast his eyes back on the skyscrapers of New York, white, luminous buildings soaring up against a sky he had not seen so vividly blue since he was in India. A sky as blue as amethyst and the air fresh with the breezes from the sea. The liner gave a huge blast of farewell from one of its funnels and Freddie was smiling now. He looked out at the Atlantic Ocean and wondered how Cynthia Field would respond when he asked her to marry him.

Thirteen

It was on the boat sailing back to England that Freddie really decided what course he wanted his life to take from now on. Having decided that he would leave the newsreel team and sell out his ownership in it, he examined the possibilities of moving from London to one of the counties in the UK, and working for a newspaper. He would maintain his contact with the Companions of the Circle, but would work from the seclusion of a country retreat.

In his youth Freddie had attended school in Somerset, a place that held mixed memories for him of a lonely time away from home as a boarding pupil, yet also of a time when his senses and intuition were heightened to new levels. The county that mostly attracted Freddie was Cornwall. On his visits there in his younger days he had been captivated by the magic and allure that was Cornwall. On arriving back in England, if Cynthia was still seriously interested in him, he would tell her of his plans and propose to her.

The course of Freddie's life was about to change through his own making. For Arthandur Palmai in Austria his life too was about to change. However, for Arthandur and his family the changes in his life were not self-initiated, it was the circumstances that were thrust upon him that changed his whole situation.

An open newspaper lay spread-eagled on the table in the lounge room of the Palmai household. The front page of the tabloid was graphic and brutal in its description of the explosion of the *Hindenburg*. When Arthandur had first read the news he had been horrified and appalled. Then when he had recalled that Baroness Christina von Harstezzen had been on board, he felt his spirits plummet downwards like a huge weight pulling him down into a feeling of defeat.

He had walked straight out of the house and into the solitude of the mountains on hearing the news. He was aware that he had now fully assumed a colossal weight of responsibilities in his capacity as the new leader of the Companions of the Circle. But for hours and hours he sat on a crevice away from people where he could be alone with his thoughts and his grief. In private he had wept openly for the Baroness and he realised that he loved her as closely as a near and dear relative.

Marlene had found the newspaper on the table and realised straightaway why Arthandur's absence from the house was noticeable. She had noticed the front door wide open and knew that Arthandur would be thinking things out in solitude. Marlene knew her husband's instincts. She knew that he never wanted to burden his family with the worries of his responsibilities. She also knew that whenever he had a difficult decision to make or when he was experiencing a mood of despondency, he would walk to some secluded part of the mountain paths and find isolation. For his family Arthandur felt that he must only give them a face of cheer, an appearance of serenity and understanding. It was not always easy.

He had been gone a long time when Marlene began to get concerned. It was late afternoon, soon the shadows of the evening would be falling and it would start to cool off rapidly. This prompted her to go out and find him. Nathan was playing in the house next door and she started out to console her husband.

Through the village she began to walk, past the chalets glistening in the afternoon sunshine, with the families together in their tiny little gardens, past the shops where the proprietors were getting ready to close for the day, and past the tavern where the owner was preparing for the throng of customers that would flood the tables in the evening. The local Austrian villagers, the men from the fields, the stores and the outlying farms would come in and gulp their steins to quench a furious thirst after by their long hours of toil.

On the mountain path Marlene walked up, looking left and right with worry. She had never known her husband disappear on his own for such a long time, and her mind was a cluster of worry. It was getting darker how. It was slightly eerie as with the changing of the tone of light the local rock formations took on a different shade of colour.

Grey rocks became luminous. Dark green became pitch black as the shadows stretched out across the varying clumps of vegetation, and the path that she was treading on led into blackness.

Suddenly, she was startled by movement. She felt her heart jump.

Something ran out of a clump of bushes at her. She stepped back in a moment of terror and then the shockwaves subsided as fast as they had been pulsated. It was a mountain goat leaping and clambering on its own way. She paused for amusement at the way she had been startled. Then she was shocked again even more with double the effect.

"I'm over here, Marlene," came a familiar voice from up ahead in the shadows. She could only identify a silhouette standing up in front of her but even in the dark the figure was clearly that of Arthandur.

"Oh, you frightened me!" She stammered, holding her chest in a minor fit of shock. Arthandur moved out more clearly into view. The moonlight seemed to capture his face and it was as if in a matter of hours all the pressures in the world had caught up with him. He appeared drained and disconsolate, and tearstains were evident on his face, but, despite the obvious, he still managed to smile at her warmly. He came down towards her and hugged her.

"We have lost Christina," he said softly. He looked at her sadly. The red veins in his eyes and a downcast look in them made it clear how he felt. "You know I came up here to think."

In the darkness as they walked down the path Marlene listened to her husband as he spoke of his sadness of the loss of their close friend. Down below them the village looked a picture of fairy tale lights sparkling in the blackness of night. Going through Arthandur's mind was the thought that this picturesque retreat may be under threat sooner than previously envisaged. For the first time since he had begun in participating in the activities of the Circle the fear invaded the privacy of his mind, that with the loss of Baroness von Harstezzen, good may not triumph over evil. Realising the great task of keeping the networks of the Circle together he suddenly found himself in possession of doubts. Doubts that he may not be the man to head the Circle.

Arthandur stopped walking for a moment and stood looking at the village far below.

"I feel such sadness." He said, turning to his wife. Marlene looked at him reciprocating the ever-loving patience and understanding that never left her. "Of course for all the passengers and their families. But Christina – Christina! Why?" His voice was tortured. "She of all people. It was through so much of her efforts that many of our people have begun new lives elsewhere, free of persecution."

"You must not torment yourself. The fact that so many of our people from Austria and Germany are free is a living testament to her work. More people will be free because of her efforts. If war does come there will be much resistance from the underground groups she has formed. There will come a time when she may get recognition as a humanitarian. Arthandur you must not brood."

"I find it hard not to do so. I had a very deep feeling for her. When I first saw the overwhelming response to Hitler in Berlin and Vienna, I was frightened – and I feared – I felt terror. Then when I was introduced socially over dinner in Berlin to Mrs von Harstezzen, and I learned of this secret group she had formed, I felt a great sense of purpose. I felt that with her aid and the Companions of the Circle, we could all come through."

"We will come through, all of us. Besides, the entire weight of the Circle does not solely depend on you. You should not take on the worries of the world. You did say that Freddie Miller's associate, Colonel Brindmarsh, would take over much of the operations."

Arthandur acknowledged this fact and they began walking home again. "You know, Marlene, I expect to be hearing from both those gentlemen at some time."

"I expect you do. He was a good man. I liked Freddie. He seemed reliable; the kind of man who would be there if you needed help."

Arthandur smiled at the mention of Freddie. He had great affection for the man. He had not forgotten the time of their meeting in the café in Berlin the year before. The letters that Freddie had written to Arthandur since then remained a treasure as a valuable communication from one good friend to another.

His mood of sadness was lifting a little now. He was not quite so pensive.

"I might even write to Freddie myself," he felt inclined to add. Thoughts had been occupied elsewhere. He thought how strangely fatalistic life could be sometimes. He remembered with an alarming suddenness that before her departure the Baroness had given him a huge bundle of documents detailing all the private and personal details of the members of the Circle. It had been purely a matter of routine, of course, but even so it was merely proof to Arthandur of how forward thinking the Baroness was. She never left a stone unturned. She never missed a practical detail and she always prepared well in advance for any unexpected circumstances. Thinking of this Arthandur said unexpectedly, "Christina must have had a premonition."

Marlene looked at him surprised. "What do you mean?" She asked. "A premonition?"

"Before she left she gave me a bundle of papers. They were the records of our fellow members in Holland, Belgium, France, Freddie in England, of course, and the others here in Austria and Germany. I think that as soon as it is clear that Brindmarsh has all the names on record then I will burn the details so that it will not fall into unsuspecting hands that could possibly betray our networks. And then do you know what I will do, Marlene?"

"I am only here to listen to you, my husband," she replied knowingly to him.

"Then I will write to Colonel Brindmarsh and tell him of my desire not to be the centre of the Circle, not to be the leader but just a fellow Companion. Not the man who runs the risk of having the lives of his family threatened but just to be another operator in the shadows. I will ask him to break the Circle up into regions."

"You mean such as Holland and Belgium to be on their own for example. France and Luxemburg as a separate region perhaps."

"Yes, and Germany and Austria, and Colonel Brindmarsh can pull the strings from his office in Whitehall."

"I think, Arthandur, that would be a step in the right direction."

"And one more thing, too, Marlene."

"What is that?"

"We must plan for Nathan."

The quickly enthusiastic mood paled off significantly almost instantaneously. Marlene new exactly what Arthandur was talking about. The subject of the kibbutz in Palestine had reared its head once again.

"I know what you are talking about," She reassured him.

"Tomorrow with all the other tasks I have ahead of me, I must write to the appropriate authorities and prepare for our beloved son's departure on an agricultural scholarship to a kibbutz in Palestine. He must go early next year as soon as possible after his sixteenth birthday."

Marlene nodded to him. Now she too was feeling sad, although this was for different reasons. It was too painful for them to think of Nathan leaving them. This would be another loss that would be hard to bear.

Fourteen

True to expectations Arthandur received letters from both Freddie Miller and Colonel Brindmarsh within a few weeks since the *Hindenburg* had exploded. Freddie's letter was postmarked with an American stamp. Arthandur could see that Freddie had been quick to write so soon after the event. He was wary of opening it but, by now, a month had lapsed since Freddie had posted it and Arthandur, after some deliberation, opened the letter.

> *May 7th 1937*
> F R Miller
> St Ettienne's Hotel
> Lakehurst
> New Jersey
> United States

Dear Arthandur

By now you will have heard the tragic news of the Hindenburg. I do not wish to dwell on that event or the loss of our mutual friend, Christina. It is all so terribly painful. I was there at the airfield with my cameramen and I can only tell you that it was as dreadful as any newspaper headline you may have read. My heart goes out to you at this time. I know how much this great lady meant to you. She was a person of great compassion for those who needed it.

Arthandur broke off from the letter for a minute. Freddie had obviously suffered a dreadful trauma as an eye-witness to the incident at Lakehurst. To have been so near to Christina and yet so far would have been a huge pain that would tear a man's emotions in two. Arthandur continued reading.

> Apart from the great loss that we have been subjected to by the loss of Christina, I realise that the pattern of our mutual concerns will take on a new direction.

This was a cleverly written letter, Arthandur conceded. In case the letter should fall into the hands of any high-ranking German official, even slightly suspecting the good doctor of anything offensive, the wording disguised the hidden meaning. The words 'mutual concerns' referred, of course, to the Circle and the 'new direction' was an obvious reference to Colonel Brindmarsh, who would be in contact shortly no doubt.

> From now on our interests will probably not coincide as they have done previously, but undoubtedly as friends we can communicate regularly. I would like to know how you, Marlene and Nathan are getting on. Please remember my offer to you, Arthandur. If I can be of any assistance in helping you and your family, should you wish to take up residence in England, please let me know.

Arthandur was touched by Freddie's offer, but inside he knew that he wanted his own family to be settled in Palestine for this was really the land that held promise for the future.

> I have informed our mutual friend in London of Christina's passing. Knowing his proficiency in most matters, I can advise you that the said person in question will be in touch with you either directly or by letter. I will write to you again, Arthandur. Please pass on my best wishes to Marlene and Nathan.
> Once again, I must add that to witness the Hindenburg disaster, especially knowing that our fine friend was aboard, has been all too hard to bear. Look after yourself old friend. My thoughts are with you.
>
> Yours faithfully,
> Freddie

Just a brief letter, but in its short length it was so much to the point. The 'mutual friend' in London was Colonel Brindmarsh, who had written promptly too. Less than a fortnight after Arthandur had received Freddie's letter, Colonel Brindmarsh's correspondence arrived. To Arthandur's amazement, it was brief, merely stating that Colonel Brindmarsh would be arriving within a week for a private visit. Presumably, Arthandur pondered, for matters of urgent consultation. He was becoming so used to the magical weaving of words that constructed all manner of inventive phraseology, and to large examples of the vocabulary that disguised hidden meanings and clandestine secrets all so unique to British Intelligence. To a German the English language was quite difficult to learn to begin with. Now it seemed he would have to scour certain aspects of letters that he received from British agents to try and learn any deeper meanings that were immediately obvious. For one moment Arthandur asked himself if it would have been easier for them to write in Hebrew.

Colonel Francis Brindmarsh arrived in the little Austrian village five days later. Dressed in civilian clothes, a very dour grey suit with a matching tie and a brimmed hat, he arrived by taxi at Arthandur's house. He did not make his presence obvious or give away his try identity. True to his profession he posed as a German tourist giving his name to the receptionist in the doctor's surgery as Ardun Steiner and told her he was passing through the village but wanted a check up in relation to his blood pressure, which he said was invariably high.

The wait in the doctor's surgery gave the colonel an opportunity as an outside to see how Arthandur operated privately. He saw, just as Freddie Miller had done so in the previous year, how warmly Arthandur was greeted by each of his patients. It was obvious to Colonel Brindmarsh that here was a well-liked man. Upon first sight of Arthandur, the colonel determined how deceiving a first appearance and a judgement on immediate viewing could be.

Then, after several patients had been consulted and despatched, it was time for the colonel to enter Arthandur's surgery. Purely as a matter of politeness, Arthandur greeted him with a handshake, and a cordial greeting in German, to which Brindmarsh, highly conversant in that language, replied amiably. There was a quizzical look in Arthandur's eye because he could see in the man's complexion and hearing his pronunciation of certain syllables of the German dialect that this gentleman may have been an outsider.

Arthandur carried on speaking in German to Colonel Brindmarsh as he tested his blood pressure, but he was listening carefully to his patient's dialogue. He was pretty certain of the true identity of the man, yet he was careful not to give away his suspicions.

Arthandur had realised that he was going to be paid a visit by Brindmarsh. He quite admired the way the colonel had crept up on him unawares. In a moment, with good humour, he would turn the tables on him. He told the gentleman, who professed to be Ardun Steiner, that his blood pressure was fine and that he was in excellent health in German. Then Arthandur leaned back in his chair, clasped his hands together on the top of the desk, and looked at his patient, smiling almost benignly. Brindmarsh caught the change in attitude and stared back at him wondering what the next response would be. The silence of a few seconds puzzled him.

"How is the weather this time of year in England, Colonel Brindmarsh?" Arthandur spoke at last. The colonel, surprised he had been found out, smiled back at him.

"Very good," he complimented Arthandur at his discovery. "How did you know?"

"In your dialogue, Colonel. If I may compliment you, sir, you speak German with a fine tongue and a remarkable pronunciation too. However, I have a keen ear for languages. I could hear the tones of a Scotsman in some of your words. Your skin and complexion, too, is that of a man who has spent much of it in English weather."

"You are an observant gentleman!" remarked Colonel Brindmarsh. He bristled his moustache, a mannerism that was at times maddening to watch as he did it so often. "My friend and colleague Freddie said you were sharp. Now I know just how much so."

"It is good to meet you, Colonel. I know that we can help each other in the most efficient of ways. You realise that I am working. I take it you wish to talk to me in private away from my surgery."

"Indeed I do, Mr Palmai. Away from earshot, and in a secluded spot. Could I suggest one of those mountain tracks leading up from the village? Freddie has told me of your fondness for walks in that area, When you finish your day's surgery perhaps?"

Arthandur glanced at his watch quickly. "I have a couple more patients to see. Say half an hour, Colonel?"

"Half an hour will be fine, Mr Palmai," Colonel Brindmarsh agreed.

The two men met up after Arthandur had finished his day's surgery and walked along the paths that led up above the valley.

"No wonder you chaps are so damnably fit. All this clean mountain air and arduous walking," Colonel Brindmarsh joked. "Now, Mr Palmai, first I must say how sorry I was to hear of the loss of your friend, Mrs Harstezzen. From my conversations with Freddie, I was aware of the enormous contribution she made in the activities of your organisation."

Arthandur lowered his head sadly. "She will be missed, Colonel. Be in no doubt as to that, not only for her leadership and her organisational capacities, but as a friend too."

"I understand that," said Brindmarsh sympathetically. He then quickly he reverted to the business side of things. "I must qualify a few things about your organisation, the Circle. If I could just tackle the subject of – shall we describe it as undercover emigration? By that I mean the transportation of refugees through falsification of documents." Arthandur nodded acknowledgement to him. This was one of the more controversial areas of the work of the Circle. "His Majesty's government cannot recognise this, whatever the circumstances. Even if the refugees in question are screened by your side, we are still running the risk of accepting infiltrators. Do you understand our position on this, Mr Palmai?"

Arthandur looked concerned. But he could understand the reasoning behind this.

"Regretfully I do, Colonel. What is even more regretful is that I agree with you on that aspect. You must forgive me if I seem grave in appearance. I still held out hopes that we could help far more people."

Colonel Brindmarsh sighed reluctantly. He had an official stand to take on his duties, but they did not cover areas of emigration. He felt compelled to explain. One could not deny the sincerity in his gentle Scottish tones.

"Mr Palmai, it is understandable how you feel. The area I work for is a department primarily concerned with the prevention of war and establishing networks of agents throughout Europe who can end any conflict through their assistance to servicemen and resistance groups. I regret to say that the provision of fake documentation for refugees is not part of our work. It is also not part of our policy."

"But Colonel Brindmarsh, I believe our friend, Freddie Miller, sought out leading members of the Jewish community who could provide temporary accommodation to German and Austrian Jews."

"Yes, he did. And if I may say so, he did a fine job. He has established connections for many of your people in the East End of London, North London, Leeds, Manchester, and Coventry. Even in my hometown of Edinburgh, I may add. But I must stress this is for official migration on official documentation."

"I understand completely and I will abide by your wishes." They both walked in silence having agreed in spirit to that particular point and then Arthandur thought of something else that merited a special mention.

"Before Christina left she brought to my house the entire documents that she had in her possession of the membership of the Companions of the Circle. Originally I was going to burn them. However, I think that you may wish to take it back to your office in Whitehall. I believe it would be far better for you and your men to have the entire details in your possession; the lists of agents, their occupations and their addresses."

Brindmarsh smiled. "It sounds as if it would make interesting reading. I'll take it back with me. Is it my understanding that you wish my men to coordinate the activities of the Circle? By that I mean you don't wish to be the successor to leadership of the Circle."

Arthandur breathed a sign of relief. He had wanted to shed himself of the responsibility of leadership as the tension and stress attached to it was affecting his health.

"To use a British phrase, Colonel. There you have it in a nutshell."

"So be it then, Mr Palmai. My men will officially take charge. You will, of course, remain in the Circle. We need your expertise."

"Of course, Colonel."

"Now, Mr Palmai I have a little bit of news for you concerning our friend Freddie."

"Oh!" Arthandur looked concerned.

"My goodness, no; nothing alarming. Freddie has resigned from his newsreel team and he's moving to Cornwall on the coast. He's going to work for a newspaper and he's going to get married."

"Well I'm pleased for him. You must pass on my best wishes to him." There was real pleasure in Arthandur's voice at the news.

"Freddie's connections with the Circle will remain. He'll still be working with us. From now on I will personally look after the Companions of the Circle from Germany and Austria in order to maintain careful scrutiny of their activities. I trust that will meet with your implicit approval?"

"I would be pleased. From what Freddie has told me your efficiency is unparalleled."

Colonel Brindmarsh beamed with pride.

"If I were a man of ego I would not hesitate in agreeing with you," he said good-humouredly, "but believe me, in this kind of work, everyone has to pull together. It's united performances that count. Not solely that of the individual."

"And what of Freddie? What will be his role from now on?"

"Well, as I said, Mr Palmai, he will still be working with us but because of his new location in Cornwall he can work in his spare time with some of our radio operators in that area. They are in touch with some of the Circle's French operators. He can monitor the French agents of the Circle from his home."

"I see," said Arthandur, and he felt almost a sense of loss when he realised that Freddie would no longer be working with the members of Germany and Austria. He did feel happy though that Freddie would communicate with him as a friend. At least he would be in touch with him on a personal basis. That was something. "Regarding the papers of the agents, Colonel Brindmarsh, shall we go and get them unless there is anything else you require to know?"

"No. First of all I need to give you some private codes and the names and addresses of some of my European contacts but, apart from that, there is nothing else. When we have established this, and you are well acquainted with our methods, then we will get all the papers you have in your possession."

This was it. Colonel Brindmarsh was now in command of the activities of the Circle in Germany and Austria. Arthandur was relieved of the immense responsibilities of co-ordinating the entire organisation. He was free to work on his own, helping the various people he came into contact with, and also a number of his own relatives. Through the many connections Freddie had set up in England, Arthandur was able to assist some of his friends and relatives to new lives in the British Isles. For his own part Arthandur was able to carry on as a doctor in the village and the greatest joy of all was that he could also devote so much of his time to his beloved family.

Nathan Palmai's agricultural scholarship was arranged to begin in the early part of 1938 and, knowing that his departure to Palestine was only a question of months away, Arthandur spent a great deal of time with his son. It was this time that benefitted Nathan in many ways for his father treated him like an adult, speaking on a manner of subjects, bringing him to a mutual understanding of Arthandur and a maturity that far outweighed his youthful years. There was something about Arthandur's voice. It was beautifully warm. It enveloped the listener of it in a feeling of deep sincerity. Arthandur spoke lucidly, softly and gently. Nathan loved his father greatly. In future years Nathan was to appreciate that few sons had the opportunity at that time in history to know their fathers, not only in the normal father-son relationship, but as an adult would know a close and intimate friend.

For the rest of the year the Circle in Europe operated under a great clandestine veil of secrecy, transporting a trickle of Jewish families to the British Isles. Arthandur still took a deep interest in what he had helped to build with the late Baroness Christina von Harstezzen. Many families who had journeyed from their homeland would have a huge debt of gratitude to Arthandur and Christina, for as events would unfold in the mysterious annals of history, they would realise just how fortunate they were that the Circle had helped them to reshape their destinies.

Sometimes in the middle of the night Arthandur would wake up suddenly and realise he had been dreaming. He would realise with a shudder that he had been dreaming of Christina. He would then look at his wife sleeping peacefully with that wonderfully, unworried countenance of hers. Arthandur would often wander the house in the early hours thinking of the Baroness. He did love her. He knew that. It was clear. But it was not the kind of deep love that a man has for his own wife or brethren. It was the kind of love that could only be defined in the terms of a great friendship and a deep, abiding respect for a human being, who despite the riches of monumental wealth and prestige, would risk it all for the sake of preservation of human lives and freedom. One day people would know of this great lady's compassion and strength.

In the coming months Arthandur received frequent letters from Freddie Miller and they were a joy to read. Freddie had married Cynthia Field in London one happy day in 1937 after many years of a friendship that had begun in India in the 1920s. Arthandur was overjoyed for Freddie, who wrote that the girl he married was one in a million and he sent a number of photographs to the Palmai's. Marlene remarked that Freddie's bride was a very beautiful woman with humour in her eyes. Arthandur could only smile with admiration at her friendly features and of that laughing face which almost leapt out to greet him.

Arthandur also read with interest the details of Freddie's new lifestyle. Having resigned from the newsreel team and sold out his share, Freddie had moved with his new wife to a delightfully picturesque village called Mousehole in Cornwall. In the various photographs of Mousehole that Freddie had sent, Arthandur could see a village by the sea of thin, narrow twisting lanes and olde worlde style cottages. Freddie did not describe it in any particular literal style. He merely expounded that both he and Cynthia thought it was 'heaven'. He also added how good life was working for a Cornish newspaper, writing articles on local events instead of trailing around the world in search of news with a camera team.

Often in Freddie's letter he would ask Arthandur how Marlene and Nathan were progressing. Nathan had obviously impressed Freddie, and Arthandur was only too pleased to write back and give an adoring description full of the boy's scholastic record. After all, Nathan had the best two teachers in the world: A lady who appreciated books, the arts and music – his own mother, Marlene. The other teacher was a man of wisdom, a man of medicine and a lover of the experiences of life itself, which he in turn considered were the greatest tutors of all. Arthandur was naturally that person. Two better teachers in the world that could not be surpassed.

Music played a big part in Nathan's life. Marlene would play the piano in the chalet with all the vigour and the enthusiasm of a concert virtuoso performing to a spellbound audience in a huge concert hall, perhaps in her own imagination in one of the huge cities of musical appreciations such as Berlin or Vienna. Her eyes would sometimes appear to be staring at something no one else could visualise. Often Marlene's thoughts would be far away. She would appear wistful and detached and her fingers glided with such a professional ease over the keys playing a slow enchanting melody. It was almost as if she would suddenly realise her thoughts were a long way away and she would snap herself into a more concentrative mood. Marlene would then look at her son and smile a beautiful smile of reassurance at him which was so lovely it would almost bring a cloud of tears to Nathan's eyes for it was this embracement which would strike a chord in him that he was loved so deeply by his Mother.

It was this same music played on the piano early one cool morning a few days after his sixteenth birthday in 1937 that woke him up from a very deep slumber. Rubbing his eyes, he knew that they were red with moisture for he had been crying in the night. Today he would be leaving his home for ever. The day had finally come when he would leave the village in the valley to travel to Palestine to begin a new period of life in a kibbutz.

The feelings that he had within him were a mixture of overwhelming sadness, and nostalgia for his life but strangely there was also another new feeling he had never known before. A sense of exuberance and excitement for something new to be experienced.

On that morning in 1938 – a morning that he would always remember for every intricate detail and which would stay embedded in his memory like a photographic portrait for the rest of his life – he washed and dressed and then stopped to look at the contours of his bedroom. He stopped still like a frozen statue. He remembered the day he had woken to find a bird watching him inside and he remembered how his Mother had told him to let the bird fly out. With the music of the piano being played in the main room, over the top of the haunting chords, Nathan could hear his Mother's words that day. "One of God's messengers, Nathan. He came to show us there is beauty in the world." Then, with his heart feeling heavy, he gazed at the view from his window, looking across to the mountain that his father had once climbed in his youth. Finally, the other feelings that propelled him to rise above his sadness at leaving home took over and he picked up his bags that had been packed the night before and walked out of his bedroom forever, to the new life that awaited him in Palestine.

Nathan walked into the room from where the sound of the piano music emanated. The enchantment of the slow drifting melody pulled him with all the effects of the pull of a magnet and, as he gently pushed the door open, he was astounded by the sight that befell him. Arthandur stood behind Marlene as she played the piano. His arms were on her shoulders and the two of them were both smiling, but these were smiles of pride in their son. Then Nathan stood aghast, for the rest of the room was filled with many of the Jewish community that lived in the village. Even the Rabbi was there in all of his splendour. It was awe-inspiring for Nathan because he knew he was the recipient of so much love and good will. No amount of happy faces could hide the sadness of the day, and his own emotions choked. His face ran with tears. That instant there was a flood of voices. "God be with you, Nathan." "Our thoughts are with you." "Say a prayer at the Wailing Wall for me." "We will miss you." A great flurry of voices confused and bewildered him. His mother and father hugged him. There seemed to be faces of all ages surrounding him, smiling and beaming and some evidence of moisture in their eyes. "Jerusalem is not far away, my boy." Who said that?

That morning after a breakfast with so many people, the most people he had ever sat down to a meal with, Arthandur said a few words and various people stood up wishing him well. The Rabbi said the prayers for the occasion, delivering his words in a curiously deep voice. The love of the day was so overpowering it had two effects on Nathan. One was to make him feel such sorrow in leaving these good people. The other effect was that he was being given such a warm departure that he wondered if he would ever know great love like this in his new land.

Soon the time was drawing close to the moment he had to leave the village. There were hugs and handshakes and more tears and more smiles, and more words of goodwill. Suddenly Arthandur said something.

"My boy, take one more look at the mountains," he said softly as they stood by the car. Marlene pointed to a precipice high up. The morning although cold was clear and the sky a crystalline blue and where Nathan's mother had pointed there was the unforgettable sight of a good friend of his childhood standing against the horizon. The other villagers also stood and stared.

Nathan smiled and waved to his friend who stood high above the village that had always been his home. The sunlight seemed to capture the imposing figure of old Wilf the goat herder who waved back. His goats flocked around him, diversifying in all directions along the ledges.

Nathan would never forget dear old Wilf or his friendship and the yodel. When the car was moving out of the village with Arthandur driving and his mother sitting beside him he suddenly had the overwhelming compunction to put his head out of the window and look back. It was at that moment as he gazed back that the sound of Wilf yodelling across the valley enhanced his final memories of life in an Austrian mountain village. Wilf raised his hat in a farewell gesture.

Fifteen

It was on the boat bound for the port of Jaffa that the news of the Anschluss of Austria came through. The captain relayed the message over the loudspeaker system to the dumbfounded passengers most of whom were German and Austrian refugees. The news understandably shattered them for they nearly all had families and friends left behind. With the suddenness of it all the atmosphere on board became a buzz of worried conversation. The absorption of Austria into German rule would mean the policies of the party in power would become part of the way of life there and further discrimination would continue.

The expectation and thrill of the journey so far turned to sadness for Nathan in the flash of an instant. After the initial sadness of saying farewell to his parents at the train station in Vienna, he had settled down to the train ride down through Italy to Naples where the boat sailed from. He had enjoyed talking to many of the other people who were also travelling to Palestine from Austria. In addition to Nathan there were several other youngsters of his own age who had also been given an agricultural scholarship.

The changing scenery throughout Italy had excited him and when the train had briefly stopped at Rome, he had felt quite breathless about it all. Naples, where his land journey terminated was exciting and noisy, scruffy and glamorous. With Mount Vesuvius rising up in the background over the Bay of Naples, it had an aura all of its own, so different to the cities of Berlin and Vienna that had played so prominent a role in Nathan's life. The main feature of this city was the life that it breathed. It wasn't the life of a grandeur portrayed against the backdrops of Berlinese or Viennese regency buildings and a long inherited culture. It was the life in the streets of Naples. The sounds of people clinking glasses in outdoor cafes, the never ending stream of traffic and car horns pressed down hard like one long rehearsed sustained chord in an orchestral piece. There was colour even in the tiny streets where washing hung across in rows and rows, and with the roar of the traffic, there were people bantering in the market places, and the smells of pasta and fresh baked bread intertwined with those of fruit and fish on the stalls.

It wasn't until the boat pulled away from the quay at Naples that the full realisation of what was really happening took its full effect on Nathan. He was not only leaving European soil behind, he was leaving a lifetime and beginning a new one. His parents, Arthandur and Marlene, were further away now than they had ever been. So too was Wilf, the old goat herder, with his embellished tales. So were all those warm-hearted people of his own religious upbringing who had bid him farewell so cheeringly and with such feelings of love.

The looks of the Jewish immigrants on board the boat as they stood at the rail watching the shoreline recede told the full story. Would they ever return? Would there be a time in their lifetimes when it would be possible to do so?

Once out on the Mediterranean sea the water looked a deep and luscious blue, and the sky in contrast was of a lighter shade but complemented it in its varied contrast. The smell of salt air was overpowering. The sound of the water being ploughed by the bow of the boat thrilled him and he moved into a different part of his life, and the sound of the seagulls in the sky came together like the finale note of a great concerto. It must have been Nathan's musical education by his mother that always compelled him to relate the sounds of the world to that of melody or symphony.

To add to the excitement there had been a short stay in Limassol in Cyprus and after this the last breathtaking lap of the voyage to Palestine. Nathan wondered if his mother and father would make exactly the same journey when they came a few months later. But one morning on the boat had put the fear in him that they may never make this trip away from persecution.

The Captain's voice sounded taut. His words were spaced and, with his deliverance of them, could not conceal the fears he held within him, for he too was of the chosen race. The news had been relayed to him on the ship's radio and he felt it was his duty to inform the passengers.

Nathan overheard some of the elderly passengers talking in sombre tones. One man said to another that there would now be 'widespread migration'. Just the mere mention of it suggested that there were reasons to worry. Nathan could recall Wilf telling him, "That man in Germany – that is why you go away." He suddenly felt a dreadful longing and a fear for his parents and friends back there in that village. He could only go to the rail and look back at the sea in the direction from which he had come. Never had he felt such concern before. It weighed on him enormously.

The worries he had newly acquired diminished slightly a while later when the ship came within its first sight of Palestine. The passengers leaned over the rail in anticipation of finally arriving in their new homeland. The Promised Land, at last. The Land of Ceasarea and the Garden of Gethsemane in all its splendour. This was the land where the refugees aboard could dwell in peace.

When the ship docked at the port, Nathan studied the first sign of the throngs of people milling around the wharf. There were instantly recognisable people of the Jewish race in beards, black tailcoats and homburg hats, which were worn as part of their religious discipline. There were men with donkeys and typical style dress worn by the residents, some carrying fruit in baskets, men in flowing robes and there were children jumping up and down, and men with camels. The most obvious thing was the feel of the place. Even the air seemed different. The scent in the air seemed mystic and alluring. The buildings at the port seemed unusual in style and far off in the distance were gleaming ice white structures. There were palm trees and cedar trees, and through some of the soil surface the colours of mixed orange and auburn over which ran cars and bicycles and overfull buses. It was exciting to be here at last in Palestine.

Not long after disembarking from the boat, the refugees were shuffled into a shaky bus and the long drive to the various kibbutzim began. The migrants would be dropped off according to the areas where they were to be settled.

On the long meandering drive Nathan could understand, by viewing the countryside, why agricultural scholarships were awarded to so many young people. Although the land was beautiful in its aridity, it looked in dire need in some areas of a huge cultivation programme. Some land was spartan. Vegetation seemed to be non-existent in places. There was a certain beauty, a certain attraction about it and Nathan felt truly captivated when he thought of the history of this land. He thought of the Torah and the Old Testament and wondered what Palestine would have been like in the times of long ago.

When Nathan had been aboard the vessel en route to Palestine, he had listened to the sound of the sea as the boat made its journey and at night he had lain awake in his cabin at times buoyant with the thrill of seeing this land. The passengers on board had linked arms in more jovial spirits and danced on deck occasionally thanking God that they were going to this land called Palestine.

And now they were here. The bus was travelling this land. Nathan was soaking up every sight and sound, which his memory would recall with a huge intricacy in many years to come.

His companions in the bus also seemed excited. The sadness of leaving families behind had been replaced with a spark of new interest igniting the features of their faces and giving them a more wide eyed keener look whilst eagerly observing their new found surroundings. The countryside flashed past in varying shades of green, auburn, orange, and the level of the road changed from flat and undulating to hilly and occasionally rolling sweeping plateaus. Even in the bus the strange scent that a person first experiences in a newfound land persisted in the air. Palm trees came into view, more hills, pastoral land, green agricultural fields. Crops. The sort that could not be determined at a long-distance glance seemed to rise up in an instant. There were men picking oranges from trees and donkeys with packs on their backs. Little villages were passed, sleepy and quiet in their appearance. There were glassy lakes, a deep azure blue; so clear the reflection was like that of the reflection of the finest mirror..

Soon the sight of the first of the kibbutzim came into view. Nathan had been told by the driver that the kibbutz he was going to would be the very final destination that the bus would arrive at and so he settled back at each stop waving to the various people as they left. Each kibbutz he saw looked approximately the same in size, shape and layout. They were more or less rows of huts and buildings set on different types of land, where it became obvious that the content of the crops and produce varied enormously from the last one he had stopped at. It was almost nightfall when the bus arrived at the Kibbutz Jezarat nestled far away in some distant hills.

The sky was too dark and seemingly impenetrable for normal vision. Only the faint outline of the kibbutz buildings could be identified.

Nathan, together with the few remaining on the bus, were greeted by the leaders of the small community, and then after a warm meal and a wash, they were shown to their quarters. Nathan fell into a deep sleep, the exhaustion of the day finally overtaking him. He felt his weight creak the surface of the bed and then sleep came.

When morning arrived the rays of the sun streamed through the beams of the hut, pouring light over his youthful face. The brilliant sunshine lit up the dour surroundings of his room and with a sudden curiosity he rose from his slumber and gazed out at the window. The sunlight was so powerful it soaked everything in sight with an incredible radiance, like a God-given light, bringing all the colours of the land to a greater enhancement. Still clad in his nightclothes, he pushed the door of his room and stepped outside. The sight that greeted him enthralled him.

In the first rays of sunlight of the morning, before him stretched orange hills on one side and on the other fields of crops to be tilled and cultivated. It was almost noiseless apart from the squawk of poultry in a nearby run.

So this was Palestine and a new life on the Kibbutz Jezarat. His eyes, so sensitive in their appraisal of everything, conceded the beauty of it all but beneath the gaze there were clouded emotions: he was alone, his mother and father were in Austria, and for a moment, the moisture glistened in his eyes. He wanted to weep and weep, and bawl like a newborn baby, but something stopped him inside and he controlled his emotions. He had to get on with his life. There was much to be discovered in the new environment he found himself in.

The first few months of Nathan's new life at the Kibbutz Jezarat were the start of a new education for him in many different fields; not only in his learning of agriculture or his Talmudic studies but in his communications and relationships with people. He found himself thrust amongst commune workers of all ages, different personalities and intellects. Surprisingly conversation came easy. Although he was one of the younger members of the community, he found that he was accepted and treated as an adult. He suddenly felt a confidence develop within him he had never previously realised. This was not only his spiritual awakening, but the introduction to his mental capacities of a new maturity.

He was beginning to develop his character, outspreading his physical and metal abilities to new horizons. His work in the fields was long and arduous, starting early in the day, but it was physically rewarding. He was exercising his muscles to limits he had not known he was capable of extending himself to.

He began this day tilling the soil, turning the ground over and looking at the daily progress of the varied crops. Under the guidance of the kibbutz leader a group of young trainees worked very hard in the fields.

Nathan found himself working not only with Jewish people from his own lands of origin, but with those from other countries such as Poland, Ukraine, Hungary and France. He also found himself in contact with those who were *Yeshiva* and deeply orthodox. Conversation was not limited to purely that of a religious context. It was wide and deep on a manner of subjects, which were diversified in their nature. It seemed that the kibbutz for many of its inhabitants was purely a ground base for them to jettison to a world outside, where they could make a greater contribution. Some talked of medicine, others of the legal profession, the business world and finance, and a very popular subject that always crept into the conversation, the arts. Nathan's inherited love of music was something he could always converse so knowledgably on, in a manner that would often surprise his peers. It was in these conversations, normally held over the spartan tables of the main recreation area of the kibbutz, that Nathan began to wonder at such an early stage of his life in Palestine if agriculture was his true vocation.

It had surprised Nathan that farming and agricultural professions attracted people of his own race. Even as a child before the political change of events in Europe, most of the people who had been friends of Arthandur and Marlene had all been in commercial professions, and as far as he could remember none of the skills of the tradesmen or the apprenticed in industry were featured. When Nathan had been entered into an agricultural scholarship it was an area of work he had never even dreamed of. It had more or less been chosen for him by his father and in the circumstances that existed in Europe he had never questioned the decision that had been made on his behalf. But now, after a few months in Palestine, he was beginning to consider just where the course of his life would take him.

Arthandur and Marlene were never far from his mind. At night in his room in the kibbutz he would often lay awake, staring at the ceiling and thinking of his mother and father. There were moments in the dead of night when the haunting piano music that he heard on the morning of his departure from Austria would circulate in his mind. He would think of his mother's voice and the tones of his father's voice, so splendid in their enunciation and phrasing of words.

A few letters had arrived from Arthandur and Marlene. Then there had been none forthcoming. Rumours were circulating around the kibbutz. Nathan had heard them one day when he had been working amongst the crops in the middle of a very hot day, he heard two workers discussing what had become of many of the relatives of various families ensconced in the kibbutz. There had been talk of the camps. 'The camps', it had a harrowing ring to it. In years to come when the full brutality and horror of the camps would be fully revealed in all of its terrifying detail, it would be a subject to be slotted into the back of the mind, rarely mentioned but never forgotten. On that hot day Nathan wiped his brow and moved nearer the two workers talking of the internment of thousands of Jewish people in Germany and Austria.

"Is it true?" Nathan asked, his voice tinged with horror. The two men looked at him sympathetically. One of them had deep brown eyes that assessed Nathan's age, judging that he had relatives in Europe.

"Your mother and father?" the man asked Nathan, concerned.

"Yes," he replied, lowering his head sadly.

"I am sorry," said the man. "Your parents? They are in—"

"They are in Austria." This time Nathan's voice was cold and his eyes were frozen like ice. "I hadn't heard from them for some time."

The two men looked at him, not knowing how to console him. They were obviously at a loss as to know what to say but then Nathan dropped his agricultural tools and turned around and walked away. He could feel the heat of the sun stinging his face and drying the tears that trickled down his face as fast as they flowed. He was feeling a deep and terrible pain inside, a feeling that would never evaporate over the years. The deep emotional pain hurt and hurt and hurt.

He just wanted to be alone in his grief. In the turmoil and confusion of his thoughts he found himself wishing that he had resisted his father's good intensions and stayed in that far away village.

For a long time afterwards Nathan became solemn and withdrawn. He was often alone in his thoughts. Beyond the tones that passed for polite civility, he seldom engaged in conversation with anyone. Many of the people in the kibbutz had relatives too in Europe but they had taken the news in their stride and sought to carry on with their lives in a more positive manner. It was obvious to anyone though that they too were heavy laden with worries over their relatives.

Nathan seemed to drift for a while. When attending Talmudic studies he would stare into space. His eyes focussed somewhere in a place of memory. Sometimes things didn't register with him. He would be carrying out hard, demanding physical work in the agricultural area of the kibbutz and people would speak to him three or four times before he realised that their voices had been directed towards him. It was as if he had given up on life.

His melancholy mood had not gone unnoticed by the kibbutz leader, Shirom Banai, who indicated to a few of the younger people to try and pull the young man out of his shell of isolation. Slowly and surely Nathan began to respond to their friendship. The olive branch of warmth attracted him. Soon he was his good self again, talking deeply on numerous subjects, playing a part in the running of the kibbutz.

Shirom was a kindly man, rather thoughtful-looking, quietly spoken, but with a voice like honey that encouraged Nathan to participate more in all the activities of the community. There was no doubt that Shirom wanted all the members of his kibbutz to be happy. One man unhappy could cause great dissension at Jezarat. No one was ignored. If they had a problem they were encouraged to talk about it.

The art of conversation at meetings of the committee running the Kibbutz Jezarat was practiced to its finest degree. The actual running and organisation was not a difficult task. It was from these conversations that deeper discussions originated. Knowing that his father had been such a fearless advocate of Zionism, Nathan would listen intently. Time and time again the future of Palestine came to the fore. Often there would be mention of the Balfour agreement. There was fear that this declaration may never be fully implemented to the letter. This was a hotbed of discussion.

The education, versed in all things traditionally Jewish, continued. This took the form not only in the readings of the Talmud but in the singing of deep patriotic tunes in which the kibbutz populace would sing with great gusto and passion. Stage plays would be presented with a strong emphasis on the Jewish character, seeking to give a clear outline of the strengths and weaknesses of the individual.

In all these plays Nathan noticed a familiar cast member. Always there would be the same girl who attracted his attention. She would have been approximately the same age as Nathan, yet her character was boisterous and charismatic. Her face was full of great expression. When she strode on to the stage, she filled it with an aura all of her own. Nathan had not spoken to her previously yet he was determined he would do so, for she was beautiful. Her eyes shone, she seemed possessed of a great confidence and appeared to be lacking in inhibition. She dominated her performances by the deliverance of her lines in such a manner that one could not doubt she had talent and poise that destined her for some celestial height in her lifetime.

All the time it seemed Nathan was learning about life, about people. He was learning about being self-reliant. By far he was learning how to find an inner satisfaction in life from the art of debate, pleasant conversation, books and study, wisdom and good will. He observed his fellow kibbutz companions and developed a rapport with them he had never known possible.

So this then was his new found life? A combination of gruelling hard work that rippled every muscle in his body, and a new mental awareness in his life. Although he was slow to recognise it, he had in fact inherited many of the traits of his father. The distinct difference in his life now was that his own qualities were being developed totally devoid of parental influence. There were some alarming signs that he came to realise. It had occurred to him that in many ways by living in the kibbutz his thinking was becoming almost regimented. It struck him that he was living in the confines of a Jewish world. Beyond the realms of the Kibbutz Jezarat, the rest of the world might not have existed. Everything in his life seemed to be steeped in the traditions of Judaism: his dietary habits, prayer and teachings, plays and discussions, all these centred on the basis of his own religion. Yet he conceded how advantageous in other ways this had shown itself to be. He considered that in Germany and Austria being proud of his own faith, which indeed he was, could have been detrimental. Here in Palestine, they could deeply bathe in the full splendour of their religion. He knew he was lucky to be the recipient of an agricultural scholarship.

Nathan could not have cared overly for the sewing of cotton, the reaping of a harvest of vegetables, and the texture of soil that, when blended with varying weather conditions, could yield diversified crops.

He respected the man on the land. He realised the hard work it entailed and how heartbreaking it could also be, but at the same time he knew this was not his life's work. He found work purely the necessity to bide the time of day until be could mix with the other people in the evening. There amongst all the other nationalities he could know the friendship of people of all ages, from rich and poor backgrounds, and be on equal terms with all. If truth be known, the kibbutz in its curious way was a classless, perhaps even socialist, society where the common bind was a respect for their fellow companions. For the first time in his short life Nathan was living in a community where there were no divisions, no barriers. No one was downtrodden or scorned. The atmosphere was, for the best part, one of harmony. Even in discussions, the most heated of debates never tilted towards the point of being stormy. Everyone's opinion was of value.

Shirom Banai thrived on the success of the Kibbutz Jezarat. At first glance Shirom did not seem the man of authority and decision, as one would have expected to keep all sections of the community working harmoniously together. First impressions did not give an accurate portrayal of this man. He seemed aloof, conservative and detached from a brief study. In fact he was a deep thinking man, a lonely administrator. Yet he was very much the father figure of the kibbutz, a man who was ultimately respected and as with shy people, often misread as aloof. He was genuinely caring of his compatriots and sought to see that the self-sufficiency of the community was constantly maintained. He involved himself without imposing too much.

He did not mind getting his hands dirty turning the soil. Nor did he mind meandering around in the poultry and livestock. He spoke to everyone, never forgetting anyone's name. He would let the various steering committees operate independently without interference. When the delegate of these groups would present their recommendations to him, Shirom would listen politely. If he was in disagreement with any points, he would strive gently with them to arbitrate a mutual consensus.

One day Nathan was enjoying himself immensely driving a tractor over a previously untilled plot of land when he saw Shirom in the far off distance coming towards him. Shirom's shock of grey hair caught the gentle breeze in the air. He waved affably to Nathan who responded in the same manner. Nathan stopped the tractor and climbed down to meet him.

"Good morning, Shirom," he said politely. Shirom smiled warmly and leaned against the tractor. He studied it admiringly.

"Ah! A fine machine is it not, Nathan?"

"Yes, it does the job well."

"That is good," said Shirom warmly. Then he looked at Nathan inquiringly. "You are happy here, Nathan?"

He hesitated slightly before answering not quite knowing what to say. "I am," he said finally.

"But you miss your mother and father?"

Nathan's eyes seemed to change expression instantaneously. "I have tried not to worry, but the talk of the camps is so distressing. I do worry so much, Mr Banai."

"Shirom," he corrected Nathan. "Always by my first name." Then he became serious. "I know how you feel, my boy. There are others here also with family who are interned. You must try not to distress yourself. Oh! I know it is easier said than done, but I pray that the international pressure brought to bear on that Nazi party may soon secure their release. We must have faith. Always have faith, Nathan."

Nathan averted his eyes momentarily to the ground then looked back at Shirom squarely. He managed a half smile.

"I will try," he said, even his voice sounded an effort to produce.

"Good. You must," Shirom said quietly. "I have come to ask you if you would like to make a trip to Jerusalem with some committee members."

"I would be delighted," Nathan said, surprised. He felt flattered to be asked and he could not help but glow with pride at the privilege of being considered for such an important assignment. He knew straight away that this was as part of a delegation for an important conference that had been much talked about at Jezarat. He beamed happily.

"This is a particularly important conference. No doubt you have heard many here talking about it." Nathan nodded in reply. "I have heard from our friends and teachers here that you have a very inquiring mind and a good head for discussion," Nathan smiled. At such a young age he had never been complimented to quite this extent before. It was almost as if Shirom could read the young man's mind and he made a remark straightaway to keep him on the ground. "Please Nathan. I am complimenting you. You show promise but don't get a swollen head my boy. In later years the kibbutz will need good men to run it. Men who have an understanding of people, and the initiative to build on the dreams that we of the chosen race have for this land."

Nathan continued to listen. Although Shirom, and Nathan's own father Arthandur, were light years away in appearance and terms of character, he could sense a great similarity between the two men. It wasn't just in their quintessential Jewishness, so vivid and striking, but in their manner of phrasing words together. The substance was almost the same, yet the voice and character were different. But in a contrasting manner they were both father figures: one a natural father, the other fatherly in an authoritarian role.

"What do you wish me to do, Shirom? I feel honoured that you've asked me."

"At this conference there will be leading Rabbi's, politicians from here and abroad, diplomatic observers, and members of the steering committees of a number of major kibbutznim. They will be discussing the future of Palestine." He hesitated for a moment. "And, of course, the situation in the world today." Shirom looked stern. Nathan knew straightaway that Shirom was speaking of Europe specifically.

"I just want you to go along with several other young people as an observer. Not as a participant. Just to listen and look at this stage. When you return I would like to hear your impressions. You have a keen mind. A good ear, and this is your land now. You have a part to play."

"I understand, Shirom," Nathan said humbly.

"You leave tomorrow. Be ready to join the others first thing tomorrow morning." Shirom was just about to walk away when it seemed as if he had a further point to add. "Oh – and one more thing Nathan."

"Yes," the young man looked up with interest,

"I believe you are a great reader of literature."

"I do read many books. I have done since I was young. My mother was – is – a school teacher."

Shirom caught the rapid but unsure change of tense in Nathans words, and as if to allay any doubts he moved the conversation on to a surer footing. "Who are your favourite authors?"

"Steinbeck, Pasternak, Kipling."

"Kipling?" Shirom was interested. Why would a conservative and colonial author like Kipling appeal to a kibbutz worker? "I am interested. You surprise me constantly young man."

Nathan smiled rather shyly. "Oh, I like his stories of India, of a long time ago, and there is a poem he wrote that always stays in my mind. It was almost a code to live by."

"Really!" Shirom looked bemused. "What is this poem?"

"It's called 'If'. There's a line in it you would enjoy."

"I know the poem, Nathan. Don't think I am versed only in the world of Jewish affairs. My mind has stretched to English literature and the works of Rudyard Kipling. I too know the poem. It begins; 'If you can keep your head when all about you'."

"That is right. You will know the line then. 'If you can meet with Triumph and Disaster and—'"

"'And treat those two imposters just the same'. Yes, it is a great poem, Nathan. One man's own personal philosophy, mind. You won't find it in the Talmud!! But I must admit to an admiration for the content of it." They both smiled at their mutual feeling for the poem. "You will be accompanied by a couple of others of your own age to the conference, by the way. Melissa and Leon will be going with you to Jerusalem."

"Melissa and Leon." Nathan repeated the names. The names did not register with him. But he had a slight inkling who Melissa may be. At this stage of his life at Jezarat, he did not know everyone by name.

"They both show promise too. Definitely I see leadership potential in Melissa. Her work in the kibbutz plays has been outstanding. Like you she is not afraid of hard work. She is in charge of poultry and livestock. Melissa has come up with some good suggestions that the committee plan to initiate shortly."

Nathan now knew who Melissa was. He felt excited. He realised that Shirom, having mentioned the kibbutz plays, could only have been referring to the girl he had seen in a number of them. Her performances for a sixteen year old were absolutely electric. Melissa! So that was her name. Nathan felt a glow within him as he eagerly anticipated meeting her. It was fortunate that such circumstances would fling him together with such an attractive and charismatic young person. He did not realise it at the time but Nathan was feeling the first pangs of youthful love. He was experiencing the magnetism of attraction to the opposite sex for the first time in his life, and during the remainder of the day, he had felt a zest for his work and an eagerness for the next day to come.

He was not wrong in his assumption of who Melissa was. The next day in his keenness and enthusiasm, he was one of the first to board the ramshackle old bus to go to Jerusalem. Some of the elder members of the kibbutz boarded soon after. He sat at the back of the bus waiting for a glimpse of Melissa. He was not to be disappointed. Melissa and Leon were the last to board. Nathan stared at her. His eyes must have caught her attention for as she boarded the bus and took the front seat with Leon, she beamed a warm uninhibited smile at him. Nathan felt entranced by her attention. It made him feel ten feet tall and he felt a surge of confidence within.

There was something that caused a slight flurry of panic in him. Melissa and Leon had taken the front two seats of the bus. Was it purely in Nathan's imagination or was there something stronger about the relationship between the couple at the front. Nathan could not figure it out. During the course of the bus journey he seemed to spend much time watching Melissa and Leon talk.

Leon must have been eighteen or nineteen. He seemed to match Melissa for every details of description. Leon was in essence her true counterpart. He was brash, vain, confident and oozing with that magical aura that sets some people apart from others, purely by nature if not the content of their character. There was something about him that Nathan did not like. Even at a distance Leon seemed to have an aggressive edge to him, so different to the many gentle people that Nathan had known. Nathan really wondered just what Melissa found so attractive in Leon. It was only then he realised that he was feeling a twinge of jealousy. All the same he could not take his eyes off Melissa. He was perhaps dangerously infatuated, or maybe feeling even more stronger emotions.

It was only when they arrived at Jerusalem and were shown into a huge building that the formal introductions were made. Nathan found himself sitting next to Melissa and Leon. Far from being the person he had envisaged Nathan found Leon quite amiable. Leon leaned across Melissa and shook his hand. The two young men smiled at each other politely.

Strangely it was Melissa who was slow to respond. Nathan found her quite reserved. He thought that this would be because she was not her on-stage personality. Nathan thought that in a play Melissa's bubbling persona was purely the skill of a consummate actress and that in reality she was in fact a much more demure person than he previously realised.

In this assumption he was correct. Melissa, at such a young age, already possessed a devastating talent and threw herself into every performance with an unbounded energy and enthusiasm that perhaps would one day win her acclaim. However, Nathan was not to know that Melissa was trying to sum Nathan up in much the same manner as he was.

Although Melissa held Leon's hand, the evidence of the first flush of a youthful love, she was intrigued by the gentility and softness of Nathan's manner. On each side of her, she had young men of opposite characteristics. Leon, a Polish Jew, whom she could liken to a being of fire, someone whose character blazed and crackled like the flames of a runaway fire completely out of control. In Nathan she saw only the still waters of his personality. He would be a person who only in time would reveal his real strengths and weaknesses. For the moment she smiled meekly and in a limp handshake bade politeness to Nathan. Her eyes flashed ahead of her to the stage where the speakers were preparing themselves for the conference. Yet occasionally Melissa would glance quickly sideways at Nathan. She was curious about Nathan. Of that there was no doubt.

During the course of the conference as speaker after speaker orated on the future of Palestine and the world situation, Nathan felt a feeling of some exuberance within him. Just the touch of Melissa's hand had triggered his emotions. Melissa was the type who, as she grew older, would excite men by her sensuality.

The topics that the speaker brought up in the conversation revolved around the history of Palestine as relative to the future of the country. It was a detailed discussion of the reasons behind the need for the Jewish people to have a land of their own. Much of the information was new to Nathan and he listened with great interest to the men who put forward their views. He was impressed by the sincerity and conviction with which they stated their case.

To justify their beliefs, the speakers referred to the immigration of various groups since the early centuries of mankind. It was fascinating for Nathan to learn that a mixture of people originally occupied Palestine after the Arab conquest in the seventh century. These comprised of Muslims, Christians, Jews, Druses, Egyptians, Turks, Kurds and Caucasians. Many of these groups had been nomadic who moved in and out of the land as they felt the mood.

It was an invigorating experience to be there at the conference listening to emotionally charged speakers coming forward with different views and facts that were now history. There were kibbutz leaders speaking with great gusto on the huge contribution these communities could make in turning arid land into good quality farming produce. Each leader of the kibbutz spoke in the belief that the young people of these communities would develop character and qualities of leadership that could one day be applied on a greater scale. After all, the young farm labourers of the day, who toiled so vigorously in the fields by day and adhered rigidly to the principles of the Torah, would one day be in a position of authority, and their knowledge and their teachings would cover a far greater audience.

Some of the elder speakers mentioned their backgrounds. In any migrant country there is the second generation growing up with a background of the two cultures; their own and that of their parents. One talked of his family leaving Russia in 1882 and travelling to Palestine, where they had enrolled at an agricultural school near Jaffa known as the Mikveh. This was relevant to the context of the conference, for after expressing their views on the benefits of a mixed migration in Palestine, the subject of present day events in Europe was discussed in great depth. There would be much more migration now; the floodgates would surely be opened widely to welcome all refugees.

By the time the conference had drawn to a close Nathan felt keyed up. The acquisition of knowledge he had gained was beneficial in moulding his character. He was interested in the thoughts of the cross section of speakers. One point became clear to him: every man has a story to tell and every man has a point of view. Without realising it, the key to Nathan's real future had been subconsciously introduced to him at the conference. Nathan pondered in his mind how, if he had been on the stage, he would have expressed his views in defence of a homeland for people of his race. Then as his mind drifted, he thought of the work of a lawyer in comparison to a speaker at a conference. Public speaking suddenly had a lure to him. He considered how persuasive he could be in a debate, or in fighting for a cause, if he armed himself with the facts and a detailed knowledge of the subject matter.

Melissa and Leon had enjoyed the experience too. Particularly Leon. Leon's character was showing its real colours now. When the three of them had left the conference centre to return to the bus, Leon was aggressive in putting his point across. It was obvious to Nathan that Leon was undoubtedly a hardliner in his view. Nathan felt great patriotism, but preferred a milder, steady-as-she-goes approach in the creation of a new nation. Leon was all for doing things quickly and with force if necessary.

If Nathan had learned something special today, it was that there is a great power in the use of words. He had particularly admired the passion with which people at the conference had put forward their beliefs. In all of the debates, Nathan had noted that the speakers had not used empty rhetoric but had stayed on facts and figures and used historical examples to emphasise their desires for the future of Palestine. In any argument, debate or verbal conflict, a spontaneous battle would not yield a winning side. It was obvious that technical research would be necessary. Nathan felt that with some knowledge and a good grasp of his subject matter, he could be a competent public speaker. How to apply these techniques to a career was another matter, but as he sat on the bus returning to the Kibbutz Jezarat, he entertained the thought that he could become a lawyer.

Nathan looked at Melissa and Leon at the front of the bus. They were obviously immersed in each others company. It would be hard to win favour with Melissa. He virtually conceded in his own mind that his fascination for her was purely that. It would probably not eventuate to anything stronger.

Tomorrow it would be back to the work of the plough and the tractor. Yet now he had a goal to work to. He would serve his time usefully on the kibbutz, learning the profession he had been awarded a scholarship for. His private hours now would be spent in voracious reading and intense private study that would contribute to his dream of becoming a lawyer.

Nathan knew that his mother and father would not disapprove of him taking this direction in life. Then suddenly he felt a great wave of sadness engulf him. He knew that his parents were being detained in a camp in Europe. He prayed that one day he would be reunited with them. He had not given up hope that they would be released.

Sixteen

Shirom Banai was interested in the observations of Nathan, Melissa and Leon. He listened intently as they discussed the major points of the conference, and there was no doubt that he was impressed by the keenness of their youthful minds. To Shirom he felt that his people were on the verge of a new chapter in history but the contents of the pages were yet to be fully defined. There was doubt in the world. The growing European crisis was the predominant factor. Even in Palestine there was unrest beginning to ferment. There was talk of the gates of Palestine being slammed to Jewish émigré's fleeing the Third Reich.

All three agreed that this had been the most disturbing aspect of the conference. Surely with the mistreatment of the Jewish people in Europe, some representations must be made to the government of Great Britain. Although Shirom was angry at the possibility of this, he was quick to point out that this was only a rumour at this stage. Just speculation. But Shirom would approach the Jewish agency, the governing body of his people, to press for some details on this matter. He knew that rumours of this nature did not circulate without foundation nor would it be mentioned at such an important conference as a matter of chance subject. Shirom loved this land. Surely the people of his race who wished to share it could not be denied the opportunity to come here and make new lives.

He thanked Nathan, Melissa and Leon for their comments and they left for their separate quarters. Each of them had their separate interests. Apart from the one uniting bond of their religion, they had their own ambitions that only they knew. The three of them were essentially private people, although in the characters of Leon and Melissa there were strong giveaway signs that revealed their real aims.

For Nathan seeing the speakers on stage at the conference had provoked in him a real admiration for the way in which an argument or debate could be presented. Since his return to the kibbutz he had sought out every available textbook he could find relating to the subject of law. He had found some British books that covered his needs. They had been in Shirom Banai's own personal library and Nathan had read them all with a hungering for knowledge. He found the books covered the diversity of law, including the Constitution of Great Britain, the rules on which the Houses of Parliament and the Commons abided with. Then there were the subjects of criminal law, bankruptcy, petitions for divorce, enticement cases, children's custody cases; the law as applied to the corporate and business world. He read on with a real desire to improve his knowledge. If he felt inclined he could specialise in Industrial Relations representing either trade unions or the management to state the case of the particular party. It was a wide and illustrious area but Nathan decided he would chart a course of private study to enter the profession of the lawyer.

Melissa's own ambitions were obvious although she did not make a point of telling anyone. To any onlooker, Melissa's work in tending chickens and poultry was only the daytime hurdle to the evening when she would enthusiastically participate in the kibbutz's own private theatre. This young girl seemed to go through a metamorphosis when she stepped in front of an audience. The girl, that Nathan had discovered to be really quite reserved, was flamboyant and expressive on stage. She also had a rich singing voice of excellent clarity and an ability to sustain notes for an admirable length of time. So far all her thespian performances had been in traditional plays of a Jewish nature. Beneath the surface, Melissa had one burning ambition: to act in a Shakespearean play. When she had been a child in Berlin she had been taken with her parents to see an English touring theatre stage Hamlet. The production had completely mesmerised her and she dreamed of one day performing on stage in London, in the West End. She did not foresee a future in Palestine. In her room she read many of the plays that had been performed at the Old Vic in London in recent years. What a dream it would be to appear in Shakespeare's plays: Hamlet, Othello, Twelfth Night, Macbeth, and there were many other plays that captured her imagination.

Leon was proud of two things, his nationality and his religion. To be Polish and Jewish was to be strong and privileged. The reasons for his sharp temperament and aggressive nature soon became clear. He did not like to be downtrodden. The people of Poland had suffered terribly over the years. It had been their kindred spirit, their inbuilt tenacity that he had inherited. With good reason he wanted to lead and to overcome opposition. His own family had known hard times in his native country, not just in recent years, but right throughout his ancestry. Leon had often heard tales of how his grandparents had suffered under the oppressors that came in from foreign lands.

The ambitions of Leon were in dogged contrast to those of Nathan and Melissa. Whereas their futures lay in the areas of self-development and personal achievement, Leon's dream was to be a spokesman and an envoy for his nation and the Jewish people. One day he would be a member of the Palestinian parliament, stating the case for his people, defending their rights to be a nation of their own, and developing the people's own destiny. In short, his ambitions were not for himself, but as he saw it, for the people of his own faith and their homeland.

So determined had Leon become to achieve these aspirations, that he had not ruled out force as a combatant to overcome all opposition to the creation of the Jewish nation. Leon had become involved with the secret army the Haganah, which had been conceived to protect the Jewish people of Palestine. He had regularly made secretive trips to attend armament practice. The Haganah had amongst its ranks members as young as fourteen and many of its commanders were then in distinguished positions. The formation of this underground force had not been initially designed as an organisation of attack. It was one primarily of defence against outside forces. The existence of it was almost contrary to the very nature of the Jewish people. To carry arms and engage in skirmish was not in line with the gentle outside forces. The existence of it was almost contrary to the very nature of the Jewish people. To carry arms and engage in warfare was not in line with the characteristics of most of the people living in the land who only wanted a peaceful life.

Leon had become an enthusiastic advocate of the Haganah. He recognised that lightning attacks could occur without notice and fully believed in its purpose as a defensive force. The British government had effectively given the organisation its blessing and had even provided training to its members. In later years the whole character of the private army would change. It would become an organisation of attack and, regretfully, would find itself in conflict with the British army in the struggles that were to follow nearly ten years later.

At that particular period in 1938, it was still operating as a secretive and defensive force. It needed more volunteers to boost its membership. Leon had looked towards the possibility of recruiting Nathan and Melissa, but for the time being he kept his own participation in the Haganah private.

The Kibbutz Jezarat was in a sense not big enough for each of them. They would have to move further afield in the not too distant future. The circumstances of a changing world would ensure that their lives would take the varied courses for which they were befitted. Although each had begun to shape their own destiny by their own hands gradually, slowing and cautiously.

Nathan had occasionally ventured from the kibbutz when the opportunity had arisen. He had begun to explore the rest of Palestine with a great deal of interest. There had been trips to other kibbutzim to study how the various communes functioned and what could be learned from the progress of each. On each of these reconnaissance journeys a great deal of distance would be covered and, from Nathan's childhood studies, much of the Torah and the Old Testament came to life before him in the countryside that he visited.

The desert areas of Palestine stirred him. Unlike the cultivated land surrounding the Kibbutz Jezarat, the desert, quiet and still, echoed with the history it evoked. On this very area of spartan ground, Mary and Jesus had walked, as well as John the Baptist, Abraham, Joseph and Moses. To Nathan who was a keen compiler adherent of the Talmud, he had also extended his thirst for knowledge to the Old and New Testaments and with every place that he visited, be it Ararat or Ashdod, he would be able to relate a biblical story to its existence.

At Gaza, close to the border of Palestine, he observed the infrequent palm groves and the camels that grouped together and he would study the Arabs who lived in plain huts and simple dwellings. Then he would realise that this was, in biblical times, the land of the Philistines.

Nathan once visited Jericho. He was awed to be there. He thought of Joshua's campaigns and the crashing walls – the walls of Jericho. His deep readings and studious studies in Austria under the guidance of his mother had not been in vain. Now he had so much more awareness of his surroundings. In his own mind he had created visual images of biblical happenings and implanted them on the scenery that lay before him, or at the ruins of a certain place that had once yielded a tumultuous moment in history. He was determined that he would not miss anything and he savoured every sign, every sound, storing it away in his mind, never to be forgotten.

It was not enough for Nathan just to be disciplined to live within the rules and conditions of his own faith. That he was proud of it and his background could not be denied, but he wanted to know more about other faiths. He wanted to understand them and in a curious manner he wished that all the faiths of the world could be as one, so that there not be divisions and factions. Why could there not be peaceful coexistence?

The field of learning for Nathan was wide. At the kibbutz there had been very comprehensive study of the Talmud, the combined body of Jewish law and legend that comprised the Mishna and the Gemara. He was highly knowledgeable of the Pentateuch, the first five books traditionally ascribed to Moses, and its objective of Hebrew instruction. He understood the latter part of the Talmud with its commentary on *Mishna* known as the *Gemara*.

Like the other members of the kibbutz he had been brought up to abide by the rules of the Torah, the revealed will of God and Mosaic Laws. But now, living in a country of a mixed population comprised of Arab and Jewish peoples, he began to wonder and question himself. Why could all people not live harmoniously, whatever their faiths, whatever their religious disciplines?

When Nathan saw the Arabs from time to time, he would think of the book on which their own way of life was established, the Koran. One day he would read it so as he could understand the other people of Palestine. He knew that the Koran was the sacred book on which the religion of Islam is based. He also knew that the Arabs spoke in different dialects, were fierce warriors and great trackers and nomads. Beyond that there was not a great deal he knew about them. He would have to make the effort to learn about them.

Back at the kibbutz, Nathan had embarked on a correspondence course designed to bring him up to the standard required for entry to a university where he would be able to qualify as a lawyer. This was quite intensive and had left him little time to participate in other activities, but one night, after hours of gruelling study, he decided to put down pen and paper in his quarters and breathe some of the night air.

Nathan strode out from his room and gazed at the deep night sky. It was a brilliantly clear night. The stars twinkled effervescently in the colours of night. The air was fresh and filled with that wondrous scent that seemed to evoke Palestine in much the same manner that the mountain vapour had done so in the Austrian village where Nathan had spent much of his life.

Nostalgia was aroused in him with a sharp suddenness. The thoughts of walking along the mountain paths and looking across at the snow-capped mountain filled his mind. If only he could see his mother and father again. More to the point, if only he knew where they were. He lowered his head in great sadness. Nathan felt so downhearted and despondent that it was as if a weight had descended on him deadening his spirits and enthusiasm. A gentle voice shook him suddenly forcing himself to get a grip on his senses.

"You are looking troubled, Nathan."

He turned to find himself facing Melissa. She was wearing a plain coloured dress and carrying a book under her arm. Nathan glanced down quickly, identifying the title, *The complete works of William Shakespeare*.

"I – I was just thinking," he stammered, "What are you doing out here?"

"It was a nice night. I thought I would read out here for a while." She looked at him. There were still the signs of hurt evident in Nathan's eyes. Melissa felt compelled to pursue her original question. "I did not mean to be inquisitive at all, Nathan. You looked sad as if something has hurt you greatly. I would understand if you told me to go away. But you don't talk about yourself very much. Can I help you?"

Nathan felt deeply touched. Melissa was a genuinely caring person. There was warmth and concern in her voice. He felt comfortable with Melissa, and gave her a mild smile of acknowledgement. She was definitely someone Nathan felt he wanted to know a great deal better.

"My parents, Melissa, that was what I was thinking of, and my home in Austria. I miss all of it. My parents are being detained and I am so worried for them. I fear for them so much. It is the fact of not knowing where they are and what has become of them."

Melissa listened to him sympathetically. Nathan realised he may have ignored the fact that Melissa's own parents were in the same predicament. He strived to change the subject. "Come, let us sit down. I'd like to hear about your life." They both sat down on a mound of earth and stared ahead of them into the night. "I was being self-centred. Your parents – they are also in the camps?"

It was Melissa who now looked hurt. She looked into his eyes, pausing before simply replying, "Yes" to Nathan's question. She chose to expand on the subject freely. "Yes. My mother and stepfather were taken away and I too do not know of their whereabouts. I cannot understand why. They were just ordinary people; they weren't offensive in any way, they were just ordinary people. My stepfather was a theatrical agent and my mother a secretary. I ask you, Nathan, how could they be detrimental to the German government?

Nathan's eyes showed deep understanding. "I know how you feel. My father and mother saw the things that were coming and left Berlin for Austria. They thought it would be safer there." He rubbed his chin, pondered, and after a short pause he said in a low hushed voice, "But how wrong they were."

There was now a mutual understanding between the two of them that had not existed before. Melissa saw in Nathan, that there was more to that man than just the still distant figure she had imagined him to be. Nathan was finding out about Melissa too. Not only was she attractive and gifted, but also she was warm and caring. Nathan continued in conversation with her.

"My parents intended to come to Palestine soon after me. I cannot understand why they did not leave with me. They could have gone to Switzerland or England." An alarming thought raced through his mind torturing him badly. "We could all have gone together! I just do not understand. Does anyone, I wonder? Perhaps we were lucky, Melissa."

"Perhaps," she said softly. "My stepfather said to me one day, 'Melissa Heiletz, my girl, there are problems here that will destroy us. You must go to Palestine.'" She smiled at the memory. "He was a cantankerous old man but delightful at times. I miss him as I do my mother. My parents – they did not even imagine –" Now her voice was changing "– could they have ever imagined that such action would happen? It makes me so angry that our people are singled out for such punishment."

"We must not dwell on these things Melissa. It is painful enough as it is." Melissa recognising the sincerity of his words, unselfconsciously gripped Nathan's hand sending a bolt through him. The feel of her hand was electric. Just as quickly she removed it not realising how the tenderness of her touch had excited Nathan.

"Could I tell you something?" She said quietly. Nervously she glanced round to see if there wee any eavesdroppers. Satisfied that there weren't any she continued. "I am thinking of leaving the kibbutz."

The revelation stunned Nathan. He was just beginning to get to know Melissa and now she was considering moving from Jezarat.

"Why?" Nathan asked, although already he thought that perhaps he knew the answer.

"I am not yet eighteen, Nathan. I have not been here in the kibbutz that long either. Yet I am not sure that my life is here." She waved one hand to indicate the length and breadth of the land before her. "You have probably noticed how my enthusiasm changes as soon as I've finished my day amongst the chickens and the fowl. I was thinking of becoming a professional actress; maybe joining a theatre in Haifa."

"You are very good, Melissa." Nathan reassured her. "I have watched you on stage here in the plays. I think you have a beautiful singing voice too."

Melissa's eyes were shining at the compliment. She turned to face him and smiled sweetly. It was encouraging to be the recipient of such a smile. Then while Nathan still seemed to be the possessor of the winning hand he added a further remark.

"But isn't it a bit early to be thinking of leaving? I too have my dreams. Surely it would be sensible to stay on here for a while until you are really sure. I have started to study. I sent away for a correspondence course from the college in Jerusalem. And when it is finished I hope to qualify for the University. I would like to become a lawyer."

Melissa looked surprised. "A lawyer? You seem so… so reserved for a lawyer, but then Leon Zielinski has said you are a good debater and have a great way with words. Leon said that you have presented good points at the committee meetings."

Now Nathan was enjoying being complimented. He was surprised that Leon had been generous towards him with praise. He now felt in good spirits. It was strange how the company of a woman and her compliments could uplift a man from the doldrums.

"I like the power of words, the use of expressions and the way in which a phrase can be used for emphasis. You know I really admired the speakers at the conference that you, Leon and I went to. I could feel the power behind their arguments. The way they put forward their case for our homeland and its future. Do you know what else, Melissa?"

"Go on." She was now listening with great interest.

"I admired the sincerity in their voices. They believed in what they were saying. They used facts and figures for justification. Imagine being in a courtroom. Imagine representing a client, someone you believed in, someone whose best interests had to be defended. The challenge would be enormous. The power of words would be so important."

"By the determination in your voice, I would be surprised if you did not achieve your dream. For me becoming an actress in the theatre would be a real challenge. I have been reading much of Shakespeare's works lately." She indicated to Nathan the book she had been studying. "I find acting a role takes research. Acting is taking on another person's personality. To use your phrase, acting is the power of words."

"And you seem to be very successful, Melissa. Here, talking to you now, you are so different to when you perform with the kibbutz theatre. You are a different person, much quieter. On stage you are so alive."

"I thought much the same about you, Nathan." Melissa surprised him. "At the meetings of the kibbutz organisation you are more alive too, in debate especially. I can see why Shirom chose you to go to the conference. The only difference between you and Leon is that Leon is always forward, he is always opinionated. He is always pushing his ideas. I suppose." She smiled, "you have noticed his manner."

"Oh yes." Nathan nodded, acknowledging the fact that he had always been well aware of. "I think Leon knows where he is going and he is determined to get there no matter who he treads on. He is like the mountain goat leaping from crag to crag."

Nathan had recalled the words once said to him by his old friend, Wilf the goat herder. Melissa did not understand him and had to think twice about what he meant.

"I'm not sure how Leon would feel about being compared to a mountain goat."

"When I was living in a village back home in Austria, my family used to know an old goat herder called Wilf. He was a bit of a philosopher. He told me once that he could see the behaviour of human beings in some of his goats: there is the natural leader of the herd who is the self appointed one, a goat who thinks he was born to lead." Nathan laughed as he thought of the memory. "Wilf told me there is always an ambitious one. That is the one who steps on those blocking the way and eventually takes charge of the herd. He is the one who leads by example and the flock will follow of their own free will."

"And which one are you?" Melissa inquired, her eyes sparkling with amusement.

"Me? I am neither." Nathan thought of that day Wilf had talked to him. He remembered it so clearly. "I think I am the one that wanders away from the herd. The one that tries to make a life of its own."

"Austria, goat herds, snow on the mountains – I wonder when I shall see them again." Melissa sighed and looked up at the stars in the sky. The night was pleasant. She was enjoying being in Nathan's company. More than anything there was something about Nathan in his voice and his character that made Melissa feel she could confide in him. There was something Melissa wanted to speak about. She desperately wanted to talk about it to a good listener. She turned and looked at Nathan side on. Perhaps he would listen. "One day I must return. It is important that I do."

Nathan caught the change in her voice. He turned and looked at her.

"Why? Are you telling me something that is private to you? Do you want to tell me?"

"Yes. You seem like a person I could entrust a secret to. You are troubled about your parents. I am too. But there are things of my past life that I did not know until recently. Such as the identity of my real father."

"I will listen, Melissa, but that is all I can do."

"When I was a child in Berlin, I was also a curious child. I always played where I should not have done. I'd climb trees. I'd climb walls and fall down. Once I climbed into the attic of our home. I had always been forbidden to go there for reasons known only to my mother. One day curiosity got the better of me and I went into the attic and discovered an old trunk. I opened it to find many letters and photographs of my mother with a man I did not recognise. I started to read them and my mother came up behind me and smacked me hard and told me never to go there again. She shouted! She was angry! I did not realise that she was hiding a secret from me. There was something about her past that she did not want me to know. Later on when we moved to Vienna and I was fourteen, I remember thinking I would choose my time carefully and look inside the trunk again. One day I stood at the window of our apartment in Vienna and waved as my parents drove off to visit some friends for the afternoon. I was supposed to be studying. I did study, but not my homework. Instead I studied my mother's letters and photographs inside the trunk."

Melissa stopped as the torturous memory came back to her. Her voice had sounded haunted and racked with doubts. It was as if she had begun to feel deep misgivings now about telling the story. Her face looked grim.

"When I looked at the photographs of my mother with this man I, at first, wondered if he was an uncle of mine or a relative of my family's that I did not know about," Melissa's voice began to falter. She took a grip of herself.

"I discovered the man in the photograph was my real father. I read the letters to my mother. It seemed that in the village where my mother lived, she met this man, but could not marry for some reason. In the letters that my mother had from him it was clear that he was a man of ability. He wrote well but there wasn't any address or signature."

"So you know that your mother kept this from you."

"Yes, but it was for a good reason that I feel sure of. My mother married my stepfather – who I had always believed to be my real father, shortly after leaving the village in 1921. She did not realise that she was expecting me. The man who was my real father offered to look after us when he was told. My mother must have written to him and told him she had married. So there, Nathan, I have to live with this."

"A difficult thing to live with, I agree. Melissa, did you never ask your mother about this?"

"I always felt I should wait until I was older. When I was more mature I would ask her. Then when things got gradually worse in Europe I came here. I couldn't ask. It was so emotional leaving. I did not think that things would happen the way they have in Germany and Austria. I always thought that perhaps I would see them again."

Nathan felt a little embarrassed at her outpourings. He was surprised that Melissa had opened up to him. He put this down to the fact that the Jewish people were always a demonstrative people, who were scrupulously honest and never feigned in their affections. It was strange that this young girl of seventeen carried such a weight on her shoulders. Nathan felt almost duty-bound to reassure her and accept her confidences.

"Melissa, you and I, because of things that have happened to us, are more mature than many others of seventeen. I think that you should not let the past trouble you. Can you just accept things for what they were? Your mother and stepfather – were they not good to you?"

"They were wonderful to me," she replied without hesitation. "I could not have asked for better parents."

"Then nothing else matters, does it?" Nathan said firmly.

"Not for the moment I feel." Melissa appeared to be in concurrence with him.

"Maybe one day I will look into the matter. But for the moment I will try not to let it bother me." She gripped Nathan's hand momentarily again. "I am sorry I embarrassed you. I should not have bothered you with such a thing. You will not speak of what I have told you to anyone, will you?"

"Of course not," he murmured, and then he added. "I have enjoyed talking to you."

Melissa smiled brightly at Nathan. It was a rerun of that first smile that had bedazzled him on the bus to Jerusalem.

"We must talk again." She said softly. "In the meantime I must go and study more Shakespeare plays. I am studying the part of Viola in *Twelfth Night*, a good, light-hearted role. Goodnight, Nathan."

Nathan smiled at her and watched her walk away. He could not sum her character up. Melissa was a more complex girl that he imagined. On the one hand, she was warm and uninhibited. It was true that her personality on stage was exciting, bursting at the seams with life, and vibrant. All the expressions of the human being she could somehow characterise and bring to the fore. Her voice on stage was full. It could boom to full resonance. When she laughed, it would shower the audience with sparks. If she played a downcast role she would act the part of a tragedian with such conviction that the other members of the kibbutz would listen in hushed silence. Melissa Heiletz was a spellbinder.

Yet here on that crystal clear night when Nathan and Melissa had spoken so deeply of their lives, another side of her personality had come to the fore. It was the first time Nathan had really spoken to her in depth. Certainly Melissa away from the awnings and the greasepaint was a different a person as could be imagined. She was quietly spoken but effective. The most notable thing to Nathan about Melissa was that she was haunted and insecure.

Haunted by her illegitimacy and insecure about who her father really was. The social stigma was not something to dwell on. Nathan's father had always taught him to accept people for what they were and how they were found to be. He was fascinated by Melissa and concluded that her insecurity was the reason she had clung so often to the company of Leon.

Often in the days that followed, Nathan and Melissa would talk pleasantly when their paths crossed in the course of their day's work. Although they never did talk again quite so intimately as they had that night. If anything the distance between the two did become quite wide again as it had been before. He wondered if Leon had been privy to the confidences Melissa had shown Nathan when she had spoken of the past.

By this time Nathan was spending every spare moment working on his correspondence course. He began to realise that his own mother had been an excellent teacher. Much of the subject matter of his course had been covered in private tuition with Marlene. His studies of the French and English languages were complete in that he was highly fluent in both. Not only was his mastery of the language above average, but he had taken to the literature of both languages with a passion. He was already knowledgeable of the works of Rudyard Kipling and Robert Louis Stevenson. He now extended his love of books to Victor Hugo's *Les Miserables*, and the writings of Balzac.

Nathan did not overly care for the study of sciences but as a par for the course, he made himself read the books pertaining to Physics and Chemistry. He needed to be proficient in these subjects to gain qualifying passes for the level he required. So, very grudgingly, he forced himself to understand the workings of the combustion engine, the four stroke cycle, the theory of electricity as applied to Ohms law, and many other formulae and solutions that covered a whole amalgam of principles. He understood force and velocity, chemicals and their scientific composition, and the mathematical calculations that were related to this.

Science subjects were his weakest point. The rest of his studies came with ease. He was an avid historian, particularly where his own faith was concerned. He could speak freely on every event affecting the Jewish people throughout the centuries. Modern, political and ancient history came within his grasp easily. Geography stirred in him the desire to travel so much further than he had done already in the short span of his life. He was progressing well independently with his studies.

Above all, Nathan was mature beyond his years. His continually changing life had already generated this maturity. He had come to terms with himself and his position in the world. He acknowledged the fact that being Jewish in the present day climate of the 1930s was not an easy existence. But he believed that he and the chosen race would survive. After all he was privileged to be free and living in Palestine.

The changing of the seasons in Palestine had brought with them a freshness and a vigour for the landscape that surrounded him. Winter in Galilee had been crisp, the hills were a deep luxurious green at that time. Travelling through the country as Nathan often did, he would notice such things. The summer months gave the land wide blue skies and flowers that grew in a dazzling array of colours and scents. It was all so beautiful to the human eye.

One day in early November 1938 Nathan was toiling away in the green fields, hard at work, his muscles and intentions precisely performing the tasks he was required to do but, as usual, his mind was far away involved in his academic studies and his law ambitions. From out of the former of his eye he saw Leon Zielineki approaching him. He turned to greet him.

Leon's training in the Haganah had made him physically fit. He was broad and muscular and with his work in the fields and he was almost glowing with good health. His tanned skin against his jet-black hair made him a dashing figure. That combined with his strong personality made it easy for Nathan to realise why Melissa was so captivated by him. The ensuing months had mellowed Nathan's opinion of Leon. At first he had disliked his pushiness and his aggression but now, after having got to know him well, he found that Leon was quite an amiable person beneath the brashness that lay on the surface. When Melissa had told Nathan that Leon had admired his ideas, he had warmed to him.

"Nathan, you have heard of the unrest in the hills?" Leon was straight to the point as always. He was direct and he was about to bring up a subject he had always avoided up to now, but the situation had arisen where the Haganah needed more volunteers. It had even been rumoured that the leader of the kibbutz, Shirom Banai, was a secret commander in its force.

Nathan looked perturbed. He sensed that something was wrong.

"I have heard," he replied, stepping back and looking at a vegetable patch he had been tending.

"What is it?" asked Nathan with concern.

"Would you be prepared to take up arms?" Nathan looked stunned at the question. "To defend the kibbutz," Leon felt inclined to add. "There have been several random attacks by marauders at a kibbutz near the Jezreel Valley."

"I find the idea repellent," said Nathan in a firm but not unpleasant manner. "Besides," he added, "I have never handled a rifle in my life. It is contradictory to anything I believe in."

"For the defence of the kibbutz, Nathan! You do not think words will stop a gang, do you?" Leon's old character bubbled to the surface again, not bothering to hide his displeasure at Nathan's apparent rejection of the idea.

"Why the sudden concern? Are we under immediate threat?" Nathan sharply came back at Leon in a manner that quite surprised him.

"Ah, so you can snarl like a tiger, Nathan, when you feel like it," Leon grinned. "I was beginning to think you weren't human. So there is a fire beneath the still waters." Nathan cooled down as quickly as he had flared and looked at Leon with a slight smile.

★★★

"Perhaps we are not under immediate threat. It is good to be prepared for such a thing."

"I understand that. Do you foresee a need though, Leon?"

"Yes, of course. I wouldn't be asking you would I, my friend? You have heard of the Haganah?"

"Now I understand," Nathan said with a deep certainty. "Are you a member?"

Leon did not reply but the look on his face, and the glimmer in his eyes, were answer enough.

"They will need volunteers – many more volunteers. We live in isolated conditions and while we live here at Jezarat we are under the constant possibility of being attacked."

"Leon, if we are ever under attack, and I mean if we are under attack and not the ones attacking, then I will take up a rifle and standby defiantly alongside you. If there is war and our race is under threat – as I believe there will be war and that our race is threatened – then, and only then, will I take up arms. Until then I will remain a pacifist."

Leon admired the way Nathan had spoken. He reached out and patted Nathan warmly on the shoulder.

"I like you, Nathan," he said warmly. "I wish you well."

"And I you, Leon. I have the feeling that one day you will be a Member of Parliament in more peaceful times perhaps."

The sound of a motor vehicle engine roaring suddenly became loud in the distance. The two turned to gaze at the oncoming car.

"Something is badly wrong. I feel it in my bones." Leon had spoken quietly and coldly. Nathan could sense it too. It was as if the brisk November air was generating vibrations.

The car came speeding towards them on a dirt road between the rows of crops leaving a spiral of black smoke and strewn up earth behind it. Nathan and Leon stood to one side as the car hurtled towards them and came to a screeching halt throwing earth up over them as the tyres grinded to a standstill. The driver wound the window down and put his head through.

"You drove like a maniac. What on earth is it?" Gasped Leon. The driver was one of Shirom's closest confidantes in the running of the Kibbutz Jezarat. He was obviously distressed.

"George," said Leon, recognising him, "you would not drive like the devil if something wasn't terribly wrong."

"You are right," stammered George. "I cannot tell you now. I have to find everyone. Shirom is holding a meeting in one hour. Everyone must be there."

The driver did not wait for their replies and immediately put the car into gear, moving off at a frantic pace to alert the other members of the commune. He drove off at such a speed that it left Nathan and Leon as to no doubt of the urgency of the situation.

"Well obviously it couldn't be one of the attacks you were telling me about, otherwise we would not have the breathing space of one-hour."

"No, Nathan. But I fear. I fear my friend." The two looked at each other in alarm. "Come, we must go and hear what Shirom has to say."

Nathan downed his tools and walked back to the huts with Leon. On the way back they saw many of the other kibbutz workers putting down their agricultural tools and leaving the crops. Soon there was a whole throng of them walking together as if part of one great pilgrimage destined for a holy shrine.

This did not go unnoticed by Leon who remarked to Nathan, "We walk together like pilgrims," and then looking up at the sky and at the cultivated fields around them, he further added, "a clear sky, a potentially good harvest. What can be wrong with the fates?"

Back at the huts of the kibbutz all of the people of the commune gathered together inside to hear Shirom Banai speak. They sat down at the chairs and tables provided. Shirom rose to speak. He looked pale and drawn. The silence before he spoke was deafening. He looked from left to right to ensure that everyone was there. They were all and keen to listen.

"My people," he began. "I have brought you all together to tell you of some news I have received today." Shirom's voice was hushed but controlled. Every word stung in the stillness of the room. From where he stood, he could see the emotions registering on every face. "Please prepare yourselves." He raised his hand in a gesticulating fashion, brought it to his face, pinching his forehead and then continued. "On the night of November 9th through to the morning of November 10th 1938, a date we will always remember, I regret to tell you that some dreadful things happened throughout Germany and Austria." Shirom hesitated before carrying on speaking. He allowed a pause to let the cold impact of the words sink in for the preparedness of what was to follow. The members of the kibbutz stared at him in expectation of the worst to come. "The figures I have been given are still to be confirmed, but it is my melancholy duty to tell you that gangs of thugs went on a rampage attacking many Jewish homes, property and institutions." Horrified looks spread over every face. Melissa Heiletz reached quickly for her handkerchief as her eyes filled with moisture. Nathan covered his face with one hand. Leon ran his hands through his hair and appeared to close his eyelids and open them quickly; he was thinking that this could happen in his beloved Poland. "It is not easy for me to tell you this," Shirom continued, struggling for ways to lower the impact of the news. The poor man had rehearsed this over and over in his mind for the previous hour. No matter how he had thought about it, the words were still going to hurt enormously. "It has been estimated that something like," Shirom looked twice at a piece of paper he held in one hand on which he had written down the details, "seven, eight, maybe even as many as nine thousand shops belonging to Jewish people were looted and smashed. Nearly two hundred synagogues were burnt and gutted.

It was reported that while this was happening crowds of people stood by and watched and did nothing to extinguish the flames. I cannot believe this; this is supposed to be a more humane age. The twentieth century has not shown us good fortune." Shirom felt anger rising in him. He controlled his temperament. "Further I have to add that approximately two hundred Jewish homes and apartments were torn apart." Tears began to fill his eyes rapidly. The last part of his announcement filled him with enormous pain. "Twenty thousand of our people. Twenty thousand were arrested and detained – for what we need not speculate. Their arrest and detention is enough sadness in itself." Then in the coldest delivery of all Shirom told them the worst news of all. "If all that I have just told you is horrifying then what I have to say now is the worst I have ever had to tell anyone Over three thousand of our fellow brethren were struck and beaten up. Fifty of them were murdered."

Gasps of horror broke out amongst them. Several of the young girls broke into fits of sobbing, and had to be consoled. For a few moments everyone let loose with their emotions and their anger. How could they bear such tragedy? It was beyond such limits of pain. The room was full of mixed feelings of grief and a wild fury.

Leon did not show any signs outwardly. Inwardly it was different. He was doing something that he had never done before in his life. He was suppressing his anger and his disgust and his fury at what had happened. He clenched his fists, controlling himself when really all he wanted to do was rage with every emotion that he could muster. He wanted to pick up a chair and smash it down on the floor in his deep anger and frustration.

"Shirom," he called out above the buzz of conversation and the crying. Shirom looked over to Leon. "What will happen now?"

"Representations have already been made to the agency of our people. The violence has brought international condemnation. Undoubtedly there will be more countries that will be swift to join the rest in condemning the violence and the government. Obviously, for those of you with relatives in Germany and Austria who may have been caught up in the events, I have spoken to you of, the mere condemning of such – such unprecedented action – will be of little comfort to you all." Shirom knew that he was the centre of all attention and that 'his people' as he referred to them, were looking towards him as the symbol of leadership and inspiration. He could do little but console them. It was an unenviable position for any man to be in. "I must ask you all to be strong." He said to them. "The pain and the despair that we feel for our friends and relatives is enormous, I know. We have to go on as best as we can. Our continued survival is vital. A positive attitude to carry on is the most important thing for us all. It is paramount that we must never lose faith in ourselves – that we never lose faith in our own faith, strange as that may sound to you, and above all that we never lose faith in the rest of the more humane countries of the world, who I still believe will come to our aid in times of crisis."

The commune members looked a sombre group, stunned by the news he had brought them. A voice came from the back of the room addressing him. "Shirom, will you be able to obtain a list of the casualties from your source of information? God forbid it, but I fear that some of us may have relatives who could have been caught up in this."

Shirom nodded to the young man who had asked the question. "I shall do my very best at the earliest opportunity. I cannot promise you swift answers but I will try, believe me."

Another voice echoed across the room. This time it was a young girl. "Will the Jewish agency continually monitor the situation from now on?"

The kibbutz leader responded gently. "I feel absolutely sure of that. I can assure you that as soon as they received the news they would have been swift to react. Their protest will be loud and clear and they will be seeking support from the civilised nations to bring immense pressure on the German government." Shirom looked around him. The expressions of everyone there that day were downcast and diffident. "Any more questions?" he asked in a voice that was barely a whisper. "Tomorrow we will not work. Instead we will mark it as a day of respect for the Jewish people who are affected so terribly by these events. We will take prayer in their memory and for the wellbeing of the many who live under such cruelty." The words that Shirom had uttered seemed to float above everyone. He had to rouse them and get them back into a fighting spirit in attitude alone if not instincts. He looked at them hard, his eyes blazing and his mind in a quandary as to what to do. They were all so quiet and despondent. "Are you going to dwell on such despairing news?" He asked them. There was an uplift in the tone of his voice. It was not a voice impressive in volume but its tones were caring and inflamed with passion, energy and a positive certainty. "Are you going to be dispirited and mope in sadness? I love you all, my people. We must rise up from our despondency. Come on, my friends! We as a people have always survived. We will continue to do so." Several of the people began to raise themselves from a state of crumpled and sagging spirits, and sat erect and alert listening to every word. Shirom pushed on and he felt relieved when he saw the changes coming over them. "Where are your spirits that are so powerful when we sing our traditional songs together?" They were all looking up at Shirom now. He realised he had got to the heart of them all. In an enthusiastic voice he beckoned, "Come, sing." Several people stood up. The rest followed and joined hands in kindred spirit. Shirom outspread his hands demonstratively, beamed a smile and said to them in a carefully modulated voice, "Come sing with me, my people."

One man started to sing an old Jewish song, which the others immediately recognised and joined in enthusiastically. The mood of all of them had been dramatically uplifted. Their voices of all different timbres and tones came together in one splendid rousing harmony, almost lifting the roof of the hut wherein they stood.

Nathan was spellbound by the sound of such enthralling voices. There were many moments in Nathan's life that had been memorable, many cherished memories but this night was one he would never forget for the sound of all around him was that of a downtrodden people who would rise again, their spirits constantly rejuvenating. Yes, they would always survive.

Leon, Melissa and Nathan must have been the possessors of telepathic senses for they all seemed to turned their eyes to each other, noting the expressions of each. Leon had such remarkable presence about him. His eyes sparkled and flashed as he sang in that wonderfully heavily Polish accented voice of his. He seemed to generate pride and strength in every syllable of the lyrics. Melissa's face was possessed of a deep love. Not the love for one individual but the love of being alive and of her faith. At the front of all the throng of Kibbutzniks stood Shirom totally in charge of them who with barometer-like precision had conducted their moods carefully orchestrated to the heights they were ascending now.

Nathan felt as if he was part of some great celestial body singing their praises to an all time high. They sang with all the latent energy they could find for the dispossessed, the downtrodden and those that had suffered.

For Shirom it was a gigantic sense of relief he was experiencing. He had retrieved his people from plummeting to the depths of sadness and self-pity. His people were coming back now, stronger than ever.

★★★

The unbearably tragic events in Germany and Austria of the nights of 9th and 10th November 1938 soon passed into history. It was referred to as the *Kristallnacht*, 'The Night of Broken Glass'.

Seventeen

Far away from Palestine in a picturesque village in Cornwall, Southern England, Freddie Miller stamped around the pathway along the cliff-top walk between Mousehole and Lamorna. It was a route that he always enjoyed taking. Clad in his wellington boots, a pair of baggy trousers and a fisherman's thick woollen pullover he was every inch the country gentleman. He would often wander along the rugged coastline before breakfast every day looking at the sights around him.

Sometimes at the crack of dawn he would see the men on the trawlers sailing out to a cold and inhospitable sea where they would drop out huge nets to bring in hauls of fish. In the cove at Lamorna there would occasionally be the lobster potters in tiny boats who must have had the patience of a saint whilst waiting for their catch.

The waters of the channel always looked murky and grey and when the weather was wild and windy the waves would crash against the jagged rocks of the cliff faces with a tremendous force, the creamy surf surging over furiously. Freddie always had great admiration for the salty stubble-bearded Cornish sea dogs who made their living ploughing their vessels through such turbulent conditions.

But in spite of the often-fearful weather in Cornwall, Freddie's new life here had opened up an entirely new world for him. Happily married to Cynthia Field for over a year now and with a new occupation writing for a local journal, he had eagerly accepted his new surroundings and got to know so many of the villagers, he felt as if he had lived here all his life. The villagers at first, in their curious way, had at first been slow to open up and accept this 'posh' London couple, but as with the passing of time and the lowering of inhibitions, they began to fit in to the pace and style of this lovely old village called Mousehole, but pronounced 'Muzzal' by its inhabitants.

Freddie had found that there were a number of characters in and around his new home. There was a woman affectionately called the Cat Lady by the locals. One day he and Cynthia had met this colourful lady at a jumble sale in a church hall and had been asked to come to tea one night. More out of inquisitive feelings than to enjoy the company of this eccentric old lady in her seventies, they had gone along to see if the gossip about her was justified. After all Freddie had met Gandhi and Clark Gable why not meet the Cat Lady of Mousehole as well? They were stunned when they were shown into her cottage. There were cats literally everywhere. Stretched out across the carpet and rugs, on the mantelpiece and the bookshelves. There were cats sleeping on the tops of wardrobes and one was even giving birth to kittens in the kitchen sink as the old lady filled up her old tin kettle to make her guests some tea. Cats dropped out of windows and jumped on to chairs and the settee as Freddie and Cynthia tried to make polite conversation. Filming in the Spanish Civil War had been fraught with difficulties but considerably less than taking tea and a clotted cream scone in a house where Cynthia counted twenty-two cats and more, multiplying by the hour.

There were other fascinating characters, slices of local colour that Freddie couldn't resist getting to know. Billy the Blacksmith was a man of immense stature and gigantic physique. He had huge muscular arms, massive biceps which, combined with the steely gaze of his vivid blue eyes, curly jet-black hair and a two-feet-long pointed beard, made him look a formidable figure in anybody's book. If his appearance was not stunning enough, a display of his strength was simply overpowering. Freddie looked on in awe, wishing that he had a cinecamera to record the scene. For the benefit of Freddie and Cynthia, Billy, without any apparent discomfort, lifted a horse above his head in full view of the villagers. That certainly was a sight to see. But it was no ordinary horse. It was a massive carthorse – and what was more, it had a man mounted on its back.

The Hermit, as he was known, was another interesting figure on the landscape, who remained silent to such an extent that many people wondered if he had a voice. He didn't speak to anyone, he didn't appear to have any friends and lived alone, except for the company of a couple of old dogs, in a hut not any bigger than a garden tool shed, without the advantage of electric light or running water. This figure of isolation wore day-in day-out the same clothes, a black beret, a long trench coat and gumboots. His face, submerged beneath its constantly unshaven appearance, was one of blank expression. He never seemed to spend money in any of the shops. He was never seen in a public house jarring with the locals. So who was he? The hermit's true identity was only revealed accidentally by the local policeman who, after a more than convivial night celebrating his promotion to the rank of sergeant, confided in a close friend with the utmost confidence. Needless to say this close friend could not constrain himself, revealed all and the rumour went around like wildfire.

This man they nicknamed the Hermit was a living piece of Cornish history. In truth, it seemed he owned much of it. Even his name, Runus Trevere, sounded like something from a fabled legend. Apparently he was descended from a family who, a couple of centuries ago, were smugglers of note. Over the years, through the accumulation of goods beyond the normal excise boundaries, their wealth had grown to staggering proportions in Cornwall. The Trevere family had become legitimate. They had bought into several tin mines, property, a farming community and a coupe of fishing boats. Needless to say all their wealth had been passed from generation to generation until it had finally arrived in the hands of the somewhat miserly and eccentric Runus. Why he would choose to live in an old shed without any luxuries, when he could have been living in the best comforts that money could buy, was one big mystery. But the villagers thought nothing of it; if that was the way old Runus wanted to live, let him be free to do so. He wasn't doing anyone any harm. He certainly wasn't spending any of the money his family's investments were bringing in.

One marvellous old character that Freddie enjoyed talking to was a man in his sixties of regal bearing and resounding voice who had once been a sea captain. He seemed to exude an aura of effortless superiority. In the centre of a public house he could hold the attention of all those who were interested in listening to this fascinating raconteur – and there were many, because he was incredibly entertaining with his vivid descriptions of his life as a mariner. When he spoke in hushed whispers of sailing across the cold Atlantic and circumnavigating Cape Horn, he did so in a manner of a professional storyteller luring his audience in, piece by piece, until he brought the story to a crescendo with all the impact of the waves crashing down on the Cornish coastline. He was never dull and his stories improved with every retelling.

These were the type of magical figures that Freddie Miller had been brought into contact with in his life in the village. He and Cynthia had developed a great rapport together and he was happy in his way. His surroundings smacked of the old time adventure of sailing ships of another age with long masts from where pirates would attack and plunder for bootie. It was easy to imagine the days of a bygone era when smugglers would bring in great quantities of illegal rum, 'baccy' and trinkets from exotic lands. There were the old gypsy camps tucked away in a remote corner where there would be coloured caravans, long with round roofs and strong horses that pulled them put out to pasture, while the occupants lived their own individual lives. The gypsies themselves were colourfully clad in bright apparel and the ladies seemed to possess huge metallic earrings that caught the glow of light from the moon and, when they realised they were being stared at or admired, would respond by defiantly putting their hands on, more often than not, slender hips and glaring back with bright shiny eyes that disturbed a stranger by the entrancing quality of their focus. Sometimes the gypsies would dance around high burning yellow fires, and sing strange songs from another land. They were a community until themselves.

If people and history in Cornwall were a fascination for Freddie and Cynthia, then too was the landscape. Occasionally in their long, slow meandering walks across coarse green moors from which bright yellow flowers would flourish in the most unexpected of spots, they would encounter the ancient ruins of a druid temple or the weather-beaten remains of a castle of Plantagenet times half remaining like a wedding cake where the reception guests had left in a hurry. They would look at these ancestral ruins and wonder. Did the druids long ago make their sacrificial gifts here in this very spot? At the old castle ruins where Freddie mounted a lookout turret in the pose of a great thinker for a photograph taken by Cynthia, it was a test of imagination to envisage knights on horseback in gleaming shiny armour on stallions of uncontrollable zest and energy.

Then there was always that lovely walk from Lamorna to Mousehole. Freddie and Cynthia would spend hours just sitting in silence on the cliff tops just watching the sea and the waves cracking and spilling. It was a peaceful escape away from Freddie's taxing new job as a sub-editor on a Cornish newspaper. He had got the job mainly because of his incredible diversified experience running a cinecamera news team and his impressive firsthand knowledge of current affairs.

Sometimes the two of them would go along to any one of the several village pubs and, amongst the copper pans and brassy shiny plates and mugs placed intermittently on the oak beams above them, they would enjoy a pleasant glass of ye olde English cider and chat to the various customers. Often the trawler men would come in talking about the day's catch and that wonderful Cornish accent would roll and dip like the surf. The barmaid would invariably use the expression 'ow are you, me 'andsome?' when politely addressing a customer which at first, to an outsider not conversant in the local idiom, would be a bit disarming until one got used to it.

Freddie and Cynthia lived in the main narrow winding street of Mousehole, in a house that looked like a tiny doll's house from outside. The outside appearance was very deceiving. In fact the house was as long as it was high. Cynthia at first thought it a condensed cottage but with her womanly touch she had added a flourish of taste and colour to it, without the original character of the home being disturbed in any way. It was here that they wiled away long cold evenings sitting in front of a warm fire, arms around each other with a dog at their feet, and they were at their happiest. The sound of waves or the squalls of seagulls could be heard and when there were fierce electrical storms with massive yellow streaks of lightning emblazoning the sky, they would sit in the comfort of their own home and watch through the window.

Whatever happened in the future they would have these moments to remember. For Freddie he had found real happiness with Cynthia. She was in essence a typical girl of the 1930s. Cynthia could not have been of any other age. She was fun, flirtatious, but gentle and her appearance seemed to jell with country cottages and roses. Cynthia was by now acquainted with her husband's association with the Companions of the Circle. Knowing the life Freddie had lived she was not surprised.

One night before they were married, Freddie had sat down with her and told the full story of how he had met Arthandur Palmai in the cafe in Berlin and about all the things that had happened since then. At first it had all seemed so fantastic to Cynthia, but as she learned of her husband's deep commitments, she became more and more impressed. How fascinating, she thought, that Freddie could roll off the names of Colonel Brindmarsh of British Intelligence, and Baroness Christina von Harstezzen – the late industrialist who had formed this widespread group, the Circle, of which all its members were referred to as Companions. It seemed to Cynthia that her husband, Freddie, was well-connected in the cloak and dagger aspects of another world, worlds apart from their home in a pleasant fishing village in the South of England.

Since their marriage and their subsequent move to Cornwall, Freddie had maintained his links with the Circle by monitoring the comings and goings of agents working in France. Freddie had set aside one room in his house for the purpose of using his radio equipment to regularly speak to the French agents of the Circle who advised him of their new addresses, their work, any change in their circumstances that might affect future operations. Once a week Freddie would supply a report to Colonel Brindmarsh, who since the death of Mrs Harstezzen had co-ordinated much of the Circle's clandestine work. There were other separate resistance groups that would be operating on a widespread scale in France upon the outbreak of war. The Circle was one of several groups indirectly controlled by British Intelligence with a growing band of agents now firmly established in Austria, Germany, Holland and France.

On many cold nights Freddie would disappear upstairs to the place he nicknamed the radio room. From his window he would look across the sea and the grey skies to Brittany and Normandy and speak to various agents through the airwaves and chat cheeringly as if he was a relative on the telephone. Secret agents when speaking over the line or airwaves spoke in code hence double talk and pseudonyms. It was clear that the co-operation of the French agents would be essential in future years

Freddie did not miss the life of a roving cinecameraman. The years he had spent behind the lens of a camera filming the history of the times had been rewarding. Yet he had never really found peace within himself. He had always been constantly on the move filming the events of war and tragedy, depression and politics, invention and disaster. He had met the popular figures of the movies and the national leaders of many countries, but Freddie always realised his head was in the clouds much of the time and that he needed to keep himself on a sure footing with reality. Everyday he drove to St Austell to work at the newspaper offices of the Cornish *Courier-Recorder* where he wrote articles on a variety of subjects, including foreign affairs and military matters. Freddie wrote with a degree of authority for he had experienced much of what he wrote about. Colonel Brindmarsh approved too as he saw Freddie's new occupation as the perfect opportunity to put forward certain views of the changing course of events in Europe. The views that Freddie expressed in his articles did not always coincide with that of the *Courier-Recorder* editors, but even they grudgingly acceded to the point that this journalist who was a former army officer and cinecameraman, and still on the reserve, was very well placed to make such judgements.

The *Courier-Recorder* newspaper tried to base itself on some of the more influential London dailies, but it had a fairly limited circulation and as a result did not come to national prominence as a voice on foreign affairs or the changing fortunes of politics. It intended to concentrate on activities in the West Country with occasional forays into national issues. Although Freddie was content with his lifestyle at the moment, he was aware that if it were not for the expected advent of war in the coming year, he would have to advance his new journalistic career on a better, well-known newspaper. While talk of the coming war persisted he would continue in the most leisurely pace of life he had known for many years.

There were times on weekends when Freddie and Cynthia would jump into their open topped MG and drive to Land's End, Truro or Camborne where they would visit friends at Rosker Villas. In many ways life in Cornwall bore similarities to the style of country-living that both of them had known in their youth.

Freddie often thought of his childhood, long ago as a youngster on a farm in Hampshire. His parents, who had both died within a couple of years of each other, had been humble people and very hard workers. When they died Freddie had felt very much alone and he still missed them enormously. The memories of long childhood summer days when the days seemed long and the fields of Hampshire always seemed green, tended to evoke in Freddie feelings of nostalgia. His life had been extraordinarily successful in terms of his diverse experiences if not in material gain for which he had a fairly healthy disrespect. He put this down to a modest upbringing.

Cynthia was a girl of the utmost fun to be with. She was well aware of the power that a woman has simply by being feminine and in this respect with her rich flirtatious eyes that bubbled with humour she used her charm on Freddie well and truly. They were both madly in love with each other. Cynthia had loved Freddie for years and intended that he knew it.

Her own early life had begun in Malaya, where she was born of Hampshire parents who were working on a rubber plantation out there. Brought back to England as a child of five, she had been raised in Bournemouth and had loved growing up there with the attractive countryside all around. When she was only eighteen she had gone to India and worked as a civil servant in a remote outpost called Jawapindoo where, as she continually liked to point out, she had asked lieutenant Frederick Miller to dance and as he loved to remind Cynthia, how could he refuse? This lovely flirtatious funny lady was now his wife. What luck!

Such happiness had been a gift to them both. They realised that the time of their marriage and the happiest moments of their life so far had been caught up in the scale of time that would tip forward from the relative security of peacetime to the anguish and uncertainty of war.

One night when a heavy storm was erupting over the Cornish countryside, Freddie was unable to sleep because of the howling wind, the cracking of thunder and the torrential rain pounding down on the windowpane. He lay there watching the lightning and glanced quickly at Cynthia. Even in her sleep she looked beautiful, warm and comforting.

"That blessed Cornish lightning, Freddie," she said in an amusing but drowsy voice as she rolled over to look up at him. Her smile always brought out the warmth in him.

"And at three o'clock in the morning too," chuckled Freddie. "I'll make you a cup of tea, Mrs." Freddie had just got up when the sound of the downstairs telephone ringing caught them both by surprise. "Good grief! Who can that be at this time of the night?" Freddie reluctantly went downstairs to answer it. "Hello," he said. It was a member of the local lifeboat team at the other end.

"Tommy Boas here, Fred." There was a sense of urgency in the burr of the man's voice.

"Tommy?" Freddie was startled. "What is it?"

"We've just had a report from the coastguard. There's a French tanker in trouble a few miles out to sea."

"What sort of trouble?" Freddie was instinctively alarmed. He knew just what this would mean.

"It seems there's been an explosion in the boiler room on board. Ripped half the side out and it's sinking. It'll be down in an hour." He sounded breathless. "Look there's a handful of crew and a couple of guests in dinghies. We're going out in the lifeboats to guide them in but we're short of a couple of blokes. You wouldn't mind—?"

Freddie cut him short. "I'm on my way Tommy. I'll be there in a few minutes. Immediately Freddie began to change his clothes frantically. He had changed from his pyjamas into some good strong clothing, thick boots and he placed a woollen cap onto his head.

Cynthia appeared at the top of the stairs, aware that something was drastically wrong. She was surprised to see Freddie dressing. "Where are you going in this filthy weather, darling?" she gasped.

"That was Tommy from the lifeboat team. There a tanker in trouble. I'm going out with the lifeboats."

"Oh, Freddie. Do be careful." She was understandably concerned.

Freddie ran up the stairs and kissed her quickly. "I'll be all right. I'll have that nice hot cup of tea when I get back." Then just as quickly, he dashed out of the door, casting a backward glance at her and winking good-naturedly, before going out of the house into the street. Goodness, the weather was terrible. He only had to dash a couple of hundred feet or so to get to the lifeboat station but the rain was cold and heavy, and a freezing cold wind was blowing straight off the sea onto his back. He was wet and soaked already.

One lifeboat was just going out to sea as Freddie arrived and as the other members saw him running through the rain, they began to start pushing the other one out. He ran towards them and got behind the lifeboat pushing it out as well. The cold seawaters soaked straight into Freddie's legs sending a chill right through him, and as soon as it was floating he scrambled into the vessel and frantically grabbed one of the large paddles rowing furiously.

Once out on the water, the turbulent sea thrust the boat sideways and forwards and the power of the waves literally threw it into the air. The men in the lifeboat team were all very strong, well trained and powerfully built, all very capable of handling the situation. Waves spilled over into the boat. All around huge bright yellow streaks of lightning lit up the pitch-black starless sky creating momentary flashes of daylight. They were getting further and further out on a dangerously rough sea.

The men used all the power they could muster to keep the boat going in a forward direction. The wind was blowing at gale like force. The huge waves beneath them were tossing the boat up towards the sky at an angle and then bringing it down hard quickly so that water filled up each time. It was an enormous strain on the arms of each man to keep the boat level, but Freddie was the least experienced of the crew and he was feeling the agony and the chill of the sea more than the others. Every time the boat lurched forward with sudden rapidity it seemed to make him feel dizzy. It was purely the spray of the sea and the rain beating on his face combined with the icy chill of the howling wind all around him that kept his senses in gear.

It was so black in front of the lifeboat that visibility was almost non-existent. They were practically reliant on the short, sharp burst of lightning that virtually illuminated the way ahead of them. Somewhere in the pitch blackness the silhouette of a French tanker would come into view.

A gigantic swell took the boat to an unprecedented height, virtually forcing it to a forty-five-degree angle slope. The impact was terrifying. For a split second the crewmembers came perilously close to losing control of the vessel. Then as they regained their ability to manoeuvre the boat level again, it became obvious to Freddie they had been close to being overturned and thrown into the freezing cold grey waters.

Far out ahead of them the sound of someone shouting, "Heave, lads!" could be heard. It was the other lifeboat. A flash of lightening revealed their whereabouts. They were less than a hundred yards ahead. The leader of the crew in Freddie's boat cried out loudly in response. "We're right behind you, boys."

There was a strange stench of smoke and burning beginning to reach the nostrils of each crewman. Then through the blackness a thick spiral seemed to stream over them. It stung their eyes. Freddie shook his head and blinked his eyes quickly as he felt his face covered in rain and black smoke.

One of the crewmen shouted out loudly. "Where's the tanker?"

A voice from the other boat in front replied, "To the left. About four hundred yards away." He had hardly finished his words when there was a tumultuous clap of thunder, another massive streak of lightning spread-eagled into separate veins diversifying in all directions like a huge yellow tree with unkempt, outspread branches rising high into the sky.

This time the light did not dissipate. In front of the two lifeboats there were flames streaming upwards. The smoke that had reached them earlier was being blown from the tanker by the wind. The sinking vessel was now clearly in their view.

The tanker was tilting badly to one side. It could not be long before it would be submerged. Much of it was burning. There was so much flame and smoke going across the bow. The wind seemed to be carrying the flames forward despite the rain that should have been heavy enough to extinguish the fire.

"Where are the survivors?" yelled one of the crew.

"To the right," came back a quick reply from a member of the boat at the front. Freddie looked urgently to his far right. There were two luminous white dinghies with the group of people from the tanker, well-wrapped up and hanging on for dear life.

"Move to the right, lads. Come on, boys, hard down now." The leader of the boats had a voice of discipline that the men responded to immediately. "Them poor souls will be freezing," he added, indicating the people in the dinghy. Freddie, despite the cold and the chill, felt a sense of mirth. *What about us lot?* he might have asked. They were freezing too.

Freddie hardly had time to enjoy his own private joke. A terrific current oozed across the water raising their lifeboats with sudden pressure but not in the same manner as the wild waves. There was something different this time. Ripples kept spreading out across the water and the rain soaked crewmen turned their heads to see the most terrifying sight some of them had ever seen.

Amidst the storm and the rain the tanker was sinking. The front of the bow tilted upwards. It was beginning to slide downwards. The flames were being extinguished as it began to be submerged by water. There was crashing and creaking and the sound of something exploding. Then suddenly there was a strange gushing sound. Before anyone could gather their thoughts together, the tanker slid down into the waters of the channel and disappeared from view. It had been an incredibly dramatic sight, the sinking of a ship, and Freddie turned his head away. He had been witness to an horrific sight of a different sort once before in Lakehurst in the USA when he had seen the Hindenburg explode.

A brutal streak of lightning flashed across the sky and in that instant Freddie saw the looks of horror in the other men's eyes. It was only the huge waves throwing the lifeboat up with a sudden lurch that made the crew constrain their grip and then they began frantically pulling hard on the oars, heading in the direction of the dinghies. Behind them the sea cascaded across the point where the tanker had been.

This whole escapade seemed to be taking an eternity. The two lifeboats rowed away frantically trying to escape getting caught up in the section of the whirlpool created by the now fully submerged tanker.

Freddie's whole attire was drenched by icy water, so penetratingly cold it seemed to be chilling his very bones. Tommy Boas and his team of Cornish lifesavers were a tough breed of men. They were full of an indomitable spirit and grit that kept them forging ahead even though their own muscles and limbs were probably numb by now.

The two dinghies were becoming closer now. They were swirling around and around on the waves, out of control, and the twenty survivors of the tanker seemed to be getting further away as the strong currents started to widen the distance.

"Harder, lads!" yelled Tommy Boas. The crewmen of each lifeboat rowed even harder than they had done. The strain on their arms was enormous. Freddie's own arms felt as if the blood had run cold in them. It must have been pure psyche and willpower that drove them on.

Still the white dinghies seemed to be even further away. The distance between the boats was increasing. The lifeboats could not bridge the gap. A massive wave took Freddie's boat up suddenly and it came down with all the impact of a carriage in the big dipper at a funfair. Freddie's stomach seemed to rise up around his throat. It was becoming unbearable.

"Listen, lads, I'm going to throw a rope to one of the dinghies," called out Tommy Boas, his voice roaring above the sound of the waves and the wind. "Hang on there." With just one man down it was now becoming a test of human endurance to keep rowing. Tommy grabbed a rope and leaned forward at the front of the boat to direct his aim. He was a plucky fellow. No doubt about that thought Freddie.

"Grab hold of the rope and we'll pull you," he cried out to the people in the dinghies. Then he stood up with one hand on the side of the boat and tossed the rope to the nearest one. The rope was hurtled through the air, almost aided by the wind. It fell short of its target by several yards.

Immediately the people in the dinghy began trying to paddle frantically to reach the rope. With a mammoth effort they fought furiously against the power of the sea to reach it. One figure practically hung out, attempting to grab it. Once they tried. The rope was slipping away fast. The second time the same person tried, but it was just too difficult. Freddie tried hard to identify the person. Surely it was a sleek feminine figure who was struggling so valiantly to grab at it.

Suddenly the person practically leaped forward and a couple of crewmen held her or him by the legs for support. The poor soul was almost taking a bath in the cold seawater. It was not in vain. The rope was snared and the people in the dinghy pulled the person back quickly, all of them then tugging in hard

Tommy Boas instantaneously pulled the rope at his end, the crewmen had control of the dinghy and it was brought in by a few extra hands in the lifeboat. Signs of genuine relief came from everyone in the boat. The Cornishmen, coming together to make a gladiatorial effort, brought the people from the tanker closer to them. Half of the men in Freddie's boat were pulling on the rope with Tommy, while the others rowed valiantly. Then as it came closer they began to scramble from the dinghy to the lifeboat while Tommy Boas aided them.

The lifeboat ahead of theirs was performing the same tasks. Their job was made easier by the fact that the distances between the vessels was not as great as had been the case with the one in which Freddie was situated.

The crewmen of the French tanker eagerly took their places in the boat beside the Cornishmen, muttering, "*Merci bien, monsieur,*" and, "*Quel mauvais temps!*" and one high-spirited man, probably oblivious to the fact that no one could understand him, looked up at the sky and grimaced saying, "*Sacré bleu! Vents trés forts! Pluies abondantes avec du tonnerre et des échairs! Sacré bleu!*"

For the first time in the hour or so since the crew of the lifeboat had been afloat Freddie had to nod his head and laugh. The Frenchman was saying how terrible the weather was.

"Did you understand him, Fred?" asked Tommy, noting the grin on Freddie's face.

"He said the weather stinks!" replied Freddie, his humour holding intact.

Tommy looked amused and then said, "OK, lads, hard to your right now and back home." The crewmen immediately dipped their oars to the right and began to turn the vessel round in a one hundred and eighty degree turn. This time instead of riding against the powerful sea currents, they would be riding with the tide to the coast.

All of them looked thoroughly exhausted and drained. It had been the most physically demanding rescue attempt that even the most experience lifeboat men had known for some time. There were welcoming lights on the coastline in front of them and the beacon in the lighthouse far off was like some celestial guiding light bringing them in.

Freddie's teeth chattered. His face felt like a plate of frozen ice. The tips of his fingers and the movement in his limbs felt as if they weren't there at all. The icy wind seemed to penetrate his forehead. The wet clothes clung to him so tightly that it was as if the garments had become part of his own body. He shivered and shivered and shivered. Still the night was nearly over. A heartening thought added a touch of warmth to his frozen demeanour. What a privilege to have rowed with such a hearty breed of men. They had so much strength and guts to cope with incidents such as this on the coastline. They were admirable fellows.

"Lights are blazing brightly, boys," shouted out Tommy. His strength was unbelievable for a man of his age, which Freddie estimated must have been close to early sixties.

The Frenchmen sat huddled, although a couple were helping out with the rowing, Freddie was intrigued by the gallant person he had seen from the distance who had grabbed the rope thrown by Tommy Boas. They had boarded the boat in a black duffle coat with the hood up and sat in the row in front of him.

The wind changed direction with a sudden ferocity taking the duffle coat hood off backwards. A woman with long tawny dark hair and a vital glowing skin was revealed. She had deep sensitive eyes that showed signs of tiredness from the exhausting night that they had all endured. *Who is this young woman?* Freddie wondered. *What was this olive-skinned creature doing on board a tanker with a bunch of roughneck Frenchmen?* Just a curious thought that was passing through his mind.

These fine men who manned the lifeboats were the very embodiment of Cornwall. They were gravel-faced, sharp eyed, good-natured men who worked at physically arduous jobs by day in the tin and copper mines, and on the fishing boats. At a moment's notice they would go out on these really rough and stormy nights to risk life and limb to save human lives. One thing that came across to Freddie repeatedly was that these Cornishmen were people who cared.

The little harbour of Mousehole was becoming closer. The two lifeboats were gliding in on the waves sweeping towards the coastline. All along the front of the harbour side was a single row of lights flickering backwards and forwards. The rest of the villagers, and the wives and girlfriends of the lifeboat men, stood side to side, each of them holding a brightly glowing lantern. *God bless the lot of them,* thought Freddie. On nights like this when the lifeboats had been out on a mission of rescue, the villagers, almost as if by tradition, had hot soup and tea and towels at the ready for the men who had braved the elements and the people they had brought back.

The two boats were getting close to the shore. Oh, and it had been such a long and weary night. Nearer they came, over and down the waves, gliding up and gliding down. Nearer and nearer: less than a hundred yards to go.

Suddenly above the roar of the sea crashing down on the coast and the wind blowing, the people waiting in Mousehole harbour broke into a spontaneous bout of cheering and handclapping. By God, it brought tears to the eyes. And there was Cynthia waiting with all the others.

Within seconds of each other the two lifeboats thudded against the sand, and everyone was jumping out and dragging the vessels clear of the water. Freddie's legs went practically numb. He was conscious of being unable to hold his balance. He swayed around for a few seconds before stabilising himself. The weather, the wind and the rough ride on the sea had shaken his whole metabolism.

"Well done, me lads," Tommy Boas called out to his colleagues. The lifeboats were dragged away to some sheds, and the people immediately began to disperse, the crew going to join the families and the French crew were attended to by some First Aid officers. Cynthia came down from the footpath to the bay where Freddie was beginning to make his way.

"Where are the French crew being taken?" he asked her quietly.

"They'll be all right Freddie," replied Cynthia taking Freddie's arm. She was surprised at how cold and wet he was. "After the doctors have had a good look at them, the publican's have got some rooms organised for them, and some warm food I believe." She looked at him lovingly. "And for you, my love, I've got a warm bath and some piping hot soup for you." Freddie suddenly felt very cheerful. His wife always had a way of making him feel good. They made their way home in the rain and the wind.

Eighteen

The day after the devastating storm, Freddie lay in his bed luxuriating in the absolute warmth and comfort of it all. The pillow beneath his head felt soft and secure, the sheets and blankets that he moulded himself into were warm and comfortable. After that stormy, ice-cold night, Freddie just wanted to be warm. He had slept so well. It was not just the sleep of tiredness but one of total exhaustion. After Cynthia had given him some hot soup and put him in a hot water bath, he felt a bit more life pulsating in his arms and legs. He had barely made it to the bedroom when the effects of several rigorous hours on a fierce sea took over and he fell into many hours of a very deep sleep. When he woke it was after midday on a placid Saturday.

Staring through the bedroom window Freddie could see what the effects of the storm had taken. On the coarse green landscapes spreading around the perimeter of the bays and inlets near Mousehole, trees and bushes had been uprooted, and in some cases completely overturned. Fences had been blown down. Gates had been loosened and were hanging off by their hinges. Branches and twigs littered the narrow roads. Out on the sea a number of private boats had been propelled away from the shore and were floating aimlessly. Some boats had run aground and some were smashed. The sea was testimony to the events of the previous night for it yielded the evidence of wreckage of a large boat. Freddie gathered a pair of binoculars and studied the floating signs. Sure enough there were life belts, pieces of masts, cabin doors and amazingly enough still intact, and bobbing upright just north of Lamorna were the two white dinghies from which the crew and the passengers of the French tanker had been rescued. The sea, restless and fearful yesterday, was bouncy and serene that morning.

It was a much more calmer day. The sky, although still grey, was clear and the rain had gone. There was just a gentle breeze instead of a wind of gale force nine ferocity, and everywhere looked so peaceful unlike the early hours of the night before.

Yesterday, thought Freddie, he had been part of one of the village's unique establishments, the Lifeboat Institution. It was unique to many of the villages in Cornwall and the West Country in general. He prided himself that, even though he had a milder, quieter life, he could still be a participant in activities that required a certain amount of stamina. But goodness, last night had been tough out on the waves.

Inevitably Freddie compared life in this village to the one in Austria where he had stayed with Arthandur and Marlene. There were similarities of course. Although one village had a mountainous backdrop and the other a rugged coastline, there were certain characteristics that were a common denominator to them both. Both villages had an atmosphere about them that was evident in the air. The freshness of the salt spray rising with the wind and the squawk of seagulls seemed to suggest the character of Mousehole. The almost perfumed breezy air and the fragrance of the incandescent flowers were of an Austrian village now another time ago. Freddie could compare characters too. Wilf, the old Austrian goat herder with the deep belly laugh and the crimson cheeks, was a raconteur much in the same tone as the old sea captain in Mousehole, who too could be broad and expansive in his embellishment of an ageing yarn, and content of the story forever improving.

He thought about Arthandur, Marlene and Nathan. He did not realise that Nathan had gone to Palestine. Since the Anschluss of Austria, there had not been any contact from the Palmai family, and he had feared the worst. Freddie had contacted Colonel Brindmarsh and asked him to try and trace the location of the Palmai's through the intelligence networks he was in contact with, but so far in their inquiries they had come up with absolutely no details at all except to say that they were probably being detained, although where was a mystery.

Cynthia came into the room carrying a tray of food. She smiled pleasantly at Freddie when she saw him at the window looking through the binoculars. She placed the tray down on a table and moved up behind him spreading her arms around him and resting her head on his back.

"I was so worried about you last night," she said in a resigned sigh. Freddie turned around in the hold of her arms and squeezed her and then kissed her slowly and passionately. Her eyes were dancing with delight.

"That made it all worth it," Freddie said gently, as he drew back from her, stroking her soft hair. "You know all my life, except for when I was a child on a farm in Hampshire, I've always been on the move. If it wasn't being away for the time at Somerset Grammar School, it was when I was in the army. Then I was always moving around as a cameraman and I must say that when I evaluate my time here with you this has been one of the happiest times of my life. I only wish—" and then he cut off abruptly as if there was something he wanted to suppress, but Cynthia caught his hesitation and quizzed him.

"What do you wish?"

"I wish that we had spent a lot more time together." He squeezed her tightly again as he said that. "Just seeing you waiting for me at the quay in the pouring rain when I was in the lifeboat yesterday made me realise how lucky I am to have you." There was real sincerity in his words. He looked at her warmly. It was true. He had never known such happiness in his life, and all his years of adventure and travel as exciting as they had been, did not give him the satisfaction or the warmth that he had known in one year of his marriage to Cynthia. Always in the back of Freddie's mind that, like so many other things in his life, the feelings he enjoyed now were only of a temporal state. He feared that something catastrophic like the advent of the pending war would drive a wedge between them, perhaps separating them and changing their feelings for each other. Maybe even war could mean premature death for one partner. In a rare moment of revealing his true feelings, he broached the subject cautiously. Looking down into her twinkling eyes and holding her gently on the shoulders he said, "If anything ever happens to me, Cynthia, and the Lord God forbid that it does, but we can't ignore the possibilities that there might be a war this year, you would carry on, wouldn't you? You would be positive about your life and try to be happy. I love you so much. You're so good to me. I just want happiness for you."

Cynthia put her fingers on Freddie's lips to stop him rambling. She was very perceptive. "Oh, Freddie," she gasped in dismay at such sombre talk. "I think this is such a downbeat subject."

"I know it is," Freddie agreed. "I was trying to be realistic. I am still on the reserve. I would almost certainly join up on active service. Besides Colonel Brindmarsh has indicated there would be a place for me in intelligence." He adopted a more serious tone in his voice to emphasise the gravity of the matter. Brindmarsh had only recently told Freddie in a telephone call that, with his knowledge and experience, he would be needed. "When I told you of my role as a Companion of the Circle, the Palmai family and Baroness von Harstezzen, I wanted you to understand just what I'm involved in. It's a daunting commitment. The end result could be the prevention of untold suffering for many people. I'm knowledgeable of various resistance groups, agents and code names. There would be operations to be worked out. Escape routes to be determined; the transportation of refugees. It's very involved; very complex."

"I realise that, Freddie. I understand, and I just hope that you never need to use that knowledge. I hope that the warmongers of this world never get their way." Her voice had risen sharply. "I'll be dammed if I'll lose you after having waited around nine years for you. Now! Enough of this clichéd talk. If you go out on any more lifeboat escapades like yesterday, you won't be fit enough for army service."

Her wry retort brought a smile to Freddie's face. His efforts at a serious conversation with Cynthia were thwarted again. She could always be relied upon to bring humour to any situation.

"Trust you to bring the conversation down to earth, darling," he said amused by her dry wit.

"And after you spent three days rehearsing that little speech too, you better eat that meal before it gets cold." She walked to the door and winked at him mischievously. "When you've finished perhaps we could take the dog for a walk along the beach."

He looked at her admiringly. "Righto, tiger."

Before she left Freddie to the privacy of his meal, she added one final comment. "You know your trouble, Freddie?" She said with an engaging smile. Freddie hung on to her words. It sounded as if, for the first time since he had met her ten years before, he was about to be criticised, But he wasn't. She paid him a subtle compliment that seemed to sum up his life aptly. "You're one of the last of the Elizabethans."

For a while afterwards Freddie sat and wondered what she meant by that. *One of the last of the Elizabethans.* In a way, Freddie considered that what was actually meant by that phrase was a man who love the swashbuckling side of life yet still had a love of the ordinary simple things. Even if the remark was slightly tongue in cheek, how intriguing it was to be placed in the same category as someone like Sir Francis Drake; an Elizabethan of such adventurous breed.

After Freddie had finished his meal, he dressed and took the tray downstairs to the kitchen. He had just walked through to the living room when he saw that Cynthia was sitting in an armchair with their dog sitting at her feet. Cynthia was talking to someone who sat directly opposite her in another armchair with their back towards Freddie. The dog ran to Freddie, greeting its owner with affection.

"Freddie, we have company," said Cynthia. "This lady has called to see you."

The person in the chair stood up and turned to face him. It was the young Frenchwoman who had been rescued from the French tanker along with the crew. She was a striking young woman. In the light of day she was even more charismatic than she had appeared to be in the lifeboat when all the elements of the weather had been striking her. She was tall, at least five feet eight inches, with long tawny hair parted in the middle, and a glowing tanned skin that must have bedazzled the local Cornishmen with a shade not seen in this part of the world very often. Her eyes registered a deep sensitivity about them. This combined with her good looks gave her a girlish charm and an appearance of a woman in need of protection. Her skin, if heavily suntanned, was clear showing not a blemish or a wrinkle. Freddie judged her to be about eighteen or nineteen years of age.

"My name is Francine Macé" she said, speaking English beautifully in a crisp French accent. When the French speak English they make the words sound so attractive.

"I recognise you from last night," responded Freddie, taking her hand in a limp handshake, "You were on the tanker." Freddie sat down at another armchair. "Did we rescue everyone?" He was concerned because it seemed to him that it had more or less been taken for granted that all the crew and survivors had been on the two white dinghies. In actual fact the radio operator on board the tanker had fully briefed Tommy Boas before the lifeboats had left their station. Although the rescuers had left very quickly they were actually advancing from a well-prepared position. The men in the lifeboat were very well trained and skilled in rescue operations.

"Everyone," she replied. "All of us who were on the dinghies. That is why I came to see you. I just wanted to thank all of the lifeboat men personally. I got a list of names and addresses from Mr Boas. I've been calling in to see the men all day. I have had so many cups of tea to drink, Mr Miller, and so many scones! And two of the men's wives insisted I stay for breakfast. They were so kind. I didn't want to offend them, so this morning I have had bacon and eggs twice, about half a dozen scones and a dozen cups of tea. I feel as if I were the Queen of England visiting."

Both Cynthia and Freddie laughed. Francine had a delightful maturity about her. "Well it was very nice of you to come, Miss Macé. I'm quite relieved that everyone on board was rescued. Tommy told me a boiler blew a hole in the side of the tanker. Is that correct?"

"I believe two boilers. It was an old tanker anyway on a final voyage to Liverpool from Calais. It was frightening when the boilers exploded. What with the rain, and the wind and lightening, it was terrifying. Luckily all the crew and myself, we were sitting in the – er, how you say, recreation room when the explosion took place. It was an enormous sound. We were told to abandon ship immediately. Our own lifeboat was blown apart by the explosion. We were so lucky to have had the dinghies, otherwise we would have gone down with the ship."

"My God, you certainly did have fortune on your side," said Cynthia, sounding shocked.

"And thank heavens too for those good men in the lifeboats," continued Francine, "I admire them. They were so tough – and – and brave to go out in such weather."

Freddie thought for a moment how her admiration for the lifeboat men would undoubtedly have been returned. No wonder Francine felt like the Queen of England basking in the limelight. With her looks and a sensual French accent that almost purred, she would have set a few Cornishmen's hearts racing that morning. In an area of the West Country where the complexions of people were normally lily white or pink, Francine's suntanned figure would have singled her out for attention anyway.

"As a matter of interest, forgive me for sounding serious, but what were you doing on the tanker?" asked Freddie, "If you were a deckhand, you'd be a little different to the normal run-of-the mill deckhand."

Francine smiled, and when she smiled her whole face lit up. She had a fine set of pearl white teeth. "My father worked on the docks in Marseille, and the captain was an old friend of his, and I happened to meet him in Paris a few weeks ago. I have been planning for a while to come to England. My mother lives in Yorkshire."

"Really," remarked Freddie, surprised.

"Yes, and the captain offered me a cabin. I was originally going to go across from Liverpool to Leeds where my mother lives."

"Is your mother a French woman?" Cynthia asked, curious about Francine's background, having noticed the obvious separate locations of her parents.

"No, my mother is a Yorkshire lass," Francine replied, jokingly trying to emulate a Yorkshire accent which was made all the more amusing because of the French tones that still managed to surface. "In her youth my mother was a dancer at the City Varieties Theatre in Leeds. When she was a little bit older she went to London and performed at a few of the Theatres there. The Hippodrome, I think was one of them. The Chiswick Empire and the Victoria Palace and Drury Lane were others. And after that she joined a troupe that toured Europe and Russia and some countries in the Far East, I believe. She left the troupe in Paris and danced for a while at the Folies-Bergère and the Lido and she met my father in that city. He was a sailor on leave at the time. They got married and moved to Marseilles, my father's hometown, where he got work on the docks. I was brought up there. Believe me, the South of France is a good place for a suntan."

"So I see," remarked Freddie. "Your suntan would be the envy of many of our girls." Then, realising that Francine's background was interesting listening, he said to her diplomatically, "Sorry. Do go on. You were saying—" Freddie lit up his pipe, a habit he had recently acquired. "Your father still works on the docks?"

"Sadly, no," she answered, and the shine in her eyes seemed to dull immediately as it brought to her mind recent memories. "My father died a couple of years ago. My parents were already separated. My mother went back to Leeds to look after her sick father a while back. I've been in Paris studying Art at college."

"I'm sorry about your father," said Freddie apologetically. "It's hard to come to terms with these things. I lost my own parents some years ago and there is never a day that I don't think about them."

"Yes, it is difficult," Francine agreed. "I was so sad when they separated. Still, as people tell me, the path of life is strewn with the sad and the beautiful." She was silent for a moment and then said, "Do you know Paris well, Mr Miller? Your wife said that you spent some time there."

"I have been there on a number of occasions," said Freddie. "I once had a friend who lived there." He was referring to Tillie, one of his lost causes of the past, and then he added, remembering the address vividly, "Number 17, Place Vendaux, Malakoff."

Francine's eyes seemed to light up like beacons. "Malakoff!" she exclaimed "Why that is where I was living! What a coincidence. I was staying with cousins of mine in Rue Robespiere. Joelle and Dany Macé."

"Well, I never," mused Freddie with astonishment. "Perhaps we passed by each other many times and here we are. How amazing!"

"What are you going to do here, Francine?" asked Cynthia, slightly nervous but not alarmed at the closeness between her husband and the young woman. She knew Freddie was a great studier of women yet she knew their emotional attachment was enormously strong and could be stretched to the greatest of limits.

Francine seemed to ponder before she answered. "I have not seen my mother for a while. I would like to spend a bit of time with her. She lives at a place called Harehills, and then I am going to join the Women's Air Force. I am going to become a WAAF, as they say."

Freddie was suddenly very interested. "In any particular area?"

"Oh, I was thinking of perhaps becoming a radio operator."

An idea suddenly flashed through Freddie's mind. He thought about it for a moment then decided to keep it to himself.

"Why do you want to join the WAAF? Forgive me, I'm continually asking questions." Cynthia's nature was always cheerful. Her words never sounded possessed of any intent.

"I think mainly to be near my mother to begin with. But with all this talk of war I will join up before the queue begins to enlist. I would like to start learning some sort of skill now. Perhaps later on I may continue my work as an artist."

"Well I wish you well, Miss Macé," said Freddie. "Where are you staying at the moment?"

"In the pub in the village."

"Would you like to stay here for a while?" asked Cynthia, glancing hopefully towards her husband.

"Yes, we'd love to have you here," agreed Freddie. "We have a spare room, and we'll help you with your journey to Leeds."

"That is so kind of you, Mr and Mrs Miller." Francine was obviously touched by their thoughtfulness.

"As a matter of fact I have some radio equipment here you might like to look at. I could give you a little bit of knowledge in advance that might be useful if you are joining the WAAF.

"That would be most helpful. Are you a coastguard operator, Mr Miller?"

"Er – indirectly speaking, yes." Freddie replied, not revealing the real reason for the radio equipment he possessed. "Perhaps we could come to the pub where you're staying sometime tomorrow and bring you here. Would that be fine with you?"

"It is nice of you both. I will not impose on you for too long, I assure you. Just a few days until I know where I am going."

"Stay a few weeks," insisted Cynthia. "While Freddie is working, I can show you some of the English countryside."

Francine ended up staying with Cynthia and Freddie for three weeks. They were to be a most happy time for her. She warmed to the Millers immediately. Although there was a difference of ten years between Cynthia and Francine, they developed a great rapport between them. In many ways they were women of the same fun living cheery spirit who enjoyed many of the same things. Both had a keen intelligence and awareness of things and an amiability and love of people that endeared them to nearly everyone they met. If Cynthia was a very attractive lady who could be defined as 'typically English', then Francine, in spite of her mixed parentage, was very definitely French. She was – to use a word not current then – sexy, without realising it. Her voice was enough to break a man's heart and captivating so as to send a thousand pulses beating beyond the rate of normality.

When Freddie was working at the newspaper office during the day the two girls would travel to different spots in Cornwall. They would drive to Land's End or join Freddie for lunch at St Austell. Sometimes the two would go to Penzance and Mounts Bay, to Lizard Point and Falmouth Bay, where they would walk along the beach, barefoot, laughing and joking about various moments they had enjoyed in their lives. Often they would drive further afield to Plymouth, or to Looe, Polperro and Mevagissey, where they would chatter away merrily while drinking tea and enjoying clotted cream scones in old antiquated cafes.

During the evenings Freddie would show Francine the fundamentals of radio operations without giving away the reality of his main mission in life. She was a good pupil and swiftly understood the different frequencies that were used. In the future she would be most conversant in the new skills she had acquired which would put her a step ahead of her colleagues when she enlisted in the WAAF.

Francine talked in detail about her life in Paris. It was obvious that she knew most parts of the city. She loved to paint in oils; her paintings, which had remained with her aunt in Malakoff, were many and varied. They had included street portraits of people, capturing the caricatures of the contrasting personality of the flamboyant city of Paris. Toulouse Lautrec was the artist from which she drew the greatest inspiration. So inspiring had his influence been she had sought to capture the same sort of atmosphere in the flourish of her painting. There was the high-kicking extrovert style of the ebullient Parisienne nightclub dancers. The whistle-blowing gendarme policeman directing traffic in the boulevards, his cheeks blowing up different shades of crimson as he adapted to the changing inflow of cars and traffic around him, the Sacre Coeur in Montmatre, and the view of the rooftops of Paris spreading out from the top of its steps. All this had been represented in the style she had expounded and at such a young age, Francine's paintings had already been exhibited twice and she had been further compounding her talents in this direction by her studies at college.

Apart from her passion for Art, her other great delight was swimming. Indeed her physical shape was representative of a girl who had spent much time in aquatic sports. She spoke of her early life in Marseilles as an only child in a humble household on the docks, her days spent on the beach just soaking up the sun, and her parents whom she held in the greatest of esteem.

When the tanker on which Francine had been travelling from Cherbourg had sunk off the coast of Cornwall, she had lost a suitcase of her clothes. All her other possessions had, luckily for her, stayed behind with her aunt in Paris. But in Francine's coat that very fierce night, she had managed to salvage from her belongings a portrait photograph of her as a young child with her parents behind. She showed it to Freddie and Cynthia, who looked at it with interest.

Francine's father was a dark-haired man with more Latin looks than those of a Frenchman. Her mother had a pleasant matronly face with a jolly neighbourly look about it. It was easy to see where the characteristics she possessed had evolved. The real sadness for her had been in her parent's separation when she was fifteen. It seemed that her hardworking father had been seeing a local café owner's wife very discreetly for some time. When the café owner had heard of this, he had gone down to the dockside at Marseilles and challenged Francine's father to engage in fisticuffs. The result was a no-holds brawl, which had the whole town talking for a long time afterwards. The two men had swung their fists at each other for a long time, leaving each other truly battered and bruised. When Francine's mother had seen her husband arrive home in a truly bloodied state, she had demanded to know what had happened and why. Her father, on telling his wife, received a long cold stare and an icy silence and then, without saying a word, she had walked straight out of the house and down to the café to confront the opposition.

Walking with intent through the rows of tables and chairs, she headed straight to the back room where the proprietor was nursing his wounds. She found him being comforted by his wife. There was no stopping Francine's mother; she was made of the stuff of legends. The woman who had come between her and her husband received a sharp right hook, knocking her into a row of cupboards and putting her into oblivion. The poor old proprietor after his bout on the docks received a sharp left from the wronged woman. It just hadn't been his day. To be laid low by an angry Yorkshire woman was about the last thing he would have expected.

Francine had seen the commotion from the street and had gone to console her mother whose fury had now turned to tears. It was a heartbreaking sight for Francine seeing her mother so upset. Until then her parents had always seemed so happy. It had taken one infidelity to wreck the marriage. Back at the house there had been angry words between Francine's parents. There had been pleading by her father not to separate, but it was in vain and Francine's mother moved to another suburb. A short time afterwards Francine enrolled at an Art College in Paris and went to stay with her aunt in the suburb of Malakoff. Francine occasionally went back to visit her father, who had become very remorseful that his philandering had cost him his marriage. Francine's mother had by now returned to Leeds to look after her widowed father in his late eighties and for the young Frenchwoman she remained in contact by mail with her mother. After the sudden death of her father from a heart attack, Francine had made the journey to England.

She had been looking forward to being reunited with her mother. There was a sadness about her that came to the fore now and again. Having lost her father and been estranged from her mother for so long, she had become quite self-reliant and independent; she had an air of maturity about her that gave her an edge beyond her years.

Finally at the end of the three weeks Francine came to the time when she would journey to Leeds. Cynthia, who by now had become firm friends with Francine, took the car and drove her to the station at St Austell where she would take the train to London and then make another connection to Leeds. Freddie waved to the two girls as they drove off and then he went inside the house to make an important telephone call.

Colonel Brindmarsh received the phone call from Freddie. In the conversation that followed Freddie told him of the young lady he had just met, she was heading up to Yorkshire to enlist in the WAAF as a radio operator and knew Paris really well. Freddie told the colonel that not only did Francine speak French and English fluently, but at her school in Marseilles she had also learned German and spoke that language quite proficiently.

"It could be that Francine might be able to help you in the operations of the Circle or may be even in another intelligence capacity. With her firsthand knowledge of Paris, she could be a great asset in the backroom directing the agents."

Brindmarsh was definitely interested, but not in the capacity that Freddie had suggested. The ever-astute colonel considered the possibility of perhaps using Francine in an operational capacity amongst the Circle agents in France. He was wily enough not to admit it though.

"Well, I'll keep that in mind, Freddie. If and when she joins the WAAF I'll get her supervisors at the radio operations training school to send me a detailed report on her progress. There's a Wing Commander I know, I'll be in touch with him during the week and I'll get him to keep an eye out for her."

When the colonel put down the phone he smiled to himself. He had deliberately misled Freddie who he knew would be angry if he knew the real intentions he had in mind for Francine. Always assuming of course if war begun. There was so much talk about it. In his profession he had to prepare himself and his colleagues well in advance for it.

Francine travelled on to Leeds where she had a very happy reunion with her mother. She found her mother living in a terraced house in Harehills. It had been the home that Francine's mother had spent the earliest years of her life in Leeds. The house itself was pleasant enough, and had a warmth about it. It was hard for Francine to imagine her mother as a child playing on this cobblestone street, and running up and down the coal slag heap at the end of it, getting covered in dust from head to foot until her own mother got cross and would order her down.

The house had two floors with a very steep but short staircase. The front room had a hearth fire permanently burning it seemed, with a settee and armchair on one side and dining room table and chairs on the other. There was a snug feeling about the fire that seemed to echo the warmth of the whole house and her mother's character. An old crockery cupboard in the same room held cups, saucers and plates dating back to the age of Queen Victoria. There was a door in this room that led out to the cobblestone road on the other side. It was always unlocked. At breakfast time the milkman would knock, then enter, and place the milk on the sideboard, tipping his hat politely and saying cheerily in the broadest Yorkshire accent of all, "G' morning all, right dreary day. Nice t' see you all. Bit o' sun t' morrow, wiv a bit a luck. Cheerio now." *They were delightful, these Yorkshire people,* thought Francine.

Her old Granddad, getting close to ninety and as deaf as an oak tree, sat by the fire all day. Poor old fellow. Every time Francine's mother spoke to him she would have to repeat herself several times. Sometimes the dear old man would give a reply that had nothing to do with her mother's question. One day she heard her mother say to him at least four times, "Cup o' tea, Dad? Would you like a cup of tea, Dad?" To which he replied, "No, thanks, I've been twice this morning."

Francine was further amused when her mother told her that in the fierce winter days when the snow was thick and heavy on the ground outside, that her old dad for fear of catching a chill in the draughty upstairs bathroom, would sometimes in the morning sit in the tin bath in front of the fire and would greet pleasantly the milkman or the insurance man carrying on a conversation about how Leeds United played the previous Saturday. From his tin bath Francine's mother pointed out that the old man could talk in his younger days on any subject from soccer to politics with the impassioned oratory skill of a labour politician like Aneurin Bevan.

The Yorkshire people that Francine met were hard-working and very good-natured people. She got on well with them as she had done the Cornish villagers. Sometimes Francine's mother would speak with sadness about the breakup of the marriage and the death of her husband. When she had first greeted Francine, her first words apart from, "By gum, lass, it's good to see yer," had been, "Ah, I never noticed till now just how like your French dad you are. You've got his good looks t' be sure." In this her mother seriously underestimated her. Francine had inherited her Yorkshire mother's genial nature and a good sense of proportion about things in general too.

Unaware that on joining the Woman's Auxiliary Air Force, her every moment would be studied, Francine went ahead and enlisted being accepted as a radio operator. She was stationed in Bridlington and often in that year of 1939 went to Leeds on weekend leave to be with her mother. The two would often go and visit relatives in Scarborough, Bradford and Barnsley. Francine found that apart from several aunts, uncles and cousins, she also had quite a few great-aunts and great-uncles to get to know. It was all new and invigorating to her.

The Wing Commander that Colonel Brindmarsh knew had been alerted to the fact that he had a potential intelligence agent within his ranks. During the months heading up to September 1939, unbeknown to Francine her career was well-documented. Francine's superiors were studying her far more than the usual recruits. She had initiative and a quiet authority that would have marked her for a position of responsibility, that was easily identifiable by her officers. The remarkable thing was that Francine managed to retain her essential femininity at all times. Even that was a quality which, used correctly, could be an asset for the tasks that Colonel Brindmarsh had earmarked her for.

Then came the day that everyone had dreaded. In September 1939 Germany troops entered Poland. People everywhere waited in trepidation for the outcome. The British Ambassador to Germany, Sir Neville Henderson, upon instructions from the Prime Minister

Neville Chamberlain delivered a message to the German Foreign Office demanding immediate withdrawal of German troops from Poland. It was bluntly put. It read clearly:

> "If His Majesty's Government has not received satisfactory assurances of the cessation of all aggressive action against Poland, and the withdrawal of German troops from that country by eleven o'clock British Summer Time, from that time a state of war will exist between Great Britain and Germany."

★★★

In Palestine on the Kibbutz Jezarat the news had been greed with anger by Leon, who complained bitterly to Nathan and Melissa. "My beloved Poland," he roared with fury. "For how much longer must people and my country suffer!" Melissa and Nathan could only sympathise as Leon staggered away into the fields, his fury raging through him like a blazing scrub-fire.

★★★

Freddie Miller, in anticipation of the coming conflict, had not waited for the inevitable. The previous month he had rejoined the army and was now, for the second time in his life, a Commissioned Officer in his Majesty's forces. He was home for a few days on leave with Cynthia, and the two of them sat together in their cottage in Cornwall waiting for the wireless broadcast that Prime Minister Neville Chamberlain would be making in response to the situation.

Colonel Brindmarsh sat in his flat resting his chin on his hands that were clasped together. He hoped that all his planning, organisation and strategies would never be used for in his heart, although he was a sound military man, he was very much an anti-war officer. He believed more in the role of the army as a peace-keeping force and a defensive organisation. He disliked war and the resulting consequences of it, now a broadcast would commit the world to the conflict.

Francine was also at home on leave with her mother. The young Frenchwoman looked splendid in her air force uniform. Far from a uniform diminishing her haute couture European appearance, it, in fact, enhanced her greatly.

Then Neville Chamberlain began to speak to the nation. In their separate locations on September 3rd, 1939, the small group of people whose destinies were invisibly linked listened to the sombre tones of the British Prime Minister.

"I am speaking to you from the cabinet room of 10 Downing Street. This morning the British Ambassador in Berlin handed the German Government the final note stating that, unless we heard from them by eleven o'clock that they were prepared at once to withdraw their troops from Poland, a state of war would exist between us. I have to tell you now that no such undertaking has been received and, consequently, we are now at war with Germany."

Brindmarsh sat at his desk staring straight ahead of him and then looked up at a chart of Europe on the wall alongside him. There would be positions to be plotted and names to be added to the chart. It was going to be the start of the imperious activities of the Companions of the Circle.

Freddie Miller looked at his lovely wife, Cynthia. After one of the happiest periods in both their lives they were to be parted. Freddie stood up almost in a manner of salutation. Now he was a colonel in the British Army Intelligence Corps who would be, once again, in the thick of things. It was an ominous thought. What lay ahead now? Would it all be over in a matter of months? Would it drag on for years? And looking down at Cynthia, one other question troubled him: would his marriage survive? She was a jewel in his life.

★★★

In Leeds, Yorkshire, Francine, her mother and grandfather had all been listening intently. Francine's mother had switched the wireless off at the end of the broadcast. It was at that instant that the grandfather stirred dozily in his seat by the fire. His deafness and weakening perception of things as usual made him misinterpret the announcement by Neville Chamberlain.

"Is the Kaiser stirring up trouble then?" The poor man still lived in the past.

A slight smile crept over Francine's lips. Her mother raised her eyebrows towards the ceiling with an amused look on her face. "Nothing for you to worry about, Dad," she said, tapping him gently on his shoulder. "Dear old fellow your granddad," she remarked to Francine as she poured each of them a good strong cup of tea. She handed Francine a cup and then stood back and looked at her. For a moment her eyes seemed to be brimming over with tears. Then, in the quiet of the room, the only noise being the beat of a large wall clock, she spoke to her daughter in a voice that quivered slightly indicating hidden emotion. "Lass, I'm so proud of you. You've grown into a fine young lady. Better than I ever dreamed a daughter of mine would." She sat down in the armchair next to Francine. "You know I always loved your dad, don't you?" Francine nodded. "Yes, he was a bit of a lad your old French Dad. Swept me right off my dancing feet with his charm, and that voice of his." There was sadness in her voice. "I right loved him, I did." And then after a pause she said, "Well, lass, it's just you and me and your deaf old granddad there. When the war starts proper like n'all, promise you'll take the damndest care of yourself and come home safely from wherever they send you."

"I promise, Mum" she said gently, and then with a tone of chirpiness she added, "I'm not the daughter of a grand Yorkshire lady for nothing." With a wink in her eye, and a dash of humour, she said, in a mock Yorkshire accent that she was very fond of emulating, "Bah gum that's rairt you know, lass."

★★★

At the Kibbutz Jezarat when the news finally arrived there Nathan, Melissa and Leon stood huddled outside gazing up at the night sky. In the light of the events of the past decade the only surprise was that it had taken as long as this for the conflict to eventuate. Melissa was the first to echo her sentiments.

"I knew that this would happen, but I feel such disbelief that it really has begun."

Leon was more scathing in his remarks. "After the first war you would have thought they would have learned their lesson. But no! The bastards still make war. And the people of the world who least offend, the people of Poland, our race – the Jews, and the innocent onlookers, we are the ones who ultimately suffer."

"We must bear up," said Nathan. "History has shown that the downtrodden races are the ones who continue to survive. For the sake of humanity we must."

Leon looked at him with undisguised affection but there was doubt in his voice. "You speak with such certainty, Nathan. Well, we will see my friend. We will see what history has in store for us all," and then as he had spoken the night air seemed to take on a sudden chill.

Nineteen

1940-1945

"We shall fight on the beaches, we shall fight on the landing grounds, we shall fight in the fields and in the streets, we shall fight in the hills; we shall never surrender." The stirring words came from the new Prime Minister, Winston Churchill, on June 4th 1940. He had spoken after the evacuation of Dunkirk had taken place and thousands of British troops had been brought home by all manner of boats. The German Army had swept across the Low Countries gradually swallowing France up under its grasp.

Cynthia heard the speech at Yelverton in Devon where she was now a WRAF driver. With Freddie away in London working with Brindmarsh in operations, she had decided to make her own contribution to the war. During the coming months Cynthia saw many of the RAF pilots come and go. The nights before the fighter pilots flew out were always memorable. In the NAAFI many of them realising that there may not be a tomorrow evening, always lived that night as if it were their last. For some it would be. Someone would take over the piano and play like a virtuoso. Someone else or a group of excited aircrew would gather around a WRAF, kiss them, consume a beer and in a smoky NAAFI canteen above the tinkle of a piano and the chorus of voices, the drone of aircraft engines leaving the airstrip to go into conflict would soon be heard.

For purposes of morale the surviving aircraft did not return to the same air force station. If the raid had been one in which many victims had been claimed, the sight of a few bombers returning would not be of inspiration to a new aircrew about to outgo on a new mission. Therefore it was always a mystery to Cynthia when she thought of the pilots who had been merrymaking in the NAAFI, the night before. She wondered how many of them had survived.

One morning Cynthia was driving a lorry close to the airstrip when she saw some of the ground staff attending to an aircraft of another squadron that had returned that morning from a mission. One man was literally washing out the back cockpit of the aircraft, which had been shot to shreds. The hosepipe water that was being flushed around the cockpit was dripping red in colour from the fuselage. That glance at the aircraft disturbed Cynthia immensely. She shuddered at the thought of the fearful duels that would have taken place over the English Channel the previous night, and she put her foot down on the clutch to change gear and park the lorry.

Cynthia entered the canteen on a very cold and wintry morning. The wind seemed to howl across the airstrip that day. She suddenly felt very dizzy and took a hold of herself. Her appetite was ravenous that morning too. These were a strange combination of feelings she was experiencing. The symptoms were so obvious. Ever since Freddie's last leave a few months before she had wondered about her condition. Now she was certain that she was pregnant.

Taking a plate of healthy-looking bacon and eggs, she made her way to a table. She had almost demolished the food in a matter of minutes, as hungry as she was, when she saw a WRAF enter the canteen who she recognised instantaneously. It was Francine who looked absolutely superb. A couple of RAF officers and some aircrew men were right behind her like wolves poised to pounce on their prey.

Francine seemed to turn so that her eyes directly met Cynthia's. The two women smiled with delight and embraced happily. They sat down, eager to talk once again.

"Why, I had no idea you had joined up too," Francine said to Cynthia.

"Oh, yes. Just over a year now. I've been driving trucks."

"And Freddie? How is he?"

"He's with British Intelligence in uniform, of course. Up at Whitehall most of the time, although it is rumoured he's to be sent to Cairo."

The two women appraised each other mutually. From being girls of the feckless 1930s to servicewomen of the 1940s, there were changes in them. Cynthia seemed to sum up Francine in a very concise statement.

"There is an absolute rightness about you in that uniform. It suits you so well. Even the colour too, Francine."

"Ah, it is not the style they'll be wearing on the Champs Élysees at the moment." She replied, referring to the recent occupation of France by the Nazis.

"That is true. At least your mother is near you."

"I have enjoyed meeting her and my granddad in Leeds, and so many other relatives I did not know I had. I felt quite at home there. It's strange, you know, when I heard I was being sent down here, I thought I would surprise you with a visit and now you have surprised me instead by being here. I am here only for a short while, I believe. Two weeks, possibly longer. Just for an operator's course."

"You'll like it here. It's lovely countryside and there are some lovely old pubs around." Cynthia stopped short of telling Francine something she was bursting to tell someone. Finally she could not resist it any longer. "Guess what?" Francine looked at her curiously. Cynthia's face was as bright as an orange. "I think I'm going – going to have a baby."

A look of exaltation spread across Francine's face. She was obviously delighted for her friend. "How wonderful!" She leaned across the table and kissed her friend on the cheek in a congratulatory fashion. "Have you told Freddie yet?"

"No," Cynthia smiled. "I'll be ringing him tonight. It'll be quite a surprise for him! But I'm delighted. A pity though in a way, as I've just got used to driving so many trucks here. And I feel, in my own way, I've been making a little bit of a contribution to the service."

"The role of women in the Armed Services should not be underestimated, Cynthia," Francine said, almost defensively. "Everyone is making a contribution. You have probably done a great deal in your own way."

Cynthia felt some pride well within her at Francine's comments. "Thank you. That is a nice thing to say. Oh, I'm not selling us females short, my darling." There was a tone of joviality in her voice. "My goodness me. No! I'm a bit far ahead of my time in my belief that in war we are on equal terms with our men, and by golly, heaven knows we need to be. We need to support them with every fibre we can muster. I've seen some of those fighter planes coming back from missions with the guts shot out of them. This morning before I came in I saw a plane that had half the tail hanging off. Only God could have guided that one in." In her own way sensing as she always did when a conversation was becoming too serious Cynthia quickly added a dash of humour. "Talking of women, and *they* are," Cynthia acknowledged some pilots and a navigator at a nearby table giving them admiring glances. "I think they're mentally undressing us." They both grinned broadly. "No, seriously, talking of women, one day there will be women pilots and equal pay and equal grading in jobs, believe me."

"You sound like that suffragette in English history. What was her name – er?"

"Emiline Pankhurst."

"Of course. I read about her in a book at my mother's home."

"I think one of those officers there has rather taken a liking to you," Cynthia whispered, her eyes sparkling with wicked amusement.

"What are these men like here?" asked Francine curious about the aircrew on this station. "I have only met people in administrative jobs so far. These airmen. The officers?"

Cynthia now became more serious and was genuinely sincere. "They are good men. The best," she paused to admire the many men who were pouring into the canteen and then she turned her eyes back to Francine. "Years ago when I was a teenager and out in India in the 20s, going to dances and functions with all those spoiled brat officers, all with high opinions of themselves and low opinions of everyone else, I wouldn't have given twopence for any of them. Freddie was the only one who was worth his salt because he came up the hard way from a humble background. But now when I look at some of these fellows who go out night after night on ghastly missions never knowing if they're going to see another day or not, these officers have got more courage than I have ever imagined. And I'll tell you what, God bless them all. Like the song says, Francine, and I don't want to sound hammy or clichéd, bless 'em all. The long, the short –" Cynthia smiled at one of them passing by, "– and the tall."

For the next few weeks whenever Cynthia and Francine had the chance, and when their respective duties allowed, they spent time together. Cynthia would have to leave the force soon and return to Cornwall to have her baby. It had been only a brief reunion but a pleasant one. Over a pint of beer in one of the locals one night, Francine told her friend that she had been asked to report to Whitehall the next week, although the purpose of her posting there was unknown as yet.

"Whitehall?" Exclaimed Cynthia. "Gosh, you'll be able to say hullo to Freddie before he leaves for Cairo. Now what on earth will they need you for in Whitehall? Must be something special?"

"Oh well, I will just wait and see," Francine murmured in a so-so manner, taking a sip of a strong Devonshire brew in a pint mug. It was obvious though that she was a little bemused by her apparent posting to this important area.

Twenty

At Whitehall the following week when Francine reported for duty she found herself allotted with several other WRAF radio operators to an operations office under the watchful eye of a Wing Commander. She didn't realise that in the office where she was situated, not only her immediate supervisor was watching her, but through a double faced mirror so too were the uniformed figures of Colonel Brindmarsh of the Special Operations Executive of the Secret Service and Freddie Miller, now a Colonel also but in the British Army Intelligence Corps.

The two men studied her with interest. Several times Francine came very close to the mirror to pick up a codebook or a map reference and she would gaze into the glass completely unaware of her observers. There was a look on Brindmarsh's face that Freddie couldn't comprehend. He was given to wondering just what the wily Scotsman was thinking. One thing was abundantly clear to Freddie, however, and which was obvious to him: Brindmarsh had something in mind for Francine other than mere background work. He looked at Freddie in a way that was prompting him to say something.

"What are you thinking?" Freddie probed him gently.

"Exactly what I have thought all along." Brindmarsh answered him in a short sentence that was infuriating to Freddie for it revealed nothing. They turned around and began walking to another office.

"You have something else in mind for Francine, don't you?"

"Look at it this way," said Brindmarsh, opening the door of an office and closing it behind Freddie. "Francine Macé knows every contour of every side of Paris. Why, you told me yourself that she's a painter whose speciality is capturing every striking feature of Paris on canvas. She is fluent in French and English. She has a few relatives in France, knows her way around and her appearance – marvellous! That young lady has a look of vulnerability about her, but as I suspect, with so many sensitive people, a great strength beneath the surface."

Freddie was beginning to get impatient. "Look, Frank—"

Brindmash interjected sharply. He did not like being interrupted. "And she's a trained radio operator. I want to interview her and see if Francine Macé is the stuff of which agents are made of."

Freddie was stunned. "Good grief! When I recommended her to you, I thought she would be useful in helping to plot details for your Parisian people."

"I am going to put the idea to her." Brindmarsh sat down at his desk and reached for the telephone. "I'm going to have her sent down to me. Would you wait in the next room but listen in to the conversation."

Nodding to himself in bemusement, Freddie went into the next room and sat in a chair beside the door. He heard Brindmarsh say, "Have Francine Macé sent down to me." Brindmarsh put the telephone down and shortly afterwards Francine came along to the office. After the formalities of saluting, Brindmarsh said to her, "Sit down, Miss Macé, I would like to talk to you on a job that I'd like to offer you. Please relax. Feel at ease to ask questions if you feel the need."

Francine eyed the Scottish colonel warily. Since arriving at Whitehall the day before she had sensed a purpose for this posting. Freddie listened keenly from the other room. He could only imagine the expressions on the faces of each of them. Brindmarsh didn't beat about the bush. He came straight to the point "I'd like to ask you, Miss Macé, if you would consider an operational job with the Special Operations Executive?"

Francine's face became quite hard. She was gathering her thoughts before she could relax her composure. "What would this involve, sir?"

Brindmarsh leaned across the desk and gave her a reassuring smile. "It would involve working as a radio operator in occupied France, providing us with information and being the link between a certain resistance group and the Special Operations Executive."

"I – I am quite taken aback, sir. You must forgive me. This is quite a shock. Do you mean that I would, in effect, be an agent?"

"Yes." He looked at her. Francine was still trying to understand the substance of the matter. "Yes, Miss Macé, that is exactly what I am suggesting. It's entirely your decision but your credentials for the job are excellent and your background knowledge of Paris is perfect. This is a confidential matter, you understand. Not a word to anyone, please. If you decide to accept this position there will be some vigorous tests to undergo. Believe me, your help would be in the national interest." Brindmarsh was silent for a moment to allow the impact to sink in. Then Francine spoke.

"Sir, I do not have to accept this job, do I?" She sounded firm and in control.

The colonel showed a distinct look of disapproval. "No, you do not," he said in a voice that clearly echoed his feelings.

"Well, sir, I would like to consider the matter. Would I be transferred from the Air Force to your staff in the event of my acceptance?"

"You in fact would become a member of the SOE. I would arrange for you to sign the appropriate enlistment papers."

Francine gave the impression that she was thinking hard, and then she brought up a few points that were on her mind. There could not be any doubt that as Brindmarsh had previously assessed to Freddie that same day, beneath Francine's very attractive veneer, was a woman of great strength. "Sir, I think that in all probability I will accept this appointment." Brindmarsh's expression changed immediately. He was undoubtedly pleased. "However, I realise that my life would be in danger constantly."

"That is correct." Brindmarsh answered her honestly. "If you are caught by the enemy you must expect the worst. I cannot pretend anything else."

"I have a widowed mother in Leeds who gets by on a very small amount. If I die during the course of my duties," Francine was leaning forward in her chair looking directly into Colonel Brindmarsh's eye for an honest answer to the point it was disconcerting, "would any pensionable rights, gratuity pay, and any benefit be transferred to her name?"

The colonel, normally ice-cold, showed signs of sympathy. "That will be arranged."

"Before I say yes or no to this job, I am not foolish, know someone chose me for this job or put me forward to you.

"You are stuff that agents are made of!" Brindmarsh exclaimed at her inquisitive nature. "I can see I've made a good choice. But to answer your question it all began when you were rescued from the tanker that sunk off the coast of Cornwall."

"You know about that?" Francine seemed surprised.

"Oh yes – and you stayed with a couple called the Millers in Mousehole for a while."

"That's right. They were nice people, Freddie and Cynthia. I liked them very much."

"Freddie and I have been friends and colleagues for many years." A look of surprise appeared on Francine's face. Brindmarsh instinctively knew just what the young French lady in front of him was thinking. Francine was asking herself, had she been used? Were Freddie and Cynthia not merely the friendly people she thought them to be? But Francine was put at ease by the colonel who had realised she would be considering this fact. "Freddie is a man of integrity. He did not use you in any way. They were genuinely fond of you, I know that from various conversations I had with Freddie. He was working for me in a civilian capacity – monitoring the activities of a particular group of agents who shall be nameless at this stage – and he mentioned to me that he had a French lady staying with him who had expressed an interest in joining the Woman's Royal Air Force as a radio operator. Freddie did say that you could be of help in our backroom operations. It was actually my idea that we could use your abilities in an operational capacity."

"I see." Francine believed him for he projected sincerity.

Brindmarsh rose from his seat and walked to the door behind which Freddie has been listening to the conversation.

"Freddie was as surprised as you were when I told him that we could use you in an operational role. You can ask him for yourself if you like?" and with that Brindmarsh swung the door open to reveal Freddie Miller standing there in his uniform. He smiled meekly at Francine who stood up in surprise.

"It's true, Francine," he said. Then, as if to emphasise the options that were available, Freddie added, "As Colonel Brindmarsh said it is entirely your decision. You do not have to if you don't want to. The choice is yours."

Francine did not show any signs of annoyance at having been singled out for this assignment. In fact her feelings were exactly the opposite.

"I would be very proud to go." She said, beaming with pride, and the tone of her voice and the look on her face, left neither of the two men as to any doubt that she meant it. At this stage Francine had looked on the assignment more as an adventure than anything. In her own mind she was quite unprepared for what lay ahead. The series of tests and exercises that the Special Operations Executive put her through soon changed all that. In the latter months of 1940 she learned of the responsibilities that she would soon be facing.

Just before Freddie's departure for Cairo, he informed Francine of the 'certain resistance group', as Brindmarsh had so aptly put it, that she would be liaising with in occupied France. Francine would be working with the French section of the Companions of the Circle whose role in wartime had obviously changed from its peacetime manoeuvres. Whereas in peacetime the group had worked for the safety of the Jewish people, now that Europe was embroiled in war, they still had the same intensions but, in addition to this, the Circle was also helping allied servicemen and members of other underground forces. Brindmarsh was directing much of the operation from Whitehall.

After being made fully conversant of her new duties, Francine prepared herself for her journey back to her homeland of France, now under the grip of the German Army. She spent some leave with her mother and grandfather in Leeds and then travelled down south again to an RAF station just outside of London from where she would fly across to Northern France.

It was early in 1941 when the aircraft left London. Down on the aerodrome many of the ground staff stood around in great coats blowing cigarette smoke in the frosty night air and stamping their boots up and down, and rubbing their cold hands together. For Francine this was a night that would be indelible in her memory. Freddie Miller was now in Cairo, but had sent a personal message through Colonel Brindmarsh, which he delivered to her on the night of departure. Francine was warming herself with some hot soup and talking quite amiably to the colonel who she had never felt any animosity too. To be exact Francine quite admired Brindmarsh. She found him to be a gentleman and rather than being annoyed at having been plucked from relative obscurity to perform a job of national interest, it was exciting and thrilling for her, and she felt privileged to have been chosen.

Colonel Brindmarsh, a man not given to showing emotion, still managed to give the appearance of being slightly cold but his guard dropped when after saying to her, "Good luck, my dear," he felt inclined to clasp her hand with both of his and add, "God bless you, my dear." An unusual remark, but somehow it only managed to emphasise the gravity of this mission.

The aircraft was soon flying away to its destination, and the RAF station at Northolt from where she had departed soon disappeared from view. It was a short flight across a blacked-out Southern England, and an English Channel the colour of black metal. When France came into view, one of the crew fitted her out with a parachute. She was the only person aboard the tiny aircraft apart from four other crewmembers.

"Nearly there now. Brace yourself, sweetheart," said the RAF corporal who had strapped the parachute onto her. The plane began to drop in altitude now. The change in the engine was noticeable and for the first time Francine felt slightly nervous. Almost spontaneously the crew yelled out, "We're here now. Your checkpoint is below. Good luck, God speed." Francine was standing up, ready to jump. Down below in the fields one of the members of the Companions of the Circle was waiting behind a clump of trees to greet her and escort her to Paris.

The corporal opened the hatch. Francine looked nervously left to right and then she jumped. The air came whooshing up around her and she felt the bitterly cold night air sting her face. She fell with all the velocity of a lead weight and she reached for her ripcord. No sooner had she pulled it than it seemed as if the sudden jerk as the parachute opened had created a cushion of air for her to ride down upon.

It was only a short time afterwards that she hit the ground. From out of the shadows of some trees a member of the French Resistance came rushing out to help her. For a moment the two looked up into the dark night sky as the aircraft did a complete circle and headed back to England.

Once Francine had been released from the parachute, she and the Frenchman ran quickly from the open exposed field into the shadows. Francine's mission had now begun in earnest.

Twenty-one

Cairo was a fascinating city filled with colour and people, sights and sounds that made Colonel Freddie Miller ache with nostalgia for his days as a newsreel cine cameraman and commentator. In 1942 there were a diversity of foreign servicemen there. Everywhere there were the British soldiers of various regiments and the forces from the dominions. Along with the fez, and the djellaba, could be seen the army beret, the glengarry and the slouch hat. There was quite a mixture.

The public transport seemed to be bursting at the seams. Freddie was being driven by a soldier in an open-air jeep, and in the busy traffic of the Cairo thoroughfares he caught sight of a bus so full that some Arabs were literally falling off.

The markets were bustling and the traffic was chaotic, coming seemingly from all directions. A camel wandering loose with an enraged owner in tow walked in front of the jeep forcing the driver to slam the brakes with a sharp suddenness. Immediately behind a whole line of busy traffic began pressing their horns and shouting in Arabic. Freddie grinned as the wandering camel now became stationery and refused to move. Several irate Egyptians attempted to move it before the traffic became free flowing again. Then the jeep continued its journey.

Freddie gazed at the minarets and the mix of white, silver and grey buildings. When he had been told of his transfer to Cairo, he had been enormously surprised and indeed devastated. He had envisaged that his knowledge of the Circle would have merited him remaining at Whitehall for the duration of the war and working with Brindmarsh directing that area of intelligence. However, Brindmarsh was keen to co-ordinate that part of the work himself and had decided that Freddie's sound abilities would be beneficial in operations in the Middle East.

Here in Cairo Freddie was responsible for intelligence work in the Suez Canal and Ismaila zone. It seemed that there had been some intrusion into the work of the British Army in that area and some spies had been relaying information of the defence capabilities to the enemy in Berlin. Through a complex network Freddie had tracked down the German agent, who had turned out to be an Egyptian employed by the British on one of their bases. Without deliberately blowing the man's cover he had arranged to keep the man informed. Although the secret agent, who had strong sympathies with the axis power, was unaware of it, the information he was now being supplied with was completely false, and he happily supplied his superiors with the details. Every move he made was being monitored carefully by Freddie's staff and it would only be a matter of time before that complete espionage ring would be rounded up in one carefully rehearsed operation.

Brindmarsh had been delighted with Freddie's planning and the deceptive information he had passed on to the German forces. It was possible that Freddie could help operations in the Far East. Singapore had fallen under the onslaught of the Japanese military and there had been fierce fighting as far afield as Indonesia and New Guinea. Strategies and plans needed to be blueprinted to put into action attempts to save the lives of thousands of British and Commonwealth servicemen held in Prisoner of War camps under the fearful dominance of the Samurai. After a year in Cairo, Freddie was now expecting to be sent to Colombo in Ceylon where he would begin work on the Far East operations.

For the time being now that his work in Cairo was drawing to a close after long days and nights working he was enjoying the opportunity of looking round the city. So far he had seen some of the biggest mosques and minarets. He had been to the Pyramids and the Sphinx, and spent a day looking around the huge museum. That same afternoon he had to attend a meeting in another part of the city to arrange with some senior officers the final details for taking into captivity the spy ring who had been under surveillance.

The jeep turned a corner slowly and as it began to accelerate along a very narrow street Freddie saw a British Army private walking on one side. The private on seeing an officer saluted smartly. Freddie returned the salute and got a brief glimpse of the soldier's face. There was something startling familiar about the young man's face. Those features; surely he had seen him before. It was strange because the army private showed recognition of Freddie too, but the jeep had long gone past before each other's memory had been jogged.

Freddie after a moment of thought racking his brains to recall the man uttered to himself, "It couldn't be."

"Sorry, sir?" said the corporal driving the jeep.

"Only speaking out loud," smiled Freddie and then a thought flashed across his mind. "Tell me, corporal. That solder we passed, where would be he based?"

"I think with the regiment based a stone's throw from here, sir."

"I know him from somewhere. He's familiar. Do you know what time they have parade roll call in the morning?"

"Same as us, Sir."

Freddie pondered in his mind who the man was. He knew for sure, yet it all seemed so incredible. What was he doing in a British army uniform here in Cairo?

If they had slowed down in the jeep and bothered to stop, Freddie would have got the shock of his life for the young man in the uniform was Nathan Palmai. How Nathan had joined the British army was a story in itself.

★★★

In October 1941 Nathan was still working on the Kibbutz Jezarat when the British army, who had established themselves in Palestine, began to ask for volunteers from the various communities. With the possibility that the German army might invade, the offensive had to be built up and with thousands of Jewish lives at stake, the British regiments found themselves inundated with many volunteers. There were Austrians, Poles, German Jewish, all now party of the British forces in the Middle East.

The British army were accepting volunteers from the Kibbutzim of the age of nineteen and over. Service was to be for the duration of the emergency and for one year after the finish of the war.

To Nathan it was a superb opportunity to once again expand his horizons and with so many of his friends on the kibbutz joining up to protect the interests of their race, he took the initiative. He had been surprised when his regiment had moved to Egypt. It had given him the opportunity to study much of the history of the Arab people. He was forever learning. He had spent many days looking around the big museum in Cairo studying the preserved mummies, trying to understand the objectives of the Koran and learning about such things as Tutankhamen. Walking around the many winding streets he looked at every building and stall, every bazaar, and every landmark never missing a thing.

The sight of the officer had momentarily thrown him. He thought hard trying to recollect where he had seen the man before. If he had only known that the officer in the jeep was doing exactly the same.

The sun was scorching that afternoon and it was the type of heat that easily burns. Nathan could feel the effects on his soft white European skin. In his time in Palestine and then in Egypt he still had not got fully used to it. His face looked a golden brown in colour and very healthy in appearance.

During his service so far Nathan had at first felt a bit awkward at being a German Jew in a British regiment, but as time had worn on he had acclimatised himself to his unusual situation, and had made many friends amongst the soldiers. He espied one of them walking up some steps towards him mopping his brow. Nathan smiled at the solder who he called Private John for some reason. John was a cheerful Londoner who he had always found easy to talk to. Nathan had met him first in Palestine and here in Egypt, the two had been at the same barracks in Ismaila before coming up to Cairo. On free days the two had often gone for a ride in a jeep along the Suez Canal area and they had become quite good friends.

John at twenty-two was a couple of years older than Nathan. He had light brown hair cut in a typical Army short back and sides fashion. He was easily six feet in height and he had a big toothy smile and an infectious laugh that tended to be contagious in a group. A butcher by trade from South London, John had proved to be a model soldier. He smiled back at his friend and greeted him in his usual warm and friendly manner.

"Hullo, Nathan."

"Hullo, Private John. Warm, isn't it?"

"Cor. Blinkin' warm it is. I'm parched. Fancy a cold drink somewhere?"

Nathan licked his lips. He was feeling the heat too. "I was just thinking I could do with a nice cold lemonade."

"I tell you what, I'll buy you one. There's a bar just over there." He pointed out a small bar in an alleyway and they walked over to it. Once inside they found that apart from a few locals it was filled with servicemen cooling down beneath rotating fans and consuming lashings of drinks. John nodded to a couple he knew, a British solder and an Egyptian woman who was strikingly beautiful and sitting in an enclave at one side of the bar. He made his way through the rising cigarette smoke and the uniformed figures to get himself and Nathan a drink.

When he returned, he and Nathan sat at a table in one corner sipping on their drinks. Nathan looked round at the people in the bar. Turning to John and pointing to a group of soldiers, he asked, "Tell me, John, who are they?"

"You mean the couple over there?" John responded, thinking Nathan meant the couple in the enclave. "That's Charles and Alitat."

"No, not them, John. The soldiers at the bar making all the noise. I don't recognise the accent."

"Oh them," John grinned as he sipped his beer. "They're Aussies. Yeah you can't mistake them." There was a good nature in his voice. He obviously liked them. "The Australian blokes like a few drinks and a good time."

"Australians. Oh, I see," murmured Nathan, assessing them.

"I met a lot of them in Tobruk," said John. "They were a hardy bunch." Nathan looked at them intrigued. The Australian soldiers were noisy but jovial, and the conversation was so loud that virtually everyone in the bar was listening. They were talking about a wide range of subjects but the idiom, the slang, and the vocabulary they used, was unlike anything Nathan had ever heard before. The Australians were talking about 'the bush', the outback, the big wet, abo's going walkabout, stockmen and drovers. All of these suntanned, well-weathered men fitted out in Khaki shorts and shirt, and the slouch hat so identifiable with the diggers as they were affectionately known, were talking in a blaze of nostalgia about their homeland. They had all been convivially drinking and were in that particular state between merriment and inebriation.

An English solder from another table went to the bar and ordered some drinks in a broad Geordie accent. Next to him a digger turned round on hearing the accent and said, "Bloody pom!"

The Geordie glared back at him. "Who asked you, big mouth?" In a couple of seconds the two men began throwing punches at each other. Then it seemed as if all the English and Australian soldiers in the bar decided now was the perfect opportunity to liven up proceedings.

All and sundry joined in, fighting each other not so much in a vicious fashion, but more like a bunch of teenagers letting off steam at a dance hall on a Saturday night. It seemed to be a pretty evenly matched fight. A few Scotsmen decided to get in on the act too. They seemed to be enjoying themselves immensely trading punches.

Nathan and John sat in the corner watching with amusement. John took a sip on his drink and remarked with a chuckle, "Don't worry about it, Nathan, they're just rehearsing for the real thing."

Nathan just half smiled and said, "Oh," although there was a gleam of humour in his eyes. The two of them were sitting by the door and an Australian sergeant from the AIF came in, grinning broadly from ear to ear. He stood by the table where Nathan and John sat and smiled good-naturedly at them.

"Hullo, you blokes," the sergeant said cheerfully. "Sitting out of this one then, boys?" They smiled back at him. The man stood with his hands on his hips observing them all and nodded his head from side to side. "What a pack of drongos!" he chuckled, "I'll wind this one up, I reckon," and then he shouted out at the top of his voice cupping his hands together around his mouth, "C'mon, you blokes! C'mon! C'mon! Knock it off! Knock it off, you blokes! There's some military police down the road! You don't want to ruin a good afternoon's drinking, do you? What are youse? A bunch of dills?"

At this the fight broke up and the men started shaking hands, tousling each other's hair and buying rounds of drinks. The Aussies and 'poms' suddenly became good mates!

"Geez, Serg, you're a spoil sport," said one of the Australian soldiers jokingly. The sergeant laughed and got himself a drink. He wandered back to where Nathan and John were sitting.

"Would you blokes mind if I joined you?" He asked pleasantly.

"Feel free," said John, and at this the Australian soldier drew up a chair and sat down. The soldier was about twenty-eight with sunburnt hair the colour of straw and brown eyes that looked straight at the person he was talking to. He had a pleasant manner about him. Yet when he spoke in an accent that was more related to colour – chocolate brown so Nathan thought – he spoke with a gut feeling and directness that was almost abrasive in its tone.

He took his glass of cold beer and sank the complete contents in a few seconds it seemed without swallowing. He wiped his mouth and said, "Geez, I needed that. The name's Ted McTaggart." Shaking John's hand, he asked him, "You'd be?"

"John – John Dunn is the name," replied the Londoner cheerfully.

"Well, I'm pleased to meet you, John. I know you're a pom obviously, but where are you from then, mate? You'd be a Londoner, would you?"

"That's right. I was born in Wandsworth, brought up in Clapham, although my old man was a butcher and we moved around a bit. I spent a lot of time down in Worthing on the coast of Sussex, too. That was a nice spot. I used to be a greengrocer's delivery boy there. I used to ride a bike around the Sussex Downs taking groceries to a lot of the local villages. Between '36 and '39 right up to the time I joined up, I was living in Ealing, fairly close to London. I was a butcher. Then the war came."

"Is that right?" Ted McTaggart was genuinely interested in his new acquaintances. "I s'pose like most pommies you're a soccer fan, are you?"

"I was a Brentford supporter. You know about English football then?"

"Oh my word! I've seen games on the newsreels when I've been to the movies in Australia. Wouldn't miss it for the world. I know all about Chelsea and Tottenham Hotspur and Arsenal, and a lot of the great players. Me, though, I follow the rules game of footie in Australia."

"Rules?" inquired John, "What sort of game is rules?"

Nathan was sitting quietly listening. He hadn't escaped the notice of Ted who glanced at him occasionally as he spoke.

"Rules, John, is a bloody great game. It's played in my home state of Victoria. I come from Melbourne, you see, and the team I barrack for is the mighty Hawthorn. It's a combination of kicking, throwing and passing. There's a lot of skill in it." He turned to Nathan and smiling he shook his hand saying pleasantly, "I'm sorry, matey. I'm being real enthusiastic about my favourite subject, footie, and I haven't even asked you your name. I'm talking away with John here. What's your name mate?"

"I am Nathan Palmai." He replied.

"Nathan Palmai?" Ted repeated. "Doesn't sound like a pommie name to me. Come to think about it neither does your accent. Where are you really from, mate?"

There was a strange look of suspicion on his face as he studied Nathan. John was quick to see this and quickly cut in to speak for his friend. "Nathan joined us in Palestine. He is—"

"Let him speak for himself, John," said Ted abruptly but not impolitely.

"I was brought up in Berlin, Austria and Palestine. I joined the British Army in Palestine. I was sent from my home in Austria to a kibbutz before the Anschluss."

"Geez, that's interesting and you're—"

"Yes, I am Jewish." Nathan anticipated Ted's line of questioning.

"And where are your parents, matey?" Ted signalled to a passing waiter to replenish the drinks of the three of them.

"My parents, as far as I am able to make out, are in concentration camps. They were arrested and taken away at the time of the Anschluss of Austria. I was on my way to a kibbutz in Palestine at the time. Despite repeated efforts to find out, I have no idea where they are, or even if they are still alive."

"That's really rough," said Ted with considerable sympathy in his voice and by the look on his face there was no doubt that he meant what he said. The waiter came back with the drinks and each one took their glass. "Well that's no flamin' good at all. I'd like to toast you blokes. John, it's nice to meet you." He clinked his glass with John's. "To you, John. I'd like to wish you the best and all the safety through this war, and God be with you, mate." John and Nathan smiled then Ted turned to Nathan and said in a tone of absolute sincerity, "And to our mate here, Nathan, I don't know what life has in store for you but many of us, my mates over there, and all the blokes fighting in this war – we all know what you're up against. And in spirit at least we'll be right behind you all the way. That's what we're fighting for. Freedom for everyone." Ted raised his glass to Nathans. "To you, friend, your family and your people. God bless you, me old mate."

Each of them clinked the other's glass and took a sip. Nathan looked very touched. He was impressed by the depth of Ted Mctaggart's compassion and conviction in his words.

"Thank you, Ted," said Nathan. "I feel I am with two fine men here. My friend, John, and you from Australia."

"You've got a Scottish name though, Ted." John pointed out.

"Yeah, I've got a bit of the Celt in me all right, that's for sure. My old man was a Scot from Glasgow. He fought in the Boer War. He met my mother – who was Irish incidentally, from Dublin – in Camden Town in London. They came out to Melbourne in 1910. Dad worked on the trams for many years. He drove trams on the St Kilda route mainly."

"Your home is still in Melbourne?" asked Nathan.

"Well, like you I moved around a bit. My mum and dad and my two sisters are still in Melbourne. I got a bit of the wanderlust when I was in my teens. At the time there was a Depression on and it was tough going trying to get work so I moved on up to Sydney. Well this was back in '31 and things weren't a lot better there. I'll never forget it: thousands out of work, blokes queuing up for work, people sleeping out in parks, factories laying people off every day. By a stroke of luck I managed to get some work as a packer in a meat works in Auburn. This lasted till '32 when I literally walked off the job. The drongos who ran the place were telling us who to vote for in the state election. The Premier of the State then, a bloke called Jack Lang – they used to call him the Big Fella – got into a little bit of strife and the governor sacked him. I forget what for. I think the Government had a loan from the Bank of England and because of the Depression he wanted to delay paying the interest. Something like that. Anyway an election was called and in our pay packet the flaming management of the meat works enclosed a note telling us if we vote for Lang there wouldn't be a job for us. Well, I'll tell you what I couldn't give a bugger for any political party but I'd be blowed if I'd be told who I should vote for. So I walked into the office and told the boss what he could do with his job. And he says to me, 'Where are you going to work then, son? There's a Depression on.' And I said I'll survive. The next thing I know I'm heading up to Queensland. I ended up getting work cane cutting in a place near Rockhampton. After a while I moved on from there and I worked on a cattle station in the west of the state."

Nathan and John were listening intently. They had never met a character like Ted before. "What is this place Queensland like?" asked Nathan with a burning interest.

Ted's eyes shone with delight. "Queensland? It's my home now, mate. It's a beaut place. Yeah I've been a cane cutter, a cattle drover in the West and for a while, before the war, I was a linesman with the Postmaster Generals Department in Cairns. I always enjoyed living in Queensland, mate. Sometimes I'd get up in the morning and the sun would be shining so bright and I'd go down the back garden and pick a banana off the tree. There's so much there: cattle, sugar cane, tobacco and dairy farming. There's pineapples, and citrus fruits, and fish! You should see what they've got in the way of fish along the barrier reef. Marlin, Coral trout;

it's a fisherman's paradise." Ted blew a ring of smoke from his cigarette. He had been delighted to talk to someone on a subject he was so fond of.

Nathan had been impressed by the detailed description of his land of which he had previously known nothing. "You are a great ambassador for Queensland, Ted."

The Australian was the centre of attention and enjoying it. "Not only Queensland. I've been all around Australia and I reckon it's all right. I was over in England in '40, and Syria, Crete and right across North Africa, but there's no place like Aussie to me. Mind you," he turned to John with a smile, "I like England, John, and I like the poms – especially some of those rosy red-cheeked sheilas with the white, fair skin. Can't let you off free, though. I can't stand your beer, I don't like your weather and, even more, I don't like your cricketers. I found the poms a cheerful lot, though. Even after the Blitz and all the bombing, the English were out there giving each other a hand, pulling together like one big bloody family and I admired that, I really did. I found myself saying, 'Good on em a thousand times'. It's not fashionable to say it but by geez the poms are a brave, sturdy lot."

John could not help but admire Ted even though he had been slightly offensive in a jocular fashion about English weather and English cricketers. It was impossible not to warm to Ted McTaggart. He was open, honest, brash, friendly and humorous. Nathan could see similarities in the two men. Whereas John was a slightly shyer man, he too had a warm and friendly manner given to occasional brashness and earthy humour. Despite the difference in their accents, the Englishman and the Australian who sat with Nathan that afternoon were so similar in their ways and yet so diversely different people.

"Did you visit Glasgow when you were in England, Ted?" John asked.

"I had to," said Ted. "I wanted to. There was a lot of things I wanted to know about my mother and father. Where they came from, what their background was like." Ted was more pensive and thoughtful about his words. "I had some leave and I went up to Scotland to have a look at where my dad came from in Glasgow. It's strange, y'know, but I had no idea how tough it was. My old man was quite a straight sort of a bloke. I reckon that came from his upbringing. When he was a lad he joined the 1st Glasgow Boys Brigade, the first company in the world, it was run by the founder of the Brigade, Sir William A Smith, and my dad would often talk about it. For a bloke who liked the occasional drink, loved all kinds of sport and football, and had fought in the Boer War and years later went through the Gallipoli landings, he was a very moral man. He used to tell me what the object of the Boys Brigade was. They used to say it at parade meetings." Ted paused and recollected. "The object of the Boys Brigade shall be the advancement of Christ's Kingdom amongst boys and the promotion of habits of obedience, reverence, discipline, self-respect and all that tends towards a true Christian manliness." He was silent for a moment remembering. "Quite a fellow, my old dad. He was with the British Army in South Africa and four years after he went out to Australia, he joined the diggers in 1914 and fought at Gallipoli and in the trenches in France. He worked really hard all his life. He was a tram driver in Melbourne, and a staunch trade union man."

"He sounds like a good bloke," remarked John, "You say your mum came from Ireland?"

"A Dublin girl she was, from the slums and a real lady in her way. When I was over in England I went across and had a look to see where she came from. Like my dad's home suburb in Glasgow, the area she came from was pretty run down. It's a funny thing, fellas, my mum and dad came from the poorest backgrounds you could have imagined but, by geez, they were the salt of the earth. They'd do anything for anyone and I couldn't have asked for better folk."

The nostalgic tone in Ted's voice had struck a note in Nathan's memory. "My parents were like that too. I could not have wished for better."

Ted could sense how Nathan was feeling. "Well, Nathan, we'll be keeping our fingers crossed for them." His eyes showed sensitivity. "When I am back in Aussie my thoughts will be with you. When this show's all over I hope you have a good life."

It seemed strange to Nathan how a man as brash and direct as Ted could also be a man of compassion. Before this meeting Nathan had never met an Australian and, in spite of all the vast reading he had done, he was incredibly ignorant of Australia. He made up his mind to read up on this land.

It had stirred interest for John too. "I wouldn't mind going out there one day," He said.

"To Australia, John?" Ted said with surprise. "Oh, you'd like it." Turning to Nathan, he said, "And so would you." Nathan looked up curiously. "It's got so much potential. There's a place there to suit all tastes."

"I have spent all my life in Germany, Austria and Palestine," said Nathan. "But I am lacking in knowledge of your country, Ted. Until I met you I knew nothing of Australia or Australians. I am very interested. Tell me, what are the cities like?"

Ted shuffled in his chair like a university professor positioning himself more comfortably to give a lecture. He was obviously enamoured and spoke with great authority about the subject he loved. He was almost beaming with pride.

"Each city in Australia has got its own character. I mean I'm in a pretty good position to know: I was brought up in Melbourne, I've lived in Sydney, I've been out in the bush, and I spent some of the happiest times of my life in Cairns. Well, Melbourne is graceful. It's got big wide streets like Collins, Bourke, Swanston and Elizabeth. I've heard people who've been to Paris say they're like the Boulevards there. There are lots of parks too: Treasury Gardens, Fitzroy Gardens, and the Botanical Gardens. It's real nice. There are some hills just outside of Melbourne. I used to go up there a lot as a kid on bush walks. The Dandenong Ranges. Now they were nice."

"And Sydney?" Nathan pursued. He was quite engrossed and he listened attentively.

"Oh it's dynamic, mate. Its got this magnificent harbour and a bridge like a coat hanger. It's a city for sun lovers, for living in and enjoying life. On a day when it swelters the beaches are crowded, I'm telling you, boy. There's not a square inch at Manly or Bondi to be found when the suns out and the surfs up. On some days when everyone's heading to Bondi, the old trams are so full with people, they shoot through every flamin' tram stop. There's an expression in Sydney people use when they see a bloke rushing somewhere, they say he shot through like a Bondi tram."

"You make it sound so interesting. Perhaps one day I may ride a tram to Bondi." Nathan liked the sound of it, the sun and the surf. Perhaps one day he would go out to that land which had previously been an unknown quantity to him.

"I'm not rattling on too much am I, you blokes?" asked Ted modestly.

"Not in the slightest," said John. "You've got me hook, line and sinker.

Do you know since I've been in the army the only Aussies I've met are the ones I've been in punch-ups with in bars from Cape Town to Benghazi. You're the first one I've had a decent conversation with."

"Oh, there's plenty of us, mate," grinned Ted. "Some of us could yarn for a living!"

"I was wondering what life was like when you worked on a cattle station," John looked at Ted closely, almost urging him to continue. Ted recognised the hint and reached for his beer. He drank half the contents of the glass with a speed that surprised, if not amazed, John and Nathan. Ted was obviously a connoisseur in this area because in the various rounds of drinks that followed that afternoon, he managed to stay pretty much in control of himself without slurring his words.

"The cattle station was a high spot in my life," he continued, "and boy I had some experiences out in the bush. I remember one time when me and my mate, Bobby Maylor, were out droving in the far west. We rode out to round up some of the stock that had wandered way off from Quentin Downs – that was the name of the property I worked on – and we had practically gone into the Northern Territory where the sun was really beginning to take its toll. Strewth, it was bloody hot! We'd been riding for quite a few days and I was well and truly saddle sore. And when I say sore, I mean sore. Cattle country is pretty flat all the way until you get into the more tropical climes where the vegetation starts to spring up. It's as flat as the palm of your hand for as far as you care to look. Well, me and my mate Bobby were dying for a wash. Four days in the saddle, in the same clothes, and with the sun making you sweat buckets all the time, even the horses won't talk to you! Then like a mirage in the distance we could see a clump of trees. We figured where there are trees there must be water. Would you believe it, there was? Me and my mate stripped off and we're splashing around making the most of it, and then we could hear laughter. I couldn't believe it. From out of nowhere there were some Aborigines in the trees laughing at us. Well there we were, stark bollocky, and they're pointing at us laughing their heads off. I thought perhaps they knew something we didn't."

"The Aborigines – they are wanderers?" asked Nathan.

"My word. They can survive where a white bloke can't. They're an ancient people with tribal rites and customs of their own. Put them smack bang in the middle of the desert and they'll find water."

"Any more stories, Ted? I find you quite entertaining," said Nathan humorously.

"Me, entertaining? There's a turn up for the books eh. Mate I've got hundreds of them, let's fill the glasses up, boys." Ted got up to get some drinks and as he did so the couple called Charles and Alitat, who John had spoken to earlier, passed by the table. Ted gave her an admiring look over, which she returned with a coy smile. "See there, you blokes," chuckled Ted, "she fancies me. It must be my hat and the accent." He laughed and went to the bar. There was no doubt that he was a popular boy. At the bar the other Australian soldiers greeted him and slapped him on the back good-heartedly. He could hold court anywhere it seemed. He was the centre of attention laughing and joking with the others. One of the soldiers took a mouth organ from his pocket and said, "Let's have a song, fellas," Someone else said, "How about the 'Road to Gundagai'," and that was it; the whole place echoed with a group of Australians singing in a rowdy happy fashion.

Many hours and drinks later Nathan, who had kept rigidly to sipping lemonade that day, walked back with John and Ted and a group of Australians through the streets of Cairo to where they were billeted. That afternoon and evening Nathan had been on a verbal travelogue of Australia. He was fascinated by what he had heard from Ted. In the space of hours, Nathan's appetite for travel had been whetted considerably. For all of his twenty odd years of life, albeit filled considerably with experience already, he had never considered what lay beyond the confines of the lands he had already lived in.

The surf and the sun, the bush, the cities of Melbourne and Sydney, the cattle stations and nomadic Aborigines; they had a romantic ring about them and it was something so enormously different from Berlin and Vienna, and a mountainside village in Austria, something so different to his life on a kibbutz in Palestine. Even that, which for him had been such an exciting and invigorating time, seemed to pale in comparison now. For too long Nathan had found himself looking back and reflecting on much of what had happened to him. He was beginning to look to the future now. He had not given up hope that his parents would eventually be found. But it was his future that concerned him. Ted had done enough talking about Australia to convince Nathan that it would be a fine place to live. Perhaps Nathan would ride a tram to Bondi one day.

Twenty-two

The next day Nathan lined up the usual parade roll call. Even at such an early hour in the day the sun was already high and it was warm. By midday it would be a temperature similar to the heat from an oven grill. There was no doubt that the British Army were an efficient lot. Parade inspection was always detailed. Not a button or a buckle was left unexamined and if so much as a tarnish or scuff to the boots could be found then the sergeant major would let everyone know. *For such a little man*, thought Nathan, *the RSM had an all-powerful, almighty ear-piercing voice that at its incredible range of decibels could surely shatter glass windows.*

For a few days rumours had been circulating round the barrack room that a number of the troops would be moving out with the Long Range Desert group for a rendezvous somewhere in the desert. The announcement was made by the sergeant major that same morning. Tomorrow they would be moving out in a stream of tanks, jeeps and armoured cars to meet up with some SAS troops at an oasis on a particular desert route from which they would mount an offensive on some oncoming German panzer divisions.

After the parade had been dismissed Nathan was just walking away to attend to his day's duties when the sergeant major called out to him. "Private Palmai, come with me." He shouted in his shrill voice. Nathan turned, very surprised, imagining he was about to be singled out for some unpleasant duties like cleaning the billets.

"I have done something wrong, sergeant major?" He asked with clearly a hint of worry in his voice. The sergeant major, who away from the parade ground and regimental life was really a good sport, smiled at him.

"I don't think so, old son. One of the officers in military intelligence section wants a little bit of assistance for an hour or so. He needs some help, preferably from someone who speaks a bit of German. And you being who you are he asked for you by name."

Nathan looked a bit bewildered. In all of his time with the British Army he had not become acquainted with any officers personally. Apart from inspections and a little bit of driving duty, he did not know any officers except by sight. He was puzzled as to why he had been selected. The sergeant major noticed that Nathan was looking confused and in a gruff manner he said, "Come on, lad, smarten yourself up." Nathan stood to attention quickly. "Private Palmai, by the left quick march." The two men started to march towards the huge building that was actually the centre wherein intelligence and strategic operations were planned. The parade ground they marched across was in fact a converted recreation ground belonging to a top Cairo school but for several years it had been used by the army. "Moving out tomorrow, eh, lad – looking forward to it?"

"Very much, sergeant major, a chance to see more of the desert."

"Take a little bit of advice, son. Keep your bloody head down when you hear the fire of rifles." Nathan realised that there would be a lot of action ahead and before he could pass any comment the sergeant major said, "Left wheel, Private Palmai" and they marched into the building, the heels of their boots clinking in time as they took big steps along the corridor. Rotary fans spun above their heads and the sound of typewriters from different offices could be heard, each one sounding as if they were in competition with each other.

They marched along until they came to one particular office right at the very end. "Private Palmai," The sergeant major drew a breath, allowing Nathan a chance to prepare himself and, directly outside the officer's room, he gave the command, "Halt!" and then said, "Just wait here for one moment, Private Palmai."

Nathan stood still for one moment. He heard the sergeant major rap on the door with his baton and a voice from within say, "Enter!" The door closed. It must have been three long minutes before it opened again. The sergeant major, holding the door open, said, "In you go, Private Palmai," and as Nathan entered the door was closed behind him. He stood to attention in front of the desk. The officer in the room stood with his back to Nathan, staring out of the window at the maze of minarets and the traffic going past. Nathan was acutely conscious that the officer was deliberately stalling for time, delaying turning around before facing him. For a desperate moment he feared something ominous.

In the silence of the room broken only by the swish of the fans he glanced around him. On the wall there were three pictures hanging with faces that he distinctly recognised; King George VI, Winston Churchill and the Commander of the 8th Army, Bernard Law Montgomery, whose visage almost set the tone of the room. On the other side of the room was a map of the entire length of North Africa. The officer's desk had a bundle of files on top of it and a photograph mounted in a frame of a woman with a beautiful smile. Nathan had just relaxed his gaze on the photograph, admiring the woman's composure, when the officer adjusted the shutters and blocked out the powerful rays of the morning sun. The room was shady and cool unlike the outside where it was uncomfortably hot, but the palms of his hands were perspiring nervously.

The officer turned around slowly and faced Nathan. The mutual recognition between the two men ignited in their eyes. Nathan knew that this man, whom he had seen briefly just the previous day, was who he had believed him to be.

"Do you recognise me?" the officer asked. But it was a question asked in vain for the answer was inscribed all over Nathan's face.

"Mr Miller," exclaimed Nathan. "You are – Mr Miller. You stayed with us in Austria many years ago."

Forgetting the distinction between an officer and a private in the forces, Colonel Freddie Miller came from behind the desk and there was a great feeling of relief evident in his face as he shook Nathan's hand warmly.

"How good it is to see you again. I am so happy to see you." There was genuine delight in his voice. "Take a seat, Nathan, please." The two men sat down. The shock of seeing each other again was still registering. The pleasure was overwhelming. They both appraised each other. In the six years since they had last met, there had been tumultuous changes in both their lives. Nathan had moved from being a studious teenager to a mature adult with poise and an understanding of life's situations. Freddie had always lived a full life and experienced many things. Although still in his thirties there were flashes of silver in his hair and he had recently been trying to come to terms with a tragedy in his life. For the moment he tried to put it to the back of his mind and concentrated on Nathan, who he was so thrilled to see after all this time. "I saw you yesterday. The moment I saw your face I was, to put it mildly, damn near dumbstruck. I'd heard that there were many Jewish people in Palestine serving in the British Army. I didn't dream for one moment that I would ever meet you again in such circumstances. I was watching from the sidelines this morning at roll call. When I heard the name Palmai, I could not believe it. I especially asked for you."

"It is good to see you again, Mr Miller. I was lucky to leave when I did. I was on the boat to Palestine at the time of the Anschluss."

There was a look of deep concern on Freddie's face. "I'm glad you got to the kibbutz." Freddie looked hard at Nathan and thought of the young man's parents. There were characteristics about Nathan that reminded him of Arthandur and Marlene. He would wait before broaching the subject. "Did you meet some good people at the kibbutz?"

"Some of the best." Nathan thought instinctively of Leon and Melissa. Since he had left Jezarat he had not heard what had become of them. *Melissa. Oh, Melissa.* He still thought of her now that she was far away; she had become a distant, unattainable dream. Melissa was someone who to Nathan was like an exotic temptress of fabled legend. But now she was still in Palestine and he was in Egypt. He continued to answer the question. "I was fortunate to meet so many good people from whom I have learned a great deal. I have learned much about my homeland, its history, the mixtures of peoples who have lived there, and I have read many books and even studied law which—"

"Law!" interrupted Freddie. He was genuinely surprised.

"Yes." Nathan smiled at Freddie's surprised look. "I want to be a lawyer after the war. I intend to study at the university."

Freddie was obviously pleased for him. "Good luck to you, Nathan. I hope you achieve your ambition. I know your parents would have been pleased for you." Freddie stopped silent for one moment realizing he had drastically slipped up by speaking of Nathan's parents in the past tense. He looked at Nathan whose eyes had registered with emotion at the thought of Arthandur and Marlene. Freddie carried on in the hope that he could divert the subject. "You certainly came from the right professional background for that. With your mother being a teacher and your father a doctor, you certainly have the influences to be a distinguished man. I also hope that—?"

"Mr Miller!" Nathan interrupted this time, raising his hand sharply There was just a chance that Freddie might know something about what had happened to the many people who have been interned in the concentration camps in Europe.

"I think I know what you are going to say ,Nathan. But do go on."

"Almost immediately after I arrived in Palestine I had a few letters from my parents. Then… then nothing. There are stories being told constantly, of rumours and talk about the concentration camps. It is frightening. I met someone at the kibbutz who had escaped from one of the camps. He told me that in my home village when the Nazis came that nearly everyone was taken away. I asked Shirom Banai, the leader of the Kibbutz Jezarat, if he could find out anything but, in spite of his many attempts, he just seemed to meet up with a brick wall of silence." Nathan's voice had faltered slightly. It was indicative of the feelings of frustration and despair he was enduring. He looked at Freddie in an almost pleading fashion, urging him to answer. Freddie could not for he felt great empathy for Nathan who, he knew, was experiencing a deep mental agony. "Mr Miller – you are an officer. You must know something about what is really happening in the camps. Surely you, as an intelligence officer, must know something."

Freddie appeared worried and confused. His face was stern and grave when he spoke. "I have heard about the camps. My colleagues in Europe have not at this stage managed to break down the facts from the fiction. But one or two of our agents have extracted some details. If they are true then I regret to say, Nathan, I fear the worse. The Red Cross and the various intelligence services, and our contacts in resistance groups and the underground, have all tried desperately to locate the thousands upon thousands who went missing or were taken into custody. I wish that I could give you some reason for hope. I really do. I put out a special request it might interest you to know, on the whereabouts of the Palmai family. Your father mentioned to me in a letter that you were due to go to the kibbutz. Not long afterwards Austria was absorbed into German rule and I never did hear from Arthandur again either. I admired your mother and father greatly." He looked downcast for a moment then raised his eyes and focused them on Nathan again. "Nothing in the world would please me more to know that they're still alive. I have to be brutally honest with you, Nathan, to give you false hope would be wrong."

"I appreciate your frankness, Colonel Miller." Nathan said, and although he did respect Freddie's word, he did allow himself the suspicion that maybe, just maybe, the Englishman knew more than he was willing to divulge. Nathan considered that this might be because Freddie was not insensitive to other people's feelings and that he did not want him to offer any more pain than he had done already.

There was a thought that occurred to Freddie in a momentary grappling of words. To ease the pain that Nathan was feeling, perhaps he could pay tribute to Arthandur's great skills and organisational ability with the work of the Companions of the Circle. Freddie got up from the chair and walked to the window. He adjusted the blinds slightly and turned around again.

"Did your father tell you much about his work?" Freddie asked in a curious vein.

"Oh, just about the various patients and their complaints. My father did not really bring his work home with him. He was very devout, very religious. The family and the faith were of the greatest importance to him."

Not only that, thought Freddie. "No, I didn't mean that sort of work," Freddie said, quietly and seriously. Nathan had a strange look about him that seemed to suggest what other sort of work could his father have possibly been involved in.

"I don't understand. Work? He was a Doctor of Medicine." Nathan said naively. Freddie felt an undercurrent of unease within him. Was it possible that Nathan had never learned of Arthandur's work for the Circle?

"I know he was a doctor, Nathan. And a very fine one too. Very caring of his patients. I spent a lot of time with you father in his surgery and I could see he looked after everyone with the utmost care. His love of his people – the Jewish race – extended far beyond a doctor's surgery, though. Through the Companions of the Circle he helped to save many people who would otherwise be in the camps."

Nathan's face was an absolute blank. It was clear that he did not know of his father's work in this area.

"You don't know about this, do you?" Freddie asked gently.

In a hushed voice betraying astonishment, Nathan said, "You must tell me, I know nothing of this."

So, Nathan did not know after all. Strange that Arthandur and Marlene had been able to conceal so many clandestine activities from Nathan, yet in consideration of the enormous secrecy of it all, perhaps it was not surprising after all. Freddie knew in his heart that it was important that Nathan knew the truth, and he weighed up in his own mind Arthandur's achievements. Although Freddie at thirty-seven was sixteen years older than Nathan, he found himself adopting a gentle fatherly approach to the young man. It was a difficult thing to tell someone that their father had lived a double life. But Freddie knew that Nathan would be proud when he learned what his father had really been doing.

"Your father made many trips to Berlin from your home, didn't he?"

"Yes. He used to go there every few weeks. He was keen for my aunts, uncles and cousins to leave, but they wouldn't go."

"On those visits, Nathan, he used to meet some of the members of the Circle. Let me tell you about the Companions of the Circle. It was formed by a lady called Baroness Christina von Harstezzen." Freddie felt a note of sadness when he thought of her and, looking up at the rotary fan twirling around with great rapidity, he could almost visualise the tiny propellers on the *Hindenburg*. He thought of it crashing and bursting into flames on that fateful day a few years before. "Christina was the widow of Rieber von Harstezzen, a German Industrialist who had no political links whatsoever. On Rieber's death, Christina took over the helm of these industries. They had wine fields, factories producing auto parts, steelworks, I believe, and armaments. An enormous variety of industries. Christina came into contact with many people including a consortium of European Jewish businessmen. They expressed their concerns to her about the rise of the Third Reich and the fear they held for their own people."

"I remember this lady," Nathan felt inclined to comment. "She came to the house in Austria. I thought she was just an acquaintance of my parents. I did not realise why she came. I recall she was beautiful and she wore a perfume that seemed to stay in the room long after she had gone."

Freddie remembered that perfume too. It had been evident in a letter he had once received from her. "Christina von Harstezzen and these gentlemen decided to form a group that would assist the Jewish people in Europe. They established a network with people in Holland, France, Austria and just about every country where they could find sympathisers. Your father recruited me in Berlin at the time of the Olympic games. You see, long before I became a newsreel cameraman and a journalist, I was an Intelligence Officer in the Army – much the same as I am now – and obviously with my links your father could see the merit in recruiting me."

"This is all so unbelievable. I find it hard to believe." Nathan was puzzled. "You are either a great actor or else this was one of my father's most well kept secretes."

"It had to be a well kept secret," Freddie emphasised. "Your father was virtually Mrs Harstezzen's right-hand man. He organised recruits for her; people in all walks of life who would lobby foreign governments about the Nazi threat. He organised sponsors and sponsorship for many of your people so that they could start new lives overseas, many of them are alive, thanks to the efforts of your father and that magnificent woman, Mrs Harstezzen." Freddie wanted to make the last point utterly clear. "Your father is a man that you can be proud of."

The effects of Freddie's words stunned Nathan into a silence that hung over the room. It was so shattering to have learned this. It was amazing to think that his father, whose demeanour was gentle and humorous, was also a man of the backroom tactics. In that short period of shock and surprise the rotary fan was the only sound in the room as it swished around and around. It diverted Nathan's thoughts for the very sound of it reminded him of the waves breaking every few seconds. Waves were engulfing him. but waves of a different kind. Shock waves. In all of his life he had never been more stunned and surprised by such news. His face which had looked a picture of shock now relaxed slightly. If his father had indeed helped many people in this way, then he most certainly was a man he could feel immense pride and admiration for.

Freddie went on to talk about the role he had played himself. He talked of Mrs von Harstezzen and how she had died in the Hindenburg disaster. He went on to talk about so many things involved with the Companions of the Circle. In short, the revelations were stunning. Freddie was so exasperated by the scope of the Circle he mentioned to Nathan of one of the latest agents they had recruited.

"We have one young lady, a French girl of about your age actually, liaising with other Circle members in occupied Paris at the moment," and then he added in a wistful manner, "She was a dam fine young girl too. I hope she's looking after herself. God knows what she's doing at the moment."

★★★

Francine Macé was certainly looking after herself. At that particular time she was busy in Paris painting portraits of the city highlights, but in reality she always had a microphone carefully wired up near her, from which she would talk to members of the resistance, whilst watching the comings and goings of Nazi officers. Under the guise of painting a scenic view of the rooftops of Paris looking down the Seine, Francine kept one eye on her work and the other on an apartment building that housed German officers. With the swish of her brush, she applied colours of light and shade to her portrait of the city she loved. Her microphone was cleverly concealed within the pallet that contained the oils and, as she painted, she would lean forward to speak to one of her contacts giving descriptions of various officers for future reference.

For one quick moment Francine, with sleight of hand, disengaged the wire leading to the microphone. Out of the corner of her eye she was acutely aware of several German soldiers walking towards her. They stopped by her and studied her work over her shoulder. If they lowered their eyes they would have caught sight of the small box transmitter leaning against her easel. Francine turned around and looked at them directly, almost expressionless. Her beauty entranced them and momentarily diverted their gaze. The solders said something in German that she interpreted as being relative to her painting and moved on, casting a backward glance of intense admiration of her.

It was hard not to be absorbed by Francine's looks. Her height and suntanned figure was striking enough. Her legs looked as if they belonged to those of a lido dancer, and the beret, half slanted over her head, gave her an air of mystery and allure. She made a very good agent in her day-to-day role as a painter, but the real test would be yet to come.

Colonel Freddie Miller realised this. In Cairo he thought of her in her capacity as an agent and felt responsible that his suggestion to Brindmarsh had resulted in her being used in this manner.

"Yes, she was a dam fine young girl," said Freddie, repeating himself. "And many of the people working for the Circle are very fine human beings. I have great respect for them all. Believe me when this time is over your father's name will be held in high esteem. Oh I know it's not much of a comfort but always remember many people are alive because of your father and Mrs Harstezzen's efforts."

Nathan seemed to understand and nodded meekly. He averted his eyes from Freddie's gaze and rested them on a photograph of the young woman situated on the desk. "Who is that lady?" he asked out of curiosity.

At this a lump appeared to produce itself in Freddie's throat. He looked deeply saddened and there were red veins in his eyes; emotions of a longing for something gone forever shot through Freddie's inner soul. It hurt and hurt and hurt. This was the tragedy Freddie had been trying to overcome in his life for some time.

At last he brought himself to answer. "That's Cynthia." His voice sounded even in the two words as if it might break with emotion.

"Cynthia?" queried Nathan, "I recall my father saying you married a lady called Cynthia. She is your wife?"

Freddie hesitated before answering for the pain would not go away. "She was," replied Freddie. "I spent the happiest times of my life married to that dear lady." His voice was distant and quiet, so much so that Nathan had to lean forward to listen. "Cynthia was killed in a motor accident in Cornwall some time ago. Stormy weather one night, I understand. A wet road and the car took a bend too fast. To make matters worse, we were expecting a child too. She had just gone home on weekend leave." Freddie controlled his voice because he could feel his emotions taking over and then he looked directly at Nathan. "So, young man, both you and I have lost people we have loved."

"I – I am sorry. This war is hard for many of us."

"Yes, Nathan, it is." He rapidly changed the subject. "Your CO tells me that your platoon is moving out tomorrow. I too am moving out although in a different direction; I'm going to the east, to Colombo. I don't think our paths will cross again during our time with the services. But whatever life holds for you I can assure you that it is my heartfelt wish that the years ahead for you will be happy." He stood up and stretched out his hand to Nathan in a warm handshake. "I must let you return to your duties now."

"I'm pleased that you were honest with me. It is hard to come to terms with the realisation that my parents have gone. But I agree with you, the truth is better than false hope. I am still shaken by what you have told me about my father and the Circle. It is all so amazing."

"And it's all totally and absolutely true, Nathan," emphasised Freddie.

He walked to the door with Nathan. Before he opened it he felt inclined to volunteer some more information. "I know, because I was part of it in the years before the war, I lobbied the government of the day. I organised petitions. I even arranged sponsorship for a number of Austrian and German refugees before the gates were slammed. There was much more we could have done had time and events not restricted us. Right up to 1939 I was in touch by radio to the Companions of the Circle in France. It was an enormous task."

Nathan absorbed the words. He was still stunned by all that he had learned that morning. "I have learned much this morning," he said quietly. "Sir, I should just like to say again that I am deeply sorry about your wife."

Freddie acknowledged him with a deeply sensitive look in his eyes. "Thank you, Nathan." Then he opened the door for the young man. "Perhaps we may meet again," he murmured in a hopeful voice. "Good luck." He shook his hand warmly.

Nathan took one step back and saluted smartly. Freddie returned the salute and smiled warmly at him. Nathan marched off down the corridor in a highly presentable manner. *I wonder what he's thinking,* thought Freddie. *Did the news come as a compete surprise to him? Apparently it did. Surely there must have been telltale signs that would have been evident in Arthandur's day-to-day life.* But no, it had all been carefully concealed from Nathan, and as he strode out onto the parade ground with the full effects of the sun and the heat bearing down on him, it felt as if he was emerging from a dream. It felt as if the details of his father's secret life belonged to the pages of a mystery novel. Nathan felt dazed and confused. He found it utterly incredible.

From now on Nathan would not only think of his father as a gentle and loving man, but as a member of a secret organisation dedicated to the preservation of freedom and religious beliefs. He yearned to see his father again, and to tell him how proud he was to be his son. In another place beyond this earth perhaps?

Freddie returned to the work in his office. By the middle of the day the operation he had mounted to identify the spies who were passing on information about the size of the British forces in Egypt, would be over. Operation Akib, named after the Egyptian sympathisers who were working for the Germans, would effectively come to an end when the whole ring would be arrested by members of the military police. It had been a smooth-running piece of work very professionally dealt with. The whole operation had taken a great deal of patience and application.

Over the telephone Freddie uttered the words, "Operation Akib. Please complete all procedures." Within minutes the order would pass down the line and Freddie's work in Cairo would be complete.

No sooner had he put the phone down then he felt a great wave of relief go through him. He had finished some complex intelligence work and he was delighted that Nathan Palmai was alive and well. His eyes rested on the photograph of Cynthia. What a loss to him her death had caused. The heartbreak and grief caused him such deep pain and mental anguish.

In a quiet voice choked with emotion he talked to the picture. "Cynthia. Oh God, how I miss you." He put one hand to his forehead and gripped it hard. "Oh, Cynthia, why did you have to leave me, why?" He lowered his hand to the front of his face and he began to sob gently. Alone in the privacy of his own office, he shared his grief with no one. He could hear the words Nathan had said earlier going around in his mind. *This war is hard for so many of us.*

Twenty-three

Operation Akib was successful. Akib and his associates were arrested in one fell swoop. When they realised that they had been fed with false information, which they had passed on to their German contacts, even they had to concede that there was great ingenuity in Freddie Miller's scheme.

Freddie left soon after for Colombo on the Island of Ceylon where he would work on intelligence operations in the Far East. With Cynthia's death still on his mind, he threw himself into his work to blot out the pain.

Nathan left Cairo immediately after the day he had been reunited with Freddie. In the best traditions of the British Army, the various platoons had left in separate convoys to travel across the desert regions but they would all converge at a particular oasis from where they would mount an offensive on the oncoming forces.

The desert of North Africa opened up yet another world to Nathan. Just as his time in Palestine had been an education, so too was this period in the wilds of the 'Garden of Allah' as it had been referred to by some Arabs he had spoken to in Cairo. To travel across such a spartan land at first held little magic. It was not until Nathan fully experienced the stillness, the quiet and the far-reaching horizon, the smell of date palms in some remote oasis, that he came to realise just what a scenic wonder the desert had proved itself to be.

The departing convoys had all left in different directions. Each one was comprised of the same make-up that included a number of open-topped jeeps, tanks, lorries and trucks, all of them fitted out with the same armaments as a precaution against the oncoming onslaught.

In the depths of the Libyan Desert the Long Range Desert Group, a special unit formed from the SAS, would meet up with the troops travelling from Cairo. The convoy that Nathan had been attached to travelled in a south-westerly direction going as far down as the Sudanese border before moving up towards the centre of Libya.

Nathan found himself with his friend, John, and some of the toughest soldiers in the British Army; some of them, he was to discover later, came from impoverished backgrounds, and service life had given them a purpose that they had not experienced in the civilian life of the Depression years during the 1930s. Nathan's friend was an example of this period of history. John Dunn, although shy and quiet on first meeting, had worked tremendously hard during his teenage years in an assortment of jobs and he had an almost continuous cheerfulness about him. He had begun the war as a paratrooper and had transferred into the Long Range Desert Group after a spell in Palestine. A bout of malaria had laid him up in Cairo for a while, and after he had been deemed fit he was enthusiastic to be rejoining the elite group again.

The journey through the desert has been one of mystery. Their commanding officer advised the direction they would travel and the other vehicles followed on in response to the command. The tracks that they made were not in too straight a line. They zigzagged from point to point, guided, it would seem, by the point of a compass and the stars of the desert sky.

Sometimes the route would take them over almost everlastingly flat plains. It was not the desert of legend but a barren wilderness; a scrubland of curious colours of brown, orange and yellow. Occasionally, it would be broken by a rock formation or unusual grey and white monoliths that would rise in the distance as they crossed further and further towards the spellbinding horizon line behind which the sun would rise and sink so distinctively. In the dark of night an ice-white pillar of rock would gleam like silver as the moon cast its beams through the purple shades of a desert so still and so lifeless. One could never forget that characteristic of the desert and the sound of the silence.

By day the convoy travelled on what seemed an uncharted journey. From one extreme of desert the group moved on to the more expected scenery, that of constant rolling bright yellow dunes, clumps of tall, handsome palm trees, and sand that gave way beneath the weight of motorised army vehicles.

Nathan and John were in a jeep that underwent a lot of punishment in the course of its day-to-day action. Both men were wearing regulation shorts and khaki safari shirts. They had both taken to wearing the headdress worn by the Arabs to counteract the daily effect of the sun's rays beating down on them, which had come close to bleaching their hair blonde and their skin a deep glowing bronze. They had not had the opportunity in days to wash and shave and they looked generally unkempt. Yet even in a state of untidiness Nathan felt like a wide-eyed Conradian adventurer travelling over unexplored land with a zest and curiosity for every unexpected change in the landscape that would occur with an amazing suddenness.

The dunes were the substance of a romantic imagination. They were sweeping and rolling and the real life discovery of it at the wheel of a jeep was far more breathtaking then seeing it in a cinema movie. It was hard for Nathan to realise he was here.

Sometimes the convoy would pass by groups of wild camels clustered together: a sign of reassurance that there was at least another form of life in existence in the desert. One day when it was glaringly hot and the sun hung in the sky like a blazing beacon, the mood of the men in the convoy was one almost of apathy. Even the pace of the vehicles began to slow down as the commanding officer at the head of them deliberately slowed his jeep down to accommodate the men who were feeling tired and exhausted.

Nathan mopped his brow. His eyes felt heavy as if he could drop into a deep sleep, but it was the buzz of flies that stung his face that kept him awake as he moved to wave them away. John was virtually driving one-handed when out of the corner of his eye he saw several figures standing beneath the shade of some tall palms. "Look!" John exclaimed, pointing sharply to the right. Nathan's bleary eyes became wide open with alarm.

It was the first sign of human life they had espied in days. Another jeep from behind came up beside them. One of the soldiers in the other jeep called out to John, "They're Touaregs, mate."

"Touaregs?" John looked at Nathan who shrugged his shoulders. He didn't know any more than John did. But it was the solder in the other jeep who added one further comment that enlightened them.

"Touareg Arabs. We're not far from a place called El Djemina. We might get some fresh water there."

The other vehicles slowed down to a complete standstill and halted the jeep. The jeep next to them drove over to the clump of trees stopping where the Arabs were standing. A commissioned officer stepped out and began conversing with them. He was obviously fluent in the Arabic dialect as there was much hand waving and pointing. No doubt the man was capable of making himself clearly understood. After a few minutes of animated conversation the officer came back to his jeep and the Arabs came with him. He beckoned to a few of the drivers, including John, to bring their vehicles over and they immediately responded to the command.

Drawing close to the Touaregs Nathan could see them at close proximity. They too equally studied the newcomers with interest. The officer gave them instructions, "All right, gentlemen, we're going to pay a visit to an Arab village at El Djemina about fifteen miles from here. We might be able to get some water there and treat ourselves to a scrub up while we're at it. These fellows will be coming along with us for the ride." He said something in the native language of the Touaregs and they immediately swarmed all over the jeeps. Two got into the back of Nathan and John's jeep and jumped up and down like children loose in a candy shop. A ride in a motorised vehicle was obviously a novelty to them.

The jeeps revved into action and rejoined the convoy. Then they were off again on their journey. The route now was flat and the palm trees and vegetation more frequent.

Nathan could hear the Arabs talking constantly behind him in a garbled conversation that was virtually non-stop without taking a pause for a breather. He turned around in his seat and studied them, their caricatures and their dress. These desert warriors had a strange manner about them. They looked fierce and hard. One of them became acutely aware that he was being watched and stared back at Nathan. The silence that befell him was sudden. His smile spread across the Arab's face revealing a couple of missing teeth and he began to laugh. Nathan twitched his eyebrows. The Arab said something to the other one and he too began to laugh.

"I wonder why they laugh, John," Nathan said, smiling back at them.

"I wouldn't have a clue, Nathan," chuckled John. "Perhaps they've never seen people like us before!" As he spoke he put his foot down on the accelerator, pushing the jeep to its limit to catch up with the other vehicles in the convoy, which were now gathering pace.

The sight of the Touareg village at El Djemina came into view although it was far away on the horizon. A shimmering haze on the desert partly obliterated it and as the vehicles approached it the features of the village became obvious. Nathan could see houses that were not so much houses but dwellings moulded together from a clay mixture. With the sun sinking in the horizon on an orange-yellow landscape, the dwellings of a downcast grey colour looked strangely out of character in its harsh setting.

These desert dwellers were so remarkably different than their city counterparts that Nathan had met in Alexandria and Cairo. Here their homes were something out of a legend. *In fact,* thought Nathan, *something out of another time.* It was as if the village belonged to an era of time in the first centuries of the earth's existence. Tanks, jeeps and lorries with artillery rumbled into the Arab village and came to an abrupt halt. It was a strange cacophony of twentieth century modern warfare and desert warriors.

Nathan looked around him in awe. At one end of the village there were several bearded Arabs making pottery by moulding clay with their bare hands, which, indeed, looked powerfully strong. To obtain a good shape and finish, the makers of these articles heated them over what appeared to be a burning furnace, and then further shaped them against a grinding millstone that another man operated on a mechanism of pulleys. It was fascinating to watch. Even in the wilds of the desert far away from any well-worn track a form of industry was taking place. An inquiring thought entered Nathan's head: presumably the making of such pottery was for local use. The marketability of such products would surely be limited here.

Many of the locals stood gasping incredulously at the sight of the convoy. The Arabs who had been given a lift back to El Djemina jumped down from the vehicles and started conversing with their friends. It had obviously been a great novelty to them.

Close by to them was an open waterhole from which the villagers dredged up water buckets and emptied them into their own containers. The women in El Djemina wore strange robes tightly strewn around them and veils across their faces. One woman, obviously intrigued by the military visitors stopped directly in front of Nathan and John and eyed them curiously. Only her eyes could be seen in the midst of all the robes that were swathed around her like bandages, but they were eyes of mischief that could be recognised easily. She looked at them closely and then moved away. She made a sound that sounded slightly like a girlish giggle as she moved into one of the clay dwellings.

There was some semblance of animal life there too: a couple of donkeys, a few camels, some chickens and a strange breed of dog that Nathan wasn't too sure about.

But goodness there was something eerie about this place. The people eyed the soldiers with looks of puzzlement but said nothing as the men filled their containers with water and treated themselves to a much-earned all over wash. It was only when Nathan had lathered himself all over and thrown cool water over his perspiring body that he realised just how disgustingly filthy he had become. When he washed his hair and his ears it seemed he had accumulated much of the desert sand in them.

No sooner had the men scrubbed themselves and filled their containers, than they were once again on the move, heading further and further west. This had become the normal pattern of their movements in the past few weeks and it continued in this manner for some while.

Some nights they would camp out or sleep in their vehicles while various soldiers took watch. Often there would be great camaraderie amongst the men around a fire in the open as they talked about their lives and made jokes amongst themselves. On occasions like this Nathan would feel very much the odd man out. The soldiers he was acquainted with came from a mixed background. His friend, John, a down to earth Londoner, traded jokes and friendship with the Scots, Lancastrians, the men from Surrey and Sussex, and the odd Irishman or two, who all formed part of this group. But Nathan was a German-born, Austrian-raised Jewish refugee, whose homeland was Palestine and he felt strangely out of place in his present situation. By nationality he was certainly the odd man out. But he was never made to feel so and one thing he was grateful for was the way in which the soldiers accepted him as a friend and were well aware, if not openly so, of the difficult life from which he had emerged. They were good men who had treated him as an equal and for this he was thankful.

Their commanding officer, although prim, proper, well-bred, haughty and polished in style, was not lacking in good humour or spirit. Around a campfire at night he was very down to earth, and enjoyed talking to the men and listening to their stories and being part of them, but never losing their respect. One night when the shadow of darkness had fallen on the desert sands like an impenetrable veil, he aroused in them some humour.

"You!" He said sharply to one soldier. "Sing!" The bemused soldier catching the smile on the officer's face, and realising what he was up to, began to sing the lyrics of 'Bye Bye Blackbird'. Turning to another soldier he ordered, "And, you! Shuffle your feet in the sand like Fred Astaire or Jack Buchanan." The soldier, grinning broadly, leapt into action immediately. "The rest of you – play your mugs with your cutlery like drums, play the spoons on your elbows and arms, sing like the barber shop quartet, slap your thighs and whistle like you would on a Saturday night at the Rose and Crown or wherever you go boozing in the British Isles."

These were the sort of moments that Nathan would always remember in his life of diversity. The sight of those solders enjoying themselves in the middle of the desert was one he would always remember. Someone was playing the spoons from the top of his cranium right down the length and breadth of his arms. John conducted them all with the flamboyance of a deranged orchestra conductor. The funniest sight of all was the soldier who had been ordered to dance, shuffling around kicking sand in the air. They were a great bunch, these fellows, who had a sense of humour and courage that would carry them through in any walk of life. Always in times of adversity the British could find humour.

It had been so hot that particular night most of the soldiers had slept out in the open, stretched out with their guns close by. When the watch was changed every few hours or so, everyone had to take their turn at some stage. For Nathan it was thinking time. The desert at night was so quiet he would have to resist the passion to shout into the sky. Truly at night it would sound like a thunderclap. Thinking time offered its dangers to Nathan. While he was with people he would be actively engaged, his concentration on the job in hand; alone, he would drift back in time and, looking out at the desert sky at night when it was a lush deep violet blue, the type of clearness when the constellation of the stars could be seen in all its true evidence, Nathan would think of his mother and father and ponder as to what their fate might have been.

It had been such a shock to him when he had been reunited with Freddie Miller in Cairo; to have learned that his father was instrumental in the running of a group that saved many Jewish lives. His admiration for his father had increased tenfold knowing now of his total commitment to the preservation of human life. *Perhaps it is one of the tragedies of life,* thought Nathan, *that sometimes the people in our life do not reveal their great strengths in life, and it is only when they are gone, that the truth is revealed – when it is too late to express the great love and respect that they are entitled to in life.* These thoughts crowded Nathan's mind over and over gain. When his time on watch finally came to an end he gratefully returned to the comfort of his bed on the sand beside the smouldering embers of the campfire and closed his eyes to dream in the peace and solitude of a desert night.

Hours later after a fitful night's sleep Nathan woke slowly. Already the sun was up and the desert air was warm. He shielded his eyes from the sun's rays that were already quite powerful. There was no noise whatsoever. Everyone except the soldiers on watch were sleeping peacefully. He rolled over on his side and looked at the scenery before him. Nathan froze in his position. He could not move. He was not sure how to react. Not more than a few feet away from him, moving through the sandy scrub in a stalking almost stealthy manner, was a jet-black scorpion; its tail quivering, poised to sting. Nathan was obviously the intended prey. His thoughts raced: to leap up instinctively would almost certainly risk the scorpion moving quickly. One sting would be fateful. To reach for his gun would involve a fast movement, which again might propel the scorpion to race forward.

Nathan felt cold even though it was a warm temperature. He could not work out what to do. Just one bite from the tail sting and that would be it. He stared in a decidedly frozen manner. Then to his horror the scorpion, not more than four feet away, seemed to elevate itself as if it was about to pounce. Suddenly it seemed to spring across the sand.

Almost as suddenly something came down sharply, trapping it in the sand. Nathan reeled back, his heart beating so hard it seemed to echo in his eardrums. He jumped to his feet and saw that the scorpion had been trapped in a metal tin that closeted its hapless victim.

"You were lucky there, boy," said a friendly voice. Nathan turned to see Charles, one of the soldiers he had met in Cairo who was also in this convoy. "Deadly little beast, isn't he?" he added. The noise of the commotion had woken up some of the other soldiers.

"I thought I was gone then," murmured Nathan mopping his brow. "I must thank you, Charles."

✱✱✱

"That's all right, mate," said Charles. "Lucky I went to do a little bit of early morning motor mechanics. Question is, how do we get rid of him?"

A soldier walked up and staring through his sunglasses at the victim picked up some embers of fire and began to strew it around the metal rim. At the sight of the flames the scorpion stung itself in a flagrant act of suicide. It was almost a brutal instinctive action. Nathan twinged with fright as he realised that he could have been the recipient of such a lethal sting.

Shortly afterwards, the journey continued and a few days later the convoy came into the last stretch of their trek. On the map that John had shown Nathan, the army vehicles, in order to steer clear of areas where it was known the German army were operating from, had literally zigzagged and double backed along some routes. Finally, they came to a place where water filtered through the sand and palms grew readily along the route of the flow of the downstream trickle. The men greeted the sight of an oasis as if it was a country pub in England on a warm summer's day.

John browsed over the map. "My guess is," he said with predictably, "that we are only a short way from meeting up with the rest of the Long Range Desert Group." He had no sooner spoken than all the vehicles began to align with each other and the word was passed down the line that now was an adequate time to bathe in the waters while they had the chance.

Very soon all the men had stripped naked and were enjoying the soothing effects of the water running over them. It was clear in this display of nudity just how burned by the sun everyone had become during their time on the desert. Everyone looked lean and hard; so powerful had the rays of the sun been, that even the darkest head of hair had taken on a lighter shade of colour.

The men dipped and splashed in the water, refreshing them immensely. It had been a luxury to roll around in the water beneath the shade of the palms. Nathan felt good all over now and emerged to dry himself. In just a second he received another powerful shock that made him pale visibly. A different type of tank from that which had been travelling in the convoy was positioned at the end of the water. Nathan stood there naked, almost gasping in horror. For one moment he thought it had been an enemy tank. He was soon put right in that thought when a familiar face emerged from within.

"Wel, well! If it isn't the big bad boys of the SAS caught with their pants down!" The others came up from the water. John grabbed his towel and wrapped it around his waist.

"Hullo, Nathan! Hullo, John!" said the man inside the tank. "You blokes haven't got any girls down there have you?" The man was the Australian soldier Ted McTaggart who leaped out of the tank and shook hands with each of them. "Now listen here, you two blokes, if you know of a pub round here and a place where we can latch on to a few sheilas, don't keep it to yourself. You're certainly dressed for the occasion!"

They all laughed. Ted was a bright light with a sense of humour as colourful as the desert sand.

"What are you doing here, Ted?" asked Nathan, a bit bewildered.

"Oh geez, there's a few of us Aussies here. Apparently we're advancing together to push all our opponents into a corner. "We've been here a couple of days hiding away, waiting for all you blokes to show up. Well I'll be blowed, eh! Fancy meeting you fellas here!

"Bit of a surprise for us too," said John, as they walked back together to where the long line of jeeps and tanks were situated. It seemed that the Australian contingent had also travelled a somewhat unorthodox route to get this far. When they had dried and dressed back into their uniform they stood talking for a while about some of the sights they had seen on their travels. Ted produced a couple of bottles of beer, which tasted delicious in the middle of the day. While they were chatting, a solder nearby pointed out a cloud of dust generated by motor vehicles approaching them rapidly.

"Looks like some more of our blokes," remarked Ted. But there was something drastically wrong. The commanding officer of the platoon put a pair of field binoculars to his eyes and then with one hand waving frantically in a backwards motion to signify everyone to stay back, he turned round sharply.

"Get to your guns men! Come on move it!" There was no doubting the urgency in his voice. Charles moved over next to where the other three were standing and looked through is own binoculars.

"Stone the flaming crows! It's a panzer division!" No sooner had he spoken than everyone was racing to their jeeps and tanks and preparing themselves for the inevitable onslaught. This frightened Nathan perhaps even more than he realised. This was to be his first encounter as an active serviceman. He remembered the time in Palestine when Leon had urged him to take up arms in the Hagganah. Now he was in the position where he was compelled to do so.

The panzer division came nearer and nearer. "Get ready men!" The CO's voice boomed across the sand. Every soldier had his finger on the trifle. Nathan was so nervous he could feel his finger quivering and perspiration of a different kind, other than that induced by heat, began to drip down from his forehead on to the butt of his rifle.

In an instant there was one mighty roar as a shell exploded a hundred yards or so away and, almost as if in response, the once peaceful serenity of the desert became a noisy firework display. Bullets cracked and there were bursts of rifle fire. Bazookas fired, tanks geared up into action, machine guns rat-a-tatted at a frightening pace.

"I don't blinking like this much," muttered John, who was normally constantly upbeat. Nathan ducked several times. It was uncomfortably close to action that he had, until then, only heard about. Being in the thick of it with bullets soaring all around was no fun. He fired so often from his rifle that the mechanical working of the bolt became a repetitive motion that he hardly knew he was performing. Except for the pain in his right shoulder caused by the butt going back sharply as he fired, it was all a natural movement.

The skirmish went on for a long time. There is nothing glorious about a battle. The only victory is when it is all over. Several trucks received direct hits and blew up in smoke and flames. There was nothing but the sound of bullets for what seemed like a never-ending hail. Nathan remembered the advice the Regimental Sergeant Major had told him one morning on the parade ground about keeping his bloody head down when he heard the sound of rifles. Never in his life had he heeded advice so well.

The Germany army panzer division had remained at a distant position firing at full blast. Neither side advanced their artillery. This was entirely intentional on behalf of the British CO; he knew that the division of the German army would limp away,, only to be rounded up by another Eighth Army contingent further out in the desert.

Ted and his other slouch-hatted Aussie mates fought on to an amazing extent. They ran out from the front of the lines firing machine guns and actually exposed themselves to the full attack of the enemy guns.

They didn't have to bare the full brunt of it for too long. The panzer division began to retreat and head out towards the centre again. The burned out vehicles lay smouldering in the sun, the smoke pouring black across an azure sky. The wounded soldiers were picked up and taken to the vehicles that were leaving the scene of the attack. The CO waved to all the soldiers to halt their fire.

"Stop firing, lads." The order was passed down the line, and the scene became one of quiet. In the distance the German artillery sped away.

"Let them go, lads," said the CO. "The rest of our men are advancing north of here." He strode along the line of British and Australian soldiers who were all standing in silence watching the group disappear into the horizon. "No need to worry, men," continued the CO, "We're winning through. It may not seem like it, but this is only the beginning of the end of the war in North Africa at least." The men relaxed the grip on their weapons and stood in silence looking ahead.

Nathan watched the departing vehicles. It was hard for him to realise that he had been firing on people of his own nationality. But then he reminded himself that the enemy in this case had not been people who had been sympathetic to the Jewish race. Somehow this saddened him even more than the thought that he, a concerned pacifist, had taken part in wartime service.

Twenty-four

The convoy proceeded north to the Akaja oasis without any further attacks. Considering that they were on the edge of more confrontation with the enemy, and the possibility of further dramatic battles, this part of the journey was remarkably quiet. It seemed to be a difficult thought to swallow for Nathan, but the attack had put paid to the impression he had acquired that the North African desert belonged solely to the Arabs, the camels and the Eighth Army. He had tasted the harshness of engaging in a fierce battle and this trip of discovery had become clouded by the realities of war. Somehow the beauty of the desert – and it was beautiful in a breathtaking fashion – had been disfigured by the smoke and the fire that had emanated in battle.

At Akaja there were many vehicles congregated together from the various patrols that had traversed the desert routes from Cairo. Not only were the British Army there in its full might, but also the Australians and the New Zealanders. Eventually these British and Commonwealth troops would move out to join even more soldiers at El Alamein, which would become of the most decisive battles in history. For now though, the troops regrouped in the desert.

There were a number of addresses to the troops by senior officers mainly with the intention of keeping morale high in the ranks. Nathan stood with all the other soldiers watching and listening to the officers who stood on the front of jeeps echoing their words to all and sundry.

In more leisurely moments while they waited for other patrols to arrive, the Australians would play a game called Two-up. Nathan watched with fascination as the diggers took part in this game, which involved betting money on the spin of a coin. It was a relatively simple game. Ted McTaggart was at the centre of the action. Around him in a circle were rows of Australian soldiers putting all forms of currency notes and coins on a small rug that someone had placed strategically near the centre of the ring. Ted rolled a tailor-made cigarette as the bets were laid and, as soon as they had all been placed, he picked up a small board of wood. On this Ted placed two coins. From somewhere in the crowd, someone said, "OK, fellas, ya all set to go?" No one urged him to stop and the same voice said loudly, "Come in, spinner!"

Ted flipped the coins into the air and they spun high and dropped noiselessly on the soft carpet of sand. There was a momentary silence as all the heads moved downwards to see the result of the throw.

"It's heads, you blokes!" came a voice.

The men moved forward like cattle stampeding and eagerly divided their winnings. Over and over they played the game in an enthusiastic manner ever keen to break the monotony of their desert location.

Nathan had been joined by Charles and John, who were also intrigued by this game. It was noticeable how the piles of money at the feet of the soldiers increased and dwindled constantly. All this was totally reliant on the spin of a coin. When the game had finished, the three soldiers were walking away when Nathan saw an officer from their own convoy approaching them.

"Ah, just the three chaps I want to see," he said in an amiable manner, but it sounded pretty ominous, almost a forewarning in fact.

"Yes, sir" said Nathan meekly. He could sense the Lieutenant was going to ask them to volunteer for something. It would be difficult to refuse because it would then become a command, which could not be disobeyed.

"How would you like to volunteer for a job?" He knew it. Nathan just knew it. The officer had such a way of putting things. The three soldiers looked at each other waiting for the other to respond.

"What would you like us to do, sir?" asked Charles reluctantly.

The officer looked bleak suddenly. "We're all here except for two small patrols. I've been talking to some of the other patrol leaders and we are just about ready to move out. The two patrols – they're only a few lorries and trucks in each, but they're a real worry. Before we move out we want to be sure that nothing's happened to one of them. They could be delayed or else they could—" he broke off his words sharply. Strange how sometimes when a person says nothing, the look on their face betrays exactly what they are thinking "Well you were in that attack further down the track so you know what I am talking about."

"You want us to look for them, sir?" Charles broke in.

"Exactly. I want the three of you in one jeep to travel south west for about thirty five to fifty miles in a circular manner." He leaned down in the sand to demonstrate what he meant by pegging out the direction with a stick.

"Check out tyre marks on the tracks. See if there are any signs that the patrol might have been there. If you meet up with them travel quickly back here. Head back up northwest and then rejoin us here. Well arm yourselves – see the munitions officer before you go. Any questions?"

"When do you want us to go?" Nathan asked.

"As soon as you're ready, please, men. Good luck."

The officer walked away quickly. In the short time the three soldiers drove away from the relative security of the camp at the oasis and back out to the fierceness of the dessert. Charles sat in the back positioned by a rotary gun ever ready in case of an unexpected meeting with enemy troops. John drove fast while Nathan kept an eye open for the tyre tracks of the two missing convoys.

There weren't any indications that other convoys had passed in the direction in which they were travelling. In fact it was back to a pretty deserted ride again. The rides that Nathan had undergone in the jeep would provide him with many prolific memories of travel in this part of the world. He was amazed at the punishment it had undergone in the course of its journey. It had travelled over sand dunes, scrubland, rocky ridges, stone tracks, routes of loose stones rocks and boulders, and it was still incredibly intact. Not to mention it had been driven hard and fast and at times seemingly beyond its capabilities. The jeep had been a trustworthy vehicle to travel the desert in, almost indestructible it seemed.

For miles ahead they could see that they were pretty much alone. Yes, it was unbelievable really. Out in that vast expanse lay their opponents lurking in hiding somewhere ready to attack. The German and Italian Armies would clash with the Eighth Army at some stage. The earlier attack had been indicative of this.

Some hours later, after they had travelled in the southwesterly direction, that the lieutenant had asked them to do so, the sky seemed to be throwing up shades of a different colour in the distance. It was as if there was a furious gust of wind blowing up around them. John began to slow the jeep. He was aware what was happening. All around him sand began to blow in mounds.

"Sandstorm!" he gasped.

Sand was beginning to swirl and swirl in a twisting motion. It was covering them from head to foot in a matter of seconds. Each of the men were wearing sunglasses, which was only a fair protection from the twisting sand that was accumulating all over. John brought the jeep to a grinding halt.

"Jump in the back, lads," shouted Charles. The noise of the sandstorm was more frightening than could be imagined. "If we lie under the canvas, we should be all right." Nathan and John jumped into the back of the jeep and pulled a huge tarpaulin sheet over them and they lay down on the front of their chests. Charles sneaked a quick glance from out of the canvas at the storm.

So powerful was the full fury of the storm that the jeep was actually rocking from side to side. The sand that was being blown around was gathering on the top of the sheet that they were lying under. It was beginning to become heavy.

"By God, it's furious," murmured Charles as he raised his head to look at the storm.

Somewhere in Nathan's widely read mind he recalled the name *Sirocco*. This was surely an Arabic word that was relative to this type of fierce desert storm. Or was it? *Sirocco*. What did that mean? It kept going over and over in his mind. *Sirocco*. He could not recall its meaning. Then another noise other than the sounds of the storm disturbed his train of thought. He listened. It was undoubtedly clear. The sounds of ignition and exhaust were so distinctive.

"I can hear a motor-engine revving," he uttered,

John raised his head slightly. "Yes – yes. So can I," he agreed.

The vehicle belonging to the motor engine was obviously stuck in the sand somewhere close to them. It was impossible to see through the whirling sand. Visibility was poor. Nothing but sand blew before them.

"They need help," said Nathan in an almost urging tone. "It must be our men."

"Hang on a minute," Charles beckoned. "Their voices – wait till we hear their voices."

"There are more," said John sharply. "I'm pretty sure of it."

In spite of the sounds of the storm the revving engine managed to come through. That one particular engine became louder. Then another one, and another. Nathan estimated that there must be several vehicles outside. It was obvious that the trucks could not move from their positions. The sand must have formed around the wheels of the trucks bogging them down in an unmoveable position

"Let's wait before we do anything," said Charles. "If I could just hear the noise of one of them. If they're our blokes, we might be able to do something."

Nathan suddenly moved himself sharply from the jeep.

"I'll have a look," he whispered, and disappeared into the swirling sand. He ran along quickly trying to go in the direction of the engine sounds. The sand beneath his feet felt heavy and laden. Through the mists of swirling sand he looked left, right and behind him. He could not see anything at all. He ran on a bit further. Still nothing. He could hear garbled voices. He could hear the sounds of a wheel going around and around but going nowhere. The sounds were coming somewhere to his left. He ran on and glanced left sharply. At that very instant he ran hard into something. It felt as if he had run directly into a brick wall. The full effects sent him tumbling back sharply. He rolled down a sand dune aimlessly and virtually unconscious.

It took him several minutes before he realised just what had happened. He rolled over on his back and straightened his glasses. The sandstorm was beginning to dissipate. Up above him at the top of the dune was a tall palm tree. Nathan had run flat bang into the palm and had almost knocked himself out. He scrambled up on his feet quickly. His head had taken a fair old bang. Blood was streaming from his forehead. Grabbing a handkerchief he mopped his brow quickly and straightened the Arab headdress he had been wearing.

Nathan struggled up the dune. Something made him stop. All the vehicle sounds had stopped and now he heard clearly the voices. It was the enemy, no doubt about that whatsoever. His head was hurting enormously. He tried to concentrate. He could hear the accents that were reminiscent of his youth. Slowly he ascended the dune carefully going in the direction of the voices. Just a few yards on and he would be able to steal a glance.

The sandstorm was dying away. It was clearer. The sand had settled in mounds all over. He trod softly as he came to a ridge in the dune. If he could peer over the edge he could see the German troops down below. Just a few more steps then he fell to his knees and began to crawl quietly.

The voices rose up from below. Nathan leaned over the dune edge and studied the sight. There must have been fifteen heavily armed trucks and jeeps below. True to form the sandstorm had caused a huge build up around the base of the German convoy. The soldiers were moving their transport clear of the sand. There was a good harmony between the men.

Nathan thought to himself, *They are the enemy but they are people from my own birthplace*. What a strange situation life had placed him in, to be observing the enemy from a distance who were people he shared the same country of origin with. He could have stayed on for ages just watching them and thinking, but he would have to get back. He turned around and began to walk back to the jeep where Charles and John were waiting.

His heart missed a beat. Coming towards him was a German soldier.

My God, thought Nathan, *what do I do now?* The soldier was armed with a rifle. He brought it up in a sharp and violent action pointing directly at him. An idea flashed through Nathan's mind. He called out a greeting to him in German.

"Stop. I am German. I am one of your countrymen."

The soldier recognised the dialect instantly, but he appeared puzzled and bemused. He could not understand why this man in British Army uniform spoke in such crystal clear German. He lowered his rifle slowly. Nathan took a step forward. The soldier brought the rifle back up sharply with a vengeance.

"Who are you?" He demanded of Nathan in a sharp accent.

Nathan looked closely at the face of the soldier. It was a remarkably boyish face. He could not have been more than twenty years of age. His eyes showed a hint of fear beneath their stony gaze.

It was a strange situation. Two young men of the same age, and the same country of birth, but they were of a different religion and on opposing sides. Each one stared at the other. Neither quite knowing what do to.

"I am a soldier like you," said Nathan. He took a short step forward. What to do now was the question. The German soldier would surely shoot him if he attempted to do anything. If there was a scuffle the noise would almost certainly bring out all the soldiers down below.

"Why do you wear the khaki of the British Army?" he asked.

The sun was beginning to go down and the change in light gave the soldier a sinister, almost menacing appearance.

Nathan gambled on the hunch that the soldier had not determined from his characteristics the faith to which he belonged. Nathan's hair, face and sunglasses had sand all over them; he assumed this to be another disguising factor in the lie he was about to perpetrate.

"My patrol was attacked and lost." He spoke in his keenest German. "But I took the uniform of a British soldier that we found in a burnt-out vehicle." Nathan lied with remarkable clarity. His gaze over the soldier's shoulder was startled suddenly. Not more than a hundred yards away he could see Charles and John peering out from behind a mound of sand. If Nathan could only keep the soldier talking.

"What is he doing?" John whispered to Charles.

"It looks like that soldier is about to frogmarch Nathan away," replied the other.

"My bet is that there's a whole bunch of German soldiers over the dune. I bet you a day's pay that Nathan saw them and he bumped into that bloke coming back."

"I bet you a day's pay, you're right. What do we do though?" He looked at John for inspiration.

"I've got an idea," John whispered. "I'm going to run like a panther to the jeep and drive like the bloody wind back. You cover Nathan. Sneak up behind that soldier, push him over really quickly and you and Nathan jump on the jeep as I come cruising along. Get on the blinkin' gun quickly as soon as you get on, I'm going to move bloomin' fast and I'm not stopping for tea and crumpets with the enemy."

"You better go for it then, my son," said Charles in a hushed voice. John turned around and moved quickly back to the jeep. Charles began to edge himself forward. He crawled on his belly very slowly.

Nathan was still spinning his unbelievable yarn to the soldier, who was listening intently. The man was virtually convinced now. Without giving too much detail away about his life, Nathan talked of his boyhood in Germany and Austria mentioning place names that aroused his attention.

Charles moved closer now. Nathan kept talking. He tried not to let his gaze nervously divert from the soldier's face. He kept on talking.

John had made it back to the jeep and he attempted to start it. Damn it! Blast and damn it! It wouldn't start. He tried again. The noise of the accelerator would sound like a thunderclap on the desert enough to wake up the entire German and Italian forces in North Africa. He jumped down and lifted the bonnet up. There was sand smothering the engine. So powerful had the sandstorm been that it had got into the engine. With his bare hands he scraped it off and blew and blew until his cheeks turned crimson. He got back in and tried again.

Nathan had never talked for so long in his life. He spun out his story a bit longer, then, from behind him, came two German soldiers marching up the dune. He heard their voices and spun around in horror. Charles was still creeping up behind the other soldier when they came into view. Nathan turned round and looked at Charles horrified.

"Get down, Nathan!" Charles shrieked loudly.

Nathan went down to the ground like a tree lobbed at a great height. The young soldier turned sharply to receive a sharp uppercut from Charles that knocked him over the side of the dune and sent him rolling down the sand.

Charles picked up the young soldiers, rifle and went racing towards the other two. He was fast, that boy, so fast he took them by complete surprise and, using his boot and rifle, he pushed them back down from where they had walked up. One of them came back and reached for his pistol. He was too slow. Charles had not been a boxer in his youth for nothing and a sharp left sent the man tumbling down the sandy hills.

Nathan picked himself up and ran up to Charles. "Are you all right, Charles?"

"No problem," he gasped. "Let's get out of here." They began to run and Charles cast a backward glance. "Oh no!" His voice was tinged with agony. There behind them were about fifteen enemy soldiers scrambling up the dunes. They ran like Olympic sprinters to get away, bullets were splaying all around their heels.

A God-given distraction suddenly appeared. Driving like a racing car driver on the final lap of a high-speed circuit, John manoeuvred the jeep over the sandy hills with a skill he had never realised he had. The jeep came flying over the dunes; its wheels not touching the ground as it shot into the air. It came down with a thud and raced along the edge of the sandhills. John was stunned to see the German soldiers in front of him. Putting his foot down hard on the accelerator he drove at them.

They jumped like they had never jumped before to get out of the way. He steered his jeep off in the direction of Charles and Nathan. He slowed down beside them. They both leaped in with John pushing the jeep into high speed again.

"Where have you been? Did you meet a bird or something?" Charles roared in a good-humoured and cynical fashion.

"There was sand all over the blasted engine. I couldn't get the thing started."

"A likely story!" Charles shouted as he propped up a machine gun in the back of the jeep. They had hardly sped away over the sand when in the space of five minutes, the sound of another engine roared from behind: they were being chased by a German armoured car. It obviously hadn't taken their opponents long to spur themselves into action.

The two vehicles hurtled across the desert tracks at a great pace. It was staggering the punishment they were both taking. The German armoured car began firing and firing, but its shots fell short of its target. John weaved the jeep in and out and at angles to avoid the shots that were being taken at them.

Charles hung on for dear life trying at the same time to aim fire from the back of the jeep. "Slow down, John. I want to take a shot at them." He called out.

John's sense of humour never seemed to desert him. "I'm not hanging round here, Chas. I haven't had my blinkin' dinner yet."

There was no stopping them now. The jeep began outpacing the armoured car, which seemed to be dragging in its pace. Eventually it lagged behind to the extent that it gave up the chase.

That was perhaps the most memorable time of the war for Nathan. He was never to forget those experiences on the desert and particularly that day when he had come face to face with the young soldier.

On that same day Nathan, John and Charles, returned to the camp at the oasis to find that the two patrols they had gone in search of had arrived together within an hour of their own departure.

The forces that had gathered together at the base moved out to take part in the monumental battle at El Alamein. Years later in conversation Nathan was to recall how ironic it was for him, a man bitterly opposed to war, to find himself in the midst of one of the biggest campaigns of the Second World War. Nathan was always able to remember his time in the desert of North Africa with almost a passion for detail. He could remember the colour, the atmosphere, and the sunsets with affection but, perhaps most of all, he cherished the memory of the friends he had made: Charles, John and the Australian soldier Ted McTaggart. It was one of the most significant times of his life.

Twenty-five

While Nathan was in North Africa, Freddie Miller was in Colombo working on intelligence operations. His abilities in this direction were being tested once again to the limit. It was a totally different area for Freddie to work on. Together with a number of his colleagues, he had been planning missions in the Far East. With the Japanese forces occupying much of the East a number of attacks had been organised on military installations.

Freddie had been responsible for working out how to minimise the effectiveness of the forces of Japan by blowing up bridges, destroying ammunition and supply trains. He had applied himself to his tasks rigidly. Several teams comprising of a few volunteer soldiers and some locals had penetrated the jungles of Malaysia, Burma and Thailand. When the people on these missions had not returned, he knew that he would have to embark himself. It was a great worry to him. There were thousands of British and Commonwealth troops held in captivity in Japanese Prisoner of War Camps and their welfare was at stake. Freddie would have to enter the fray himself.

Since Cynthia had died, Freddie had been grief-stricken. Even now there were times when he would wake up in the morning and it would be moments before he could get his thoughts together; then he would realise with a heavy heart that he had not woken from a nightmare, Cynthia really had gone forever in this lifetime. That was such a bitter blow to him.

If it had not been for his work, he would almost certainly have gone under. It was only the huge responsibilities of his intelligence work that kept his mind and thoughts in gear. Both in Cairo and Colombo he had put in many hours planning missions and reconnaissance trips.

Beneath his industrious mind he felt totally dispirited. When this war was finally over he realised that he would probably be forty years of age and totally alone in life. He had no other relations. He doubted that he would ever marry again. He knew, too, that so many things had happened in his life that his character had changed with the acquisition of experience and the passing of the years. Never again would he be the freewheeling young bachelor of the years between the wars. That man belonged to another life.

Part of the reason that Freddie had volunteered to go on a very dangerous mission was that he simply didn't care anymore. He had lost Cynthia; he didn't know what he would do when the war ended or where he would go. If he was going to do something heroic he might as well go for broke. Damn it all! He had filmed war in Abyssinia and Spain, he might just as well participate in an almost impossible mission somewhere in Indonesia where the objective would be to blow up Japanese supply depots; a hard task – almost one for someone on the edge of insanity.

Now that Freddie had volunteered, he was beginning to wonder if he had made the decision when his mind was still on a precipice brought about by Cynthia's death. The day before he was due to leave Colombo he drove to the Mount Lavinia Hotel to meet another officer for drinks and last minute talks about his forthcoming mission. It is strange how, at a certain time in one's life, when they are about to embark on a journey possibly of no return, the beauty of the world immediately at hand is increased tenfold. Freddie's surroundings were enhanced by the feeling of just being alive and being there to appreciate it.

Sitting on the veranda of the Mount Lavinia Hotel, Freddie toyed with his drink. It was a splendid day, the sun was warm and it really did feel good to be there looking out at the sparkling blue waters of the ocean. Tomorrow it would be the drone of aircraft and into the breach once more. He sipped his drink and pondered in his thoughts.

Moments later an aristocratic officer joined Freddie and in the sunshine they talked deeply about the coming mission. They exchanged a few ideas and then took the subject of conversation to a more moderate plateau discussing different things and places they had been to in their lives. Finally after a while the officer mentioned that prior to his posting to Colombo he had been on Brindmarsh's staff in London. Freddie pricked up his ears with interest. He listened keenly for a while then interrupted and made mention of the fact that he also had worked for Colonel Brindmarsh.

By a coincidence the officer was well-informed of the operations of the Companions of the Circle. Freddie then pursued the subject of Francine. Seeing he had been indirectly responsible for involving Francine in the work of the Circle, he was eager to know how she was progressing. The officer unfortunately couldn't throw too much light on the matter. He had not been involved in that side of things for some time and as such he couldn't inform Freddie of any recent developments in Paris. It was not until the war was over that Freddie was to learn of the extent of Francine's career with the Special Operations Executive.

★★★

Francine was in her element as a member of the Underground forces. Using her abilities as an artist she disguised the real mission in her life with great skill. Her radio transmitter was hidden beneath a pallet of oil paints and a tiny microphone would be carefully wired up behind her portable stand on which she placed her paintings. So far she had made observations of the Nazi officers at their headquarters as they arrived and departed, and made estimations of their numbers and noted their descriptions for future use.

The movements of the Circle operatives were constantly relayed back to Brindmarsh at Whitehall, who kept in touch with developments as they occurred. There were many people who were being protected by the Circle in Paris and their safety was of the utmost concern. They were all Jewish people who feared for their lives if their whereabouts were disclosed. The Circle was concerned for them and the entire energies of this organisation were devoted to looking after their interests. There were other resistance groups in Paris, also directed by Whitehall, but their function was different to that of the Circle's. The resistance groups comprised of people who possessed the kind of spine-chilling courage that became legendary. The figures of the resistance moved in a shadowy world, always aware that capture would mean instant death. From these groups came people whose heroics were outstanding amongst them, such as Noor Imayat-Khan, known as Code Name Madeleine, and many of the brave individuals without whom the fate of the world may have been very different.

Francine had formed a close attachment to her Circle colleagues.

Amongst the tiny group she worked with they included several fiercely patriotic Frenchmen: Claude Renalier, Jacques Simeon and Jean Venual Each of them were men of character and strength. Except for Jean, who was a business man in his thirties, the others were all in their twenties. Claude was unofficially the leader. He had more or less the stronger personality of the group and tended to show initiative and direction when making decisions. He was cool and confident in his manner, and in his appearance well-groomed, tall with dark hair slicked back and permanently shiny. Jacques was a quiet moustachioed man who never seemed to remove his beret. The only hint of his real personality was in the manner of his continual chain smoking. Jean Venual was different altogether; he was bald and overweight but very astute and quick thinking.

Every so often they would meet up in a smoke-filled room somewhere and transmit the latest information to Brindmarsh. Then they would talk and plan their next manoeuvres. Every time they met, at some interval along the way to their meeting place, each one would carefully check to see if they had been followed. For hours they would work out their procedures and aims, and then in the dark of night depart for their respective apartments.

After these meetings Francine would make her way back to her cousin's flat in the Rue Maximilien Robespierre in Malakof. Francine's cousin was working for the Free French somewhere in the country and she had allowed her the run of flat. From there she would radio her contacts in Whitehall giving them the latest details of the movements of the Circle. It was a nerve-racking task of transmitting the information from the seclusion of the flat. She lived in dread of a knock on the door and being visited by the Gestapo. It had happened before to various resistance agents. The awesome possibility that it could happen again was not to be ruled out.

Claude had more than a passing interest in Francine. He made no pretences about it, but didn't impose on her too much. The work of the Circle had more importance attached to it than mere emotional matters. Claude and Francine were a contrasting couple in their personalities brought together by their wartime commitment. Sometimes in a bar they would talk over a few drinks and discuss in confidence things that were happening within their group. They had become very close friends.

By day Francine carried out her pretence of a professional artist, speaking to her colleagues on the transmitter that she carried with her. The response that she got from her opposite number in Whitehall was normally pretty straightforward, usually just a simple exchange of information. In Paris she spoke internally to her Circle comrades. The whole operation had been going smoothly for so long that it seemed as if it would always be the case.

One day when Francine had been painting a scenic view of Paris from the Left Bank, through her hidden microphone she had been trying frantically to get in touch with one of her associates. When he had failed to return the transmission call, Francine had become worried. Several other associates of the Circle also had not answered the call. Something was definitely amiss. Francine immediately walked to a nearby café and made a telephone call to Jean Venual. There was no answer. Francine was now getting very concerned. What had happened to all of the Parisian operatives of the Circle?

It was beginning to rain now and Francine sat inside the café wondering what to do next. Francine got up from her table and made a call to Jacques Simeon. The phone rang and rang at the other end. Then there was an answer. Jacques answered saying only "Hullo". Just as Francine was about to speak, several German officers walked into the café. Before continuing to speak she drew a breath letting them pass.

"Jacques," she spoke very quietly, "I have been unable to contact anyone. Where are they all?"

"Claude is here with me," he replied. "We must meet – the three of us, say in half an hour at the Place du Figaro. I cannot tell you now. Something has happened."

Francine replaced the phone and stared at the floor in shock. The Circle was highly important in its Paris operations in protecting prominent Jewish citizens and aiding other resistance groups. The failure of this organisation here would be disastrous for many people. Effectively the demise of the group in Paris would almost certainly lead to the end of the work of the Circle in the other countries where it was operating.

Not a moment was to be wasted. Francine left the shelter of the café immediately and went out into the street. The rain was pouring down in heavy torrents. She pulled her beret down tight on her head and buckled her raincoat tightly. It was a precarious time in occupied Paris to be an agent. With so many Nazi officers around, conversation on matters to do with the resistance were always conducted in whispers in public places. Telephone calls were always brief, always directly to the point, saying nothing more, nothing less than need be said. At times it was thrilling, even exciting to be working undercover but it was tinged with a very real danger. Now it seemed that something wildly wrong had happened. Francine felt a real dread about the present moment.

By the time Francine had arrived at the Place du Figaro, Jacques and Claude were waiting nearby in a parked car. Francine caught sight of it. She ran across the road splashing in the puddles and got into the back of it. No sooner had she entered the car than Jacques, at the drivers wheel revved the car into action and started speeding away.

"Where are we going?" Francine asked full of alarm. "What has happened?"

It was Claude who answered, swivelling around in the seat to face Francine. "To the country, there is a farmhouse we must stay at. We cannot go back to our apartments for the moment."

"But why?" exclaimed Francine.

"Because we have been betrayed." Jacques had answered. His voice was as cold as ice. Betrayed. The word sent a shiver through the spine. The rain pelted against the windshield of the car as the journey out of Paris progressed. Francine felt fear of the future suddenly.

Before she could ask another question Jacques added to what he had said earlier, "When we get to the farmhouse we must sit down and work out a number of things. There is a radio there. We'll radio Brindmarsh straight away."

Some way out of Paris the car went down many narrow winding country lanes, finally arriving at a secluded house backing onto acres of arable fields. Once inside the three of them dried themselves and lit a small fire. From a hidden trapdoor in the floor Jacque brought up a radio transmitter. Claude was obviously well-acquainted with the house for he made straight for a cupboard that housed a few bottles of port and rum. He produced a bottle and three glasses, pouring the contents into all three.

Jacques toyed with the radio. Then he placed an aerial in a bush outside of the window. Wireless frequency sounds came across the microphone. Jacques adjusted it and began to transmit. An English voice with crisp modulated tones came across.

"Please give your code name."

"Code name Companion 14. Come in, please." The static on the line was annoying. Jacques persevered, "Come in please."

There were a few breathtaking moments as Jacques waited for a response. Then the voice of Brindmarsh came on the line. "Chief Companion." This was the disguised title that Colonel Brindmarsh was referred to as. Jacques signalled to Francine and Claude. "Keep watch on the front and back doors while I talk." He called out. "We don't want any surprise visitors."

Claude grabbing a pistol moved quickly to the back door of the farmhouse, while Francine covered the front door. Jacques communicated with the Colonel telling him all that had happened and with a pen he wrote down details furiously taking note of his instructions. Within ten minutes Jacques had passed on the new and garnished fresh information and advice upon which to act. He called to Claude and Francine to come inside. He immediately disassembled the radio transmitter and placed it together with the outside aerial beneath the trapdoor on the floor.

When Claude and Francine returned to the room they found Jacques looking particularly grim. He still managed to half smile but appeared stern though.

"Well, my friends, you better reach for your glasses of rum. I fear the news is grave." Almost as if commanded they each took a sip of the drink. "I am afraid, Francine, that when you were trying to contact the other members of the Circle today, they had all been rounded up by the Gestapo and taken away to 84 Avenue Foch."

The news delivered a fatal body blow with all the impact of a force eight gale. 84 Avenue Foch! The name seemed to strike a severe nerve because that was known as the address of the SS headquarters in Paris.

"How did this happen?" gasped Francine totally unnerved for she knew that this meant they were probably known by name to the enemy now.

"As I mentioned earlier, someone has betrayed us," retorted Jacques with anger rising in his voice. "I went to meet up with several of the men yesterday. On each occasion an observer of ours contacted me first to tell me that the Gestapo had rounded them up. I tried to get in touch with the others when it was clear what had happened, but I was too late. They had all apparently been arrested, all except one."

"You mean one got away!" exclaimed Francine.

"Not exactly," said a subdued Clause topping up each one's glass. He cast a knowing look to Jacques. "We think it likely that Jean Venual betrayed us. The observer saw him go to his office and return, but, if all the other Parisian members of the Circle have been arrested, why did they not find Jean? If the three of us had returned home tonight, I am pretty sure there would have been men waiting for us to arrest us. But Jean was seen going to and from his apartment completely alone."

A stony silence followed as they took in the news. Obviously shocked. Finally Francine said in a voice that did not hint any deep concern at this stage, "If Jean has revealed the workings of the Circle that could mean the end of its operations not only in France but in its underground role in Holland, Austria and Germany. It would be destroyed completely."

"That I am only too well aware of, mademoiselle," remarked Jacques. "When I spoke to Brindmarsh he said the only course for us to take is to find out who the betrayer is. Brindmarsh is going to contact the Circle elsewhere in Austria and Holland and the other countries that you mentioned. They will cease operating until we are clear here."

"But they must know who we are," Francine pointed out.

"That is what we must find out, Francine." Jacques slurped the contents of his glass and brought it down to the table aggressively. His eyes blazed furiously. "One of us must make contact with Jean. But we must not even give any hints that we are suspicious of him. We need someone to gently probe him, feel him out for any clues. Anything that might indicate just what he knows." His gaze shifted directly to Francine. "Can you do it, Francine?" he asked. "Claude and I will be close by in the car at all times, I promise you."

Francine's eyebrows rose in astonishment. "Me?"

"Yes, because you have femininity on your side to begin with," replied Jacques, filling up his glass again. He was a hardened drinker thought Francine. "And –" he added, "It is mademoiselle, a psychological advantage. Jean is more likely to respond to the coolness of a woman, more so than the aggressive nature of his fellowman."

"You are not asking me to use the allure of womanhood are you, Jacques?" Francine questioned, and this time there was clearly distaste in her voice and annoyance on her beautiful face.

Jacques was swift to respond sensing the line Francine had interpreted.

"No not your beauty," he purred making it clear he understood her. "Just the cunning and the instincts of a street brawler, which we all have."

"Very well," she grimaced at the thought of it. "What shall I do?"

"Tomorrow we shall go back to Paris," said Claude this time. "We will wait in a café near Jean's apartment. When we see Jean enter his home you must telephone him immediately. Tell him everyone of the Circle has gone missing including Jacques and I. Make it clear that you want a meeting with him at another café in about an hour at the Boulevard Henri Lamont. Before you arrive Jacques and I will check it out from a distance. It is quite possible that if Jean is the betrayer or is being used in any way, there may be members of the SS there. From our studies before, and our observations on their headquarters, some of their men may be there."

"You must stay in the café near Jean's apartment," stressed Jacques. "When I have checked out the other café at the Boulevard Henri Lamont, I will ring you to tell you to stay or proceed."

"And if it is safe?" Francine filled her own glass to quell her nervousness at the prospect the coming day would hold.

"If it is safe," began Jacques, stopping to knock back his glass and wipe his mouth with his sleeve, "if it is safe, test him. Probe him. But do not on any account even indicate that we know all the Circle members in Paris except us have been arrested. Do not let him know that some of our observers from other resistance groups were watching the arrests. That was until now, only known to Claude and I, and now you. We have to have some sort of protection that was private to us."

"I see," mused Francine astonished at the turn the conversation had taken. Then it became obvious to her that Claude and Jacques must have agreed on the plan earlier. It was not a spur of the moment thing. "This was well thought out, was it not, Jacques? Eh, Claude? You both worked this out before I rang you in Paris, didn't you?" Francine was angry now and she didn't care who knew it. The two men were surprised at her indignation and said nothing. "Kindly remember that I trusted you and that we, as part of the Companions of the Circle, should always work together and not in secrecy from one another."

The measure of her words had taken the desired effect. "I think you are right, Francine," said Jacques realising the truth in what she had said.

Francine began to fill up the two men's glasses and then when filled she took one in each hand and before handing them their drinks, she said,

"I will carry out the job tomorrow, gentlemen. Next time, tell me!" She tossed the contents in the face of each man.

Despite the drenching Claude managed to smile. "You are most definitely a French woman!"

"And dazzlingly beautiful in your anger." Jacques said in a voice that sounded a little sarcastic.

★★★

In Paris the next day the trio returned in their car and sat quietly within view of Jean's apartment block. Jean returned at about midday totally alone. There was no one around who looked suspicious. Claude and Jacques knew the faces of certain high-ranking SS officers, and after careful scrutiny they gave the all clear for Francine to make her phone call to Jean. Francine walked carefully to a nearby café and rang Jean Venual.

"Jean. It is Francine."

"Francine!" Jean's voice expresses genuine surprise.

"Where is everyone? I tried all day to contact our colleagues., but nothing."

At the other end of the line Jean mopped his brow. When he was nervous his forehead tended to perspire in floods.

"I don't know. I was busy at work yesterday."

Even at this distance over the telephone line Jean's voice sounded false. It was clear that he was not telling the truth. The observers employed by the Circle to keep watch on the agents; in the case of Jean had observed him going in and out of his apartment all day.

"Jean, we must meet in one hour's time at Sylvester's café at the Boulevard Henri Lamont. Be there! Goodbye."

Francine had not been sharp or angry in her manner of speech to Jean but she had been clearly direct, leaving Jean with no alternative. Francine had disengaged the line abruptly. In agony of spirit, Jean replaced the receiver, and turned to face the SS officer who had forced him into such a difficult position. The man looked at Jean in a sharp, curious manner.

"Well, you heard the lady, Monsieur Venual." He was standing over Jean, menacing him. "One hour's time. Sylvester's café, The Boulevard Henri Lamont."

Jean looked back at him with disgust. "Under threat of death to me and my family you push me to such limits. You may destroy the resistance but you will never win the war."

The SS officer did not say a word. He just glared at Jean but a sarcastic smile crossed his lips.

Back in the car Francine reported to Claude and Jacques.

"The meeting is arranged," she said coolly.

"How did he sound?" asked Claude.

"Distraught, surprised. He was lying. I could tell that, I am certain there was someone in the background."

Jacques looked round sharply from the front seat. "Why do you say that?"

"It was as if – as if I could hear someone breathing."

"Probably breathing down his neck I bet," retorted Jacques. "I think it likely that Jean's cover has been blown and that he is under pressure to reveal all. I did not think he would be a willing betrayer."

"You must keep the meeting, Francine," said Claude.

Francine lit up a cigarette and began to take long breaths in order to calm her nervousness. For a young lady of twenty-two she was a remarkably charismatic person, even the way she smoked her cigarette had a manner of seduction about it.

Forty-five minutes ticked by. They watched Jean Venual leave the block. He was obviously nervous. He looked around him sharply and started to walk in the direction of the Boulevard Henri Lamont.

"I will follow him," said Jacques. "Go and wait over there in that café." He pointed. "Wait for my phone call there before going to Sylvester's café."

They both left immediately while Claude waited in the car. Jacques walked down the street with stealth in his footsteps, following Jean down to the proposed meeting place. Several times Jean turned around as if he was aware that someone was following him. Jacques always moved carefully into the shadows if he was too close. Then Jean turned into the Boulevard Henri Lamont and walked across to Sylvester's café.

Jacques stopped close by and stood at the edge of the street studying the people in and around the café. He froze in his tracks. Jean was sitting at one of the outside tables but close by, in normal every-day clothes, sat several SS men. It was obvious what was happening. The trap had been set. For as soon as Francine entered the café there would be simply no escape. Jacques glared intensely at the SS men. They were known to him from contacts he had made. Jean was obviously being used as the pawn in the attempts to checkmate the movements of the Circle.

Jacques turned around and made his way to the nearest telephone but as he began to move down the street he was aware that something also was wrong. From out of a side street several men with hard looks stopped to bar his way. In a single moment of horror he realised that he had been trapped. The SS in their bid to round up all the members of the Circle had obviously planned on moving behind Francine, but their specially laid trump card had caught another ace instead – Jacques Simeon.

"Ah, monsieur Simeon I believe," said one of the men. But there was frantic interaction suddenly. Jacques reached for a pistol. He never had time to squeeze the trigger. One of the others was quicker off the mark and Jacques was struck down in his tracks.

At the other end of the Boulevard the sound of the shot that had felled Jacques caused Jean to stand up with dismay. When he realised what had happened Jean produced his own gun and in the middle of the café he shot two of the SS men before he, too, was shot down. Two of the Circle's best men had died in a bloody confrontation. It was all so quick and terrifying.

Jacques lay dead at one end of the road and in a café Jean and two others lay spread-eagled beneath several overturned tables. A short way away, totally unaware of what had happened, Claude remained in the car and Francine sat in another café waiting for the phone call that would never come. By now Francine was getting anxious. Every couple of minutes she glanced at her watch until she had waited nearly half an hour. Around the corner Claude sat at the wheel of his parked car. He, too, was worried that Jacques had not yet returned, but he was not compelled to move just yet. In the world of evasion and subterfuge patience was not only a virtue; it was a highly developed skill. Impatience could destroy a plan and put lives at risk. He decided to light up a cigarette and as he blew the first ring of smoke, Francine tapped on the window. Claude unlocked the door and Francine came inside.

"Where's Jacques?" he asked.

"It's been nearly half an hour, Claude," she groaned, "and he still hasn't called."

Claude looked deeply concerned. "It wouldn't have taken him half an hour," he said in a worried tone. "Not to check out Raymond Sylvester's café. He started the car. "Why is it that on this job I can pick up the vibrations from several streets away? Come, we'll take a drive along the Boulevard Henri Lamont."

The car moved into the centre of the road and Claude manoeuvred it through the city traffic. Considering this was occupied Paris, movement around the city was still remarkably free. The girls still looked to be devastatingly attractive, although Claude felt that Francine was the pick of the bunch. When Claude's thoughts were not concerned with the Circle they were heavily involved with Francine. Claude had barely the time to let his thoughts drift away to the feminine side of life when he steered the car into the Boulevard Henri Lamont. A German soldier stood in the middle of the road diverting traffic.

"What is it?" Francine whispered.

Claude slowed the car right down as it turned in the direction of the diversion. He glanced sharply to his left and quickly towards Raymond Sylvester's café. The evidence of the shootings was clear. A cluster of figures stood around the bodies at each end of the street. When Francine saw what had happened she let out a gasp of horror.

"Oh it was, Jacques," she cried dismayed.

"And Jean too," Claude pointed out his own utterance filled with shock. He pushed his foot down on the accelerator. His face looked a picture of fury. "Oh why, why, why!" He shouted, enraged. "Two good men dead! I am sure Jean must have been trailed. The SS must have set this whole thing up."

Francine's beautiful face was now a saddened composure. She looked horrified now as she realised that the fate that had befallen Jacques could have been hers.

"If I'd gone—" she began.

"I know, Francine." Claude cut in sharply and he took one hand off the wheel and gripped her reassuringly for a moment. "But it wasn't you, was it? No matter how cold it sounds, Francine, that was part of war. If it hadn't been Jacques and Jean, it would have been us."

She stared back at him knowing it was true.

"What now?" asked Francine, still shocked at what had happened.

"Back to the farmhouse and radio Brindmarsh, I think," replied Claude, although he was thinking hard and suddenly he added, "I think we better stop off at your apartment. Pick up what you need. We may need to operate from the farmhouse now, at least for a while, anyway. Then when Brindmarsh hears from us we must work out how we can regroup the Circle in Paris. What worries me is just how much Jean revealed to the enemy. And now we shall never hear it from Jean's own lips. I only hope the Circle will survive in the rest of Europe."

"Even if I am caught I can tell you this, Claude, I would not reveal the slightest thing. I would be tight-lipped to the end."

"If anything does happen and you are caught I would not like to guess just what would happen to you. I dread to think of their methods of interrogation."

"You should not underestimate me because I am a woman."

Claude appeared to smile briefly at her remark. "I don't." He said. "Believe me, I don't."

They drove on quickly through the busy Paris streets. It was like being on the edge of a precipice. Suddenly everything was laid bare and the workings of the Circle were common knowledge to the occupying forces of Germany. Even to go back to their separate apartments was in itself a tremendous risk for Francine and Claude, as surely their identities had been established, since the Gestapo had obviously put Jean Venual under fierce interrogation.

When they arrived at Francine's home in the Rue Maximilien Robespierre in Malakof, they waited outside the apartment block for some time as a matter of caution; there was the possibility that somehow another trap may have been laid to ensnare Francine.

"Do you think it's clear?" Francine asked with some trepidation. They both sat in the car gazing up at the windows of her apartment trying to see if there was any sign of life, any movement, any slight ruffling of the curtains. There was nothing suspicious at all.

"It looks to be fine. Go quickly, Francine. Don't take too long. Be careful. Check for anything that looks suspect before you open the door."

Francine immediately sprang into action and made her way into the apartment block. Once inside she took the lift to the floor where her rooms were situated. Walking along the hallway she felt a nervousness in her stomach as if she was expecting something drastic to happen. At the door of her apartment she examined the edges of the door around the lock for any signs of scratches or missing wood, indicating that it might have been jemmied open. When she had checked that out, she put her ear against the door to listen for any movement. It was quiet. There was not the slightest ruffle of noise. Slowly Francine put the key in the lock and turned it quietly. She opened the door very gently without a shudder or a hint of nervousness. With the door pushed wide open she breathed a sigh of relieve, for the room was empty. There was not a sign that anyone had disturbed the room. Drawers were unmoved; books were in the same place. Francine relaxed herself immediately. She went to her bedroom door and opened it. It was in that split second everything changed.

There was nothing Francine could do. The room was full of SS men. Francine found herself in a position that she could not move from. She was frozen in her tracks. The SS men grouped round her and moved her out of the apartment. But they did not leave by the front entrance. Instead they took her out down the fire escape at the back and into a waiting car. From there they drove to 84 Avenue Foch, the SS headquarters,

For Claude waiting outside in his car, he was beginning to get the same feelings he had experienced earlier on before discovering what had happened to Jacques and Jean in the Boulevard Henri Lamont. After a quarter of an hour of anxious waiting, Claude could stand it no longer and made his way up to Francine's apartment. When he got to the room the door was still ajar. Sensing that something was wrong he held his gun in his hand as he entered. Looking around the flat he realised something drastic had happened and he knew in his heart that Francine had been caught. How she had vanished from there left him puzzled. Leaving the apartment he caught sight of an opened door at the fire escape. He walked in that direction and looked down at the alleyway in the back. There was a patch of oil where the car had been. He felt absolutely dismayed that he had not accompanied Francine back to her apartment. There was nothing for it now but to drive out to the farmhouse and radio Brindmarsh in London. For the Companions of the Circle in Paris the operations were going steadily downhill.

Claude could simply not drive away from Paris straight away. It was too cold-hearted. It was lacking in humanity for the individual agents. The rest of the operatives had been rounded up and, out of the controlling body of Jacques, Jean and Francine, Claude was now the only one at large. He had to remain elusive yet he felt an overwhelming concern and love for Francine, and he was worried of the torture and torment that she would go through. His fears were well-founded. He had heard some frightening stories of what had happened to some members of the resistance who had been caught.

Rather than drive through Paris, Claude decided to make his way through the city by public transport and see if any other members of other resistance groups could work out a way of rescuing Francine from SS headquarters, On meeting up with them, he was told bluntly and honestly that it would be a difficult and almost impossible task. Heavily laden with regret Claude at once left to go to the farmhouse in the country and contact Brindmarsh with the sad news.

For Francine, now a captive of the SS, she genuinely expected the worst to come. In the car with the SS men it had been a silent trip to 84 Avenue Foch. All the way there she was thinking of the amazing spiral of events that had somehow propelled her to this suspect fate. If the tanker on which she was travelling from Calais to Liverpool had not gone down off the coast of Cornwall, she would not have met Freddie and Cynthia Miller, and her association with the Circle might never have begun. However, she had to remind herself that when she had been recruited by Colonel Brindmarsh, it had been stressed to her that participation in these activities was strictly on a voluntary basis. Yes, she had volunteered, that was true. She had just never envisaged being caught. Francine had been so confident, and perhaps so naïve, that she had really imagined that the cat and mouse game of this shadowy world would last the duration of the war. In this she had been horribly wrong and she was now about to face the stiffest test of all, survival under pressure. She steeled herself for the worst.

The interrogation at SS headquarters began in a mild fashion. Francine was seated in a room of only half-light and her interrogators sat opposite her. If she had not known their aims and intentions, Francine would have thought them pleasant looking enough. Even when she was asked the simple question "Tell us about your work, mademoiselle," it had been asked in a manner that did not depict anything malicious to come. Francine almost relaxed again determined to remain numb. Yet it was a false alarm for these men asked her over and over again. They asked her different questions. They asked her the same questions in a different frame. Their voices changed from a normal tone to a harsh tone. Hours and hours of interrogation followed. Still she did not break down.

"Who are your contacts?" One voice screeched at her. The man's face was angry and totally unsympathetic.

"Who are you working for?" The new voice was vindictive.

Another fierce-looking man glared at her. "We know your name, mademoiselle. You are Francine Macé. Tell us about your contacts in the underground."

So many voices seemed to be shouting at her; so much noise and fury in the room. There was no end to this interrogation. Finally when she felt on the edge of breaking down completely she was taken to a cell. She could not believe what a nightmare the past few hours had been. The nightmare of reality had induced in her exhaustion and she fell straight down onto the bed in the cell and fell asleep.

In what only seemed mere minutes later but was in fact a couple of hours, Francine found herself being dragged out of bed and taken into another interviewing room. This time she faced only one man. It was somehow one of those curious fatalistic coincidences that often occur in lifetimes with surprising regularity. Francine Macé's new interrogator was Verner Burnhoff, who himself would have been amazed if he knew how he was already indirectly linked to this young woman. His manner was not in any way abrasive. In fact it was exactly the opposite. This did not impress Francine at all. She knew that perhaps what had gone on before was just a mere prelude to far worse things that were to come.

"Mademoiselle, I admire your courage." He had spoken in a genuine manner. Francine ignored the comment fearing the worst. This man was too charming, too easy-going to be true. "You stood the test of the last few hours much better than many men would have done. To that part of your courage I pay you great tribute."

Francine had undergone a mentally exhausting few hours. She was tired and bedraggled and she was truly a picture of exhaustion. At Burnhoff's comments she could somehow manage a half smile, buoyed up by the thought that there was not much else in the way of harm and interrogation that could be done to her, Francine decided to meet the main square on.

"You obviously know what I have been doing and why. And you obviously know who all our agents are. I know you have rounded them up. Our observers said the Gestapo did the swoop. You must know everything by now. You can torture me some more, put me through absolute hell, but I will never reveal anything to you. I saw what your men did to Jacques and Jean. I was in a car in the Boulevard Henri Lamont after the shooting."

Burnhoff looked at her almost in sympathy. It was sympathy because he knew that Francine would have to undergo more torturous interrogation. He admired her. He had always liked strong women. He had a deep feeling of conscience that he felt guilty about. This young Frenchwoman, who was possessed of an extraordinary beauty and a strong will, was the sort of person that he wished he could have been on friendly terms with. Since Burnhoff had transferred from his duties as a career soldier to this line of work, he had wished that he was back in the line of fire again, rather than being a participant in the cruel and brutal treatment the Gestapo had dished out to individuals. He looked at her in a cold, icy stare.

"It is a pity you do not cooperate with me. There will be far worse for you to come. I hope for your sake you will change your mind."

"I won't."

"You could tell me one thing. Who was the instigator of the organisation you worked for?"

Burnhoff was walking around the room, and Francine turned her head to follow him.

"I don't know what you mean by that," she remarked. When she spoke now she was much more composed and she didn't speak with any defiance or aggression in her voice; she was puzzled by the question.

"The instigator," Burnhoff repeated, "yes, that is what I mean. The founder."

Francine thought for a moment. It was strange but even though she had learned much about the operations of the Companions of the Circle, she was really not conversant with its history. It was also a leading question that Burnhoff slyly asked, for to answer it in one manner would almost certainly indicate the origins of the Circle and its indirect control by British Intelligence.

"Even if I knew I would not tell you," said Francine coolly.

Burnhoff then said something that surprised her. "Because I believe I know. I have long had my suspicions, perhaps you might confirm them. My belief is that this organisation of yours – this underground movement – was started by a certain person who was well known in the German industrial world. Several of the men we have taken into custody are not ordinary people of an insignificant background or a poverty stricken upbringing. They are men of skill and trade and commerce, who are businessmen in their own right, factory managers, shareholders of large companies that dealt directly with the Harstezzen industries. The Harstezzen industries that were run by the late Rieber von Harstezzen, who, passed on the reins to his widow Baroness Christina von Harstezzen upon his death. This person – a fine lady, I add – who by a trick of fate was a friend of mine, I regret to say that she perished as a passenger on the *Hindenburg*."

Suddenly a thought came into Francine's head. She recalled that when she had been staying at Mousehole in Cornwall, Freddie Miller had mentioned in conversation that he had been a newsreel cameraman who had actually filmed the *Hindenburg* disaster. Francine looked up at Burnhoff sharply as she realised the connection there. She knew that it was obviously no coincidence that Freddie had been there on that occasion. Had it not been for the explosion of the Hindenburg, Freddie and the Baroness must have planned to meet at Lakehurst, probably to discuss the work of the Circle.

"You are telling me things I have no knowledge of," said Francine truthfully, although she could clearly assess the details.

Burnhoff did not say anything for a minute. The silence in the room was deadly. Then he turned and looked at her intently. It was a look that frightened Francine. She was not disposed to show her fear, but within her she could feel herself on edge.

"Very shortly, mademoiselle, I will leave the room and some others will take my place." His voice was cold and every word was spaced breathlessly. "They will undoubtedly try a more, let me say, a more psychological approach. Very persuasive methods. It would be terribly—"

"Enough!" Francine snapped. It was not out of anger, but, for the first time, out of fear. Her voice trembled with real fear. "I will not tell you anything." Then she made a comment in a quiet effective voice that surprised Burnhoff. "I ask only that you have me shot as quickly as possible."

Burnhoff remained unmoved. "I am afraid it will not be as easy as that. Just tell me am I right in my earlier suspicions. Was Mrs Harstezzen the founder? Were her business dealings with people who helped her cause? You only have to nod yes. Was the group that you work for designed to protect and transport leading Jewish figures to their safety? You only have to nod, mademoiselle. What do you have to lose now?"

Burnhoff did not give up. He prodded and goaded and asked questions over and over again. He walked round the room. He sat directly opposite her. He stood behind her and spoke in her ear. Then he shouted and the pitch of his voice rose and he unleashed all the rage and fury he could muster. For three long, exhausting, gruelling hours, he put Francine through mental torture and torment. Francine did not break. She was close to breaking down. Tears flowed from her eyes. She shook with nerves. Then when it seemed as if it was all over, Burnhoff left the room only to be replaced by two gruesome-looking characters.

The ordeal that followed was even worse. Hours of ill treatment and torment drove her towards excruciating pain until she was on the edge of revealing the details that her opponents wanted. But miraculously, at the precise point when she was just about to crack up under the immense strain of it all, her interrogators decided to end the session and return Francine to her cell. It had been a close call. Just a few minutes more of the harshness would have effectively ended the work of the Circle in Paris. By God's grace it seemed Francine had suffered through this crucial test, endured the cruel interrogation and not exposed a single facet about the work and the details of her underground contacts and operations.

In her cell Francine lay back on her bed trying to recover her senses and her resolve. The interrogations had been a nightmare. The whole experience had taken her to the brink; yet she was still intact, exhausted and nerve shattered perhaps, still capable, however, of handling the next course of events. She thought of the many Jewish people who had been transported to safety and protected by the Circle, and for a moment Francine felt a twinge of guilt that under pressure she had come so close to endangering the operations that assisted them. Whilst lying on her bed gathering her thoughts, Francine was staring up at a fanlight in the ceiling of the cell and then with a sudden rush of enthusiasm she realised she was staring at her escape route. She sat up suddenly. Directly below the fanlight was a bar, if she could only prise it loose she could stand on her chair and manoeuvre herself through the gap eventually onto the roof.

Francine got up from her bed slowly. She knew that a guard was outside of the cell. She would have to be as quiet as a mouse. To reach the fanlight Francine would have to stand on a chair and stretch her arms to full length to manoeuvre the bar. It was not easy standing ill at ease on a wobbly chair trying to balance and pull the bar out which was fastened so securely. Desperately she looked around for something to force the bar out of its bracket. Then she spotted the knife and fork on the plate on which she had eaten a meal in her cell. Grabbing the knife she began to chip at the cement around the bar. Nervously she kept listening for the sound of the guard – or even worse, more interrogators – coming for her again. Hurriedly, she scraped at the end of the bar. With her other hand she pulled hard at the bar. It was loosening. Just then she heard footsteps coming down the hallway outside. She jumped down from the chair and pushed it away. She lay down on the bed again, her pulse racing until the footsteps had passed and she heard the cell door next to her being unlocked. For a few minutes she listened anxiously. At last the footsteps could be heard going in the opposite direction away from her cell. Francine got back on to the chair, this time continuing her task more frantically.

It took far longer than at first thought but Francine finally managed to free the bar. She pushed it down and began to release the fanlight. Outside of her cell Francine could hear voices. She carried on regardless, chipping away at the foundations around it. Finally she dismantled it and lowered it on to her bed, the way out was clear now. She would have to manoeuvre herself up into the ceiling now. It was going to be a tense escape. Francine stretched her arms up to an absolute limit and positioned her fingertips around the rafters in the ceiling. She gripped the splinter wood beam and tried to pull herself up. It was enormously difficult. From the chair she had to raise herself. It was a test of strength. She pulled at the beam and brought her knees up to the rafters. In a moment of sheer agony, she managed to bring her shoes up around the beam, well clear of the floor. Another minute later she was up amongst the beams and rafters and crawling on her hands and knees in a precarious manner.

Francine could feel the dust in her throat. It was black inside the section and her hands and face were covered in filth and dirt as she scrambled around trying to find some way out onto the roof. There was a draught coming from somewhere. This was surely a sign of a crevice or way out. Francine crawled along the confines of the roofing. With plaster and beams beneath her she crawled and crawled along taking each yard as it came and trying desperately not to make any noise. Finally she came to a small ventilation grill in the wall. She felt the bricks around the grill. She looked above her. Then in the darkness she saw something metallic, which despite the soot and dirt around her still managed a gleam. Stepping across the beams and rafters very cautiously, Francine realised that it was a wall ladder leading up to a trapdoor in the roof.

A feeling of exuberance came over her. With the adrenalin pumping through her, she began to ascend the ladder. Approximately ten feet above the bottom rung of the ladder, she finally touched the trapdoor. There was a long bolt securing the trapdoor to the roof. Francine tried to pull it back. It felt as if it was rusted in. She was beside herself trying to force it back. She swore and cursed under her breath as she tried to pull it free. Just to get this far and not to be able to open it was the most frustrating thing of all. Then with a gush of relief it came back. Forcing back a rusted bolt was difficult enough. The most arduous thing of all was trying to push back the trapdoor. It was virtually rammed in. She pushed up hard. It was moving but it was tight. She could feel her arms hurting as she tried to raise it. It could have only been the anger of her feminine temper that finally forced her in a furious moment to dislodge the trapdoor and pushed it open. Dirt and plaster rained down on her as she pushed it right back. Francine could hardly believe it. The breeze was blowing in and she had a full view of the rooftops of Paris.

She raised herself onto the roof and found that she was in a difficult position. There was a sheer drop if she miscalculated her footing. It was lucky for Francine that it was night-time otherwise she would have been exposed, enough for the guards below to see her. She manoeuvred herself across the roof treading in a tiptoe fashion. Beneath her a tile came loose. She was slipping and sliding, trying to keep her balance. Frantically she grabbed at something. She managed to get hold of some guttering. She was hanging over the edge trying to manipulate her way back. The pain of it all was enormous. The muscles in her stomach tightened up with tension, she closed and opened her eyes several times not daring to look down. Her eyes were streaming with tears from the pain.

Francine had no sooner got her balance back when the air raid sirens wailed loudly. She had to hide. There was the sudden sound of the German air raid observers rushing to their posts. Francine had no other choice. She could only go down and she risked fatal injury to climb down a drainpipe. Vertigo spun over her as she clambered down to the ground. The descent felt as if it would take forever. She made it to the ground and found that she was in a courtyard where cars were parked intermittently. With the sounds of aircraft zooming above her, Francine took cover behind a car. The sound of voices came from one side. In a moment of horror, Francine realised that she was in the German Army

Officers' car park. She had to hide, but where? The men were obviously about to get into the cars and drive away. Francine tried the boot of one car. It was open. She clambered in, but once inside she held it lightly ajar.

From within she could hear the noise outside. Her imagination could only visualise just what was happening. German voices yelling and shouting filled the air. Engines revved. Car doors slammed. Up above aircraft flew. There were the sounds of gunfire and machine guns. Francine could only sit hunched up in the boot in silent sufferance. The opportunity to close her eyes was irresistible. The ordeal she had gone through had been terrible. Somehow she had come through.

It was a long time before the noise outside dissipated. When after a while the raid was over and things seemed to be normal again, Francine was tempted to open the door of the car boot wide and fully, but a sixth sense seemed to stop her. The voices of two men speaking in German became apparent. One of them she recognised; it was the voice she could not forget for it belonged to Verner Burnhoff, one of her earlier interrogators. Francine could only stay where she was, frozen in fear, transfixed in the notion that if by any chance the boot of the car was raised and she was discovered, she would almost certainly face another terrifying ordeal – this time, perhaps, even worse.

A thud of the car sent a shock wave through her. Francine realised that the car door had been slammed shut. She heard the sound of the car starting and felt the sudden jerk beneath her. The car was moving. Francine hung on for dear life as the car moved forward. It slowed down as it came to the exit and she heard the voice of the driver speak to someone, obviously a guard. But the voice of the driver! She was startled beyond compare. Francine was in the car of Verner Burnhoff!

A moment later the car started up again and Francine dared to raise the lid of the boot. The first sight that greeted her was the early morning view of the Paris streets. *I've escaped*, she thought. At the first opportunity she would leap from the back of the car and make her way to the farmhouse on the outskirts where she hoped and prayed that Claude would be hiding out.

Early morning Paris, how good to feel the pulse of the city. From a nearby café the car passed by, the smell of croissants and coffee came in the air with the breeze. She was hungry. The thoughts of being free and enjoying the simple pleasures that life could offer was something she would never take for granted again.

The car was moving much too fast for her to leap from. Francine would have to wait until it slowed right down. It was hurtling along at a very fast rate. Several times Francine raised the boot lid and glanced out quickly. It seemed as if the car was heading out of the city towards the countryside. At this, for the first time in a while, Francine allowed herself a smile. Her interrogator was unknowingly giving her a lift in the direction she wanted. It was worth the discomfort to sit it out until she was close to where she intended to go.

Several times the car stopped at intersections. Francine was wise enough not to take the opportunity to jump out at these points. More often or not the German Army would have a checkpoint there. She could hear Burnhoff talking in German. Then after several tense moments the car would move on again at a great pace.

Francine kept peering out at the passing scenery. The car was travelling down a country lane now. She would have to make her escape soon. The opportunity was not long in coming. The car began to slow down, eventually coming to a halt. There was the sound of sheep bleating and baaing around the car. A flock of sheep had spilled out on to the road. Francine raised the boot lid. She could see the sheep spilling around. This was it. Her escape had to be done now. Quickly she stepped out of the back while at the front of the car Burnhoff pushed the sheep out of the way. Francine pulled the boot down quietly and made her way into a clump of trees at the side of the road

From the security of the trees she peered round, watching Burnhoff get into his car and drive away. It seemed absolutely impossible, an incredible story, but Francine Macé had escaped and one of her interrogators had aided her. Who would believe her when she told her story? However, when she looked down at herself, she felt her appearance would tell its own story. She was covered in dirt and scratches from her experiences. The moment she found a stream or a water pump she would treat herself to a wash.

She began walking across fields to get her bearings and work out how to get to the farmhouse. Ever since the tanker had sank off the coast of Cornwall her life had become an amazing series of events that seemed to have happened to someone else. The whole thing had been breathtaking. Even her escape had been a fantastic episode. She convinced herself that this was wartime and that in times such as these, the immense pressure and circumstances that brave individuals found themselves in brought out their greatest qualities.

Some time later Francine found a stream and cleaned herself up. She was surprised at just how much cleaner she felt after she had doused herself with the cleaning qualities of cold water.

Further on she found a small village nestled away. She worked out just where she had to get to and, in order to get there more quickly, she stole a bicycle from outside of the local library. From there she rode along some of the lanes in the direction of the farmhouse. At one stage of her journey, coming towards her on the opposite side of the road, was a German soldier on a motorbike and sidecar. He passed Francine by without incident. She looked up at the heavens with a sigh of relief. Surely it was only the intervention of divine providence that had guided her through all this.

It was nearly midnight when Francine arrived at the farmhouse. The farmhouse was hardly visible in the dark of the night. Only the moon and the starlit sky illuminated the way to her destination. The farmhouse was dark. Not a single light was on. She put the bike to one side and walked up to the entrance. Francine felt on edge. *Was it at all possible*, she wondered, *that the Gestapo had discovered this address too?* She pushed the door open slightly. It creaked as she pushed it. Immediately she reached for the light.

From out of nowhere a hand grabbed her shoulder and spun her round. So great was the shock that Francine fainted. It was Claude who picked her up and carried her to a settee. When she came too, Claude was smiling at her, delighted to see her again. Francine sat up and embraced him. They hugged each other with feelings of real joy. There were tears in Francine's eyes.

"It's all right, Francine," Claude reassured her taking his own handkerchief and drying her eyes. "But – how did you get away?"

Francine recovered herself, for despite her young age and vulnerable beauty, she was in possession of a great strength. The ordeal she had gone through had sapped her energy level to the point that she was near collapsing again. It had not sapped her humour. Through her tears and tiredness she managed to smile.

"Remind me never to volunteer for anything again," she murmured, and then the effects of near exhaustion and lack of sleep took over. She lay back on the settee and fell into a deep sleep. Claude looked down at her shaking his head from left to right gently.

"Mademoiselle, you are a most courageous young lady," he said gently. He took a blanket and placed it over her. Claude was incredulous that Francine had escaped.

He listened to her story over a breakfast of croissants and coffee the next morning. It was a stunning piece of information. Claude listened, horrified when he heard of the methods of interrogation that had been employed to Francine. At times it seemed like an improbable story embellished beyond all reason, but he knew Francine. Claude knew she was sincere and honest as the day was long. He felt empathy for all that she had been through. After he had listened, he sat deep in thought pondering over all that he had heard.

Finally he said, "I must tell Brindmarsh." He took the radio from within the trapdoor and set up the outside aerial. Within a short time he was in contact with Whitehall eventually speaking to Brindmarsh.

At the London end Brindmarsh felt a mixture of delight and distress, delighted that Francine had escaped and distressed at the ordeal she had endured. He briefly spoke to her congratulating her on her courage and ingenuity, and then Claude spoke to him again getting more information and instructions. Claude wrote down the details and he signed off. He dissembled the radio, took down the outside aerial, and placed all the components beneath the trapdoor.

Francine watched Claude as he moved around the room. She could tell by the expression on his face that something of undue urgency had occurred. When Claude sat down again Francine, from her corner of the room, looked at him square on.

"Well Francine," he began after drawing a short breath, "It's all over." Francine looked at him curiously. *What did he mean?* Claude lit a cigarette, inhaled and blew a ring of smoke into the air. He offered the open pack to Francine who declined. "The Companions of the Circle are no more. When I was talking to Brindmarsh moments ago, he told me that after our colleagues had been rounded up in Paris – including you – because so much of the groups whereabouts have been identified by the Nazis, the Circle as it had been operating up to now must be disbanded."

"I cannot believe this," gasped Francine, "our work here is so important in saving the lives of so many Jewish people and transporting them to safety. We cannot stop now."

"Our work will not stop. The work of the Companions of the Circle will continue. Its members in Austria, Italy and Holland have already integrated with the underground forces there. The same will happen here. The few remaining members will remain, although they will work with the resistance. The Nazis know too much about the Circle, and as Burnhoff informed you during your interrogation, they know who the founder was – Mrs Harstezzen, no less a personal friend of Burnhoff, who deluded him so successfully – and from that they could determine her business associates and work out their leads from there."

"Some will go into hiding for the time being then, Claude, and carry on when we have merged with the resistance?"

"I will," said Claude. He looked at her sympathetically. He was conscious of the fact that despite all Francine had been through, she was determined to fulfil her commitment. "Brindmarsh is going to send an aircraft to pick you up and take you back to England. He feels that with the ordeal you have been through it would be difficult for you to continue."

Francine slid off the end of her chair; anger was rising in her, but it was not directed at Claude or even to the motives of Brindmarsh. More than anything she felt angry because she realised the highly important nature of her tasks. Francine was expressionless for a moment as she considered what to do. Then to Claude's surprise a huge smile appeared on Francine's face, a smile so dazzling that it puzzled him.

"What is it?" he asked.

"I am staying," she replied defiantly. "I will work with the resistance."

"You cannot. Brindmarsh wants you back."

"Claude, my friend, in a few days time I will be twenty-three years of age. I am a grown woman capable of making decisions. I have survived so far, haven't I? I believe in what I am doing. What is more, this is my country and I have a duty to it. I'll work with the resistance. I'll carry on helping our people."

"I must confess I am surprised. I am also secretly delighted. I like working with you, Francine." Claude took the opportunity to point out how he felt about Francine. "You know how I feel about you."

She was touched. Her eyes showed a flash of vulnerability beneath her usual steely gaze. "Yes, I do." She gripped Claude's hand for a moment. Without taking her eyes from Claude's face she added, "Get the radio out. Set the aerial up, and I will talk to him. I cannot believe he wants me to go back. I am sure he would prefer that I stayed on to work with you. They need radio operators here; they need people in the resistance. The Circle may not exist in name anymore, but its work must go on."

"No wonder you smiled. I think you are as brave as you are beautiful," Claude took her in his arms and held her tightly. His admiration for this young woman knew no bounds. Francine Macé was certainly one of the true heroines of the war. Her work was far from finished. During the remaining years of the war Francine and Claude, together with the other brave men and women of the resistance, carried on their work. Using the farmhouse as a base, the two operated with the underground carrying out daring missions and providing help to the Jewish people they had originally been assigned to protect. In addition they also gave assistance to British and allied servicemen they found amongst their ranks.

Then in 1944 France was liberated. The fight in that country was over. It was a wonderful time to be there at the liberation. Francine and Claude held each other's hand as they stood in Paris with half a million other French nationals. They had survived. To be free again was the most wonderful and exhilarating feeling. To sip coffee in a sidewalk café and feel the breezes blowing in freedom across Europe and to see normality returning to the lives of so many was a luxury.

Francine's efforts did not go unrewarded. For her work with the legendary Companions of the Circle and the resistance she was awarded the George Cross and the Croix de Guerre. After the liberation Francine did return to England where she again worked for Brindmarsh. Although this time with her status very much enhanced by her outstanding work, she was given a top administrative job in the upper echelons of Whitehall in the operations section.

The war finished peacefully for Francine. It was in complete contrast to the experiences she had endured earlier. For the man who had indirectly introduced Francine to the Circle, his war was more prolonged. In the Far East, Colonel Freddie Miller was a prisoner of war held by the Japanese.

Twenty-six

When Freddie Miller had left Colombo on his mission to the Far East, he had anticipated a difficult reconnaissance assignment. It was, to him at any rate, unknown territory that he was traversing in 1942. The objective of his mission was to blow up lines of supplies to the troops of the imperial Japanese forces in Southwest British Malaya. But there had been incredible setbacks in his duties; from the time he had started this job, things had not run smoothly.

Freddie and a team of four men had parachuted into Malaya, but the navigator of the plane was way off course. They had immediately found themselves behind enemy lines. Then to make matters worse they had been subjected to days of continual tropical rain, which had made trekking through the jungle a tiresome ordeal. Every so often they would hide in the vegetation when the team heard Japanese troops talking. So close were they it would have been possible to touch them. They would stand in the undergrowth peering through the tropical fauna, trying not to loose their balance or make one solitary human sound that would give their position away.

The team of soldiers were accompanied by some local Malays, who guided them through the difficult terrain. In order to pitch themselves against the enemy Freddie Miller and his men normally played tactical hit and run raids against Japanese ammunition dumps and supply points and then disappeared into the blackness of night as quickly as they had struck.

The weather for such raids was fearful. The heat and the torrential rain made the going so much harder. All of his men were feeling the effects and Freddie himself was coming down with some sort of fever. It was making him doubly sweat and he was short of breath especially at the peak of the day when it was at its most tepid.

Several times Freddie's men suggested to him that now might be the perfect time to concede the mission. But Freddie counter-fired by insisting on one last raid. The men admiring of Freddie's gallantry although wary of taking such a risk especially with all of them feeling so unfit, reluctantly decided to carry out this last valiant attempt.

The objective of the mission was to destroy a rail track that ran over a high tableau. Once this had been done the men would escape by travelling downstream on the river that was nearby, where the Malays would be waiting in some dugout canoes.

Detonators had been set and it would mean waiting for the fuse to ignite when the track would be effectively dismantled. At the dark of night Freddie, despite his feverish condition, ascended the hill and planted the explosives. The fuse was lit and a few minutes after Freddie had scrambled to safety the track was blown sky high, permanently disrupting ammunition and other supplies from reaching the enemy target.

That was it as far as Freddie was concerned. The exhausted men would have to rest up now in a Malay village downstream. Freddie and his men got into the dugout canoes and let the drift of the water take them away to more peaceful places.

Freddie was very sick. The constant raids and heavy rainfall and the tropical environment had well and truly taken their toll on him. He had a hardy constitution, undoubtedly from years of outdoor activity, but he conditions he had gone through now put him to his limit.

Somewhere between boarding the dugout canoes and departing downstream he had blacked out. When he regained consciousness some days later he found himself in a Malay hut laying flat on his back and being daubed down by some local girls with water. He was sweating constantly. His mouth was as dry as a dustbowl. When one of the Malay girls gave him a dish of water he could feel the cold seep into his hot body.

"Hang in there, sir," said one of the soldiers. Freddie could hardly raise a smile and just managed to twitch an eyebrow before he felt himself sinking into oblivion again.

This time there were faces and places that flashed through his memory as his mind subsided into a quiver of dreams. His mother and father, hard at work on their farm in Hampshire, waved to him from some timeless distance. Then he was a schoolboy at Somerset Grammar School hitting four runs off a beautiful linseed-oiled cricket bat that made a hollow thud as it deflected the awesome impact of a heavy ball. Occasionally his eyes would attempt to open in the midst of these dreams. Through the doorway, which was not really a doorway at all but a hollow in the hut, he could see a sparkling blue sea and a tall thin wavy palm. Sometimes it would be night and the stars would reflect on the water. Good God. How long had he lain there? Then his eyes feeling like lead weights would close and the memories would return.

He saw the parade ground at Sandhurst again and his dreams of the places he had served were so vivid he could almost smell the dusty peppercorn summer in India, the wind blowing off the desert in Saudi Arabia or the dockside at Valetta in Malta. He remembered his travels as a cinecameraman and those famous people he had met. Then he saw Tillie and Christina and over and over again he saw Cynthia till his eyes wept at the memory of it all. There was Arthandur and Marlene, and Nathan, and Cynthia again and again, and then there was Francine.

Finally there was the crack of thunder in the depth of night and Freddie awoke to hear the rain pelt on the hut in which he lay, and on the floor beside his bed an aged Malay couple sat cross-legged and smiled at him; a beautiful generous smile as they realised he was better. They pointed to the rain outside and said something in Malay, which Freddie did not understand, but he smiled anyway and lay back into a fitful sleep.

At dawn the rain had gone and in its place the sun, brilliantly red, rose above the blue sparkling sea. Freddie still felt weak, though he felt better. A clap of thunder came startling him. Yet, was this thunder he heard? Some tropical white birds in a flock rose suddenly into the sky. Freddie knew in his heart that he had heard rifle fire. There were people shouting. The accent was unmistakable: they were Japanese voices.

Freddie tried to raise himself. He looked out of the hut and he could see his three comrades lying dead on the ground. He gasped in horror as a wave of agony and shock passed through him. He lay down then raised himself again. This time he gasped in shock for he faced two Japanese soldiers who stared at him through the hut's entrance. Then Freddie realised the hopelessness of it all. He could barely croak at them.

"Well come and get me then," he moaned. Come on!" They just looked at him. "Come on!" His temperature rose and he passed out.

★★★

The prison camp was on an island in Borneo. Freddie never knew how the Japanese had raided the Malay village and he couldn't believe his luck that his life had been spared. The prison camp was hardly a reprieve. For the next few years it was a living hellhole, but it introduced Freddie to the finest group of men he was ever to meet.

When Freddie had first arrived at the prison camp, he was appalled by the condition he found the British and Commonwealth troops in. He immediately approached the most senior British officer in the camp who was also a colonel, but whose seniority date was, to Freddie's surprise, a few days earlier than his

Colonel John Saunders did not seem to mind in the least and agreed to work under Freddie's command. The two men shook hands and talked about the camp.

"The men here – what nationalities are they?" asked Freddie, and he clutched his chest as he spoke for he still needed some time to recover.

Colonel Saunders noticed this. "Are you all right, man?" He looked very concerned.

"No, it's nothing," Freddie said. "The nationalities of the men?"

"Oh, yes. British, Scots, Welsh, a few Irishmen, Australians, New Zealanders, a couple of Canadians, and a stray yank from the Pacific Fleet."

"Some of the men I saw this morning John—" Freddie broke off in the middle of the conversation before continuing. They walked in the direction of the hospital. "They don't look in the best of condition. In fact they look bloody awful."

"Without offence, Freddie, so do you."

"My mind is still sharp," replied Freddie without appearing to be annoyed, "but I concede I might need some medication."

Looking around him Freddie studied the prison camp in detail. The camp itself was in stark contrast to its almost paradisiacal tropical surroundings. The prison huts were made of bamboo and cane stitched together. There were a number of these huts all within a few feet of each other. The biggest building was the prison hospital. It had to be. For the number of patients who were admitted there grew in numbers constantly.

Outside of the barbed wire that circled the camp dense tropical vegetation grew thickly. In the distance blue hills could be seen. There always seemed to be tall palms swaying wherever one cared to look. The sky was so clear and radiantly blue, but within the confines of the prison camp there was an aura of darkness about it. The beauty of the tropical environment outside could not disguise the horror of the camp.

Freddie compensated himself with the thought that although he was prisoner he was at least alive. It was a miracle to him that he had been spared in the Malay village when the Japanese had arrived. Looking around him now he felt a deep concern for his fellow soldiers. He stopped and looked at the men digging and working in gangs with Japanese guards watching them and goading them even when it was obvious the men were under a great strain.

John Saunders saw the look of dismay on Freddie's face. He slapped his arm on Freddie's shoulder in an amiable fashion.

"This is how it is," he murmured quietly. Freddie said nothing and merely averted his eyes to meet Saunders. "Come on, Freddie, I'll introduce you to the men in the hospital.

Freddie was visibly stunned at the sight of the emaciated men working under great duress. In that instant it was as if the sight of such sadness had made him oblivious to his own illness. His heart was pounding fast now. Not with the shortness of breath he had experienced after the fever had stricken him. This time it was pounding with an unrelenting anger for the misery and condition that the soldiers were in.

Since he had arrived that morning he had been appalled by what he had seen. The prison hospital was also a sight that he wished he could not have focused upon. Most of the sick men were in such a bad state that they could not raise themselves. Saunders, who in outward appearance was an archetypal cold and reserved officer, glanced at Freddie who to his immense surprise was showing some signs of emotion. From the corner of Freddie's left eye rolled a tear staining his cheek. Saunders was close to frowning but then he realised that Freddie had seen far more than he could have ever expected.

Before them prisoners lay dying of malnutrition, dysentery, malaria, typhus, pellagra and dengue fever. Not only were they suffering from these dreadful illnesses, there were signs of men who had lost a limb. Heaven knows how they had survived the operation in a tropical Prisoner of War Camp, where there would not have been the facility to provide pain killing injections or anaesthetics to numb the effects of the gruelling procedures.

Freddie and Colonel Saunders walked along through the makeshift ward. It was in Freddie's nature to be warm towards people he met. Saunders introduced him to an Australian surgeon who was treating a man.

"Colonel Miller, I'd like you to meet Dr Paul Vincent from Brisbane, Australia." Freddie shook hands with the doctor who was fair haired, fortyish, with a thin moustache and a pleasant nature.

"You've got a tough job," said Freddie quietly.

"That's for sure, colonel. Men in great pain and nothing to ease it for them and every day that someone dies, two more patients seem to replace them. The worst part about it all is that when one man looks to be recovering, he's immediately hauled out again to join the working party."

"And you protested to Captain Shigoshu," Colonel Saunders pointed out with the intention of emphasis for Freddie's concern.

"My oath I did!" remarked the Australian medical officer. "After a great deal of pushing and shoving and being bullied, in return we got some medical needs, but by golly it was nothing compared to what we needed."

Freddie rubbed his chin and then his look of deep thought turned to one of frozen horror as he saw the ailment that Paul Vincent was treating his patient for. The Doctor was trying to apply a dressing and bandage to the foot of one bronzed soldier. He had never seen such injury before in his life. The solder concerned grimaced as the Doctor swathed it.

"What – what sort of injury is that?" asked Freddie.

Paul Vincent could see the unease in Freddie. Half the flesh of the man's foot looked as if it had been eaten away exposing sinew and bone.

"It's a tropical ulcer, sir," replied the Doctor.

"Are there many like this lieutenant?" Freddie asked again noticing the man's rank on his tropical outfit.

"A few."

Freddie looked at John Saunders. "I think I'll have to see Captain Shigoshu" he said in his usual controlled manner. His anger blazed in his eyes. Turning to the young soldier he asked him, "Where do you come from, old son?"

"Bermondsey, sir." The young soldier was only about twenty-two. His appearance did not belie his youthfulness. He was already sunken in the jowls.

"Keep your chin up," said Freddie sincerely. Then to Lieutenant Vincent he added, "I'll do what I can for you, Paul."

"I wish you luck, sir, but I don't fancy your chances." Lieutenant Vincent responded. Freddie obviously took that as a sign that the Commandant of the Prisoner of War Camp, Captain Shigoshu, was inflexible and unyielding.

When Freddie and Saunders walked out of the prison hospital the glare of the sun flickered across their faces. Freddie looked ashen. He looked around him and realised he would have to do something to alleviate the circumstances of the men. The war could go on for some time and in the present conditions the men would be hard pressed to survive.

"John, when the men have finished their work this evening I want you to assemble them all for me in the biggest prison hut. I want to be able to talk to them all before I encounter Capital Shigoshu. Will you do that?"

"Of course. What do you have in mind? Are you going to plan something?"

"Plan something?"

"Yes, Freddie. Like an escape."

Freddie looked towards the barbed wire encircling the camp. He wondered about the possibility of it. The Japanese had guards everywhere. Escape would be difficult. He conceded that to himself yet he did not rule it out completely.

Colonel Saunders did as Freddie had requested and organised all the men together in one hut. They were a mixed group of POWs. There were a tough bunch of men too. The experiences they had undergone since their capture had made them that way but for men who had suffered through the traumas of humiliation and ill health, they remarkably still had a very healthy sense of humour about them. Despite the conditions of the camp the men could laugh together.

Freddie studied them all curiously. Now that he was officially their leader he considered that he was closer to the men in character and instinct than ever Colonel Saunders would have been. Saunders was of a world of breeding and arrogance and a self imposed superiority. Freddie was a farmer's son for whom luck, initiative and fate had propelled him through the years. He had now to establish a rapport with the men and at the same time he needed to project an authority; an absolute sincerity and a leadership that they would respect and respond to.

He knew it was not going to be easy. Right from the outset he had to make it clearly understood that he was the leader. He looked at all the men he would be leading.

Sergeant major Thomas Griffith was the most distinctive of the group. He was every bit the Welshman of legend. He had black shiny hair and eyes to match, and a voice of crisp Welsh clarity. His physique was that of a man who had spent years in the collieries of Wales.

Freddie who was quick to recognise in Griffith similar qualities that he himself had possessed, immediately recognised a handy ally and he seized on this.

"Sergeant major introduce me to some of the men" said Freddie. He turned to the front row of men and walked down the line.

"Well, sir, obviously I can't introduce you to all one hundred and sixty of us, but I'll give you a run down." The sergeant major stopped at one tall man.

"This big lad's from Texas. Gordon Sheridan is his name."

Freddie looked up. "Ah, you must be the stray yank from the Pacific fleet, if I'm not mistake."

"I surely am," he said beaming a smile that displayed white shiny teeth.

"What did you do before the war?" asked Freddie.

"I was a drafter for an oil firm. I was a pro-baseball player, too, for a while."

The sergeant major moved on and stopped in front of a group of slouch-hatted soldiers. "These fellows are Aussies, sir." He pointed to each one. "Mulrone, Mellers, Donnelly and Glenville."

"All right, gentlemen, why don't you tell me what you did before this?"

Mulrone was the first to speak. He was a big burley man who stood with his arms folded. He was thickly set and looked hard. "I was a colliery worker in the Hunter Valley in New South Wales."

Donnelly was the next one to speak. He was lean ands heavily tanned. "Me. Back home in Perth I was a carpenter and joiner."

"I was a bank clerk," smiled Glenville.

Mellers was hesitant and just stood there until Freddie prompted him. "And what did you do?" he asked.

"Oh, I was inside," he said boldly.

"Inside?" repeated Freddie and looked at Mellers square on. "What were you in for?"

"Armed robbery," replied Mellers without a trace of emotion or embarrassment. Freddie rose to the occasion.

"Well unfortunately there are no banks in Japanese prisoner of war camps." This remark brought an onslaught of laughter. The men were obviously in dire need of some humour. "Perhaps we could find a use for your talents sometime." He looked around him and when he felt certain that he had everyone's attention he took centre stage. Anyone looking at Freddie in his tropical safari outfit and appraising his quiet but effective domination of the room would never have guessed that he still felt very weak and breathless from his bout of illness.

"All right, gentlemen, doubtless I will get to know you all in good time. I don't take airs and graces and I don't take any pretence to be something I'm not. So, if any of you lads want to talk to me about anything at all, we can cut out the bull straight away and get down to brass tacks." He glanced quickly at John Saunders to see how he was responding. "When I arrived here today I was appalled to see how badly you men have all been treated. Believe me I'm going to make a bloody loud protest to Captain Shigoshu to improve our lot here. I want to ask you men now," Freddie looked down towards the doorway where a British soldier was keeping watch. The soldier indicated all was clear and Freddie continued, "how many of you have considered escape plans, individual or otherwise. Put you hands up if you have."

A forest of hands shot up in the air. Freddie surveyed the group.

"With respect," Colonel Saunders intercepted, "we've looked at a lot of plans to escape. The problem is if the most physically fit of all of us escape, we would be leaving the very sick to an unknown fate. In the hospital this morning when we walked around you saw the conditions of the men."

"Yes, I did," said Freddie with a look of sadness in his eyes. "I saw the amputees, the malnourished and the emaciated. It's important I know from the men what they want." He moved in amongst them. "What do you want, men?"

The interior of the hut was quiet as the men looked at each other.

"No comments?" asked Freddie. He looked to Colonel Saunders. "John?"

Saunders responded. "The way I see it, Malaya is swarming with enemy troops. Escape here would be virtually impossible."

Freddie nodded in agreement. "That's certainly my view. But as I said it was important that I asked. My great worry is for the sick and for the general condition of everyone. All right for the moment, any ideas of escape must be put on the back burner. It's true we certainly risk everyone's life by attempting to escape. We're going to need to improve our lot here."

"What are you going to do about it?" asked Mellers, the Australian soldier who spoke out rather brashly.

Freddie walked up to him and eyed him. "We can all work together for a start." Then he turned away and attracted attention from everyone. "Tomorrow I will confront Captain Shigoshi and push for action for better conditions. Are you men going to be one hundred per cent behind me?"

"Too bloody right, mate!" came back Mulrone, not giving Freddie respect for his rank but as a friend, in that curious Australian manner whereby everyone no matter what their status in life was thought of as an equal.

"All the way."

"Yeah, good on you, mate!"

"Yes, sir, we'll support you."

A whole flood of voices came across the room in an array of different accents giving note to the diversity of soldiers who were there.

Freddie could see that it was a popular move destined for huge support. "Immediately after morning parade, I want you all to stand your ground when I go to see Captain Shigoshu. It could take some time so be prepared for some fireworks tomorrow. I don't know how they're going to react. I can assure you I'm not going to give in easily. I suggest, men, you all try and get a good night's sleep. Tomorrow might be a difficult day."

Freddie departed from the hut and before going to his own that passed as officer's quarters, he stood outside looking into the night sky and listening to the sounds of the insects and birds squawking in the tropical jungle. Today had been an eye opener. Before embarking on the assignment that had inadvertently led him to this prison camp, Freddie had learned of some of the fates that had befallen some of his fellow servicemen. Stories of the Burma-Siam railroad had circulated and he was well aware that if any of the men in this camp were shipped there in their present condition, their chances of survival would be slim.

The sky was almost purple that night broken only by the flickering stars that were burning embers thrown into the air by a furious fire. Freddie studied the constellations and galaxies that swirled into eternity across the deep sea of night. He heard movement behind him and turned. It was Sergeant major Griffiths.

"The Lord made beautiful nights in this part of the world, didn't he, sir?"

"Yes, he did, Sergeant Major Griffiths. It's a pity we don't have more pleasant company to spend it with though."

The two men looked towards the various watchtowers around the prison camp. Japanese sentries stood poised with their guns at the ready. Escape was damn near impossible as had been mentioned earlier. Everywhere Freddie looked bamboo was the order of the day. The prison huts were made of bamboo. The hospital was made of bamboo. So too were the watchtowers.

They were safe in the shadows of the huts. Freddie looked at Griffiths. The Welshman, somewhere in his late thirties, was a real character. He seemed to be larger than life in his physical attributes and his manner of speaking. Griffiths with his magnetism and rich soul would undoubtedly have been responsible for keeping the spirits of the men together. Freddie could see this and decided to enhance his knowledge of the Sergeant major.

"Tell me about yourself, Sergeant Major," he asked pleasantly.

"Me, sir?" He seemed genuinely surprised. "As you can gather by my voice I'm a Welshman, from a family of several generations of coal miners. I was brought up in a happy family background. I've got three sisters and two brothers you know. I had another two brothers but they died in accidents in the pits. I lost my own father in the pits as well as two uncles and my Grandfather – well the coal dust got into his chest and that was it. It seemed like I was destined to die in a pit accident or of coal dust accumulation in my system. My poor mother lost so many relatives in the mines sir that I thought I'd be safer in the Army. So here I am, sir, and by God I wish I was home in Wales singing my head off in the chapel and going home to a Sunday roast on the table. When I come through this bloody show I will never take the simple things in life for granted again. That's my story. What about you, sir? Are you married?"

The hurt was shown in Freddie's eyes. "No – not any more" he said softly. "I was widowed some time back."

"That's bad luck, sir," said Sergeant Major Griffiths quietly, and he genuinely meant it. He felt inclined to add, "Well at least you've known marriage, sir. Some people never get to know how good it can be. My mother and father were together for nearly forty years."

Freddie nodded his head and smiled. He liked Griffiths. He was goodhearted,

"The men here – what sort of food have they been getting?"

"Rice, rice and more rice. Little else. The Red Cross have dropped parcels, but, of course, when those oriental fellows got hold of them—"

"Yes, I know, Sergeant Major. It's most important we keep the spirits of the men up. I've looked hard at them. They're skeletal. Their energies are low. And I want to help them. God only knows how they'll survive this. Pity you can't get a bit of that singing going here that you Welsh are famous for. That might buck their spirits up."

"Begging your pardon, sir, but that's one thing I have got going here. I've got some of the boys singing their hearts out on a Sunday morning where we take service. A lovely bunch of voices too. Y'know it's amazing how you can get a group of men in a situation like this who probably, in any other set of circumstances, wouldn't have had the slightest thing in common with each other. Yet here they are in Borneo, all men of different backgrounds singing hymns like the 'Holy City' and that 'Old Rugged Cross', and 'Steadfast and Sure' as if they were all old friends who'd known each other all their lives. Do you know what I think, sir? I think that the harsher moments of our lives, the times when we are most troubled, under the greatest stress, it's my belief that it brings out the best in us. We Welsh are famous for our words of wisdom. Times of great hardship bring out our greatest strength."

Freddie read into the words deeply. He knew that there was much truth in what Sergeant Major Griffiths had said. Freddie's sensitive eyes showed that he understood so well.

"I think you're right Sergeant Major. Adversity breeds our characters. It's not success or failure that makes us what we are. It's the effort and the struggle. And how we cope with the end result, win or lose. Take our situation here for instance. We're up against it. It's up to ourselves to endure this and survive and show them -" he pointed to the guards "- that no matter what, they cannot break our spirit." Then he added for emphasis. "They won't break our spirit. You might try and get the men singing more often. Show our friends there that no matter what, we'll always survive."

The sergeant major agreed with him. Freddie was a man he could admire very easily. He watched as Freddie walked away to his hut. The two men were of a complete contrast. A keen observer of human nature would have known their initiatives were the same. They both had the same quiet strengths and courage that the bravest men have without being brutally masculine or making a false pretence of bravado. Sergeant major Griffiths judged Colonel Freddie Miller's character accurately. He was undoubtedly a man who could be relied upon.

Griffiths looked up at the guards. It was time he tried to get some sort of night's sleep. The only sleep one could get in cramped, stifling, over crowded conditions was slightly less than fitful. A few hours sleep then the gruelling hardship of the day would begin. Often in the middle of the night if a tool or weapon had gone astray, it would not be uncommon for a search to be conducted in the early hours, when Japanese soldiers would suddenly burst into the huts and overturn everything. The prisoners would find themselves thrown out of their beds while the search took place.

On that first night Freddie heard the commotion of a search taking place in a hut next door to his. It was about three o'clock in the morning and an angry Freddie, followed by John Saunders, stormed into the hut. They were devastated when they saw what had taken place: their captors had gone through the huts with the fury of a whirlwind. Freddie was enraged. He wanted to strike out the soldiers who had done this. They left as fast and as furiously as they had come. It was then that Freddie saw captain Shigoshu for the first time. The captain walked through the rampage of the hut with several large Japanese soldiers by his side. An angry Freddie, wearing only shorts and a vest, stepped directly in front of Shigoshu effectively barring his way.

The sight was breathtaking as the two men found themselves in a confrontation. The other POWs looked on in awe and amazement. The Texan, Gordon Sheridan, took one pace forward as if he should do something to stop the inevitable but Lieutenant Vincent held him back.

Shigoshu was an overpowering looking man. He had a massive girth that actually stretched his Japanese Army Officers uniform to its limit. His moustache was black against an almost radiantly orange-yellow complexion. He stared directly at Freddie in a look of puzzlement.

"In the name of decency man, why?" Freddie screeched angrily.

The reply came in the form of a cane from one of the soldiers who struck Freddie across the head with it. Freddie reeled back in pain onto the floor, blood dripping from his forehead where he had been hit.

This started a near riot. The POWs rushed forward, but the Japanese soldiers came striking back at them. Freddie tried to regain his senses. The pain of the cane stroke was searing but something in him compelled him to stand up again. With Freddie on his feet again, he once again stood face to face with Captain Shigoshu. The hut became filled with a deadly silence. The quiet was icy and one of stealth. Freddie turned to the soldier who had struck him and made the most fatal mistake he could have ever made. He snatched at the cane and hurled it angrily to the ground.

In the next minute Freddie was punched, kicked and dragged away out of the hut. There was outrage amongst the POWs. They could not contain themselves. Their captors, well-armed, beat them back into submission. Saunders looked up at the roof. He feared for Freddie. There was absolute uproar in the hut. The Japanese soldiers fiercely held back the POWs who swore and cursed at their captors. It was going to be a long day ahead for all of them.

When the sun rose the next morning and hit its peak at midday, Saunders, Vincent and Griffiths looked across the prison camp to a point where there was a cage positioned so that it caught the full blast of the sun's rays. It was where Freddie spent the next four days for his protest. The full force of the tropical sun could not be imagined. At the worst time when the sun's rays were well exposed, Freddie's soft white Hampshire skin was burnt almost black, his fair hair almost white. Freddie was dehydrated and breathless. He wanted to give up completely. He had not expected to survive the war and indeed after plunging into a deep grief following Cynthia's death, he had been most uncaring whether he did or not. But during those dark hours Freddie turned to prayer. Somehow being this close to the end he felt the need to pray, not only for himself but for all the people he had known in his life, and for the men outside in the prison camp.

Several times Gordon Sheridan on instructions from Lieutenant Vincent tried to get across to give Freddie some sort of sustenance in the form of a sponge of water, but the guards around that particular area made it virtually impenetrable.

Lieutenant Vincent and Colonel Saunders tried to approach Captain Shigoshu about Freddie. Each time they were rebuked by guards who would not allow them to pass. Both men angrily returned to their men.

Kindness came to Freddie early on the third day when he lay on the floor, his tongue dry and his body only gently flickering with the will to survive. The act of kindness came from the most unexpected source, a young man from the Land of the Rising Sun gave hope to Freddie that there will always be someone who will rise above the rest and show signs of humanity.

Shortly after midnight, when Freddie laying face-up, looking at the stars through the bars above him, the youthful face of a Japanese soldier appeared. Freddie didn't know what to expect; he was parched and dry and his stamina was low. To Freddie's amazement the young oriental soldier produced a small bottle of lemonade and some rolls of bread. The soldier looked around to make sure no one was watching and when he felt it was fine to do so, he lowered the bottle and the rolls to a stunned Freddie Miller.

Freddie looked up, hardly believing his eyes. Then in a moment of relief he emptied the contents of the bottle into his throat. His hot and feverish body suddenly felt a few degrees cooler. Moisture became apparent in his tongue. He coughed slightly and then with a rasping voice tried to find some words.

"Why?" It was the only word he could find.

The Japanese soldier looked down at him. *Surely,* Freddie thought, *this soldier was no more than a boy. He could barely have been sixteen.*

"I admired your courage," the soldier said in shaky English. "I saw you get up in the hut when you had been struck."

In a moment of confusion and bewilderment Freddie tried to assess the character of the young man. "What is your name? You're only a youngster. You speak English so well."

Freddie's voice was hoarse and soft. Although it was the dead of night, the tropical heat was moist and humid, and the noise of jungle insects all creating their own individual sounds intermingled together making the atmosphere of the moment unique in memory.

The young soldier answered Freddie. "I am Takahishi." His voice too was that of a controlled whisper but distinctive in its tone. "I studied European languages at university before the war."

So, Freddie thought, taking a bite out of one of the bread rolls, *this young man must be in his early twenties.*

"Where do you come from, soldier?" Freddie asked, swilling back more lemonade. He had asked the question more to keep the conversation going than out of curiosity.

"Have you been to Japan, Colonel?"

"No," Freddie replied. "Many other places, but never Japan."

Takahashi spoke in broken words, pausing slightly between each word. "I am from a place called – Hiroshima."

Freddie just nodded. He had not heard of the place. He was still bemused by this show of decency from one of his captors, who were not known for making concessions of this nature.

"You must go," said Freddie suddenly. "Your superiors will treat you harshly if they learn what you have done tonight. Takahishi?"

"Yes?"

"Thank you."

"You will be released tomorrow, Colonel. I know that. You will have strength to face the future. I must ask you to pass the empty bottle to me. If a guard finds it—"

"Yes, of course," said Freddie realising the consequences for both of them should the remnants of the brief sustenance be found. Then as Freddie raised the empty bottle of lemonade his eyes froze. The label on the bottle was an English brand name. "Takahishi, where did this bottle come from?" he asked with sudden alarm.

"From a Red Cross parcel."

The words had an immediate effect on Freddie. He felt violently angry inside. He had been informed by the Welsh sergeant major that Red Cross parcels had been dropped to the prisoners, but the guards had seized them and failed to distribute the contents.

"Takahishi. These parcels from the Red Cross – why were they not given to our men? The other prisoners are starving."

Freddie waited anxiously for an answer. Somehow the anger within him was dissipating fast for he realised that he was on the receiving end of an act of kindness from the most unusual quarter. At last Takahishi answered. "You must not mention to Captain Shigoshu what I have told you."

"I won't," Freddie assured him. "But I'd like to know if there are any other parcels from the Red Cross here."

"I must go," Takahishi said softly, and with a scurry he moved away quickly leaving Freddie gazing up at the stars through the bars of his small prison. He lay back and closed his eyes and prepared himself for the next day. He took deep breaths and tried to sleep to vent out his mixed feelings.

When morning came so did the feeling of being free, at least being free as far as was possible in a prisoner of war camp. The lock from the cage was removed and a couple of Japanese soldiers slid back the door. After several days Freddie was finally released from the confines of the cage. He came outside and the sudden rising of the sun forced him to shield his face from the glare of the day. His legs felt stiff and sore and he suddenly realised how terribly sunburnt he had been during the few days. Freddie ran his hand around his bearded face. Gosh, he thought, what a sight he must be with his skin burnt black, his hair burnt white, and he felt hot, sticky and dirty. There was a dreadful dry-eyed feeling around his eyes from not having slept properly for a few days. It was hard too for Freddie to stretch his legs and retain his balance. Yet somehow he managed to find a smile to spread across his lips, even if his face stung from sunburn and to contort his facial muscles for even the slightest expression hurt him.

The two Japanese soldiers positioned themselves on each side of him and indicated to him to march in the direction of Captain Shigoshu's hut that doubled as an office. Freddie gritted his teeth and began to walk in a marching fashion. So anxious was Freddie to encounter the captain that he walked several paces ahead of his guards. From out of the corner of his eye he saw Takahishi standing on sentry duty with a rifle over his shoulder. Freddie cast a quick glance at him. He carried on walking and as he neared the huts where all of the prisoners were usually housed, he suddenly realised that all of the POWs were standing on parade. Sergeant Major Griffiths suddenly yelled out a cry of, "Atten-shun!" and he spun around to salute Freddie.

"Bloody good to see you, sir!" he said, not bothering to conceal his delight that Freddie, despite his confinement, was in fine form.

Freddie too was sparkling and returned the salute with a smile of confidence, "And a bloody good parade too, Sergeant Major! A bloody top show!"

Freddie had no sooner passed by, than the men broke into a spontaneous cheer and applause for him, astonishing even the Japanese guards. From the sick bay Colonel John Saunders and the Australian medical officer, Lieutenant Vincent, stepped forward and saluted. Freddie felt slightly phased by the support he had been given by his men. More than just phasing him, it had touched him enormously. They had come right behind him. It was his duty not to let them down now at any cost and he knew that he must strive to get better conditions for his men, even if it meant more tumultuous confrontations with the camp commandant.

Inside Captain Shigoshu's office the guards closed the door behind them as they left. Freddie faced Captain Shigoshu across the table in silence and for a few seconds each tried to anticipate the reaction of the other. Finally, the Captain motioned to Freddie to take a seat. Freddie sat down, removed his hat and stared directly at the Captain, who was quick to determine that he meant business. Over the next couple of hours, the two men talked and argued in a most stormy fashion.

"What the devil is he doing in there?" Colonel Saunders said to Lieutenant Vincent outside as they both looked up at Captain Shigoshu's office. The long wait was chilling in its suspense.

It was several hours before Freddie finally emerged. When he did the POWs who were by now hard at work stopped to see him walk to his quarters. Before he entered his hut to shave and shower for the first time in a few days, Paul Vincent and John Saunders encountered him. Freddie looked dazed and definitely bedraggled.

"Sir, are you all right?" asked Paul Vincent, plainly concerned about the colonel's health.

Freddie managed to ignite his eyes with a spark of humour. "Nothing that a decent shave and wash, and a good night's sleep won't put right."

"What went on in there?" asked John Saunders bursting with curiosity

"Gentlemen," replied Freddie, smiling through a stubble bearded face, "I have Captain Shigoshu's word – a word that I have every reason to believe he will keep – that he will distribute the contents of some Red Cross parcels to the men tonight. And Lieutenant Vincent, I might add there will be some medicine forthcoming."

The two men were aghast. They stared at Freddie in disbelief, not knowing whether to laugh or cry. It was Saunders who echoed the only note of pessimism "Seriously Freddie, I'll believe it when I see it. Those chaps don't make concessions."

Freddie pointed with one finger behind Saunders. "Take a look. Take a look."

Several Japanese soldiers, including Takahishi, were walking towards them carrying parcels.

"How did you do it?" Paul Vincent murmured.

"It was simple. After a lot of arguing, a lot of shouting and a test of nerves on both sides, I reminded Captain Shigoshu of the rules stipulated in the Geneva Convention. I told him that at the war's end he would be tried as a war criminal. He wasn't convinced. He seemed sure that this was the beginning of a hundred year reign by Japan. But he acquiesced when I reminded him there is such a thing as human decency, and that if we didn't get decent food and medication once in a while the whole bloody lot of us would be dead in months. Now, gentlemen, see to it that everyone gets their share. I'm going to treat myself to a wash."

With that Freddie walked inside the hut. Vincent and Saunders looked at the food and medicine parcels being taken into the hut. The men would eat better that day. The sick would get better attention. From close by Sergeant Major Griffiths beamed with admiration for Freddie's endurance and efforts. Freddie had shown magnificent grace and courage under enormous pressure and tension. His quiet strength and dignity led the men through the remaining three years of the war.

Never once during the next few years did Freddie give up. It was as if the death of his wife, Cynthia, had propelled him to take more risk-taking missions, thinking he had nothing to live for. By fate and misfortune he had found himself in charge of that mixed assortment in that hellhole in Borneo. The very negative, couldn't-care attitude that Freddie had possessed at the outset of the mission gave way to a more positive way of thinking. Now that he had the men to lead, the new responsibility gave him a renewed vigour. He knew it was up to him to keep the men together in body and soul and he did not flinch from this duty. Time and time again Freddie stood up to Captain Shigoshu demanding better conditions and respect for the prisoners. It became a massive contest of nerves between the two officers, with Freddie being returned to the cell three more times. Freddie only became tougher and more resilient, and the more he stood up to his captors, the more his own men rallied behind him.

The prisoners became intensely loyal to Freddie and they in turn, particularly the Australians amongst them, generated a wonderful spirit and sense of humour despite the humiliation and cruel treatment that was inflicted upon them. Freddie developed a fondness for the Australian contingent and for Seargent Major Griffiths, who he was convinced was the mainstay behind the men. Griffiths often rallied the men into song. Singing brought out the latent spirit in the men and roused them out of their apathy and their low moods. On a Sunday morning when they took service they genuinely felt they were thanking God for their continual survival.

Not everyone survived the next few years. Many died from sickness and wounds that were not properly treated. Freddie and Paul Vincent continually fought a verbal battle with Captain Shigoshu over this and occasionally they were successful in getting the medication required, but it was always a major battle to acquire it. The graveyard in the camp became bigger as many soldiers died, the victims of disease.

Not all those who died had suffered disease of one kind or the other. Four Australians attempted to escape one night and only one escaped. Mulrome, Mellers, Donnelly and Glenville attempted to break out in the early hours. Donnelly managed to evade capture. The other three were shot by a keen lookout. What became of Donnelly was something of a mystery. After that, escape was never attempted again. The men kept together and gave each other enormous support to ensure that they would survive this dreadful ordeal. Friendships were born out of the experiences of the camp. The Australians and the English, who are by nature standoffish to begin with, developed an enormous camaraderie between them and found they had far more in common than they would normally have been prepared to admit. All the men were strong in spirit at least and pulled together to the very end.

It was in May 1945 that Freddie, John Saunders and Paul Vincent were called to Captain Shigoshu's office. They had been informed that Shigoshu had some news for them. When they left the office after being told the news, they walked out in the tropical sunlight with smiles of absolute disbelief on their faces. The war in Europe was over. It could only be a matter of time before war ended in the Far East.

Far away in London, victory in Europe was being celebrated. VE day was one that Nathan Palmai would always remember. After his service in North Africa with the British Army he had been sent to England to a base in Essex. Nathan had come to London that day to join the huge crowds that were expected to swell in the centre of the city. Everywhere Nathan looked there were servicemen; English, American, Canadian, Australian, soldiers, airmen, marines and civilians. There were people climbing lampposts, statues and buildings draping flags, streamers and victory stickers.

People were dancing the conga and the Lambeth Walk. All along Piccadilly and Oxford Street there were thousands upon thousands of people converging, and Nathan simply drifted with the crowd. It was impossible not to be caught up in the thrill and hysteria of it all. People sang, they danced and, servicemen of all nationalities used the occasion as an excuse to grab the nearest girl and give her a long passionate kiss. Nathan did not see one girl object.

He stumbled along with the crowd. Then in front of him he saw one young woman misjudge her step and slip over. Nathan rushed forward and helped her to her feet. She turned and smiled at him. Nathan was stunned by her attractiveness.

"Thank you, monsieur," she said pleasantly.

Nathan was completely taken by her appearance. He did not realise that this was a particular moment he would remember all of his days; for he was gazing at Francine Macé, a girl who would be prominent in the future years of his life.

"Are you all right?" he asked.

"Fine – I slipped. These are new shoes. I am not used to them."

"You are French?" Nathan queried. Her accent was so obviously French and her looks so compelling that he wanted to pursue the moment for all that it was worth.

"Yes I am," she said casting an equally admiring gaze at Nathan.

"You wear a British soldier's uniform, but you are not British?"

At this Nathan appeared downcast. "I am a Jewish refugee from Austria, I joined the British Army in Palestine and when I am discharged I intend to stay here and go to university and study law."

She remained silent for a few seconds giving him a quizzical look, then said, "Well good luck, monsieur," and in the flash of an instant she gave him a delicious kiss on his lips, and just as quickly she disappeared into the crowd. People surged up behind Nathan and he felt compelled to move with them. He had a wide smile on his face. What a lovely encounter that had been. She had been a welcome intrusion on his life.

Soon Nathan had gone with the crowds along the Mall towards Buckingham Palace. There on the balcony were the Royal Family, King George VI, Queen Elizabeth and their daughters, the young Princess Elizabeth and Princess Margaret, and the fiery old statesman himself, Winston Churchill, who had led the nation through the war to this ultimate victory. When Churchill waved, a huge roar of approval went up from the crowd. Nathan looked up from amongst the crowd and realised that this was a moment in history to be cherished and remembered. The joy of peace in Europe had spread through the nation.

It was still not the end of the war. Nathan listened to Churchill's speech when in the words that flowed the Prime Minister mentioned that Japan was still at war. The joyous festivities taking place in London were far removed from the POW camps in South East Asia. For the imprisoned soldiers there the pain still continued until later in August when something happened that terminated the war with a suddenness that reverberated across the world.

On one morning early in August at the prison camp in Borneo, where Freddie Miller and the mixed group of POWs were housed, there was a sudden cooling in the air like a breeze blowing away the scattered leaves of a fallen tree branch. The change in the atmosphere was not only noticeable due to the cooling of the tropical heat, but for the sudden downbeat feelings that were so apparent in the Japanese guards.

Freddie was the first to notice this. On rising from a totally sleepless night, during which he had lain in deep thought, half-closed eyelids occasionally blinking, he had wandered from the hut at the break of dawn and, looking up at the watchtowers around the camp, he saw that one was totally empty. He was immediately puzzled by this. He looked around him and saw groups of Japanese soldiers talking. By the looks on their faces there was something happening. Freddie did not have any feelings for his captors. He had seen too many of his own men suffer and die at their hands. He had seen too many of his men overworked while starving and fed only rice. Then with a sudden twinge of conscience, perhaps an old biblical passage reaching from his childhood past into his mind, told him not to be bitter, not to hate his captors, for he realised with a sudden ferocity that bitterness and hatred are the most destructive components in a man's character. No matter how badly he and his men had been treated, Freddie somehow had to remove this from his system. There and then he decided that the hardships he had endured and seen would not scar him. He would overcome, but he knew he could never forget, nor would be ever allow himself to do so.

But what was it that had troubled the guards? Why were they not pushing everyone to work? From behind him Saunders, Griffiths and Vincent approached. They too were surprised by the somewhat apathy of their captors.

"What's going on here?" asked Saunders. "What are they doing?"

Freddie seemed perplexed. "As far as I can see, John, they're just talking. It's what they're talking about that worries me."

"Well I might only be a sergeant major," cut in Griffiths sharply, "but it's in my nature to understand men and they look concerned. Is it possible, sir?"

"Do you mean is the war over?" Freddie mentioned.

"Yes, that's what I'd like to know," added Vincent, also curious as to the strange mood of the guards.

Takahishi, the young soldier who had once shown Freddie kindness when he was imprisoned in a cage, walked away sharply from the group. The young man's face looked as if it was tear-stained. To Freddie it was a complete surprise. His captors had not shown signs of emotion or sensitivity before. He knew that something had happened.

"Excuse me, gentlemen," said Freddie, "I'm going to find out."

Takahishi was walking in the direction of the graveyard. Freddie followed him and found the young Japanese soldier staring at the crosses. Before approaching him he stopped short of a few yards away from him. Freddie was alarmed to hear the young man sobbing and then in a fit of fury and unhappy anger Takahishi fell to the floor thumping and hitting the ground and wailing uncontrollably. It was more than anyone could bear to see this young man's terrible agony.

It was some time later that Freddie returned to the other men. Now he looked a stern and saddened figure. The two other officers and the sergeant major looked up at him for an answer. Freddie looked down at the ground before answering them.

"I just spoke to Takahishi, the young soldier—"

"And what's happened?" Saunders quickly interrupted.

"Let me finish, John," Freddie said raising his hand momentarily. "Takahishi comes from a place in Japan called Hiroshima. Two days ago, something devastating happened there." The men looked at each other totally astounded by what they had heard. "It caused enough widespread destruction to end the war. I think you can safely say that it won't be long before this is all over."

"What else did that young soldier say?" queried Vincent.

"He wasn't really in the mood for talking as you can imagine. However, if that doesn't signal the end of the war, heaven knows what will. Tell me, Paul, in conversation once, you told me of a special day in Australia when the fallen in war are remembered.

"Yes its called Anzac Day. Normally held on the 25th April. It begins with a dawn service held at the cenotaph in each capital city, followed by a march of the ex-servicemen through the streets."

"We won't be doing any marching. I do propose to hold a dawn service tomorrow morning with all the men on parade who are fit enough. Is that all right with you men?" The others nodded. "Sergeant Major Griffiths, perhaps you could think of a couple of hymns suitable enough. I don't know what all your religious beliefs are. I know that something has kept us going. Something, some spirit, be it that of the men or something beyond our comprehension, has pulled us through. It's not been without terrible cost. We've lost good men. We've got men here who've lived on rice for a couple of years and haven't had a decent meal since God knows when. I want to show our opponents that we've survived, and not only have we survived but come through with strength."

"It would be fine by me, sir," Griffiths responded with enthusiasm. "We'll sing our hearts out. By heavens we're still alive and we'll sing like angels!"

"Good stuff, Griffiths," Freddie said in reply.

On that day the prisoners rested. They were not spurred into action by any guards; it was a rare day on which they could rest without fear of mistreatment. Later in the day Freddie was called into the office of Captain Shigoshi, who officially gave him the news. Even at this stage Shigoshu still did not make concession for the pain that the men had suffered.

The dawn service took place as planned the next day. All of the men including some in the sick bay came out to pay homage to the comrades who had died at the camp. It was a stunning sight: a group of English, Australian and American servicemen all standing erect, shoulder to shoulder, and yet it was very sad for even in the early morning hours before the light emerged, the hunger and the tiredness on each man's face was so obvious.

The American soldier, Gordon Sheridan, brought the bugle to his lips and in the lustrous navy-blue darkness of a tropical morning, as the bright red sun forced its way up behind tall palm trees sending a flicker of early morning light flashing through the treetops, he played the 'Last Post' and 'Reveille'. It was an emotional feeing for each man, realising that they had survived and that in the camp graveyard many lay with a cross as their only testimonial of their suffering. One minute's silence was observed at the cessation of the rendering of the 'Last Post'. The sound of the bugle had spread throughout the camp. Even Captain Shigoshu and Takahishi in their quarters had woken at the sound of it, and unintentionally they seemed to observe the silence that followed almost as a tribute to the men. One brief minute passed, and Sergeant major Griffiths sang in a poignant welsh voice the opening words of the hymn, the Holy City, and the men slowly joined in singing with all the heart and spirit they could muster. The words *'Jerusalem, Jerusalem, lift up your gates and sing'* seemed to make an emotional impact on every man as they sang. From out of the darkness the light of early morning suddenly flowed across the men. Every man's eyes were moist with emotion. Even the hardest men had tears on their leathery faces.

At the end of the hymn, they took prayer. In the midst of saying the Lord's Prayer, the sound of aircraft engines up above broke the spell. The men looked to the sky with a shock. Freddie too was fearful, then he broke out a sigh of relief and he looked at the men whose expressions were a mixture of tears and happiness. Several more aircraft flew over dropping leaflets and parcels. They were allied aircraft. The leaflets merely had the words stating that the war was over. Everyone began to cry with relief. That same night all of the Japanese guards disappeared and a few days later allied troops came and took the weary POWs to ships and vessels to get them to happier destinations.

In September 1945 Freddie found himself on a boat bound for England. This ordeal was now finally over. A new journey in a world of peace had begun for him.

★★★

For Nathan peacetime would bring him a distinguished career, travel, love and real achievement. He would be successful wildly beyond any plans that he had chartered for himself.

Life for Melissa too would bring its twists and surprises. Her talent, beauty and tenacity would almost certainly ensure success in her chosen field. It did not guarantee for happiness however. But the life she was destined to lead was the stuff that dreams were made of.

Francine also began a new life in peacetime Europe before extending her horizons further afield.

Freddie Miller, somewhat emotional and battle-scarred by the events of the war years, could never quite abandon a lifestyle that contained a certain amount of risk. An office desk or a quiet, safe life was not for him. In the post war years, he became a journalist of international repute.

Somehow, though, as each person set about their own lives, none of them could have envisaged that their destinies would continue to be linked.

Twenty-seven

1983

The more eventful the life, the stronger the memories. For both Nathan Palmai and Melissa Campbell, the night had re-awoken a past life full of adversity. They had talked strongly of the years leading up to the end of the Second World War.

In the time that had passed, they had both had illustrious careers and lives full of activity. For a few moments Nathan and Melissa sat in the wonderful silence that old friends could afford as the impact of distant memories sank in.

Nathan gazed at Melissa in wonder. Here was a beautiful, vibrant, exciting and talented woman who rivalled such screen immortals as Elizabeth Taylor, Joan Collins and Jean Simmons. Melissa's voice had been compared to that of Judy Garland; rich in timbre and immaculately controlled, she could sustain notes powerfully in any octave it seemed. Yet for all this, to Nathan, she was still the young girl who had caught his eye in a play performed at the Kibbutz Jezarat so long ago.

Melissa too sat in silent analysis of her old friend. Her thoughts were of a similar nature. Nathan had once been a shy, sensitive young man. But determined – oh yes, definitely determined! She always knew that his industriousness, his attention to detail and the electric drive beneath the still waters would propel him to the heights he so desperately needed to reach.

At last an impulse within Melissa compelled her to break the silence. "It's good to talk like this, Nathan. You have such a good memory of things. I can see now why you have done so well as a lawyer." She allowed herself a tiny smile and added, "I wish you had represented me in Hollywood in some of the legal problems and contractual disagreements I have found myself embroiled in from time to time over the years."

"Ah – yes. I have read of those," Nathan said casually remembering the particular incidents. In fact Nathan had kept scrapbooks detailing her career and notices. He was well acquainted with Mellissa's marriages and show business accolades.

"Just a small price I have had to pay for my fame," said Melissa.

Nathan remembered how he had once wanted to marry her. There was something he wanted to ask Melissa. Considering how well publicised her life had been, Nathan was curious to know.

"I have always followed your life through the newspapers," Nathan commented almost proudly. "One thing I am simply bursting to know…"

"And what is that, my old friend?" she asked with interest.

"You and I… we are both old time émigrés … people from another time and a world that is so different to the one we knew when we were young. We were caught up in circumstances beyond our control that affected us because of our faith and birth right. Today… you are an almost legendary figure in show business. I am looking at you now. I remember you as the girl on the kibbutz chasing the chickens!"

Melissa smiled at this. "So that is the question? You have still not asked me."

"It's hypothetical really," explained Nathan. "The old question that everyone asks themselves at some stage in their life… if you were to go back in time, perhaps even to the wooden shacks, the poultry and the agriculture of the fields in that land… that spiritual home of ours, Israel – is there anything you would change? Would you do it all again?"

The question seemed to throw Melissa temporarily off balance. "Do you know? That is the hardest question anyone could ever ask of themselves. I have often heard people say that we are the authors of our own lives. The authors of our own lives!" A sparkle suddenly flared into her extraordinarily expressive eyes. "I have never heard a comment that I am so violently in disagreement with." Now this was something thought Nathan. Melissa's brilliantly artistic temperament seemed to have been fired up. "You mentioned a moment ago, how our lives were caught up in circumstances beyond our control. That is often the case throughout life. Things happen! Conflicts occur! People change! My first two marriages – they were disasters, but I did not go into them light-heartedly. If I had my time again, I don't think I would change things, my old friend. I would not be able to change the things that have affected me."

"Nor me," remarked Nathan.

"So then it has been all worthwhile, has it not?" Melissa asked him now. Before he could reply Melissa felt inclined to add another comment. "I once met Errol Flynn in Hollywood. He had something of a reputation as a hell-raiser. He always seemed to be involved in some sort of controversy, but he told me it had been an exciting and wonderful life. I feel the same way about my own."

Nathan quickly glanced at his watch. "My goodness, we have talked for a long time and so far we have only reached 1945."

He realised that he may soon have to drive her back to her hotel at the Sebel Town House in Elizabeth Bay

Mellissa looked almost lovingly at Nathan. "Now the years from 1945. They are quite a story, aren't they?"

"Shall we talk about them?" asked Nathan. "Do you have the time tonight to remember?"

Melissa smiled in that old glowing manner which she had possessed in her youth. Once again, it was that young girl in the Kibbutz, not the world-weary international film star.

Finally she answered, "I will always have time for you, Nathan, my old kibbutz friend."

Twenty-eight

Nathan Palmai and Melissa Campbell had talked long into the night. There had been so much to talk about. The memories of the years had made them both feel very nostalgic about the past. In recent times since his wife had died, and both of his children had created new lives for themselves, Nathan felt very much alone. The house at Bondi held only memories for him. When Francine had died, Nathan became a lonely, crestfallen figure often walking along the beach at night thinking of her, lost in deep feelings of grief. He would gaze up into the mauve darkness of the sky at the twinkling constellations and galaxies, and for the first time in his life he found himself questioning his faith. He wondered if there really was an afterlife, somewhere that Francine would meet up with his parents, Arthandur and Marlene. The thought of a world beyond this one delighted him. How pleased his parents would have been at Francine being their son's wife. With the waves roaring in the background Nathan often wondered if the three people he had loved the most were watching him from a beautiful love filled place beyond all human comprehension.

Meeting Melissa again after all these years revived many memories for Nathan. To think that it was forty-five years ago they had first met on the Kibbutz Jezarat. One should never live in the past. One should never overindulge in nostalgia. These were positive words of advice Nathan had given himself. Nathan had let go of the past in many ways before. When Francine had died, Nathan could not live amongst the memories of his home at Bondi. It was too painful. Everywhere he looked, he half expected Francine to walk through the door. He envisaged her painting in the sunroom, sitting in the sunshine in the garden laughing with the children. Finally he could bear it no longer and he moved to his present home, a high rise luxury apartment at Darling Point, with what Nathan considered the best view in the world, a panorama of Sydney Harbour before him.

It was here in an attempt to blot out the grief of losing Francine that Nathan had involved himself more than every in his legal work, his business directorship positions and a deep commitment to community affairs for ethnic groups. In addition to this he had also regained his faith. He had devoted much of his time to the Jewish community. He was passionately proud of his origins, his family line, and of the fact that his late father, Arthandur, had been part of an organisation that had protected the lives and interests of many people of his own faith.

Talking to Melissa that night had reawakened the dormant past, the nostalgia, the pain, the love, the excitement, the struggle, the passion and achievement of his life. He had remembered everything with clarity and an almost photographic detail of people and places.

Melissa sat poised, still beautiful although showing signs of being world weary. Life had given her fame, fortune, several marriages and children. Nathan was disposed to ask her if it had also given her happiness. Her divorces, legal suits, and a nervous breakdown had only been obscured by her dazzling talent. In films Melissa acted with sensitivity and finesse. Not surprisingly she had been nominated for an Oscar, had won an award for a sensational performance she gave on Broadway, and in television she had picked up several Emmies. As a cabaret performer, Melissa was much in demand. One critic, not known for his generosity, had dubbed her a female Al Jolson – high praise indeed!

Here were two people, both German born, Austrian raised, and one time fellow kibbutzniks. The reminiscences had come back with spellbinding accuracy, and they sat in silent reflection of all that they had talked about that night. Melissa's eyes settled on Nathan as if she was about to speak. It was just as she opened her mouth to say something, the chimes of Nathan's huge antique clock indicated the time on the hour.

"One o'clock in the morning. My goodness!" Melissa remarked. "We've talked for hours. If I told you all of my life story we would be here til breakfast."

"I would love to hear your version of your life, my dear," Nathan exclaimed with delight. For his age he did not tire easily. Even though the hour was late it would have been a pleasure to hear some of Melissa's memories.

"I am going to be in Sydney for a while," Melissa pointed out. "The film I'm making is going to be a two-month shoot. Maybe when my husband and daughter arrive we could all get together."

"That would be nice," Nathan said quietly, thinking how much he would have preferred to talk to her on her own over a meal and share the memories only they had in common. "You know, I have seen most of your films over the years. I even have a few of your records that you made with your husband." Nathan pointed to his record collection mounted in a mahogany sideboard. "Your husband, he is a great bandleader. There is one radio station that consistently plays his records. I think I would enjoy meeting him."

"And he will enjoy meeting you, I know," replied Melissa rising from the armchair indicating it was time for her to leave. "Nathan, I have to do several interviews tomorrow including a television show at lunchtime. Reluctantly I must go. I'll be in touch. I have your telephone number. We'll get together again whilst I'm here. I'm staying at the Sebel Townhouse. Could you call me a cab?"

"Nonsense," said Nathan, "I'll drive you myself. It has been wonderful to see you and talk of days gone by. You have brought back so many things to me. The kibbutz – I can see you now barefoot amongst the poultry. I remember the plays and the concerts you were in." Nathan was beside himself with enthusiasm. "And then there was the time in London, you turned up without warning, at Jack and Elsie Faley's party in Ealing Green. Not to mention the times we knew when we met up out here again." He smiled at his own self-indulgence. "Forgive me I am besotted in my own nostalgia and sentiment."

"You are entitled to be. Both of us did not lead ordinary lives. They were full of characters, episodes and events. More than most people's normal run-of-the-mill existences. In my case my allegedly colourful private life vastly exaggerated by the news media, I might add, was never all champagne and cocktails. I've been married three times – not a record I'm proud of. The greatest peaks of satisfaction have come from my career and my children. I'm immensely proud of them. My daughter is doing well at the University of Hawaii. My son, from my second marriage, is a commercial airline pilot in Florida."

Nathan put Melissa's coat around her. "Mine too. They've both done well, particularly Joseph. Considering he has been deaf and speechless since birth, he has achieved extraordinary things. Like his mother, he is an artist. Not full-time. By day he works as a postal clerk for the State Public Service; at night, however, he performs with the Theatre of the Deaf, and now and again he paints. Some of his paintings have been exhibited. He has received some good reviews from art critics."

"Does he live with you?" Melissa asked curiously.

"No, he lives with his girlfriend at Potts Point. She is also deaf. They are good for each other. It is almost touching to see how they communicate their joy and affection for each other in sign language. At times I am moved to tears."

"And your daughter?" Melissa asked as they both walked towards the door.

"Anastasia," Nathan sighed. "Sounds like the name of a Russian Princess, doesn't it?"

"It was," Melissa reminded him. "She was the Grand Duchess, the youngest daughter of the last Tsar of Russia. I should know, I played her in one of my first films in Hollywood; one of several about that particular lady."

Nathan laughed gently. "I know, I was only joking. Shortly before Anastasia was born in 1955 Francine and I went to see you in that movie. It was Francine's idea. She said if we had a daughter we ought to call her Anastasia."

"How intriguing," Melissa said with a genuine sense of wonder. "Either my performance was good enough to influence you, or else the name made an astonishing impact on you and Francine."

"Both" replied Nathan. "Anastasia is married. She lives in Darwin with her husband. He is an officer with the CSIRO. Anastasia has always been the independent type." Nathan opened the door of his apartment for Melissa and they both went down in the lift to the car park.

"In what way was she independent?"

Nathan unlocked the door of his car. They got inside the warmth of the Mercedes. In minutes the car was being revved up and Nathan drove Melissa towards her hotel.

"In what way was Anastasia independent?" Nathan repeated her question. "Oh, headstrong, opinionated, and sometimes very argumentative. I suppose with parents like Francine and I, radical in our thinking but conservative in our outlook, it was only natural that she would rebel. In her teens she used to hang around with the surfing crowd, very energetic people I might add. I don't mean to be derogatory, but rather than study she would rather have stomped and surfed. I had many raging rows with her. I eventually got her to study hard. She worked for the ABC for some time as a production assistant as she originally planned. She went on location to the Northern Territory to do some filming work. Amazing how these things work out. Anastasia found herself filming Orange Tree Downs, the station I once worked on."

Melissa smiled. "Perhaps some day our families should meet up. They sound quite adventurous. It must have been our time in the kibbutz in the 1930s that bred that spirit.

"One never knows Melissa. It may well have been. Anyway, Anastasia visited an Aboriginal mission near Orange Tree Downs. While she was there she developed an affinity with them. The plight of the Aboriginal people is something I have also had feelings for. When I was working with the Law Reform Commission, there were many proposals put forward for the welfare of the Aboriginal people.

"I remember reading that Gough Whitlam, when he was Prime Minister, did much for them in the way of land rights and welfare," said Melissa who, although a resident of the United States, showed she was still conversant with things that went on in Australia.

Nathan turned the car into Kings Cross. "Indeed he did. My daughter worked in the bush after she left the ABC. It mellowed her considerably. She was on an Aboriginal station helping infant children. That's where she met her husband. I must admit I did not like him at first, but now I do. It's a good marriage."

"You are not a grandfather yet, are you?" Melissa asked.

"I am optimistic," Nathan replied with a smile. "I thought being a father was the most wonderful thing that could ever have happened to me." He drove the car to a halt outside of the Sebel Townhouse at Elizabeth Bay. "It's funny how you can aim for such heights in life, and yet the most simple things in life can give the most satisfaction."

Melissa unfastened her seat belt. "I agree," she concurred. "When one comes down to it the family is the most important thing in life. A person may be a millionaire or a pauper, but whatever their financial position it is that closeness of belonging to someone that counts for most in life." She appeared pensive and thoughtful. Eventually after a moment's silence she leaned over and kissed him on the cheek. "Well, my old friend from the kibbutz, I shall say farewell. It has been a wonderful reunion."

"Wonderful," Nathan agreed. The two looked at each other in adoration. After forty-five years since their first meeting, a loving friendship still endured. Somehow there was still a glistening sparkle in Melissa's eyes that Nathan had seen way back on the Kibbutz Jezarat. For a moment he was back in his youth in Palestine falling in love for the first time. "I shall be back next year," she added as a passing after thought.

Then, quickly, Melissa was stepping out of the car and going inside. At the entrance to the hotel she stopped, turned and waved to Nathan. In a moment she was gone.

Nathan drove home to Darling Point. On the way home he mentally summed up the evening. The myriad of memories he had stirred in his mind that night was astonishing. He felt as if he had relived all the years of his life in the space of a few hours. How eventful they had been.

Melissa and Nathan had talked much that night about their lives in Germany, Austria, Palestine and of their own wartime memories. Nathan found himself sitting in a comfortable armchair pausing for reflection. He thought of the London he first saw in the 1940s, a city that had been kind to him. It was from there that he had progressed to the better life he had lived since.

Twenty-nine

1946-1972

Post-war London showed so many of the signs of the previous years when it had been heavily bombed during the blitz. The East End in particular had taken many direct hits. Now the process of rebuilding and renovating had begun. The Attlee Labour Government had begun to implement many social programmes in a bid to re-house and re-settle the huge numbers of servicemen returning to a civilian life, as well as providing a national health and welfare system.

Living in London in peacetime after the traumas of war was a welcome relief. People were picking up the threads of their old lives, and many were beginning new ones, taking an entirely different uncharted direction from the one they had started in the pre-war years.

The de-mob suit was a familiar sight around the towns. Just about every young man at every street corner wore one of these. Nathan Palmai wore one, although it looked slightly ill-fitting on him. The sleeves of his grey breasted jacket were about an inch too long and the trousers were a little loose around the waist although they were long and baggy and the turn-ups wide and flabby. For Nathan it did feel good to be alive and living in London. At the tender age of twenty-four he had already been through so much, and now for the first time in years he felt that he was moulding his future, and that he had finally taken charge of the course of his life.

Here in London he had commenced several years of study in Law at London University. He was exhilarated by his newfound place in the world. His studies relating to all facets of the law were profoundly interesting. Criminal and Industrial Law opened up his mind to new horizons and tested his abilities in all respects.

On being discharged from the British Army, he conceded that the decision not to return to Palestine was one of risk. Yet when the studies and the resulting qualifications that Nathan had gained from his correspondence course in Palestine were presented for inspection, he was delighted to get acceptance to such a high establishment. Nathan's place of residence was in the suburb of Ealing Broadway. He had taken a room above a greengrocers shop near Ealing Green, and in order to pay part of his way he worked on a Saturday and one evening in the shop. The owners of the shop, Jack and Elsie Faley, were a lovely warm-hearted cockney couple who always made Nathan feel he was part of the family. Often knowing that he was spending much time on his own, and he had lost all his family, they would do their best to help him. Frequently he would be asked to join them. Jack and Elsie were a salt of the earth couple. Nathan grew to regard them as his adopted family.

He often thought of his own family. The years did not weather the pain. It was hard for him to accept but he invested thoughts in his studies if he began to dwell too deeply on the past.

His life in Ealing was one that he enjoyed. It was a casual down to earth existence in a very pleasant homely suburb. Sometimes Nathan would look out from his room above the grocer's shop in Ealing Green. Near him was Walpole Park where he would often sit on a bench for hours reading his books of study. Sometimes he would wander up to the Uxbridge Road where there was a church with a huge tall spire that stretched up high. He found people in the shops very chatty and jocular and as time went by he began to know so many new friends.

On a Saturday, Nathan would ride a bike on a grocery delivery round, going to nearby suburbs like Greenford, Hanwell and Shepherds Bush. The pushbike became a fixture in his life. He covered so much distance discovering the best things about London, Richmond, Kew Gardens, rides along the Thames and the Grand Union Canal. Not only did he look at the attractive parks, gardens and pleasure spots, he also spent time looking around the things of culture that abounded in London. The Natural History Museum, the Albert and Victoria Museum, and the Science Museum were all places he spent time in, as well as the Opera and the Theatre.

Being at London University for much of the time was exhilarating. Nathan genuinely wanted to learn and what was more important was the fact that it was a subject of his own choosing. The syllabus of his Law course kept him busy and well occupied. It was satisfying for Nathan to know he was working towards a fulfilling career that would one day bring him many interesting hours and courtroom dramas.

Late in 1946 Nathan returned home after a day's study at the university and found himself strolling across Ealing Broadway in a typical London fog, a heavy pea souper like he had never experienced before. When he crossed the road he saw the local forum cinema lit up brightly and the movie being shown that Friday night was *The Overlanders*. Out of curiosity Nathan moved across to read the billboard. It was a film set in Australia. Nathan smiled thinking of Ted McTaggart, the Australian soldier he had met during the war in North Africa. He could recall Ted's expansive descriptions of Australia so well. Just the name Australia seemed to conjure up the thoughts of cattle country, tropical scenery, Melbourne and the Dandenong Ranges, Sydney and the trams 'shooting through' at Bondi, all so vividly described by Ted McTaggart at the height of his descriptive powers, propelled by a few beers in a smoky bar in the wartime Cairo.

Slinging his trench coat over his arm and removing his trilby hat, Nathan decided to spend the evening at the cinema. Looking around him those demob suits were so much in evidence. It seemed at times as if every male member of the population was an ex-serviceman. In those post-war days when money was in short supply, a night at the cinema was always a cheap evening's entertainment. After the movie Nathan thought he might look into The Green Man in West Ealing, the pub where his landlords Jack and Elsie Faley often spent a Friday evening.

Sitting in the cinema Nathan found himself in the middle of the seats that British cinemagoers usually termed as 'the gods' because of their position that gave its occupants a view right across the cheaper stalls below. Then the B-movie came on, followed by a newsreel programme. Nathan sat transfixed as the ruins of Berlin flooded across the screen. A dramatic description accompanied the photo images. In the pictures that followed it showed the aftermath of the wartime bombing, the various allied servicemen who now occupied it, and the haunted faces of young children not old enough to know what all the devastation had been about. Nathan felt gratefully relieved when the news switched to more happier topics such as what the girls were wearing in civvies street, how men were coping with life after years in the armed forces, and the latest dances in the Mayfair Clubs. Attlee and Churchill came across the screen, two political opposites of contrasting character and style of leadership; Attlee now being Prime Minister, and Churchill the Opposition Leader, after his defeat in the 1945 election.

Finally the main feature film came on, and Nathan sat back and watched *The Overlanders*, a film made curiously enough by Ealing Studios whose base was within a stones throw of Nathan's flat on the Green. It had been made entirely on location in the Northern Territory of Australia. The story line involved the droving of cattle across the outback before the threat of imminent invasion by the Japanese during the war. Apart from the film's star, Chips Rafferty, a lean tough looking Australian, so much like the men Nathan had met in North Africa, the real star was the scenery. The dry dusty country depicted in the movie and the suntanned leathery characters with beads of perspiration on their foreheads fascinated him. The accents and the scenery he saw before him set his mind thinking of the Australians he had met during his army service. They were an interesting crowed of people. Already he was experiencing nostalgia.

Immediately after the film was over Nathan decided to join Jack and Elsie and their two sons who were also ex-servicemen. One had been with the Royal Navy and the other with the RAF. He always enjoyed talking to them and the atmosphere at The Green Man pub was usually convivial. On the bus going down to West Ealing Nathan was intrigued by what he had seen in the movie. The fog outside the bus was heavy. *In Australia,* thought Nathan, *there are clear blue skies, wide horizons and constant sunshine*. It was an intoxicating thought. Perhaps when he had finished his time at university, he might consider the possibility of migrating to that land.

Nathan felt extremely grateful that he was here in England. An English education was something of value. He genuinely liked England and the English, although he was already well aware of the rampant class distinctions that were so prevalent; the way in which a person's accent, upbringing, heritage and education seemed to bracket a person in a particular social grouping. *If I ever went to Australia would it be the same there?* he wondered.

Down at The Green Man Nathan joined Jack and Elsie and their sons. He was amongst friends and cherished their company. In many ways Nathan had been immensely lucky to find such good friends in Jack and

Elsie. They were typical of so many working class people of that time. Salt of the earth was exactly what they were; people who were always cheery, could always offer a word of encouragement, and would go out of their way to help anyone who needed it, even the most complete stranger. The nice thing about Jack Faley was that he was a man who would never allow himself to be talked down to or bullied or see anyone else treated in that manner. From Jack, Nathan developed a great affinity for the ordinary battler which was to last him for all his life.

The pub was certainly the focal point for meeting people. The scent of beer and the fumes of tobacco smoke seemed to dominate the air. People were playing darts, frothing back pints and chatting which became a buzz of intermingled conversation, the topic of which seemed to be someone's war exploits in one part of the world or the other. Many of the people Nathan had met in the local shops made an appearance and waved amiably to him. It was a pleasant evening for him. He had even joined in on the Friday night sing-along.

On returning to his flat on the Green, Nathan made himself a bedtime drink and switched on his wireless set. Two men were talking on a programme about the coming war trials in Japan. It was staggering! Nathan was listening to his friend Freddie Miller speaking to a BBC reporter on air. Freddie was speaking of his time as a prisoner of war and how he had been called to give evidence in Tokyo against the officers of the camp he had been held in. Nathan was stunned. He often wondered what had happened to Freddie and now he knew. The moment the interview had finished, Nathan rushed down to the telephone kiosk outside his flat and rang the radio studios of the BBC's Portland Place building.

Within minutes, Nathan was speaking to a completely amazed but thoroughly delighted Freddie. The two arranged to meet one evening when they were free to do so, at a restaurant in East Acton that was convenient for them both. Freddie now lived in Shepherds Bush.

Nathan kept the appointment, wearing the old de-mob suit which by now was getting its fair share of use. He arrived on time and was shown through to his table by the headwaiter. Nathan was slightly earlier than Freddie and he waited for a few minutes. He kept looking eagerly at the doorway waiting for Freddie to make his entrance. It had been nearly four years since they had last met in Cairo.

Freddie finally came in carrying a raincoat over his arm and wearing a double-breasted suit and a surprisingly new addition, a pair of thin-rimmed spectacles, which he removed inside the restaurant. Nathan was surprised by the change in Freddie Miller's appearance. Freddie was gaunt and thin and his hair had flashes of faded grey in them. On espying Nathan, Freddie smiled but it was not the natural smile of old and the sparkle had gone from his eyes. In them the light had dimmed. It was more a look of fear that had been transposed there in place of that spark of confidence. The change in Freddie was so enormous that the young man who shook his hand was lost for words. They began by giving each other an update of their lives, but both avoided any topic that might have been painful to the other.

Finally, Nathan felt compelled to say, "I believe you had a terrible time in the POW camp."

Freddie did not reply in words. He merely indicated in a masterly fashion by raising and lowering his eyes in a manner that obviously indicated it was a part of his life he wanted to leave out of his conversation. He was quick to change the topic.

"So you are finally here studying Law at London University?"

"An ambition fulfilled. I enjoy it. I am studying both Industrial and Criminal Law. It is a very good course. I am developing my knowledge. I am very happy with the way everything is going for me here."

"I'm glad for you, Nathan. You deserve some happiness," said Freddie, his expression one of fondness and pleasure for his friend.

And you too, thought Nathan, knowing of Freddie's personal suffering at the loss of his beloved wife. Having to endure that would have been terrible enough, to undergo several years of torment, torture and near starvation in a prisoner of war camp would have put Freddie through hell. Nathan could see by the drastic changes in Freddie's appearance just what an ordeal it would have been. He continued speaking of his new life in England.

"I have been most fortunate, Freddie. When I joined the British Army in Palestine, I did not expect to be engaged in action. I thought that as a volunteer from the kibbutz I would be just doing background duties, like working in the stores or in provisions, something like that. I found myself, to my amazement, in Egypt, where we last met in '42. What a surprise that was for me!" Freddie smiled at the memory. "After that I went through all of North Africa with the Long Range Desert Group. I finished out the war in England. I was based in Ongar in Essex and that was where I got my army discharge. I could have gone home after that, there was one big problem though."

"What was that?" Freddie looked at him concerned.

"I don't know where home is for me now. I have heard people use the expression 'displaced person'. I suppose that is what I am." He stopped for a moment realising his emotions were surfacing knowing he had a sympathetic listener. "Freddie, am I talking too much about myself? I know you too have suffered, losing your wife, and the terrible years in the prisoner of war camp."

"Thank you for your consideration," Freddie replied gently. "Feel free. I am interested in your life. I may even open up about my life as the evening progresses."

Nathan feeling relieved continued. "As I was saying, I am not sure where I belong now. In my life I've gone from Germany to Austria to Palestine, and now I am here in England. The place I feel I belong is the moment – to the present day."

"That is precisely where we all belong, Nathan. We must never forget the past. I firmly believe that. I know I never shall forget many things in my life. I do know we must not dwell on it. Do you not think that you may eventually go back to Palestine? Perhaps even —"

"I do not think so. I can never go back to Germany or Austria. Too many things trouble me. Palestine – well, I thought at first I might return. Now I have my studies to think of. I must complete those before I do anything else. I have been thinking lately of one place I would like to go to: Australia."

"Australia?" Freddie was genuinely surprised. He was also quite interested, for the years of comradeship with Australian POWs had whetted his appetite to visit that country.

"I met many Australians during my time in North Africa with the British Army. One in particular, a fellow called Ted McTaggart. He came from Melbourne but he's travelled around a lot. He lived in Queensland for a long time and he told me about Sydney. He made it all sound so interesting. When I finish my studies, I think I may well go out there. It seems like a country I could enjoy living in. The people too I liked; a bit brash, a bit abrupt but I could warm to them. They seemed straightforward."

"I can agree with that. I met quite a few at the prison camp. But as people, there was no bull about them. I have a hankering to go there sometime. In particular to see some of the men I served with."

"What are you doing these days, Freddie? Are you working at your old occupation as a cameraman?"

"By coincidence, although I appeared on the BBC as a guest, I have just applied to the same organisation for a journalistic position; although, until I return from giving evidence at the war trials in Tokyo, I will be unable to take up a position. It looks pretty much as though I'll be working there at the BBC. I think my experiences before the war were pretty much a good sort of qualification for the type of work I'll be doing."

"When do you leave for Tokyo?"

"In just over a week's time." Freddie looked grave. "It's not a trip I'm looking forward to. I think the trials are going to reopen plenty of memories of the POW camp that I have been desperately trying to blot out of my memory." Freddie looked at his watch quickly. "Nathan, I almost forgot to tell you. We're going to be joined this evening by a French couple who were with the Companions of the Circle and the resistance. I'm sorry to spring such a surprise on you but they're leaving to go home to France tomorrow. This is the last opportunity I'll have to see them before they go. You don't mind, do you?"

"Not at all. You say they were with the Circle?"

"Right. Francine Macé and her husband Claude. You'll have a chance to meet some people who were in the organisation your father started. You'll like them." Freddie took a sip of his drink and then changed the subject. "What made you decide to live in Ealing?"

"Oh, I met a soldier called John in the Army who lived here before the war, and when I decided to stay here on my discharge, I walked round everywhere asking people where I could get a room. I went into Jack and Elsie Faley's shop on the Green and they offered me a room above their shop. It's adjoining their house, the shop that is, but I can more or less come and go as I please. They are a fine couple. Often they ask me to join them for a drink at the pub they go to in West Ealing. Sometimes I have Sunday lunch with them. I work for them in their grocery shop and I do a delivery round on a bike on Saturdays. The money helps to pay my way. My course is very demanding, though and I spend a lot of time studying."

"I see," mused Freddie. "Do you do anything socially besides?"

"I have been to the soccer with Jack and his sons a few times. Jack is a mad keen Brentford supporter whilst his sons are Tottenham Hotspur fans. But apart from sightseeing on a Sunday, that is more or less the format of my life."

"No girlfriends as such then?"

"Apart from those I meet at the university, there is no one special." Nathan smiled shyly. He couldn't help studying Freddie's appearance. Freddie hardly had any of the dash or the air of *joie de vivre* that he had possessed before the war. Nathan pondered that the champagne fizz had completely gone from the man who had visited his family in Austria ten years before. He tried to avert his gaze from resting too long on the tiredness in Freddie's face, and raised them over his shoulder towards the doorway of the restaurant.

Nathan fixed his gaze on a couple who entered at that very moment. There was a flicker of recognition in his eyes. He instantly recognised the girl who was accompanied by a suave man. The girl had been the one he had helped to her feet after she had slipped over in the Mall on VE Day. She was superbly dressed and was undoubtedly the most beautiful woman he had been privileged to meet. Freddie noticing the look on Nathan's face turned around and raised his hand to the couple.

"Ah, this is Francine and Claude," Freddie said with delight and as he stood up to hug Francine and shake her husband's hand, the old sparkle and warmth returned. For a moment the old panache of Freddie Miller returned. He turned to introduce them to Nathan. *So this was Francine Macé?* thought Nathan and he greeted them both pleasantly.

"We have met before, mademoiselle," Nathan said, noticing the sudden look of recognition in her eyes now.

"Of course!" she gasped. "It was on VE day. You were the young soldier who helped me to my feet when I tripped over in the crowd. How amazing!"

Both Freddie and Claude looked stunned by the fact they had already met. They all sat down. Almost defensively, as if to emphasise they were married, Claude and Francine moved closer together. It was Freddie who brought the conversation back to a plateau of normality.

"That was certainly a surprise," he added. "Claude, Francine, you will be interested to know that the organisation we all worked for at one stage of our lives, the Circle, was in fact founded not only by Baroness Christina von Harstezzen but also with the assistance of Nathan's father,

Arthandur Palmai." There was already a bottle of wine on the table and without asking anyone, Freddie proceeded to fill up everyone's glass. He raised his own glass. "To the Companions of the Circle," Freddie said proposing the toast. "To the great work they did for freedom, and the individual, during the years of trauma and tribulation that we have all come through."

The little group clinked their glasses together. It was the start of a very enjoyable evening during which they talked over the meal about all the experiences they had known. Nathan listened to Claude and Francine as they recounted the simply amazing story of their time in France. These were the first real operators of the Circle that Nathan had met. He was intrigued to hear of the missions of the Circle's agents. It fascinated Nathan no end that the activities of this group had been partly set in train by Arthandur.

Even more fascinating was the story of how Francine had first met Freddie Miller. It was wonderful to see Freddie smile and laugh as he told of that cold rainy night when he together with some lifeboat-men rowed out off the coast of Cornwall to rescue the crew and passengers of a foundering French tanker. Freddie embellished the story and added a touch of his own humour. Francine was quick to join in and give her own account of what had happened on that occasion. Her smile and humour too was contagious. Claude was obviously a very lucky man to have married this strong and courageous woman who, despite her ordeals, had emerged well and her appearance was dazzling. Nathan had to divert his eyes from looking at her too long. It would have been obvious that she entranced him, exactly as he had been on VE Day. He listened politely as Francine spoke of her life and noted the sadness in her eyes as she spoke of her mother and grandfather in Leeds, who had both died recently.

A string quartet began to play in the restaurant. The evening had obviously gone a long way in boosting Freddie's spirits and he cheekily asked Francine for a dance, reminding Claude if it has not been for him the two probably would never have met. Claude simply laughed.

The two men watched Freddie and Francine dance.

"Fine people," said Nathan looking at them.

"The best," murmured Claude. "Mr Miller told Francine and I about you. Your life – it has been full too. You were in a kibbutz in Palestine, I believe. Do you still have friends there?"

It was time for a revelation. Nathan turned his eyes to Claude.

"Yes. I must write there soon. I was in love with someone there, but that was five or six years ago. I would dearly like to know what became of her." The admission had come out of the blue and surprised even Nathan himself by his own frankness.

"What was she like?" Claude asked interested.

"Her name was Melissa. Like your wife, she was full of talent and beauty. Her talent was of a different kind. She was an actress and singer in many of the kibbutz plays. When she was on stage she was so confident and so dynamic. I must write to the kibbutz to find out what course her life took." Even though Nathan had spoken of Melissa he found himself looking at Francine. She was quite a different sort of girl to the type he had ever met. The innate genteelness that Francine possessed covered her real drive and strength, yet perhaps this was what had reminded Nathan of Melissa. For in reality they were very similar women. Melissa had poise and beauty, and on stage generated an electricity and sexuality that even she was not aware of just how powerful it could be. Melissa in private had been insecure and lacking in confidence. Nathan remembered a conversation he once had with her on the kibbutz so long ago, which in its honesty was revealing of her true personality. In Francine he saw the same sexuality, the same type of beauty and magnetism that made her unique. He turned to face Claude. "You are a lucky man." Claude smiled "It must have been tense for you both during the war years. Francine must have been your reward for those years."

Claude Renalier lit up a cigarette and inhaled deeply before blowing a ring of smoke and then he spoke with a firmness and conviction that had been evident in the conversation that night.

"Francine was not my reward. She was my companion and friend and I don't mean companion as with the members of the Circle. After her escape and right up to the liberation we worked constantly together. We organised work with the Underground, shuffled people of your faith through every escape route we could devise. Believe me, my friend, they were stirring times to reflect upon, but the only reward for us was the freedom of France. Liberation Day 1944 was the greatest day of my life, and Francine's. We really felt rewarded when we could walk the streets of Paris in freedom again. To know our efforts had contributed to that was wonderful. When the crowd sang the 'Marsellaise' it was like a choir from heaven my friend."

Nathan filled both their glasses. Now he was reminded of Leon Zielinski at the kibbutz. Indeed, as both Freddie and Francine returned to the table from the dance floor, Nathan was reminded of the couple that had been Leon and Melissa. There was such a similarity in Francine and Claude.

"What is this?" asked Francine noting the two full glasses, "Another toast?"

Nathan leaned across and filled the glasses of both Freddie and Francine.

"Yes. Claude was just telling me of Liberation Day 1944. I would like to make a toast now. Seeing my late father Arthandur co-founded the Circle perhaps it is only right that I, as his son, who lived on, should toast two of its members. To you both and your country," Nathan raised his glass *"Vive la France."*

They all clinked their glasses and consumed the contents. A lot of wine had been drunk that night, a lot of old times and memories reawakened, and amidst the laughter there had been much emotion. Francine red eyed, and beginning to tire, felt compelled to make a toast now. She replenished all the glasses and took the situation in her hands.

"Now it is my turn. To the memory of your parents, and to your future, to use the toast of your people, *l'Chaim Chaim.*"

It was a grand toast providing a great finale to the evening. Soon it was all over and it was time to leave. Outside the rain was falling hard. They turned up their overcoat collars and unfurled their umbrellas. It was time for them to go to their separate locations. Claude shook hands with both Freddie and Nathan. Francine moved forward and gazed upward at Freddie.

"I will always remember you and Cynthia with so much affection," she said quietly. "That time in Cornwall with you both was a very happy time for me." In one brief moment she gripped Freddie tightly, and Nathan looked on wondering if the moisture on her face was that of the rain or the tears of farewell. "I hope you find happiness again, Freddie," she continued and, as she moved away with Claude, there was a warm smile to Nathan. "Good luck in the future."

"There's our bus," called out Claude, and two ran across the road to join the queue at the bus stop.

"I'll write from France," Francine yelled out. In a moment they had gone. Freddie stood in the rain with the water dripping from his hat. Something had gone from his life in that instant. His memories of the first time he had ever met Francine flashed through his mind. It had been a rainy stormy night on that occasion not unlike this night. Freddie drifted away in thought. He suddenly realised that there was no one now with whom he could share the memories of the happy years he had spent in Cornwall. For the first time he suddenly felt very isolated. The bus drifted away in swirling rain taking not only Francine but also almost a link with Freddie's previous years.

"Freddie, we are getting drenched," Nathan reminded him, noticing the far away look in his eyes."

"I'm sorry," Freddie replied. "We better walk down and catch our bus." They began to walk in the rain. "It's a funny thing you know, Nathan. We all have our journey in front of us now. I was just thinking then of my wife, Cynthia. I could talk about her to Francine because the two of them were such good friends. Now that Francine has gone I have no one to share those memories with. I dread to say it but I am in danger of beginning to feel sorry for myself. That is a sure sign of a man about to give up. At forty-one years of age I am beginning to doubt myself."

"That is not like you, Freddie," Nathan remarked. "You are a man of great achievement. Your time as a newsreel cameraman and journalist was exceptional. But your career in the army, your work with the Circle and the way in which you pulled your men through in that prisoner of war camp is outstanding too."

"You are right, Nathan. I have much to be thankful for. Much of my life has been wonderful. There is no such thing as the perfect life. I know one has to take the good with the bad. I don't think of life as being all good or all bad. Life is full of downs and ups. Some people have far more downs than ups. Other's more ups."

"I think the wine has made you philosophical," Nathan said wryly.

Freddie chuckled. "I think it has. Well I must be leaving here soon to go to Tokyo for the war trials. When I get back, we must meet up again." He stopped for a moment then started walking again. "If I may say, Nathan, you've handled your own life well. Your parents would have been proud of you."

Those words were of great reassurance to Nathan. It set him thinking of Arthandur and Marlene. The pain had begun to recede now whenever he thought of his parents. Just seeing Francine and Claude that evening, and hearing of the work of the Circle, made Nathan feel that Arthandur's life had been well spent. Hearing firsthand from Francine about her incredible escapade filled him with a deep sense of pride for his father.

The two men boarded their bus and took shelter from the rain. A few stops later Freddie shook hands with Nathan and got out to catch another bus to his home in Shepherds Bush. Nathan stayed on the double-decker that went all the way down to Ealing Green. Sitting on the bus that night gazing out at the rain splattered streets and the flickering lights of illuminated shops and neon signs, Nathan felt an easy security in his life now. He could not help thinking of Francine. In much the same way as he had felt a twinge of envy on the kibbutz at the obvious romantic attachment between Leon and Melissa, he had felt much the same that evening about Francine and Claude. His thoughts about Francine were almost verging on lust. Indeed it was not surprising. Francine had such superb tanned olive skin, gentle eyes, tawny hair rising in curls, long painted fingernails, long straight legs and even when she spoke she was unintentionally sensuous. Nathan could feel a twinge of conscience biting him for thinking such thoughts, and then he allowed himself to smile that he had been so carried away. Anyway, tomorrow Francine and her husband would be on their way to a new life in France, in a beautiful village called Avalon.

Nathan dismissed the thoughts of Francine and Claude and decided that at least out of curiosity he must write to the Kibbutz Jezarat in Palestine to find out what happened to Melissa. Obviously, Nathan must have felt that relationships in his life with women were sadly lacking for him to pursue someone from his past. He convinced himself that it was curiosity that was the real reason for him to write.

When Nathan got home that evening and before he went to sleep, he took several photographs that he possessed and placed them on the mantelpiece. There was his favourite one in which he, as an eleven year old, stood with Arthandur and Marlene with the Austrian mountains rising up behind them. Another had him with Ted McTaggart, John and Charles in the North African desert. Ted and John were smiling with such big toothy grins that looking at the picture was contagious. It prompted Nathan to smile at the memory of the time they had met up in the oasis.

There were a few others than Nathan glanced over until he found the one he wanted. It was the only photograph he had where he was not featured in one way or the other. It was a dark haired girl in a frail cotton dress tending poultry on the kibbutz. Melissa, where was she now?

Even though it was late at night Nathan decided there and then that he would write to Melissa using her last known residence at the kibbutz as the address to send the letter to. Sitting at a table by the window, and glancing out every so often at the rain pelting down on Ealing Green, he began to write a long descriptive letter of all the things that had happened to him in the past few years. He asked himself if this was a letter that would ever be read by the person intended.

Thirty

Exactly a week after his reunion with Nathan, Freddie journeyed to Japan to give evidence at the war trials. It has been a difficult task to relive some of the harrowing memories of the prison camp in Borneo. The day before Freddie's departure for Tokyo he had been delighted to learn that he had been successful in his application for a journalist's position with the BBC. The news made it easy for Freddie to embark knowing he had a new career in front of him when he returned.

Freddie was in Japan for several weeks. Once he had performed his duties and detailed the worst aspects of all the mistreatment his men had been subjected to, he felt keen to forget this chapter of his life and move forward once again into the future with a feeling of enthusiasm. Before he left Japan he had one private mission of his own to fulfil. He made a trip to the bombed out place that had been Hiroshima.

It was utterly beyond belief the terrible sight that lay before him. There was a great stillness, a sense of morbidity and eeriness about Hiroshima. The silence and the chill of what had happened here filled him with unease and what the possible further use of such devastating power could inflict on human beings. Once Freddie had studied the scene he felt tears well up into his eyes and in the midst of fallen leaves, and a mass of debris and strewn confusion of rubble and dirt, he felt compelled to pray for world peace for ever. The once career solider and military man now felt himself taking on the role of a committed pacifist.

Through his own private research, which began even before his departure for Japan, Freddie had managed to locate Takahishi, the Japanese soldier who had shown him the only shred of compassion that the captors had ever given him. When Freddie had been hanging onto the shreds of his life purely by his positive mental attitude rather than his physical wellbeing,

Takahishi had braved his own soldiers to bring the prisoner a bottle of lemonade and food.

Takahishi lived in a tiny village some way from Hiroshima. There he lived with his family, some of who had suffered terrible sickness in the aftermath of the bomb. Freddie had written to say that he was coming and Takahishi, who was very surprised, agreed to meet him and take tea with him in his own house, and to afford the visiting Englishman a hospitality far removed from his treatment in Borneo.

It was a clear morning when Freddie stepped out of a car he had hired to make the journey. Freddie looked at the house in its oriental form. There was a strange feeling going through him, he realised that he was about to meet a former opponent but yet a man who had given him cause to believe that in human nature, conscience and consideration of others will prevail in at least one person, no matter how unruly the crowd that surrounds them.

Takahishi appeared at the doorway. For a moment the two men looked at each other remembering those traumatic times, each one assiduously studying the other. Freddie was not sure how to approach the situation. He was on the verge of making the first move and shaking the man's hand. Takahishi took a short pace forward and then in the traditional Japanese manner he bowed graciously to Freddie. The Englishman immediately responded and followed in the same manner. Takahishi beckoned to Freddie and he entered the house.

Inside Takahishi introduced his parents and relatives. One man lay frail on a rolled up bed on the floor in the corner. He had suffered terrible burns and his appearance was frail and feeble. Takahishi explained that his illness occurred since that fateful August day the previous year. All of Takahishi's other relatives bowed politely to Freddie upon introduction. On that day Freddie took tea, and a meal in the traditional Japanese fashion, and they all talked about simple things. Takahishi through his study of languages was expert in English and translated Freddie's remarks for the benefit of the others who listened with interest,

Takahishi's family talked of the cherry blossom season, the dynasties that had ruled Japan throughout its history, ordinary family life and traditional customs. Throughout the conversation not a word of reference was made to the war and the circumstances that had brought about the acquaintanceship between Freddie and Takahishi. When Freddie looked at this peaceful gracious family he could not reconcile their genteelness with the brutal guards he had known in Borneo. It was a memorable day for Freddie because some hidden power within him, some overwhelming force seemed to tell him to forgive and forget his terrible experiences in the camp. To do so was an enormous effort but now looking at these gentle people he felt that he had to do so. For they had been merely an innocent family caught in the turmoil of things as so many people unwillingly had been. Some while later Freddie had to leave. Before the family bowed, Freddie took the initiative and bowed first. Takahishi and his family followed suit. For the final time Takahishi and Freddie Miller looked at each other with a mutual respect. Freddie bowed once again, prompting Takahishi to do so, and then he entered the car and drove away.

On the long drive back to Tokyo, Freddie looked with interest at the picturesque countryside and the ever-changing scenery. His lifetime of travel had continually taken him to different parts of the world and he found himself ever learning, ever trying to understand the other man's point of view. Here in Japan he could see much agricultural land. He envisaged that this land like all other nations would begin a new wheel of progress. Perhaps in due course much of this attractive countryside before him would yield new cities and a new generation of commercial and industrial enterprise. Most of the major countries in the Western world were rebuilding their shattered economies, and Freddie's premonition would one day prove to be correct, because the Land of the Rising Sun was beginning a new era, and would swiftly move forward with technology.

Hardly had Freddie returned to London after his sojourn in Japan when he began his new position with the BBC. Freddie's first assignment was ironic: it was to take him back to Berlin. Freddie could not believe it at first, but his supervisor, aware of his new journalist's early cinematographic achievements, saw this as the perfect opportunity for him. The objective of this particular assignment was to look at the Berlin of today and to visit the forces in the occupied zones. When Freddie was told that this was to be his first assignment, he almost felt like declining. He could hardly refuse to go having just begun this new position, so reluctantly he went.

When Freddie flew over Berlin it had been ten years ago since his previous visit. He was stunned when he saw below him the remnants of this place that had once been something of grandeur. It held so many memories for him. In his various visits there in the 1930s it had been a city of curious trends and political changes. Below the aircraft was now a place that would need completely rebuilding. Freddie did recognise one particular construction as the plane began to slope on its descent. The Olympic stadium was still standing. The memories came back with a shuddering suddenness: the cheers, the propaganda, the athletes, the ceremonies.

It was ironic that the last time Freddie had been in Berlin he had been in charge of a newsreel camera team. This time he was again part of a camera team, albeit in a different role. He took his new responsibilities as a journalist very seriously. Before setting off each day to cover a different story, he drafted many notes using his previous knowledge of Berlin as a guideline. During his time there he interviewed visiting US congressmen, military chiefs from the allied forces, people in the streets and other journalists of international standing. Freddie toured the city in a jeep with an American Army General. They talked incessantly of their own remarkable lives and swapped anecdotes and stories.

Was it really ten years since he had last been here? The content of those years had been diverse. They had taken him from covering the 1936 Berlin Olympics to the snow-capped mountain peaks of Austria where Freddie had first met the Palmai family. He had met Baroness von Harstezzen and formed an association with the Companions of the Circle. Then fate had taken Freddie and his newsreel team to the traumas of the Spanish Civil War. From there he had returned to England and renewed links with British Intelligence who had taken great interest in his new found friends, and had set about acquiring his knowledge of the Circle's operations. Then Freddie had taken his newsreel team to the United States where, whilst filming, he had been witness to the explosion of the *Hindenburg*; on board had been Baroness Van Harstezzen, the founder of the Circle. Upon her death the leadership of the Circle had passed into the hands of Arthandur Palmai, who in turn had handed over control to Colonel Brindmarsh who directed its operations from Whitehall. Freddie had returned to England, married Cynthia Field, a girl he had known from his army days in India, and moved to Cornwall where he had become a journalist. There, whilst assisting the local lifeboat team, Freddie and Cynthia had befriended Francine after she had been rescued from a foundering tanker. Francine had later become a member of the Circle on assignment in France. Then had come the years of war, the death of Cynthia in a car crash, his time in service in the army and the terrible time in the POW camp and the war trials in Tokyo. Now Freddie was back in the city where his life had been set in a different direction after that first meeting with Arthandur Palmai in a café.

Looking around he could not reconcile that time with this. There was hardly a trace of familiarity from that era. Freddie wondered about the girl in Berlin he had once loved. Tillie – where was she now? So many things had changed. So many buildings were but mere rubble now.

Surprisingly Freddie found the ordinary people to be cheerful. The ordinary Berliner seemed to have a sense of relief that they were alive and well, and for them too a new chapter had begun in their lives. There would be an upsurge in building programmes, which in itself could only generate work and increase production levels, thereby creating a resurgence in a stagnant, shattered economy. In peacetime there would be a new industriousness applied to the work ethic here, Freddie felt sure of that, and in his correspondence for the BBC, he was quick to note this. Freddie, whose primary emphasis in his journalistic career, especially during the pre-war years, had been on foreign affairs, now began to take an avid interest in economics and the role of industry. On all of his bulletins to London he was able to detail information relating to German industry.

Often he would tour factories where workers toiled on the production line in conditions that were not at that stage regulated by any strict rulings as laid down by unions in other countries. It was in one factory that Freddie finally found out what had become of Tillie. It came as a staggering surprise to Freddie that he found her working as a supervisor in a food factory. Before making a camera study of the factory production, Freddie had to work out what to say in his journalistic role. He asked the factory manager if he could film the various stages of process and production so he could remark on it as a camera followed him along the line. The manager took Freddie along to the supervisor's office and introduced him. When the woman behind the desk rose to greet him an incredulous look spread across Freddie's face. He was facing Tillie.

Tillie was slow in recognising Freddie but when she did it was with such shock and amazement that she was totally lost for words. It was minutes before she could talk. The two just stared at each other blankly. There had been a decade in between the time the two had last set eyes on each other. They were both mummified. Finally when the astonishment had subsided, they both agreed to carry out the filming in the factory and meet at a tavern in the evening where they could talk of the intervening years.

It was a particularly cold and damp night as Freddie made his way to the tavern. Several American soldiers passed him by, blowing spirals of smoke into the misty night air. It was so cold Freddie wrapped his long coat around him firmly and put his hands into his pockets tightly. With his hat sitting squarely on his head, he looked more like a local businessman than a British journalist.

At night the Berlin of late 1946 was a city of shadows and flickering figures and military uniforms of different nations. Once it had been raffish and colourful but one could not see the character that had been there in the 30s when the atmosphere evoked a sense of dread of the coming years. It would be interesting to keep returning to Berlin throughout the future to see how the city would develop.

Freddie eventually found the tavern and entered, removing his hat and unfastening his coat. The smell of beer, smoke and people crowded together came rising up to him. It could have been ten years ago thought Freddie but only the uniforms were different, summing up the changes that had taken place. Freddie espied an English soldier he had met on his assignments as he made his way to the bar.

"Good evening, major," he smiled at him shaking his hand. "A little spot of recreation, eh?"

"Even officers like to have some leisure time, Freddie old son. Bit of a change since you used to come here in the 30s to do your newsreel reports." The major noticed the astonished look in Freddie's eyes. "Oh, it's all right. I used to see your reports quite regularly before the war. Pretty hair-raising stuff from what I remember. You did one in Spain, back in '36 wasn't it?"

"That's right," said Freddie, recalling the particular newsreel.

"Are you waiting for someone?" asked the major, noticing Freddie's eyes wandering towards the door.

"I am as a matter of fact," replied Freddie, and as he spoke he noticed Tillie come through the door. Smiling again and shaking the major's hand, he said politely, "Look, I'll drop by before I go back, Major. Good to see you again. You really must excuse me, my date has just arrived."

"Certainly, old man," remarked the major jovially. "Don't let me hold you up." The major turned to look at Freddie's date and felt inclined to express his admiration. "I must say she cuts a fine dash, doesn't she?"

Freddie nodded in agreement and moved forward to greet Tillie. She kissed him on the cheek and they both moved to an out of the way table in a secluded corner. Freddie ordered some drinks from a passing waiter and they sat in silence looking at each other, remembering their love affair of another time. Tillie sipped her drink unaware that Freddie was thinking exactly the same thing as her. They were both summing up each other's appearance.

Tillie, who was slightly older than Freddie at forty-five, still 'cut a dash' as the major remarked, but lines of worry were evident in her face. She had a beautifully creamy coloured skin, luxuriant ashen-blonde hair lined with streaks of grey. She had acquired weight, especially around her waist. This did not dispel her looks at all. On the contrary it gave her a more matronly look. Freddie assumed that she must have borne children in the past ten years to have taken on this appearance. Before Cynthia Field this had been the only woman he had loved. Yet he knew in his heart that this was only a friendship he was renewing, the more emotional side of things could never take on the same meaning.

"Tell me, Freddie, how the years have treated you," she said quietly, noticing the changes in him. "Or how the years have mistreated you perhaps?" She was direct. "I know we are both getting older, and I know there has been a war. You are different, though; I do not see the happy young man who I once dared to run in front of the bulls in Pamplona."

This comment engendered surprise in Freddie.

"So you still remember," he replied, the surprise in his voice so obvious.

"Of course. There have been changes in my life too. Before I tell you my story, you must tell me yours. I cannot believe that a man of your love of life and travel did not experience excitement at least in the past years."

Freddie admired her perception. Tillie was still a shrewd woman in summing up people. Freddie decided he would tell her about his life, although one subject would remain secret. That would be his involvement with the Companions of the Circle, and also he would gloss over his military career prior to his time as a POW.

"Obviously a lot has happened, Tillie." He began and as he started to tell Tillie all that happened, in the background of the tavern a band started to play a tune called Auf Wiedersehen. It seemed to be music for the mood. Even as Freddie spoke of Cynthia, his life in Cornwall, and the years of the war, he was aware of Tillie's perfume. Tillie always wore perfume on her dates with Freddie. All these years later and she had still not forgotten.

"What was Cynthia like?" Tillie asked suddenly, curious to know about the woman who had replaced her in his affections after she had rejected him.

"That's coincidental," mused Freddie, "She once asked me the same question about you. I told her you were stylish, sophisticated, very intelligent, beautiful but intense, deep-thinking, and I felt the political climate of the time had changed you, as it did with many of your people."

Tillie raised one eyebrow curiously. It was a mannerism that she had never quite conquered, for it always betrayed her thoughts, whether they be impatience, annoyance or a slow burning anger bubbling to the surface.

"You are both flattering and accurate in your judgement of me," she said mildly, and Freddie immediately saw that she had mellowed. "But you still have not told me what Cynthia was like."

"Cynthia was a fun girl, she enjoyed life, she was happy and a devil of a flirt." At this Freddie grinned, remembering how often she had teased him. "Being married to her was fun. I loved her. She loved me. And I believe we both made each other enormously happy. When she died I was so wrapped up with grief." He stopped talking, realising the topic was sad and in danger of lowering his emotional spirits that night. He raised his glass to his lips.

"I would say that Cynthia was your match in every way. Your description of her as fun, enjoying life, happy and a flirt, that was you all those years ago. Now I see you as a weary man. When I knew you then, you were Freddie Miller, Army officer. Then Freddie Miller, cameraman. Now you are an ex-Army officer again, ex-prisoner of war and journalist, still travelling, still going through life but going more slowly. The wisdom of the years perhaps? The feeling that maybe you have seen it all and you don't know what is next. Am I right, Freddie?"

"I am just older, Tillie," said Freddie quietly. "Older, yes. Wiser, certainly. Yet one thing I know and that is for my experiences I am certainly more knowledgeable. For my worst experiences I am more tolerant. I understand the intolerable hardships and humiliations that are inflicted on human beings by other human beings simply because I went through several years of absolute hell. In many ways if I look at my life, which until the war had been a mish-mash, a pursuit of adventure and travel, and unattainable women – no disrespect intended to you – I believe my finest achievement was to have survived the hell of that prison camp without bitterness. Indeed when I was in Japan recently I visited one of the guards who came to me one night with a bottle of lemonade and bread when I was in a virtual prison cage. No, probably until then I did not realise the really true values in life: compassion for others, and helping other people when they are down. The men I served with were such a wonderful bunch. I shall never forget their courage and humour.

"You underestimate yourself, Freddie," Tillie pointed out. "You were always a man of compassion, and I do not think your life and career was wasted. You look at life from a different angle. Only your values have changed." She appeared to reflect on her words and then gazed into the depths of her wine glass as if she was thinking of something further to add. Tillie was always direct. Whenever she spoke to anyone she always stared directly back at them. "Like you, Freddie, I have changed. Matured is the word I believe. I was married also." Freddie looked up sharply. "To the officer you saw me dancing with at the night of the ball." Freddie immediately remembered the night when he and his newsreel team had filmed the proceedings of a post-Olympic ball where Hitler had been present. He recalled how his cinecamera lens had captured Tillie and her beau at a moment of great surprise to both of them. "I am a widow now," she continued. "My husband was killed on the Russian Front. I am a mother of two sons also."

Freddie appeared sympathetic. "I see. It must be hard for you with two young sons."

"I have help. My neighbours look after them when I am working. They are good boys, too young to understand what the past years have all been about, too young to understand why the city they live in is in ruins, or why I and many others are so – so regretful of all the terrible things that were happening. Neither my husband or I knew of the horrors of the camps. I feel such shame. I should have listened to you all those years ago."

There was real regret in her voice. Freddie felt that he wanted to divert the subject. He could see that she was sincere.

"You must not dwell on these things. You have a duty to yourself and your sons to keep on with your life. It is the future that counts now. I know it sounds simple but we all have to make the effort. All through our lives there will be influences of good and bad, public figures putting forward idealism and propaganda. It is up to us to recognise and to separate them. Now the world looks with horror at what has happened."

"I will educate my boys to love," said Tillie. "To love people."

"I am puzzled by your occupation. With your education what are you doing as a supervisor in a factory? I thought a commercial job would be more suited to your talents."

"I have to work," she said almost defensively. "I have two boys and no husband and I need to look after them. From what you can see, there is not much industry left. I was lucky to get this job. The general manager is my uncle, you see. I think you could say I used some family influence. And it is not just a job, I enjoy my work. We are looking at methods of efficiency and better means of production, and how to make the best use of machinery and plant. I look at our factory now as being the leader in a chain. I think it will be a booming business, eventually catering to many new markets and providing more jobs for many people."

"And your husband? What sort of man was he? You did ask me about my late wife. Was he good to you?"

Tillie eyed him with that curious look again. It was so hard to tell with Tillie whether she was annoyed or not. The look broke into a smile as she remembered her husband with affection.

"Very," she replied. "A good father to the boys. My husband was a serious man, not without humour. He was always serious. I suppose he and I were well matched, perhaps in the way that you and Cynthia were." Tillie stopped for a moment as the band in the tavern began to play an old familiar tune. It was 'Lily Marlene'.

At this point the people began to sing along to the music. There was a clear mixture of voices, young and old combining to make a distinctive sound in the enclosed atmosphere of the tavern. They stopped talking to listen. The tune was so indicative of a time gone by. It matched the mood of the evening.

"Strange how they all sing together," continued Tillie, as the song drew to its conclusion. "They sing for the future, not for the past. If my husband were still alive, he would have felt that. Towards the end of the war he began to realise how misguided he and his fellow officers had been. When he spoke of this publicly he was sent to the front. And he never came back. So now I am a widow in post-war Berlin helping to manage a factory, and all the dreams of splendour have given way to the cold hard facts of reality. I look back to my education at the Sorbonne and the times of the 20s. We were a free generation then, living on the credit of dreams and irresponsibility, rolling along on the tides of change, but now that the debts have been run up, it is time to honour those cheques. Forgive me for speaking in clichés; I simply cannot put it in any other way. In many ways I prefer my life today: I have my children, I have my work, I have the memories. One should never try to resurrect the past."

"That is one of my problems," admitted Freddie. "I have to leave the past where it is. I sometimes yearn for that old time freedom I had before the war, and I yearn for some of that glamour: That touch of excitement, the passion of a love affair once gone. The war took my wife, and it took a lot of me too. When I saw you in the factory today, I remembered so much in the space of what just seemed an instant. Before the war came you and I really were fortunate to know the times we did. Carefree days, of a reckless carelessness that could have only occurred in the 20s and 30s, when one half of the world lived in relative affluence and the rest fought with the Depression. I remember when my newsreel team filmed some of the conditions of the mines in the heavily industrial areas. It was round about the time that Edward VIII remarked that something must be done, after he had gone down one of the mines. I always had a social conscience after that."

"Not only for working conditions," pointed out Tillie. "But also for politics."

"That was my job. Filming the front line issues," emphasised Freddie. "Even after the luxury of a commissioned Army officer's life, I managed to live well as a cinecameraman. True I was in most places filming life as it occurred. I saw the starving in India, the rich in Hollywood, the Jarrow marchers, the battles of Abyssinia and the Civil War in Spain, and yet my position then was always one of comfort, always returning to my home in England, away from everything that I had seen. And then for me the day of judgement came when I was taken Prisoner of War. The experience instilled in me a deep sense of reality. It's strange coming back here and seeing you again. Have the years changed you?"

"Not so much the measure of the years, more the substance of the years. I wept when I learned of what had happened in the camps. I wept when I learned of what we had been part of. Now I resolve to leave the past where it is for different reasons. You understand what I mean. I am ashamed that I was swept away by it all. For me, my family is my sole purpose of fulfilment. Nothing else matters, they are the most important thing of all. I intend to spend my years giving them my undivided attention. I want to be true to myself. Not a person caught up in passing phases and changes."

"And do you think that in time you may remarry?"

"No, Freddie, I do not." Tillie was most definite in her reply. "You? Will you marry again?"

"Perhaps not. I don't see how I could ever find that kind of happiness again."

The band started to play another tune and for a moment they sat listening to the music. Tillie glanced at her watch. She looked up at Freddie and gripped his hand for a moment.

"I must go," she said.

"I understand," said Freddie, "you have a family."

"Will you walk with me a little of the way?" she asked pleasantly.

"Of course." They rose from the table with Freddie taking her arm gallantly.

They quickly left the tavern and walked out into the cold night air. The change in atmosphere from the warmth inside was extremely noticeable. A chill had firmly set in that night, and the wind blew across the fragments of the buildings that remained. Freddie and Tillie walked along just talking of simple things. A street car rolled past with a suddenness, breaking the silence of the night.

Many people scurried to their destinations in this once great habitat of grandeur. Uniforms of American and British servicemen were dotted everywhere, and the voices that passed by in the night were of a varied cosmopolitan mix. From a nearby café the aroma of sauerkraut and onions rose into the air making Freddie feel hungry, and with some astonishment, he realised that his day had been so busy, he had not found time to eat since breakfast.

"When do you go back to London?" Tillie asked him.

"Oh, very shortly. I'm sure I'll be back here on assignments with the BBC from time to time," he responded adopting a hopeful tone.

Tillie said nothing in reply, which disappointed Freddie, for he was in fact a little hopeful that they could remain friends and meet up again. Although the area they were walking in was in ruins, Freddie recognised a number of familiar sights and he recognised the area. The last time Freddie had been in Berlin in 1936, he had visited Tillie in an apartment block close by.

"Do you still live in this area?" Freddie asked automatically assuming that she still did.

"No, not any more," she replied coldly. There was a definite change of tone in her voice, but before Freddie adjusted to her shifting moods, Tillie said suddenly, "Come, let me show you the old building where I used to live," and then they were walking across the road and down narrow side streets, and across piles of bricks and rubble. Then they stopped. In front of them the bombed-out devastation of the apartment block remained. It was amazing. The stairs winding up to individual rooms remained. The lift shaft, open and exposed, was clear to see, but the rest of the building had the appearance of a child's dolls house with the roof and walls ripped away leaving everything in full view.

Tillie stepped forward from Freddie and walked towards the crumbling structure.

"Where are you going?" Freddie asked almost stupidly when it was blatantly obvious that she was going inside.

"Come on, Freddie," Tillie called back without turning around. Freddie meekly followed her more for protection than anything. Tillie ascended the stairs and came right to the top of the building. She stood motionless staring out at the city of Berlin. The wind blew up with a sudden flurry sending her beret flying into the sky. Droplets of a gentle rain stung her cheeks and her hair rose gently as the wind blew. She turned to Freddie who had come up behind her.

Down below car horns tooted in the streets, the sound of motor vehicles roaring in the far off distance could be heard, and from buildings that were still standing in good condition, lights flickered and twinkled in the dense black of the night. Many of the fragmented buildings glowed luminously in the dark.

"Well, what do you think of Berlin now?" she asked Freddie, lighting a cigarette and blowing a ring of smoke that seemed to dissipate instantly in the air.

"The view here is like observing the wreckage of an empire that, thank God, was never able to reach its full might. For you the view must be hard to come to terms with especially when one considers this is a city, that this block of apartments was once your home. I predict that this city will flourish again. Oh, new buildings will go up. New industries will develop, new lifestyles will evolve, and the horrors of the Nazi regime will fade into history."

"I was here in my apartment with my two boys when the bombers came," Tillie said quietly in reflection. "We knew it was the closing stages of the war. I heard the sounds of the bombing and from here I saw the buildings go up in fire and smoke, and the noise. The noise! I could hear people shouting in the other rooms. I knew then how the people in London must have felt at the time of the Blitz. My whole body trembled. I was white with shock. I had lost my husband. The only thing I cared about were my little boys who were crying. Then I grabbed a trunk and I filled it with everything valuable to my memory, photographs, my diploma from the Sorbonne and even a doll, Freddie, one that you bought me in Spain. I threw it out of the window into that road down there. I grabbed my two boys and I ran out into the street. We took shelter while all hell broke around us. Fire and falling buildings. People running. When the bombing had stopped, and the noise had gone, my boys and I had survived, and I just had a trunk of bits and pieces. That is all I have of old Berlin. An old trunk."

"You have a lot more than many people, Tillie. A family. Your career seems to be of importance to you. Treasure those things. They are absolutely precious."

"We've both learnt a great deal in the past ten years," she said turning around and indicating she wanted to leave the shell of this building. Freddie began the downward walk and in a rare moment of affection he put his arm around her and pulled her close to him.

"Times remembered, Tillie," he said in a whispered tone. "Perhaps we should meet up in another ten years?"

"Perhaps we shouldn't, Freddie," Tillie said in a strict emphasis. "I will always remember Paris and Biarritz, Pamplona, the times we swam in the bay at San Sebastian, and when we walked along the pathways winding up Mount Igueldo. They were good days."

Tillie and Freddie walked down to the roadway. A taxicab came hurtling past and Tillie hailed it. The cab stopped within a few feet of them.

"They were good days," Freddie repeated softly, realising Tillie was leaving again.

"And I shall never forget them," said Tillie. They both held each other tightly as if there had never been ten years between their last meeting. Tillie released her grip and she stepped back and entered the cab.

"Goodbye, Freddie," she said softly and she put her hand on his for one moment offering him a final gesture, and the taxi started up and moved off leaving Freddie standing alone on the road watching from the position of solitude, he always seemed to find himself in. The scent of Tillie's perfume seemed to remain in the night air long after the cab had disappeared from view.

"Why is it I always end up on my own?" he murmured to himself.

Thirty-one

From Nathan's bedroom overlooking the the Green at Ealing he could always observe the changing of the seasons. In winter snow fell thickly, giving the grass a white carpet effect set against a background of dark barren trees and grey buildings, the clash of colour was not unlike the composite of a black and white negative. Children would build snowmen, throw snowballs, and slide on the ice. In the springtime the flowers, the leaves and the grass grew densely and lushly in a mixture of iridescent colours. People always seemed to whistle in the spring. The finer weather seemed to make the English more cheerful and enthusiastic, and in the summer months they were positively beaming. The flowers looked radiantly beautiful, the lawns were spectacularly green and fine in shades of texture, and people looked happy. The summer evenings were long and pleasant, and even though there was austerity and still rationing, it was nice to be here in England. Nathan enjoyed the autumn months most of all.

Jack and Elsie Faley and their sons, Ron and Mick, almost adopted Nathan into the family. It was hard not to be moved by their constantly overwhelming kindness. The Faleys were a humble family, very straightforward in their way of life, never seeking too much, and always working very hard for every penny they earned. It was the only life they knew. Frequently Jack would ask Nathan to join them for a Sunday lunch if Ron and Mick were home too. Sometimes the meal would be simple and sweet. Something like a scrumptious steak and kidney pie beautifully prepared by Elsie with tender loving care, and as Jack would cut a knife into the soft puff pastry, the delicious aroma of the meat within would rise up in a steam. The Faleys were good cooks and being real battlers, knew how to make food go a long way in a time of austerity.

Often on a Sunday morning Jack and his sons would be out in the garden digging the vegetables up from a particular patch set aside for that purpose. Remembering his time on the Kibbutz Jezarat so long ago, Nathan would join them, not only to help them but also out of curiosity to relive his memory of work on the land. Elsie would be singing in the kitchen as she prepared the Sunday roast and in the garden Jack would examine his produce with pride. From his garden he had runner beans, potatoes, tomatoes, string beans, shell peas, apples and rhubarb. Any of these could be used to supplement the Sunday roast They would sit for hours shelling peas from the pod into a strainer to give to Elsie who would serve them up a while later with a slab of butter and some mint leaves added for effect. To Nathan food prepared freshly from the garden, and made with such pride and care, tasted so much better than anything he had ever tasted in a restaurant. For the effort that went into it there was more true value than anything he'd known. There were times when Nathan found their lifestyle appealing for its simplicity and pleasantness.

Nathan studied long hours and rarely did any socialising apart from the occasional university function. It must have been the influence of the Faleys that always kept Nathan in perspective. At university Nathan found himself studying alongside ex-servicemen, nearly all former officers, unlike himself, who had never risen in the NCO ranks let alone anything else. There were also an entourage of former public schoolboys who had not tasted real life, or the feel of independence under pressure of continually trying to survive on meagre amounts of money, as Nathan had found himself in a similar position. Nathan considered that this would be a plus in the run of his career because he would be more easily able to identify with people to whom struggle was endemic.

It was almost as if Nathan wanted to isolate himself from many of the students. He could not relate to the better off category. He found friends few, but not lacking. Those he befriended were always those he felt on equal terms with, and those with whom he felt the most comfortable.

Nathan would often look back to the past, in the lonelier moments of his life. He had written several letters to the kibbutz, but he had never had a reply from Melissa or Leon, and he concluded that they had probably moved on as he himself had done and commenced new lives elsewhere.

Freddie Miller often dropped by if he was in the area. Nathan had great respect for Freddie. For the journalist had fought himself up on his own merits, and yet in Freddie, Nathan saw a man of gentle old fashioned good manners, but quietly possessing strength and conviction, and one who never failed to acknowledge his humble background. Freddie was liked too by the Faleys, although they were worlds apart in terms of lifestyles. It was interesting how Jack and Elsie could converse so well with Freddie. If truth be known, in fact, there were strong similarities in them as people. Jack's sons, Ron and Mick, had both met people during the war who had been imprisoned with Freddie in the POW camp in Borneo, and the stories of how he had personally waged a continuous battle with the Japanese for the welfare of his men despite being very sick himself, had circulated and he had engendered great respect.

When Ron had announced he was having a twenty-first birthday party and celebrating his engagement to a lovely girl called Jill from Greenford, he had no hesitation in asking Nathan to tell his mate Freddie Miller 'to drop by for a beer.'

The night of Ron's twenty-first was late in 1947. It was quite a party held at the Faleys house at Ealing Green. Nathan came home from his delivery round to be met by Elsie in the corridor, as he was about to ascend the stairs to his room to change and join in the fun.

"Hullo, luv," she greeted him cheerily. "Coming down and joining us, are you for Ronnie's knees up?"

"Most certainly, Mrs Faley. I wouldn't miss it for the world. I've got a present for Ron and his fiancée."

"That's nice of you dear."

"I'm just going to wash and change and I'll be down."

"All right, dear. I'll let 'em know you're coming. Your friend – that nice Mr Miller – is already there with Jack. He's a nice fellow y'know, isn't he?" One knew she really meant it. "Oh! Incidentally..."

Nathan stopped at the top of the stairs instantly.

"Yes, Mrs Faley?" He looked a bit alarmed as if he was about to get some bad news.

"Nothing bad, luvvie. Don't look so surprised," she smiled cheeringly. "You're a bit of a dark horse, ain't yer?" Nathan really did look surprised. What did she mean by that? "A lovely young lady called by this afternoon to see you. She said she was sorry to have missed you, but I told her to drop by tonight. She was a smashing lady. Said she wanted to keep it a surprise; wouldn't tell me her name. She'll be here later." Elsie winked at him mischievously.

Nathan looked a bit perplexed. He could only wonder just who on earth this young lady could be.

"Now I really am surprised, Mrs Faley. I shall wait and see," he grinned. Nathan went to his room and washed and changed. Just before he went downstairs, he looked at his reflection in the mirror. At twenty-five years of age he had matured well. He cut a fine dash with his dark hair and bushy eyebrows, and his glowing eyes that could give rise to sparkles of humour or sadness from something within his soul that would remind him of something that happened to him in the past. His physique was still slim but not under developed, and if on the surface he came through as a rather shy person, he was confident and sure of his abilities.

For Nathan to go to a public gathering or even a party was at first an ordeal. Once he had gone to a particular occasion he would throw himself into whatever the situation happened to be, and make an effort to mix and socialise. Tonight's party for Ron Faley's twenty-first birthday and engagement would be one such occasion. When Nathan was sure he was dressed decently in a nice shirt and trousers, he went downstairs to join in the revelry.

He knocked on the door and it swung open to reveal the room already filled with people. Freddie Miller was talking to Ron and Jill, and they smiled at Nathan as he entered. Nathan nodded and smiled to all the other guests who were people he didn't know. There was plenty of food on the tables: sausage rolls, Cornish pasties, pies, cakes and there was enough to drink to suit all tastes ranging from soft drink to beer to a huge bowl of punch.

Nathan shook hands with Ron and kissed Jill politely on the cheek. "Congratulations, Ron. Best wishes to you both, Ron, Jill." Looking around he couldn't see Jack or Elsie. "Nice to see you, Freddie," he said to his good friend and then turning to Mick, he asked, "Where's your mum and dad, Mick?"

Mick tousled his soft brown hair and chuckled. "Just wait till you see 'em, mate! They're getting dressed up, something spectacular."

"I'll wait with interest," he said.

Over at the piano in the corner, a lady sat down and tested a few keys for sound. A few other people in party hats came in carrying a keg of beer. Generally everybody seemed to be having a good time chatting away to each other. To Nathan this type of party with a group of happy-go-lucky Londoners, was a new experience. Nathan's background had been one of quiet Jewish gatherings, normally conducted with dignity, and his upbringing had introduced him to the arts and classical music; so different from the Swing and Big Band sounds that Jack and Elsie Faley played at the Green. Freddie Miller was in his element talking to different people as if he'd known them all his life. That was the remarkable thing about Freddie; he had the ability to fit in anywhere.

Nathan talked to Freddie about Berlin. He was interested in the observations that Freddie had made on his recent journey to that city. The conversation between the two was just becoming engrossing when the door flung open, and Jack and Elsie Faley made a stunning entrance.

"What do you think, ladies and gentlemen?" Jack laughed. He was sparkling. Literally sparkling. He and Elsie were wearing the outfits of a pearly king and queen. It was quite a startling outfit. They looked like something out of a vaudevillian music hall era. Jack wore a flat cap with make pretend pearls strung across, and a cut away jacket and trousers, all decked out in the same style. Elsie wore a wide-brim hat with plumes of coloured feathers, and a two piece ladies outfit also strung with glass imitation pearls. Everyone looked on with amusement.

"Blimey, Dad!" gasped Ron. "I know it's my twenty- first, and I'm getting engaged, but you didn't have to dress up like a pearly King and Queen for our sakes!"

"We're cockneys, my son! At least your mum and I, and what do cockneys do when they get together with their relatives and their friends? They have a sing-song and a party, don't they?" Jack then doffing his hat in cavalier fashion and, smiling a huge smile revealing some startling teeth, called out to everyone in the room, "So what are we going to do?"

About half the room replied in unison, "We're going to have a sing-song!" Nathan found himself exposed to rough, warm-hearted London humour. He watched them with fascination as Jack took centre stage at the party. Jack was brash, a man of good humour who enjoyed himself enormously at gatherings like this. He moved over to the piano where the lady sat poised at the ready to play. Jack was in his fifties, with a good head of lush grey hair, a very toothy smile and all the boyish charm of a juvenile.

"Speech, Jack!" someone called. A few other people called out in agreement. "Speech!" Speech!"

Jack waved his hand. "All right I'll say a few words now that everyone seems to be here. First of all, ladies and gents, I want to thank you all for coming to what is a very special evening. You all know why we're here. My son, Ron, is twenty-one today and he's getting engaged to a special girl called Jill. Ronnie's done a lot in his twenty-one years. Back in the war, despite his mum and I asking him not to, he put his age up and enlisted in the RAF. We worried about him a lot but he came through and with flying colours. I'm proud of both my boys, Mick and Ron. They've grown well. Well it's Ron's day today – and it's Jill's too. It's my wish they'll be as happy as life can be for them—"

Ron interrupted. "Come on, Dad! What about that sing-song? I'm getting a bit embarrassed here."

"Okay. Enough of the words for now, we'll have a few speeches later on. This here's my sister, Ruby Anne, on the piano. Rube, give us a couple of notes, darling. It's time for me party piece. Twinkle your fingers across the keys, Ruby." Ruby played a few notes, "Lovely eh?" Jack chuckled. "Who said you can't find an answer to Hoagy Carmichael on Ealing Green?"

Ruby played a key and in a monotone voice to the setting of an occasional piano note, Jack espoused the words of a cockney monologue.

> "I'm not a squire of the shire with a mansion and some grounds,
> I'm just an ordinary fellow whose friendship knows no bounds.
> I'm not a wealthy man from up West with a team of horses and a sailboat or a yacht,
> I come from London's East End and I don't pretend to be something that I'm not,
> Because I'm a Cockney.
> Because I'll not make concessions to pretension or false dimension to condescension.
> I ain't a toff from Mayfair,
> And I was always taught to play fair,
> In whatever I do or try to do.
> Now a lot of us who were there took the full blast of the Blitz,
> And through times of terror our East End hearts and spirits took us through all of this,
> You'll see us at King George Docks, Petticoat Lane and Canning Town,
> Cheerful, hardworking, as the day is long from morning to sundown,
> Because we're Cockneys.
> On the day that I was born the Bow Bells rang, they nearly deafened me,

Me dear old muvver, God bless 'er heart, she advised me wisdomly,
Go forth, my son, do your best, be of good heart, enthusiasm is the name of the game,
Never feel sorry for yourself when things don't work out the way they should 'cos it's apathy that makes you lame,
Because we're cockneys,
And we're proud of it. We're a cheerful, chirpy, perky bunch, who'll always have a go,
So remember that, my friends, wherever you may go."

Ruby placed the last note down concluding the short monologue. Everybody clapped and cheered Jack, who threw his hat up in the air. Then Jack, in a jovial manner, roared, "Let the dancing commence!" Ruby, demonstrating her skill on the piano, burst into a rendition of 'Knees Up Mother Brown'. Everybody in the room started to dance enjoying themselves so much that the floorboards started to shake and the walls began to vibrate. Nathan stood this one out for a moment grabbing a glass of punch. Not for long though. One girl grabbed him and pulled him laughingly protesting into the thick of things. These Londoners liked a good time.

There was a loud knock on the door prompting Jack to interrupt a conversation he was having with Freddie, and wandering across with a pint of beer in his hand, he opened it to find himself confronted by a neighbour in his pyjamas.

"Hullo, Sid," Jack said affably. His next-door neighbour Sid looked at Jack in his Pearly King outfit with absolute astonishment.

"Bleedin' hell! You're done up like a mad dog's dinner on Christmas day, ain't yer? What you doing then? Having a flippin' fancy dress, are you?"

"No, it's Ronnie's twenty-first and he's getting engaged to his Jill today too."

"Cor. Well you're aint arf making a blinkin' noise in there, eh?"

"Well, I tell you what, Sid," said Jack. "It's a special night tonight. We've got pies, pasties, sausage rolls and jellied eels, and cakes and beer, and everyone's invited."

Sid looked at the tempting food on the nearby tables and the great quantities of beverages available. A smile creased his lips from ear to ear.

"And you say everyone's invited?" he asked.

"That's right," said Jack.

"Leave the door open, Jack, I'll get me missus!" Sid raced off leaving Jack with a wide smile on his face. Sid and his wife had no sooner returned than there was another knock on the door. The party was in full swing, with Ruby playing a variety of different tunes on the piano. Jack went to the door again, this time to find a policeman standing there. Almost at once the music died away and the place went quiet as the policeman came in taking off his helmet. He looked at Jack sternly, who looked at him equally sternly.

"I understand you're having a bit of a knees up," he said to Jack, who suddenly looked as if he was trying to bottle up a laugh. "I'm here to make an apprehension."

A few people looked deadly serious, including Nathan. Then Ron, Mick and Elsie started to laugh uncontrollably.

"Hullo, Uncle Harry," laughed Ron. "Apprehension? My foot it is!"

"I'm here to apprehend a beer and a dance. Come on, Rube! Flash those dazzling fingers, luv!" Harry grabbed a pint mug and joined in the fun.

They all laughed and everybody began to dance madly again. It was a happy party. Freddie had a dance with a couple of ladies. Nathan danced too. Several times that night they had a sing along in which everybody joined in.

Freddie and Harry who must have both been about the same age had a conversation together, and were seen laughing loudly at a joke that one of them had cracked. They both moved across to the piano where they said something to Ruby. Freddie raised his pint, took a sip and began to sing an old favourite, and Harry and Jack started to sing along. The song was *'I want a girl just like the girl that married dear old dad'*.

Nathan looked on at everyone singing this popular song. All he could do was smile and laugh as he didn't know the words. Thinking of his already somewhat worldly background, he suddenly felt very isolated amongst all these nice people. He tried not to show it on the surface, though. Jill and Ron were a lovely couple. Jill was a pretty girl who was about five feet four in height with medium brown hair that was cut in a sort of pageboy style. She seemed like a girl born to be a mother and wife, she had that kind of look about her. She constantly looked at Ron with eyes that revealed such love for him. With their arms around each other, one had the impression that they never wanted to let go of each other.

The words of the song seemed to float around and around the room. *Dear old Dad*, thought Nathan, and he momentarily thought of Arthandur and Marlene. With a twinge of alarm he realised that it was now close to ten years since he had last seen them. He envied Ron and Mick in the fact that they, as young men, still had their father and were at an age when they could not only be sons but friends and confidants to that lovely man, Jack, who seemed to ooze decency and cheerfulness. Nathan heard a knock on the door but didn't look up to see who this next guest would be. He busily helped himself to some punch.

Ruby had now taken a temporary respite from the piano and this time she had put a soft music record on the gramophone turntable. It was 'Music for Lovers' and Ron and Jill moved slowing out into the middle of the room followed by everyone else. Someone had turned the main lights off and put a half lit standard lamp on instead, giving the room the desired effect of soft music and soft lights. Nathan was still looking at the wall sipping his punch occasionally glancing around but not for long and not too much.

Jack had answered the door. In the dim half-light it was impossible to see across to the other side of the room to see whom Jack was talking to.

"Yes, love, what can I do for you?" Jack smiled at the girl who stood outside. He was quite taken by her attractiveness and her dark features. On eyeing her he sensed that she was not English.

"I like your outfit," she said in an admiring tone, her voice clearly indicating her European upbringing. "You look like a man I saw on stage recently at a music hall."

"Well, it's one of the old Pearly King's outfits, love, passed on to me by my dad. He used to do a turn on the pub floor now and again when I was a lad." He noticed her peering over his shoulder at the people dancing. "You know someone here, do you?"

"Oh, I came here this afternoon. I saw your wife, Elsie—"

Jack snapped his fingers in memory. "That's right, of course. Elsie mentioned that you know our lodger, Nathan, don't you?"

"Yes, I do. Is Nathan here?"

"He certainly is, darlin'. He's in there somewhere. You go on in and find him and join the party, sweetheart. Help yourself to any food and drink you want."

"That is very nice of you," she said happily and she moved into the room moving through the dancers who were all in romantic moods swaying to the lush strings of the orchestral music. She looked over to the food table and she saw Nathan replenish his glass of punch. He turned his back to the party and pretended to look at a picture hanging on the wall. In reality he felt isolated and remote at the party. Nathan took a slow sideways glance and turned his eyes away again. Almost as quickly he turned his eyes back, just as quickly, to absorb the view of the girl before him. His face showed absolute disbelief. He was so shocked he could hardly croak her name. Just as quickly as he had looked at her, she came rushing forward and they hugged each other. It seemed impossible that this girl could be here.

"Melissa!" Nathan finally blurted out softly. "Melissa," He said it again. "Melissa." His voice was full of such shock. He could hardly speak above a whisper. "I – I – I just cannot believe it. I just cannot believe that you are here."

Melissa pulled him into the middle of the room and they swayed together in time to the music. Nathan studied her; she had blossomed.

"Nathan. I am thrilled to see you, my old friend."

"What – what in heaven's name are you doing here in England?" he exclaimed and as he looked down into her eyes he saw they were clouded with tears of joy.

"It's a long story," she sighed. Her normally controlled emotions could not disguise her unremitting joy at seeing Nathan again. "Your letters…"

"Yes," replied Nathan. "The ones I sent to you at the Kibbutz Jezarat?"

"They were sent on to me here in London," she stated. She saw the surprise in Nathan's face. "I have been living in England for several years."

"Several years?" Nathan repeated blankly. The soft music in the background wound down before moving on to another track. "Look, let's sit down. This is no place for a conversation, on our feet dancing." They sat down in two chairs in a corner of the room. "You have really been here all this time?"

"Since 1944 to be exact," she stated proudly. "After you had joined up in Palestine, Leon decided to fight with the Haganah. During the war it became known as the Palmach. It was supposed to be an illegal organisation but, of course, the British Army trained much of its men for special missions. There were a number of Palmach men at the kibbutz: Leon, George and surprisingly Shirom."

"You mean Shirom Banai?" asked Nathan. "He seemed such a tranquil man."

"He was. He was also a patriot and, like a patriot, he came out in defence of his home. To continue, there were a number of British commandos working with the Palmach and for a while they actually lived on the kibbutz and trained the men. One day, for the benefit of the British soldiers stationed at Jezarat, this unit from ENSA – you know the entertainment section of the army – came to the kibbutz and did a concert show featuring Stars in Battledress. There were a lot of British film and theatre people in the ENSA group, and during the show I asked one of the actors if I could sing a number. He was a little taken aback but I went on stage and sang a song from the musical Showboat." She was basking in the memory of it and her eyes were radiant and shining even in the half-light of the room. "I sang 'Old Man River'. I had a standing ovation after I sang that song; it was wonderful. The British soldiers were my first real test of an audience outside the kibbutz. I sang several more songs after that, and then a private with a mouth organ played the 'Battle Hymn of the Republic'. While he played I spoke the words out loud and do you know I could see tears in several of the men's eyes. I was thrilled that I could move an audience to that extent. One of the principal players was a theatrical producer and he asked me if I would like to join the ENSA group. It was an offer I could not resist. So for three years I toured with ENSA. We went everywhere. We did concerts on the Ghaza Strip, all over Palestine, and across Africa and Europe. In 1944 I went with them to England and this is where I have lived ever since, apart from a concert tour of Berlin appearing before the allied troops."

"How interesting," observed Nathan. "I was in North Africa for much of the war. It was a wonder we did not meet up. What have you done here in England these past few years? I still cannot believe that after all these years we are sitting here talking in England. Those nights in the kibbutz when we sat and discussed our lives it is as if it were yesterday."

"From your letters you said that you had achieved one of your ambitions: to study law. I too have achieved an ambition. I am an actress."

"Really!" Nathan was pleased for her.

"Really! Really!" she laughed. "The same producer in ENSA recommended me to his agency in London and when I came here I signed with them. I have been working mainly with provincial repertory theatre. I appeared in Lady Windermere's Fan in Birmingham for a while. I was in Lovers at Midnight in Coventry and I was in a musical show in Blackpool." Melissa laughed at the memory. "When I was in Blackpool, I stayed at this theatrical hotel, digs they call it, where all the performers who are in town stay at. It was so funny. At breakfast a man would throw fish from the table to some performing seals." She laughed again. Nathan found Melissa's laugh contagious. "There was also a tap dancing knife-thrower there and a couple of acrobats. That show only lasted a month and then I appeared in Liverpool in a Shakespearean play. From there I went to where I am now."

"And where is that?" Nathan asked still laughing at the story she had just told.

"The Old Vic," Melissa replied on a serious note. Nathan appeared to be impressed. Indeed he was because the Old Vic was the most prestigious theatrical company in England. "I have been with them for over a year now," Melissa added.

"The Old Vic. My, you have done well. Is that not the company that is led by Sir Laurence Olivier?"

"Yes, I still can't believe it. How fate has taken me from being a dreamer in Vienna to Palestine where I still dreamed of becoming an actress. And now I am on stage here in London in Olivier's company."

"His wife, Vivien Leigh, is also wonderful on stage, I believe."

"A wonderful actress. She has such presence. I am performing and watching Sir Laurence and Vivien Leigh, the two greatest theatrical stars in the world. It was a bonus to receive your letters by the way." She looked at him affectionately. "I have kept in touch with one or two people in the kibbutz. I was so surprised when they forwarded me your letters. I rarely have any time. I am so busy but I would have come to see you earlier." She broke off to look at the people chatting and dancing. She turned her eyes back to him. "I was sorry about your parents." Nathan felt heavy hearted. Melissa touched his hand reassuringly. "Mine too died in the camps."

After a pause Nathan said, "We must not think too much about that, however hard it hurts. Tell me, where are you living?"

"I share a flat with three other girls in Maida Vale. At least till early next year when I will be touring overseas with the Old Vic for some months."

"Overseas?" queried Nathan. He felt a slight panic rise within him. After all these years he had been reunited with Melissa and now she was travelling overseas.

"Early next year Olivier is taking the Old Vic on a tour of Australia and New Zealand. I am really looking forward to going."

"Australia! It is a country I am very interested in." Nathan sounded almost exuberant. "I met many Australian soldiers when I was in the army in North Africa. In fact I have been thinking that when I complete my course in law I may go out there to live. You must write and tell me all about it."

"I shall do, Nathan," Melissa said.

"Melissa, I must introduce you around to everyone here," Nathan said suddenly.

"Please do," she said, "and then we must dance again."

Nathan really felt proud that evening introducing Melissa around to everyone. Freddie Miller was particularly taken by her, and she by him. They had an engrossing conversation about each others career and places that both had visited. When Jack Faley learned that Melissa was an actress and singer, he insisted that she sing a song to the accompaniment of Ruby on the piano. Even at a party Melissa had the firmament of a bright star and when she sang in a closed room, all those who were there could never have foreseen that she would one day rise to celestial heights in her chosen career. Just about every man at the party had a dance with her. Rather than being annoyed Nathan was very impressed and felt proud that his friend seemed to command such attention.

Looking at Melissa as she was now and remembering her as she was on the kibbutz, Nathan could see how the years had improved her appearance. It was Melissa's clothes that made her look so different, yet otherwise physically she seemed to have grown more beautiful. Nathan realised that in the time they had spent together on the kibbutz, he had only ever seen her in the most austere of clothing, which was usually a hand-made cotton dress or a shawl. Melissa in modern European clothing was something to behold. When she walked her long dress seemed to swirl and rustle, and the heeled shoes she wore gave her a more polished look. Nathan had only ever seen her in sandals in Palestine.

At last Melissa returned to his side after she had spoken to everyone at the party. It was their time to dance once again. In silence they danced but it was the look in her eyes and the feel of her soft hands that thrilled Nathan. In his heart Nathan was asking himself if this encounter could possibly lead to something deeper. Perhaps even something permanent.

Later that night, he felt inclined to ask her about their mutual friend Leon Zielinski. Nathan was curious to learn of Leon's progress in life and how his ambitions had eventuated.

"Leon," Melissa smiled at the mention of his name. "That old firebrand! He should have been a movie star with his explosive personality. I think the stage wasn't big enough for him. Politics is his stage. Leon greatly admires David Ben-Gurion, which is hardly surprising. They are both Polish, a few generations apart, but men of a deep similarity."

"I am not surprised," said Nathan. "Leon was born to debate and orate. His whole personality crackles with fire. Perhaps we may see him as Prime Minister of Eretz Yisroel one day."

"Israel," Melissa corrected him releasing her grip. "I must leave now. Would you walk me to the station?"

★★★

Throughout the remainder of 1947 and the early part of 1948 Nathan would meet up with Melissa when time allowed for both of them. Melissa was extremely busy rehearsing for the Old Vic's theatrical productions. Even in conversation Nathan sensed how besotted she was with her profession. Any man competing for her love and affection would have to compete with the theatre, which was of far greater importance in her life than any romantic interest. When he could, Nathan would divert the subject on to their past lives especially their mutual years on the kibbutz. Deep down Nathan had an overwhelming need and desire for Melissa, but somehow this want of her love was never to be satisfied. Her career always came first.

They would meet in the city or backstage at one of her plays. Sometimes they would walk through Hyde Park to the Serpentine and throw bread to the swans and the ducks. Yet anything more intimate than a kiss on the cheek, or handholding, never came to fruition.

Nathan never gave up hope that he could make her fall in love with him; even up to the day that Melissa left with the Old Vic on its Australian tour. It seemed somehow fittingly ironic that the day of her departure was February 14th, 1948, Valentines Day, and a particular occasion festooned with all the romantic feeling that such a day brings.

Before Melissa had left her flat that day there had been a card and flowers delivered to her. Strictly in accordance with the anonymity that was traditional to Valentines Day, the card was not signed. Melissa recognised the writing on the card. *Dear Nathan*, she thought. She took the mixed bouquet of flowers and put them in a vase. It was touching and romantic. Melissa hugged each of her three flatmates, all pleasant English girls she had developed a great affinity with, and then with her two suitcases she entered a waiting taxi to take her to Euston Station. From there Melissa would travel by boat train with the entire company of the Old Vic to Liverpool and sail from there on the long voyage to Australia.

Nathan had been waiting at Euston Station for a couple of hours in the hope of seeing Melissa just one more time before she left. The importance of the occasion could not be underestimated. It was a Saturday and there were crowds of people waiting to glimpse Sir Laurence and Lady Olivier and members of the Old Vic Company. Nathan anxiously looked around for Melissa. He could not see her. He could see the stationmaster, resplendent in top hat, obviously enjoying the day. There were photographers eagerly flashing their cameras non-stop at virtually anything that moved. There were the dignitaries and celebrities in attendance and relatives and friends fare-welling the members of the company. Nowhere was Melissa to be seen. Nathan was just about to give up and leave when he saw her walking through the crowds at the station. He breathed a sigh of relief and moved forward to greet her.

"Here, let me take those," he said, reaching for her cases.

"Thank you for the flowers and the card," Melissa said. Nathan said nothing but looked at her admiringly. It was then that Melissa put her arms up around him and kissed him gently on the lips.

"You look splendid, Melissa. Absolutely splendid," he said, absorbing the moment for all that it had been worth. "I shall miss you while you are away. It has been so good to see you these past months. I really feel that I've recaptured much of my life seeing you again."

"I have felt much the same."

"Are you excited, Melissa? Excited to be travelling again and so far?"

"It is going to be so thrilling. I will write to you, I promise, Nathan."

"We better go," said Nathan, and he picked up the cases and walked with her to the platform.

"Incidentally, Nathan, for professional purposes I have changed my surname. I am no longer Melissa Meiletz; I am Melissa Campbell. I think my agents feel the name is better remembered when I am cast in future stage and film productions."

"Melissa Campbell. I will look for that name in the future," said Nathan pensively. They stopped at the platform, and some film and television cameramen came charging past. The object of their intentions was to record on film the presence of Sir Laurence Olivier and Vivien Leigh, who had arrived amidst all the people at Euston station.

"What a remarkable couple they are," observed Melissa. "Even here they generate such presence." Turning to Nathan she embraced him. "Goodbye, Nathan. Thank you for coming to see me."

"Goodbye, Melissa. You are a wonderful woman." He had no sooner spoken than he was the recipient of another kiss from Melissa. There was such a sense of finality about the moment that Nathan couldn't interpret it. All of a sudden Melissa had raised her cases and disappeared into the crowd on the station. Nathan watched as the train pulled out, bound for Liverpool. By early evening Melissa would be on board the *Corinthic* with the members of the Old Vic bound for Australia. The *Corinthic* would berth in Fremantle, Western Australia, in four weeks time where the tour would commence.

Melissa wrote to Nathan often during the next few months. The first letter that Nathan received was addressed from Capetown, South Africa, where the ship stopped over for two days. It was not so much a letter, more a hastily written note in which Mellissa briefly described the city and how she had gone to the top of Table Mountain, but every communication from her was important and Nathan felt encouraged that she had taken the time to write to him. The next piece of correspondence he received from Melissa was postmarked Perth, Western Australia. It was a descriptive letter that Nathan felt inclined to read over and over again. Melissa described Perth as a "bright, sparkling city with beautiful trees, parks and gardens, and the most wonderful blue sky". In the same letter Melissa went on to write about the reception afforded the Old Vic's production. The Australians were, she wrote, the most wonderfully responsive audience, especially when, on the final night in Perth, the members of the Old Vic at the finale of the play burst forth into a rendition of 'Waltzing Matilda', which sent the audience into a mood of absolute delight. Nathan smiled at the thought of this for he knew from his meetings with Australians how patriotic a people they were. Melissa closed her letter by saying how she would write as the tour progressed through Adelaide, Melbourne, Sydney and New Zealand.

Even though Nathan was fascinated by Melissa's travels, he tried to stop his mind from wandering, and he put aside all nomadic thoughts to concentrate on his studies. At the university Nathan had befriended a young man from Africa's Gold Coast, of his own age, whose company he always found enjoyable. They often spoke to each other not only of their studies but also events occurring in the world today. Tony Landero, the son of a Lawyer, had a car and occasionally on a Sunday they would drive out into the heart of the English countryside. The Sussex Downs were a particular favourite with Tony as he had a friend from Africa who worked at some nurseries in Lindfield.

Often they would drive down pleasant country lanes on balmy summer days when the trees and the Downs looked a luxurious velvet green set against a mid blue summer sky. After a meal in a pleasant olde-worlde village pub where flat-capped villagers chatted in a wonderful Sussex burr, while Nathan and Tony enjoyed a traditional ploughman's lunch, they would then leave these amiable oak beamed, trinket littered surrounds and drive to the top of the Downs. The view from the top spread across to the seaside villages of Worthing and Goring one way, and in the other direction outspread beautiful green and orange fields with the appearance of being cut in neat rectangular shapes. Nathan and Tony sat at the top chewing cuds of grass and absorbing the view.

"I love England so much," said Tony in a moment of revelation. "I have found it a delight to be here. It is giving me a worthwhile education and days like this that I shall always remember when I go back to Africa. I think that my coming here was a sort of predestination."

"Predestination?" inquired Nathan puzzled by the usage of that particular word. "What do you mean Tony, when you say predestination?"

"Predestination. Predetermination, Nathan," mused Tony. "It is a school of thought that I believe in. It means the belief that our destinies in life were determined by God; that we are not so much the determiners of our goals but the predetermined, the passengers being swept along by circumstances and fates that we are relatively powerless to avert."

Although the words seemed to belong to a deep thinker and an intellectual, Nathan could relate to them. It was easy for him to interpret their meaning in the sense that it applied to his life.

"You believe then that you were meant to come to England to study?" said Nathan without humour.

"In my way I do," Tony agreed. "The colonies abroad that belong to the United Kingdom produce the raw materials that I see so often here: stationary, pencil lead, coffee, tin, meat, metals. I see so much merchandise from colonial origins. If our colonies in Africa are to produce the wealth, then the producers of it must have a good education and training, and that is why I am here. You know, Nathan, it is not only the engineers, and the plantation managers who need an education but also the lawyers and the economists. Our education here will be of benefit to Ghana and the work of our industries in Ghana will benefit England."

"And what happens when your country gains independence, as I'm sure it will one day?" asked Nathan out of curiosity. He was interested because only recently Nathan's spiritual home, Palestine, had been declared the Independent State of Israel by Prime Minister David Ben-Gurion on May 14th, 1948.

Tony chewed a long straw of grass and thought carefully before answering. "When that day comes," he said spacing the words out in a definite tone, "I am sure that once the initial negotiations and decisions are made, then it will be simply business as usual. It will take some getting used to for both sides."

"Hmmm," Nathan murmured. "I was thinking of Palestine. At least it was Palestine then. Now it is Israel, and it has not become Israel without pain. Its struggles are not over yet. I wonder if ever they will be. I lived there for some years, perhaps the happiest years I have ever known. Yet I fought for the British and I am being educated here in this lovely country."

"One should never get too involved. The politics of one area often clash with another. I hope that eventually there will be leaders of pragmatism and rationalism, who are able to communicate with each other," Tony emphasised.

Nathan chuckled quietly to himself causing Tony to look at him with surprise. "What's so funny," he asked, a smile creeping over his face.

"Your fascinating usage of words, Tony," he replied. "Pragmatism and rationalism. I must do more reading."

"Also schools of thought," Tony pointed out. "I have studied them in great detail. There is existentialism, the doctrine I most believe in – that is the freedom of human beings to make their own choices and to accept the end results. Pragmatism, I see as being a particular behavioural outlook. In another interpretation, I see it as the method of putting an idea into plan, and the results that stem from its practical use. Rationalism is the most down to earth Philosophy that I can think of. Reason is the only real source of true knowledge. In future years when my studies are finished and I am once again in my home in Africa, if and when I have become successful as a lawyer, I may enter the political realm with a view to applying those theories."

"Why is it, I wonder, that lawyers often consider politics as a career after Law?"

"That is something I too have often wondered about. I wonder if it is the thrill of debate, the power of oratory perhaps. That is not the appeal to me, though. What attracts me to it is the cross section of work performed in a constituency; trying to understand the problems of the community."

Nathan smiled at him understanding his friend's motive. "Looking at this beautiful countryside, I think the Member of Parliament who has this area as his constituency is a lucky man."

"I agree," concurred Tony. "Come, let's go back to the car and drive around some more."

The two walked down the slopes of the Downs to where the car was parked and drove on. It was a pleasant day for them both.

They had a typical British afternoon tea of scones and jam in a village called Arundel, which had a castle and a high street littered with antique shops, and old style coffee houses set in beams that must have been structured in a bygone Elizabethan age. Further on at Amberley, Nathan and Tony sat by a pleasant estuary where the only sounds were of children and families laughing together as they took picnics on the banks. There were the sounds of occasional ducks or geese and the slow dip and splash of pleasure craft drifting along the fresh clear water. On the other side of the bank some village cricketers played in splendid gleaming white kit enhanced even more so by the power of the sun. Cricket was a game that Tony enjoyed enormously and one that Nathan had learned to love during his years in England. There was something tremendously exhilarating about the sound of a solid red cricket ball thudding against the linseed-oiled surface of a bat. Even more fascinating to Nathan was the organisation of eleven players, who occupied so many positions on the field with such intriguing names as 'third man' and 'silly mid on'. It was all so marvellously peaceful that afternoon that it seemed to Nathan almost like heaven. Another village called Storrington that they stopped at was a picture postcard.

Living in England, Nathan had grown to be aware of the huge depth of tradition, history, celebration and occasion in this country. In addition to his studies in Law, Nathan had read widely of England's history with a particular interest in the results of the Industrial Revolution as well as the biographical details of such varied people as Winston Churchill, Florence Nightingale, W G Grace, General Gordon of Khartoum and William Shakespeare. He had noted how Royal weddings and traditional anniversaries were celebrated with great enthusiasm, and how sporting events such as the FA cup, the Cricket Test matches, the Wimbledon Tennis finals, and the Oxford versus Cambridge boat race were observed with unflinching interest. Yet still with all of its universal appeal, Nathan knew that he wanted to try a new way of life.

In the evenings at Ealing Green, when Nathan sat and pondered over his studies, he would often have his wireless switched on to a programme such as ITMA Variety Bandbox, or one of the shows featuring the hit parade when the voices of singers such as Vaughn Monroe, Frank Sinatra or Perry Como would rise from the speaker. There was a jovial bandleader called Billy Cotton, and another man who sang, 'I've got a lovely bunch of coconuts'. There were also bandleaders like Edmundo Ross and the Victor Sylvester Orchestra. Tunes that Nathan would always connect with a certain time and place.

Letters came continuously from Melissa during the many months she toured Australia with the Old Vic. They came from Adelaide, which Melissa described as a city of churches, cathedrals and beautiful surrounding countryside with green rolling hills and blue mountains. For two months the Old Vic performed in Melbourne, which Melissa felt most at home in. Melbourne to her was a leafy, handsome, well laid out city with rolling green boneshaker trams, and the best parks she had seen with beautiful flowers and tropical vegetation. Her descriptions matched almost word for word that of the Australian soldier, Ted McTaggart, whom Nathan had met in Cairo. When Melissa got to Sydney the letters that came from her were full of description. Sydney, to Melissa, was a glamorous, sparkling edifice surrounded by water and attractive bushland that swept down the foreshores of the harbour. It was, Melissa wrote, a city where light seemed to saturate every building, tree, plant or person. Her glowing descriptions of warm summer days and the beaches of Manly, Bronte and Bondi, almost radiated a visual image from the pages of her letter to Nathan. Just the very thought of the places Melissa wrote about created an intoxicating feel. A real desire to see that hot, burning land; that wondrous sunburnt country.

Some while later Nathan received a letter from New Zealand where the Old Vic was completing the final part of the tour. Soon they would be returning to England. The thought of seeing Melissa again thrilled him. From the land of the long white cloud, the company would soon be sailing on the long voyage home. Nathan had wondered if in the six months or so that she had been away if there would have been any desperate longing on her part to make the relationship a more meaningful one, rather than the close friendship it had been up to that time. Would there have been a realisation on her part that she may have loved Nathan far more than she knew? Nathan realised that this was probably wishful thinking.

A few weeks later Nathan received another letter from Melissa with a postmark from Sydney stamped on the envelope. This surprised Nathan, because the date of the letter was a fairly recent one, and by now Melissa should have been close to completing the voyage home.

It had been raining heavily outside as Nathan entered his flat at Ealing Green with the letter tucked under his arm. Removing his trench coat and kicking off his shoes, he sat down and began to read it with interest. The first words of the letter seemed to strike him down with a curious impact.

'Dear Nathan, I have decided to stay in Australia…'

This surely was not possible. Nathan couldn't believe what he was reading. Surely Melissa would not leave the greatest theatrical company in the world to stay down under in a sunburnt country known more for its sporting achievements than any culture it may have had. But as Nathan read and re-read the letter it was clear that Melissa was in love with the easy-going Australian lifestyle, the people whom she found warm and refreshingly direct, and most of all she felt that, as the country was so young, it could spawn a new film industry and theatrical companies. Melissa wrote that there were opportunities to her there that she had never previously envisaged. Already she had obtained an agent in Sydney who was in the process of booking her work in radio plays in both Melbourne and Sydney, possibly a role in a stage musical, and also the chance of putting her wonderfully rich singing voice to good use in a series of engagements as a vocalist with a big band.

When Nathan had fully absorbed the contents of the letter, he walked across to the window and stared out at the London rainfall splattering itself on the windowpane. Melissa was far away the one woman that Nathan felt he truly loved and had always loved. The sun would be shining brightly in Sydney where Melissa would be starting her new life. Probably at this moment she could well be 'shooting through' on an over-packed Bondi tram as Ted McTaggart had once spoken of. Nathan smiled at the thought of it. It was now late 1948. In just under a year's time he would complete his Law studies. Looking at the rain, Nathan announced to himself quietly, "Now I shall definitely go to Australia when my studies are over."

Thirty-two

In 1949 Nathan finished his studies in Law at London University. It had been a long and tiring course of study, but it had been a profoundly rewarding four years. The course had prepared Nathan for a career in law, which he felt immensely proud about. Having had an unsettled boyhood being shuffled between Germany, Austria and Palestine, and having had to study at home with his mother before the war, and again by correspondence at the kibbutz, Nathan's success had been a real achievement. It had been a sense of self-help, and his own motivation, that had carried him through. Even after the end of the war, when he had finally accepted the realisation that his parents had died in the concentration camps, Nathan desperately tried to burn out the deep depression he felt by plunging headlong into his studies. He had virtually worked his way through the course by doing the delivery round for Jack Faley's greengrocer's shop. It had been Nathan's own efforts, plus the wonderful opportunity to study at an English university that had charted his course for the future.

Almost at once after passing his final examinations, Nathan prepared his way to travel to Australia. Now that Melissa had stayed on in Australia after touring with the Old Vic, it was almost an added incentive for Nathan to go out there. Melissa had been appearing in radio plays in Melbourne where she was now living, but very shortly she was to tour the States of Queensland and New South Wales as a big band singer. In her latest letter to Nathan, Melissa wrote that the agent had been true to his word and all of his plans for her had come to fruition

Nathan had scoured through Australian newspapers, which he had obtained from the High Commission in London, and had written to several firms of lawyers to establish references and possibilities of employment in Melbourne. Less than a month after applying to emigrate, Nathan was accepted and given a sailing date. It had all happened so quickly. yet it was thrilling to be going and so very sad too. In the last four years Nathan had become very fond of Jack and Elsie Faley and their sons, Mick and Ron. On his delivery round Nathan had got to know many nice people and he had grown to love the English. He saw Freddie Miller occasionally. Freddie was so often abroad on assignments that when he did return, he usually had little time to spare as he was so heavily embroiled in his work. Tony Landero, Nathan's fellow law student from university had become a close friend. Now Nathan was to say goodbye to all these fine people.

There is always something deeply sad about farewells. Nathan had said goodbye so often before in his life that it almost seemed par for the course. He could never forget the day he left the village in Austria to travel to Palestine. He had been so young then, a mere boy of sixteen, and the circumstances were different. He had been going reluctantly, although in response to his father's wishes. This time Nathan was leaving on his own accord. The decision was entirely his own, and he was twenty-seven years of age, entirely in charge of his own life.

Everyone turned up at the Green Man pub in West Ealing for Nathan's farewell. Jack and Elsie were on form laughing and joking and their sons, Ron and Mick, two of the kindest, friendliest people Nathan had ever known, were also in good spirits. All of the local people Nathan had met also turned up to say goodbye, and it was a surprise to him just how many took the time to wish him well. It seemed to Nathan as if everybody on his delivery round, from pensioners to people who worked in the local butchers and bakery, had come along, and he was almost moved to tears by their thoughts of kindness and compassion.

At the end of the evening Nathan walked home with Jack and Elsie, Ron and his adorable, sweet wife, Jill, who was by now several months pregnant, and radiant and glowing with it. Mick who was really a younger version of his dad walked with them, cracking a joke every now and again to lighten up the course of the evening which, although on the surface was filled with happiness and good will, was in reality a sad occasion.

Nathan stopped as they came to Ealing Town Hall, not far from where they lived. He turned to Jack and Elsie and the others.

"What is it mate?" asked Mick, slightly apprehensive of the change of expression in Nathan's face.

When Nathan spoke his voice almost quivered with emotion. He eyes looked as if they were about to brim over with tears.

"Jack, Elsie," he said quietly, "I can never thank you enough for the many kindnesses you have shown me. You have treated me so well. You have been like a second mother and father to me." Jack and Elsie looked moved as well. It was not in Nathan's nature to forget anyone. He turned to Ron, Jill and Mick. "Ron and Mick, you two have been so good as well. Jill, I hope you have a wonderful child." Jill smiled that wonderful warm smile of hers.

"It's getting a bit emotional for me, son, I ain't really one for farewells," said Jack good-naturedly. Then the tone of his voice changed to one of really deep sincerity. "But I'll tell you this, Nathan, old mate, you're a good fellow, and Els and I, we wish you all the best. We like you."

"And from us, too," agreed Ron. Nathan smiled at him as acknowledgement. They started walking again and a look of mischief came across Jack Faley's face.

"See that lamp post?" said Jack pointing it out.

"Yes," came a surprised reply from Nathan.

"Well I'll race you to the top of it!" He said jovially, and in a fit of fun, Jack and Nathan in a joking mood both ran to try and climb the lamppost. The others laughed while Jack, the obvious victor, pretended he was climbing it.

"Cor, nearly up it," laughed Jack. From out of the shadows a bemused policemen appeared "Now then, what do you think you're up to?" The policeman inquired. To the others this was even more amusing as the policeman was obviously a decent sort of man, not lacking in a sense of humour.

"Just having a bit of fun, mate. No harm intended," chuckled Jack coming down from the lamppost. The two men looked at each other in wry amusement.

"Grown man like you," said the policeman, "I dunno, you're as bad as a drunk I saw one night." By the way the policeman spoke, the others could see he was leading up to a joke. "Yes, he was banging on the lamp post yelling out, 'Let me in, let me in.' I said, 'Don't be silly, nobody lives in there.' He says to me, 'Course they do, there's a light on upstairs!'" The others laughed at the policeman's attempt to crack a joke. "Go on get out of it," he said in jest, pointing his thumb back in the other direction.

They moved on wards the Green feeling very jovial and in a very happy mood. That night would be the last one that Nathan would ever spend at Ealing Green. Tomorrow he would be sailing away to a new land and a new life. He had developed such an affinity with that suburb, the people he had met in his years in England, and rather than feeling excited about his forthcoming voyage, he felt more as if he was mourning a great loss in his life. Jack and Elsie and their sons had been so kind to him that his heart ached from the compassion and goodwill he had been the recipient of for so long now. Nathan had talked with Jack and Elsie until nearly two o'clock in the morning, and then fallen into bed feeling exhausted.

When Nathan woke after a smooth six hours of sleep, the birds were singing in the trees outside of his window. He rose and pushed up the window and looked at the plants in a window box. They were withering now and the petals had fallen. He would not be in England to see them bloom again next summer and the thought made him feel momentarily sad. Down below in the street, a red double-decker bus on its way to Richmond flashed past. Even that made him feel a little sad too, for it was the bus he had often taken with Jack and the boys when they had gone to see the game at Brentford Football Club. Car horns beeped in the early morning Saturday traffic, the sounds of accelerating engines of Morris Minors and Austin A40s hit the air, and so too did the sound of gear crunching and lorries revving up. Nathan absorbed it all that morning, memorising every last detail. The aroma of newly baked, fresh bread rose into the air from a local bakery where its employees were busy rolling and kneading the dough. From next door, the smell of sizzling bacon and eggs carried through the air. He knew that was Sid's wife preparing his breakfast before he went out to work as a cable jointer for the GPO.

Down the road, Nathan could see Jack walking his pet dog: a small playful brown and white haired terrier, who he too had grown fond of. Jack was, in essence, a working class gentleman. When Nathan had first met him, he had never been quite sure what to make of him, but now, as time had gone by, he saw in him all the old school qualities: honesty, decency, sincerity, good humour, and being a hard-working man who loved his wife and family above everything else. Nathan knew that Jack had lost his shop during the blitz in the war, and despite that he had moved from the East End to Ealing Green to take over a run-down old shop and, with the maximum of effort, had turned it into a thriving greengrocery business. Jack was certainly a man to be admired.

"Good morning, Jack," Nathan called out to him, waving.

"Hullo, Nat old son," Jack called back, doffing his flat cap and sparkling that old cheerful grin. "Another few hours mate and you'll be catching the boat train to Tilbury, eh? You'll be leaving this lot behind." The words seemed to catch Nathan suddenly and he felt overwhelmed by the sadness of leaving. "Els is laying some breakfast on for you. You better have a good hot meal to travel on. Come on down as soon as you're ready. Ron, Jill and Mick have all got a little present for you. By the way, your mates Freddie and Tony both rang this morning. They're going to drop in and pay their respects. I told them to drop round for breakfast, why not?"

"Thank you, Jack, that is so good of you," replied Nathan, and he put his head back inside and started to get ready for his journey. Once it had been Austria that he was leaving and Palestine that he was going to. Once, there had been Arthandur and Marlene, and the people of the Jewish community of an Austrian village, who had bid him farewell. Now it was a whole world away in England, and the Faley family were farewelling him on his voyage to Australia, and suddenly he could feel a rush of enthusiasm in him. The feelings of excitement seemed to blot out the sadness.

Downstairs, as Nathan pushed open the door, he had not anticipated that he would be greeted with the same sort of reception he had known the day he left Austria eleven years ago. There was such a similarity to that day; only the faces and the voices were different. It was as if Jack and Elsie Faley had been the spirits rising of Arthandur and Marlene. Only in the room before him were Jack and Elsie, Ron and Jill, Mick, Sid and his wife, Ruby, Jack's brother, Harry, and a whole host of friendly faces including Freddie Miller and Tony Landero. Nathan kept swopping images in his own mind. He could see the people in the Austrian village, then he could see the Faleys and their friends, and the similarity and the contrast between those two days triggered his emotions.

Jack stepped forward. "Here's to a jolly good fellow. C'mon everybody, hip-hip!" Three cheers of "Hooray" immediately followed on, and there was some hearty backslapping and handshakes. Nathan was almost in tears but he kept his reserve. "Better get your breakfast, son. It's a long way to Melbourne," said Jack showing Nathan to a place at the table.

Elsie had gone to a lot of trouble to cook a beautiful breakfast of lamb chops, eggs sunny side up, mushrooms, tomatoes, and some toast and marmite. Knowing Nathan's faith restricted the eating of certain meats, Elsie, as she had always done in the past when inviting him to eat with the family, had always been careful about the choice of cuts she had served. It was only a further example of the never dwindling thoughtfulness of the Faleys. There was good humour all round. Jack did his bit, joking and playing the perpetual jester. Freddie and Tony mingled happily, and then the jokes and the humour and laughter came to an end. It was time to go.

Young Jill, always pretty as a picture came forward with a large bag. Inside there were some shirts, a huge farewell card signed by all of Nathan's friends and a couple of books.

"This is from all of us," she said and she kissed him gently on the cheek.

"I don't know what to say. I am so deeply touched," Nathan wiped a tear away and he was a genuinely sensitive man moved emotionally by the warmth of human beings when they are at their kindest.

"Don't say anything, luv," said Elsie, who was holding back her emotions too. "Freddie and Tony have got a cab outside. They'll go with you to the station."

They were all outside on the pavement now and Nathan was shaking hands with everyone. Even Jack's little dog ran outside. Nathan bent down and stroked it. Today seemed to be the day for him being touched by even the slightest sentiment.

"Time to go, Nathan," said Freddie picking up his young friend's cases and putting them into the taxicab. Nathan shook hands with Ron and Mick, hugged Jill and finally found himself facing Jack and Elsie. The feelings were indescribable. Jack looked at him, with a look more of concern, but it was a mixed emotion he was experiencing.

"Well… well, goodbye, old son," Jack stammered, shaking his hand, and then forgetting his embarrassment, he moved forward and embraced Nathan in the type of hug a father gives to a son. "We're going to miss you, Nat," he said softly. "I reckon your old man would have been damn proud of you if he'd known how you've battled it out." Freddie, who was the only one present who had met Nathan's father, agreed with the sentiment. "Son," continued Jack in a voice that slightly faltered, "if you ever come back—"

"I will come and see you. That I promise," Nathan replied in anticipation of what Jack was about to say. He turned to Elsie and hugged her.

"Goodbye, luvvie. You take blemin' good care of yourself, eh!" she said, her eyes becoming slightly tearful.

Nathan stepped back and looked at everyone for the last time and somehow he managed to beam a warm and loving smile at them all. In the next moment he was in the taxicab, the engine was starting up, and he was sitting with Freddie and Tony waving to everyone on the Green for the last time. Jack stood with his arm around Elsie, and Nathan was waving to them until the cab moved to a road turning and he was on his way to Tilbury to board the boat and sail to Melbourne, Australia.

On the drive through the London streets, Nathan looked at the people and the traffic, and he genuinely felt that for his education at University here, he owed this country a great deal. In truth the past few years had been a very happy time for him. It was only his desire to travel abroad to a land that had long fascinated him, that was the real impulse for his departure, plus the fact Melissa, now in residence in Melbourne, was an added incentive.

At Victoria train station Nathan said his farewells to Freddie Miller and Tony Landero. This time Nathan did not feel as if he was saying goodbye forever to Freddie. Their lives had crossed in twists of fate in the past eleven years. Something prophetic within him told Nathan they would meet again. After shaking hands and promising to write to each man, Nathan boarded the boat train and headed off to Tilbury.

That same afternoon Nathan stood on the deck of a huge P&O liner as it sailed down the River Thames at the beginning of its six-week voyage. The boat was thronged with British migrants heading for a new life in the sun. There was a great sense of excitement about starting this journey and it seemed to manifest itself amongst the passengers who watched their home country recede into the past. The liner sailed out of the mouth of the Thames. During the course of it's voyage it passed by the North and South Forelands and the White Cliffs of Dover as it sailed from the darker, colder waters of the North Sea and the English Channel to the warmer climes further south.

In the next few weeks, the voyage was filled with new experiences and places for Nathan. Throughout the journey there were different shipboard functions beginning with the Captain's Cocktail party. There were shipboard fancy dress balls, a talent contest, a number of classes conducted by travelling immigration officers, which introduced the passengers to various facets of what life would be like in Australia. At the point where the ship officially entered the southern waters beyond the equator, a Crossing the Line Ceremony took place with a made up King Neptune and his Queen in flaxen curls bowing honours on the passengers. During the six week voyage the clocks seemed to be adjusted continually to make up the respective time differences accrued by the immense distance the ship was covering. More than once did Nathan hear the words, "Oh God, not another bloody hour," as the immigrants struggled to keep themselves in tune with the ever changing time scale.

Amongst the passengers Nathan was not unique in his nationality status. There were also Poles, Czechs and Scandinavian migrants who had found their way to England at the end of the war, and who were now amongst the British immigrating to Australia. From observation of his fellow passengers, Nathan concurred that it was a vastly cosmopolitan influx who were going out to make a new home in that great southern continent. Obviously there was something immensely appealing about Australia if it could attract such a diversified array of nationalities. What were the prime attractions? Nathan pondered this many times. Was it the fact that Australia was a relatively new land, untarnished by war and internal conflict that had been the way of many other countries? Was it the image of the bronzed friendly genial digger who'd fight like mad for a good cause and his mates, yet underneath the surface was a good-hearted bloke with a rough diamond, Galahad approach to most things? The fact that it was a peaceful, sunny land, still young and with potential for the individual with a sense of self-motivation and independence, must have outweighed all other considerations. Nathan knew in his heart that, providing he could accept his new situation and work to improve it, he would be able to make a great life ahead for himself.

Some idea of the distance between England and Australia could be measured not only by the six-week time span of the voyage but also the varied ports of call they visited en route. When the P&O boat had sailed from Tilbury after a meandering journey down the English coastline and into the channel, there had been a stormy passage through the Bay of Biscay. Then after passing the coastlines of Spain and Portugal, the boat passed through the straits of Gibraltar on an immensely clear day. The first port that the boat set down at was Marseilles in southern France. The passengers had a whole day and an evening to spend there. Marseilles was an attractive quaint port with fishing boats bobbing up and down the gentle tide. Nathan recalled from his meeting with Francine Macé, that this had been her hometown and it only added to his curiosity as he looked around Marseilles trying to envisage that golden suntanned girl spending her teenage years on the beaches and the waterfront.

A few days later the boat stopped at Naples. This reawakened old memories within Nathan. He had last been here eleven years ago when he had boarded a boat as a sixteen year old to travel away to a kibbutz in Palestine. It was so strange to be here again after all these years. The vibrancy had not changed in the busy Neapolitan streets: the car horns still beeped constantly, the washing still hung across the narrow streets, the pasta still abounded in the markets, and the streets were still crowded with throngs of people. Eleven years before he had only really passed through but the sights and sounds of then remained with him now. This time he had more time to spare and he made a quick trip in a taxi to the ruins of Pompeii, observing the sparkling grandeur that it once was. The same taxi driver, a chatty, jovial man, then took him to a vineyard high above Naples which could only be reached by a funicular travelling up a steep incline. Nathan spent an hour or so with the driver sipping red wine and looking at the view.

After Naples the boat glided through the familiar waters of the Mediterranean Sea on a long stretch to Port Said in Egypt. Again, Nathan's memories were stirred going back to his army service there. The passage through the Suez Canal took place on a limp and humid day. On either side of the canal great expanses of golden desert stretched for a seemingly infinite magnitude. On one side lay the Sinai and on the other Egypt, which Nathan had travelled across by jeep many times during the war. Occasionally, on the far horizon a camel and its rider could be seen. There was something magical about the sight of the lone rider in the desert. Nathan stood at the rails of the ship for a long time taking in the view and remembering the times he had been there. The liner steamed past Ismailia, a city he had once been stationed at, and he looked at it with interest. Once, he and his friend from the army, 'Private John', used to drive along the banks in an open topped jeep.

Beyond Ismailia and Lake Timsah, the liner continued its slow voyage south along the canal, towards the port of Suez at the mouth of the Red Sea. Surprisingly, the western bank changed contrastingly in its scenic appearance. There were many date palms and distinctive trees, and the bank was a beautiful deep green in texture. Agricultural land, yielding arable crop spread out in an orderly fashion where men toiled away in the heat of the day. Men in long robes rode donkeys along the banks, and Arab children dived into the waters for coins thrown by passengers from the boat. After passing through two more lakes along the canal, the Great Bitter Lake and the Little Bitter Lake, the boat eventually docked at Suez.

Not surprisingly, it became warmer and warmer as the boat travelled further south. In the Red Sea Arab Dhows sailed past and the hot sun above seemed to hang there taking its full toll on the passengers. At Aden where the ship docked, it was even hotter and Nathan tied a handkerchief over his head as a protection against the sun, not caring in the slightest how silly he looked. Aden was yet another eye opener to Nathan. Every port of call had different characteristics about it, different sounds and accents, smells and people.

The next port was Colombo in Ceylon. The island looked beautiful as the ship cruised into the harbour. The coastline was fringed with tall waving palms, and the beaches were of clear white crisp sand. Vegetation was a deep lush green, and the waters of the rolling Indian Ocean were an iridescent sparkling blue. In Colombo itself there were white buildings; the streets were filled with bustle. The Ceylonese women wore beautiful coloured saris. Men, also in bright apparel, walked along with goats and livestock. Nathan was intrigued by a snake charmer he saw in a market. At the same market he purchased, as a souvenir, some woodchip elephants to be used as a mantelpiece. Having heard that Ceylon tea was the finest in the world, Nathan bought several packets that had come straight from the plantations at Kandy and Nuwara Eliya.

When Nathan had mentioned to Freddie prior to departing that Colombo was a port of call his friend was quick to recommend a spot he had visited during the war. Freddie mentioned Mount Lavinia, and Nathan made a journey outside of Colombo to this place. He took lunch at the Mount Lavinia Hotel, which was a huge colonial building overlooking the attractive coastline. It was almost too soon to leave this island of enchantment and mystique.

From Colombo the liner sailed south on the final long stretch to

Australia. The days passed with the constant, endless sunshine. Many migrants sat up on deck all day to obtain a good suntan before they disembarked in their new land. Sometimes other ships or strange fishing vessels passed by.

Eventually, their destination came into view. Just before breakfast one morning the early risers amongst the passengers sighted the North West Cape of Australia. It was a strange shade of orange and brown intertwined together depicting the aridity of the barrenness of that part of the country. The returning Australians aboard spoke of the scent of eucalyptus drifting from the shore. It took nearly two days for the ship to cover the complete coastline to Fremantle, an indication of the immense size of Australia.

Fremantle, Western Australia, was Nathan's introduction to his new country. The boat was guided in by some tugs on a warm Australian summer's morning. At the wharf a lone bagpiper played 'Waltzing Matilda'. Twelve thousand miles Nathan had come and this was his first welcoming sound: the squawk and drone of bagpipes. 'Can ye no hear the pipes?' A Scotsman leaning over the rail asked Nathan who nodded. There were tin warehouses lining the wharfs. It was only when the ship pulled in close that an abundance of people could be seen waving from the passenger terminal at the dockside. At long last they had arrived. It felt good to be in Australia. On that first day there was brilliant sunshine. The sky was wide and deep blue, a more-deeper shade than Nathan had ever seen in Europe.

At Fremantle many of the ship's passengers disembarked for Perth. The ship had a whole day there. Nathan spent it looking around this attractive well laid out city. It was Nathan's first taste of an Australian city, and straight away he took to its easy-going feel. The wild flowers were out in full blaze in Kings Park, the waters of the River Swan sparkled clearly in the resplendent sunlight, and the Black Swans glided along in their distinctive manner. After looking around the city centre, Nathan took a bus through some of the pleasant suburbs such as Subiaco, Melville, Claremont and Cottesloe where Nathan saw his first Australian beach. It was a day when there was an enormous swell and the surf rose incredibly high, crashing down into splintering waves. The sand was golden and so soft Nathan felt it could sift like flour through his fingertips. He sat there on Cottesloe beach, a long time just taking it all in, the smell of salt spray, the sound of the waves rolling in on the beach, the squawk of the seagulls and the laughter of sunburnt little children playing with their families. He was a newcomer to this land after all, and everything he saw tended to make an impression on his ever alert, ever absorbing mind.

But that first day was wonderful because he saw in a glance so many of the good things that Australia had to offer before he had time to equate and measure its material benefits. Environmentally it was superb, clean and unspoilt. And it was warm, not just in the golden sun climate but it was warmth from the people, the good-hearted Australians who even in the every step of their daily walk along the sunny Perth streets, seemed to generate the goodwill that Nathan would know for years to come. There was a definite easy-going atmosphere that came through immediately. City businessmen made their way to their destinations wearing sunglasses and light office clothing, and more often than not, shorts and long socks. Office girls wore light cotton dresses, and in the heat of the day their suntanned skin and coiffured hair made them look absolutely spectacular. After a time of rationing in England, to sit in a Perth café and eat a huge T-bone steak and some rich cream cake was a sudden switch from austerity to pampered luxury.

Back on board the ship Nathan reflected on the day. It had been a simply stunning introduction to his new country. There was something so good about what he had seen in Perth. The boat continued its journey sailing across the Great Australian Bight to Adelaide. Every night on board there was community singing. It seemed as if the whole ship's passengers and crews wanted to celebrate the arrival down under.

Adelaide in South Australia was a very beautiful city, although it was a city in stark contrast to Perth. Nathan was to discover that each of the major Australian cities had a character of their own. In Adelaide Nathan saw a combination of architecture with strong English influences. Many of the churches and older colonial type buildings seemed as if they had been transplanted from England. The parks were a deep green with an array of flowers and palms. Strolling along King William Street, office and government buildings soared on each side, with people scurrying along to work. Nathan took a tram to Glenelg beach, and after a few hours there he returned to the boat for the final leg of his journey.

In just a little over a day's time Nathan would arrive in Melbourne. It was beginning to excite him: the prospect of a new life, all the different experiences he would soon know, and seeing Melissa again. He had written to Melissa from London. At the time he knew that Melissa had been touring Australia as a big band singer, and just where she was domiciled was anybody's guess. Nathan had written to her last address in the suburb of Prahran in Melbourne in the hope that his letter would reach her.

The night before the ship arrived in Melbourne, it seemed as if everyone on board wanted to stay up and enjoy their last emotional farewells before disembarking. After Melbourne the ship would carry on its voyage to Sydney and Brisbane before returning on exactly the same route it had come but this time it would be taking home migrants who had not settled, and Australians travelling on their first trip to Europe.

News had been received that there were dock strikes in Melbourne and Sydney. The passengers travelling to Sydney and Brisbane would have to wait in Melbourne for some days before the dock dispute was resolved and the ship was able to continue its journey.

When Port Philip Bay came into view it was at the point in the evening as the sun began to sink and darkness fell, so Nathan arrived in Melbourne at a time of an almost golden autumnal sunset. From the boat it had a pleasant appearance about it.

The dock strike created a delay for disembarking passengers. It was up to the ship's crew to unload the passengers' cases and crates of furniture and all their worldly goods. There weren't any cranes being operated on the wharfs to unload all the passengers' cases. The whole disembarkation process was very low. To cap it all, rain had begun to fall heavily. It was not until very late that night that all the passengers leaving the ship at Melbourne finally were able to continue on to their destination.

Nathan boarded a bus that had been sent from a migrant hostel to take many of the new arrivals to what would essentially be a temporary home while they established themselves in their new land. The bus started up and soon they were travelling from the dockside area of Port Philip to the outer suburbs where the migrant hostel was situated. It was raining so hard outside that Nathan could see little of his port of arrival.

Just after midnight the bus arrived at Brooklyn migrant hostel in the suburb of Footscray. The rain was still falling heavily as the newly arrived migrants were shown to their quarters in the black of night. Nathan found himself tramping through the mud to a tiny spartan box room where he put his only suitcase on a creaking wooden bed. He looked around him at the drab surroundings. It was bare and austere, but for the time being it was home. Unpacking his suitcase he looked at the minimum belongings he possessed. They included some shirts and books the Faleys had given him, his de-mob suit, a few pairs of baggy trousers, a leather zip up flying jacket, his law books, professional certificates, documents and an album of photographs, a light fawn jacket, assorted ties and underclothes, and eleven pounds two shillings and sixpence.

Tomorrow he would start looking for work. For the moment, he felt excited. He had at last arrived, and he was enthusiastic to get going. When he got into bed that night he listened to the sound of heavy rain pelting down hard on the corrugated iron roof above him. He smiled to himself, as he thought that he might shortly see Melissa. Perhaps there would be sunshine tomorrow.

Thirty-three

Brooklyn migrant hostel in Millers Road, Footscray, was a Nissan hut complex. It was not untypical of migrant hostels throughout Australia at that time. There was almost a feeling of desolation about it. It was situated in an area where there were few houses, although many were in the process of construction. The nearest beach was at Altona, which was either a long walk or a bus ride down Millers Road past a huge refinery that flared up into the sky. To get to the city centre was a combination of bus and train travel.

Early the next morning Nathan looked at his new surroundings. The rain had stopped. It was a clear, fresh sunny morning without a trace of cloud in the sky. The grounds surrounding the hostel were still densely muddy. Almost conspicuously amongst the huge shed-like dwellings was a luminous tree spreading out against a periwinkle blue sky. It was in an odd position between the hostel buildings, but its sole presence seemed to indicate isolation. There was a canteen where the migrants entered to have breakfast. When Nathan sat down with the other migrants he found himself seated alongside the Poles, Hungarians, Italians, Greeks, Irish, Scottish, English, Yugoslavs, German, Dutch, Austrian, and people from the Baltic region. There was not a European nation it seemed that was not represented in the hostel. The breakfast was most prolific. It comprised of a T-bone steak, two eggs, enough to fortify Nathan through a day when he was going to call on the various law firms he had written to from England.

With some directions he had obtained from the manager of the hostel, Nathan made his way into the city of Melbourne. Coming out of Flinders Street railway station, he was at once struck by the Anglo-European influences well entrenched in the city buildings and thoroughfares. Even Flinders Street station looked as if it would be equally at home in Paris or Berlin. Green trams filled to bursting point rattled down the wide streets of Swanston, Elizabeth and Collins, big wide boulevards teeming with shoppers and businessmen. In the huge department stores of Myers and Buckleys Christmas shoppers packed into an already overfilled area in stifling hot temperatures soaring around the hundred degree mark.

During the course of that first morning Nathan visited several law firms regarding the possibility of work. Neither the first nor the second firm he went too could offer him anything at the present time except words of encouragement and welcome. On his third attempt Nathan was greeted by an Hungarian lawyer who had come out to Australia before the war, and who knew the trials and tribulations of a European making his way in a new land. He was a man of kindly disposition. He spoke to Nathan for a long time, inquiring into the details of his background and education. The Hungarian was very impressed when Nathan told him of his efforts to learn at home in Austria under the guidance of his mother. Nathan went on to speak of his self-motivation in studying through a correspondence course in Palestine, and how he had worked his way through university. Realising it would be a while before Nathan could begin a career in chambers, the senior partner offered him a temporary administrative job with the company lasting several months after which time he could jettison himself to another firm with the knowledge he had gained. Although the job was purely of a clerical nature it seemed the ideal answer in his present circumstances. Without hesitation Nathan accepted the position and agreed to start the following Monday. He felt delighted that he had at least acquired some work in the short-term which would undoubtedly be a stepping stone to something bigger and better in the future. It would give him an opportunity to make inquiries to other law companies.

Nathan thought that he would call in at Melissa's last known address later on in the afternoon. First though he thought he would acquaint himself with his new city and he spent a while looking around at some of the parks that Melbourne was famous for. Crossing over Princess Bridge, which spanned the River Yarra, Nathan walked through the Botanic Gardens. The grounds looked beautiful in the sunshine. He walked past the gates of a huge, imposing house that looked for all the world like a stately home. It was in fact the official residence of the

Victorian Governor. Walking in another direction, Nathan found the Shrine of Remembrance. On Anzac Day, when Australian servicemen in that city remember the fallen of the two previous world wars, wreaths were laid by the President of the Returned Serviceman's League.

On St Kilda Road, which ran virtually parallel with the Botanical Gardens, Nathan boarded a tram to go to Prahran where Melissa had last written from. Nathan was bitterly disappointed when he arrived at the flat to be told by the new occupant that Melissa was still on tour with a band in Northern Queensland, but would be going to work in Sydney on a radio play after the final engagement. Melissa's agent had moved there and all her future engagements would be handled in Sydney. It would be a while before Nathan could get to see her again.

With the disappointment inside of him, Nathan went back to Brooklyn migrant hostel. He stopped at a milk bar-come-delicatessen opposite the hostel with the intention of buying a few household items. Behind the counter, an amiable cheery-faced man greeted him. Nathan bought some soap, toothpaste and milk and looked around at a few other things on display. His eyes rested on an old wireless on a shelf. He knew he couldn't possibly afford it but he thought he would ask anyway.

"How much is this?" Nathan asked the shopkeeper, who was watching him inquisitively.

"That?" said the other sharply. "It's not for sale." He paused momentarily.

"No, mate, it's not for sale. You're from that hostel, aren't you?"

"Yes. Just over there." Nathan pointed across Millers Road.

"And you've just arrived in the country? I guess you haven't got much of the old cash, eh? No wireless either?"

Nathan was a little disarmed by the man's frankness. "That is right," he said quietly.

The shopkeeper picked up the wireless and gave it to him.

"This is yours, mate. Welcome to Australia."

Nathan was a bit dazed by the man's sudden splurge of generosity. He did not know what to say. The man was smiling at him, almost as if he himself was thrilled to be giving this new migrant a helping hand.

"The name's Mac," he said, outstretching a huge hand. Nathan guessed the shopkeeper to be about fifty. He had a warm, friendly face with a sparkle in his eyes, and thin hair the colour of straw.

"That is very generous of you. Thank you. I must give you something towards it." Nathan reached into his pocket but the shopkeeper stopped him

"Nah, don't worry about it. Well what do you think of Aussie, then? She's a beaut, isn't she?"

Nathan looked at his newly acquired wireless and then at Mac. "Yes, she certainly is."

From then on Nathan thought all Australians were marvellous. Mac went out the back and returned with a bottle and two glasses. He filled both of them and toasted Nathan. It was Nathan's first taste of an Australian beer. Since Nathan had left Palestine, although he in spirit was still faithful to his Jewish upbringing, he had more or less followed the rule of living like a local wherever he was. It wasn't until many, many years later that he returned to his orthodox origins.

He sipped beer with Mac on that first night in Melbourne, and they talked about so many things. Mac was a lovely man. He was kind-hearted and cheerful. Nathan was to learn later on that Mac had given help to many newly arrived migrants at Brooklyn hostel. Often when immigrants had stepped off the boat penniless, Mac had let some of them have whatever they wanted on a 'pay me when you've got it' basis. It never failed to impress and delight the new migrants, who always came back finding Mac such a kindly and cheerful man. Mac was truly an unsung hero.

Nathan grew to love Melbourne, and its people. It wasn't a city of an international feel like the places he had known. It didn't fail to live up to its expectations. Ted McTaggart had described it to Nathan during the war in almost accurate detail.

In the golden Australian summer of 1949 and 1950 Nathan commuted to the city each day from the hostel. He began putting all of his knowledge he had gained from his law studies at London University to practical use. The lawyers at the firm were impressed with his capacity for hard work and his attention to detail. Nathan was not a person to whom class or status meant much. It didn't worry him starting at the lower end of the scale in a clerical position because he appreciated that dedication and hard work would bring the results. Besides he was in an ideal position to learn. He didn't demean his own position. He remembered his father Arthandur telling him many years before that all men who worked hard should be given respect, whatever their profession, no matter how humble. In his own position he didn't have the huge responsibility that a lawyer carries. His job was to provide the research details, certain facets of law, references, and any other information that might be required by the lawyer in court that day.

Nathan put his heart and soul into what he was doing. 'Enthusiasm is the name of the game,' Jack Faley had once expressed in a monologue. Nathan always remembered that. He truly believed that even the most menial task could be made more interesting and satisfying if a person approached it with enthusiasm.

At the hostel a number of migrants had found second jobs. Not far from Brooklyn hostel, there was an industrial estate at Footscray. There was so much work available that many of the factories had evening shifts starting round about five-thirty and finishing at ten-thirty or eleven. In the interim seeing the opportunity to get a good start in Australia, Nathan found work in the evening as well. He went straight from his job in a city law firm to the factory, changing into overalls as soon as he arrived.

The factory obviously relied on immigrants for its continuous turnover of labour. The work was hard, damned hard in fact. It involved working as part of a team on a production line manufacturing oil drums, canisters and containers. Depending on the requirements of the evening's production, the men were shuffled from line to line. The moment the production line started to operate it was sheer solid hard work. Long before the science of ergonomics had entered into industrial operations, it involved stretching, placing, securing, closeting pieces together as the line operated at high speed. If anyone made a mistake causing a bottleneck in the system, the production line would have to be stopped and cleared before it could continue. For the period of the breakdown the workers would be deducted an equivalent from their wages. There was absolutely no room for error.

By the time Nathan got back to the hostel before midnight he would be feeling aches and pains in his arms and legs from having stretched himself to such a physically arduous limit. No sooner had he got into bed than he fell fast asleep. By day he was stretching his mental capacities and by night he was exerting his physical attributes.

From this start, Nathan was able to get a great understanding of the problems facing migrants. He understood how tough conditions and a limited knowledge of the English language could take its toll particularly on migrants from non-English speaking countries. He could also see the great advantages too. At that time, the boom years were beginning. After the Second World War the immigration minister in the Labour government of Ben Chifley had begun the scheme that was to bring boatloads of migrants to Australia The minister, Arthur Calwell, had presided over the initiatives with great delight as the migrants began to swell the workforce and give an added impetus to post war production. The Liberal government of Robert Menzies, which had recently defeated Ben Chifley in the 1949 elections, had continued on with this plan.

To the newly arrived it really did seem that if anyone wanted to work the opportunities were there. It was not a condition that would always prevail but those in the work force, as if sensing this, took full advantage of it while it lasted. Nathan was surprised at just how quickly he had managed to accumulate a cash reserve from the combination of two salaries.

It was a long and tiring day for Nathan, but he thrived on it. He found that he could manage on less than six hours sleep. He was glad that at the end of the three months he would have some experience and knowledge of the judicial system. Beyond that time he would have to find some alternative company to carry on in the field he had chosen. For the moment he was content to continue with his two jobs. In fact so keen was he to accumulate a substantial nest egg that he found a third job. On a Saturday and Sunday evening, he worked as a waiter in a plush restaurant in Toorak.

Nathan's eloquent manners, and gentle nature, were an asset in this job. He had seen the job advertised in one of the great Melbourne dailies and had tried for it even without having had experience in waiting or having any knowledge of silver service and catering formalities. His first few months in Melbourne were becoming a time of learning and experience for him. He was learning the practice of law during the day, understanding the life of a working man in a factory by night, and on weekends he was serving the wealthy set of Melbourne in one of its most expensive and luxurious suburbs.

The restaurant in Toorak oozed wealth. Its seats and tables were finely polished and laden with shining silver and candelabra. Each chair had built in cushions and quilt back lining. The carpets were patterned, luxuriantly soft and Persian in design. The curtains were lined red and could be swept across the window if so desired by the tug of a cord. It reminded Nathan of a film set of the great house Tara in Gone with the Wind. Often, while serving, Nathan would casually eavesdrop into the conversations of the diners. They talked about a coming economic boom, the war in Korea, stocks and shares, and often there would be judges and barristers who were, for Nathan, the most interesting people to listen to as they discussed cases and law reforms that were needed.

Nathan had been chosen for the job more for his striking looks and good manners. Before commencing he always conversed with the headwaiter about just what to say if he was asked to recommend a good wine, the house special, or to give an opinion and description of the various courses of the menu. He was gaining knowledge all the time, and learning how to relate to different types of people.

When he travelled back to the hostel late at night, he was staggered at the world of difference and class between where he lived and where he worked. Even here in Australia there were class divisions. He prided himself that he could transcend those barriers. On a Sunday night he would be wearing a white bow tie and a dark waiter's suit and he would be service Chianti and turkey. The following night he would be in a Footscray factory stretching, straining and sweating as he worked on a production line. In the tea break in the factory he gratefully consumed a couple of doorstep sandwiches and a mug of strong stewed tea. During the day when assisting lawyers, he would plough through volumes of legal cases and references. Nathan thought only here in Australia could one have the opportunity to cover so much ground in so few months. He had the sort of opportunities to work that he could never have had anywhere else.

Nathan was so busy with his three jobs that his free time was virtually non-existent. Except for a Saturday and Sunday morning, every other part of the day was occupied. He had not made any friends apart from Mac, the shopkeeper. On New Years Eve at the hostel, Nathan had befriended a few Scotsmen who, although many thousands of miles away from home, had been determined to carry on tradition. Armed with lumps of coal – a strange part of that tradition, but an essential one – the band of Scotsmen, together with Nathan, made a point of calling in at every room in the hostel and having a social drink with everyone there. It was eventually about five o'clock the next morning when a group of weary, jovial revellers finally made it to their beds. In those first few months in Melbourne that was Nathan's only attempt at socialising. There were few at that time at the hostel who weren't doing a second job.

Melissa was constantly on his mind. Nathan seriously considered the possibility of going to Sydney after his stint with the law company had ended. He had enough money saved from his three jobs. He was in a good position to do so. Nathan's appetite to see more of Australia had been considerably whetted.

One Saturday night when Nathan was waiting at a table at the restaurant, he listened to the conversation with great interest. The headwaiter had told him privately beforehand that he would be serving an oil magnate and a cattle station owner from the Northern Territory. The two men would be there with their respective spouses. Nathan felt a twinge of guilt as he listened. He realised that he was being what the English term a 'nosy parker'. However, he didn't let that bother him too much. The oilman spoke of how he and a team of men had uncapped hidden reserves in the bush of Western Australia and expanded their operations considerably. When Nathan heard the share price he hastily jotted down the details in the kitchen in between courses and decided he would purchase a few.

The cattle station owner was Ed Mitchell, a man whom the headwaiter had described as a legend in his own lifetime. Nathan found the man to be quite unassuming. He had the face of a countryman, lined and suntanned, with his remaining hair a soft silver white in colour. His physical characteristics were that of the true territory man. He was strong and well built. When he spoke it was in a quiet slow paced voice Ed Mitchell had strong powers of description as he spoke of his huge property situated somewhere between Alice Springs and Mt. Isa. When he spoke vivid images came alive of cattle mustering, a property the size of England, and huge sweeping plains. It sounded almost breathtaking. Again Nathan took note of the company controlling the property, the Orange Tree Downs Proprietary Limited. Hearing that shares were available he made another note of the name. It would be interesting to investigate the prospect there of buying shares also.

More than anything the conversation reminded Nathan of Ted McTaggart's description of his own droving days. Before going to Sydney to see Mellissa, Nathan toyed with the idea of travelling to the Northern Territory.

After four and half months of working at three jobs, Nathan decided to drop his evening and weekend work. He only had a few weeks left at the law firm. For the first time he had leisure on the weekends. Sometimes he would walk down to Altona beach and spend a few hours there. More often than not if he was there earlier in the day, he would find himself the only one on the beach. He would walk along the fringes watching the waves cascade and looking out to sea where there would often be early morning yachters grappling with the varying weather conditions. Without his additional jobs, Nathan began to appreciate just how long and lonely a day could be. When he returned to the hostel at the end of the day he found a lot of comfort in the old wireless that Mac had given him. He would listen to the commercial radio stations and the Australian Broadcasting Commission. There was plenty to listen to: innumerable radio plays, live band broadcasts and overseas sports reports.

One Sunday evening Nathan sat alone in his room in the Brooklyn hostel. He was half listening to the wireless whilst writing a couple of letters to Jack and Elsie Faley, and Freddie Miller. The announcer on one radio programme signed off of a chit-chat and music show with a cheery "G'night, ladies and gents, it'll be a sweet tintara tonight." Then another announcer introduced a show called the *Drama Hour*. Nathan chewed on the edge of his pen as he wondered how to complete his letter to Jack. He was caught by total surprise when the announcer on the wireless spoke the words, "Ladies and gentleman, tonight the *Drama Hour* proudly present 'The Story of Mata Hari'." Nathan stopped to listen with interest. He had heard of the legendary World War One spy. The announcer continued the introduction. "And the lead role of Mata Hari is played by Melissa Campbell."

Nathan dropped his pen in surprise. Melissa Campbell! His friend, and love of his life was on the radio. Nathan listened as Melissa came across the airwaves. It was now 1950 and Nathan had not heard that voice since 1948. Melissa spoke her lines in a provocative, sensuous accent. Somehow that particular role seemed tailor made for her huge thespian talents. She delivered her lines in a thoroughly professional fashion that only served to demonstrate the skill she had acquired from her years in the theatre. The play was being broadcast live from Sydney, just five hundred miles away. It was almost as if listening to that broadcast was the deciding factor for Nathan. In another couple of weeks when his stint with the law firm was over, he would travel up to Sydney.

Thirty-four

Nathan had befriended an English couple called Gus and Jean who came from Staffordshire. They lived in the room next door to Nathan at Brooklyn. They were a very friendly couple with a twelve-year-old son called Robert. Both in their late thirties Gus and Jean were a little homesick at times, but they made the best of their lives. Gus had a love of anything mechanical. A motor mechanic by trade, he was currently employed as a long distance haulage driver. He was often away from the hostel for several weeks at a time when he would drive a vehicle across country, sometimes travelling to the real heart of the bush. When he was home at the hostel he would spend a great deal of time fixing up the cars of other migrants. There wasn't anything about cars that Gus didn't seem to know; from fixing the ignition timing to replacing the gearbox, Gus could do it all. They had a small car of their own: a well conditioned Ford Popular, which they would take out on weekends. If Nathan was free they would extend an invitation to him to join them.

Sometimes they would drive up to the Dandenong Ranges, and have a picnic in a quiet spot where the grass grew high, and they could view the city of Melbourne stretching to Port Philip Bay. There were other pleasure spots that Nathan would always associate with those early days in Melbourne; they visited Sorrento, Portsea, Werribee, Ninety Mile Beach, and drive along the Mornington Peninsula to Dromana and Arthur's Gate. If they ever went further afield it was to places like Glenrowan where the legendary, some would say infamous or notorious, bushranger Ned Kelly made his last fatal stand wearing a metal helmet and armour covering his body.

When Nathan had been working at the restaurant on weekend evenings, he had always been given a lift by Gus and Jean to his place of work on their way back from visiting a particular place. Now that he was entirely free of weekend commitments, they would drive to Ballarat, Bendigo or Geelong and not come back until fairly late when the days seemed long and sunny. On one of these weekends Gus confided in Nathan that he and his family had booked passage aboard the passenger ship Mooltan for England soon. Jean had recently lost her father and badly missing the rest of her family in Staffordshire, decided she wanted to go home. Gus, who had grown to like Australia, felt a bit disparaged at first. However, being a man who adored his wife and always put his family's welfare ahead of his own, after only two years here had decided to take Jean and Robert home. Before he left Gus was going to undertake one final long distance journey as a driver. One Saturday afternoon as they strolled around the old historic gold mining town of Bendigo, Gus explained to Nathan what he was going to do.

"We're all going home in about eight week's time. I booked passage on the Mooltan for us all. Jean misses her family and since her dad died she's been worried about her mum. I don't really want to go. Home is where the family is though."

"A shame you are going so soon," said Nathan in sympathy. "I am going to Sydney fairly soon. For a while at least, anyway; I have a friend up there I'm going to see."

"You're in a pretty good position to go," said Gus. "You must have saved a bob or two from those three jobs you were doing. Gosh, you put in some hours, didn't you, over the past few months? I'm off to Darwin the week after next on a long distance driving job. It's going to be my last fling here in Aussie before I go home."

"My job at the law firm finishes then. I've finished up on my job at the factory and the one at the restaurant. I never realised how long the day is. I shall be off to Sydney when you are on the way to Darwin."

"Why don't you go to Sydney the long way round?" suggested Gus, suddenly thinking of an idea.

"What do you mean, Gus?" inquired Nathan.

"Why don't you come up with me to Darwin in the lorry? It's a long way on my own. I'd love to have some company. I've often picked up passengers on the way. If you wanted to, maybe you could stay up in Darwin for a while. Or else, you could work your way across to Queensland and down to New South Wales. It's only a suggestion."

Nathan thought of the opportunity before him. It was a great suggestion. He could cover so much distance in the one journey. It would give him the chance to see much of the country that Ted McTaggart had told him of in the army.

"Gus, you've got yourself a passenger," said Nathan eagerly.

In the next couple of weeks Nathan finished up at the law firm and armed with some references, he prepared himself to continue his career possibly in Sydney if he decided to stay there. He made a point of thanking the Hungarian lawyer who had given him the chance to work there. The man wrote Nathan a special letter of reference, and told him to keep in touch.

On the day that Nathan left Brooklyn hostel, he went across with a present for old Mac, the shopkeeper; the man who had shown Nathan a great kindness on his first night in Melbourne by giving him a wireless set.

Just a while later Gus drove the lorry to Millers Road from the point of pick up. It was enormous; practically the length of one and half trams.

Upon its arrival, Nathan went into his room at Brooklyn and picked up his suitcase. When he had arrived there, he had little money and now, several months later and three jobs later, he had over two hundred pounds. From eavesdropping at the restaurant he had learned of some shares at a good price from the conversation between the oil magnate and the owner of the Orange Tree Downs cattle station. With every consideration that he was taking a hell of a risk, Nathan had bought nearly seventy pounds worth of shares in the two companies. He was leaving the hostel considerably better off then when he had arrived.

Gus kissed his wife Jean goodbye and said a few words to his son, Robert. When he came back to the hostel from Darwin, the family would be preparing for their voyage home to England.

Nathan clambered aboard in the passenger's seat of the lorry. Gus returned to the driver's seat and they started to move on the course of their journey to Darwin. It was a nice feeling to be on the move again, leaving city life behind. They drove from Melbourne through Geelong and Bordertown to Adelaide. There was a brief stop there where Gus had to take on a load. They then drove out of the city heading out into the wilds of the state into wheat country, scrub and bushland. The next stop was at Port Augusta where Nathan and Gus stayed overnight.

After leaving Port Augusta, the scenery became harsher and more varied, and suddenly the feeling of experiencing the expanse of the Australian bush became apparent. It really was breathtaking, not only for its size but for its capacity for bewildering the onlooker with its beauty, its harshness and its arid desolation.

Gus and Nathan pulled into Coober Pedy early one morning for breakfast. Even though it was just after the crack of dawn, everything in this opal-mining town had the appearance of being white hot. They took breakfast in a ramshackle roadhouse with a fly screen and several rotary fans swishing around trying to create a cool air in the already humid, tacky atmosphere.

It was a particularly long and dusty drive after they left Coober Pedy and drove through South Australia. The scenery became a mixture of red dust, green bush, scrubland, purples, yellow and spinifex, and as the day wore on, it became hotter and hotter. Often on the journey Nathan saw overturned burned out cars in the bush, beef cattle from a nearby station, itinerant Aboriginal workers, and the very occasional bridge or road working teams. On one occasion several big red Kangaroos bounded across the horizon. The desert of Australia had an entirely unique character of its own.

Crossing over the South Australian border into the Northern Territory, the heat was tremendous. When Gus decided to stop at one place comprising a pub and a petrol station, which hardly merited the title of town or village, Nathan felt gratefully inclined to consume a couple of ice cold beers. It was so hot that the beer literally exploded on the palate of the mouth, and cooled his insides with a soothing impact. *How could anyone live in the Northern Territory and not drink a glass of the amber liquid*, Nathan wondered?

Eventually Nathan and Gus arrived at Alice Springs, a town of grey bungalows, tree lined streets, a drifting Aboriginal population, wide deep blue skies, and a burning heat that didn't seem to dissipate even at night. Gus had to unload some goods there and take on a new freight. While Gus was busy Nathan took the opportunity to look around this frontier town, which Australians had, and still have, the greatest affection for. It was a town that conjures up in the imagination the pioneering spirit of the Territorians. Nathan climbed to the top of Anzac Hill, and outspread before him were the sprawling bungalows of the town. From this town a Flying Doctor base operated, ready to transport patients from outlining homesteads for medical treatment at a moment's notice. Into the town Jackaroos from the local stations rode in on horses. Nathan was impressed by what he saw. In 1950 it still had the hallmarks of a frontier town, although, as the years progressed, it would undoubtedly become a huge metropolis. Alice Springs was situated on the Todd River, except that the Todd was a dried up riverbank only filled with water after a period of torrential rain. Along the banks of the Todd Nathan looked around at the luminous trees and listened to the sounds of insects buzzing in the trees in the torrid burning heat.

Meeting up with Gus, the two of them had a massive meal of roast lamb and vegetables followed by syrup pudding and custard, and a pot of tea, at a hotel in Todd Street. It was the only meal available on the menu and despite the heat they ate the warm food. Nathan had to follow up with a glass of ice-cold beer to cool him down. He felt certain that he would burst from the heat otherwise.

From Alice Springs, Gus and Nathan drove to Darwin at the far north tip of Australia; they passed through places such as Ti-tree, Tennant Creek, Three Ways and Dumbaba. The Northern Territory could surprise constantly: red dust, green trees, huge lorries ploughing their way on dusty roads, cattle, artesian wells, lizards wandering out into the road with colourful scales, and gradually changing scenery with Buffalo and dusty drover's riding in the hazy sunset with dust streaming up behind them. The scenery changed from red dust to tropical vegetation the further north they progressed. There was a stop at Katherine, another frontier-type town with Aborigines and stockmen, and there was the occasional stop at places like Pine Creek and Adelaide River, or some far flung outpost of old tin shacks and bungalows. They drove further through cattle station country and finally came into Darwin, a bright clean looking town, with white buildings, tropical houses on stilts and an intense sweltering head.

Nathan helped Gus unload the entire contents of his lorry, and then bought the Englishman a meal of seafood at an outdoor café. Gus was only to stay for a couple of days, as he would have to collect another load and drive back to Melbourne. Nathan and Gus liked this cosmopolitan town enormously. During the war it had been badly bombed. Since finely reconstructed, it now looked superbly out across the Timor Sea. It was a thriving, friendly town with a heart as big as the Territory itself, and a population comprising Timorese, Chinese, Aborigines Indonesian and a great proportion of mixed Europeans. Darwin was noted for its superb seafood and in the sauna bath heat, Gus and Nathan tasted its delights.

A few days later they returned o the same route. This time however Nathan went down only as far as Three Ways. From there he would try and catch a lift across to Queensland and then eventually wind his way down to Sydney. At the roadhouse the two sat and had a couple of final drinks together before they each went their separate ways. Gus stepped down for a moment and looked outside at the lorries and road vehicles outside. He looked for the group of drivers who were having a meal, and went and asked if any of them could take a passenger. Gus came back ten minutes later with a big muscular man wearing a blue vest and a broad-rimmed hat. The man was unshaven and sweating profusely, but when he spoke it was in a good-natured, affable voice.

"G'day mate," he said, slightly pinching the rim of his hat, "Fella here says you'd be wanting a lift. I wouldn't mind giving you a lift. It's no trouble. I'm heading east towards Mount Isa, would that do you?"

"Yes, that would be fine," replied an exalted Nathan, knowing that Mount Isa was in Central Queensland, and halfway to his destination.

"Okay, matey. I'll be pulling out in about half an hour after I've had a bit of brekkie. I'll sees ya outside then. Oh, I'll be making a bit of a detour on the way."

"A detour?"

"Yeah, I've got to drop into a big property run by a bloke called Ed Mitchell. Runs a place called Orange Tree Downs. You mighta heard of it."

The mention of it brought a smile to Nathan's face. He had a chance to see the big station he had bought a few, if not substantial, shares in.

"I have heard of it," grinned Nathan, "and it will be a pleasure to travel with you."

The man smiled at him and walked off to continue his breakfast. Nathan carried on chatting to Gus until it was time for him to leave. The two men shook hands and Nathan watched Gus pull his lorry into action and move off. A few minutes later Nathan joined the other driver in his road tanker, and they were moving in another direction towards Queensland. The driver was an easy-going man only too happy to chat. He began telling Nathan about the owner of Orange Tree Downs.

"Yeah, old Ed Mitchell – he's one of the real characters in the Territory.

They reckon he was a bit of a boy in his younger days. Started work on the waterfront in Melbourne. Bit of a pro-boxer before the First World War, I believe. Naturally the legend goes on. Course he was a soldier at the Gallipoli landings. That adds a bit of dash to the story, doesn't it? Well when he came home from the war he went bush, and lived with a tribe of Abos up in Arnhem Land, so the story goes. Then he got work on Orange Tree Downs in the '20s when it was only a fledgling property. Ah yeah then he went on to become a ringer. He married the station owner's daughter, Roslyn, and when her dad, old man Jarvis, died, the two of them inherited the lot, lock, stock and flamin' barrel and turned it into a flourishing enterprise. Would you believe they found mineral deposits up there too? Now they're into mining and getting bigger all the time."

Nathan smiled to himself. The shares he had bought in Orange Tree Downs, although minimal, could be a huge boon in years to come. At once he chided himself because he realised that he was in danger of getting caught up in the ever-winding spiral of making money his God. It could become self-destructive. He was curious about Orange Tree Downs, and was interested to know a little bit about its history.

"Do they employ many people on Orange Tree Downs?" Nathan asked.

"My word they do," answered the driver. "My mate Alec Taylor's the foreman at Orange Tree, and he tells me they employ altogether, including the staff on the mines, a good hundred or so. Big turnover, mind you. Blokes coming and going all the time. Old Ed's got a big heart. He's a real hardened fella. I s'pose that comes from his hard upbringing, but I'll tell you what, sport, back in the Great Depression when the people without jobs were going bush and looking for work, if any of them turned up at Orange Tree Downs, he'd always take a bloke on, give him a feed and some work, and some good quid in their pay. Oh yeah, old Ed he's hard in so many ways, but in others he'll always give a bloke a fair go. I'll tell you, mate, if you turned up there and asked for work he'd find something for you."

Nathan turned to look at the driver quickly. An idea flashed through his mind.

"Do you think I could get work there?" Nathan asked, astonished at the prospect of working on a cattle station.

"Sure! No problem. I mean, they're always looking for blokes. I could ask my mate Alec what they've got going. I'm not being a doubter, but you don't look like a bloke that's done outside work."

"I used to work on a kibbutz in Palestine," Nathan intercepted quickly.

"A kibbutz? What's that?" The driver quizzed him.

"A kibbutz is a farm. A community working together to produce crops collectively. I used to sow crops and drive a tractor, and I know about poultry. It was one of the happiest times of my life."

Nathan was very convincing. The driver looked impressed.

"Sounds like you'd be right then. I'll tell Alec when we get there. He might be able to fix you up with something."

The journey continued and the combined heat of the bush and the lorry engine caused Nathan to feel drowsy, and as the day wore on he grabbed some sleep where possible. Several times he roused himself, blinked his eyelids and stared outside at the barren landscape. It seemed to be so flat with only the occasional tree spaced at unequal intervals. The driver was whistling to himself and keeping his eye on the horizon. Nathan slipped back into a sleep again.

Half an hour or so later, Nathan was jolted out of his sleep by the driver shaking him. Nathan stirred quickly. The huge lorry's engine was still reverberating under him.

"What is it?" Nathan asked, rubbing his eyes.

"Outside," the driver indicated. Nathan swivelled in his seat and looked out at the flat green scrubby land with numerous cattle grouping in herds. "And this is only the start of it," the driver continued. Nathan looked bemused. The driver recognised the look of bemusement on Nathan's face. "This is Ed Mitchell's property. This is Orange Tree Downs."

Nathan looked out again and he studied the scene before him. It was broad, dusty and expansive. Red dust and green scrub, and an incredible white glare that made the eyes squint. The sound of cattle mooing, and whips cracking as jackeroos on horseback struck the ground with their stock whips forcing the herds to move in a particular direction, was a rousing spectacle. Nathan remembered the movie *The Overlanders* he had seen one fog filled night at Ealing Broadway a few years before. It was unbelievable to him to be here in the very scenery he had seen on film.

For the rest of the trip Nathan talked to the amiable driver. The man was right. This was only the start of Ed Mitchell's property. The size of Orange Tree Downs was simply beyond comprehension. It was not until one was on a cattle station this size that a person could realise the thousands of acres that had to be controlled by the owner. The distance to the actual station quarters itself took almost another day to reach from the time they had first entered the boundaries of Orange Tree Downs.

The property house and the quarters for the employees were quite striking when they came in view. The house where Ed Mitchell and his wife and family lived was of a large colonial design. There was a veranda completely around its perimeter. The house was three-storeys high and it had an atmosphere of supreme grandeur about it, almost an air of nobility. To Nathan the house was a strange structure to be situated in such a barren country as this. Nearby the windmill-type fans of artesian wells rotated at a creaking pace in the hot stillness of the desert air.

The jackeroos quarters were some way from the main house. They were less austere, a series of light wooden huts painted white and gleaming in the sun. This was where Nathan would live if he found work here.

The driver pulled the lorry into the property grounds. He and Nathan unloaded the contents onto the ground outside and then the driver went inside to one of the huts to see his friend, Alec Taylor. Nathan stood and looked around him. It was the silence of the North African desert, but the smells and the colours were different. Obviously everybody was out working. There was no one around. Nathan stood wiping his brow when the sound of a couple of voices came across from the background. He turned around and saw the driver in the distance talking to someone who he automatically assumed was Alec Taylor. The driver pointed to him, obviously mentioning to the foreman that Nathan was seeking work. Alec was nodding his head, smiling and laughing, and a few minutes later the driver returned.

"I told you, didn't I?" said the driver cheerfully. "Said you'd get work here."

"How did you get on?" Nathan could see that the man had been as true as his word.

"I told Alec your story. Said you'd done a bit of work on farms in Palestine. He wanted to know if you rode a horse. Couldn't remember you mentioning it, but I presumed you did, so I said, 'Yes, he's a rider'. Yes, Alec's got a job for you if you want it. They need a few blokes to ride the boundaries. On a station this big the boundaries are pretty flaming long, I can tell you."

"What would I do – riding boundaries?" inquired Nathan.

The driver grinned at him. His passenger wasn't acquainted with much of the jargon and the phraseology he had used on the journey.

"Well – see, a boundary rider, he's a bloke who rides along the fences of the station boundaries. What he does is fix any broken fences, y'know, where the cattle have broken through and wandered into the station next door. You might have to round up some of the stray cattle and bring them back. Course, you'll check the cattle by the station brands. Wouldn't want to be sneaking off with any of the other station's cattle. Goes on a bit, I know. They call it podgy dodging. But anyway you'd be out riding a boundary for days on end, maybe weeks. You'd be packing a bit of tucker, and camping out, but it's decently paid, and once you're on your own, you can take it as it comes."

Nathan considered it for a moment. The apparent solitude of the job quite appealed to him. It had almost a romantic lure about it; the thought of being a lone rider set against a burning desert landscape filled him with excitement. He could do this job for a while. Gather more experience of life in the process, and to live in the Territory would surely be an interesting episode to look back on in future years.

"Youse still considering it?" persisted the driver, noticing the pause that Nathan was taking to make up his mind. "I'd grab it if I was you. You're still a young fellow. Could be the chance of a lifetime."

"What do I do?" said Nathan.

The driver pointed to one of the huts. "Go down to that hut and sign on with Alec. You'll have a whale of a time here at Orange Tree Downs. They're a good bunch of fellas here. Go on, mate. Alec's down there waiting for you."

Nathan reached into the cabin of the lorry and pulled out his only suitcase. He looked around the station and mused at the fact that he had a few pounds worth of shares in this property.

"Now I shall be a boundary rider," Nathan said with almost a chuckle in his voice.

"And it'll be an experience you'll never forget," replied the driver in a jovially predictive manner.

Thirty-five

Life at Orange Tree Downs in the Northern Territory was different. It was a man's life, something far remote from a day's work at any office or a factory, or a period of study at University. Here on this massive property the men were big hearted and hard-working. The day started before dawn as the red sun rose in the horizon and the silhouetted figures of jackeroos on horseback began to muster cattle. They rode across the horizon like men from another time. It was easy to see why a man could grow to love this land and its solitary lifestyle. Nathan believed that it took a special kind of man to live here. The Territorian's were a special kind of people. Without being chauvinistic or dismissive of city people, for a man to live here uncomplainingly would take a certain amount of tenacity, a love of isolation and quiet, and rigidity to nature's harsh contrasts.

Nathan took this new experience with all the zest of a swashbuckling conradian adventurer. For the moment anyway his studies in law and his desire for Melissa happily faded into the background. His life on the cattle station presented him with the thrill of exploring the Northern Territory by horseback. That in itself was a rare gem amongst the shinier jewelled moments, which had been the composition of his life so far.

Clad in a broad-rimmed hat and typical jackeroo boots, shirt and trousers, he looked the part. Riding a horse had not been the problem he envisaged. He had taken to it really well and developed a love of horses. He had needed to; on the long rides by the boundaries, a horse was his only companion. Out there in the real dead centre of the bush, a horse was given great respect and affection. Treat the beast well and it would serve its master all of its days.

To begin with Nathan had been shown the ropes by several of the older jackeroos. They had ridden with him showing Nathan the great length of Orange Tree Downs. After a while he was ready to embark on the long solitary rides himself. Often at the station Nathan would return to his bunk in the dormitory that berthed the jackeroos, and he would listen to the yarns spinning. The ringer himself always told tall and highly embellished tales of times gone by, almost as if it was his duty to do so. They told stories of legendary horse-breakers, chance encounters with a mate in an outback pub, the characters that were the cooks who came and went on different stations. There were stories of long spells of droving over great distances, talk of the 'largest cattle drive ever' – 'was it back in '46 or '33?' Nathan listened long and hard to these big muscled men of the Territory, and all the time he noticed how their eyes glowed with enthusiasm as they spoke, and he laughed happily with them as a master storyteller liberally laced his anecdote with a raunchy rough style of humour.

Long hours of sleep were necessary if a man was to survive the rigours of the day. The days were long and arduous, but they were full and exciting; this was the real Australia, the stuff of dreams and imagination. At night the exhausted men would tumble into their beds and put a mosquito protection net over them, and all too soon, their energies, sagging from the day's toil, would send them into slumber almost immediately. In the very early morning before dawn on the day of Nathan's first solo boundary ride, Alec Taylor, already up and dressed, strode into the dormitory banging a tin plate loudly.

"Okay, you blokes. Rise and shine! C'mon, everybody up! This is not the Hotel Australia."

Sleepy jackeroos stirred from their slumber, some with faint smiles of amusement as they looked at Alec exercising his foreman's authority.

"C'mon boys. C'mon gents. Brekkie's good this morning – beefsteak and eggs. That's worth moving your backsides for. Where's that new boundary rider?"

"Over here," replied Nathan sitting on the edge of his bed tousling his hair.

"Righto, Nathan – it is Nathan, isn't it?"

"Yes."

"Okay, Nat. Your first ride on your own. See the cook before you go and get him to give you a fair bit of tucker before you shoot through. You'll be in the saddle a few weeks. Make sure your water containers are full, but don't forget there are quite a few waterholes along the way.

You'll be meeting up with a bloke called Joe Patterson at Spearhead Creek. He's been camped up there for a while in a makeshift humpy. Joe's been chasing up some of our wandering stock. I'd appreciate it if you gave Joe a bit of a hand and stayed up there for a few days."

"I'll do that."

"Good, Nat. You've got your maps and your route sorted out?"

"Certainly; the men instructed me where to go and what to do if I needed help. I should be fine."

"That's good, mate," Alec said slapping Nathan firmly on the back and moving off quickly to rouse all the men.

There was one big communal shower, which all the men entered. Nathan had been more than a little embarrassed to walk naked into a huge shower room with everyone totally starkers. It reminded him of one of the Roman orgies he had read about except that no one seemed to notice the other's nakedness. They were all too busy trying to scrub up a lather. That was difficult as the outback water was hard and it was not easy to create soap bubbles. It surprised Nathan that the heat, even at such an early dawn hour, was already of a high temperature. When he had turned the cold-water tap on, to his surprise the water was more than just lukewarm, it was hot. He didn't dare risk turning the hot tap on.

Breakfast was taken in another area, a hut strictly set aside for meals. The morning 'tucker' at such an ungodly hour of five-thirty was a bit hot and heavy, but knowing the hours of toil ahead of them, the men on the cattle station wolfed down cereal, steak, eggs, tomatoes, damper bread, and pots of tea with a hearty appetite. Soon afterwards they mounted their horses and rode off in search of the stock.

Ed and Roslyn Mitchell, after a lifetime of living at Orange Tree Downs, were early risers by nature. They were up and on horseback, and watching the men move off in the early morning light. The Mitchells kept themselves to their own confines, and were rarely seen by the station staff. There was no doubt that Ed and Roslyn were a formidable team, running the station and its associated companies with a rod of steel. Roslyn was tanned with a leathery skin, and most of the time she wore trousers, a white shirt and a hat. Her appearance was hard, she had a steely gaze, but the sternness of her profile could change quickly. If something amused her, Roslyn was capable of breaking out into laughter, and her hardness would turn to mirth. Ed always seemed to be so quiet and deep in thought.

Even when Ed spoke a person would have to lean forward to listen to him. It was hard to believe that such a quietly spoken, genteel man, could have led such a varied knockabout life, and that he was considered by many of the Territorians, not only to be a shrewd businessman, but also something of a legend.

Nathan rode out soon afterwards, his saddlebags weighed down with only the bare necessities for his long horseback ride. He considered it all so unbelievable. To actually be here and in this sort of situation was something of a fantastic journey. What would his parents, Arthandur and Marlene, think of the curious and mixed life he had led so far?

The boundaries that Nathan rode on that first journey were to take him through some of the most beautiful, harsh and varied scenery he was ever to travel. Many miles of flat undulating country were covered fairly easily without any problem. The sun was the only intruder. It seemed to hang there with such glaring light that it could constantly make both horse and rider squint their eyes. Dust and flies were the only other accompaniment on the long ride in the first day. If Nathan stopped momentarily to drink from his water bottle the flies suddenly swarmed up in droves and his horse would shake its head angrily. He would then jerk his horse into movement rather reluctantly.

The flat, bare, orange-green distance seemed to stretch for infinity before him. He did not realise that this would be the normal scenery he would survey for several days, until slowly and gradually, rocks, palms and vegetation would rise up and the view would be something quite different. For the first part of his job there were few sections of the fence that needed repairing. Until nightfall when the stars twinkled in a purple sky, it was a slow, casual, meandering ride. At night Nathan camped by the side of the fence boundary of Orange Tree Downs. There was something romantic about the quiet of the outback at the peak hours. With a blanket roll bed he unfurled and lay down on, it had a touch of individuality about it that could only belong in the yarns of the bush.

In the early hours Nathan would rise from his makeshift bed, and have a bushy's breakfast comprising of some tea boiled in a Billy can and some food cooked in a tiny pot over a charcoal fire. He had already been forewarned by some of the stockmen how easy it would be to start a bushfire if a person was careless. Nathan watched the flames like a hawk aware of the danger that one stray spark could create even on flat scrubland like this.

After tending to the horse, Nathan continued on his journey, repairing broken fences where necessary and checking for any wandering stock that might have crossed over into the adjoining property – an equally big station called Alexandria Downs. This was his routine for several days.

At long last the scenery before him started to change. Before him there were rocks and ridges in shades of red, brown and auburn, and there were tall palms and graceful spectacularly ice-white ghost gums. After days of riding across so much rain-starved earth it was like encountering an oasis. Nathan checked the maps that he had been given before he embarked on his journey. He discovered that this point was a place of significance, a waterhole, where he could bathe and refresh himself. He cantered on, diverting slightly from his fixed route along the property boundaries.

Riding into the shade of the palms and the gum trees he found a crystal clear valley of water not huge in depth or length but of a substantial size. The banks of the waterhole were a reddy-brown in colour and, with the surrounding green and white tones of the trees and the flame red of the cliffs and rocks, the sun's rays produced a startling reflection in the smooth, unrippled surface of the pool.

Nathan let his horse drink from the waters. He sat there in the shade, which even now was a staggering temperature hovering around the century mark. He felt the beard growth around his face. Nathan realised that he was filthy and dusty and in only a few days of riding his clothes had accumulated much red dust from the desert air. He leaned forward and looked at his reflection in the waters. His face looked sunburned, brown and dusty, and was he imagining it or were there lines beneath his eyes. He was only twenty-eight years of age, too young for age to show. Not bothering to sit uncomfortably any more in the hot temperature, Nathan removed all his clothing and soaked it and hung it out to dry on the branches of the gum tree, and then he entered the refreshingly cool waters of the pool. He was amazed at the red dust that came off his naked body. It had almost become ingrained in his hair and skin. Taking a bar of soap he cleaned himself from head to toe, and using a razor he shaved the beard from his face. The water was so cool and luxurious that he splashed around in it, and dipped up and down for ages creating ripples in the pool that, with its crystal clear reflection, had previously been like a still life colour composition of the surrounding scenery. The temptation to stay longer was enormous but he knew he had a job to do, and very soon he was back on track repairing fences.

On one occasion he found several cattle that had recently broken into the next-door property. The Orange Tree Downs brand on the cattle's back was unmistakable. Nathan rode after them and chased them, yelling and shouting and brandishing a stock whip that he struck on the ground until the stubborn creatures responded and headed back into their home property. Swiftly afterwards Nathan took the precaution of securing the fences tightly.

There was no doubting the size of Orange Tree Downs. By horseback the realisation of its magnitude was obvious. A week after leaving the property Nathan found himself in the absolute wilds of a hot big distance, the shimmering haze of the sun's rays playing on the horizon line and the infrequency of gum trees. His horse was beginning to tire, plodding along at a slow pace. Nathan rode the animal under the shade of one of these trees with huge outspread branches, and with a container of water he filled a carrying pot for the horse to drink from. Nathan removed his hat and mopped his brow. To his amazement in the wavy heat lines in the distance he saw something move far away. It was an animal of deep red in colour about six feet tall.

Nathan stopped and stared blankly ahead of him. All of a sudden several chocolate brown figures with jet-black hair seemed to emerge in stealth-like movements from the shade of other trees. Nathan stood fascinated by what he was seeing. He was watching several Aborigines wearing only loin clothes creep up towards a big red kangaroo. He held on to the reins of his horse and stood in the shade, absolutely still and silent. The Aborigines were of a remote tribe who wandered across Arnhem Land and the Barkly Tableland. They lived on their wits and their natural impulses. The diet of Aborigines would not have been to Nathan's liking. He understood from what the stockmen at Orange Tree had told him that the nomadic tribes ate witchetty grubs, kangaroo meat, lizards and goanna. They had a fierce look about them, and their physiques were lithe and slim. Nathan could hear them speak in their tribal dialect.

In one of the more curious moments, one of the Aboriginals stood directly in front of the kangaroo rubbing his stomach in a movement that the animal immediately began to imitate. It was a clever ruse designed to lull the kangaroo into a false sense of security. Immediately it was caught off guard as another man from the tribe lunged forward with a spear. Within minutes the dead kangaroo was carted away. From the trees and the enclosing vegetation sprang up about fifteen Aboriginals, men, women and children. The kangaroo's carcass was roasted on an open fire; it was obviously the big meal for them all. Nathan stood watching with interest. He was quite intrigued by these people, and was totally absorbed in his concentration.

A hand suddenly gripped his shoulder. His heart almost stopped beating with shock. Nathan turned round sharply to find himself facing one of the Aboriginals. He was tall, lean and fuzzy haired. He had painted markings, wore a thin rag around his middle and carried a spear. He said something to Nathan that he couldn't understand, naturally enough because the language was in an Aboriginal dialect. Nathan could however interpret the gist of the words. The tribesman was asking Nathan to follow him in the direction of the feasting. He decided to follow apprehensively, and pulling his horse behind him, he joined the small entourage.

One of the Aborigines, upon seeing Nathan, tore off a piece of meat and handed it to him. Nathan felt a bit bemused. The others virtually ignored him apart from a couple of stern-faced nods, although some of the young children smiled at him. Nathan took the meat and reluctantly ate into it. He did not like it at all. Yet, having no wish to offend his fellow diners, he chewed it, and made pretence that he was enjoying it. He stayed for a while, communicating in sign language. He tried to understand the nomadic tribe by watching the expressions on their face and trying to decipher the meaning of their words by the tone of their voices, and the intonations in their syllables. He was not successful, but he did manage to obtain one distinct impression. It appeared that malnutrition was rife amongst them. A few of the tribe looked distinctly sallow and ill. When he returned to the station he would have to ask someone about the welfare of these people.

Nathan eventually left the group, and took up on his ride again. His brief meeting with this Aboriginal group had made an indelible impression on him. It was something he would always remember.

Just over a week later, and very much further on, as he was nearing Spearhead Creek where he was to meet up with Joe Patterson, there were huge rocky ridges on one side of him. The colours were bronze-red, interspersed with purple shades and green trees rising up the escarpments. Again, curiosity got the better of Nathan and in order to assuage his fascination with this land he rode up and onto the ridges. He was above a wide craggy canyon with boulders perched perilously on the edges. Down below there was a gaping chasm and a mixture of broken rocks and trees growing in tufts of breakaway earth. It was almost as if an earthquake had once occurred, and the huge gap had not sealed. He rode cautiously along the tops of the ridges. He seemed to be riding higher and higher until the top began to level out. He rode around two massive boulders, and then he jerked the reins of his horse sharply. There was a vast empty space before him. Nathan had ridden the horse right to the very edge of a precipice. Manipulating the horse back slowly, he dismounted and led the horse away from the edge. He took the reigns and carefully tied them around a rock. For a few moments Nathan stood at the pinnacle of the ridge gazing out at the view before him.

Visibility was excellent. Beyond his vantage point he could see the great expanse of Orange Tree Downs stretching to Spearhead Creek some miles away in the distance. Now Nathan knew why that particular spot was called by that name. From above, the water flow created a shape that looked exactly like a spearhead. The water flow came from the trickle of an estuary, which in turn was connected to a river. So clear was the visibility that one could see that the river flowed from the Gulf of Carpentaria. Nathan checked his map.

"Ah ha, so that is Spearhead Creek," he said to himself with a smile. Looking around himself, he thought that tonight he would camp up here on the ridge. He considered it an ideal spot. The shelter of the rocks would make good accommodation. *A bank robber or an escaped convict would have envied this place*, Nathan thought to himself with some amusement. He still had a long ride to Spearhead Creek, but it was within a day's ride now.

That night he settled down on the top of the ridge and boiled a Billy, as he had so often done on his solitary journey. He had gotten so used to having meals in this way that he was beginning to enjoy the solitude and peace of the bush. Here all the worries of city life dissipated completely. There wasn't competition, crowded traffic, fear, or the continual chase of great material wealth, prestige or position. It was spacious, free, peaceful, sometimes unforgiving, and desperately lonely. Yet Nathan knew that as he sat by a small fire, drinking a mug of tea with only the flames rising and the twinkle of the stars igniting the dark night sky, he felt completely at peace with himself.

He thought of the Aborigines he had met about a week before. They had been the only sign of human life he had encountered in his journey. He couldn't stop thinking of the condition they had appeared to be in. Nathan recalled that one of the elders had obvious signs of glaucoma. The whole group of the Aboriginal men, women and children, all looked as if they had been suffering from a great degree of malnutrition. In the future Nathan would become an advocate of better care and help for the Aboriginal people.

Before going to sleep that night, Nathan walked around the various caves between the rocks. In the moonlight some of the caves seemed to glow with the powerful beams playing on the mixture of rock formation colours. On the inside of one cave there were more contrasting colours. Nathan stopped to inspect it. This one was different. There were engravings and paint markings on one side. He stood absolutely mesmerised by what he saw. He was in a cave that an Aboriginal tribe had once used, perhaps generations before. In this timeless land he saw before him an example of the traditional artistry of the Dreamtime people. It had been painted with a unique style. The shapes of animals, trees and tribesmen had been descriptively drafted into the rock. All the shapes had been portrayed in an acutely accurate manner with a colouration that would have matched its real life counterparts almost exactly. These wandering nomadic men, who lived almost primeval lives by city standards, had unusual talents in the fact that they could paint the ceremonies and activities of their people. Their artwork was a craft of its own.

It was eerie being in the cave. Nathan felt as if he had trodden the hallowed ground of some forbidden territory. He took a last look at the painted rocks and then returned to his camp bed. He lay down and looked straight up at the remarkable night sky that seemed to stretch forever and ever. The accumulated tiredness of the day caught up with him almost at once. He closed his eyes and began to dream. He dreamed of Austria and the old goat herder, the snow-capped mountains, and Arthandur and Marlene. No matter how far he had travelled, no matter how great the extent of his isolation and loneliness, even out here in the Australian desert memories of the past could still affect him.

When morning came it brought the squawks of a flock of birds flying over the desert. Then Nathan squinted as the rising sun flickered into his eyes and the morning glare cut low down so that he had to shield his face with his hands. His dream of bygone days in a mountain village in Austria had been terminated. He wasn't a boy climbing the mountain paths in that far off pre-war time. Instead he was a bearded, itching boundary rider alone in a vast expanse of a hot dry, breezeless scrubland. How much he desired another shave and a dip in another cool waterhole. Nathan sat up and pondered for a moment or two. How sad that the early childhood days of his life had gone like a streak of lightning in the sky, that he hadn't cherished these more. The reality of life as an adult, compared to the naivety and dreamlike existence of a childhood world, were at such diametrical opposites with each other. Even now Nathan found it hard to believe that his boyhood in Austria was a whole world away and that it was actually him waking up on a ridge in the wilds of the Australian desert. He stood up and gazed out into the distance.

The outback was God's own country. It was a wild harsh beauty. At least that was what authors with great descriptive ability had glamorised and romanticised, but to Nathan Palmai, with red dust in his hair and sweat soaked clothes, this land was God forsaken and bore no comparison to the one that supposedly flowed with milk and honey. The stark reality of it was so clear to his eyes now. It was harsh, brittle, coarse, a combination of red-yellow ground with an occasional shrub, and if there was a beauty in this rugged land it was clearly a personal view in the eyes of the beholder. Yet, if truth be realised, Nathan adored it, and even he was at a loss to understand just why.

For miles ahead there seemed to be ground of the same rain starved earth with only occasional tropical vegetation allotted around at infrequent intervals. To the eyes of the boundary rider he could sense no validity, no purpose, no promise for this dusty moonlike surface that lay before him. Unless one enjoyed solitude, a trenchant fierce sun, and a scarcity of water, he could see nothing that would be worth meriting a mention of in some far off bar where people made easy amiable conversation. At once Nathan's conscience caught him off guard. How could he think like this? On the surface the country was lonely, frightening even with the silence that was more effective than the noise of the rumbustious cities on the coastline. The harsh rays of the sun beat down on the wide, vastly exposed, land that lay unchanging for an infinity. It was almost a land in suspended animation, unchanged since primeval times.

But if one could not solely judge the scenery of its harshness there before him was some of the finest cattle country in the world. It was resource rich, with innumerable mineral deposits, as yet to be yielded to its fullest potential. It had a history of which had been made by unique explorers like Burke and Wills who had perished in their attempts to cross this land. This had long been the home of the Aborigines. The people of the dreamtime had survived in such conditions, roaming across the territory surviving where others would find it impossible to do so. In all of its great wilderness and splendid magnitude, it was a magnificent country.

It was time to start travelling again. After a breakfast in the shade of the rocks on the ridge, he rode down the escarpments back to the final part of the track that led to Spearhead Creek. This morning it was unbelievably sticky and humid. The perspiration ran from Nathan's forehead like a waterfall. There was the aura of an oncoming storm about.

By the time Nathan reached Spearhead Creek the humidity had reached an uncomfortable peak. In the distance he could see many head of cattle drinking from the water leading to the creek. All he had to do now was find Joe Patterson, who he knew would be pretty close by. He rode along the banks of the creek until he saw a stockman on horseback some way away riding amongst the cattle. The man acknowledged him with a wave and rode up to him, a wave of dust streaming up behind him as the horse pounded its hoofs.

"Joe Patterson's the name," he said with a friendly smile. He was in his forties and tanned so deeply, his skin was almost mahogany in colour.

"Nathan Palmai," replied the other. "They told me at Orange Tree Downs to give you some help for a few days."

"I sure can do with it," said Joe. "Let's round up a few of these fellas and we'll put a brand on them, and afterwards we'll try and herd them together, and get them close to where the good feed is; can't have these boys without a decent meal."

In the next couple of days Nathan tasted his first real piece of stock work. This was something straight out of *The Overlanders* to Nathan.

He enjoyed riding after the cattle and rounding them up. In his heart he was convinced that every man has the latent spark of adventure within him just waiting to be ignited when the opportunity arose. Nathan felt that this was his time, and he made the most of it. Branding the cattle was a tough job. Joe was obviously well versed in this area. It still took a lot of skill for two men to use all the strength they could muster to manoeuvre the cattle into a position where they could brand them. For Joe's age, he was a remarkable carefree rider. He took amazing risks riding at a pace that would have frightened many younger men.

Joe Patterson was a versatile man. He told Nathan of his early life. Joe had always worked on sheep and cattle stations apart from his army service and there was little about this way of life that he didn't know. All day long they worked very hard without any let up. Even in such tremendous heat, Joe carried on relentlessly doing the one thing he really knew how to do, work hard. Nathan followed Joe as they did everything that was necessary.

After Nathan had been there for a few days he prepared himself to go back to the main property at Orange Tree Downs. Joe needed some help in droving some of the castle to an area that they could put the stock out to pasture, and Nathan agreed to stay on a while longer. He didn't mind. Joe was agreeable company.

Sitting on the banks of the creek that night they talked of many things. If Joe was basically a simple man, he was very straightforward and honest as well, he was also well read. He revealed to Nathan that he seldom rode anywhere without a book of poetry. Somehow poetry didn't seem to fit in with the hurly burly of Joe's character. In this, Nathan was pleasantly surprised. Obviously amidst the toughness of Joe's bush ways, beneath that character lurked a man with a sentimental heart and a soft appreciative nature of gentle words linked in prose.

Joe drew on his cigarette and blew a ring of smoke into the hot night air. He talked of his past, his real sensitivity to life adding a touch of humility to his lean laconic appearance. It was a vulnerable side of Australians Nathan had not seen before.

"Yeah, I always recall when I was a kid in Adelaide how hard life was for my family. Dad was a true battler. There were eleven kids in our family, but it was a happy home, you know. Even though we were in dire poverty we still had a lot of laughs. I guess that's the way it is with a lot of hard up families. Funny thing but up here I've a lot more than I've ever had in my life, even out here in this wilderness." He swept his hand out. "I spend so much time on my own that I've almost forgotten what it's like to relate to people. So I read a lot. Always get a few books when I'm in town to bring back with me to read out here. Why I say I've got a lot more now than I've ever had is because I learned at a late age some of the good things in life that I didn't appreciate when I was younger. Sometimes I read poetry out loud here. Even write a bit."

"You write poetry?" Nathan asked with surprise.

"Fair dinkum! Don't look so surprised," Joe replied with a smile. "Had a bit published in a book of bush poetry. Read quite a bit of the work of some of the Australian poets. People like my namesake, Banjo Patterson – he wrote 'Walzing Matilda'. Henry Lawson, Breaker Morant and Will Ogilvie. When they write about the bush, the mulga and Johnnycake, you can almost smell it. I wrote a piece about swagmen and sent it off to a publisher in Sydney. My word, I was thrilled when I get a letter back saying they'd publish it."

"I would like to read it sometime," Nathan said with enthusiasm.

Joe reached across to a saddlebag and pulled out a book. He raised it up in front of Nathan. It was the opportunity Joe had been waiting for.

"Bush poetry," he smiled and thumbed through the pages. The moonlight seemed to illuminate his face. "I'll read you my poem." He opened the book to the correct page and showed Nathan. "There you are," Nathan looked at the page. It was titled 'The Way of a Swagman' by Joe Patterson. Joe beamed with delight. It was his absolute pride and joy. He began to read, and as the night hours began to fall the depth of colour made a huge difference to the whole rock structure of the desert and the vegetation, as dark shadows began to merge with the iridescent glow of the sand and the white gum trees creating a much more startling and sensuous landscape. A deep red sky intertwined with the purple blackness of the night and the chandelier sparkle of the stars gave the country an added touch of prosaic beauty that could have come from the brush of the most distinguished of artists. In fact the thoughts entered Nathan's mind that perhaps God was the artist and this strange harsh land merely an experiment for his portraits. Somehow Joe's rich voice full of timbre and resonance as he read this poem matched the background perfectly. The words of Joe's poem drifted into the night air, every phrase, and every intonation was as clear as the creek water.

"*Where go I that I may go, in peace and solitude,*
That I may find life free of worry, devoid of tension, free of strain and struggle,
unhappy anger, sadness and upset,

If I could be a wandering man not tied down by city life, by mortgage, dept or spouse,
But free to walk the lonely track where once the pioneer did road,
And to recreate the legend of a valiant man looked down by some and scorned by others,
Yet this man is noble, honest and solitary, he carries his blanket roll and billy can and makes his bed beneath the stars,
Works for a meal, lives for the day, finds the night a comfort, the dawn introduces him to a new horizon,
The gentle swagman winds along the lonely track across land made of a sedimentary rock and fire coloured earth,
To different towns and faces and every day as the day before is just a faded memory,
Oh where that I go, may I go like the swagman with blanket roll and billy can,
That I may go too in peace and solitude."

When Joe had uttered the last word he put down the book and looked at Nathan for approval. Nathan smiled his regard for Joe's literary efforts.

"Were you ever a swagman, Joe?" Nathan inquired.

"For a while I was, back during the Great Depression," Joe replied. "It was a tough time. I was a shearer in those days in South Australia. When the lay offs came I couldn't just go back to the city. There wasn't a job going spare then. So I trekked around the countryside. In '31 and '32 I was a plain old carthorse. I did backbreaking work like picking tomatoes and grapes at about six bob for every ninety-odd flaming buckets, would you believe? Geez, up here my life is a luxury compared to that."

Nathan immediately remembered a conversation with Ted McTaggart, who had told him of his experiences in the Depression.

"When I was serving in the British Army, I remember an Australian soldier I met who told me how he struggled through those years. Matter of fact, it was a station near here, Quentin Downs, that he worked on for a while."

"Quentin Downs? Yeah I know it." Joe re-lighted his cigarette. "I used to know a few blokes who worked there. I had a good mate there. He and I met up on the track a few times when we were swaggies in the bush. We met up cane cutting in Queensland and when we were both droving near where the station boundary lines crossed, we'd meet up and spin a few yarns and throw a bit of bull like most mates do up here."

"The soldier I met, his name was Ted McTaggart."

At this Joe's face lit up in a blaze of laughter.

"Well, I'll be. He was my mate! Old Ted, eh! And where did you meet Teddie then?"

"It was in a bar in Cairo. Ted was with the AIF and I was a volunteer from Palestine in the British Army. We met up again in the North African desert when the convoy of the Long Range Desert Group that I was in, met up with an Australian regiment. He was a fine fellow."

"For sure. He was a great mate of mine before the war. Last I heard of Ted he was in Cairns. Well that has to be one of those million to one chances you read about and wouldn't expect to happen in real life. Well, just fancy that!"

Nathan was smiling to himself at the fantastic chance of it all. He looked out at the desert and listened to the sounds of insects buzzing in the trees. He looked at Joe Patterson still exuberated by the coincidence and the sheer fate of both having had a mutual friend that the other had met at opposite ends of the world.

"Joe, you know Ted told me about the great Depression in this country," continued Nathan. "He told me of the homeless people living in the parks and on the outskirts of the cities. I can see when you write about swagmen how you write from experience."

"It was character moulding," said Joe with an air of conviction. "People who've never struggled, never known what it's like to be out of work, hungry and broke, they'll never know how much stronger and tolerant it makes a bloke when things get better." Nathan thought for a moment that there was an edge of bitterness, almost malice, in Joe's voice. But Nathan realised that the Depression and the war had hardened many people. "I'll tell you another thing too, Nathan, it makes people more compassionate. In the bad times people will pull together like we should do all the time I reckon. A lot of the things I've learned came from my mum and dad. They were the tops for battling their way through difficult times. I remember when I was about seven years of age, would have been 1915, me and my brothers and sisters were in this rambling old house we lived in, at the beachside of Port Adelaide. We were all sitting down at the table for the evening meal one night. My dad was looking really stern and moody. And he looked at us and scowled. I guess we all looked like grubby, untidy kids. Then dad growled almost in his moody voice that rarely revealed the generous, forgiving and encouraging spirit that was contained in his heart. He said, 'I honestly don't know why I bother sometimes. Your mother goes to a lot of trouble to keep you kids decently clothed, and you all come home as if you've been in a scrap. It's not a fair go, is it?' Then I could see a faint smile flickering across his face and Dad's voice had a different tone in it. More like warmth." Joe chuckled at the memory of it. "He then says, 'Look after the clothes you've got. Your mother and I are doing the best we can to make ends meet. Don't forget there's a war on, and I might have to go if that happens –… well, those clothes you've got are going to have to last you for quite a while.' My old man generally acted the part of the stern father. He cherished us kids I know." Nathan continued to listen politely. He knew that Joe had spent so long on his own that he was probably glad to talk in depth to someone. "There was another night I remember. Dad had a bad day at the factory and mum's day hadn't gone too well either. I was only seven. I was standing in the doorway watching them have one hell of a blue. They didn't see me standing there. When Dad told Mum he'd lost his pay, two nerves on edge went over the brink and there they were, accusations being flung from one side, insults thrown from the other. Dad was saying, 'Well, what the bloody hell would I do with it? I keep telling you, Nancy, some lousy bastard copped off with it.' Mum didn't believe that. I don't think she wanted to believe that. Poor Mum. She said in a shrill and angry voice, 'I s'pose you went and blued it on a flaming horse that ran last.' 'Geez, Nancy! For God's sake, Nancy, some lousy bastard joker whipped it!' The row became something worse than the normal. Venomous words crept into the insults. Two fiery tempers bubbled over the brink erupting into violent rages!" Joe paused for a moment. He had realised he was dwelling too deeply on something that had happened in the past and his eyes appears red and moist. When he continued speaking there were melancholic tones in his voice. "Anyway my dad in agony of spirit, puts his hat on and marches down the passageway, calling back to mum 'I'll be back later! I'm going to plead with one of the boys down at the pub to shout me a few beers – because by golly I need them.' Dad walked out, slammed the door, and he made his way off in the direction of his favourite pub. I knew he'd make it in time for the big swill and get a few beers inside of him, before the drinkers all staggered out onto the pavement in a drunken stupor. Poor Mum! Her eyes produced a flood of tears and as she cursed herself for having lost her temper, she suddenly realised I'd been watching. I'd been witness to the row. Being so young I had been a bit bemused by what I'd seen, what I'd heard. I was not quite sure what to do but I went to my crying mum and I did all that a little boy could do to console her. 'Mum, don't cry,' I said almost pleadingly. By this time I was crying too.

"My mother seemed glad of the assurance and she hugged me gratefully. All the rest of the Patterson kids were out playing. I'd found myself the witness to one of my parents' infrequent blazing rows. Now and then Jim and Nancy would have a blow up and then all would be calm and peaceful and the family would be happy. Mum gazed at me through her tears and forced a warming smile for me, and then she said in her sincere way, 'You shouldn't listen to us when we argue. Your dad and I – we have a row now and again. It's nothing really. Go out and play." Joe relit his cigarette, and looked at Nathan and smiled. Nathan was listening politely and was genuinely interested. "I'll never forget that night," said Joe quietly. "I guess I must have been really hurt by what I'd seen. I was showing a combination of hurt and I was trying to be understanding. But I didn't like to see my mother and father hurt. I liked the happier times when my family laughed together. I remember going out the door but not going out to play. In a mood of childlike responsibility towards my mother, and a great respect for my father, I went down to the pub where I knew he'd be. I stood outside the hotel listening to the drinkers inside racing against time to drink as much beer by closing time, when the clock struck six o'clock. I knew my dad was in there. I thought maybe I could go inside. Maybe, I could call him through the doors. I was too young and confused to know. I only wanted to mend the row between my mum and dad. A crucial climax seemed to build up inside me and I pushed the door of the bar open and stepped inside the hotel. I'd never seen a scene like it before, the six o'clock swill. There were seething paralytic drinkers surging forward, crushing against the bar, eager to fill their glasses. Some big burly bastard says to me, 'You can't come in 'ere, sonny, piss off out it! Go on!' Well I said defensive like an all, 'I'm trying to find me dad.' Through the many rugged faces in the bar comes one face I recognised. It was my old man. I always remember it. He had a glass of beer in his hand and a real pained depressive look on his face. 'Dad—' I said. That was far as I got. 'What are you doing in here,' he say's to me. He was real astonished at my presence in the bar. I can tell you. My dad, he exploded! 'I ought to tan your bloody backside red, white and blue!' All I could say was, 'Mam's crying, Dad. I don't like it when you and Mam are unhappy.' The whole of the proceedings, of course, are being watched by every man in the bar and the bustle's completely died away. Dad gripped me, oblivious to the fact that he's got an audience and he groans, 'Oh, you silly, silly little bugger.' Yet his eyes were red with tears that I reckon he felt too manly to produce, but I'd like to think that he also had a feeling of pride that I could show genuine concern for him. He was obviously embarrassed at seeing his little boy in the pub and I could see the humiliation swelling up over him. One angry bloke snapped at my dad. 'Take your kiddie home, fella! This is no place for a kid!' Dad spun round to him like the wind and gave him that growl of his. 'All right, you mug!' And then he turned round and winked at me but his voice was softer, more understanding."

Joe looked up. Nathan was listening. He felt some compassion towards Joe who he felt was something of a real loner. Joe was glad of someone to talk to. Nathan noticed the pause as Joe reflected on his childhood past. He beckoned him to continue.

"Then what happened, Joe?" he asked.

"Dad turns to me and says, 'You're a good kid, son. I'm glad you care about your mum and me – but if you ever come into this pub again when I'm here you'll get such a flamin' tanning from me. Let's go home, shall we, son?' Well Dad and I departed from the bar and, as we closed the door behind us, I remember the silence that we'd left behind grow into a real uproar. A little way from the pub dad found a park bench and we sat down and talked. It was a cold night. I remember Dad talked to me in a way I'd never known him talk before. With a real sympathy and understanding, I didn't know he had."

"In what way Joe?" inquired Nathan, realising that he was viewing the really finer characteristics of Australians that rarely transcended overseas. Too often in books and films Australians were portrayed as Larrikins from the bush. In Joe, Nathan saw a quiet pragmatism that came through with warmth and gentility. It was a great quality of so many Australians.

"Was there something beneath the front your father maintained so strongly?" Nathan pursued.

"Oh my very word there was," replied Joe. "Y'know we sat down on that park bench and he really spoke to me in a way I've always remembered. Time and time again I've sat out here in the desert with no one to talk to and for some reason – I don't know why – but I feel you're a bloke I can open up to. You seem like a bloke that might have been hurt really badly in your life at some time or the other. Am I right?"

"You are right," Nathan said quietly and he felt the further need to clarify. "I was sent to a kibbutz from my home in Austria. I was only sixteen. My parents and all my relatives died in concentration camps. I have battled ever since to make my way in life. You and I are, I suppose, kindred spirits of a sort. It is curious, is it not, how things that happen in our childhood still make an impression on us when we reach adult age. I think I too am a loner, probably an isolationist, frequently looking back to my childhood, my parents, when I should be looking forward. I too think constantly of my father's words to me when I was young—"

Nathan broke off. He could see Joe looking at him sympathetically.

"You've had a real rough life, mate," said Joe to Nathan. "But it's the making of you. I honestly believe that tough times breed people with a real capacity to survive. You know on that night after the row at home, my dad and I sat out in the park and he said to me, 'Listen, son, I felt quite proud that you came in the pub to tell me about Mum. It made me realise you respect us – and love us – that's good, son. There is nothing greater in this life than the power of love.' He went on to say, 'Joe, your mum and I – well, we have a little blue now and again, but it's nothing. It blows over and everything becomes fine again. Mum and I gripe at you now and again, Joe,' he said, 'and we might give you a hefty clip round the backside but it blows over and we're all happy again.' Then he said the words that stay in my memory. They've become almost a principle, a code of honour, if you like that I've always strived to live by."

This was interesting. Nathan listened curious to know what hidden faith and objectives drove this stockman in his long day of loneliness in the bush.

"Well dad said to me, 'Your mum and I, we think the world of you and all of our kids, and we just want the best for you all. We want you to grow up to be good people, nice people, polite, cheerful, y'know, and to be triers and hard workers, and always in there giving it a go. What I hope for you kids is that you'll try hard at whatever you do in life, whether it's schooling, your work when you get older, that you'll always have a decent sense of fair play. And when you meet people, be nice to them, son. Ask them how they are, how they're going and when you meet a stranger, you'll shake their hand.' And do you know what else he said to me, Nathan? He said, 'I'd like you to be a tryer, son.' Could you think of better advice?"

"A tryer," repeated Nathan. "What more could anyone ask?"

"Yeah, and that's all I've ever been." Joe sighed wistfully. "When Dad got up from the park bench that night, he lit a cigarette and the sparkle of the match seemed to illuminate his craggy face. It was like I was seeing a side of him I'd never seen before." Joe smiled remembering. "He grinned at me and he said, 'You're a good kid, son.'" Joe's voice changed slightly, the tone lowered as he continued. "Not long afterwards I came home from school to find the house in Port Adelaide filled with aunts and uncles and the neighbours breaking into bottles of beer and the gramophone with a record of Peter Dawson's playing and there in the middle of the room was dad in khaki and slouch hat dancing with Nancy. Dad went away to Egypt, Turkey and the fields of France. I was sitting in the classroom at school one day. The teacher was giving us a history lesson telling us about Captain Cook's voyages. She was trying desperately at the same time to keep the attention of the class. Us kids were always mucking around. The poor lady's voice was interrupted by the sound of boots outside hitting the surface of the road with an impeccable timing. There was a military band playing outside the classroom. They were playing 'Waltzing Matilda'. What else could Anzacs march to? The schoolteacher's attempts to pacify the class were wasted. All of us kids rushed to the windows to look at the battalion of soldiers marching away. It was amazing how emotional we got at the sight of the diggers in their puggarees and slouch hats, and a brass band playing with a lot of oomph. I heard one of the kids say, 'My dad's one of them.' He must have summed it up for all of us. So many of our fathers answered the Little Digger's rallying cry and went—"

"The Little Digger?" Nathan did not understand the reference.

Joe sought to put it into perspective for him. "The Little Digger. That's a nickname they bestowed on William Morris Hughes, better known as Billy Hughes. He was Australia's Prime Minister during the First War. Fiery old bugger. He's still alive; in his eighties, still sitting down there in the Parliament in Canberra. As I said so many of our dad's responded to him. I came home one night after school and mum was being consoled by my brothers and sisters. Dad wasn't coming home. He was only thirty-four. The Somme was where he saw action. I couldn't believe it; the man who'd once said to me, 'I'd like you to be a tryer, son' was the object of a telegram. My father, whose stern moody appearance had once been revealed in the space of seconds in the park that night was really a bloke of concern and worry, and hidden love and generosity, had gone. I never forgot that one conversation in the park that night, the advice he gave me."

A silence followed as both men reflected on Joe's story. It was still uncomfortably hot that night, and Nathan mopped his brow.

"Some years later," Joe suddenly continued, "I took off for the bush. And I went through the Depression years like so many. I did it all, shearing, fruit picking, cane cutting, droving, and I did my army stint up to 1945. I was on the Kokoda trail; couldn't wait to get back here. It's wonderful country here."

Nathan just nodded and smiled. He was in agreement with Joe but probably for different reasons.

"I have enjoyed listening to you Joe," he said. "I have probably learned more about Australia by listening to you than if I'd read many books on the subject."

Joe smiled. "Thanks pal. I hope I didn't bore you. There are times when a bloke's got to talk about himself. I guess I've been up here for so long on my own, that it's good to have someone to talk to."

"I know the feeling," said Nathan. "Riding the boundaries I can understand why one would feel so isolated. Why have you been up here so long Joe, on your own out here?"

"Rustlers." Joe replied emphatically.

"Rustlers?" Nathan was surprised. "In this day and age?"

"You'd be surprised what goes on round these parts." Joe stood up and brushed himself down. "Yes, mate. A lot of blokes from who knows where come sneaking in at night and make off with a dozen stock when they think no one's looking. Ed and Roslyn were pretty concerned about this. They asked for volunteers to come up to different parts of the station and keep an eye open for any of those rapscallions. I'm a peace-loving bloke myself. Thought the seclusion would do me the world of good. That's why I'm here. There's a few blokes scattered round like me. We've actually managed to cut down on some of the stock going missing. Reckon it's probably working in the long run."

"I think I might get some sleep now," said Nathan stifling a yawn.

"Me too," reiterated Joe. "Are you going to sleep out here in the bush?"

"That's all I've been doing on this ride," answered Nathan.

"Well I reckon I might bed down in the humpy there," Joe pointed to the small wooden cabin that he was housed in. "By geez it's warm tonight. Okay, Nat, well I'll see you in the morning. Reckon you'll be all right out here?"

"No problem."

"Get a good night's sleep then. We're going to have a real hard day tomorrow," said Joe as he walked towards the wooden hut that was his home in these parts. Nathan considered that it would probably be cooler outside than in there. He lay out his blanket roll and attempted to get some sleep.

Several hours later he awoke at the sound of a huge clap of thunder. The noise shook him. The thunder continued and it was immediately followed by great flashing yellow streaks of lightening, which violently brightened the sky. Huge torrents of heavy rain cascaded down suddenly. Nathan immediately rushed for the cover of the wooden hut. He could hear the sounds of the cattle moaning.

It was Joe who rose very quickly at the sounds. "My God," he gasped. "It's like a bloody tropical storm. The cattle are going to be all over the flaming place if we don't keep them together. They'll be racing off breaking fences."

"What do we do?"

The two stood in the cover of the hut. Outside the rain was falling heavier and heavier. Nathan had never seen rain quite like it before. The thunder was cracking continuously, and the lightning flashed with long yellow streaks lighting up the night sky.

At long last Joe spoke. "We're going to have to round them up, Nathan. If we lose them—" It was too late, for as Joe had spoken the herd began to disperse, and suddenly took off in a stampede. The rain was falling with all the full power of a tropical storm behind it. "Let's go!" shouted Joe, and in the next instant both he and Nathan ran to their horses and mounted them.

The pair of them took off after the stock, trying desperately to round them up. Not only were the cattle frantic, but it was also a hell of a job to control the horses. Joe was the expert in these matters. He rode like the wind after the cattle lashing his stock whip on the ground furiously attempting to get the stock to change direction. It was a near impossible task, and the weather seemed to get worse and worse, not only were they competing with the rain and the thunder, but they now had cyclonic winds to contend with.

Nathan tried his best, but to no avail. The cattle were out of control, beyond the control of two men. In the heavy rain Nathan tried to emulate Joe in rounding up the stock. He shouted and thrashed his whip on to the ground. It was useless. The rain fell so heavily that everywhere there was running water. The creek water was beginning to overflow. It was such an incredible contrast to what had been only hours before. In a country that was used to conditions of drought, the tropical storm had created a flood.

The horses could not run in this weather. Their hoofs became bogged down in the soggy conditions. Nathan tried staying on the horse. He could not control it; it reared up and threw him. Nathan was thrown to the ground, and he found himself rolling down the creek bank to the rising waters. He landed with a splash that threw up filthy sandy water all over him. He desperately tried to get a grip on himself.

"Hang on, mate!" Joe called out from above. He had seen Nathan's plight and struggled down to help him. All at once Joe seemed to lose his grip. Within seconds he hurtled into the raging waters. Now the two of them battled to keep themselves up in the water. Above the cattle stampeded well and truly out of control. The horses had bolted. It was just the two men struggling to get their grips on the banks and force their way back up.

With the rain and the thunder and the lightning and the cyclonic winds hurtling from the Gulf of Carpentaria, and the water rising steadily in the creek, there seemed to be no relief in sight. Joe scrambled up the bank with a sudden rush of energy and tried to get his footing. Nathan followed as best he could, but his boots slid in the mud and he found himself face down as he slipped. Again and again he fought back to the top, until Joe stretched out his hand and pulled him up. The men drenched to the skin and by now totally exhausted turned to run for the cover of Joe's wooden cabin. Joe's face looked totally aghast.

"Oh no!" he gasped horrified. Nathan turned to look at the cabin. It had been completely smashed by the power of the storm. "It's no good, mate!" Joe moaned angrily. Nathan looked around for some sort of cover. It was then he saw the creek water was rising fast and spilling over the banks.

"Joe, look!" he cried, as the water began to flood everywhere. Nathan was stunned that the weather could show such contradiction going from dry and parched to one of flood conditions. The water was swelling rapidly and alarmingly. There was only one thing the two men could do. Joe pointed to the trees.

"Come on, pal, to the top of the trees!"

Nathan looked in awe. There was simply nothing else he could do; the last thing Nathan ever dreamed that he would be doing in the Northern Territory would be escaping a flood. It just didn't seem possible. He and Joe ran towards a tree and climbed up as the water flooded around the bottom of the trunk. The tree was strong and firm and its branches, thick, long and outspreading. Even so, the tree shook and swayed as the rain and the wind hurtled at full gale like force. Nathan climbed to the security of the peak of the tree. Joe perched precariously on another branch. The two could only hold on to the tree as best as they could. Down at the base of the tree, floodwaters swirled.

All around the skies were ignited by the streaks of lightning. Thunder raged and raged. Rainwater lashed the two men's faces. The cyclonic wind crashed against them. It was an agonising night for the two men. For Nathan perched up in the tree, the night seemed like an eternity. It was the noise of the cyclone that made the most impact. To be caught up in the midst of the howling sounds, and to be completely exposed to its full force, was an experience that neither man would wish to repeat. Nathan rested his head against the trunk and closed his eyes. He feared that lightning might strike the tree at any time. All he could do was to hang on for dear life. He gritted his teeth and held on tightly to the tree.

Hours and hours followed while the storm took its full effect. In the morning as the first light of dawn creaked through the blackness of the storm, Nathan and Joe saw the full, amazing wave of turbulence that had occurred during the night. The dissipation of the storm brought with it the familiar early morning outback silence. The dawn light revealed the humpy completely smashed to the ground and many bushes and trees virtually torn out of the ground. In the creek the water was lowering. Joe looked at Nathan. There was a faint smile on his face.

"Geez, looks like some drovers got paid and had themselves one hell of a party," he said with a rough humour.

Nathan forced a smile. The realisation swept over him with a fearful sense of urgency that they were now totally on their own. Their horses had gone during the night. All of Joe's food stored in his humpy had gone with the floodwaters. They had no form of communication with any of the out-of-the-way homesteads, or the main station at Orange Tree Downs.

It was surprising how densely green this part of the Territory looked. The rainwater had subsided leaving everything muddy and steamy with the humidity already high at this time of the morning. The Northern Territory contrary to all myths was not totally desert. Much of it was tropical with dense trees and carpeted with a rough texture of grass unlike the plains that Nathan had ridden across earlier. It was with some relief that Nathan realised the country was not quite an inhospitable as it might have been, and that after last nights torrential downpour, there would not be an absence of water holes.

After revelling in the calm and silence of it all Nathan felt his clothes, and ran his hands through his hair. He was damp from head to foot and his face and hair were coated in sand and mud. The heat and the humidity intermingled with the perspiration that was running from his body made him turn his head sharply. He knew how disgustingly filthy he must be.

Joe was still surveying the scenery from the branch of the tree. "That's the Territory for you." He said matter-of-factly, "It's either a drought," and then, after an immaculate pause, "or – or else one enormous flood." He knew it was time for some sort of affirmative action. "Nathan?" he called up to his friend.

"Yes, Joe?"

"See that countryside in front us? That great long stretch for miles and miles?"

"Of course I do Joe."

"That's what we've got to walk across friend. To the nearest homestead."

"How far is that?"

Joe was very slow to reply. Nathan could sense that the answer was not going to be an easy one.

"Mrs Geeves has got a place some way from here. She's got a store there, and there's also a pub and a roadhouse."

"But how far is it?" This time there was a tone of impatience in his voice.

"About sixty miles, son," came back Joe's reply. Nathan was absolutely speechless. Sixty miles! By foot! He looked out at the great distance before them. It was awe-inspiring. To walk sixty miles in this heat without food would surely be dangerous. He gazed down at Joe who eyed him, recognising the worried look in Nathan's eyes.

"Don't worry, fella," he said reassuringly to Nathan, "We'll make it. We'll get there."

★★★

The trek across Arnhem Land in blistering heat and under a hot, burning sun was an ordeal for any man. Both Nathan and Joe had lost their hats in the storm the night before and they were well exposed to the fierceness of the elements. To stop for too long a time would make it harder for them to keep going. To walk too fast would drain what little energy they had left. The two men were psyching themselves up to keep plodding along, covering as much distance as they could at the easiest possible pace they could maintain.

The storm and the torrential rainfall had made the ground muddy and damp and the heat rose in a quivering haze. There was limestone and rainforests and swampy ground to cross. It was not an easy journey to tackle. All the two men could do was to trek on in silence. Above them tropical birds flew in unusual formation. On the ground a lizard would suddenly scurry away in front of them. Rocky escarpments rose and fell in the distance. Thin palms motionless in the intense still head stood sentry like on the horizon. Spinifex and dense moisture consuming vegetation luxuriantly green, soared out over the surface of the ground. A deep red sun sat before them like a glowing lantern.

It was gruelling. Nathan and Joe were aching from the walking. They were burned from the full force of the sun's rays. They were dehydrated. Their throats were parched. The perspiration trickled from their bodies and dried out just as quickly as it came. Mile after mile they walked. Every step forward was one step less of this endurance test.

Joe was quiet, occasionally glancing at Nathan to check how he was coping. Nathan could only look back at him. Words were not needed. To put his thoughts of urgency from his mind, Nathan let his mind wander. He thought of a dish of Austrian strudel and a large glass of lemonade. By concentrating on the immediately unattainable he was effectively blocking out the circumstances of his present situation. It was surprising how the steps he took were the more gainful as he diverted his attention elsewhere.

He concentrated on this aspect for a long time until the two encountered a rock lagoon, formed by water seeping from a creek riverbed. Nathan and Joe scampered down a rocky ridge towards a clear freshwater pool. The water looked absolutely inviting. Nathan began to unbutton his shirt and prepare himself for a swim.

"No you don't!" Joe said suddenly grabbing Nathan's shoulder with a very firm grip. Nathan looked at him startled. Joe shook his head in a manner that said, *No. Absolutely no.* Joe pointed to the other side of the pool. A saltwater crocodile slid down a bank into the pool. "I think we might give this one a miss," said Joe with a look of wry humour.

"I think I agree with you, Joe," a stunned Nathan spoke in a low hushed voice, clearly evident of shock at what he had seen. The two men turned around and continued their trek.

The next waterhole they came too was less auspicious. Even so Nathan explored thoroughly around the banks for any scaly predators that might also consider using the availability of the pool. Joe was amused at Nathan's concern.

"Don't worry," he said trying to reassure him, and he entered the pool naked. Nathan soon followed at Joe's example. He was glad he did. The water really was fresh and reviving.

That night they slept by the rock pool. In the middle of the night Nathan woke with cramps in his leg. The walking, the damp and the humidity had taken a severe effect on him. He massaged his legs before going back to sleep again. He longed for the luxury of a soft mattress bed. Walking an average of twenty miles a day another two days would see them at this homestead. Two more tortuous days of walking in the incredible heat. The thought appalled him. He closed his eyes and attempted to recapture some sleep.

In the morning they continued their walking. The sun was high, the ground was flatter and more exposed, there were considerably less ridges and escarpments, although it was still densely green, but the vegetation was thicker and there were more palms. It seemed to be getting hotter and hotter the further the two men walked. Neither man had eaten in the previous two days. By now they were beginning to feel real pangs of hunger. It was becoming a question of which was the more desirous, water or food. Water was obtainable from the rock pools that occasionally appeared. There were long stretches where there wasn't any fluid sustenance. At times Joe would reach down to a shrub or bush and absorb the moisture from the leaves; it was an example Nathan followed. For food he once again reverted to concentrating on the hypothetical, and he thought longingly of a dish of Austrian strudel.

Another night in the bush followed: one final, humid night laying on some hard boulder slabs, attempting to sleep rough. It was really only a pretence of sleeping. Nathan just closed his eyes, but even though he was weary, drained and exhausted, he could not get comfortable or relax in a position where he could manage to sleep. Even the thought of sleeping on a blanket roll again seemed like a luxury compared to this. That blanket roll seemed almost as if it had all the splendid comforts of a huge four poster king size double bed, with satin sheets and feather pillows. The present situation brought a flicker of amusement into his mind when he realised he was longing simply for the basics in a life such as a shower with soap, a good bed to sleep on and a simplistic nourishing meal.

Joe and Nathan, by now walking zombies, wasted little time as soon as the dawn broke on the third day. They were up and walking on the final stretch. Sixty miles on foot in unbearable humidity, a heavy oppressing sun, a hungry belly and being continually dehydrated, is no mean feat. It was one that Nathan had no wish to repeat in his lifetime ever again.

Relief finally came on that day when in the haze and glare of the sun there were flickers of movement before them up ahead in the trees and bushes.

"I said we'd get here," said Joe in a tone of voice that sounded as if he was trying to convince himself more than Nathan.

There were aboriginal children running and jumping in the distance. Beyond them Nathan saw a homestead, actually a bungalow, surrounded by sprawling grounds and a huge artesian well with a windmill rotating in slow motion. On another side was a flat-topped building, glaringly white in colour, outside of which were parked a number of motor vehicles including jeeps, long distance trailers and petrol carriers. Immediately next-door was a pub where drovers on horseback rode up to the front and tied their horses to a barrier like something out of a wild-west movie.

"I take it," murmured Nathan breathlessly, "that this is Mrs Geeves homestead."

"You're bloody right it is, Gunga Din!" Joe exclaimed in a moment of exhilaration. "Come on!" He said slapping Nathan on the back. "I can taste a couple of ice-cold beers from here."

The two men gathered all the stamina they had remaining, and plodded the last couple of hundred yards to the bush pub. When Joe swung the door open, he almost fainted with the relief of being there. A flood of faces suddenly turned to look at the two badly sunburned men with mud dirtied shirts and trousers, several days beard growth and rips in their clothes. From behind the bar came a sharp female baritone voice.

"Bloody hell, Joe! What have you and your mate been up to?"

Joe was swift to reply. "G'day, Mrs Geeves. You wouldn't have a couple of cold beers would you, luv?"

"What happened to you two?" the astonished woman asked filling up two glasses with some draught beer from a tap. Mrs Geeves was a plump woman in her fifties with snow-white hair and a wrinkled leathery skin. She had seen drovers come into her bar in a filthy state before, but she'd never seen Joe and Nathan, two untypical jackeroos in ragged clothes, and so filthy and hot.

Before anyone answered, Joe and Nathan reached for the two glasses and emptied the contents down their throat, the beer swilling over from their mouths, dribbling down their chins. The coolness of the beer assuaged their thirst. It felt to Nathan like a cleansing process as the beer soaked into his hot perspiring body.

"Two more please, luv!" gasped Joe, relieved to be here in this pub. Mrs Geeves had second-guessed Joe on his request, and immediately replaced two more full foaming glasses in front of the two men. Immediately they consumed the contents with the same speed as before.

"You look like two blokes who've walked forty miles in the hot sun," Mrs Geeves observed.

"Try sixty," Joe said dryly, a glint of humour in his eye.

"Bulldust!" Mrs Geeves said with a snort. "Sixty miles! Go on with you."

"It's bloody true, me old darling!" Joe replied aggressively. "Me and my mate – this is Nathan, by the way – we got caught in that cyclone, storm, call it what you will, back there at Spearhead Creek—"

"Spearhead Creek!" somebody in the pub repeated.

"Yeah, Spearhead Creek," Joe answered forcefully. "And the cattle stampeded and the horses bolted leaving us stranded while the rain was pouring down nonstop in buckets. We stayed up in a tree all night long while it was flooding beneath us. In the morning when it was drying out after the big wet, we had no choice. We had to walk. Isn't that right young, Nathan?"

Nathan looked back at Joe and in a phrase that was alien to him, and not normally a choice of words that he would be associated with, he summed the reply up eloquently.

"Too bloody right, mate!"

Mrs Geeves amazed at what she had just heard refilled two more glasses. "You boys better have a couple more beers," she said slamming them down in front of the two men. "Don't worry about money, Joe. These are on the house."

"Thanks, Mrs Geeves," replied Joe. "I haven't got any anyway. My pay cheques have gone into the bank at Alice Springs since I've been up here the past couple of months."

Mrs Geeves let out a chuckle of amusement. She was a good-hearted sort.

The other people in the bar looked on as Joe and Nathan treated themselves to copious amounts of beer. Normally Nathan would have keeled over by now from drinking so much alcohol. Strangely enough it was having no effect on him except for cooling him down considerably.

"Mrs Geeves, Nathan and me, we've walked our legs off. We're tired. We're hot. We're filthy. We look like a couple of hobos on holiday in a hovel!"

"You're telling me," Mrs Geeves chortled.

"And we'd appreciate it you could find us a couple of spare beds and a meal and a bath – with soap. And can I use your radio? I need to get in touch with Alec Taylor at Orange Tree Downs to let him know what's happened."

"Sure, Joe," Mrs Geeves reassured him warm heartedly. "I'll fix you up with a couple of rooms in the house. Would you like me to fix you up with a couple of dancing girls as well?"

Joe winked at Nathan and sipped on his drink.

★★★

Some hours later Nathan woke up in a bed with crisp sheets and a soft pillow. Before going to bed, he had shaved, shampooed and soaked in a long hot bath. Mrs Geeves had given them both a warm meal that they had eaten so quickly that they hadn't realised the extent of their own hunger. He had then gone to sleep for ten hours. Over the past few weeks the long boundary ride, the spasmodic fitful hours of sleep, together with the endurance and lack of nutrition they had both come through had finally taken its toll. Nathan felt the springs of the bed creak beneath him. It was ten hours later that Nathan was awoken by the sound of someone coughing in the room next door.

Nathan listened. The cough was deep and shattering. It stopped as quickly as it begun. Nathan realised with a sudden jerk of alarm that it was Joe who occupied the room next door. He rose quickly wrapping a towel around his waist, and went to Joe's room and knocked on the door.

"Joe," he called. There was no reply. "Joe," he called again. Nathan tried the door. It was open. He pushed the door wide. Joe stirred in his bed and rolled to one side.

"Hullo, mate," he said cheerfully. Joe looked drained and sallow.

"I heard you coughing. You sounded terrible. Are you all right?" Nathan looked concerned.

"It comes and it goes. I guess it's the damp and the humidity."

"You should see a doctor, Joe," Nathan insisted politely.

"No problem, cobber," Joe spoke softly. "I'll be all right." Joe did not sound too convincing. "Nathan, I managed to get on to Alec over the radio. He said if you take the mail plane at three o'clock tomorrow afternoon the pilot will put you down at Orange Tree for you."

"But what about you?"

"I've got a bit to do up here. One of the boys from round here'll give me a ride in the jeep to catch up on all the stock and those two flaming runaway horses of ours."

"As long as you are all right, Joe."

"I'll be fine, Nathan. Look, I've got to get a bit of sleep now."

"I understand, Joe," Nathan said instinctively, and he went back to his room to continue his sleep. When he lay down he felt that perhaps Joe was not being totally honest. Nevertheless, Nathan would not pursue the issue, but he still felt concerned. Joe was a good man, undoubtedly one of the best.

The outback mail plane arrived a few minutes ahead of schedule the next day landing on the ground that passed as an airstrip. Nathan was waiting with Joe. The two had talked for some time, Nathan had promised to order another book of bush poetry for Joe in place of the one that had been lost in the storm. Even at this stage Nathan still felt he had to make a final comment to Joe.

"I really don't know how you stand this isolation," he remarked.

"It's my way of life, Nathan," Joe said almost defensively. "I'm used to it."

"I know that. But I still think you should see a doctor about your chest," Nathan reminded him.

"You better get that plane," Joe said stretching out a handshake to Nathan. "Good luck, pal."

"And you, Joe," said Nathan turning and walking to the plane.

A few minutes later he was airborne looking down at the few spartan buildings belonging to Mrs Geeves. The aircraft proceeded across Arnhem Land and the Barkly Tableland. The aerial view of the journey he had undertaken by horseback and foot gave him an insight into the rugged terrain he had covered. Nathan experienced a feeling of security looking down at the scenery beneath him. Somehow the last few days had brought home to him just how dangerous the harsh beauty of the Territory could be. It was diverse and intoxicating, and beautiful. To Nathan, it was impossible not to feel a deep affection for this part of Australia. But most of all he felt a genuine admiration and respect for the Territorians, and their strength and resolve in their pioneering lifestyle.

Inside the Dakota aircraft there were a few passenger seats. Nathan occupied one and a couple of elderly people sat at two in the aisle way opposite him. The mail plane was filled with bags of parcels and envelopes all bound for various stations and homesteads throughout the outback. The plane would have to stop at each of these before touching down at Orange Tree Downs.

Nathan sat back and relaxed in his chair. It would be easy to drift along in his present adventurous lifestyle. He had been so fully absorbed by the situation he had found himself in that his interest in a law career and a future with Melissa had almost been forgotten. With the aircraft engines chugging and throbbing beneath him, and the scenery from his panel window remaining a fascinating aerial view, Nathan diverted his mind to the decisions he would have to make. This job had originally been purely just another experience for him at first. In fact his time here had been something he would always remember and cherish.

Thirty-six

Nathan did stay on at Orange Tree Downs for several more months after that first boundary ride. He did not traverse the same route again. He rode along the southern most parts of the station which were more flatter plains, and less interesting to look at. The first journey had been eventful. If that had been any the less spectacular it would still be the one ride, he would remember.

Finally, Nathan decided the time had come for him to move on. Sydney beckoned to him. The thoughts of Melissa made the prospect of going to Sydney far more appealing. One day at the end of a long and tiring boundary ride, Nathan announced his intentions of resigning to Alec Taylor, and advised him that he would be leaving the station in three weeks time.

Before Nathan left Orange Tree Downs, a big outback rodeo was held one weekend. Ed and Roslyn Mitchell presided over this day with absolute delight. It was a very special day in these parts. People came from miles around to join in the fun. From the nearby stations of Quentin Downs and Alexandria Rose came skilled riders to compete with the best of the men at Orange Tree. There was camel riding, a race in which the humpbacked ships of the desert galloped at breakneck speed around a dusty circuit, while an eager bush bookie ran a tote giving odds inscribed on a blackboard. There were side stalls and barbecues, and a great fun filled atmosphere.

From the Country Women's Association and local Graziers Societies, there were representatives who mingled with the influx of people visiting Orange Tree Downs. Ed Mitchell, decked out in his best R M Williams gear, walked around shaking hands with many people. Nathan was surprised when Ed on espying him watching a horse race came across to acknowledge him. In all the time on Orange Tree Downs,

Nathan had never seen Ed Mitchell mingle with too many people. Ed had seemed remote and aloof, but on this day he was proving to be a popular mixer.

"How are you, young fella?" Ed asked affably, patting him gently on the shoulder.

The stock in reply when asked by someone how they were, in these parts always simply seemed to be 'Good'. Nathan followed true to form. "Good thanks, Mr Mitchell."

"Recovered fully from that storm episode up at Spearhead Creek?"

"I have," replied Nathan.

"That's good," said Ed removing his hat momentarily to scratch his balding pate. "I'm sorry to say your mate, Joe Patterson, has not been too well." Nathan turned to face Ed with alarm. In the background the horses cantered over the finishing line. "Yeah, I'm sorry to say Joe's had bad chest problems for some time. If Rosyln and I had known about it earlier we would have brought him back to the station a while ago"

"I am so sorry to hear that." Nathan was very sincere. "I liked Joe a lot. He was a good man. Seemed very strong. I think he liked the isolation of the bush a lot."

"That's true," agreed Ed. "He was always a loner. Had a few close friends. Not too many, mind. Anyway the upshot of it is that Joe's in a bush hospital up at Pearl Waters. Roslyn and I, and a few of the boys are flying up tomorrow morning to see him. I know you two were pretty close on your first ride on the boundary. Have you got a message for Joe you'd like me to pass on to him?"

Nathan was quiet for a while as he thought of something warm to fell Joe. "I have a message – yes. Tell him he is a fine man. Tell him to get well soon. And tell him – tell him to write more bush poetry, like that man who is his namesake. Banjo Patterson."

"You know about Joe's bush poetry?" asked Ed with an element of surprise in his voice.

"Yes. He read me one of his poems at Spearhead Creek. It was about swagmen." Nathan recalled that moment and he thought of the long conversation that had followed when Joe had talked for a long time about his own childhood in Adelaide.

"I'll be sure to pass your words on, Nathan," Ed returned. "Well, young man, I'll leave you to enjoy the day. How have you enjoyed it?"

"It's been a great day," Nathan responded. "I did not know that station life was as good as this."

"For sure," exclaimed Ed. "The annual Rodeo's a big thing up here. We get people coming to see the country racing, the camel racing, the rough riders, and the stock on display. We have a top barbie going too, so everyone can have a munch on some good tucker. There's not a lot we miss out on." Ed changed the subject quickly. "Alec Taylor tells me you're leaving in a few weeks time."

"I'm going back to city life. I'm heading down to Sydney."

"To the life of a city gent eh?" Ed mused amiably. "Funny thing, fella, when you first came to work here I said to Roslyn that the new boundary rider's got a familiar face. Rosie agreed. She said that you looked familiar too. Where might we have met you before?"

Nathan smiled at the retentive memory Ed must have had for a face. He had to tell him; although he had to draw the line on the fact the occasion had prompted Nathan to buy shares in the Orange tree Downs proprietary company.

"You have never actually met me before," pointed out Nathan. "I think, though, you probably recall my face from an occasion when you were visiting Melbourne. I used to work on weekends at a restaurant in Toorak. I served you and your wife when you were dining with a man who had something to do with oil."

Ed immediately remembered the night. "Ah yes – Sir Bill as we call him. That's who I was dining with. Remember the night now. So that's where we've seen you." Ed smiled slightly. "I've got to do a bit of mixing. Don't worry about Joe too much. He's a pretty sturdy fellow. I'll pass your words on."

"Thank you, Mr Mitchell," replied Nathan. He watched Ed move off into the crowds of people obviously enjoying every minute of the day. Nathan had felt slightly perturbed at the news of Joe. It had seemed to him Ed had been speaking of Joe in the past tense almost as if there was some definite finality about his condition.

***

It was late the following afternoon that Nathan was sitting on the edge of his bed in the dormitory writing a few letters to his friends, Freddie

Miller, and Jack and Elsie Faley. Some of the men were playing cards up at the end of the room. Nathan could see Alec Taylor and a few of the men who had visited Joe that day at Pearl Waters, come into the dormitory. They all removed their hats on entering and crossed over to the men playing cards. Alec looked particularly downcast. He couldn't hear what they were saying but by the expressions on their faces, he knew. He just knew.

A short time later Alec came down towards Nathan. By the look on Alec's face, Nathan prepared himself for what he was about to hear.

"Hullo Nat," Alec said glumly.

"Hullo Alec," Nathan replied. *Tell me gently*, he thought. *Don't make it any harder than it is*. Alec appeared to take a deep breath before he spoke.

"Nat, me and some of the boys, and Ed and Roslyn – we've just come back from the hospital at Pearl Waters. As you know Joe's been helluva bloody crook for a while. Kept it to himself y'know until that cough of his gave him away." Nathan shuddered at the memory of it. He remembered how the noise of it in Mrs Geeves home had woken him up. "I'm sorry to tell you, there were some complications." He paused. "Joe passed away this morning."

A tremendous feeling of sadness engulfed him. Nathan was absolutely speechless. He could only look up at Alec with sadness in his eyes. Alec in turn looked red eyed and his sharp rugged face looked vulnerable in return. He struggled to continue, his voice clearly emotive.

"He was our mate. A private sort of man, but he had a big family of brothers and sisters in Adelaide. Did he tell you about that?"

"Yes, he mentioned that to me," Nathan said sorrowfully.

Alec continued. "The boys are going to have a whip round for Joe. His family in Adelaide have requested Joe's body be taken home for a private burial. Poor Roslyn was in tears. Joe was liked by her a lot. Ed is organising a bit of a service for Joe the day after tomorrow. A minister from the bush Church Council will be conducting it. Everyone from Orange Tree is going to be there. You'll come, of course?"

"Of course."

"Pity I can't think of more of Joe's friends away from Orange Tree Downs. Did he mention anyone to you? You don't know if he had a girl stashed away?"

"Not to my knowledge. I do know that Joe and I had a mutual friend in Cairns. He was a man I met when I was a soldier who used to know Joe before the war when he worked on Quentin Downs."

Alec's eyes seemed to light up. "You're talking about Ted McTaggart, aren't you?"

Nathan looked equally surprised. "That's – that's right. You know him?"

"Sure I do," Alec said with a glimmer of a smile broaching his lips. "Before the war I was a jackeroo on Quentin Downs. I knew Ted pretty well. I last saw Ted – oh, about a year ago – I bumped into him when I spent a week in Cairns." Nathan leaned forward interested. "Thanks for reminding me. So you know Ted, eh?"

"From army days in North Africa."

"When I got back from the war I found my old job at Quentin wasn't available. Old Harper there wasn't too reliable an employer. When Ed took me on here I was well pleased, and I didn't meet Ted again until last year when I had a few beers with him in Cairns. You know what? He and Joe were real mates. I reckon I'll give him a call."

In the sadness of the moment hearing of Joe Patterson's death, there was also some brief joy in knowing he would see Ted McTaggart again. That was the only bright light on an otherwise devastatingly sad day. Nathan discontinued writing his letters. When Alec had gone, Nathan sat on the edge of his bed for a log time afterwards just thinking of Joe. Poor Joe, the quiet man with an abundance of writing talent and a love of the bush, and isolation, had gone. He could not have been more than forty. How sad when Joe had so very much to live for.

The service for Joe Patterson was held early in the evening two days afterwards. All of the staff of Orange Tree Downs came along to pay their final respects to Joe. Some of the men from Quentin Downs and Alexandria Rose were also there. Ed and Roslyn Mitchell stood at the front of all the mourners as the bush pastor delivered a eulogy in tones of absolute sincerity, expressing genuine feeling for the loss of a fine man.

There were so many there at the service it had to be conducted in the open air in front of the house where Ed lived. It was a dusky twilight evening at that particular instance when the sun begins to set and the temperature reduces a few degrees. For these men and women of the bush mate-ship held the most important priority in their lives. "He was our mate." The words had come first from Alec when he had told Nathan the news. This time they came from the white robed pastor who went on to speak of Joe's life as a give-it-a-go Adelaide boy who had been all things in his life, from a shearer to jackeroo, and a bush poet to boot.

Nathan stood with all the mourners, his hat in his hands, listening intently to the pastor's words. He was conscious of hearing a jeep drawing up in the background, and a door close. Then he turned his attention back to the pastor who said a prayer on behalf of Joe and his family. Nathan looked up slightly and some way away he saw Alec Taylor and another man walk from the jeep to take their positions with the assembled staff. The man with Alec removed his broad-rimmed hat and at once Nathan recognised him. There was no mistaking him. He had slightly thinning hair, a good-natured face that always gave the appearance of having an inbuilt smile although, for obvious reasons, he looked grave, as he took in the sight of all the people assembled to say farewell to Joe. It was Ted McTaggart.

Ted had not changed a great deal in the eight years that had passed since 1942. A few more lines, slightly thinner hair, but he still held his age well. Nathan stared at him in disbelief. It was incredible how circumstances and coincidence had created this incredible situation. By a twist of irony, Nathan found himself looking at the man who was indirectly responsible for him being here in Australia. Almost as if Nathan had sent a message by telepathic thought waves, Ted turned his head to the right. He noticed Nathan's face immediately. He flicked his eyes back quickly to the bush pastor then, almost as quickly, he turned back to look at Nathan. Ted knew he had seen Nathan before and from within the confines of his memory, he struggled to remember where he had seen him before.

After the memorial service for Joe, the mourners went into the huge house to drink and eat and to talk of their old friend who had left them. It was not the sombre occasion Nathan had imagined that it would be. Most of the people who had appeared sad and moist-eyed at the service now looked happier as they talked of Joe Patterson, the man they had known and loved.

Nathan stood in one corner talking to a couple of people. On one side he could see Ted McTaggart shaking hands with a few men and women he had obviously known during his days in the Territory. Ted's presence was clearly a bonus and a light on this sad occasion. Nathan watched with fascination as Ted met old friends. He must have been a popular boy when he had lived here. Roslyn greeted Ted with a hug, and Ed shook his hand with a firm grip. Ted had livened up the proceedings considerably. Various people came up to him to talk of old times. Nathan did not want to disturb Ted in his reunion, and left the house to go outside and stand under the veranda. He would try and talk to Ted when the opportunity arose.

Well, Joe, thought Nathan sadly, *you are with your father now, perhaps you can finish that conversation he started on that park bench in Port Adelaide*. Nathan looked up at the stars shimmering up in the dark night sky. For some reason, Nathan said the first words of Joe's poem about swagmen. He murmured to himself, "Where go I that I may go in peace and solitude—" He broke off overcome by emotion. He turned around to go back inside the house; at the doorway stood Alec Taylor and Ted McTaggart.

"This is the bloke I was telling you about," Alec said to a grinning Ted who now knew just where they'd met before.

"Hullo Ted," Nathan said softly smiling at him. "Remember me from Cairo?"

"Fair dinkum! You could knock me down with a flaming feather!" a surprised Ted gasped. He was stunned but delighted to meet an old acquaintance from his army days again. The two men talked for a while, each bringing the other up to date on their lives since leaving the forces.

Ted was amazed to hear how their chance meeting in a dusty old bar in Cairo had triggered off Nathan's desire to come to Australia. Nathan talked of his life in England as a student at London University, the Faley family at Ealing Green, his friendship with Freddie Miller, and his life in Australia so far. Ted hadn't lost any of his comic sense of humour. When Nathan mentioned Melissa currently working in Sydney as an actress, Ted was quick to drop into a line of Aussie vernacular.

"Geez, does this sheila of yours – Melissa – scrub up pretty well, does she?" Nathan still had not got used to much of the Australian strine. Scrubs up pretty well. What on earth did that mean?

Ted went on to talk of his own life. He was very happy. Since leaving the army Ted had resisted the temptation to go bush again. He had rejoined the PMG as a linesman, a job that he had held briefly before the war. In recent months, Ted had been promoted to gang foreman. In his private life he was also very happy.

"I married a sheila I met at a woolshed dance in Cairns. Lovely girl she is. We're expecting our third child in a few months. Got a place up at

Atherton outside of Cairns: Weatherboard house with big wide verandas and a view across the Atherton Tablelands. Listen mate, if you're on your way to Sydney why don't you come back with me? You're welcome to stay at my place. My missus wouldn't complain."

"I'll do that, Ted," Nathan replied without hesitation. "I'll talk to Alec about leaving earlier. I'm pretty sure he won't mind."

"Good on ya, Nathan. The missus won't mind at all. She'll be interested to meet someone who knew me all those years ago. Guess we shouldn't forget what we're here for. We'd better go back inside in a minute." He sighed and inhaled a breath of the night air. "By gosh I was sad to hear about Joe." He seemed pensive. "Did he talk much about me?"

"He mentioned how you'd both been around the bush together. He talked of how you both used to meet up at the boundaries where Quentin Downs and Orange Tree Downs meet."

"Those were wonderful days," Ted smiled in reflection. "Joe and I were two of a kind. Yeah, we'd get together, smoke a few tailor-mades, spin a few yarns about things we'd never done, girls we'd never known, place's we'd never been. And we'd have a lot of laughs. We'd forget about the worries of the world. Up here in the Northern Territory it's like being – well, like being a long way from hardship and worry. There are a lot of good people up here. I tell you what, it's nice to shake hands with a few old mates I haven't seen in years."

"They were glad to see you," sad Nathan, thinking of the reception Ted had got in the house. "It is strange how you and Joe were such good friends," he pointed out. "Joe was a lonely man. He seemed to be the opposite of you in many ways. Joe loved isolation and talking of his past. He did not need people. But you, Ted, are a bit of—"

"A fun loving larrikin," Ted suggested with a grin. They both laughed.

"No, I know what you mean, Nathan. Joe was a lonely bloke. But he didn't need people. He loved the bush; he loved the smell of it, the feel of it, the solitude. He loved it so much he wrote poetry about it. Don't think Joe was always serious. He had the driest sense of humour of any man I've every known, drier than parched wood in fact. And I'm not always the joker in the pack. My word, I've got strong feelings on some things too. It's just that I see the humour in life more often. With Joe, he could live without people. For me all I need is my family. They're the biggest security I've got."

Nathan could not help but respect and admire Ted. Like his friend Joe, although possessing contrasting traits of character, he was all that was good in an Australian. Ted was sincere, a good companion, good-humoured, fun to be with, and straight as a die with a take-me-as-you-find-me attitude.

"It's all decided then?" asked Ted. "You'll come back with me to Cairns to stay with me and the missus."

"Certainly Ted," Nathan replied enthusiastically.

"Right-oh, Nathan," said Ted. "Now we've got that sorted out we better go back inside.

★★★

Just a few days later Ted and Nathan left by plane for Cairns. Nathan left Orange Tree Downs with mixed feelings. It had been a time he would always remember. In all of his life his time here had perhaps been the most central experience to top the years that had encompassed so much; beginning with a childhood in Berlin, a youth in Austria, teenage years on a Palestinian kibbutz, army years in North Africa, culminating in study at London University, and his time so far in Australia. Nathan didn't realise it, but as he flew to Cairns in far North Queensland he was journeying on the final home stretch to the most settled life he had experienced since leaving Austria for the kibbutz at the end of sixteen. His time as a boundary rider for Orange Tree Downs had been his last big adventure.

Thirty-seven

Ted McTaggart did his best to ensure that Nathan enjoyed his stay at Atherton. That part of North Queensland was everything that Nathan had imagined it to be. In fact it was much better. After the virtual wilderness of the outback to be in that exotic tropical scenery was nothing short of ecstasy. Ted was obviously as blissfully happy as any man could be and with the lifestyle he led, it was easy to understand.

Every morning Ted took breakfast on the veranda of his weatherboard house with his wife, Ann, and their two young children. Ann perfectly complemented Ted in every sense; she was blonde, if rather matronly, and had a good sense of humour. Both were in their early forties and being around them was fun. They were always laughing, always joking. To some extent they reminded Nathan of Jack and Elsie Faley. The same characteristics were evident. In a way, they were the Antipodean equivalent of Jack and Elsie.

Ted would drive off to work wearing only the lightest of clothes, a grey rimmed hat, a pair of shorts, some protective shoes and a light PMG shirt. He did so much work around Cairns and the nearby places like Mareeba, Port Douglas and Tinaroo, that he was virtually a well know character in the area. When he drove Nathan to Cairns, Ted would be constantly waving and saying, 'G' day' to people he passed by.

Cairns was a place that Nathan took a liking to immediately. Its surroundings were a potpourri of scenery, high rolling green-blue hills, cane fields, endless palm trees with copra, coconuts and breadfruit. The people in town dressed casually to suit the weather and there was a slow easy going feel about the place. Walking along the Esplanade with its tall swaying palms, exotic water views with blue hills in the background and yachts on the gentle blue tide, Nathan absorbed the clear fresh salt air. It really did feel good to be there.

On one occasion Nathan took the Hayles company ferry across to magical Green Island, which was tiny but picturesque. It was so small that it could be walked around in no time at all it seemed. From the island's jetty Nathan took a glass-bottomed boat across a portion of the Great Barrier Reef. The water was crystalline clear, blue but transparent. Lots of different multi-coloured fish of all shapes and sizes swam across the coral, the underwater vegetation that strained in the direction of the current added a dash of exotic colour and clams, man o' war and a mixture of elements of the reef were easily identifiable.

On another day Nathan, together with Ted, Ann and their children, took the scenic train ride from Cairns to Kuranda. Nathan couldn't help but make a comparison of the staggering contrast between outback and coastal scenery. The train ride took in a diversity of scenery, going across the Barron River, through cane fields, over Freshwater Creek, up a winding ascent over some colourful mountainous scenery, through a number of tunnels, past rainforests, sugar plantations, Barron Falls, Stoney Greek Falls, across grey-bouldered monoliths, and within view the green tablelands stretching out below to the sea. The train finally terminated its journey at an antiquitous, long red-roofed station at Kuranda and from there it was a drive to Ted's home at Atherton.

There was a pub that Ted would frequent occasionally. A few times Nathan accompanied him. It was an old style pub where someone would get on an accordion, someone else would play the harmonica, and a few people would start to sing. Nathan saw that Ted had lost none of the old camaraderie and communal spirit he had on that first meeting in Cairo back in 1942. Except for the change in clothes, it could have been a replica of that occasion. Then Ted had been a sergeant in the AIF singing 'The Road to Gundagai'. Here in Atherton with a few people he was singing 'The Wild Colonial Boy', and as ever he was always popular.

Sometimes Ted and Nathan would spend long evenings sitting outside the house just talking late into the night. Ted was far more aware of things than he had ever previously indicated. If ever the conversation drifted to politics or the state of the world, Ted would express his opinions with an unrelenting conviction. For the most part he was engaging company. He tried never to be too serious about life. He was happy with the simplicity of being able to live a casual pleasant life in this tropical part of the world.

Being able to gaze out at the Atherton Tablelands from his veranda was like being at the pinnacle for Ted and his family.

Nathan could have gone on forever in Northern Queensland. It was all so idyllic: waking up to streaming sunshine and the scent of the tropical flora and fauna, putting on nothing more than a pair of shorts, an open neck shirt, and sandals. Surely this was how life was meant to be, free and easy without the burdens of huge responsibility weighing down heavily. Perhaps it was all too easy to opt out of the pressures of city living. A nagging conscience forced Nathan to leave He did not want to waste his training in law, and he wanted to see Melissa again. One sunny day Nathan bade farewell to Ted and his family and boarded a bus for Brisbane.

At Brisbane Nathan changed from the bus and took the train south to Sydney. On the train there were a group of roistering cane cutters coming down to the city to work between lay offs. They were celebrating the end of the season and spoke to each other about the good time they were going to have in Sydney, after months of back breaking toil. The cane cutters were simple men plainly enjoying the beginning of the lay off. Nathan thought how the past months had made him a man so similar in style to them. He was dressed in a chequered shirt, bush trousers and shoes, had a countryman's hat, and all his meagre belonging were no longer carried in a suitcase but in a huge canvas bag that he could strap to his back.

The reality of his journey to Sydney struck a chord within him. The past months since he had boarded the boat at Tilbury seemed to belong to a dream. Nearly a year had passed since then. It had begun with hard work at three jobs in Melbourne and taken in much romantic adventuring throughout the Northern Territory and Queensland. Now he would have to attempt to find work in his chosen field of law. He would now attempt to forge a new life for himself in Sydney. In many ways the new challenges he was facing thrilled him. Nathan was returning to city life with an unusual pattern of experiences behind him and he felt that they had enriched his character enormously.

After an overnight journey the train pulled into Central Station in Sydney early in the morning. Nathan pulled his things together and moved out into the crowds of people surging through the station. He really did feel like the boy from the bush who had just arrived in the city. Only his strong dark facial features earmarked his European origin and his faith.

Before Nathan set off to find a place of residence, he decided to take a look around the centre of Sydney. Outside Central Station Nathan took a tram as far as the Town Hall. From there he walked along George Street in the direction of the Harbour Bridge. It was a pleasant sunny day with a slight breeze in the air, just enough to ruffle the hair gently.

In less than a year Nathan had already seen most of Australia. The claim by Sydneysiders that their home was Australia's leading city was not without foundation. Sydney was a mass of colour; a beautiful swaggering city pulsating with life, cosmopolitan influences and bustling crowds. Amidst the rising office blocks of concrete and glass there existed tranquil old colonial buildings with green and copper domes. There were shops, restaurants and milk bars that were clearly owned by European migrants. The whole city had a flavour of life about it. Always there was the feeling that the waters of the blue Pacific were never far away. Occasional flashes of blue could be glimpsed where the city joined the harbour.

Nathan walked down to the ferry terminal at Circular Quay. To the left of the quay the Sydney Harbour Bridge spanned the waters in all of its magnificence. Since its opening in 1932 it had been providing access for eighteen years from the city to Sydney's North Shore. Ted McTaggart had told Nathan of the story of its controversial opening, when the Premier of the day, Jack Lang, had been upstaged at the ribbon cutting ceremony. An eccentric man on horseback, a Captain De Groot of the New Guard Movement, had ridden forward and cut the ribbon with a sword before Mr Lang, a noted battler for the under privileged, had officially opened the bridge. It was a striking symbol of Sydney.

On the blue waters of the harbour, wooden ferries travelled to their destinations from Circular Quay. They travelled to suburbs such as Kirribilli, Neutral Bay, Cremorne, Mosman Bay and Manly. People thronged through the gates bound for their city offices.

Seagulls squawked as they flew down on the side of the Quay. That day Nathan began one of the most passionate love affairs anyone could ever have. He fell hook, line and sinker for the city of Sydney and its people.

Out of curiosity Nathan had continued to look around Sydney. He had taken a tram from the quay to the raffish suburb of Kings Cross. For a while he sat in a coffee house sipping a cappuccino and reading the major metropolitan newspaper, the *Sydney Morning Herald*. It was close to the middle of the day now. Nathan had already studied the job vacancy lists scrutinising the columns for anything related to law firms. He had found a few possibilities and made note of the places he would contact. The next step was to find somewhere to live. Not being backward in coming forward Nathan explained to the waitress that he had just arrived in Sydney and was looking for somewhere to live. The waitress told him of an address in the suburb of Surry Hills that he jotted down.

Surry Hills was the first suburb that Nathan lived in upon his arrival in Sydney. When he arrived there after taking the tram from Kings Cross, the place he found was a brash, generous, colourful suburb. It was only a short walk from the city and close to places like Darlinghurst and Kings Cross. The suburb had a mixture of people from varied backgrounds. There were those of Irish descent, and names like O'Connell and Shaughnessy proliferated. There were the genuine working class battlers who leaned over the back fence talking to their neighbours. Cooking smells from various kitchens rose with the breeze. Children played in the street; it had a homely feel about it.

The address Nathan had been given was a huge three-storey terrace house. From outside it had little appeal. It looked in desperate need of a coat of paint and some restoration work. The house contained a number of self-contained rooms. At this stage Nathan needed little more than the basic comforts. He contacted the landlord who was a beer-bellied, string-vested white-haired man called McDonald. Nathan did not take to him at all. McDonald cared little for courtesy; once Nathan had given him the key money deposit, McDonald slapped the keys in Nathans hands telling him to 'make sure he paid his rent on time each week or he'd be out on his arse'. McDonald barely spoke, except by monosyllabic grunts, and he was abrasive.

Nathan found his room. It was surprisingly a very comfortable bedsitting room. He had access to just about everything he needed. With a sense of relief, he felt he had somewhere from which to advance upon the world. From the window of his room Nathan could see much of the 'Hills' as it was known. The area was filled with terraced houses, old style apartment blocks, markets, pubs and cafes. It was also the centre of the rag trade. Clothing and textile firms abounded. A huge proportion of migrants lived there giving it an added dash of colour.

In the house the other rooms were occupied by a variety of people.

Nathan was to get to know them all in time. Directly opposite him lived a family called the Hoolihans. They were nicknamed 'the fighting Hoolihans' by some of the neighbours. The reason for that was obvious. Johnny and Madge Hoollihan scarcely seemed to go a week without some monumental row – over money, usually – a row which would echo throughout the house until their nineteen-year-old son, Terry, would intervene. Terry himself had a reputation as a scrapper and street fighter. He worked out as a potential lightweight boxer at a gym in Newtown. With his short hair and cuts above his eye, Terry looked hard and fierce, but it was a wrong impression. When the Hoolihans weren't fighting each other they were a united and gregarious family who would open their doors to anyone.

On the floor below there lived a Russian family called the Kiminskovs. Abria and Maviel Kiminskov, together with their young baby daughters Irenika and Miraska, were quiet and did not socialise. Abria and Maviel, although Moscovites by birth, had long lived in Harbin, China, where there had been a small Russian community. They had recently come to Australia and both spoke little English, but had battled hard to make a life for themselves here. Abria worked long hours at a local hardware store for six days a week, allowing himself little luxuries in life. The only pleasures he allowed himself were two bottles of beer on a Friday night with his record player playing some rousing Russian music in the background. His other luxury was to take Maviel and his daughters to the Botanical Gardens for a Sunday picnic. Eventually Abria hoped to be able to buy a house for his family, but in the meantime his needs were simple.

Opposite Abria and Maviel, lived a Greek family. Spiros Ossmassis was a lively Athenian in his mid-thirties; he worked by day as a motor mechanic in a garage in Crown Street and at night he worked as a cab driver. He had a great love for anything mechanical, and motorbikes and vehicles. He was also a terrible flirt with the ladies. Despite being happily married to his wife, Kristos, and the father of a young son and a daughter, with his matinee-idol looks he would constantly smile and roll his eyes at the girls.

Beneath them lived McDonald and his family who occupied the entire first floor and were oblivious to what everyone else in the house did as long as they paid the rent. The only person McDonald seemed to tolerate was Johnny Hoolihan. Johnny was in fact the local SP bookie's runner and McDonald was not averse to having a flutter when he was sure that the odds were in his favour.

This house was, with its curious mix, Nathan's introduction to life in Sydney. From here he ventured forth to find work with a law firm. For several days he went on what seemed to be fruitless interviews presenting himself, his qualifications and his enthusiasm for a career in law. After a week of negative results, Nathan returned home to consider looking for alternative work. When he entered the house McDonald shoved a letter in his hand.

"This came for you today," he growled, handing him the letter with one hand, a wad of betting slips in the other. He looked at Nathan's suit in distaste.

Nathan smiled courteously, although inside he was wondering what it was about McDonald that always prompted him to treat his fellow human being with such damnable disinterested contempt. Halfway up the stairs Nathan opened the letter and he let out with a cry of elation. The very first law firm he had approached had written to him offering him a position. He was delighted. Luck was with him. He was especially pleased, as the firm offering him work was a multi-discipline practice. It was also on the point of a merger with another company that would make it one of the largest legal firms in the country. With a chance to become a versatile practitioner, Nathan suddenly felt good about his future and himself.

He simply had to tell someone about his good fortune. He knocked on Johnny Hoolihan's door. Johnny came to the door smoothing back his shiny mane of hair.

"I've got a job, Johnny," Nathan said excitedly. Johnny's eyes twinkled. He could see the excuse for a party coming on. "I'm gong to work for a law firm."

"A law firm!" Johnny sounded startled. Being the local SP bookie's runner, he felt a little amused at the irony of it. He laughed out loudly. "Now I'll know where to go the next time the coppers run me in! Come on in. We'll have a drink." He called out to his son. "Terry, go down and ask Mr and Mrs Ossmassis if they'd like to come up. Ask Abria and Maviel, too. Tell them we're going to have a bit of a hale and hearty to celebrate Nathan here getting a job."

Terry went down and brought the neighbours up. Everybody brought some food with them: Abria and Maviel brought a few dishes of Russian food and Spiros and Kristos brought some Greek cuisine. It was touching. Johnny and Madge were very hospitable; they were at their best with people around them. Looking at them now, Nathan found it hard to believe that the two of them could create such a raucous when they hit bad times and would argue like crazy.

Everyone in the room sat round talking and laughing. Something struck Nathan sharply. Just about everyone in the room was a battler with practically nothing, yet they were sharing what little they had. There was quite a clash of cultures in the room too: there were the temperamental Irish-Australian Hoolihans; the zest-filled Spiros and his family; Abria and Maviel, who were so quiet and gentle but charming; and Nathan, who had drifted from his origins, although retained fundamental loyalty to his faith. At any other time all these people by the very nature of their personalities and backgrounds, would have had little in common. Yet here they all were laughing and joking in a spartan room, sharing food dishes from around the world, with Johnny eagerly filling up everyone's beer glass. Madge was a feisty redheaded woman, but Nathan could see that she was taking great pleasure in being a hostess to her guests, no matter how humble her surroundings.

Nathan felt a glow within him. He hoped that everyone here would achieve their dreams or else experience a magnificent stroke of good fortune that would lift them out of these drab rooms. Everybody talked about their lives. Abria and Maviel were in their forties and had experienced much in their years in Russia and China. The pride of their lives were their daughters, both born in China, each less than five years old and who would grow up to be bilingual, speaking both Russian and English. Spiros, who had served in the Greek Navy like so many of his fellow countrymen, worked tremendously hard. Hard work and his lively nature would undoubtedly bring him and his family prosperity. Even if it did not, Nathan envisaged that Spiros would be a man who would enjoy life whatever the outcome.

It was Johnny and Madge that gave Nathan the most concern. He had lain in bed a couple of nights listening to them argue. The word money always seemed to be mentioned. This was interesting because Johnny was the local SP bookie's runner and for their efforts they could reap a good financial cut. The answer was revealed one night in a row the Hoolihan's had, the words of which spilled through the walls of Nathan's room. Sometime before Johnny had set up a business with another Irish-Australian family, who lived in the hills, called the Tooheys. The business had been a disaster. When the Hoolihans weren't fighting each other, they were engaged in battle with the Toohey family.

There was far more to the fight than just money. Both Terry Hoolihan and the Toohey's son, Patrick, were both in love with the same girl, Rose Penny, who worked as a local flower seller. Rose's dad worked on a fruit barrow at some of the nearby markets. Nathan had picked up this interesting snippet of gossip from two waitresses, Geraldine and Bernadette, who worked in a café that was actually a cover for a sly grog shop.

Nathan began his new job as an articled clerk for the law firm known as Price Rayne, Easton and Westwood. He would have plenty of chance for advancement to lawyer. In order to achieve this for the next year he would have to supplement his qualifications by some part-time and evening study at Sydney University. On his first day at the firm he was introduced to another young man close to his age who went by the name of Harry Masters. The two men worked together well and became great friends.

Harry was a larger than life character. He had a commanding theatrical voice, which had been the result of Harry's interest in dramas and plays. Harry revealed that for a while in his home city of Melbourne he had been employed as an actor by one of the local radio stations, appearing in plays by night while studying by day at university. Nathan mentioned his friendship with Melissa. Harry was quick to recall having acted with her on a play in Melbourne. It did seem all so coincidental. Harry was a rather formidable figure; educated at Melbourne Grammar, he wore well cut clothes and had a slightly patrician air about him. He was witty almost to the point of being sarcastic. There was no doubt that with all these abilities, in addition to his sharp legal mind as a courtroom lawyer, he would be a fierce opponent. Nathan could not have foreseen that one day he and Harry would be partners of their own legal practice.

A few days after starting work, Nathan was coming home on the tram when he flicked through the pages of an evening newspaper. In the latter part of 1950 there were the usual articles on sport, politics and the Korean War. Glancing down at one page, Nathan saw a caption entitled *'The Changing Face of Radio'*. Since coming to Australia Nathan had become an avid listener of the wireless. The set that Mac had given him on that first night in Melbourne was well appreciated. Nathan listened to the various commercial stations and the major networks of the Australian Broadcasting Commission. He read the article about new radio programmes. That very same evening a show called *Band Hour* was being transmitted to a live audience from the Macquarie Auditorium. Anyone wishing to watch the show live could go along to the studio tonight. The article went on to state that it featured the up and coming actress and vocalist, Melissa Campbell, who would be singing a few numbers with the Bob Simmons big band. *Melissa*. Nathan smiled at the thought of the girl from the kibbutz. He thought that he would surprise Melissa by turning up unexpectedly just as she had done at the party in Ealing Green a few years ago.

Nathan alighted from the tram in Oxford Street and walked down to his room in Surry Hills. It was a pleasant, light afternoon and it surprised Nathan that even some of the most colourless buildings here looked attractive in the afternoon sunlight. Several of the pubs were already filling up to bursting point as the drinkers arrived to beat the hands of the clock before it struck six. People on bicycles rode home and mothers called their children in from playing in the street to their afternoon tea. Nathan was feeling quite happy at the thought of seeing Melissa tonight. Passing by a flower shop he decided that perhaps a single red rose and card of greeting would not go amiss. He would surprise Melissa with the gift.

Inside the flower shop Nathan looked at the reams of bouquets and mixed flowers that were all neatly placed in arrangement. He was at a loss where to select his rose for Melissa.

"Can I help you?" a female voice asked from behind the counter. Nathan turned to find himself facing a pleasant young girl of about nineteen or twenty. She had a damned attractive face, short cut fair brown hair, bright blue eyes and soft lips. Her skin was fair. Although she wore plain clothes the girl was the type who would look attractive in anything.

"I was looking for a rose and a greeting card," Nathan said, realising he was giving her a studiously admiring look. The girl in turn looked at Nathan with a smile as if he was a man she would like to know a lot better.

"No problem, mate," the girl said finding Nathan a single red rose in a plastic transparent box and a box of greeting cards. *Funny how even girls call a person mate*, thought Nathan, looking through the cards until he found the one he wanted.

"This is fine," said Nathan, giving her the card together with the flower. She wrapped it up and handed it back to him. Nathan gave her several pounds of which she returned him some change.

"You from round here?" she asked. There was a great deal of warmth about her. The girl could have been about five feet four in height, but her shoes elevated her a little bit more. Beneath her plain grey dress was a pleasant figure. A thought entered Nathan's head: *Could this girl be Rose Penny, the one for whose affections Terry Hoolihan and Patrick Toohey had been known to square off at each other over?*

Nathan replied to her, "I recently moved to this area. I've been working in the Northern Territory since I came from Europe." She looked impressed. "I live just down the road in Braithwaite Street. I've got a room in a big house there."

"Yeah, I know it. You must be Terry's neighbour," she said matter-of-factly. *Ah, so this was Rose Penny*. Nathan could see why the two boys fought over her. "Gotta bit of a mix in that house, haven't they?"

"Terry had obviously told you about me, I suppose. But anyway getting down to introductions, I am Nathan Palmai. And you are…?"

"Rose Penny's the name," she said proudly, stretching her hand out to him. Nathan took it in a limp handshake. "I'm Rose who sells roses."

"Rose Penny," Nathan repeated. "That's a name I won't forget." He had been curious about her, knowing Terry was plainly obsessed with this girl.

"Can you dance?" Rose asked him out of the blue.

"Can I dance?" Nathan repeated the question in surprise.

"Yeah like this, mate," Rose mocked him innocently shuffling around on her feet as if she was dancing with an imaginary dancing partner.

Nathan was even more amused by her. "Well I think Fred Astaire can sleep easily, but yes, I can dance, a little."

"Well, if you'se not doing anything on Saturday night, Terry's taking me dancing at the Trocadero. Come along if you like."

"I'd like that." He smiled at her; he was flattered by her attentions.

Rose had a wicked sense of humour. Fluttering her eyelids self mockingly, and with one hand on her hip, she said jokingly, "If you're lucky, I might have a dance with you. I'm not a bad looking sheila when I get dressed up."

"I'll let Terry know," Nathan said with a farewell smile. "Goodbye, Rose."

Nathan had just got to the door when Rose called out to him. "Hey mate!"

"Yes." He turned to face her.

Rose was standing at the counter with a tongue in cheek look, her eyes glimmering with humour. "See you around, mate," she said provocatively, her voice at least a decibel lower, and she winked at him cheekily. Nathan winked back at her and went on his way home. *No wonder Terry and Patrick were in love with her.*

He was so keen to get to the show this evening that he arrived nearly an hour earlier. Nathan was just about to go and have a cup of coffee at a nearby café, when he saw his law colleague Harry Masters walking towards him. The two men smiled at each other amiably.

"Hullo Harry. What brings you this way after a hard day's work at our legal firm?"

"Nathan, dear boy," Harry boomed at him. "I would say precisely the same reason as the one that careered you in this direction of the Macquarie Auditorium. To see my old thespian colleague, of course, Melissa Campbell, from my days as a Melbourne radio actor by night and law student by day. And indeed from what you told me at work, your long time friend from pre-war kibbutz day's."

Harry always had an expressive theatrical manner about the way he spoke.

"I take it, Harry, you read the article about radio in tonight's paper," inquired Nathan. "I'm an hour early."

"Indeed I did," he retorted. "But actually, my dear fellow, I was already coming along this evening to take in a radio play beforehand. The fact that the *Band Hour* is following on immediately is an absolute plus ten. The fact that Melissa is appearing as a vocalist makes it a double plus ten. Why don't you join me for the play and stay on for the show afterwards? The play starts in a few minutes."

"That is a very good idea, Harry," said Nathan and the two of them entered the building to take in the play and the *Band Hour* programme.

Nathan had come to realise just how powerful the medium of radio was in Australia since his arrival. In those post-war years the Australian public gathered around their wireless sets, relying on them to bring news, entertainment and sports broadcasts into their living rooms. Before the advent of television in 1956 the wireless provided drama, comedy and pathos through live radio plays. There were a number of shows that had their regular listeners. Amongst them were Dad and Dave, the Grace Gibson Hour, Blue Hills, the Lux Radio Theatre, and quiz programmes with enormously popular comperes such as Jack Davey and Bob Dyer.

It was the first time that Nathan had ever seen a radio play performed live. In the auditorium he watched the actor's crowd around studio microphones and perform their lines with vigour. It was not only dialogue the actors delivered. To add more to the impact an actor would demonstrate his versatility by imitating the sound of a train, tapping out the noise of a man running, or any other sound effect that might have required recreating. The whole hour was an enjoyable experience. It led up nicely to the commencement of the *Band Hour* programme.

There was a ten-minute intermission, during which time the musicians of the band took their place in the auditorium. Nathan and Harry sat waiting for the show to begin. People took their places while the musicians tested the chords of their instruments. The musicians were all decked out in uniformly red evening jackets, bright shiny shoes, dark trousers, white silk shirts and bow ties, except for the leader of the band who was distinctive by his gleaming white outfit. When the musicians were all in tune, the band leader tapped his baton on the platform, the house lights dimmed, the audience hushed and the voice of an announcer came across from an unseen microphone.

"Ladies and gentlemen – welcome to the *Band Hour* programme. And here is your host for the evening together with his big band, will you welcome Mr Bob Simmons."

The bandleader in the white jacket turned completely around to face the audience who in turn responded with applause. The band started up playing a 40s-type swing number. When the tune had finished, because the programme was sponsored, there was a commercial performed by several female singers who espoused the virtues of a certain product. The band then played several up-beat numbers before the first guest vocalist was introduced. Nathan sat on the edge of his seat with his gift of a rose for Melissa. He had fully expected Melissa to be the first guest. Instead it was a stunning tall vivacious singer from New Zealand called Annie Sprinkle. She was a superb vocalist who handled her numbers well. In those days of the big bands, the vocals had to be skilful, and full of range and dexterity, in order to blend in perfect consummation with the instruments.

Nathan enjoyed the show. Even the commercials were entertaining. The live performances for a product such as Vegemite, Aeroplane Jelly, Colgate, Palmolive or Persil were every bit as important to the show as the featured artistes themselves. Finally in the last fifteen minutes of the *Band Hour* the time came for Melissa to be introduced. Nathan steeled himself. This was the girl he seemed to be ever reaching for.

Bob Simmons took the microphone to introduce the next guest that Nathan knew would have to be Melissa.

"Ladies and gentlemen," Bob Simmons began. "Versatility is a word we often use in the entertainment business. When you hear an announcer say he or she is a versatile performer, that's a pretty good description of someone who has talent in various areas of the performing arts; it was never more true of my next guest. When I say she's versatile, boy, is she ever! During the war she was a European living on a kibbutz in Palestine. She used to sing and act in kibbutz plays. An ENSA group saw her perform and took her on tour playing to the troops in battle zones. In England she performed in musicals and repertory theatre. She joined the Old Vic and toured here as a member of the company on that famous tour of 1947 when Lawrence Olivier and Vivien Leigh thrilled us all. Well, she liked it so much here she decided to stay. Since then she's appeared in numerous radio plays, toured as a vocalist with my band, and just recently she appeared in her first screen role with the American actor Gary Markel. What more can I say? Ladies and gentlemen, how about a great welcome for the highly talented actress singer, Miss Melissa Campbell."

The audience gave out spontaneous applause. Nathan looked sharply to the wings of the auditorium and then onto the stage came the one girl he had truly loved. Melissa looked fabulous. Nearly three years had passed since Nathan had last seen her. She had come a long way and there was no doubt she still had heights to ascend. Melissa was comparable in looks and style to some of the great screen beauties of the day such as Elizabeth Taylor and Jean Simmons. With her figure endowed in a sparkling white gown that constantly caught the flicker of the lights, she greeted Bob Simmons with a carefully rehearsed embrace and kiss on the cheek, and positioned herself in front of the microphone radiating charisma in abundance.

Melissa sang several powerful songs, which stretched the range of her voice to its most powerful. When she sang 'Old Man River', she did so with a power, clarity and an expression of the words that amazed Nathan. This all-enchanting, sparkling star before him had once been the young girl on the poultry run at the Kibbutz Jezarat. That had been light years before it seemed, and Nathan now wondered with sudden alarm if there would ever be a place in her life for him now.

When the show ended the audience gave the performers a standing ovation. Bob Simmons put his arms round the enchantingly delightful Annie Sparkle and the spellbinding Melissa. There was no doubt who the star was in Nathan's mind.

Harry and Nathan remained seated while everyone else left the auditorium. When it was totally empty Harry turned to Nathan and asked him, "Are you coming backstage to see Melissa then?"

Nathan looked at Harry and then he said, "Harry, would you go in and see her on your own. Take this flower and card and tell her I am here."

"I shall do, my learned friend," Harry replied, acceding to Nathan's request and taking the gifts for Melissa. He left Nathan sitting alone in the empty seats while he went inside. Ten minutes later he returned with Melissa by his side. Harry pointed out to where Nathan was sitting. Melissa beamed a smile towards her old friend who promptly rose from his seat to greet her. The two hugged each other in a genuine embrace of affection. It was marvellous to be reunited.

Close up Melissa looked wonderful. At twenty-eight years of age she had matured wonderfully. Her eyes sparkled, her hair looked shiny and well conditioned. Just to hold her in a warm embrace was for Nathan a dream come true.

Together with Harry Masters they decided to spend the remainder of the evening at a restaurant. At Romano's in Castlereagh Street, Nathan told Melissa of everything he had done since arriving in Australia. When Nathan talked of how he had worked at three jobs in Melbourne, and then travelled on to the Northern Territory, Melissa looked on in awe. Nathan's story of how he and Joe Patterson had trekked across sixty miles of desert seemed unbelievable. If Melissa had heard anybody else tell the same story, she would have dismissed it out of hand as a yarn of ridiculous proportions; but because it was Nathan, a man whose honesty she knew, it was all the more interesting. If each could have read the other's mind, they would have been incredulous at the similarity of each other's thoughts.

Melissa was thinking: could this well-travelled adventurous man of such refinement and experience really be the same quiet person she had known on the kibbutz? Nathan's life had been one of hard graft and reality. In a sense Melissa felt that her life and career path had taken her out of the real world into one of fantasy; the semi-real world of show business. More than anything Melissa felt that Nathan had grown away from her and that apart he was mature. Nathan belonged to a business and legal life. Melissa belonged to a life of theatrical first nights and the applause of an audience. The two could not mix. Their careers and lifestyles would render them incompatible.

Nathan had realised this when he had seen Melissa perform on stage at the Macquarie Auditorium. She had been born for this life; he knew it at that moment. The same time he had made the realisation that his long-held obsession for her had been exactly that – an obsession. In Romano's that night Harry, Melissa and Nathan talked over the excellent food that the restaurant was justifiably renowned for. The course of the conversation tended to lapse into frequent nostalgic reminiscences of Austria, the Kibbutz Jezarat and the party with the Foley's at Ealing Green. Harry, as if sensing he was imposing on the two old friends politely excused himself to go home, leaving Nathan and Melissa to talk of times and people they knew.

"Harry's a nice man, isn't he?" Melissa asked Nathan watching Harry leave the restaurant.

"Yes. He has a strong personality, a splendid lawyer's voice. I should think he will be as successful in his profession as you have been. I remember when I first saw you perform in a kibbutz play; you were good then. I did not think you could become better than you were then. I am astonished. Your voice, your appearance, the way you hold the stage. You're so – so professional."

"I am flattered by your remarks, Nathan." In fact Melissa looked more embarrassed than flattered. "If I compare my life with yours I think I have had good fortune; perhaps more than you. I was, I suppose, in the right place at the right time. From what you have told me tonight you have worked hard to get to the point where you are today."

"I think you underestimate yourself. You may have had good fortune but you have always had a unique talent. You have acted in musical comedy, drama as well as Shakespearean plays. Only someone who works hard in their career could manage to achieve all that. But the range of your voice – it is so much stronger, so much more powerful than I remember."

"Years of experience." She smiled and changed the subject. "I have just finished a film with Gary Markel."

"The bandleader mentioned that tonight," Nathan recalled. "Gary Markel, isn't he the cowboy actor?"

"That's right. He plays the part of an American rancher who comes to New South Wales to take over a property in the outback. I play the part of a European refugee he meets in the bush and eventually marries." She became serious for one moment. "Nathan," There was a sense of urgency in her voice. Before she had the chance to continue a voice was directed at her.

"Hi-Ho Melissa!" It was a cheery jovial voice.

"Hullo, Mr Davey. How are you?" she responded. A man passing by the table warmly acknowledged her. Melissa talked to the man for a few moments.

"That was Jack Davey," Melissa smiled. Nathan looked a bit befuddled. "The radio star!" Nathan at once realised who she meant. Of course, that Jack Davey! "I've appeared on several radio programmes with him," Melissa said proudly. "Wonderful man. He's so good with people."

"What were you about to say, Melissa?"

"Gary Markel has asked me to marry him."

The words hit Nathan with the impact of a sledgehammer. He was quite lost for words. In the back of his mind he had always, perhaps rather foolishly or selfishly, felt that because of their early friendship dating back to the kibbutz imagined that he had some sort of claim to her. He had never envisaged the possibility that she would consider marriage to anyone else.

"That – that's wonderful news," Nathan lied, feeling as if a lead weight had dropped within him. He felt he must not show a sign of jealousy or disappointment and he attempted a congratulatory smile.

"I haven't said yes, yet." Nathan was about to breath a sigh of relief when she confirmed his worst fears. "But I'm pretty sure I will say yes. I have commitments and bookings here for all of 1951. I hope to go to Hollywood the year after to try my luck. Gary is contracted to Warner Brothers, and I'm hopeful his agent may find work for me."

"When do you plan to get married?" Nathan still held out some hope that she might change her mind in due course.

"I'm not sure," she said happily. "That's enough talk about my romantic life. Enough talk of my career. Enough of me. I am not so interesting just because I am an actress and a singer. Your time in the British Army in the desert, and your stay on Orange Tree Downs, is far more interesting than any film script I've ever seen. I can't believe you had the energy to do those things. It goes to show that because a man is quiet and sensitive it does not mean to say he is not adventurous. You are a surprise, old friend. You are also the most interesting man I've ever met apart from your great friend Freddie Miller." Melissa reached out and gripped his hand warmly in that old affectionate gesture of hers which could still trigger off emotions in Nathan. She released her grip. "Now you must tell me, Nathan." She sat back and looked at him, smiling warmly in a curious manner.

"Tell you what?" Nathan inquired with an amused look on his face.

"About all the girls in your life." Nathan laughed at the remark. "Why so funny, Nathan? Surely a nice man like you must have a girlfriend."

"Because I have always been madly in love with you, of course," Nathan said jokingly, realising that inside that he had actually made a frank admission.

Melissa immediately took it as a joke. "So that is the real reason you came to Sydney. To seek me out and marry me!" She laughed not realising that was the very reason Nathan had come to Sydney. In fact the way she said it the irony was uproariously funny. Nathan and Melissa laughed together.

"I have always loved you, Melissa," Nathan said suddenly. Melissa wiped the smile off her face. "Yes, Melissa, I have always loved you. Like a sister perhaps."

Like a sister, thought Melissa. For him if there had been a chance Melissa might have given up her career to marry him. What price a career to sacrifice personal happiness. But no, Nathan had admitted to loving her as a sister, not for the beautiful, passionate woman that she was.

If only he had known what Melissa was thinking. *I lied*, he thought. Melissa, *I do not love you in that manner. I love you because of the woman you are. I know now you would never give up your sparkling career to be a suburban housewife. It is better I lie*, he thought. *It is better you marry this man Gary Markel and that you go to Hollywood with your bright shining blazing beacon of talent. That is the life that was meant for you.*

Melissa leaned forward and this time it was she who lied. "It's strange. I feel the same way. It must be our comradeship as fellow kibbutzim, that makes us feel like brother and sister." She filled their glasses with wine. "I hope we will keep in touch when I'm not touring."

"Of course, Melissa," said Nathan. "I have your address. You wrote it down for me. Rushcutters Bay is not that far from Surry Hills."

"Well, Nathan," she began raising her glass to his, "To times gone by. Old friends, old places, to new friends and new places. To your career. To my career. Let us not forget the toast of our people. The toast of our faith."

"*L'chaim*," said Nathan clinking his glass to hers.

"*L'chaim*," said Melissa clinking her glass and then draining back the contents.

If only each had known what the other was really thinking.

Thirty-eight

Nathan was impressed by the way Melissa had handled her career. He still admired her greatly. Melissa had grown into a marvellously confident woman, not only as a performer but in her own personality. Somehow the success of her career had helped her throw off her stigma about her own illegitimacy. Her past did not worry her, nor should it have done so. Her career had given her a stepping stone into a lifestyle far removed from the world of the battler and the businessman. Nathan concluded that they would always be friends, although in terms of career and lifestyles, they were worlds apart. In a sense Nathan felt a sense of freedom. He had always committed himself to the possibility of a future with Melissa and denied himself involvement with other women. Now that each of them had made their intentions and ambitions clear, Nathan felt independent and eager to develop his personal relationships.

When Rose Penny, the pretty young girl in the flower shop, had flirted with Nathan he had enjoyed being the centre of her interest. Saturday night he had reserved to go dancing with Rose and Terry at the Trocadero. Nathan was quite looking forward to his first taste of social life in Sydney. He had not yet enjoyed this aspect of life in the city.

On the Saturday morning Nathan was returning to his room with his lunch and some books he needed for his part time evening course. He had walked in the direction of a pub in Crown Street when he heard the sound of a commotion from within. He stopped as he saw two young men fighting each other. The two of them literally fell out of the door of the pub followed by a crowd of onlookers. Nathan abhorred violence and aggression and was inclined to walk to the other side of the road. But he was stunned when he saw his neighbour, Terry Hoolihan, one of the participants, and even more amazed when he saw the young man's father,

Johnny, rushing from one side to stop the brawl. Johnny looked distressed as he tried to break through the crowd.

Why oh why do people try to settle their differences with fisticuffs, thought Nathan, almost angrily. He was just about to go down and help Johnny when he saw a policeman make a move through the onlookers. The policeman was obviously not faint-hearted. He pushed and barged his way through the surrounding drinkers, dispersing them quickly and aggressively. He separated the fighters with his baton.

"Terry Hoolihan and Patrick Toohey, eh? I might have guessed it." He growled angrily. "Get up, you two!" The policeman pulled each of them up by the scruff of the neck. Both the young men were in a terrible bloodied state. Battered and bruised.

"Look at the state of you two. Every time there's a blue in Surry Hills, Pat Toohey and Terry Hoolihan are always at the centre of it. Bishop Street, Bourke Street, Cleveland Street, whatever flamin' street, there's a punch being thrown, you two little runts are right there in the middle of it. Now I don't know what it is about the Tooheys and the Hoolihans, that they've got to go hammer and tong at each other, but I give you kids fair warning, next time there's a brawl I'm going to run you in. Understand?" The two of them nodded. He turned to Patrick Toohey. "Okay, Toohey, beat it. You better go home and clean your wounds." The man snarled his lip and reluctantly walked away, casting a backward glance at Terry that seemed to suggest *I'll get you.*

"I'm sorry, Dad," said Terry. His father, Johnny, looked at him with a face like thunder.

The policeman looked at both of them. He waited until Patrick Toohey had gone well away within earshot of them all.

"Johnny, your kid is a bloody hothead!" The policeman said with firmness. "I meant what I said. The next time it'll be a charge. Go on, you two, get off home."

"Come on, son," murmured Johnny and put his hand on his son's shoulder. Nathan came up beside them and offered Terry a hand. Terry was limping and he had a split lip and a bloodied nose, as well as the promise of a black eye.

"Johnny, come here a minute," called the policeman,

Johnny reluctantly went back to where the policeman was still standing.

"What is it?" he asked looking a little alarmed.

The policeman removed some pound notes from his pocket.

"Got a good tip for the races this afternoon, John?" he said with a smile.

Johnny wasn't sure what to make of the policeman. He was happy to oblige him with a tip though. In his capacity as an SP Bookie's runner, he was used to things like this.

"Try Sunrise Rising at three-fifteen, eight to one for a win. It's a cert. For the three-thirty, Lightning Ride, twenty to one, for a place."

Two wads of notes landed on Johnny's hand.

"Split it evenly, John."

"Right-oh, Constable," a surprised Johnny remarked. He was amazed at the size of the bet. An SP Bookie's runner has seen a lot of big cash bets being laid. This one was surprising because of the policeman's junior rank and the salary that matched it. Johnny realised that the wad of notes must have been the lucky run from a rookie cop's weakness.

Johnny ran back to Nathan and Terry.

"I can't go to the dance tonight," moaned Terry. "You'll have to take Rose on your own." Nathan turned to look at him. "I mean it, mate. Look at my face. Toohey battered me good. The bastard!"

"Why do you two fight?" inquired Nathan, distressed that the Hoolihan family always seemed to be in conflict with each other.

"Nothing for you to worry about," Johnny intercepted sharply. "You're a damn idiot, Terry. That girl, Rose, is going to be disappointed. You were taking her to the Troc tonight. If you can't go to a couple of rounds with Rose on a dance floor, how are you going to handle your first title fight in a few weeks time?"

"Title fight?" Nathan was surprised.

"Yeah, I'm up to meet Sculler Brown at the Rushcutters Bay stadium," Terry confirmed.

"And a bloody good boxer he's going to be. All that training down the drain." Johnny was furious.

"Look, Dad, it'll be different in the ring. Toohey kicked and jabbed and did everything unfair to floor me."

"I hope it'll be different when you get up against Sculler. For God's sake don't keep scrapping with the Tooheys. It's an old fight, son. Let it die."

"Is there anything I can do?" Nathan asked sympathetically, aware of the long-standing feud between the Tooheys and the Hoolihans.

"You can take Rose to the Troc for a start," replied Terry. He genuinely meant it. Terry wasn't in any fit state for dancing.

Back at the house in Braithwaite Street they arrived much to Madge Hoolihan's despair. Madge had been used to her husband's fights as a youngster. Now it was a case of like father, like son. Nathan looked on as Terry went into the room with Madge and Johnny. The Hooliham family were as hard as nails with fiery tempers, yet Nathan knew also they were warm hearted. It was as if one drop of the milk of human kindness had never entered their lives and touched the sentimental part of their hearts that needed awakening. Somehow Nathan wanted to do something for them. In time he would.

Rose Penny was surprised when Nathan arrived on his own at her home in Boronia Street. Rose and her father, Stan Penny, lived in a couple of rooms on the first floor of a terraced house. It was a place of dwelling that gave the appearance of having once been a grand colonial terrace in the early part of the century. With some paint and handiwork it could be a vastly improved house. Nathan knocked at the door and Rose appeared. Nathan was surprised too. To use her own words, Rose really wasn't a bad looking sheila when she got dressed up.

"G'day mate," she said in a voice of delight, smiling shyly. "Where's Terry?"

Nathan studied this lovely girl's appearance. Rose was wearing a beautiful flared out dress and blouse, both in a patterned variety of colours. Her shoes were red, high-heeled and had shining leather. She had a light cardigan draped around her shoulders and her hair was shining brown with a white band in it.

"Terry is not feeling too well tonight," answered Nathan, feeling thrilled that this attractive twenty-year-old girl was his date for the evening. "Terry asked me to make his apologies. He said he hoped you wouldn't mind if I took you."

"I heard about the punch up. Me dad was one of the drinkers in the bar." Rose looked cross. "I s'pose Terry's got a bit of a shiner, has he?"

"I'm afraid so, Rose."

Rose gave Nathan a coy look. "Well, it looks like I'm your date tonight." She let out a chuckle. "How does that grab you, darling?"

Nathan responded quickly. "I think, Rose, now that you are dressed up, you are not a bad looking sheila."

Rose laughed again and held out her arm to him. "Well take my arm then, luv. We'll give it a go, eh? A fancy gentleman like you cutting a dash to make the ladies swoon, and a good-looking tart like me, I reckon we'll knock em dead."

"I think I am going to enjoy this evening," smiled Nathan putting his arm out, and being amused by his companion's brash humour.

"You think too much, sweetie. Let's get down to a bit of the enjoying," she chuckled virtually, taking charge of the situation.

★★★

On the dance floor at the Trocadero on a bustling Saturday night with lots of people crowding the place, Rose was yet again surprised. The man she was dancing with was something of an expert. Nathan danced the Tango and the Quickstep with a degree of professionalism; Rose was in awe of this quiet man, who had a number of talents yet to be unearthed it seemed. Dancing with Nathan, Rose was experiencing something new in her life. Never before had she dated a European man and, even though Nathan wore fairly conservative clothes, he had a dash of glamour about him. At the end of one dance Nathan and Rose sat down with a drink and watched the dancers.

"Where did you learn to dance, mate?" Rose asked, more curious about him than ever.

"Don't keep calling me 'mate'. My name is Nathan," he replied good-heartedly.

"All right, *mate*, where did you learn to dance, Nathan?"

Rose was incorrigible but fun. A girl like Rose was a new experience too for Nathan.

"Actually my mother taught me. My mother taught me everything." Nathan's eyes became wistful and sad. "At home in Austria I lived in a village where there were many people of my faith. Because of the things that were happening in Europe, and the restrictions placed on my people, I could not go to school. My mother, who was a trained schoolteacher, taught me at home. She taught me manners, music, art, how to speak English and some French. And she taught me how to dance."

"She did a ripper of a job, luv. Terry normally kick's me in the shin, scuffs my shoes, and doesn't so much as hold me when we're dancing but gropes me. You're a real gentleman."

"Oh, I wouldn't say that, Rose."

"Funny thing. The moment you walked into the shop I thought: now here's a nice bloke. You've come from Europe, you've' been all over the place, you talk nice, you speak a couple of languages. I haven't been anywhere. Me mum was a pom. She came here with me dad as a war bride. He was in London at the end of the First World War. He got wounded in France see, and he was in hospital in London. Met mum over there, he did. She came from a place called Stepney. Poor mum. We lost her a couple of years ago. Took dad and me a long time to come to terms that she'd gone. Mum used to say that living in Surry Hills was like living in Stepney where the sun shone a lot more. I wouldn't mind going over there one day."

"You've lived in Surry Hills all of your life then?"

"Yeah. Lived in the same house too. Known the same people as well."

"Could I ask you something, Rose?" She looked directly into his eyes as if he was about to ask something of intent. Nathan caught the change in look. "No nothing personal, Rose. I've grown very fond of Johnny and Madge and your Terry. You've known them long?"

"Yes. Terry and I went to school together. I grew up with the Houlihans as friends of mum and dad's. I knew the Toohey's too. I guess you want to know about the feud, do you?"

"I know a little bit. They argue a lot. Living next door I hear a few things. What's the full story, Rose?"

"Goes back a long time. Johnny Hoolihan and Sam Toohey were kids in Redfern and both after Madge. Sound's familiar, doesn't it? Anyway, they weren't enemies or nothing like that; more rivals you might say. So the story goes, Johnny and Sam did over a place, made off with all the takings. The coppers latched on to what was happening. Johnny got clean away with the takings but Sam got caught. Sam ended up doing bird. While Sam's behind bars Johnny goes off, marries Madge and starts his own business. Needless to say when Sam gets out he's pretty crook about it all. Couldn't blame him really, could you? Johnny married his girl, invested the takings and Sam paid the dues. Trouble was Johnny's business collapsed, so he wasn't able to pay Sam a cent. Since then Sam and Johnny have been at each other's throats. The feud more or less carried itself into the next generation. Now Terry and Sam's son, Pat, throw their fists at each other."

"And now they fight over you," suggested Nathan.

"God knows why. I grew up really close to Terry. Pat tried to shove in on my life a number of times. I keep telling him politely to piss off, but it's as if Terry and Pat see me as some sort of excuse to brawl over. Let's be honest, I'm not exactly a top-flight oil painting, and I'm hardly what you'd call a lady. I think they're carrying on a tradition like John and Sam used to over Madge."

"Rose, did you every think that there was a much more wider world out there other than Surry Hills?"

Rose seemed to become angry. "And what's wrong with Surry Hills? The people there are all battlers. They're good people. They might move their fists and their pelvis a bit more than they do in Vaucluse or Parsley Bay, but when you get to the heart of them, they're a sight more honest, decent and hard-working than some of those rich drongos."

"I did not mean it like that, Rose. I mean did you every think of travelling? Going abroad; to London perhaps, where your mother came from."

Rose smiled at Nathan. She recognised she had reacted badly. It was impossible not to like her. "I would love to go to London and Paris." Her eyes shone as she said it. "I'm just a flower seller, what chance have I got?"

"Every chance in the world, Rose. I like you – very much."

"You do?" she said with surprise.

"Yes. I admit you are a bit brash and a bit of a flirt, but I can tell you are a really good-hearted girl. I feel very proud to be your escort tonight. And you're not *just* a flower seller, what is wrong with being a flower seller? You do an honourable day's work. You say you are not an oil painting, but my goodness you are as pretty as a picture. I feel proud to be here with you. In fact I would like to take you to dinner sometime."

"No bull!" she exclaimed, obviously touched by Nathan's words.

"No bull, Rose. I know about battlers too. I have been a battler. My whole life has been a battle. Avoiding persecution as a youngster in Nazi Germany, and as a youth in Austria. Losing my parents in a concentration camp. Working on the land in a Palestinian Kibbutz. Serving as a soldier in the British Army. I struggled through university by working in the evenings and on Saturdays as a Greengrocer's boy. In Melbourne I worked at three jobs. In the Northern Territory I worked on one of the toughest stations in Australia. Do you think Rose that I do not know what it is to be a battler?

I have been one all my life. People like yourself and your dad, Stan, are people of my own spirit. Even Johnny with his wild past, and Madge and Terry, I know they are good people. I believe Rose, that people react in the way they are treated. Treat them with compassion and love and that is how they respond."

"You might be right, mate," Rose murmured softly, smiling at him and adoring him all the more for what he had just told her.

Down on the dance floor people were pouring on to it as the music played. From where he was sitting Nathan saw to his surprise Melissa join the dancers. The man she was with was instantly recognizable as Gary Markel, the Hollywood film actor she had recently made a film with. Several people on the dance floor recognised Markel and shook his hand, Nathan watched curiously enough not with the slightest feeling of jealousy as Gary Markel took Melissa in his arms and swayed with her in time with the music. There was no doubting the look in Melissa's eyes. It was one of true adoration for her dancing partner. The two of them weren't mean dancers either. Melissa was one incredible sexy package of dance movements. Gary Markel was rhythmic complimenting Melissa perfectly as a dancing partner.

"Gee that's the film star, Gary Markel down there," Rose observed not realising that Nathan had been watching Melissa and Gary for several minutes.

"I know," Nathan said glancing at her as he replied.

"Nice looking lady he's dancing with eh?" Rose said unsuspectingly. Nathan nodded at her, forcing a quick smile.

"You'd go well with a top-looking sheila like that," Rose added, admiring Melissa's style and poise.

"Not my type, Rose. I can assure you I feel more comfortable with you," Nathan emphasised with an absolute poker-faced expression. He wondered if perhaps he should tell Rose that he knew Melissa personally. Perhaps he would do later on. With relief he watched Gary and Melissa leave the dance floor for some refreshment on the opposite side. "Would you like to dance, Rose?"

"Let's go for it, Nathan," she replied enthusiastically. The two made for the centre of the dance floor. Some wild swing music rent across the Trocadero interior and they both enjoyed themselves immensely. Rose had never met a man quite like Nathan. She felt safe in his company. He in turn found her boisterous, brash and amusing. They were a contrasting couple. Almost direct opposites in fact but their differences were like two positives of alternate characteristics coming together.

When the music slowed right down and the lights were dimmed it was excellent romantic mood atmosphere style. Rose was not slow in sinking into the warmth of Nathan's arms and resting her head on his chest. Nathan looked down at Rose and saw that her eyes were closed. She had a remarkably serene loving look about her, one of peace and comfort. Nathan stretched his arms round her and ran one hand gently up the full length of her arm in a soft gentle stroking manner. She recognised the emotional feel of Nathan's hands and even though her eyes were closed, a warm smile spread across her face.

"We must do this again," she whispered.

From one side of the Trocadero Melissa held Gary Markel's hand and gazed down at the dancers. Instinctively she noticed Nathan with Rose. Strangely enough it was she who felt a twinge of jealousy. Knowing how Nathan had pursued her and yet because of each other's self doubts their relationship was purely platonic. Melissa began to wonder about the girl her old friend was dancing with. She startled herself by the realisation that she was jealous.

"Let's go and eat somewhere, Gary," she said suddenly.

"Sure, honey," replied her escort.

On the dance floor Nathan saw Melissa and Gary get up from their seats to leave. Nathan waved quickly to Melissa. Rose remained in his embrace unaware he had just waved to Melissa. Melissa in turn blew Nathan a kiss.

"Will you come to Bondi beach with me tomorrow, Nathan?" Rose asked him and then looked up at him. Nathan turned his glance from Melissa back to Rose.

"I would love to," he answered.

★★★

On Sunday morning Nathan and Rose took the tram to Bondi beach. This was the first time he had ever ridden all the way to the beach on the famous Bondi tram. It was a very hot morning on that December day in late 1950 and true to form the sun lovers were out in full force. The tram was chock a block with family's and their children, together with young surfers standing holding their boards upright. Before even reaching Taylor Square along Oxford Street, there were already people virtually hanging from the rails of the tram. It was so full the tram did not set down at any stop to pick people up until it had reached Bondi. *Shot through like a Bondi tram*, thought Nathan. Now he understood the expression.

At Bondi, Rose and Nathan changed into their swimming gear and laid out on their towels. Bondi was, and still is, Australia's most famous beach and the most well known in the world ranking only with Honolulu's Waikiki and Rio De Janeiro's Copacabana. The appeal of Bondi was strictly for the individual to discern. Some people praised it. Some people adored it and others – well others had different opinions. Nathan liked it on that very first day. The huge rolling surf accommodated the highly talented board riders catching a weave and a swell. It was fascinating to watch. The surfers performed on their boards in every position, from hanging five to going down on their knees. They were slick back bronze figures on a cascade of blue water and frothy surf.

Bondi was glorious to the city dweller who only had to travel a few miles to reach its golden sands. Nathan was quite happy to just sit back on the sand and watch the huge waves crash down spilling down surf on to the smooth sand. The whole of the beach seemed to epitomise a freedom that was unique to the Australian way of life. There were a team of lifesavers marching across the beach in step with the colours of their club being carried by a standard bearer. The lifesavers were admirable men who devoted their spare time to patrolling the beach. Without their skill many people would have lost their lives in rips or turbulent seas. The lifesavers, like Bondi Beach, were a national institution. It was hard to imagine Australia without either of them.

Rose was in many ways a typical Bondi beach girl. She played and splashed in the surf for ages before coming back out and dragging Nathan in. In her swimsuit, Rose was surprisingly slim and well rounded. Nathan realised that the clothes Rose wore normally did not do her justice. In the surf Rose was possessed of style in her swimming strokes. There was no doubting her womanly qualities. For the first time Nathan found himself looking at Rose in a different manner. He did not see her as the brash, flirtatious flower seller from Surry Hills who was an amusing, fun companion; he saw her as the bright, blossoming young woman he had not imagined her to be. The thought alarmed him. Rose hugged Nathan jokingly in the surf. But for Nathan this was the first time in a long while that he had felt his emotions drift.

When they came out of the water for a time they lay in the sun talking. Rose wore a pair of sunglasses that gave her a slight touch of sophistication. *With a bit of training*, Nathan thought, *Rose could undergo the sort of metamorphism that Professor Higgins helped Eliza Doolittle to.* Nathan wanted to see Rose on a regular basis. He felt guilty considering that Rose had long been Terry Hoolihan's girl and that Pat Toohey had fought over her. Now that Melissa had been relegated from prospective spouse to the status of being an old friend, Nathan could allow himself the pleasure of falling in love. He did not fight against it.

Rose stretched out lazily in the sun, closing her eyes. The powerful sun highlighted her brown hair. Her fair skin and complexion that she inherited through the genes of her English mother was a creamy-gold in colour.

For the time being Nathan would have to be cautious about his friendship with Rose. He was very interested in her. There were some things in life that just weren't meant to be. Intellectually Rose and Nathan were worlds apart. Somehow their styles gelled but between them and their differences of personality produced a camaraderie that could well develop romantically.

Thirty-nine

Terry Hoolihan's first title fight came up a few weeks later at the Rushcutters Bay Stadium. Moral support came in the form of Johnny and Madge, and McDonald who spruced himself up for the occasion, Rose and her father Stan, and without their wives Abria and Spiros. Nathan also came along somewhat reluctantly. Probably he came from just being curious, never having seen a boxing match before. Nathan's friend, Harry Masters, came as well. Harry seemed like the odd man out in this group of people that sat strung out in the front row. In fact Harry was very much at home. Apart from loving theatre, he was very much a connoisseur of the pugilistic arts, as well as the codes of football rules and Rugby League in which he was a passionate supporter of South Sydney. The whole row of friends waited enthusiastically for the fight to begin.

The Toohey family were also there. Predictably they sat a few rows away on the other side of the ring, close enough to be seen though. Sam Toohey, Johnny Hoolihan's former partner in the robbery, was a tough-looking man. He had a crooked nose, the result of a lifetime of brawling. Apart from that distinction he looked every bit of his Irish heritage with sympathetic eyes, black curly hair, and a strong physical build that rippled beneath his clothes. His wife, Maggie Toohey, was a sweet looking woman, almost frail in appearance. She sat between her husband and her son, Pat.

There was such a similarity between the families Nathan thought it a sadness that the two groups could not bury the hatchet. Perhaps the divisions ran too deep.

A coupe of exhibition bouts took place first of all. They were short, lasting only a few rounds each. The style of boxing was good; clean straight out jabbing without fear of causing ferocious injury. The two exhibitors moved fast on their feet and threw straight lefts and rights in which each young man was quick on defence and return. Demonstration of such speed and skill made for an interesting fight. Nathan, who normally disliked rough tactical sports, found himself admiring the two opponents. This bout purely served as a warm up to the main fight.

It was time for the fight between Sculler Brown and Terry Hoolihan. The crowd were on edge with excitement, stamping their feet and clapping their hands until the contender came out separately. The compere of the evening introduced both men amidst an amalgamation of cheers and boos from the audience. Sculler Brown sparred blows against an invisible opponent in the 'blue corner' of the ring. Even from a distance Sculler looked deadly. He was hawk-eyed, his physique was lithe and glistening, and it was obvious to anyone he could move with all the power of a leopard striking its prey. He was fearsome without doubt. What made it all the more frightening was the look of intent on Sculler's face that summed up his desire to win at all costs.

Nathan leaned across to Rose and Stan. "Sculler Brown looks to me to be a formidable opponent. How do you think Terry will go?"

Rose was clearly worried. "He'll be right – I think."

Her father, Stan, was more forthright. "I think he's got problems, Nathan. I reckon our Terry's going to get done."

"Don't jinx it, Dad," Rose responded quickly without malice.

In the opposite corner to Sculler, Terry bounded up and down working his arms and legs into preparedness. Terry lacked in physique when he was put up against Sculler. It would surely only be speed, or a lucky knockout punch, that would save him.

"Good luck, Terry!" Madge yelled out. The whole of the front row of the Hoolihan supporters suddenly erupted into cries of support. Predictably the Toohey contingent voiced their support for Sculler Brown. Nathan shuddered. The whole place seemed to be braying for blood.

Each boxer's trainer gave them last minute advice. The two adversaries were brought to the centre of the ring where they customarily shook gloved hands and glared at each other with killer instincts. The referee moved into place. Seconds out. The first round began. The bout was an awesome spectacle, a huge titanic test of strength and nerves. To Nathan it was like being a spectator to a Roman gladiatorial contest. Terry was clearly at a disadvantage. Sculler Brown rained blows on Terry before he could even aim a punch let alone make a mark. Sculler came at him again and again giving him enormous pressure. Even the Toohey family looked concerned as Terry got pushed against the ropes. Thankfully the referee intercepted, getting the two young men away from the edge of the ring back to the centre.

From there on, Terry came out fighting. He established his ascendancy immediately over Sculler Brown, moving quickly and sharply until the end of the first round.

In the next few rounds it was much more evenly matched. The crowd in the stadium roared its immense approval at the excitement of the match. Spiros and Johnny were on their feet leaping and shouting. Abria sat mystified. Rose opened and closed her eyes and clenched her fists with the tension of it all. McDonald sat absolutely unmoved by it all. Stan Penny chain-smoked. Harry Masters seemed to react to each move by changing the expression on his face. Madge put her hands over her face. Nathan continued to shudder and grimace.

Then as the fight progressed so did the ferocity of the fight. Sculler Brown had clearly identified his opponent's weaknesses and sought to take advantage of them. He could see that Terry was relying solely on his speed and his capacity to keep striking. Instantly Sculler moved on his feet like a dancer, dodging every jab and keeping a safe distance. Now that he had momentarily unnerved Terry he struck again and again. Terry began to stagger. Another punch completely keelhauled him and Terry fell to the floor.

"Oh my God!" Rose cried, rising to her feet and putting her hand over her mouth with the horror of the fight before her.

"Come on, son," Johnny yelled, running to the side of the ring.

The referee counted, "… five, six, seven."

Terry rose to his feet in time, staggering and weaving his way round. Sculler came at him again and again. Split lip. Cut above the eye. Again and again. Blows around the head.

"I can't look. Bejeezers, this is slaughter," bewailed Stan standing up and trying to look away.

Sculler was there again. Striking and striking, and then he delivered one almighty powerful blow that seemed to send Terry reeling from one side of the ring to the other. He landed on the ropes and spun round aimlessly facing the crowds. He just seemed to hang over the edge and then he slipped down the ropes and onto his back into a state of oblivion. The referee moved quickly, declared the result a knockout at the count of ten. It was the end of the bout. Sculler had won. He basked in the adulation for a few minutes but his look of delight quickly changed to one of concern as the ringside doctor rushed to Terry's side.

"A fearsome bout, old boy," Harry remarked mopping his perspiring brow.

"Something is terribly wrong," said Nathan. He glanced at Rose who was almost in tears. "Are you all right?" he asked her putting his hand on her shoulders.

Up on the ring the doctor could be seen signalling to someone at the back of the stadium. From the crowded area two men came rushing forward with a stretcher. Photographers flashed their cameras mercilessly at the sign of Terry Hoolihan lying in a fight-induced coma.

The Toohey family came up close to where the Hoolihan's stood. They looked stern and concerned. They could only look at Johnny and Madge utterly speechless, and in absolute sympathy. For one moment the Tooheys and the Hoolihans stood alongside each other. Terry was lifted on to the stretcher, Johnny, Madge and Rose moved quickly to Terry's side.

It was a long night that followed.

The doctors at the hospital worked tirelessly to save Terry's life. He had taken a terrible beating around the head and was taken into intensive care. The Hoolihans insisted on staying at the hospital all night, but they were finally convinced by a doctor to go home and rest. Nathan had stayed with them all night as moral support, and he went back to their rooms at Surry Hills.

Johnny and Madge were devastated. Terry was the one hope they had in their lives. In Terry they had invested all their thoughts and dreams, and they loved him dearly. He may have had a wild streak in him, but as Nathan had observed, he was a gregarious young man capable of great love and friendship.

Rose too was terribly distressed. Stan and Rose had left earlier at the hospital. They had returned home to Boronia Street where Rose and Stan had stayed in seclusion.

In his room, Nathan made himself a cup of tea and looked over the rooftops of Surry Hills from the kitchen window. Next door he knew Johnny and Madge were alone in their private grief. Although not overtly religious, Johnny was drawing on his Catholic faith to an extent he had never done before. Madge could not say a word. All she could do was to sit on the edge of the bed and stare into space.

Nathan tried to grab a few hours of sleep. It would not come and in the early light of day he went for a walk. It was a drab grey morning, although humid, with the prospect of rain about. The streets were almost deserted and Nathan felt uneasy when he thought of Terry Hoolihan lying there in hospital in a deep coma with a life support system keeping him alive. The doctors were astute and observant, and they would do everything in their power to keep him alive. That and Terry's own strong physique would ensure his survival.

From his home in Braithwaite Street, Nathan turned into Crown Street. He walked for ages with his hands in his pockets thinking of many things. Terry was so young with everything going for him. Why could a young man's life be shattered by so many punches in a spectator sport? It just did not seem fair play. And there was Rose who undoubtedly loved Terry despite her flirtation with Nathan. Why should poor young Rose suffer? Johnny and Madge most of all were suffering; they had led such difficult lives and it seemed the only joy of their lives, their son Terry, was on the point of being taken away from them.

These thoughts desperately troubled Nathan and he wandered down a maze of back streets toward Central Station. An early morning tram rattled past him on its way towards Railway Square. A few cars streamed past. The vehicles were the only form of life apart from the homeless people and the destitute who gathered in and around the train station. The early morning newspapers were on sale at a stand inside Central Station and Nathan deposited his change, taking a copy.

The stark reality of the headline came leaping out at him. *'Promising boxer critical. Terry Hoolihan fights for life'*. These silently read words came screaming out of the tabloids. The worst part was the photographs of the battered countenance of Terry. Nathan suddenly felt sickened by what he was reading and without bothering to turn to the other pages; he tossed the entire newspaper into a litter basket and started walking home again.

He was worried about Rose. He knew she would be deeply upset and in a state of shock. On his way back he decided to call in and see Stan and Rose. Nathan rapped on the door several times before Stan answered the door. Stan looked as if he had slept badly. His eyes were red. His hair was all over the place. His cheeks were red and blotchy. Stan wore only a pair of shorts and a string vest from which grey chest hair protruded. He was barefoot, unshaven and his stomach hung over his waistline. Stan smoothed back his hair. His brow was damp with perspiration.

"Oh it's you. Ow are yer, mate?"

Before Nathan could answer Rose's voice came from the backroom. "Who is it, Dad?"

"It's Nathan, luv."

Rose came running down the hallway. She too was barefoot, and wearing only shorts and a T-shirt.

"Any news?" she asked anxiously. Nathan looked at her face. There were tearstains where she had been crying.

"I stayed with Johnny and Madge until early this morning when we came back from the hospital. Terry was being given the best attention."

"Come in and have a cup of tea," suggested Stan.

The three went in to the living room and sat down. Nathan studied the room as he walked in. It was as colourless as the outside. The plaster on the roof was peeling. A smell of dry rot and damp permeated throughout the place. The un-papered walls had cracked paint, and the carpet was drawn, faded and stitched. Nathan did not realise that there was poverty of this sort in Australia. He did not make a verbal observation of the room, although he wanted to do so. Instead he took the cup of tea that Rose gave him, sipped it and continued to talk.

"How are you both bearing up? Rose? Stan?"

"Ah we're all right, mate," replied Stan. "It's Madge and Johnny I'm real worried about. Those two have never had a flamin' decent thing happen to them in their bloody lives. I s'pose you know about them and the Tooheys, do you? The robbery, and all that?"

"Yes I have heard the story," said Nathan.

"Back in the Depression Johnny and Sam acted like a right couple of dills. Doing over a warehouse. Reckoning they could get away with it. Things were bad then. Neither had a job. No money. No food. I could understand why they did it. Doesn't excuse it, mind. I was starving too. My late wife Joanie, God bless her, was expecting Rosie here. I didn't go out and do over a joint to get money. Course when the coppers saw two culprits going over the wall, they took flight. Johnny got clean away and Sam copped twelve months bird. Old Johnny did the wrong thing by Sam. Marries Madge, who was Sam's girl. Starts a business that he was going to operate with Sam when he gets out. But old Johnny, he was no businessman and he ran the firm into the ground. No money around for Sam when he gets through doing his stint in the jailhouse. No woman around for Sam. For twenty years the bloody Tooheys and Hoolihans have been through brawl after brawl, scene after scene. I pity John and Madge. I've got a lot of time for them. They've had twenty years of misery caused by that incident. If they lose their boy, it'll be the end of them."

"We must help them as best as we can," Nathan said with a solemnity. "Whatever the outcome," he added declaring an open verdict for he felt there was the possibility that things may not work out for the best.

"If Terry comes through," Rose said in a voice that was surprisingly weak for her normally effervescent personality, "do you think there'll be any problems? Do you think that—"

Stan was quick to intercept. "Listen, luv, we don't want to think about that now. All the Hills are praying for him I bet. And that includes Sam and Maggie Toohey and their lad, Pat. Did you see them stand up when young Terry was put on the stretcher? I'll tell you what, sport, it's been a bloody long time since a Toohey and a Hoolihan stood shoulder to shoulder. The Toohey's were as worried as the rest of us."

"This lot round here are a strange bunch," said Rose. "One minute they're dropping each other in the bar. The next thing they're all worried about someone and pulling together."

Nathan absorbed the words and thought over them for a minute. "Well I won't overstay my welcome, Stan, Rose. I'll let you know if there's any change."

"Thanks, mate," said Stan.

"I'll see you out," said Rose.

Outside the dark clouds hinted at the possibility of a thunderstorm. Nathan and Rose sat on the wall for a few minutes. Nathan felt that he needed to put their friendship in perspective; a friendship that he had briefly hoped might lead to something more. Looking at Rose now he wanted to give her reassurance and support. Both had a strong bond in their friendship of Terry.

"You know, Rose, I have enjoyed the times we've spent together, have enjoyed your company enormously. I have found you someone gloriously happy and cheerful to be with. I know now how distressed you are about Terry. I am too, I like Terry a lot. Have faith, Rose."

"I do, Nathan. If I didn't have faith I wouldn't come through. When Dad and I lost Mum it was terrible. I couldn't bear to lose Terry. I love him. Oh, I don't mean – in love – well what I mean is we grew up together. Two scruffy Surry Hills kids together; him with his arse hanging out of his trousers, me with no shoes. We grew up with Dad and Johnny almost expecting Terry and I to get married. Well, when you'se and I were hobknobbing it at the Troc that was something really different for me. I mean you'se is something different. I've flirted with a thousand blokes. Raced them all to the border line in my mind, but I really enjoyed being with you, dancing with you, being treated like one of those sheila's from Double Bay with a finger under her nose. I mean, here am I opening my heart up to you. I feel I can talk – yeah really talk-like a mate to you. I can't explain it. Maybe you were right when you asked me that night if I'd ever though there was a wider world than this. Boronia Street, Surry Hills. If I'd got out I might have met more people like you. I must embarrass you when I swear."

"I am not naïve, Rose. Swearing does not embarrass me. And you must not think that because I speak with a different accent that I am any different to the people around here. I believe there are many good people here who've never had a chance in their life to improve their lot. Perhaps it's a point about many people that they do not like to show the softer sides of their nature for fear they may display a weakness or seen to be making a concession, that could well be the way of many of your neighbours. The English have an expression, they speak of someone who is a 'rough diamond'. Another expression they use is of a person with a 'heart of gold'. Through my foreign outlook that is how I see Surry Hills today in 1950, as an area of rough diamonds with hearts of gold. When I lived in England I had a room above a greengrocers shop run by a lovely couple called Jack and Elsie Faley. In a way they too were rough diamonds. They came from an area in the East End of London, probably not unlike this one. The Faleys were people not unlike the ones around here."

"Terry thought that being a boxer would improve his lot. Now he's fighting for his life. I've seen him through so many of his amateur bouts. That was the worst I've ever seen him in."

"Rose you can be sure the hospital will be doing everything in their power to help him through."

"I know that. I can't help but worry though."

Nathan changed the subject. "I'm thinking of buying a house, Rose. When you took me to Bondi the other week, I fell in love with the idea of living by the beach. If I move I hope you'll come and see me when you can."

"Gee, you're a strange one. You've been telling me how you admire the people round here and now you're bloomin' well thinking of moving!"

"It's the beach that attracts me. Just because I'm considering moving, it doesn't mean I no longer admire the people. Don't misunderstand me. I am friends with Abria, Maviel, I adore their children, Spiros is a nice man, even my grumpy landlord, McDonald, has learned to smile now. He said G'day to me yesterday!"

"I'm sorry, Nathan. I'm just shooting my mouth off again."

"Oh, Rose. No apologies are necessary," signed Nathan embracing her. "We better both go into our homes before we get caught in the rain."

He took his leave of her and returned to him room in Braithwaite Street. For the rest of the day, while the rain pelted against his window, Nathan worked on some private law study at home engrossing himself in it, in order to block out his worries about Terry. Law still held an intoxicating appeal to Nathan. He thirsted for knowledge about the realms of the law, famous court cases and the need for reforms in many areas.

Early in the evening Nathan heard the sound of someone knocking on the door of Johnny and Madge's flat. A fearful thought entered his head. *Could it be someone from the hospital bringing the news that Johnny and Madge dreaded the most?* Nathan got up from is chair to eavesdrop, not out of sheer nosiness or inquisitiveness, but because he felt he may need to console Johnny and Madge if they were the recipients of bad news. The knocking continued. Finally Johnny's voice was heard from the other side.

"Who is it?" Johnny asked in a voice barely audible. There was a long silence. Johnny asked again, "Who is it?"

"It's Sam and Maggie Toohey," came back a male voice. It was an enormous surprise to both Johnny Hoolihan in one flat and to Nathan in the other. Nathan listened in closely. He was curious to say the least. Why had Sam and Maggie come to visit? He heard the door of Johnny's flat open.

"What on earth? What is this?" gasped Johnny in a voice of shock. "What the hell do you two want?"

Johnny's voice was neither angry, nor furious, just one that clearly betrayed surprise.

"John, you might find this hard to believe, but we just wanted you to know we're sorry about your boy."

"I – I can't believe this," stammered Johnny.

"It's true," Maggie said in a quiet voice. "Whatever our differences we know you love your boy as much as we love Pat. Terry took a hell of a beating, but he's a tough boy, Johnny, he'll pull through."

"I still don't believe this," said Johnny looking absolutely mystified. "After all our years of feuding, I don't believe this turnaround."

Sam looked as if he was trying to find the words. Then somehow he managed to make them come, and made the concessions he had never been able to.

"John, when we did that robbery all those years ago, we were both a couple of bloody larrikins. We knew what we were up against. If one of us got caught the arrangement was the other one wouldn't lag on the other. I took the dues for that one. I copped it sweet. I didn't like it at the time. Who would? And when you married the girl I had my eye on, I had a right to be crook especially as I was doing time when you got spliced to her. Then to flaming well top it all you screwed up the business both me and you had planned to run when I got out." They both eyed each other with a certain amount of aggression. "You couldn't blame me, John. The whole thing really got my goat, doing time for nothing!"

"And don't you forget, Sam, I tried to pay you back everything I'd lost! I went out and did over another place and got done! And what did I get?" Johnny was angry at the memory of it and his voice rose in anger. "Two years. Yeah, that's right. Two years. Twice as long as you! I paid too, and paid, and paid. We were crazy to think we'd get away with it. We tried to fund a business on rotten foundations. It didn't work, did it? Twenty years our families have been brawling!"

"Don't you think we're sick of it, Johnny?" said Maggie raising her hand angrily to have her say. "It's spilled over now. When you and Sam both came back from the war, I hoped that was it, the end of the feud, but now it's our boys who are carrying on fighting. They used that poor girl, Rose, as a scapegoat."

"Stop it! Stop it all of you!" Maggie appeared from behind Johnny. "I can't take this rowing. There's Terry laying there in the ward. He might not get up ever. And you lot are still fighting! Haven't we all had enough? Haven't we!"

There was a deathly silence which followed. Nathan felt a lump rise in his throat as he envisaged the scene from his side of the door.

"Sam. Johnny. You two stop shooting your mouths off." Madge's voice was controlled now.

"Sam, I know you and Maggie came here with good intentions. It's hard to believe mind. Never a better time than now. Come on in. Let's have a cup of tea."

"Is that all right with you John?" Sam asked. Even from behind the door of his flat, Nathan could see Sam and Johnny agreeing in spirit to a truce.

"Don't ask me, Sam. The missus is in charge here." Sam held out his hand to Johnny.

"Our door's open. You might as well come through."

Johnny shook Sam's hand. *It was all so easy*, thought Nathan. *Why, oh why, oh why could they have not done this year's ago?*

He heard Maggie say, "We're all Catholics here. Perhaps we could pray for your boy." Nathan did not hear the reply. He heard the door close. The Hoolihans and the Tooheys had been brought together in tragic circumstances. Surely this peace could last now for all their sakes.

It was a couple of days later that Nathan was woken from his sleep by Johnny's voice outside his room. Johnny called Nathan's name over and over again. It was still dark out in the streets of Surry Hills. Nathan reluctantly got up from his bed and opened the door. He was stunned to see Johnny and Madge standing outside, both of them with tears rolling down their cheeks. It was more than he could bear to see such a normally tough couple in such a condition. Nathan at once assumed the worst and he put his arms around them both.

"Oh, Johnny, Madge, I am sorry -"

"He's come through, Nathan," Johnny murmured in a tearful whisper.

Nathan stepped back and looked at them in amazement. They weren't crying tears of sadness. The Hoolihan's were crying tears of joy.

"We had a call from the hospital just now," sobbed Madge. "Terry's come round."

Johnny's eyes flooded with tears. "Mate, it must be a miracle. The doctors, bless 'em brought him through. Our prayers were answered."

Nathan was amazed. He could only stand there and gape. Terry had come out of his coma. It could only have been divine intervention. Johnny and Madge were beside themselves. They had come through hell during the past few days, but thank God it was all over now.

★★★

Terry never put a pair of boxing gloves on again. When Terry came out of hospital he was welcomed home with a huge party at Braithwaite Street. Just about everybody who had been friends with him, fought with him, or who was even briefly acquainted with Terry came along to pay their respects. Sculler Brown whose devastating punches had put Terry in hospital, briefly dropped by. Sculler was not expected to be welcome in the circumstances, and when he entered the room, it became so quiet that if someone had dropped a pin the noise would have created a thunderclap. The two men looked at each other in a strange manner. Then as if to shock everyone, Sculler and Terry hugged each other. For Nathan, who was an interested onlooker, he found himself witness to a demonstration of mate-ship in Australian terms: the quality that Australians have to make true friendships from those to whom they may have previously been adversaries.

The party at Braithwaite Street marked the first public reconciliation of the Tooheys and the Hoolihans. Sam, Maggie and Pat greeted Johnny, Madge and Terry in a manner that utterly bemused the Hills folk who were more used to seeing fists flying and angry voices in public. It was a sight that many people had waited years to see, and the smiles on everyone's faces were joyous.

Rose put her arm around Terry and walked over to where Pat was standing. Nathan watched curiously. Rose then put he arm around Pat, and there she stood pretty as a picture – not quite an oil painting but still worth modelling for a portrait – with the two young men who had loved her the most. Perhaps not quite. Nathan had fallen for this incorrigible, flirtatious, bouncy, cheeky, attractive young girl. He looked at her happy with the people she knew and loved the most, and he knew that Rose would only ever be a friend.

It was a wonderful party. It was the biggest and happiest knees-up that Nathan had been to since the gathering at the Faleys in Ealing Green in 1948. There were many happy people there. Apart from the Tooheys and the Hoolihans being the centrepiece of the action, Abria and Maviel showed they were no mean slouches on the dance floor, the landlord, McDonald, proved he wasn't as grumpy and as rude as he had previously been. A few beers under his belt and McDonald was as happy as a sandman. Spiros and his wife enjoyed themselves enormously in a way that only the Greeks can with their zest for enjoying life.

People seemed to pour in and out of the house. They danced the conga. They jitterbugged. They sang together round the piano. Nathan, who always found someone to dance with, took to the floor with a local factory girl. From across the room Nathan saw Rose talking to her father, Stan, Terry and Pat. Nathan beamed her a glorious warm smile to which she responded with a mischievous wink. Rose smiled just as warmly at Nathan. He could feel the warmth from across the room.

Forty

Some months later in early 1951, Nathan moved from Braithwaite Street, Surry Hills to a run-down semi-detached bungalow within a few minutes walk from Bondi Beach. The house needed a lot of renovation and decorating. When Nathan wasn't working, or studying, every spare minute was devoted to painting his first home that he could really call his own. The house and garden became his pride and joy.

Nathan had every reason to be happy with his life. His career was moving into top gear. He had his home. In barely two years since arriving in Australia he had already achieved much, probably much more than he had ever envisaged. He loved living in Bondi. Being so close gave him the advantage to take early morning walks along the beach. At night if there was a breeze or a wind, the sound of the waves rolling and crashing would carry and Nathan would lie in his bed listening to the wondrous sound of the Pacific Ocean.

One chilly winter's evening Nathan had just finished moving the furniture around in the small kitchen, when there was a knock on the door. It was unusual for anyone to call on Nathan. Since moving from Surry Hills, he had kept a low profile and had not socialised at all. Occasionally he would call in and have tea with Melissa at her Rushcutters Bay flat when she was 'resting' between acting jobs, which was extremely rare as she was very much in demand for radio plays, band broadcasts and concerts. With his colleague Harry Masters, after a long day at the office, often they would go for a meal at an oyster bar or a restaurant usually in Kings Cross where they would talk shop for hours. No one had been invited to Nathan's house simply because he wanted it to be decorated and of a nice appearance for visitors.

Nathan opened his front door and was surprised to see Rose Penny standing there smiling at him. He was delighted to see her. Rose was his first acquaintance from the Hills to come down to Bondi to see him.

"Come in," Nathan said exuberantly taking her hand and kissing her on the cheek. He brought her through to his lounge room, from the window of which gave a view of the Northern end of the beach.

"Nice place you've got here, Nathan," she said admiringly, looking around the room still in the throes of being decorated. Nathan felt almost embarrassed. His own house, infinitely modest, dreadfully run down and neglected when he had bought it, was by any standards far superior and luxurious than either Bishop Street or Braithwaite Street.

"It needed a lot doing to it. I had to paint it and restore some of the brickwork," he replied almost in justification. He looked at Rose lovingly. She really was a very pretty girl. "What would you like to drink, Rose?" Nathan asked reaching for the fridge door automatically assuming she would want a beer.

"I reckon a cup of tea'd go down the gurgler nicely, mate," she replied in her usual boisterous manner. Nathan made her a cup from a pot of tea he had already brewed, and handed it to her. Rose put one leg over the other in a manner that distracted Nathan slightly. Rose for all her cheek and bluster was a good-looking girl without even trying.

"I must say, Rose, I am very surprised to see you. Nonetheless, I am pleased that one of my friends from Surry Hills has taken the trouble to visit me."

"I really came to say goodbye, Nathan."

"Goodbye!" Nathan was startled. "Are you going somewhere?"

"Since you moved away I've been doing three jobs. I've been cleaning out jolly Geraldine and big Bernadette's café in the morning before I start work in the flower shop. In the evening, I've been working as a barmaid at The White Horse. I thought if you could do three jobs, so could I. I've saved enough for my boat fare to England."

"You are going to England!" Nathan thought that Rose must have been joking knowing how rarely serious she was. There was a look on her face that meant she was being sincere.

Rose enjoyed the surprise she have given Nathan. "I sail in a weeks time on the Strathaird. Bit of a surprise, eh! I thought I might as well see a bit of that wide world you told me about. I'm going to stay with an Aunt in Stepney. I reckon I'll probably be over there a couple of years. Yep, I wonder what some of those pommie blokes are going to make of a wild colonial girl like me."

"I must say you have the habit of surprising me." There were a couple of points Nathan wanted to clarify. "What does your dad think? And Terry?"

"Dad's real keen for me to go over there and meet some of mum's family. Dad says on the boat going through the Suez Canal and the Med I'll see a lot of the places he saw when he was a digger going over there in the first war. You asked me about Terry. We're still mates. We're not going together or anything like that. Matter of fact when Terry was in the hospital, after that boxing match, he met a young nurse. You wouldn't read about it, would you? Terry and her are engaged now. Terry gave the fight game away you know."

"I heard. I met Johnny in town one day. He told me Terry can't box any more."

"Too right! Another nasty punch up and he's in real trouble. He's got to take it nice and easy. Just as well he's splicing himself up with a nurse. Terry's working with your mate Spiros at his garage in Camperdown; Spiros is giving him the run down on motor mechanics. Even things are looking up for Johnny. He's got himself a job in a factory with plenty of overtime. He and Madge are thinking of moving out this way soon."

"And you're off to London, Rose. I hope you have a wonderful time. I must give you the address of my friends the Faleys who live at Ealing Green. They are a lovely family. I'm sure you'll love them as much as I do. Would you join me for a meal here this evening?"

Rose did stay for a meal. For a while they talked about England and places to go. Rose was ecstatic. At twenty-one with her bubbling personality and lack of inhibitions, she would surely be a hit with the Faleys. Nathan could just see her at one of Jack and Elsie's Saturday night parties, joining in all the fun with great enthusiasm. Towards the end of the evening Rose said something in good humour that could well have been interpreted as a serious suggestion.

"When I've done my travelling and been like Lady Muck on the right royal tour, I might come back and marry you! It's August '51 now. A couple of years time, eh?"

"You'd like that would you – *mate*!" Nathan said in jest.

"I was just joking. You know me. Be a bit strange though, wouldn't it.

Imagine if we did get married. Me, a flower seller, and a lawyer. You are a lawyer ain't yer?"

"Almost. Let's say I'm hacking my way through the legal jungle. Anyway, why should there be any distinction? Stranger combinations have married. Say I sold the flowers and you were a lawyer, do you think that should make any difference? Of course not! Anyway, I think that you should do the trip before you get married. It will make a difference to your whole outlook in life. Don't forget to send me postcards. Don't forget to visit the Faleys."

"I won't, mate. I'll be true to my word," replied Rose.

Exactly a week later Rose sailed on the SS Strathaird from Pyrmont Dock in Sydney. Almost all of the friends Rose had in Surry Hills turned out in the early evening to farewell her. Amongst them was her father, Stan, Abria and Maviel, Spiros and Kristos, Johnny, Madge and Terry, as well as Sam, Maggie and Pat. Afterwards they all went for a drink at a nearby hotel.

Rose was true to her word. She sent Nathan postcards from all the places she visited in much the same way as Melissa had done in 1948. It was obvious from the day Rose wrote that she was simply loving every minute of it. In England Rose met many of her Cockney relatives whom she found to be every bit as gregarious and as fun loving as herself. She visited the Faleys at Ealing and found them to be just as kind as Nathan had told her they would be. Rose was particularly smitten with Jack's elder son, Mick, and it soon became obvious from letters that the two had fallen in love.

In that same year Jack Faley died suddenly of a heart attack and a few months later Elsie died, Ron had claimed she died of a broken heart. Nathan, on receiving the letter from Ron, was enormously saddened. Jack and Elsie had been the closest people to him after his own parents and he felt the loss terribly. Ron and Mick took over the running of the greengrocers shop in Ealing. When Ron's wife Jill wasn't occupied with the two young children, she worked in the shop as well. Rose moved over from Stepney and after touring the continent, she took Nathan's old flat above the shop and worked in the greengrocer's full-time. Nathan was pleased that the Faleys had Rose as company. Rose Penny's chirpiness would help them all at this time.

One day in late 1953 Nathan came home to his house at Bondi to find two letters waiting for him. Both came from England and were filled with good news. In the first envelope he opened, he found a long letter from Freddie Miller. Nathan was delighted his old friend was coming to Australia in January 1954 to cover the first Royal Tour of her Majesty Queen Elizabeth II and Prince Phillip, due to begin in February. The good news was that Freddie would be staying on in Australia after the end of the Royal Tour for at least a year. Freddie was to send back regular reports to the BBC of events in the Pacific region. Nathan was very happy that he would be reunited with Freddie again, for he was the one link with the past; the only person alive who could talk to him of his own parents Arthandur and Marlene.

In the other letter Nathan could see from the postmark that it had come from Ealing. He opened the letter and amongst the pages of writing there was a photograph enclosed. Nathan gazed at it in amazement. It was a wedding photograph of Mick Faley and Rose Penny. He was surprised, but in a sense delighted. Mick and Rose were a good combination, both down to earth happy people, with the same sort of backgrounds. Rose looked gorgeous in a white sparkling wedding dress and Mick was beaming and happy in a bright morning suit with a flower in his lapel. Around Mick and Rose were a few of the people Nathan had met when he had been living in Ealing. The letter told Nathan how many of Rose's relatives from Stepney had come to the ceremony. Mick wrote that after the wedding at Ealing Congregational Church, all the guests had gathered at a reception centre in Richmond where, in his eloquent phasing, he mentioned 'one of the biggest bleedin' knees-up London's ever seen took place'. The thought of it brought a smile to Nathan's face. Rose and Mick, what a combination, and what a happy life those two would have together. Mick wrote in his letter that the moment Rose had wafted into the shop and said, 'G'day, mate' he had met the girl of his dreams. Mick further added, *When Rose tried to carry me over the threshold and said, "Marry me, you pommie bastard" – well I thought, here's a girl I like!* Even better news was that Mick and Rose, and Ron and Jill with their children were all emigrating to Australia. Now that Jack and Elsie had sadly gone the old house and shop at Ealing was full of memories. It was time for them to move on. They had sold the house and shop and were going to try and open their own retail business in Sydney. Rose's father, Stan, who had worked on a barrow all of his life, was going to come in with them. It was going to be a big family venture. To further make it a business with familiar faces abounding, Mick asked if Nathan, through his legal firm, could handle any matters for them relating to laws dealing with the business. Nathan wouldn't refuse the offer.

In the past few years, Nathan's career had progressed well. By virtue of experience and opportunity, Nathan had made the graduation from clerk to lawyer with ease. The company of Price Rayne, Easton and Westwood had merged with another firm. From the results of the merger the company had developed into a far more comprehensive legal firm. Not only did the work within the firm encompass areas such as corporate and commercial law, conveyancing, insurance and some aspects of industrial law, the company was expanding into the areas of family law. Nathan was in the position of working for one of the largest legal company's in Australia, and also one of the most diverse for the number of disciplines it could cover. The elder members of the firm were vastly experienced passing on not only their skills and knowledge to the junior members such as Nathan and Harry, but also their enthusiasm for their profession.

Nathan had been fortunate in his choice of firm. The lawyers who worked there were enthusiastic in a different way. They were concerned that not only should they drive to win a case for their client, but they were also concerned that the laws in certain areas should be reformed in order to show compassion for the less fortunate, and those who had become innocent victims of circumstances that had been thrust upon them. A point of mention that frequently came to be discussed was the children caught in the middle of divorce proceedings, the access rights of each parent. It was a particular issue that would be subject to much debate in future years before reforms would be initiated. Another area that the company was unanimous in agreement on was the position of the employee who suddenly found himself redundant or incapacitated with a mortgage, a sheath of unpaid bills and the unpalatable threat of creditors likely to foreclose. Nathan could relate to these problems that affected everyone and anyone. These were basic human problems which needed care, consideration and compassion. Nathan took to his profession with a deep enthusiasm spending much time away from chambers researching material from historical cases and comparing them with present day trends.

Above all Nathan learned that in the thrust and parry of a lawyer's life it was necessary to have the skin of a rhinocero's hide to withstand personal criticism, and the verbal conflict encountered from a legal opponent in the confines of a court room battle. It was also extremely important for a lawyer when dealing with a client in private to be able to handle their affair with a sensitivity comparable to handling a rose petal.

Certain cases presented different challenges, Often it would be a contest to decide whether to present a client's case in the light of it's legal or moral aspects. All in all, Nathan lived and breathed his profession, and being a lawyer was not only his career but also an all-consuming interest. Except for when he had the occasional visitor like Harry Masters or some of his friends from Surry Hills, the law took up nearly all of his time.

The house at Bondi was comfortable. It was far from ostentatious. It was not a display piece, purely a place to come home to. Strangely enough that was how Nathan had felt everywhere he had lived since leaving Austria at the age of sixteen. Nowhere he had lived, felt like home. They were just dwellings. Nathan did not realise it at the time, but in the late night hours when he would relax in his lounge with a cup of cocoa, and listen to the waves roll in on the beach, somehow it was then that company would have been nice. It would be good to talk to someone and share thoughts of love and life with. 'No man is an island' someone had once written, and Nathan realised this now more than ever at thirty-two years of age.

Both girls he had loved were married now. Melissa, after a couple of years of commuting between Australia and Hollywood, had married her long time fiancée, Gary Markel, a few months before in Las Vegas. The girl from the kibbutz had been jettisoned to the big time suddenly. Melissa had signed a seven-year contract with options at one of the big Hollywood studios. In addition to this, Melissa had also been booked for cabaret performances at some of the major hotels in Las Vegas. Melissa and Gary were returning from the United States in the early part of 1954 to farewell their Australian friends. An invitation to Nathan had been made by way of a card, which stood on the mantelpiece.

Rose Penny was now Mrs Rose Faley. That had been the biggest surprise of all. Rose who had joked that she might come back and marry Nathan had instead married Mick Faley. Nathan knew in his heart that it was a good match between Rose and Mick, and he sincerely wished them well. The new Mr and Mrs Faley would shortly be arriving on the boat from England, together with Ron and Jill and their two young children. Nathan felt extremely happy that his friends would all be arriving together.

Nathan went down to the Quay to welcome them all. Sailing into Sydney Harbour is an experience that stays in the memory for all time, especially for those seeing it for the first time, and emotionally for those Sydneysider's, who have been away and come back. Rose felt happy to be back and thrilled to be with her new husband, Mick, who was equally excited to be here. For Ron and Jill, bringing their children here was something new and wonderful to be starting life in this sunny land that Nathan had waxed lyrically about in letters.

They all had an emotional reunion at Circular Quay. Stan Penny found his new son-in-law to be a solid, reliable bloke with a good sense of humour.

"I'm very happy for you, Rose," said Nathan on greeting her. He hugged her and Jill, and shook hands with Ron and Mick.

Rose was deliriously happy, it was plain for anyone to see. "I repeated history in my family line, mate," she said with a grin. "Like me old dad here I went over and married a pom. And if you hadn't told me to go and see the Faleys I would never have met Mick. I'll always be grateful to you, Nathan."

"Likewise," Mick added. "Oh, Nat, it's funny the way things work out, isn't it? Who'd ever dream that we'd all be standing here in Sydney, Australia, together? Old friends together."

It did seem strange to Nathan. There they were standing at Circular Quay with a big white liner moored in the background against the backdrop of Sydney Harbour Bridge. Ron Faley was in so many ways, a younger version of his dad. Jill had the sweetness and gentility of so many English girls, but she was bubbling, and full of excitement at being here in Australia. Rose and Mick laughed happily with Stan. Although Stan and Mick came from different parts of the world, their senses of humour and initiatives were virtually the same.

"Words fail me when I say how broken-hearted I was to hear of Jack and Elsie going within a few months of each other," Nathan said in an offside to Ron.

"We took it badly too," replied Ron sadly, "but as they say life goes on. And we're out here now. I'll always remember the good old days at Ealing Green. Anyway we've got a new life to lead and it's great to be here. Good to see you again."

"You too," replied Nathan.

It was a happy gathering. After the Faleys had got all their luggage together they went over to Watsons Bay for the afternoon. Before the Faleys had left England, Freddie Miller had called in to see them at Ealing, to tell them that he too would soon be heading down under to be a correspondent for the BBC. With that news in mind all of them had planned a big reunion in Sydney when Freddie arrived.

The Faleys soon settled into life in Australia and they did so with ease. Ron and Mick had an advantage in that they had enough funds from the sale of the house and the business in England to get them started in Sydney. They quickly started their own grocery warehouse, which they ran with Stan Penny. In time it would become a profitable concern. Ron and Jill and their children moved to Tamarama on the southern side of Bondi and Rose and Mick moved to the suburb of Coogee. For Nathan it felt a lot more like home now that he had a few of his old friends close by.

In January 1954 the flying boat carrying Freddie arrived at Rose Bay. Nathan was on hand to welcome his friend to Australia. Of all of his friends, Nathan had the greatest affinity with Freddie Miller. Freddie had known his parents, Arthandur and Marlene. He had met Nathan as a teenager in Austria. Freddie had been part of the Companions of the Circle right up to the war years, and they shared many secrets and memories of people and places.

The flying boat glided across the dazzling blue waters of Sydney Harbour to its berth at Rose Bay. Freddie was forty-nine years of age now. He had travelled to many places throughout his two stints of army service and his cinematic journalistic career. It surprised him that even now after years of travel, he could still be excited about a journey like this to Australia.

When Freddie stepped out of the cabin, the hot sun saturated him with its heavy rays. The sky was a wide, deep blue and the scent of a foreign land filled him with the old traveller's instincts once again. If Freddie had been born in another age he would surely have been a Victorian adventurer in a gleaming white helmet and safari suit. He was every bit the quintessential Englishman abroad. Freddie's first reaction on landing was to remove his sports jacket and unbutton his shirt. It was then he espied Nathan. He smiled at the sight of his friend.

Back at Nathan's house at Bondi, he had organised a big welcome party for Freddie. Nathan had invited those that had met Freddie in England. Mick and Ron Faley were there, as were Jill and Rose, and Melissa and her husband, Gary Markel, who had recently arrived back in Australia after a sojourn in the USA. Nathan invited Melissa and Gary as a matter of courtesy. Melissa had met Freddie in Ealing and liked him enormously. Also, knowing how much they enjoyed parties, Nathan had invited Johnny and Madge. Terry also came with his new wife, and the two were seen chatting happily to Mick and Rose. Sam and Maggie came, and their son, Pat, was also there with his girlfriend Geraldine who owned the café in Crown Street. Spiros and Kristos, and Abria and Maviel happily mingled together. Stan and McDonald exchanged tips for horses racing. The food was a complete mixture of cuisine laid out on the table for everyone to help themselves. There was Australian beer, Australian wine, soft drinks and punch. Nathan had gone out of his way to make sure that everyone was catered for. It was one of those beautiful light Sydney nights when everyone spilled out into the garden.

Melissa and Gary talked to Rose for a while. Rose was surprised that Nathan and Melissa were old friends. Even more surprising for Rose was to be in the presence of Gary Markel, the American cowboy actor. He looked every inch the smiling Hollywood star with his sunlamp tan and pearly teeth. Gary was basically a B-move actor. He was destined always to be one. He would never achieve the star status of a John Wayne or a Cary Grant. It was not the case with his wife, Melissa. Before long Melissa would graduate to being one of the most in demand actresses in films.

Freddie and Nathan moved across to join Melissa, Gary and Rose. Nathan looked at Rose and Melissa together: two women he had both loved, but who were now married to other people. Rose in turn eyed him with an impish curiosity.

"You're a quiet one, Nathan," she said in her direct manner. "There was me telling you that night we went dancing at the Troc, that you'd go well with a sheila like Melissa, there. And strewth! Would you believe it? The two of you have been mates for donkey's years!"

"I was at fault there," Nathan admitted with a slight smile. "I should have mentioned it. I'm glad to see you're all getting on well. And I'm very happy for both you ladies." Nathan turned to Gary. "Well Mick married a fine girl in Rose and I think, Gary, you have married one of the best in Melissa."

Gary sparkled a smile. "I sure agree with you," he drawled in his lazy accent. It was a voice typical of numerous B-movie westerns, epitomising the hell for leather characteristics of American cowboys in just a few words.

Freddie and Nathan indulged in conversation with them for a while. Then Nathan introduced him all round to everybody. In the background the music changed constantly as someone changed the records over. On the light summer evening with the view of Bondi beach accessible, the waves rolling gently into shore, and the mixture of conversation and laughter blending together with the music from the gramophone, it became a moment of time that provided the scale of balance from one lifetime to another. The vocals of Johnny Ray, Eddie Fisher, Guy Mitchell and Frankie Laine, rising from the record player seemed to set the tone of the evening. Freddie happily mingled with everyone. Oddly enough, Freddie found conversation with the Tooheys and the Hoolihans, the easiest. There they were, such a contrasting group, all diametrically opposing characters, yet able to converse on such equal terms. The old saying that in Australia, everyone is equal, was never more truer than on this night.

"Australia has been good to you," Freddie said to Nathan later on.

Nathan appeared to think about these words. Then almost in a sense of exuberance he said, "I would say Australia has been good for me." *For me*. There was a strong sense of emphasis there. "Yes I would say it had brought many instincts out in me I was not aware of, Freddie."

"The Australians are wonderful people," Freddie said admiringly looking around at everyone at the gathering. "I have been looking forward to coming here for so long now. I have a pretty heavy schedule while I'm out here. I've a whole year to spend seeing this country and I think I'm going to enjoy it. I have so many things to get done. Apart from covering the Royal Tour, I have to conduct interviews for the BBC with some of the most prominent Australians."

"Such as who?"

"Robert Menzies, Doctor Evatt. There are two names to begin with. The Lord Mayor of Sydney Mr Pat Hills is another. Chips Rafferty, Jack Davey and Clive Churchill, the rugby player. Marvellous player. I've seen footage of him playing for his team."

"South Sydney," Nathan pointed out with a smile. "My friend, Harry Masters, is an ardent supporter. I've been along to Redfern Oval a few times to see them play. They call Clive Churchill the little master. A suitable nickname, eh?"

"I must get along and see him play. I am more of a soccer fan than I am rugby, but the rugby players in Australia are the greatest in the world, and I'm not going to miss seeing them in action."

"Who else do you plan to see? What else?"

"Oh Bradman, Frank Sedgeman. Apart from the people I have mentioned, the BBC camera team is going to travel to all of the major cities and the outback: From the Kimberleys to Alice, the Barrier Reef and some of the big cattle stations. The one mentioned in your letter is on our list. You said you were there for six months,"

"Orange Tree Downs," Nathan reaffirmed.

"Of course, I remember now. And I also have a number of personal invitations to respond to. A number of POWs I was with in Borneo are organising an RSL function I believe. I got a letter from one of them before I left England. They were good men. I'm looking forward to seeing them again. There was a real comradeship about the men I knew."

Nathan studied Freddie curiously. He managed to age well like the vintage of a fine wine. He had only put on a small amount of weight. His hair, slightly thinner, had streaks of silver grey throughout. Somehow he never lost his energy and passion for enjoying life. Even when Freddie spoke the tones of his voice emitted enthusiasm.

"Believe it or not Nathan, Freddie spoke as an after thought crossed his mind, "There is another Companion of the Circle resident in Australia."

"Really?" Nathan was astonished. "Who?"

"I might keep that as a pleasant surprise for you," Freddie grinned. "I've been in touch with them by letter constantly. When I wrote to them telling this person that I was coming to Australia, they too, on a whim, decided to come. For the past few months this former member of the Circle has been in Perth but is now here in Sydney. That's another joy about my visit here. The BBC have organised a house for me at Paradise Beach for my stay here. One weekend I'm going to hire a boat. Perhaps you could come up and meet them. We'll all go out on the harbour for the day."

"Sounds wonderful," Nathan said more intrigued, than pleased by the invitation.

A few weekends later, Freddie true to his word invited Nathan up to his new accommodation. Freddie had been provided with a contemporary wood and glass home set amongst the bush land leading down to Paradise Beach. The two men sat out on the balcony talking in depth about their lives. For Nathan, talking to Freddie was a chance to recapture some of the past. The conversation moved back to Austria, the mountain village, and Arthandur and Marlene. They talked of other people too: the Baroness Christina von Harstezzen and Freddie's late wife, Cynthia. Cynthia was still missed terribly by Freddie. It became clear to Nathan that the memory of Cynthia burned on in Freddie's heart.

Finally, it was time for the two men to walk down to the jetty at Paradise Beach. There were many boats moored out on the glittering blue waters. In the hot summer sunshine the water had the appearance of clear blue glass. The green-blue bush land of Sydney's north shore stretched down to the water's edge. It was one of those splendidly God-created days, the memory of which could last a lifetime. The trees and greenery of the nearby Pittwater Bays and inlets looked startlingly attractive.

Freddie wore a peaked yachting cap, a brightly coloured Polynesian style shirt and shorts and thongs. He adapted well to the easy-going lifestyle here. Nathan too was a complete contradiction to the professional man in a business suit that he was during the working week. He wore shorts, sandals, a striped T-shirt and a white straw sunhat. The two walked across the beach and along the jetty to where an old wooden cabin cruiser was berthed. On the side of the boat the words Taranga Princess were painted in bright red capital letters.

Nathan looked around him. He was keen to find out who was the former Companion of the Circle. They walked onto the boat and Freddie pointed to a bronzed figure sunbathing on the top of the cabin. "Right there, old friend."

Nathan blinked his eyes with disbelief as the figure sat upright and smiled at him. In Nathan's life he had experienced many coincidences that had stunned him for the incredulity of it all. Meeting Melissa in London had been one of them. Another had been working with Joe Patterson in the Northern Territory and learning that Ted McTaggart had been a close friend of Joe's. This time it just did not seem part of real life. It was all part of some romantic novel.

Above them on the cabin roof was the sleek, tawny-haired, bronze figure of a very captivating woman. It had been eight incredible years since Nathan had seen her. The two smiled at each other, and the lady clad in a swimsuit descended to the deck to greet him.

"I hope I did not startle you," she said, her French accent still as crisp and sensuous as ever.

Nathan looked down into the whirlpool of Francine Macés eyes. France Macé! How impossible this seemed. Here he was staring at the girl who during the war had liaised with the Circle, the French Resistance movement, and British Intelligence. The Companion of the Circle who had not broken under interrogation by the SS, and had gone on to make a daring escape from captivity and continued her work until the end of the war.

"This is – is impossible!" Nathan gasped. "I am amazed!"

Behind them Freddie entered the cabin and started the engines up. The boat started to move out from the jetty.

"It is good to meet you again, Nathan. I always recall our first meeting—"

"It was on VE day 1945," Nathan remembered with a smile. "I helped you up when you slipped over on the Mall. You were caught up in the enthusiasm of the occasion. I recollect we spoke for a few moments. Then you kissed me, and you disappeared into the crowd."

"Of course, in 1946, we met again," Francine reminded him.

"I was just coming to that. By one of those miraculous coincidences, or perhaps incidents, that have appeared in my life with regular occurrence, you turned up at the restaurant with your husband when I was there with Freddie. That was the night I learnt that you had been a Companion of the Circle and the French Resistance."

"It was enlightening for me too, Nathan. I learnt that your father had been one of the founder members of the Circle. Yes, that was long ago. That was the night before my husband and I returned to France to live.

"By the way," Nathan said, "where is your husband?"

Francine appeared sad and wistful at the mention of her husband. "He died young in a car accident," she murmured, and then added, "it was very hard, but life must go on"

"I'm sorry," Nathan said sympathetically, although he was at a loss as to why such a beautiful woman like Francine had not remarried. Here on a clear summer's day, Francine in a swimsuit looked not only exotic but also sensuous.

"So was I," Francine uttered. "In peacetime we still managed to have the common bond we had during the war. He became the Mayor of the village we lived in. Anyway, that is all in the past now. I took up a career in commercial art and I worked in Monte Carlo until last year. When Freddie wrote to me and mentioned that he was coming here, I decided that I would come too. So I caught a boat from Marseilles and I started off in Perth when I first arrived in Australia. Now I'm here in Sydney working for a magazine as a commercial artist. Maybe you could show me around sometime. I feel I have a lot to look forward to."

So have I, thought Nathan, as he pondered the thought of squiring Francine around Sydney. "I would love to," Nathan replied making no attempt to hide his enthusiasm at the prospect. "Where are you living at the moment?" He was eager to make the most of the moment. "On this side of the harbour?"

"I'm sharing a flat with another girl at Dover Heights. And you?"

"I've a house in Bondi."

"That is close to Dover Heights. I expect I'll be seeing you a lot."

The words were open to interpretation. Was it wishful thinking on Nathan's part that led him to believe that Francine hoped to see more of him.

Inside the cabin they joined Freddie, who was at his element skippering the cruiser along the waters of the Hawkesbury River. Freddie was never happier when taking the lead in new pastures; he was seemingly oblivious to the romance that was beginning to flourish behind him. Nathan and Francine laughed happily together. Freddie smiled. In truth he had planned it this way, knowing that Francine had come through an early widowhood a few years before and that Nathan was still single, Freddie played the role of a matchmaker. Nathan and Francine were both extraordinary people who had lived fascinating lives beyond the realms of a normal suburban existence.

Both Nathan and Francine took turns at guiding the cruiser. They ploughed along the Hawkesbury River past Lion Island and Eagle Rock, and secluded beaches only accessible by boat. There were many yachts and cruisers out on the waters that day, adding an aura of glamour to the fabulous lifestyle that many fortunate Sydneysiders were able to lead.

Later on in the morning Freddie guided the Taranga Princess to Refuge Bay, which was like some glorious lagoon with a romantic crystalline waterfall that splashed on to the rocks below. The trio crossed over to it by a small rowing boat and dipped in the warm waters. Nearby other boats dropped an anchor in the bay and soon there were lots of people swimming in the water. Francine was a born sun-lover; she stood beneath the gentle trickle of the waterfall soaking up the full effect of the sun. Nathan was convinced that if Francine had chosen modelling as a profession, with her superb looks, she would have dominated magazine covers around the world.

Francine was thirty-two years of age, the same as Nathan. She stood tall with long tawny hair, green eyes that suggested vulnerability and innocence, set against a deep copper tanned skin. Her figure oozed sex appeal, which she herself was seemingly unaware of. Nathan found it hard to take his eyes away from her. When Francine swam in the bay her long shapely legs were possessed of great strength, obviously from years of practice in the South of France.

Back on board the Taranga Princess the trio had accumulated a wide variety of food for lunch. They had prawns, salad in Greek style, a cold buffet, rolls and croissants, some soft drinks and two bottles of Champagne. It all seemed enormously rich for Nathan's blood. Then all too soon after a wonderful day on the Hawkesbury River it was time to go back to the jetty at Paradise Beach.

By the time they had berthed the Taranga Princess, darkness had fallen almost in the flash of an instant. When the boat was berthed at the jetty, the cicadas were chattering in their multitudes, the squawks of birds could be heard, even the sunset looked glorious above the trees, as they sipped warm mugs of tea.

Then from a distance Nathan saw a sight that set him thinking deeply. There was a tree in someone's garden on the river that was catching the moonlight. There were apples in the trees that looked golden and luminous in the blackness of the night and the beams of the moon. It struck Nathan how similar to the make up of life's course it resembled. Life is full of opportunities – golden opportunities. Like the apples on a tree, there are some good ones and some golden. Nathan gazed at Francine sitting on the edge of the jetty talking to Freddie as he tied the boat up at the mooring. Francine was surely a golden opportunity in his life that might never come again. Nathan had lost Melissa and Rose; he was determined that if Francine responded to him, he would not lose her.

That same night Nathan accompanied Francine to her home in Dover Heights and made arrangements to see her again. When Nathan returned to his house at Bondi, he felt wonderful as if he was on the brink of filling his empty emotional life.

Freddie Miller had his important tasks to attend to. Since he had joined the BBC he had reported on numerous assignments overseas which had included Royal visits by King George IV and Queen Elizabeth. The King and Queen during their reign had been much loved by the people of the Empire. Freddie had been saddened by the early death of the King in 1952. People worldwide mourned for the fine man who had never been groomed for kingship. Freddie always remembered a particular newsreel he had seen once of the King and Queen sitting with some boy scouts while a song about a chestnut tree was sung in the background. Then during the war when London was badly bombed in the blitz, Buckingham Palace received a direct hit. Both the King and Queen had gone out to visit the East Enders who had taken much of the bombing. It was a move that had endeared them to so many. Freddie had become an ardent admirer of the Royal Family and he considered that their positions as Heads of State must have been extremely isolated and lonely.

On November 20th 1947, Freddie had been part of a team covering the marriage of the King's eldest daughter Princess Elizabeth to Prince Philip at Westminster Abbey in London. In 1952 Freddie had been in Kenya on Princess Elizabeth's Royal Tour when the news of King George VI death from cancer had been received. Freddie had again been at Westminster Abbey on June 2nd 1953, this time for the coronation of the new Queen Elizabeth II, the beginning of a long and spectacular reign. The golden voice of the BBC's Richard Dimbleby described the occasion in a tone of clarity and perception that was moving in it's every syllable. To be there as a journalist, watching history being made, was thrilling for Freddie.

It was a marvellous warm and sunny day on February 3rd 1954 when the royal yacht *Gothic* entered Sydney Harbour carrying the Queen and Prince Philip. Freddie was on hand amongst the legion of journalists and newsmen covering the event. Amongst the hoards of people lining the foreshores were Nathan and Francine watching the commencement of a tour, which for the first time in Australian history marked the visit by a reigning monarch of the British Empire.

In future years Nathan and Francine were to remember this time for the start of their romance that would ultimately lead to marriage.

Forty-one

"Francine, what do you think of me?" The question had come from Nathan after several months of courtship with Francine. It had all been something of a magical dream to Nathan that his relationship with her had developed so well, he had asked her over dinner one night at an Italian restaurant in East Sydney.

Francine seemed ill at ease with the question. She was slow to reply and when she did it was with evasiveness. "Why do you ask?"

"Because I," Nathan took a deep breath to prepare himself, "because, I am in love with you."

Francine was caught completely off guard. At first she did not know what to say. Her face registered mixed emotions. She leaned across and wrapped her long graceful hand around Nathan's gripping it with an emotional intensity that startled him.

"I do not know what to say. I never considered the possibility that our friendship could lead to this. Since I arrived I have enjoyed your company. You have been kind to me. I know when I go home I will always remember you with much affection."

"Go home?" Nathan was startled. "You are not going to settle here?"

Francine released her hand from his and looked pensive for a moment. "I did not even consider it, to be absolutely truthful with you. I only came on Freddie's suggestion. After my husband died I moved to Monte Carlo and I lived the life of a single girl. You know I lost my mother and grandfather towards the end of the war. Mother was English from Yorkshire, which is where she was living after she and my father had separated. I had relatives in England but they were very distant. I didn't really know them. I have relatives in France too, but they are caught up in the webs of their own lives. I can't pretend that I am not drawn to you, Nathan. I am."

"My first meeting with you in the Mall in London is one of my most treasured memories."

Francine smiled warmly at the thought of it. "Since I was widowed I have been involved twice. I don't want to be hurt again. I don't want to hurt anyone, particularly you. You're a nice man; let's remain friends for the moment."

"I can understand that," Nathan remarked, and there was a hint of genuine feeling for her in his voice. "Are you planning to go back to Monte Carlo soon?"

"Not for a while, if you want to see me again—"

"Of course, Francine. Of course I want to see you again. Because you don't feel as strongly about me as I do you, it doesn't mean to say I no longer wish to see you. The two girls I was in love with, Melissa and Rose, are both married to other people now. We're still friends. I hope we will be."

Francine, who had felt nervous at the prospect of someone pursuing her with romantic intentions, suddenly felt secure in Nathan's presence. She felt that here was a man who genuinely loved her yet she could remain friends with until she felt ready to take the initiative. Her smile towards him was one of straightforward genuine affection. He returned the gesture.

They finished their meal and left the restaurant. Nathan felt gratified when Francine slipped her arm through his and strode along proudly beside him. It was a nice feeling to be walking alongside such a beautiful woman. Nathan conceded defeat for the evening as far as Francine was concerned. In the long run he felt sure that he could win her over.

He continued to see Francine on a regular basis, never imposing his very strong emotional feelings for her; always treating her diplomatically and gently. They went to restaurants together and to the theatres. Sometimes Francine would cook him a beautiful French meal at her flat. Nathan would return the compliment by cooking a candlelit dinner for her at his Bondi home. On these occasions Nathan would set the tone of the atmosphere by carefully planning the arrangement of the room. He would always have the table and chairs facing the window looking out wards the northern end of Bondi beach. The music that played from his record player would usually be the soft romantic tones of Nat King Cole or France's greatest and most emotion filled singer, Edith Piaf, of whom

Nathan knew that Francine had a distinct fondness for. Wine would be on the table, served in sparkling diamond-cut tall glasses. After the meal Nathan would always serve her chocolates. Sometimes he felt he was trying too hard. Francine never interpreted it this way.

Francine was everything in a companion that he could possibly have prayed for. Apart from her own naturally attractive persona, something she never flaunted, Francine was a bright and intelligent talker. Her personality was a combination of warmth and good humour. Never once in their many evenings together did Nathan hear Francine say a harsh word about anyone or anything. Even Francine's wartime experiences, as traumatic as they had been, did not engender bad feelings when she talked about them.

One quality that Nathan did see in her was a love of children. When Nathan introduced Francine to Ron and Jill Faley, she looked deliriously happy playing with their two young children. In one revealing conversation Francine mentioned that during her marriage to Claude Renalier, she had in fact suffered a miscarriage. She mentioned that should she ever marry again, she would dearly love a child. Nathan contemplated the fact that not only would she make an ideal wife, but surely an adoring mother too.

Francine's artistic skills impressed him no end. In her flat at Dover Heights, she had several self-created landscapes and portraits. Whilst in Western Australia, Francine had made a trip to Broome and the Kimberleys. During her visit there she had caught the fascinating colours of the bush, luminous ghost gums and whirlpools of colours, engrained in the Kimberleys, onto a set of canvasses. A commercial artist was her trained profession, but without a shadow of a doubt or discernment, her true talent lay in painting images and landscapes.

Recognising her talents in this direction, Nathan took her one weekend to Katoomba in the Blue Mountains, mentioning that this spot had an usual rock formation called the Three Sisters. It suited Francine ideally to paint this beautiful area, which she did with enthusiasm. Katoomba became their favourite spot and often on weekends, they would spend time there. They enjoyed walking along the bush tracks by the various lookout points from which they would gaze across the Jamieson Valley to the mountains, over which explorers such as Wentworth, Blaxland and Lapstone had trekked across. Nathan and Francine would stop for tea in the Paragon Café in a romantic antiquitous setting where some of the best chocolates in the world were reputedly served. Often they would have dinner in the stately old Carrington Hotel that seemed to belong to another age and era of mansion houses, ballroom gowns and dinner-suited valets. All these romantic settings proved a beautiful backdrop for their platonic friendship, which, through Nathan's gentle efforts, was becoming a calculated romance. He was slowly winning her over, and his love for her was growing stronger all the time.

Nathan introduced Francine to Melissa. It was a meeting that propelled two extraordinary women together. Melissa had invited Nathan to her farewell party. Melissa and her husband, Gary Markel, had been flying to Hollywood regularly in the past few years. Now that Melissa was contractually free of her acting and singing commitments in Australia, she was free to take up a Hollywood contract.

The big farewell party for Melissa and Gary was held at a Double Bay mansion owned by a prominent impresario. It was not just an ordinary party. It was a real razzmatazz, whiz-bang party with a jazz band, full of radio, theatre, film and musical personalities. There were coloured light bulbs strewn across the garden, which backed on to the harbour waters. A set of sizzling steaks and chops fried on an open charcoal grill in the manner of a Texas barbecue. Freddie Miller and Harry Masters were also invited and they helped themselves to some glasses of red wine and joined Nathan.

From a distance Nathan watched Francine and Melissa talking. The two women conversed pleasantly. Several times they glanced towards Nathan and smiled. What were they saying, he wondered? Francine wore a tight blue dress and high heeled patent leather shoes. He could see that he had competition that night. Several young men made passes at her and circled Francine like Tigers, poised to strike their prey. It was Freddie who rescued her from the intent surveyors. Melissa came across to join Nathan and Harry.

"Francine is lovely, Nathan," Melissa said sincerely.

"I'm glad you like her," Nathan replied.

"She told me about her wartime activities with the Circle and the resistance. She is not only attractive, but brave also."

"I told her how you entertained the troops in battle zones. Francine thinks the same of you, Melissa. You are both remarkable women."

Melissa accepted the compliment in good grace and then asked, "Are you going to marry her?"

Nathan flicked his eyes to hers quickly. Without hesitation, he replied, "That is my intention. Do you think she would say yes? You know she has been widowed. I think the thought of another commitment frightens her. I can, and do, understand that."

"You must ask her, Nathan. That is all you can do."

"Yes you are right. I must ask her. I have already told her I love her." Nathan looked serious for a moment as he pondered the future. He was not unthinking or thoughtless and he looked at Melissa. "I'm going to miss you, my dear kibbutz friend," he said and then in a moment of frankness he admitted, "You were the first girl I ever loved. I hope that doesn't shock you, or even upset you." Mellissa nodded, but appeared intrigued. Her eyes showed interest. "I remember the first time I saw you sixteen years ago. You wore an old grey dress, you were barefooted and looking after the poultry on the kibbutz. Then I would see you in the kibbutz plays and musicals. I was so shy of you, so inhibited in expressing my emotions that I could never really get as close to you as I am now—"

"If that is so, Nathan, you must not waste a moment. If you want Francine, you must express yourself. Or else you will lose her."

"I concur entirely. Let me say that before you leave for your new career and life in Hollywood with Gary, that I wish you happiness always."

"Thank you, Nathan. Don't let Francine get away. She will make you happy." Nathan knew this. He instinctively looked for Francine at the party. It was she who returned to him. Many of the people at Melissa's party were of a gregariousness and Larrikinism that Francine found overbearing. She and Freddie were quick to rejoin Nathan.

This was the last occasion that Nathan would ever see Melissa in person again until many years had passed. The only time Nathan would see Melissa over the next twenty-six years would be up on the silver screen in the various film roles that Hollywood churned out for her. A few days later Melissa and Gary Markel flew out of Sydney on board a constellation aircraft bound for Los Angeles.

Nathan was too far involved in his own pre-occupation with Francine to feel too much pain at Melissa's departure. He had lost Melissa forever. Francine, he had not. After several months of courtship, Nathan finally decided he would have to take the matter firmly in hand. He loved Francine. He wanted to marry her.

After one long hard and difficult week at the law firm when

Nathan had worked on several matters that had required all his power of concentration, he had arranged to have dinner with Francine on a Sunday evening at Bondi. He had taken special care that evening to make his home even tidier and comfortable than normal. Nathan had placed flowers strategically around the room, which gave it an added touch of romance. Candles burned softly. The background music on his record player was that of lush orchestral strings. The wine on the table was a rich French claret that Francine found suitable to her palate.

The setting was right; the atmosphere could not have been better improved. All that remained was for Nathan to propose over dinner, and then present her with the engagement ring he had carefully selected for her.

It was raining heavily that evening. When Francine arrived, she looked enchantingly French in her dress with a beret and a fashionable raincoat that was more at home in the Place Vendomes rather than North Bondi. She was soaked from the downpour and Nathan took her wet coat and hat. When she had dried herself she studied the interior of the room. A smile spread across her lips. Francine was impressed; Nathan had gone to an enormous amount of trouble. She walked up close to him and looked at him with a sense of real appreciation in her eyes.

"All of this – for me?" Francine asked, her voice so quiet it bordered on a whisper.

"Yes, my darling, all for you," Nathan replied in hushed tones. He was almost trembling inside as he gazed deeply into her eyes, which caught the light of the flickering candles in the room.

Francine was slightly taken aback by Nathan using the words 'my darling'. She leaned forward and placed both of her hands on Nathan's shoulders.

"Do you remember VE Day 1945?" she asked him quietly.

"I have never forgotten the time we first met," Nathan said honestly, recalling the occasion. That memory brought a thrill to Nathan as he remembered how in the euphoria of that day long ago, they had kissed passionately on the Mall in London.

Nathan needed no prompting. He moved forward to kiss her. Francine offered no resistance. She gripped him tightly. He in turn held her tightly and found himself immersed in the greatest love he had known outside of his family. The feelings of love Nathan had for Francine overwhelmed him completely. He suddenly realised Francine was shaking. Nathan pulled her to him, kissed her hairline and ran his hands lovingly up and down the length of her back. Francine sank into the warmth of his chest, her heart pounding against him.

With a feeling of incredible warmth searing through him Nathan held her longingly. He stroked her hair gently. Then he pushed her head back tenderly and kissed her soft accommodating lips slowly, noiselessly and deeply passionately. In a moment of suddenness he swept her up into his arms, and in a daze of confusion and ecstasy he was carrying her towards his bedroom.

What happened next seemed to be a combination of two minds, two souls and a flurry of senses coming together with a wonder, a passion, an excitement and a warmth of enhanced, heightened emotions. There were sounds that accompanied their silent passion: the raindrops tapping on the bedroom window, the roar of the waves as they thundered into the shore and the veritable explosion of the surf as it crashed over the rocks. The mattress beneath them strained beneath the pressure of their weight and they submerged into a peace and serenity, almost at the moment that the storm outside paled off into its tranquil aftermath.

Their mutual feelings of love swept them into a sense of half consciousness, half awareness as they lay in each other's arms, Francine's head resting on Nathan's chest. Love was wondrous and exhilarating; It was beautiful.

There was no way Nathan could describe his feelings. They were of an indescribable happiness. He had never realised until now just how powerful love could be. He was convinced that Francine wanted his love; that she wanted him as much as he wanted her. That night had been the consummation of their love.

In the morning Nathan stood at the side of the bed for a long time, gazing at Francine deep in sleep. She was peaceful and still. Francine had a wonderful look of tranquillity about her. Somehow Nathan could not bring himself to propose to her today. He felt that if he were to do so today, it would be the wrong time after the joy of the evening. The timing and the atmosphere would have to be impeccable.

Nathan wandered into the dining room, which he had arranged so carefully for the rendezvous that he had intended to make the occasion to propose marriage to Francine. The candles had burned out completely leaving mounds of melted down wax in the saucers on which they had been mounted. The table places were still set. The wine glasses were still full of the special claret that Nathan had bought. The flowers were still in exactly the same position mounted around the room. Nathan took one beautiful tropical flower and walked back to the bedroom with it. Francine was still sleeping soundly. He placed the flower on the pillow beside her. She roused slightly and half opened her eyes.

The scent of the flower caused her to open her eyes quickly. She smiled at the gesture and then rolled over clutching it and absorbing the scent deeply. From behind the petals she smiled lovingly at Nathan and there was real joy in her eyes. Words were not necessary. Each one's expression said it all.

That time of the early stages of their love was a very happy time for them both. 1954 was a year they would always remember with much affection. There were both thirty-two years of age with a wealth of exciting years behind them, and a host of happy ones to come. For each of them this was to be the best year of their lives.

Nathan finally got around to proposing to Francine, but it was not done with flowers, claret and soft music. It was done purely on an impromptu note. Nathan and Francine had been out dancing at a supper club in the city. The night had been memorable for the jazz band had played many varied numbers, including a beautiful version of the Bunny Berigan record *'I Can't Get Started'* with a sensational trumpet solo.

When it had been time to leave Nathan and Francine made their way to the tram stop. True to form the Saturday night Bondi tram was packed to bursting point. The two of them squeezed inside. The tram was so full the conductor could not get from one each to the other. Many people got off and on without paying, much to the conductor's annoyance.

The tram was crowded with just about every type of person available. There were men who worked late in the newspaper offices, shift workers, those who were heavily imbibed after a night out on the town, office cleaners, people who had been out to the theatres and restaurants. Nathan and Francine stood together in the aisles trying to keep their balance as the bone-shaking tram rolled and rattled its way to Bondi.

Nathan wasn't quite sure just why, but here in this crowded steamy tram, he suddenly decided that he could not delay the question any more. He put both of his hands on her shoulders and jerked her towards him. She looked bemused.

"Francine, will you marry me?" The tram rolled over a bumpy mound in the road and the sound completely obliterated his question. He started again "Francine, will you—" This time a tram going by on the other side made a loud noise that deferred his question again.

Nathan rolled his eyes towards the roof. A night cleaning lady touched Francine on the shoulder. Francine turned to look at her.

"He just asked you to marry him, luv," the lady said with a big grin of amusement revealing some gap teeth.

Francine looked at Nathan in astonishment. Nathan was just about to ask her again, when a huge trilby-hatted man in a double-breasted suit with an RSL badge in the lapel whispered some advice in his ear.

"Get down on your knees, son, and propose," he advised. "She'll be bringing you to your knees for the rest of your life! You might as well get down on them voluntarily at least once."

Nathan chuckled at the man's rough humour and took his advice. In the middle of the tram much to Francine's amazement, and the onlooker's amusement, he got down on his knees.

"Francine, will you marry me?" Again the noise of the tram hitting a bump in the road prevented Francine from hearing him.

The middle-aged cleaning lady again filled Francine in on the missing details.

"Well go on then, say 'yes', you silly flamin' sheila. He wants to marry you."

"Yeah go on, luv," said the man in the trilby hat. "Or I'll propose to you."

A speck of a tear appeared in Francine's eyes.

"I love you, Francine," he said, rising up quickly. "I don't know how many times I have to tell you. I want to marry you." There was a slight edge of frustration in his voice, as if this would be the last time he would broach the subject.

Francine's eyes flooded with tears. "I know you do," she said softly.

"Go on, sweetheart. He loves you," said the man in the trilby hat joining in good-humouredly. Francine managed a smile at the humour of the situation.

The middle-aged cleaning lady joined in once more. "Say yes, then, luv. He's a good-looking bloke. If you don't want him, I'll bloody ave im."

At this Francine let out a laugh. She was crying and laughing at the same time.

"I can see I have tough competition," Francine said wiping her eyes. She put her arms around him and hugged him. "Of course I say yes." Nathan was beaming with happiness. The people around him were smiling."

"I am so unbelievably happy," Nathan said chokingly. The old woman kissed both of them on the cheek, and the trilby-hatted man shook Nathan's hand.

Francine did not lack in humour. She gently chided him. "You smooth talker. What took you so long?"

"I wanted the place and the moment to be right," he remarked in jest thinking how he could have avoided the flowers and soft music, and the French claret. Still it had led indirectly to the first ecstatic flush of real romantic love he had every known. What a place for a marriage proposal, he thought with amusement. On a rattling old tram halfway between the city of Sydney and Bondi beach.

At the final stop at Campbell Parade along Bondi beach, Nathan and Francine were the last to leave the tram. They sat arms around each other embroiled in a passionate kiss. The tram driver and the conductor gaped in amazement.

"Pack it in you two!" the conductor exclaimed. "The tram terminates here, unless of course you want to go back to town?"

Nathan and Francine stopped embracing each other. Their golden happiness was clear for all to see.

"I have just proposed to her," Nathan said happily taking Francine by the arm. "And she has agreed to marry me. Isn't that wonderful news?"

"Congratulations!" the conductor said crisply. "I've got a little bit of news myself so to speak."

"Really!" Nathan remarked, wondering if the conductor had proposed to his own girl, and was as deliriously happy as he was feeling at that moment.

The tram conductor held his hand out. "The news is – you and your lovely lady here haven't paid your fare!"

★★★

Nathan and Francine were married at Katoomba in the Blue Mountains. It seemed to be the ideal spot for their marriage. During their courtship this had been their favourite weekend retreat. Now it was a place that would always be enshrouded in romance for them.

Their wedding ceremony was performed by a civil marriage celebrant on the lookout point with the Three Sisters in the background. Freddie Miller flew in from Darwin where he was filming for the BBC; he was delighted to be Nathan's best man at the wedding. Nathan wore a dark blue suit and white bow tie. Francine arrived with Harry Masters, who had agreed to give her away in the normally paternal role performed by the bride's father. When she arrived Nathan felt a lump rise in his throat. Francine looked absolutely glorious in a long, chiffon, iridescent blue dress and a flower in her hair. Far from looking nervous at the prospect of entering into her second matrimonial excursion she looked radiant and glowing. Her eyes shone brightly. Her cheeks were flushed crimson red and she was glowing with vitality and happiness.

It was a wonderful open-air wedding on a very hot day. The marriage celebrant's words came through crystal clear, and as vibrant as the day itself. Amongst the people who had come to the wedding were all of the old faithfuls. Freddie had performed his function as best man with utmost happiness. He felt glad that his long time friend had finally found the happy life in a good relationship that he had not known since leaving for the kibbutz sixteen years before. Harry Masters beamed with sheer delight. The crowd included Ron and Jill Faley and their children; Mick and Rose, who was now glowing being in the early stages of pregnancy; Spiros and Kristos and their offspring; the Toohey family, including Pat and his girlfriend; the Hoolihans, who loved Nathan like a member of their own family; and Terry and his new wife.

The biggest delight of the day was the unexpected arrival of Ted McTaggart from Queensland. Nathan had sent Ted an invitation card out of courtesy, not expecting it to be taken up, but just after the ceremony had begun in he strolled with that old cheeky charm and confidence, dazzling everyone, even the normally placid Abria and Mavicl.

Francine's flatmates were also there as were some of her colleagues at work. In such sunny weather and a small group of happy people, the day could only be an unqualified success.

The reception was held at the Carrington Hotel. For Nathan who never cared much for ceremony or formality, it was an odd place for a wedding reception. The Carrington still evoked an essence of grandeur, beauty and stateliness of a time gone by. In fact it was an excellent place for a wedding reception. In its heyday in the 30s it had been a wonderful honeymoon resort that held many happy memories for couples who had stayed there over the years.

Ted McTaggart was in his element as master of ceremonies for the occasion. With his ebullient comic humour and his joking manner, he had everyone in stitches of laughter as he told stories of his meetings with Nathan in North Africa and the unbelievable reunion years later on Orange tree Downs in the Northern Territory. Then for a few brief moments Ted became serious as he spoke of how proud Nathan's parents would be at him marrying such a fine girl as Francine. Ted's seriousness lasted only a short time, although a deeply sincere man, he felt far more comfortable with himself, and other people, when he was laconic and joking.

Freddie rose to the occasion when it came to his turn to speak at the microphone. He could be very witty, not as abundantly as Ted perhaps, but capable of sparkling with humour on the right occasions. He was the only person present who had known Nathan from his teenage years, charting his progress from a naïve mountain village boy to the hard-working Sydney lawyer he had become.

The party after the meal was certainly not a stiff frocked affair. It was a nice evening of good humour and dancing. The band played all upbeat happy numbers that people could dance to. Nathan felt as if he was living some kind of dream. He almost had to convince himself that he had married Francine. It was all so splendid that he could not believe his good fortune.

While the rest of the wedding guests made their way home the next morning, Nathan and Francine stayed on at the Carrington for a week's honeymooning in the Blue Mountains. They were wonderful days spent bush walking and just enjoying their deep mutual love for each other. Nathan had never dreamed that life could be this good. It was a joy to them both to sit together arms around each other, gazing out across the Jamieson Valley, in blissful silence enchanted by the fact that they were now man and wife. They both wished that the honeymoon could last forever.

Forty-two

After the brief honeymoon Nathan and Francine returned to Sydney. When Nathan carried Francine over the threshold into the house at Bondi it was the beginning of many years of happy married life for them both. They were both madly in love with each other, and for each the sense of belonging to someone again was of the most important aspect. Nathan had not known family life for many years. To come home to Francine each evening after a hard days work was a luxury that he could never be complacent about.

The security of a good marriage partner was a comforting blanket. If Nathan's career had not been demanding and responsible, he would have worked at the most humble profession to please his wife. Francine gave him the utmost support at all times. In marriage, Francine was a rarity. She was possessed of the old qualities of loyalty and faithfulness. She was a good cook in the European style, always preparing meals with care, and treating it as the occasion of the day. These were special times for them both when they could talk about the events of the day late into the night. Her domesticity and matching intellect made her the ideal marriage partner for Nathan.

Francine was very much her own person. Determined that this, her second marriage, would be long and enduring. She was supportive and loyal to Nathan. But if she was in love with Nathan, she was also in love with her career as a commercial artist. Since her early days as an art student in Paris before the war, Francine had loved her profession in all of its forms. Throughout the years since the war she had never given up studying and improving her artistic skills.

Always an admirer of the paintings of Toulouse Lautrec, Francine's tastes extended to impressionism, post-impressionism and Rococo. During her years with the Circle and the resistance, Francine had often used the impressionist's skill in sketching fleeting images of Paris at the time of the occupation. Impressionism was an unconventional art form originated in France by Edouard Manet, which spawned such famous names as Claude Monet, Auguste Renoir, Edgar Degas and Camille Pissarro. The objective of impressionism was to convey an exacting impression of a scene by the use of normal colours to recreate the atmosphere and character in its most natural style. Perhaps the most outstanding painting Francine had ever seen was Renoir's great masterpiece, *Le Moulin De La Galette*, which depicted the bustle and flurry of Montmartre in the 1870s. It showed the straw and top-hatted Parisian figures of men dancing with their girls in the fashionable clothes of the era.

Francine had tried to do something similar in Sydney's wild bohemian suburb Kings Cross, which she saw as an antipodean version of Montmartre, except that it was more racier and raunchier. She had tried to capture the detail of the characters that made up the Cross; the flower sellers, the fruiterers, silhouetted figures in the doorway, a policeman talking to someone, a Ford Popular car and an original 1949 Holden in the oncoming traffic along Macleay Street. At Nathan's suggestion she entered the painting for an exhibition at a Paddington art gallery. Much to her surprise and Nathan's delight the painting was well received critically.

It was the start of a new career for Francine. After talking it over with Nathan, she decided to become a full-time painter. Nathan encouraged her. He knew that she had a formidable talent in this direction, and he wanted her to develop her abilities. Francine knew that her husband was sincere in wanting the best for her. From the very outset of their marriage it was a mutual partnership in which each one could pursue their very different careers without conflict in the relationship.

While Nathan worked at the law firm, Francine walked about Sydney with her board and easels, as she had done in Paris years before. Using the impressionist style, Francine caught many atmospheric visual images of different parts of Sydney on canvas. They were a fascinating array of views: the surf-boarded riders at Bondi, the bustle of a Saturday morning in Kings Cross, shoppers at Double Bay, a view of ferry boats cruising the harbour as seen from a vantage point at Nielsen Park beach in Vaucluse, terraced houses and markets in Surry Hills and Redfern. On one occasion, Francine, sitting in the ladies lounge of a bathroom tiled pub, reproduced the faces of the men over the counter in the opposite bar who were drinking schooners of beer and listening to the races. Francine, in all of her artistic ability, managed to paint an outstanding image of Australian life in all of its forms.

Around their house at Bondi, Francine's paintings were everywhere. She was prolific in her output. Before Freddie Miller returned to England he paid a visit to the house to farewell Nathan and Francine. He was so impressed by one of her paintings that he asked for a reproduction for the house he had just bought in Sussex. Fare-welling Freddie Miller was a sad occasion for them both, they had liked him enormously and they would always retain contact over the years.

In that year Francine's painting were regularly exhibited in art galleries, not only in Sydney but also Melbourne and Brisbane. Nathan often accompanied Francine to these displays. He realised just what a great talent his wife had. Francine was not only interested in art from her professional role, but also the subject itself. Her knowledge of the history of art was very impressive. She could speak freely on Baroque and Rococo, the Renaissance and the works of Raphael, Michelangelo and Leonardo da Vinci. Francine did not insulate herself purely thinking of art in European terms. She was fascinated by the art world in Australia. The works of Sidney Nolan inspired her to paint landscapes of the outback. By far the Australian artist who made the biggest impression on her was the remarkable Aboriginal Albert Namatjira whose landscape paintings of the bush and the Australian desert were breathtaking.

With money coming in from the sale of her paintings and Nathan's career flourishing, life looked wonderful for both of them. Their work was satisfying. Their home life was very happy. To add to their happiness just over a year after their marriage Francine gave birth to a daughter. Nathan was overjoyed at the birth of his first child. Their daughter was named Anastasia Tamara Palmai.

It was like a dream come true for Nathan. After the years of struggle he had found a peak of happiness, he could never have envisaged. He was married to a beautiful, passionate and fascinating French woman who had given him a child, a hope for the future. He was a lawyer with a strong sense of moral values and compassion for battlers. He had a comfortable home, not austere, nor pretentious. The shares he had bought in the Orange Tree Downs proprietary company promised a good yield in future years, as the price of minerals and beef cattle increased during the boom-time of the 50s.

When Francine announced she was expecting their second child, Nathan was even more delighted than in 1955 when Anastasia had been born. Nathan and Francine had been out to the cinema to see the Australian film Jedda. During the intermission Francine had told him of the impending birth. Nathan felt convinced that his second child would be a son. He was thrilled beyond belief.

His conviction was right. In 1956 Francine gave birth to a son. But it was not a simple birth. The baby was born several weeks prematurely. Straight away the doctors diagnosed that something was tragically wrong. The baby on being delivered did not cry and it soon became apparent that sound did not register in his ears. Tragically their son initially named Joseph Arthandur Palmai had been born deaf and without the ability to speak. The only way to communicate with their son would by the process of sign language. Joseph would need a great deal of attention and patience in the coming years. Nathan had named his son after the stockman, Joe, he had known and his own father Arthandur.

Bringing up two children was a joy to Nathan and Francine. Both of them had come from loving parents who had ruled them with a firm hand, always encouraging them, but never being harsh and critical of them. The result was that Nathan and Francine although two very different people, were basically similar in nature, strong in personality, not given to anger easily, and tolerant without being impatient.

It was a difficult task bringing up Joseph. The child in his early years was curious with big inquisitive eyes and a warm contagious smile that could melt ice away. His big sister, Anastasia, was a happy laughing child who was quick in learning to speak. Young Joseph was mystified by his world of silence and why he could not communicate with his parents and sister. Sometimes the young child obviously in deep frustration would break into tears, and then it would involve Nathan, Francine and Anastasia doing their absolute best to reassure Joseph that he was loved. At times, attending to Joseph varied between heartbreak and happiness.

In the late 1950s and 1960s Australia was one of the most harmonious places to live in the world. Its easy-going lifestyle and prosperous economy made it the best country to live in, a destination for migrants of all nationalities seeking a stable, happy environment. The Liberal Prime Minister, Robert Gordon Menzies, who by his own admittance was an anglophile, an ardent Royalist and a staunch Commonwealth man, had ascended to office in 1949. His government was set for a record-breaking term, which would end many years later. Australian films of the period tended to depict country life and outback adventures, rarely entering the world of normal suburban life. People worked hard often at two jobs. Families spent weekends on the beach or in the open spaces. At that time Australia experienced some of its most golden years before the time of it's involvement in the Vietnam War, and the world economic recessions that were to plague the economy in later times.

Nathan and Francine were no ordinary couple, but neither had any aspiration to live in a wealthier suburb. They were quite content to live at Bondi amongst the mix of contrasting people that lived there. Although Nathan was a lawyer and Francine was an artist, their lifestyle was not unlike many other normal working people. Their home was comfortable enough. They did not want for anything, nor did their children. They wanted Anastasia and Joseph to grow up knowing love and charity and an appreciation of the simple things in life, instead of being brought up in an atmosphere of wealth, opulence and a craving for material things.

The determination that Nathan and Francine had for their children was well steeped in common sense. Both had come from households where they had been taught to respect all people no matter how humble their occupation. Although they could have afforded for Anastasia to be educated at a private school they wanted her to go to a normal suburban school where she would learn true values. With Joseph there was not a choice; he had to be taught at a special school for the deaf and dumb. Joseph had an excellent acumen that made up in part for the lack of his ability to speak and listen. As he grew up, Joseph developed a talent that he had inherited from his mother. He could paint perfectly refined portraits and landscapes. In another area at his special school Joseph entered the drama school performing in sign language with the other children, who had the same disabilities as him.

Anastasia and Joseph were children that their parents positively glowed with pride over. Often when they went out as a family the joy was there for all to see. Francine painted mostly at home while the children were at school but during the holidays she was like any normal mum. Francine would take the children into town for a meal at Coles, and then on a ferry ride to somewhere like Manly or Taronga Park Zoo. She was fond of tennis and if there were international contests being played at the White City Courts, at Rushcutters Bay, she would take Anastasia and Joseph with her.

★★★

The years passed quickly. They were good and happy years, rewarding at home and on a professional basis for both Nathan and Francine. By 1972 Nathan had risen to prominence as a leading Sydney lawyer. Through his professional contacts he was given two prestigious directorships: one being a nominal position for a foundation, the other for a company whose interests he had represented in a controversial court battle. The partnership of the law firm had since passed into Nathan's hands and his long time colleague Harry Masters. The work had involved much dedication and research. Nathan had sensed the need for reforms in many areas of the law; many of the reforms he thought were necessary were later implemented by the Labour government led by Prime Minister Gough Whitlam in 1972.

It was a relief to Nathan that his career had helped contribute to upgrading the law. Not only that, with his work commanding so much detail to facts and a sense of propriety, he felt that every minute of his life's tasks were truly worthwhile. He could look back on all that he had done with a sense of pride. From Austria to Australia the route of his life had been varied. There were times when Nathan looked back at the people he'd known, his travels and experiences. And the more he thought deeply about it, the more he realised that he had been a most fortunate man.

One Sunday afternoon Nathan looked out from the kitchen. Out in the garden his wife and children sat at the garden table talking and laughing. Just for a moment he smiled at the joy the sight of his family gave him. Francine was fifty and didn't look a day over thirty-five, thanks to her regular exercise and regular swimming workouts. She had truly been a prize, a friend, confidant, lover and devotedly loyal always.

Anastasia, then seventeen, took after her mother in so many easy. The two together seemed more like sisters than mother and daughter. Nathan and Francine had high hopes for her. At school Anastasia had performed well at most subjects. She was not an exceptional student, but had the same sort of perseverance that her father had. Anastasia wanted to work for the ABC as a production assistant, but Nathan and Francine had hoped she would try for a place at university.

Then there was Joseph Arthandur Palmai, sixteen years old, looking almost exactly the same as Nathan had done at that age. God had not given Joseph the power of speech or the gift of hearing; instead the young man, despite the overwhelming odds against him, had the power to translate his thoughts onto paintings. Mother and son's work were unique.

Nathan realised that when he was Joseph's age, he had been preparing himself to leave for the kibbutz in Palestine. At that age Nathan had talked to the old goat herder in the village. He remembered the conversation they had. The goat herder had pointed out different types of goats and there was one that leaped from crag to crag until it found where it really wanted to go; that was how Nathan compared his life, to the path of the true mountain goat.

Forty-three

1984

A few days after Nathan's reunion with Melissa, he was again embroiled in long hours of hard work. Undoubtedly he was trying to cope with too big a workload. He knew it was time to slow down. One man could only do so much. The worst part of it all was that Nathan enjoyed his work. He thrived on it: the committees, the preparation of legal matters, the running of the firm, the board meetings that he attended as a director, his work on the Law Reform Commission, the attendances at ethnic gatherings. He was so busy he did not have such a thing as spare time.

This had been his routine for several years. Unfortunately he was beginning to experience symptoms that were indicative of his overwork. He was tiring far more easily than he had done before. Sometimes his legs felt stiff. Occasional bouts of breathlessness struck him when he least expected it. He knew his body was receiving warnings that it was time to shed himself of many of his duties. Still he persisted in carrying on at the frantic pace he had been doing for so long.

The final warning came with an unexpected suddenness in 1984, at the time when he least expected it. At least one morning a week before going to work Nathan went for a swim and jog at Bondi beach. Whenever he did this he always felt splendid for the rest of the day. Knowing how tired he had felt recently, he was sure that if he began this regular routine he would be fit and alert again. One Friday morning Nathan drove down to the beach to begin his new format of his working day.

It was a gentle breeze that in one moment became a sudden wind jerking a little boy's kite high into the sky far above the creamy surf at Bondi. The early morning joggers were out and about. Amongst them

Nathan could see Margaret Whitlam, the wife of the former Prime Minister, and the prominent New South Wales Politician, Paul Landa. Already the surfboard riders were out trying to catch an early morning wave. At such an early hour of the day, there was a curious mixture of businessmen, housewives, public figures, obscure figures and bleach blond surfboard riders on one of the world's most famous beaches. There was also an array of pretty girls, whose sparkling figures seemed to be iridescent against a background of wide blue sky, rolling waves, splashing surf, and a stream of seagulls squawking against the noise of the crashing of the blue sea, the golden sand and the red roofs of Bondi.

There was nothing unusual about that day; nothing that seemed to hint at any stirring departure from Nathan's routine. He went for a refreshing dip, followed by a gentle paced jog along the beach. Then he drove home for a shower and some breakfast. He felt well enough apart from a general slowing down. It was on that day however that going down in the lift to his car, Nathan suddenly felt a slight twinge in his side, more like a sharp flutter that unnerved him. It lasted a few worrying moments, almost as quickly it eased. Nathan ignored it thinking that the more he thought about it, the more he would worry. He did however take one safety precaution. He decided not to drive to work this morning, as he felt that if there was something detrimental with his health, a possible seizure or attack in the peak hour traffic and could endanger people's lives.

On that particular morning Nathan boarded the train at Edgecliffe station perhaps in naivety thinking that he could continue to carry on his routine, and his very heavy workload forever if he felt capable of doing so. He was in a very reflective mood that morning. He stared out of the window as the train passed Rushcutters Bay, Bayswater Road, stopped at Kings Cross and then proceeded over the viaduct at Woolloomooloo where from above one could always see the dejected metho drinkers and the homeless men who sat in the tiny plots of the recreation ground situated between Forbes Street and William Street. Along past the shipyards at Garden Island and Cockatoo Island to the refreshingly lush green of the Domain, the Sydney Tower looming up above the approaching city office buildings like a towering pantheon. Such a city of contrasts, it always felt like an experience, more than a way of life to live in Sydney, Australia.

Nathan smiled as he read in the *Sydney Morning Herald* that Melissa was in Sydney again, this time for a concert tour.

By the time the train reached Town Hall station, Nathan was beginning to feel ill again. It seemed as if walking was a marathon effort. His legs felt heavy and stiff. He felt slow against the push and rush of the commuters thronging through the station. For a moment he felt dizzy and breathless. And then a massive tight feeling enveloped him. He clutched his chest in shock, dropping his briefcase to the floor. The sound of his slow heartbeat echoed in his ear. Nathan crumpled up and fell to the ground.

There was a sudden blur, a blue haze, faces milling around him. He felt as if the rest of the world was receding away from him. There was a sudden thud on his chest as if someone had come to his immediate aid, and tried desperately to reactivate his ailing heart. After that there were only sensations as if he was fluctuating perilously between life and the edge of eternity. There was darkness. There was light. Drowsiness. Consciousness. Shadows. Figures in a blur. A hard solid thud on the chest again. Something was happening. It was like life flowing back inside of him. He could see clearly, but he still felt weak. Nathan could feel himself being elevated. He realised he was on a stretcher being carried into an ambulance. Then he felt weak again, his eyes felt heavy. Oblivion.

"The only choice you have is for a heart transplant," the doctor was saying this in gentle tones to Nathan. He had been listening from his bed. *A heart transplant*. This was all so staggering to Nathan. Yet the doctor had left him in no doubt to the consequences if he did not take up this option. The doctor went on to describe Nathan's symptoms and the process of the operation. Waking up in hospital after collapsing at the train station had been surprise enough; to now face the most momentous decision of his life, whether to undergo a heart transplant or not, was the biggest and most crucial test he could ever face. It was virtually a choice between life and death.

Nathan listened in a fog of mixed thoughts. He was amazed, surprised and shocked at the same time. He was feeling disbelief and fear of the unknown. The doctor was telling him that a suitable donor was available. They could begin almost as soon as Nathan agreed to proceed.

"Look on it as a new experience. A second life," said the doctor lightheartedly, trying not to sound too magisterial in his tones. *A second life or an extension of the old one*. Nathan realised with absolute dismay that everything that had gone before would be part of an old life never to be returned to. If the operation was successful it would mean instant retirement from all the responsibilities he had spent his life working towards. It was a decision that would spell the end of one life, and beginning a new one.

The doctor at Nathan's request agreed to contact Anastasia and Joseph immediately to bring them to their father's bedside. Anastasia caught a flight from Darwin that night. Joseph arrived in due course. The operation was scheduled for the next day when, in the afternoon, Nathan would face the greatest test of his life. Earlier on when the doctor had mentioned in a pleasant manner to regard it as a new experience, the remark had brought a smile to Nathan. A new experience; it was one angle at looking at the most important thing that could happen to anyone since the day of their birth.

Anastasia and Joseph stayed for as long as they were permitted to do so by the doctor. They had been duly warned at the hospital of the seriousness of their father's condition and also of the impending consequences should any serious medical complication arise. On the surface Anastasia spoke warmly with her father. She tried not to show how worried she felt inside. Joseph communicated with his father by sign language, smiling warmly. It was only after a while that Joseph's inner feelings were betrayed. A tear rolled from his eye. Nathan trembled inside. His own emotions now were revealed and the next instant found the three of them weeping together.

When they had gone Nathan lay back in his bed. By his side the doctor had placed some literature about human heart transplantation. At first Nathan did not want to read about it. He felt weak and breathless, and did not have the capacity to concentrate. All he wanted to do was to wake up alive and well after the operation. The more he tried to put it out of his mind, the more he realised he was denying himself an answer to his own natural curiosity. He turned over and perused through the pages of the book.

Suddenly Nathan, despite his weakness, felt a surge of fascination come over him. He read about Professor Christiaan Barnard's heart transplant operations in 1967 and 1968. Nathan was filled with astonishment when the enormity of the operation dawned upon him: His chest would be opened, the donor's chest would be opened and the heart excised, then through the marvels of modern science and technology the new heart would be transposed. Life would continue in its normal form. It was all so fascinating that the very nucleus of a person could be changed over from a deceased donor to a recipient on death's door giving them an added bonus of years of extra living. Nathan lay back and sighed.

In his lifetime he had experienced many things. He wanted to pause and reflect on his memories. When he had recently met Melissa, they had spent an evening recounting the years almost as if it had been a preparation for the operation that lay ahead tomorrow. If for any reason Nathan did not survive beyond the next day, he wanted to remember now all the good fortune that had been his.

For some reason Nathan's thoughts drifted to a trip to Europe that he and Francine had undertaken shortly before her death. When it had become obvious that Francine had little time left to live, she faced up to her terminal illness with the courage that she had possessed during the years she had spent with the Companions of the Circle and the resistance. The two of them, making their first trip home since leaving to come to Australia, travelled to the places they held dear in their hearts. They had begun their journey in London visiting many parts of the city that had been so prominent in Nathan's life. From there they made trips to Cornwall and Yorkshire. Francine had wanted to revisit both those counties. At Cornwall she relived the night she had been rescued from the tanker by a few of lifesavers that included Freddie Miller. There were still a few relatives of Francine's alive. Some lived in Yorkshire, where her mother had come from, and there were several in Paris.

On the English part of the journey they had seen Freddie Miller for the last time. He had been living quietly in a leafy green village in Sussex. He was then seventy-four years of age, still sprightly and enthusiastic about anything to do with travel and history. He had become a pipe-smoking country villager interested in nature and, despite his worldly travels; he still had an enormous love of people and enjoyed each day as it came. Freddie knew the reason why Francine and Nathan had come to visit. It was sadness that he felt when it came for the time of farewell to Francine. Freddie realised that perhaps he had probably been in love with her at some stage of his life.

Nathan and Francine moved on through France. They visited Paris, Marseilles and Monte Carlo. Francine often appeared misty eyed as she remembered the days of her youth, the war years, and her time as a young independent woman after the early death of her first husband.

For Nathan his homecoming was deeply moving. The country of his birth had undergone an enormous metamorphosis since he had left it as a child. He did not recognise Germany in any respect; it had been separated into West Germany and East Germany. The city of Berlin, virtually reconstructed after the war, still had many of the old landmarks. Nathan looked around in disbelief. The city of his childhood fraught with tension, and the fearful rise of the Third Reich, was now a thriving commercial city full of life, bustle and industry. It had been so strange to be back there after all these years.

The place that Nathan really wanted to see was the Austrian village where he had spent such happy years with Arthandur and Marlene. He remembered the day that he returned to it with Francine. Strange how the familiar scent of the mountain air rose to greet him as he stepped from the train carriage. He and Francine stood on the platform gazing at the ice-blue mountains and the glistening white snow. It had been forty-one years since he had last been here. Tears welled up in his eyes. He felt absurdly emotional.

But there were ghosts everywhere. Walking along the mountain paths he almost expected to see old Wilf, the goat herder, greet him with a hearty bellow of laughter and yodel that would reverberate across the valley and the passages of time. Through the ages, Wilf's words rose from the past except neither he, nor the goats, were there and the young man who had listened so eagerly had long since become a man. *Dear Wilf*, thought Nathan, and he felt incredibly sad for a time gone by.

Turning around Nathan tried to imagine his parents Arthandur and Marlene waving to him from down below in a manner that they used to whenever he returned from his youthful romps. He felt heavy laden and sad. This place that had once been his home seemed desolate and empty without the figures of familiarity who had been part of his life.

Even the village itself was no more; a skiing complex had replaced the chalets and houses. Tourists now came to this beauty spot to sample the scenic views of the mountains and the peace and tranquillity of a splendid isolation amongst nature's natural wonders. The perfumed air rose from the valley floor as a gentle breeze swept up without warning. Nathan found himself caught up in a veil of memories. It was as if Arthandur and Marlene were speaking to him across the valleys of time. He could hear Marlene's piano playing, the happy conversations of the house, Arthandur's deep and warming voice secure and sincere that would always put Nathan at ease as a youngster.

With Francine beside him at that moment in Austria and the long-gone voices of his parents ringing in his ears, it was as if he had been miraculously joined by the three people he loved the most. All the years in between the time he had left, and returned, seemed to blend. He felt an incredible mixture of feelings somewhere in the middle of nostalgia, sadness and happiness, at just being here in the present, being allowed to view once again this place of his youth.

The voices continued to echo through his mind. He felt the presence of Arthandur, Marlene and Francine. He felt as if he was rising from a dark void into a world of complete sunlight and beauty. Nathan opened and closed his eyes several times. What on earth had happened? He realised his thoughts had turned into dreams. His personal reflections on his life had become immersed in the dream-like images, created by a deep sleep that could only be experienced at a time of total exhaustion. He had remembered that visit to his home in Austria, which had been of such significance in his life. Yet in that long night from which he had just awoken, Nathan could not shake off the feeling that Arthandur, Marlene and Francine had been there with him, guiding him, speaking to him. He could not see any sign of their physical being, but he had felt an overwhelming presence that he was sure they had been there.

There was something different about the way he felt. He was no longer gasping for breath. Nor was he feeling as weak as he had done previously. Nathan felt newness about his being. He felt like he had emerged from a dream-like existence that belonged to someone else. Gazing up around his surroundings he made the discovery; he was not in the same room that he had fallen asleep in. A staggering thought swept over him. Before he had time to fully absorb the shock at the realisation of what had happened, he found himself looking up into the gentle, kindly face of the doctor. The man was smiling warmly.

"My congratulations to you, Mr Palmai." The doctor's voice was reassuring with a golden texture to it that matched his friendly smile. "You have a new heart." He paused to let Nathan absorb the context of his words. Nathan opened his mouth in amazement but he could not say anything. He was stunned. "And I am very, very pleased to say that your new heart is responding well."

The incredible wonder at having come through absorbed him completely.

"How wonderful," he murmured softly. The greatest feelings of joy he had ever known in his life came over him. He realised with some embarrassment that tears were flooding his eyes and streaming down his cheeks.

The doctor leaned forward and gripped Nathan's shoulder with a fatherly reassurance. He was used to seeing reactions like this. When Nathan had eventually recovered his emotions, the doctor talked to him for some time of how life after heart transplantation would take its course. There would be daily medication, preventative treatment to follow, and a necessary change of lifestyle. But after all Nathan was starting a new life with a new heart.

Nathan found it hard to come to terms with just what had taken place. Somewhere between laying in bed remembering his European tour with Francine, and opening his eyes in another room, he had undergone a heart transplant. He found it incredible that he had literally lost the time in between. His mind and memory of the past days had gone blank. He smiled at the irony of it. He might have lost the past two days, but he had gained a whole lifetime.

Eventually he was allowed visitors. Anastasia and Joseph were the first to come. Nathan was delighted to see them. He was full of energy with his new heart and felt tempted to dance around the room. He resisted the temptation. Nathan's son, Joseph, was so pleased and excited that he communicated in sign language at a frantic speed that surely would have broken speed records. Being alive, just simply being alive, with one's nearest and dearest was exhilarating. Perhaps for the first time in his life Nathan made the discovery that life in its simplest form is the greatest creation on God's earth; that just being here no matter what a person did for a living, no matter how rich or poor, the most important aspect of life was to feel emotions and happiness at taking each day as it came.

Heart transplants were national news. Nathan knew he would have to face the media when he left the hospital. He did not shy away from the prospect of facing an entourage of newsmen. Enormous progress in heart transplantation had been made since the operation had first been pioneered. It was natural that the public would be interested in the latest developments and newest patients.

Nathan had already been a newsworthy person prior to his heart transplant. His positions as a prominent lawyer and leading public figure had always guaranteed him a certain amount of publicity. Indeed the very morning that he was due to face the press Nathan was given a copy of the *Sydney Morning Herald* in which he featured prominently. The tabloid carried a detailed description of his life under the title of *'Nathan Palmai's Greatest Test'*. It went on to describe Nathan's life in great embellishment. Truly it had all been remarkable, not at all easy. Sometimes heartbreaking and full of long and painful struggles. Sometimes exceptionally colourful: Palestine, North Africa, the Australian outback, and friends! What good friends he had known: Freddie Miller, Wilf the goat herder, Ted McTaggart, Jack and Elsie and their sons, Joe Patterson, Harry Masters. He stood at the window thinking of all these people, all of his travels. If he had known struggle then surely the fruits of his efforts had ripened with wonderful results.

Before going to meet the press, Nathan thanked every member of the heart transplant team personally. They had been wonderful and dedicated people to whom he would always owe a debt of gratitude that he would probably never be able to repay. He could only owe them his deepest thanks.

"I will never be able to thank you enough," Nathan emphasised to the leading doctor. "I wish I could find the words to thank you."

The doctor had kindly eyes. They glimmered with delight. "Your continued good health will be the greatest thanks we could ask for. The function of a doctor is to save life, to cure the sick and preserve life. Mr Palmai, you can thank us by leading a long and happy life."

"I am touched, deeply touched," replied Nathan, "and I will do my best to succeed."

The two men shook hands warmly. The doctor stretched out his hand indicating the way out. "Come, Mr Palmai. The ladies and gentlemen of the media are waiting for us."

They walked downstairs to the lobby of the hospital. There Nathan and the doctor answered questions posed to them by the press and television journalists. The questions were amiably asked. Nathan fielded them all with good humour. He was asked with some predictability if it would mean drastic changes to his lifestyle. His reply was equally predictable. Naturally there would be changes. He would not be able to carry the huge amount of responsibilities he had borne previously. He did not want to retire entirely – he still wanted to devote time to his work for the ethnic community – but, pointing to his beloved son, Joseph, and daughter, Anastasia, he stressed that his family was a top priority now. The interviews continued on the same line for a while with photographers continually snapping and cameramen rolling their film ready for the evening news bulletins.

During the course of the interview Nathan kept looking towards his children who sat close by with Harry Masters, his long time friend and business partner. Their presence was welcome. Anastasia and Joseph were a constant reminder to Nathan of his very happy marriage to Francine. At twenty-eight Anastasia looked positively radiant. Her warm smile towards her father reminded him so much of Francine. Joseph too smiled in constant happiness for his father's recovery. For one who had been born with the twin afflictions of deafness and without the power of speech, he was possessed of a remarkable zest for life. It had often been a question that Nathan had asked himself over and over again. What sort of person would young Joseph have developed into if he had not been born without two of the most communicative senses that the human being needs to make his way in life? Considering the obstacles that he had been born with, Joseph had grown well and unleashed considerable talent with his paintings and his enthusiasm for the theatre of the deaf. Nathan considered the point that he himself had started his own life with certain difficulties. Being born Jewish was a privilege. But to have been of that faith at the time of the Third Reich created enormous difficulties under which to have lived in those pre-war days.

The spiral of his life had emanated from those days. If he had not left Austria for Palestine at the age of sixteen the course of his life would have been undoubtedly very different. Here he was now a prominent figure in Sydney, Australia, being interviewed by national press, radio and television journalists, after receiving a heart transplant. It seemed strange to be the centre of such attention. Once this was over Nathan felt that he would be pleased to slip back into some sort of anonymity. Apart from his work for ethnic groups Nathan would now retire from the field of the law, step down from his company directorships and live the quiet life as a private citizen.

Before Nathan left the hospital that day, he had received a flood of telegrams wishing him well. Freddie Miller had been the first to send one; although he was far away in a country village in England, Freddie's loyalty and devotion to his friends was unwavering. Nathan looked at the telegram and concluded that his friend, Freddie, was one of the best. People like Freddie Miller were rare gems. The Faleys too, the second generation of them that is, had sent a telegram. Ron and Jill, Mick and Rose together with their own children were concerned. Abria and Maviel, the Tooheys, the Hoolihans, Spiros and Kristos, people Nathan had represented as a lawyer, one came from Ted McTaggart in Cairns. Ted McTaggart, now there was a fair dinkum bloke if ever there was one. *God love him,* thought Nathan. They had last met in Cairns when Nathan had stopped over on his way to Port Moresby, New Guinea, where he was to handle an unusual case concerning some tribesmen in the highlands. And there were many other telegrams. They came from former Prime Ministers Gough Whitlam, Malcolm Fraser and Mr Bob Hawke who had been elected to the Lodge in Canberra the previous year.

Nathan had made many friends in his life. More than he could ever have dreamed. Obviously his life had been worthwhile. The boy from the Austrian mountain village had achieved good thinks in life, yet he had never made financial gain or personal status his aim. All he had ever looked for in life was purpose, experience and an understanding of the other person's point of view. Somehow all the rest had just fallen into place naturally.

Nathan said his final farewells to the staff and patients at the hospital and then walked out into the sunshine with his arms around Anastasia and Joseph. Harry Masters walked close by. The day was beautiful; the sky was gloriously blue and the flowers and trees looked magnificent, their true colours enhanced considerably by the all-powerful Australian sun. Having been given a second chance in life, Nathan felt determined never to miss even the slighted detail. He wanted to sip and savour everything. He wanted to enjoy every previous moment. For life, with its highs and lows, is the most valuable possession of all.

He turned to Harry quickly. "Harry old friend, are you ready to take over the firm? You understand things are very different now?"

Harry looked down at the ground for a moment. "With an absolute sadness I am ready to take over, if that is what you want me to do. I say that with honesty. I've known you a long time, you're a friend as well as a colleague. Many people are going to miss you in your absence from public life. Me, perhaps most of all."

"I know that, Harry, but I'll be in touch from time to time," Nathan reassured him. The small group walked into the hospital gardens. Anastasia stopped suddenly and gripped her father's arm tightly.

"Dad, I've some news for you," she announced proudly. "I put off telling you until the operation was over. I think you can handle the news now."

"What is it, darling? Nathan asked, although looking at Anastasia's radiant complexion, he already knew the answer.

"You're going to be a grandfather," she said, her happiness contagious. Nathan's new heart missed a beat. He stood there open-mouthed and then hugged her delightedly. He turned to his son just as quickly and relayed the happy message in sign language. Joseph already knew, but in his silent way of communicating he flicked his fingers and hands indicating that he already knew the news.

"What wonderful news. What a surprise," Nathan said in a tone of undisguised delight. "This is the most wonderful day I have known in a long time."

"We have another surprise for you, Nathan," Harry remarked. Nathan looked at his friend with curiosity. *What on earth could possibly happen next on this remarkable day?* "If you'll just look to your left…"

Both Anastasia and Joseph were smiling. "Harry arranged this little reception for you," said Anastasia pointing to a group of people standing together in the gardens. Melissa was one of them. She walked across to join Nathan.

"Hullo, my old kibbutz friend," Melissa greeted him kissing him on the cheek. "I am so glad to see you. I am so happy you have come through,"

"Melissa, what is this? All these people?" Nathan was stunned. He recognised many of them as old friends of his: the Faleys and the Hoolihans were amongst them. Nathan waved to them amiably. There were also people there from the Jewish and migrant community. The group must have numbered fifty or sixty people in total.

"Dad, you have made many friends over the years. Harry suggested that I contact many of them for you." Anastasia beamed as she spoke. "But they all wanted to come. They wanted to welcome you to your new life with a new heart."

Nathan looked at his daughter. "*Oy vei*," he sighed, lapsing into a piece of Jewish dialogue that he rarely used. "I must be the luckiest man in the world today."

Melissa touched his arm affectionately. "Do you remember that day long ago on the Kibbutz Jezarat when Shirom Banai told us of the terrible night of November 9th 1936 when people of our faith had been turned upon in the streets of Germany and Austria?" Nathan nodded that he remembered, "And do you remember how Shirom told us to rise up from our despondency."

"I have always remembered that," Nathan replied.

"Didn't we rise well, Nathan?" Melissa asked in an enthusiastic voice. "To magnificent heights." She paused and smiled warmly at Nathan and his family. Then she turned and walked across to the little group of people in the gardens.

"For our friend Nathan Palmai," she said to them all in almost a beckoning manner, "Come, sing. Come sing with me, my people."

The words jolted Nathan's memory sharply. The Jewish members of the group started to sing and the words were that of a lifetime ago coming together in an enthralling, spellbinding harmony. Nathan recognised the song. He felt as if he were back there on the Kibbutz Jezarat with Leon and Melissa. Nathan began to sing too. How good it was to be there singing amidst the splendour and beauty of that most gloriously sunny day.

Nathan felt the utmost happiness. He thought to himself, *Truly life was remarkable. Come sing with me, my people.*